"MR. SOLOMON, YOUR BOOKS SPEAK TO ME IN A SPECIAL WAY. NOW I WANT TO MEET YOU AND SPEAK TO YOU IN *MY* SPECIAL WAY. I WANT TO MAKE YOU HAPPY, EXHILARATED, THE WAY I GET AFTER *READING* YOU. MR. SOLOMON, I WANT TO WRAP MY LEGS AROUND YOU AND FEEL YOU LOCKED INSIDE ME. I WANT TO PUT YOUR PENIS IN MY MOUTH *JUST TO GIVE YOU PLEASURE.* MR. SOLOMON, I WANT YOU TO DO WHATEVER YOU WANT, OR FANTASIZE DOING, TO ME."

What man in his right mind could turn down an invitation like that? Especially when it came from a ravishing blonde and nubile creature like Tippy Matthews, a totally liberated young lady who definitely meant what she said?

Certainly not Lionel Solomon, who was about to enter into fantasies he had never dreamed of —and into a nightmare from which there was no withdrawal. . . .

# SHRINKING

"BRILLIANTLY CONCEIVED AND DAZZLING-LY EXECUTED!"—*St. Louis Globe-Democrat*
"ELECTRIFYING, INVENTIVE . . . the man can write!"—*Denver Rocky Mountain News*
"An exceedingly funny novel . . . rich in comic para-doxes that delight!"—*Palm Beach Life*

## Big Bestsellers from SIGNET

---

If you wish to order any of these
titles, please use the coupon in
the back of this book.

# SHRINKING

## The Beginning of My Own Ending

A Novel by
## Alan Lelchuk

A SIGNET BOOK
**NEW AMERICAN LIBRARY**
TIMES MIRROR

This is an authorized reprint of a hardcover edition published by
Little, Brown and Company, Inc. Published simultaneously in
Canada by Little, Brown & Company (Canada) Limited.

Library of Congress Catalog Card Number: 77-28024

The lines from "The Love Song of J. Alfred Prufrock" are
from *Collected Poems, 1909–1962* by T. S. Eliot, copyright 1936
by Harcourt Brace Jovanovich, Inc.; copyright 1963, 1964, by T. S.
Eliot. Reprinted by permission of Harcourt Brace Jovanovich, Inc.,
and Faber and Faber Ltd.
Excerpts from "On Liars" and "On the Power of the Imagina-
tion" are taken from Montaigne, *Essays*, translated by J. M. Cohen
(Penguin Classics, 1958), pp. 28–32, 36–40, 41–44, 45–46, 46–48.
Copyright © 1958 by J. M. Cohen. Reprinted by permission of
Penguin Books Ltd.

SIGNET TRADEMARK REG. U.S. PAT. OFF. AND FOREIGN COUNTRIES
REGISTERED TRADEMARK—MARCA REGISTRADA
HECHO EN CHICAGO, U.S.A.

SIGNET, SIGNET CLASSICS, MENTOR, PLUME AND MERIDIAN BOOKS
are published by The New American Library, Inc.,
1301 Avenue of the Americas, New York, New York 10019.

First Signet Printing, May, 1979

1  2  3  4  5  6  7  8  9

PRINTED IN THE UNITED STATES OF AMERICA

For *Nocturne,* the literary magazine of the Brooklyn College School of General Studies (1955–1960), and for Heinz Bauer, Jack Marshall, Anthony Tommasi, the late David Boroff, and especially Arthur Edelstein.

For three teachers: Vera Lachman, Paul Rosenblatt and Sam Stetner.

For Barbara Kreiger.

*I do maintain that man creates his own illnesses for a definite purpose, using the outer world merely as an instrument, finding there an inexhaustible supply of material which he can use for this purpose, today a piece of orange peel, tomorrow the spirochete of syphilis, the day after, a draft of cold air, or anything else that will help him pile up his woes. And always to gain pleasure, no matter how unlikely that may seem, for every human being experiences something of pleasure in suffering; every human being has the feeling of guilt and tries to get rid of it by self-punishment.*

—George Groddeck
The Book of It

# Contents

# Foreword by Dr. Benjamin Lirič

I must say I am somewhat at a loss to present myself here and perform this task, since I have not willingly chosen it, and since writing an introduction is something I know little about. Healing and literature are not exactly twin arts, though years ago, in college and afterwards, I did read the great novels with a hungry interest, finding there insights and intuitions that were richer than in most other sources, including my few psychology courses. I dare say that my desire, some forty years ago, to enter the field of healing stemmed in part from my frustrations at becoming a creative artist.

My name is Benjamin Lirič, I am a doctor of medicine, I have practiced psychiatry in the Boston area for the past three decades, and I knew the missing Lionel Solomon somewhat marginally, to tell the truth. I met him for the first time in the spring of 1969, when he signed himself in at Swerdlow's Sanitarium, a small rest home some forty-odd miles west of Boston, for a four-week stay. I myself had long been on the staff there, and when Mr. Solomon asked to see a doctor, specifically an "older, nondirective type," I seemed to fill the bill and answered the request. To be sure, although I had trained traditionally in the Freudian school, and then practiced for a number of years as a psychoanalyst, I had by the 1960's enlarged and varied my methods of treatment, finding that individual cases did indeed call for a variety of approaches. (I began to question the whole idea of infant trauma and its universal applicability in view of the multitude of adult neuroses and disorders, but that is another story.) Now my talks with Mr. Solomon during those several weeks of his self-induced rest were more in the nature of conversations than strict therapy sessions; sometimes he talked and I listened, sometimes he asked me a specific question or two, and sat back and listened. He claimed this "soothed" as well as instructed him, and so I complied. (He explained how he had consulted a traditional analyst some years previously, and had quickly come to resent the doctor's stubborn refusal to speak up and offer his opinions. After my own years of considering such resentment no more than another aspect of defense mechanism, I now consider it a serious criticism.)

He had just published a novel, which was received harshly in the press, and had also just broken up with his girlfriend of the past several years. The combination punished him sharply, and he wished to withdraw from the fray, to rest up, see where he was, and recoup his energies. During the entire month of his stay, let me add, I did not judge Lionel Solomon to be characterologically ill, but rather temporarily depressed and mentally exhausted. This ought to be stated here, for the record. After he left the rest home, he continued to consult me, on an irregular basis, from time to time. He would come in to talk about particular decisions or problems facing him—about his daughter Rachel, about his relation to the university, about his critics—but never considered doing a depth analysis or sustained therapy. Nor did I think it particularly necessary. He seemed to be functioning well, with the usual amount of writer's self-doubt and anxiety, writing, teaching, fathering, living with a new woman he cared for very much. Once again, during these visits I did not judge him clinically to be a "patient." Because of certain legal and other questions concerning his situation now, I wish to state this clearly.

That Solomon himself was aware of his condition, of his own doubts and difficulties, will be emphatically apparent in his text. In this lonely and bizarre story of his affair with the young lady "Tippy Matthews," Solomon for the most part does not try to avoid the hard facts or unpleasant interpretations that face him. It is a story of illness, and it is perhaps modestly heroic that Solomon should muster the energy and the courage to confront that illness without flinching. If this does not mitigate the sickness itself, it does indicate the power of the artistic ego to try to fight off that advancing pathology, and, perhaps more, to defeat it by means of insight through art. This constant wrestling and warring, between the functioning artistic ego and the pathological drive, may be seen in the dialectic in the text itself between Solomon the actor and Solomon the observer, between the gentleman who falls prey to the woman's (and his own) actions, and the art-

2

ist who, in looking back and reconstructing those actions, constructs a running commentary upon them. This internal dialectic, apart from the actual story action, will interest the psychoanalyst as much as the literary reader; the critical consciousness becomes as much an actor as Solomon the man. Now, how accurate do I personally gauge his insights into his dilemma to be? Forgive me, but is it not enough to cite intelligence here, to cite courage—not the rather simple animal courage so heralded in our native land by popular movies and literature, but the courage of the serious mind facing squarely its own disturbing fate and consequences? Is it not enough to cite these qualities, and, for this introduction at least, forgo a professional judgment?

I think it is appropriate to say here that I personally felt affection for Lionel Solomon, respected and admired him the more I knew him, for both his strengths and his weaknesses; and as I came to read his novels, I came to admire them too, in my amateur way. I do not generally read that much modern fiction, professional duties and domestic responsibilities taking up most of my time. Also, I am rather old-fashioned in my reading habits, and find that the fiction put forward as important these days turns out to be more incidental than essential. There is a certain lack of reflectiveness in it, a certain trivial-mindedness, or else moral piety, and a baroque concern with words at the expense of content which put me off. Obviously, some of this prejudice is a result of my occupation, wherein one obtains a most special view of what constitutes "insight" into character, after listening to persons who reveal, hour by hour, their innermost secrets and private lives in the most graphic manner. The wealth of ungainly private admission is enormous; the depth of the pain bottomless; and both never fail to mystify and deject me. Thus, romantic novels (or works of nonfiction) that speak to the excellence of mankind or celebrate something called Love between adults may certainly make for virtuous bedtime reading, but they do seem to fall short of realism. The few novels of the inner life that I have read generally produce facts which are not nearly as arresting as those stated by my patients, and insights that don't measure up either with those of the patients, let alone colleagues. That is perhaps why Mr. Solomon's fiction impressed me. There was a forceful intelligence operating, and a courage too. (Not always, of course; *Rosen at Fifty* suffered to my mind from a lack of boldness, an attempt to be self-protective, which, from talking to him later on, I would suspect stemmed from his fear of more severe criticism. And *Each According to His Needs*, that earlier work, bit off more than it could chew, perhaps, more material there than digestion and understanding of it.) His characters were not miles behind my patients in terms of their experience, their turmoil, and their understanding. It may be noted here that Mr. Solomon himself is a doctor of sorts; the man who writes serious books in our time is also trying to heal something or someone—either to cure a social wound or else to heal some aspect of a person, himself included. Now during this project or search called the book, we as readers tend also to receive solace in one way or another, even if—and sometimes especially—that search entails blunder and pain, error and remorse, self-recrimination and humiliating trial. By hurting himself, and by trying to examine that hurt—to show it in its fullest detail and etiology—the writer takes upon himself the burdensome labor of a kind of collective examination, if you will: the paradox of *healing us while hurting himself*. And it should not be thought that the search and examination, which may entail, as the present one does, apparently bizarre or out-of-the-way stops is any less significant than a more ordinary probe; this is a naïve attitude, one that is not supported by the history of literature. We should recall that in most primitive societies the man who offers up wisdom is he who, in some way or another, experiences wisdom or knowledge either by vision, dream, or experiential reality; that is, *he will pass on what has first passed through him*.

Certainly the ancient Greek axiom Know Thyself has become double-edged in our time. Implied here, as I understand it, is the sense of healing and comfort that such knowledge would issue in. Wisdom itself was a form of therapy. Curiously, for us the motto has remained the same, but the implications of the journey have changed drastically. In our age, in which man has indeed come to know himself more and more, through private investigations and public witnesses, the news of the knowledge has not been very heartening. Neither the historical news of the collective animal, nor the more private accounts of the single individual, have brought much comfort or succor. Both states and souls seem to be in deep trouble. Know Thyself has become as much curse as balm, or directive. Because of this, and because of this age of intensive, pressured realism, the nursing of man has become a paramount task. Not his salvation or resurrection—those mythological hopes of times past, religious times—but the simple and deep act of nursing.

Therapy in its broadest as well as most specific senses has

sought to do precisely that. But the battle is most complicated. For at first the doctor must have his patient reveal himself, to himself, and then he must seek to allay the very fears and doubts resulting from such self-knowledge—not to mention the larger fight against consequent urges to self-destruction. It is a difficult battle, as I have said. The odds grow longer for success, furthermore, if the society's destructive powers are as ambiguous, two-sided, and subtle as they are in our homeland. In this respect, I believe, living under totalitarian regimes, with their more obvious destructive powers, presents an easier job for the doctor. So, all told, if Know Thyself becomes Distrust Thyself, Be Skeptical of Thyself, Be Terrified of Thyself—as it did in recent history, in Solomon's own history—the ancient adage for wisdom becomes a formula for pain and distress.

One of our most interesting months of discussion, I recall vividly, occurred when *Each According to His Needs* appeared, and received some harsh reviews from reviewers and colleagues; in distress and bewilderment, Solomon asked if *I* viewed certain scenes as "dirty" or "pornographic." My response, apart from inquiring into his own vulnerability on the issue, was to remind him that more than a few of the memorable literary heroes were excellent subjects for psychoanalysis; how did he think *their* creators would answer his query? Later, at another discussion, when he was calmer, I suggested that in fact the places I found weakest in his novels were those in which he seemed to be paying too much attention to his audience of critics, and, unconsciously, trying to play "the good boy" for them. (When, smiling, he asked if I might review his next novel, I said yes, in private consultation. He responded enthusiastically that Virginia Woolf had proposed that very sort of procedure for novelists, and though she had in mind literary critics for the consultation, these days analysts might indeed be a better choice.) Naturally, I realize that the above are not literary terms of praise; I haven't meant them as such. I speak simply as a professional man with an inevitable medical bias, and as a most amateur reader of a friend's novels.

I must speak here too as an executor of sorts, an emissary. The facts of the present situation are simple, and unfortunate. While on vacation on Cape Cod in August, 197-, I received a phone call from Swerdlow's on my unlisted emergency number, explaining how an old patient of mine had just been readmitted, under the care of two friends. The hospital wanted me to know about this, and about his condition: he was wearing a most odd costume, it seemed, dressed up like an American Indian, comically and pathetically so, and he wouldn't explain himself or talk at all. Now what could I do but break my steadfast rule of steering clear of all illness in August, and sticking to my serene skies and white dunes and children. So, I drove up immediately to the sanitarium, an exhausting three-hour drive on a hot summer's day, and found Solomon in his incongruous outfit and painful condition. Happily, the young lady who had brought him in had waited for me, and we had a twenty-minute talk over iced tea. The young woman, who called herself Pandora Armstrong, and who was of course the T. Matthews of Mr. Solomon's story, explained how she had come to visit "Lionel" in New Hampshire, had found him in this strange way, grew most "concerned," and extracted from him the information about Swerdlow's and myself. She thought it best if he were under "professional care" just then. And so she and her gentleman friend, a nice chap of forty-five who waited outside my office, had driven Solomon down from New Hampshire directly that day. The young lady struck me as poised, intelligent, pretty and indeed concerned; barring her Hollywood sunglasses, which she removed, she was dressed rather conservatively, and spoke openly; and her whole air was one of competence and maturity, and as I say, serious concern. I was most impressed. Perhaps too much so. Or perhaps I wanted to see Solomon too quickly, and hence hardly questioned the young lady at all, beyond the facts she gave me. She advertised herself as "a friend, and an admirer of his work," and I had no reason to question either. I said goodbye, and thanked her.

Upstairs in his room, at the window overlooking the circular driveway and lawn, Solomon nodded to me and pointed to the girl, who was by then getting into a long, fancy automobile. Speaking casually, he told me that, on the way down, with him driving his car (and the other fellow following in his) the young lady had performed fellatio on him, causing him to accelerate to ninety miles an hour and almost go off the road into a railing. "It was unbelievable," he nodded, still surprised. Then he half-smiled. "Look at her, you wouldn't think she had so many tricks up her sleeve, would you?" (No, Lionel, I wouldn't, I didn't; and I'm not sure I fully understood you.) Skeptical of his words, of his casual response to his grave condition, I remember looking at him carefully—capable and sane just a few months before, now wearing makeshift "war paint" on his face and beads around his neck, and a boy's headband with foolish feathers, the sort of getup a twelve-year-old might wear to a costume party. What had happened to him? What could his words mean? In hindsight, with the help of Solomon's text and other corroborating materials, I now understand more of what he meant about sleeves and tricks.

Although, of course, I have grown more convinced, and more concerned, about his own illness and need for care. The fact of the matter is that when I asked him to talk about the situation then, or in the next few days, he responded curtly that he was "writing about it," and that was all. I had no idea then that that was to be the only substantive remark I was to hear from Lionel Solomon during the next several months. Nor did I have any idea what he meant by "writing about it"; what I took to be a few days, or a week, meant really a much longer period of time, and silence. Well, immediately, my own vacation was shattered. August, on the surface a serene month, is also a dangerous month, for analysts as well as patients; in my years as an analyst I have had two suicides during that deceptive month. As much as one tries to obliterate such happenings, they remain, tattooed upon the brain somewhere. I was worried about Solomon, and so stayed on hand for a few days; and when I did return to the Cape, it was not quite the same. I felt *responsible* for him, the more so perhaps because he was not talking to me, not giving me a chance to see him *within*, not letting me perform my role. So, I waited for something to occur, his work to be finished or his desire to talk to emerge; unfortunately, neither did.

Nothing changed in the next few months either (with the exception of course of the actual publication of the rather astonishing article written by the young lady, in a national magazine). He talked very little, and saw very few people. He allowed one or two former students to come and visit (after their letters had been forwarded), and the little girl Alexandra, from his home in New Hampshire; but he refused to see anyone close to him—his girlfriend, his mother, good friends. He would refuse with a slow shaking of the head, and an occasional half-smile, which pained me the more I saw it. The only time he left the sanitarium was to accompany me to a baseball game at Fenway Park, where he spoke a few words to my son about Mr. Tiant's pitching, and compared that performance to Jackie Robinson's running. Not a baseball fan, I was penalized by my ignorance, and could only listen in. In any case, on the drive back, he looked out the window, smoked, and remained silent—not sullen or morose, please understand, not resentful—just silent. One should know that since Lionel Solomon was usually a very active and most gregarious man, this total quiet and withdrawal for nearly two hours was most unusual.

Through the next six months, I'm sorry to say, he stayed unusual in that peculiar way. He remained unto himself, quiet, horns tucked in, lips sealed. He took walks, listened to the radio, acted politely to floor nurses and other patients. But whenever I sought to engage him in discussion, or questioning, or talk of any sort, he shook his head, half-smiled, begged off. When at one point I suggested that without official therapy I was not sure if I could keep him on at Swerdlow's—a false threat, I must admit—he nodded, in understanding, accepting his fate. (I immediately felt badly for imposing that extra burden upon him, and was especially friendly at the next visit.) Now while he didn't talk, neither did he retreat into autistic behavior, nor, I will add, into antagonistic behavior. It was as if he were suspended somewhere, by an act of will, in a sphere between sanity and inability, or illness, between outer alertness and inner grief, between wanting to live and not wanting to be. The nurse reported that in the first few months she heard him talking to himself in the late evening in his room, but when she knocked and inquired if everything was all right, he opened the door, nodded, and returned within. She didn't bother him after that.

As I've implied, his silence was accompanied by a withdrawal from the normal outside world. There was a teaching position he held, a house and mortgage he owned, and an apartment and rent in Cambridge, and so on. There were decisions to be made, bills to be paid, responsibilities to be upheld, or explained. He withdrew, he stopped. It was only with the help of several devoted friends and associates—his lawyer and accountant in Lebanon, New Hampshire; his literary agent and executor friend in Manhattan; his loyal girlfriend (Sheyna) in Cambridge—that he remained unbothered, uninterrupted, in his room in Swerdlow's. Slowly, of necessity, we became his agents to the world, keeping his affairs in that busy place afloat. It is no small achievement to escape America as a full-fledged adult, and still live ("free") on its soil, uninterrupted. Yet, when I would tell him of a major decision to be made, of a moment of financial dilemma, say, he would look at me with head half cocked, half withdrawn, and either nod slowly, scratch his head, rub at his lips, or push back his eyeglasses. Not only was there no indication that he wanted to assume responsibility for him-

8

self, in the world, or for his property, but he seemed at times half amused at watching these decisions, as if they were, in sum, a petty disturbance. For example, there came the matter of his bill at Swerdlow's ($1,200 a month). Fortunately, he had enough money in his saving and checking accounts to cover it rather comfortably for the first six months and the weeks thereafter. But again, he didn't seem to care; he made out the check I gave him without so much as batting an eyelash, the way he made out all his checks. (At first I left him the checks, but he didn't fill in any of them. All he did was sign his name at my request, in an almost illegible scribble. It was the accountant who had to fill in the rest of the check—date, amount, payee.) Now remember, some of those money decisions were of a serious order—at one point a sale of land came in from an earlier investment, but he wouldn't have anything to do with it. It embarrassed him, it seemed. Whatever we wished and decided was perfectly fine. The world, our world, no longer interested him.

Why didn't I apply more pressure to reach him? The answer lay in his typewriter, primarily; it clacked on steadily, day after day, or rather, night after night; it was like a pulse beating regularly, a Solomon sign of life. The Morse code of the writer's heart, clacking Live, live, live! Late into the night it chattered on, the staff reported, sometimes into the dawn, with the radio on low, politely. That was it. But it was enough to keep me back, hold me off. Curiously, however—and the reader will forgive my repeated use of that usable adverb here—for all that typing, I *never saw any work*, any pages of manuscript lying about, when I entered his room. There was the pile of unopened letters on the bureau (unopened save for the two students' letters he had read); several old newspapers and magazines on the coffee table (the dates didn't seem to matter to him); and finally, the stack of empty white pages on his writing table. It was this stack, gradually diminishing, which indicated to me that the manuscript existed. Nothing else. Was he really writing? Was he destroying it as he went along? Where was it? No sign. Only after a few months did I hear, via the grapevine of maid to nurse to doctor, that he was putting stacks of typed pages in the bureau drawers, underneath pajamas, and also in boxes in the closet, much like a mother cat who deposits her kittens in secret hiding places. The room itself showed no visible signs of these nocturnal labors. It looked exactly as it had when he first entered it. Most patients in for an extended stay decorate their rooms with photographs from friends or family, or tack up something *personal* on the wall. Solomon abstained. He made not a single improvement in his room, as given him: a bed, a small writing table, a bureau and mirror, a reading armchair, the two tepid landscapes on the wall. (On my fourth or fifth visit, I noticed that the socket of the wrought-iron standing lamp had come loose, the lamp Solomon used for his typewriter light; it was I who had to have the socket exchanged. Similarly, he never once asked for a cushion for his straight-backed chair, but used a bed pillow; only when I heard about it did we purchase a seat cushion for him. On his own, *he initiated nothing;* he ventured forth not at all. It was I who thought he might like a radio in there, too, and had it installed; once there, he used it regularly.)

I have overlooked one item, the typewriter. It was the only thing he asked for, during that first week. When I offered him one of Swerdlow's, he shook his head, and suggested either the standard in his Cambridge apartment or the portable in New Hampshire. We brought him the Royal standard from Cambridge, along with several packages of heavy bond paper (twenty-pound weight). That in toto represented his imprint upon the bland sanitarium room.

Of course, in all this he knew exactly when my visits occurred—at 4 P.M. three times a week—and so had plenty of time to organize the room and clear away things like manuscript pages. Especially since he didn't commence his typing until late at night, when most patients were asleep, and had long finished by my late afternoon visits. Oh yes, his one "social" habit: at 3 A.M., once or twice a week, he played a game of checkers with Mr. Sothedy, a large middle-aged attendant who worked nights after his regular daytime job in a brewery. How did that happen? As Mr. Sothedy explained: once, in the middle of the night, he saw Solomon coming out in the hallway, fully dressed, to go to the bathroom, and himself bored, wondering if the patient had insomnia, invited him to a game of checkers. Solomon accepted, and without speaking, played a game. Such was the beginning of what became a 3 A.M. ritual. Sothedy, by the way, is in my opinion perfectly unqualified to work in a sanitarium; he is one of those fellows whose ordinary demeanor belies his simian internal life of brimming prejudice and abundant violence. But he's been at Swerdlow's for years, comes from the local community, works the graveyard shift, and therefore comes into almost no contact with patients. And yet in Solomon's case, he claims to have made a friend, the first sane "crazie" that he had ever met at Swerdlow's.

10

Of course Solomon's pervasive silence made a kind of mockery of my visits. No one, not even a psychiatrist, wishes to drive some forty-two miles just to sit and stare at objects for an hour and then leave. (Occasionally I had other patients to see, but not always.) I tried to sit and look at Solomon and remain silent myself, once, but felt ashamed, as if I were lying. Thus, I began to devise little speeches, of maybe fifteen or twenty minutes, to pass the time. Rambling commentaries taken from everywhere—current events, books, magazines—an infrequent sporting note with my cynical comment (at my son's urging I sometimes included the scores), and even notes on my own family and their doings. I felt then as if I were talking to a member of the family, a distant cousin or brother for whom I had an attachment and didn't want to give up to insanity, even though all the reports appeared dim indeed. It was a most curious challenge, those little chats; and in a way, of course, the words themselves meant little. They were simply *a reason for being there, with him.* Paradoxically, while his condition hurt and disconcerted me, his presence brought me a strange pleasure; I felt as if I were serving him by showing up, being there; in fact, I even had twinges of possessive jealousy about his presence, about those strange half-hour stays. What did he do during these times? He stared out the window, fiddled with a small object (that same "Zuñi fetish" you will hear about), occasionally glanced at me—always at the wrong moment it seemed, not at what I took to be the most interesting point, but at some other more trivial (or unguarded?) moment, which disarmed me. And even, *moved* me. Yes, it moved me. Always sitting, always in the same outfit—dungarees and pale-yellow chamois shirt, with or without pullover—legs crossed and foot shaking nervously, and whenever he looked at me, through his eyeglasses, a speck of green or gray or gray blue emerging, with what I took to be interest, why I felt . . . wanted! By this curious young man who had *withdrawn from wanting.*

And to my great surprise, after some four weeks or so of this one-sided chatting, Solomon responded. Not in spoken words, but in small notes, in my mail. The first one said, "Tell Jason to choke up on the bat more if he's facing a fastball pitcher." I was taken aback, and only after a few moments realized that two days before, I had told Solomon, in passing, about my son's concern over his "batting" at Brookline High. Now I had no idea what "choking up" meant but Jason knew immediately, and demonstrated the maneuver for me. (I had never looked upon a baseball bat as having a neck, I must say.) I grew hopeful, at last; and sure enough, in the next few weeks, I received similar notes about my miniature talks. These were always mailed to my Boston office, never hand-delivered, and Solomon never alluded to them, or discussed them when I brought them up. In other words, the notes spoke for themselves. Some specimens:

> Tell Edna to pick the tomatoes off the vines, roll them separately in newspapers, and put them away to ripen individually in a dark drawer.

> I'm not sure you understand Anarchism seriously, Doctor; have you read Kropotkin's *Mutual Aid* or Bakunin's works? (Or Carr on Bakunin?) I have always remembered his line, "All exercise of authority perverts, and all submission to authority humiliates."

> I myself find that Italian director of the movie you saw abstract and pretentious, and much prefer the movies of the lesser-known Pietro Germi, of *Seduced and Abandoned*, etc. When that gentleman died a few years ago, I felt as if I had lost a distant friend.

> If your son and friend cut the wood in the fall it will dry much quicker since the sap is gone from it then. Also, stack it in crisscross piles and let the air circulate. Don't overestimate birch, it's pretty to look at, but maple and oak will make a hotter, longer fire.

> Why encourage Juliet to study literature *formally?* If she loves it, and understands it decently enough (as she does from what you say), schools will most likely suffocate that love; why not let her pursue something else in school, and keep literature for herself (and for friends) as a private, lifelong pleasure?

And on and on. I began to feel like a teacher being looked at and graded by the student; and also, like one who was learning too. I looked forward to these notes with great interest, for obvious therapeutic reasons, but also, as a kind of reward for my patience; more than a month's worth of Solomon's silence had filled me with skepticism, and fear, about reclaiming him. Now at least, I was encouraged, and felt personally trusted.

I was mistaken as to how far I was reaching him. One day, some five months after his entry into Swerdlow's, Solomon wrote me this note:

12

Dr. Lirič,

The story of myself and the young woman is now done, as much as I can do it, for now anyway. If you shld wish to read it, would you be so kind as to retrieve it on yr next regular visit? I ask only this condition—that you take it and do with it as you see fit without bothering me about it, in any way. Can you grant me this immunity, Doctor? Otherwise I would prefer that you didn't bother with it at all. It is of little interest or consequence, I believe, except to a doctor.

L.S.

Who knew what those words meant, really? After waiting for months and months for some sort of opening up, some sort of talk *about what had happened to him* and how he perceived it, could I refuse to read it, no matter what the condition? Besides, what might *I* wish to do with it, outside of reading it? Wasn't anything that passed between a patient and his doctor permanently theirs and no one else's?

Swerdlow's is loveliest in the winter, I believe, when the snow covers the grounds and woods, and there is a sudden, absolute stillness after leaving the frantic city and highway. In Solomon's room, where the black typewriter regularly rested, sat two blue boxes, secured with a thick rubber band; on top was a slip of paper with my name on it. For the first time, Solomon was not there; Nurse Morse told me that he had gone for a walk. I accepted that, for various reasons. I took the boxes, put them in my large briefcase, visited another patient briefly, and departed. All the way home I was as nervous as a young medical student. As soon as I commenced reading the manuscript that night, I realized that the condition I had agreed to was really an enormous challenge, if not a grave error. Not to talk to Solomon about what I was reading was a deep violation, deeper than anything "moral," a violation of my own professional interests and lifelong code, a frustration of my innermost desires as a doctor. The only immediate remedy I could think of was to use Solomon's own language, and *drop him a note,* telling him that if he ever wished to speak to me about the events and/or the manuscript, I was available, and desirous, and hopeful. (I didn't add, however, that old proverbial saying Desperate Diseases Require Desperate Remedies. Especially as the latter was unknown to me then.)

I am still waiting.

The next day an event occurred which, in hindsight, had a fine logic to it. I was rung up at my office by the head nurse to ask if I knew that Mr. Solomon was leaving that afternoon. (Legally, I had no power to hold him there.) I asked if she would get him on the telephone. And if he wouldn't come, could she delay him until I got there? I waited for two minutes, feeling cheated, outraged! (You can see how psychiatrists can get possessive too, just like husbands and wives.) Here I was, just beginning to see into the tunnel, and there he was, running out the other end. She returned to say that no, he didn't seem interested in coming to the telephone, and she wasn't at all sure that she could delay him. I hung up, called up my two appointments and canceled them, strongly against my professional habit, and drove west on Route 2. I had little idea of what I would say to him. What could I say? And how could I avoid bringing up the manuscript? Moreover, I was as disturbed by my own anger, my sense of his having betrayed me, as I was at his sudden leave-taking. I was suddenly feeling all the resentment—and even jealousy—that his total indifference of the past months had provoked in me, and which I had, I saw now, suppressed. Indeed, part of me wished, on that drive, that he would have already departed by the time I arrived.

He was sitting right there, of course, in his chair, legs crossed, single suitcase by his side, in his jacket. Waiting calmly. Breathless, I poured myself a glass of water from that absurd metal pitcher used by Swerdlow's. And then, I'm afraid, I launched into a half hour or more of preaching. On behalf of therapy. On behalf of his life, his health. Though I was somewhat beside myself with concern and bewilderment (and suppressed betrayal), I tried to get through to him as soberly as possible. (Itself a comment on the comic reversal of roles just then.) "You will be doing yourself a great injustice if you leave this way. . . . You're on the way to recovering yourself, to recovering from this ghastly time of your life, so why not complete the recovery? . . . Where will you go, do you know? Do you plan to see me regularly or what? What in the world are you hoping to do? . . . If you run out on me this way, I cannot promise to keep up my end of the bargain concerning your manuscript, I can assure you!" (Ah, what a foolish threat, what a non sequitur! But you see, I did feel as if a bargain had been struck in some implicit way: he would remain in my ken and care "in return" for my not forcing upon him a discussion about his written document. So here I was, claiming aloud that if I had agreed not to bother

14

him about his words, he shouldn't be disturbing me by running off this way!) "It's not fair what you're doing, Lionel, I'm sorry to say. Neither fair nor mature nor very sane. Not fair to you or to me. We've been through this thing together for five months now, and we're just beginning to turn the corner." (Wasn't the manuscript in my hands the proof?) "Don't you agree? Go ahead, tell me if you think differently? Speak your mind, I'll abide by your judgment. What do you think?"

That simple question, however, remained unanswered; what he thought remained within; he didn't utter a word. Instead, he rubbed his lip, nervously tossed his crossed leg, gazed at me periodically, without anger or rebellion. Stared at the tall pines outside. Not a word. I felt like grabbing him and shaking him and demanding—I stayed another fifteen minutes, tried a different, softer tack, got nowhere, said goodbye. At the door I asked if he had any money with him. No response. After checking with the nurse, who knew little, I went downstairs and slipped fifty dollars into the glove compartment of his car. And departed.

My fury lasted until I was on the road again, heading east for home; then it began to dissolve. And by the time I entered my comfortable house in Brookline, and was sipping my before-dinner cocktail, the fury had become sympathy, an indescribable sympathy, as I pictured him there, writing done, silent, setting off for . . . for . . . ?

In two weeks or so I received back the fifty dollars, and this letter. There was no return address.

Thanks for staking me. I have started doing cross-country skiing again, and find it passes the time decently. The skill of the sport is more demanding than it appears, and with no one in the woods except you and the trees, it has a special quality to it. Especially when one is riding a high on marijuana as well. I smoke just enough to keep the pain at a tolerable level, and not enough to crash into a tree. I used to be most arrogant about drugs, you know; Tippy educated me, and my present condition continues the education. Now, at night, as I light up an occasional pipe of hashish or sniff cocaine—it is surprising how easy it is to obtain, even in the provinces—I look forward immensely to those several hours of drifting somnolence. The petty boredom of everyday life vanishes, the corrupt felonies of the literary life dissolve, the shameful follies of my own life fade, and in their place forms a pleasant fog, visions, unhectic dreams.

There's no place like an institution for the routine of silence and exile, is there? A place without mail, telephone, or the recourse of friends. I miss Swerdlow's and my lunar checker games. Here, in a simple house in the middle of nowhere, I have taken on an elderly lady who comes and cooks and gives the place the air of a sanitarium. (The smell too.) And, to replace the talented Mr. Sothedy, I have gotten myself a new dog, a smart shepherd-collie. I had forgotten how finely attuned to one's moods and instincts a good dog can be, without speaking a word. Don't you think that a faithful bitch is the best companion in one's solitude?

Of course I am waiting too, to see if the other one will show up, to show me her manuscript perhaps, and perhaps to view our alleged "mutual creation." I have no doubt she will find me, when she is ready, don't you think so, Doctor?

Meanwhile, there is a certain unexpected prosperity in invisibility, on one's native grounds; one feels like a traveler to the land. An un-American. The feeling, whatever it may be, acts as a counterpoint to the wakeful pain, and even, so far, a curious form of resistance to that which beckons as the only end to all pain.

What will come of all this? I have little idea, and, unfortunately little hope.

Now, some six months later, all of us concerned with Mr. Solomon have no more idea, and even less hope.

I was more perplexed than ever when I indeed looked at the manuscript and saw that it was in the form of a huge letter to myself. If you've never been on the receiving end of a two-hundred-and-fifty-thousand-word letter, you have little idea of the confusion it generates. Including at times being addressed as "sir" by one's own patient! Moreover, he had been thinking of me all along; or at least, *I* had been of some use to him, and even before the sanitarium! Once more I felt as if he had acted somewhat better than I. In a brief letter accompanying the manuscript he hoped that it wouldn't "burden" me in any way, again stressed that I should "feel free to do whatever" I wished with it; and enclosed, "just in case it comes in handy," a copy of his will. For what? And yet, that will did come in handy, in naming his literary executor (Daniel Halpern) and his agent (Georges Raymond). For without those two kindly and intelligent people, this present project would never have gotten off the ground. It was they who, once I read the manuscript and showed it to them, suggested its publication. And it was they who, perhaps in error, proposed my writing some sort of introduction. More impor-

16

tantly, they were the ones who possessed the literary assurance that the work would not taint the reputation of their missing friend's literary career. (Though that entity can mean little to Mr. Solomon anymore.)

If he has not been heard from, in person, neither has the girl. So far, as of this date (October, 197-), the young lady in question, Miss Pandy Armstrong (or "Tippy Matthews," whichever), remains out there, at large, in the great wilderness of America or beyond. One serious speculation has it that she is still down in South America after picking up Mr. Solomon's award, in which case she might have to wait for translation or paperback for this present document to take effect and "bring her to the surface" (Mr. Halpern's remark). I sincerely hope she does surface. For her sake, for the historical record, and ultimately, for Mr. Solomon's sake. The file, as it were, remains outstanding in many respects, and the young lady would be invaluable in helping to clear up a variety of questions, postulates and charges. Moral, literary, perhaps legal. As things stand now, however, the puzzle remains incomplete; the girl is needed to put together the many odd pieces and permit its final shape, and meaning, to emerge.

About the manuscript. To say the least, it was unsettling and incongruous to read that tale of misery and personal breakdown amidst the cozy surroundings of Brookline. And once again, like August in Eastham, January became disorder and disturbance. But not the natural mode of disorder for a doctor, in which he can, like a medical general, plan an attack of therapy; rather, here I was facing a situation in which I was a helpless spectator, looking in on a lost battle. It was frustrating to a punishing degree. And so, my study, usually my retreat of peace and pleasure, where I spend quiet time reviewing a patient's case, evaluating my work, writing an article, or rereading a past classic, my study became a cell where all these virtuous pastimes were now shoved aside by this strange commitment and predicament. For two disquieting weeks I read and reread the tale and pondered it. And pondered too, my whole past history with Mr. Solomon, from initial meetings and temporary conclusions, to August hospitalization and recent meetings. It was not invigorating. On the contrary, it was tormenting.

Then, reading another man's agony, his attempt to ward off approaching demons, both within and without, is a harrowing experience. And when one knows the man in life, has *treated* him, and only now perceives all that one didn't know, when it is too late to help him—this strikes me as raising

17

frustration to a near-intolerable level. *Too late.* Whenever these two small words with their vast meaning hit me, they incite a sense of great pity for the human lot, and a feeling of personal helplessness in my profession. And despite many years of professional experience and knowledge, these words still arouse guilt in the doctor; in this case, myself. Our ability to aid our fellowman in his loneliness and in his pain seems always so very incommensurate with our heartfelt desire to do so. But that is another story, a doctor's autobiography perhaps.

I see that I have been writing about Lionel Solomon as if he were dead. Perhaps he is. But if not, isn't his disappearance, or the sort of exile he has imposed upon himself, a form of death? Or is it something else altogether, something that can be understood only after reading his text? And what about that illness he claims at the end, suddenly; is it real? But the speculations are endless.

The two blue boxes actually contained two manuscripts, not one. I am most grateful here once again to Messrs. Halpern and Raymond, who confirmed the words in Solomon's note (and text) to the effect that one manuscript was clearly unfinished, while the other was of a whole. The unfinished one has therefore been sent off to the Solomon Manuscript Archives at Boston University (Mugar Memorial Library), while the second consists of the text here. The former, titled by the novelist "Last Letters," is a collection of letters, mostly suicide letters, started several years ago at that first low point in his life, and continued right on up through his present adventure with Miss Matthews; these letters were to be the raw material for his next novel. Interestingly, a half dozen or more of them show up, in one stage of composition or another, in the present story; some have been taken from past years, some have been composed during the writing of the present tale (and present low point, which accounts for the shifting tone among them). In other words, he continued to try to work on this novel while in the midst of being "interrupted" by the young lady. And it is this "interruption" and ensuing events which form the material for the current manuscript, "Shrinking." I have taken the title from the tenor of Mr. Solomon's own work; it is the tale of a young female fan and devoted reader of his previous novels, who shows up in his life one day and—but better read it. The tale, my literary friends remind me, is not unlike Coleridge's experience with his "Khubla Khan," which was interrupted by the idle visit of the famed gentleman from Porlock, and then never

18

finished. The difference here being that Mr. Solomon, though never finishing his novel, went on to tell this tale, of his "Woman from Albuquerque."

I have been speaking as if the long rambling confession were a novel. Is it? Or isn't it? Does it make a difference that Solomon calls it an actual report? Or thinks that it is? Or even that, at one point later in the text, he drops his protagonist's name and uses his own real name? In order to protect him, and also to further his interests, to have the reader concentrate on the character Solomon, and the text—I have taken the liberty of deleting the real name and continuing with the fictional one. I have not been able to keep Solomon from being his own worst enemy in life, but I have at least tried to prevent him from injuring himself further here, through his art.

# I.
## Solomon's Brief

AT THIRTY-EIGHT, MY SENSES UPSET but intact, my body sore but still capable, my will tampered with perversely—and I think irrevocably—and my other will made out firmly, I want you to know that I'm in trouble, deep trouble. And in pain, physical pain. Do you know, sir, that it exists? (My limbs ache, my upper body is a weight, my hands, precious hands, are unsteady.) What I mean to say is that before this year, this experience, I wasn't really aware of it. Physical pain was like a strange country in Africa whose name I knew and used, without knowing a real thing about it. The great illusion of names and information. Oh yes, another item, right here in the beginning. I'm dressed up, sir, decked out ridiculously, like a little boy playing cowboys and Indians, with me the Indian. Ludicrous, yes, but I am only somewhat embarrassed; by now I accept it, understand it. A just sign of my condition. Bewildered. Shamed. Writing in pain. Feeling burned, head burning. And also in limbo, waiting, waiting—for more of the same ambiguous trial and punishment? More dangerous voluptuous adventure? How odd, this fearful anticipation, this sad memory, with the sun shining upon my lovely mountain scenery, here in New Hampshire, in my own home, and—

How did I get here, in such deep hot water? While in my own element—at my desk, trying to write? And what do I "think" about it? (Doesn't that abused and senseless verb deserve quotation marks mostly, if you consider that absurd illusion it conjures up?) Would you permit me a few words, a few hundred thousand words—oh, I could write more, much more!—to report to you on these scalding illusions, these intimate follies? A report part medical, part meditative,

21

part elegaic, I think; a kind of *Merck's Manual* of the Spirit. And as I comment here, strive toward coherence and logic, please keep in mind the useful phrase *Post hoc, ergo propter hoc. After this, therefore in consequence of this.* It is an irresistible fallacy, isn't it, this searching for causality in a haystack of events. I know it's hopeless, but I'm a Pavlovian citizen here, just like the next guy, looking for reason where there's only whim. But I have given up once and for all that schoolboy notion of "learning from experience." What folly. Oh it's fine enough at Woolworth's Five and Dime store, where you're supposed to count your change before you leave. But in life? Why, the loose change cascades down like a slot machine gone wild; I fall to my knees trying to collect it all, let alone *count*—I must stay calm, in control. But please take note, in the events to come, how every time I tried to extract a bit of wisdom from an act of folly, to make it pay off later on, why I made a bigger fool of myself than before! I've felt like a monkey's brother, not uncle, with my tail live and flapping wildly. . . . Calm. My forehead sprouts feathers, my face is painted with yellow and red slashes, my wrist sports bracelets, my neck, beads—but I must stay calm, I know, to tell it. . . .

Sheyna's gone, and it's killing me. I've lost a special girl, one who has loved me selflessly for the past four years, sir. How often do you get that? And now she's gone, for good, driven away by my idiocy. my buffoonery! Tell me, how stupid can a man be? How sharply can a man act against his own best needs and interests? Would the solid achievers of the world behave this way—the businessman abandon a profit-making shopping plaza for a whim? the doctor set up shop in a jungle village where his medicine and methods counted for zilch? a critic gamble his reputation on a writer or director who was, at best, a very long-shot risk? NO. These men are practical; Rome is in their blood; certainty, not question marks, interests them! Sheyna, my brown-haired beauty, my Mozart sonata in human skin, my lovely slender swimmer, who soothed and delighted people, *plants*, nervous animals, myself especially—I've driven her away, sir, driven her to some *other* man, probably, driven her to anger and unhappiness, and condemned myself to unbearable loneliness and remorse, *remorse*. . . .

So I sit here at my desk, trying to get the story down before my visitor arrives. Everything is in order. The typewriter before me, the fold-out duo photograph of my daughter Rachel at age six, and then at sixteen, freshman at Radcliffe,

22

smiling shyly, the charmer! wearing her headphone set for study purposes. (Inheriting my sensitive eardrums for others' noise.) And there, the framed drawing of Dostoyevsky, gotten in Russia by Sheyna; how did they get the madman to sit still for so long? (And how will I?) And there, on two bulletin boards, snapshots of my friends Sidney and Daniel, Leonard and Jean, Dan and his son, Nahum and Art, Ivan and Milena, on and on. Facing them, in this condition of humiliation, hurts the most. . . .

*She* might come at any time, the only thing predictable about her is her unpredictability. What do I have, a week or two did she say? With a week like a minute in a writer's life, of course it's foolish to think that I can get much down. Why don't I run off? Where? She'd find me, in Far Rockaway or Arizona, Brooklyn or Cambridge, as she did here, so why bore both of us with needless chase? Can't we save that for the melodramas? (But isn't this one, Lionel?) Besides, I'm the one that extended the invitation when she called from that Tennessee highway somewhere. So why run?

What good will running do at such a moment? I recall your own instructive tale, told to me a few years ago at Swerdlow's, about World War II. (Even if it didn't happen, Doctor, so what? It's possible, it's utterly human. And why should I doubt you? Just because I don't trust anything as *flimsy as fact* anymore?) There you were, at the Nazi deportation camp, awaiting the train ride to one of those "work" camps in which most of your family and friends had disappeared, when you had an impulse one night and asked to see the Kommandant. There, before him, you gave your name and number, said you were seventeen and wanted very much to be a writer, and since your sole life meant little to him but a great deal to you, would he release you? Thirtyish, smoking, thoughtful, the Nazi, an engineer in civilian life, listened to the fantastic appeal of this Yid teenager, and finally noted that you had great courage. Yes, he'd grant your wish. Extraordinary. Yet I like the next moments better. He said to pack your things and be ready to leave in the morning. You thanked him, and walked to the door, but in those few steps you felt a "premonition"—I remember the way you still pronounced it with a European accent—and turned back and said you'd rather go then, right then. What about your personal belongings, didn't you want them? Some other clothes? No, you'd go just as you were, all you needed you had on. After a long minute of silence, he said fine, he'd accompany you to the front gate. And there on that walk of perhaps four

23

or five minutes, while he chatted, you didn't know if those were the last minutes and last steps of your life. Didn't know if it was all a macabre joke or a prelude to freedom. Didn't know, but feeling fear with anticipation, terror with exaltation, and yet at the same time trying to contain and shut down all emotion-systems, in the service of practicality and survival. Ah, I like that. Those same feelings grip me now, if you will. Practicality and survival I try to concentrate on, I need to, if I'm to tell all this. In your time the battle was against a large political evil; here I'm up against a more personal antagonist, a more ambiguous force. Yet I too feel most uncertain about my existence. My waiting for the girl is akin to your walking, I feel; my Tippy, perhaps, to your Kommandant. Will I be lucky like you and have the gate flung open, your hand shaken and freedom granted, your life given back to you the richer for your fabulous plea and experience? Or is there a much different fate in store for me?

Doctor, I never knew that a literary person could write with a gun at his head. I was naïve, wrong. I believe now that I would have written much more and perhaps better if the gun had been placed there before, in years past. An internal threat is not nearly as potent, I think, as a real gun. Look, it's sitting over there, across my study some eight feet away, a nice little .38 pistol set on my stand-up desk, curled peacefully like a black snake, but on guard. I purchased the gun at Barber's in West Lebanon, and the gentleman in the store asked if I needed any more guns and ammunition with the fall hunting season coming up. I smiled. How could the prey know what the huntress will wish? There it sits, potent melodrama, but real. Don't they say that most murders are of a family nature, or that intimacy spurs on such bizarre impulses? I know the feeling now, sir. It's fascinating, a whole new world of concentration.

Did you ever read Conrad's *Under Western Eyes*? (You should read more novels by the way. Why don't psychiatrists read more serious literature? Or have you started to read more since I first mentioned Stendhal to you?) *Under Western Eyes* is not a very good book, to my mind, but the opening is most memorable. I mean the moment when the pleasant but ordinary student Razumov walks into his room and is suddenly confronted by the radical Haldin, who informs him that he's just killed a man. In my case, I don't quite know whether to say to you, or to myself, "I'm about to kill a woman," or else, "A woman is coming to kill me, sir." Does it matter which way it goes, in a sense? Isn't the impor-

24

tant thing the resort to violence, to melodramatic extreme, to movie-like scenario for a man like myself? It's cruel. Degrading. Unfair. Especially as I had wanted to spend this time being reflective in my fiction, calmer in my life, Chekhovian in my spirit. . . .

Now one would have thought that on one's home turf, and in the prime of life, there was safety and protection enough. Not so anymore. (On the contrary, perhaps?) Not on the streets, not in your apartment, not even in your loved one's apartment, is one secluded, anonymous, safe. A guerrilla with a deliberate mission, be it literary or political, will easily discover your hiding place and draw you out. (Naturally, the more subtle the camouflage, a seemingly innocent and lovely creature, say, the more successful the ambush.) Remember, if the girl had struck when I was forty-eight or fifty-eight, in the grip of anxiety about prospective ending, it would have made more sense. But this way? . . . Or was the whole adventure actually the right sort of challenge after all? A serious inquiry into the meaning of full prime—ample potency and desire, adventurous impulse, physiological wit and limberness? When does a man get old, and how, where? How does a writer show he's tired, ready for pasture for a while, or for good? If one can't handle a Tippy now, at my age and in my state, when then? And it goes without saying, I hope, that I don't mean only physical stamina and condition here, but rather, emotional stamina and full ego strength. What does prime mean for a man, a writer, or is the very question no more than an invitation to defeat, humor, and humiliation?

You know, I was turned inward when the girl showed up. Inward. Easy prey, yes? The literary situation, once an oasis of taste and intelligence amid the desert of commercial America, had now become a swampland, muddy, chaotic, dangerous. The old literary standards—an exciting imagination, an education of the senses or morals, a great memorable character, an examination of the affective life—all these were now tossed overboard by the new critics, and what was left for praise was verbal gimmickry, cerebral games, soft wit and easy art. The I of advertising had replaced the ego of reflection. One could go on and on here, but I won't, Doctor. Not here at the beginning. There will be enough bursts later on, I'm sure. So I had left it. I had taken along my stock of dejection and jangled nerves, my protective narcissism and vulnerable sensibility, my literary resentment and my literary dreams, and had semiretired, in Cambridge and in New Hampshire. Me, a cityboy to the bone, a life-diver from the age of thirteen or fourteen, a puncher from the first bell, back there in Brownsville—I was in the process of pulling back. Withdrawing. Stopping in my mid-thirties. It *hurt* me, the cultural situation.

I can't help citing Literature as an Accomplice to the girl in creating this predicament. (Or is the reverse true—the girl the Accomplice to Literature? Testing me against my own old literary passions?) Writing it, reading it, teaching it, believing in it had caused me more harm than I had imagined. It's like drinking pure whole milk all your life, thinking it's invigorating you, only to discover that it's filling you with cholesterol. Believing in literature made me want the richer, more complex life over the simple; teaching it encouraged my sense of risk-taking and adventurousness to the point of extremity; writing it brought out to me its full sensual appeal and possibility, so much beyond the ordinary humdrum existence of everyday life. Literature was like a drug making you *want* more, chance more, risk more, yet all the time distorting, decomposing, exaggerating reality. Opium for the Oriental businessman, Literature for the native (peasant) boy. And there was always this Julien Sorel, that Underground Man, this Lord Jim with whom to compare yourself. It's unfair. Imprudent. Dangerous. It distorts your sense of what is real and what illusory, what healthy and what perverse, what permissible and what off limits. And once these lines are obscured, for whatever high motive—literary idealism or life-courage or whatever—there's danger ahead. Somehow or other you think there'll be redemption from the print, a catharsis from the story, but all this, I'm afraid, sets the trap tighter, digs the hole deeper.

Not that there wasn't an irony too in the special schooling provided me by girls, women. I won't go into this subject at length here because it's not my focus and because I've already written a book in part devoted to it *(Each According to His Needs)*. But I do want to say that there is no single body of people to whom I am more devoted. Beginning with one's own mother, and extending then toward others' daughters and sisters, and finally back to other mothers, a man is lucky who has been loved by women. I mean any form or mixture of their love, maternal, erotic, sisterly, rehabilitative, playful, indulgent. One starts in the bed at the nightgowned breast, moves through special scents and unmatched touches to childhood games involving prenubile lips and embarrassing embraces; through fearful adolescent pettings in clubrooms, car seats and dark theaters, to trembling experiences of or-

26

gasm at beaches and summer resorts; and then to varieties of sensual behavior in seduction rooms of adulthood, where women are older, more sensual, knowing and deeper-wanting; finally back to women one's own age, who began as little girls at the breast about the same time as you. (And even, a bit later, back to young ladies, to refresh one's memory and warm one's spirit before succumbing finally, like King David.) And through it all wafts the aroma of one's furtive past, the faint unconscious memory of care and pleasure in touch and toothless sucking, the timeless heavenly patience of the first woman's love, which invests the beginning years with a fragrance supreme and unquenchable, a fragrance everywhere and then slowly invisible, a fragrance sought again blindly the rest of one's life through how many guises and disguises? (Sought again *blindly*, I repeat now! That breast—who can resist it if it returns later in life? But the problem is the new owner!) I speak, Doctor, for those like myself who received that first act of grace, and not for the unlucky number who, back there when nuance was everything, and love, future survival, have been cursed mercilessly by a neurotic fate—director. The phrase "educated by women" actually makes crude what is overwhelmingly subtle, and describes, with a term meant for rocks or texts, the evolution of what may be the grandest human feeling. . . . Doctor, as I write this, as I breathe in that fragrance and exhale memory, I know too that that same inestimable sweetness which has nourished me has, here in this case, helped prepare my devastation. . . .

Where was I?

Does it matter? All roads, paragraphs, and digressions will lead to one place, my Tippy and Gomorrah.

Doctor, I'm messy. Chaotic. Frazzled, not at the edges anymore, but at the center. Comic too, I'm sure. . . . Forgive this, as I report to you. All my controls of the past few years have been pulled loose. Of course I see now that they were no more than surface controls, and that beneath were difficult incongruities, paradoxes—seething hurt and unappeased dangerous appetite, profound sadness and muzzled lust, literary resignation and chafing literary libido. . . . So if you see me crying in these pages, see me stopping to blunt out my pain, to voice an unreasonable anger or shriek a lament, forgive me, sir, will you? It won't be pretty literature, or pretty style, but then I'm a peasant when it comes to such stuff, as you know. . . . The most surprising thing has occurred. That entity called personality, which I had taken for granted as a

27

solid, is liquid! It—I—my concept—has been dissolved! What do you make of that? . . . a man of moods and moments . . . of particles arranged in disarray, in constant movement . . . oh, it's unsettling and dismaying, perceiving that you can be pulled this way by whim, that way by chance, way down there by unknowing cunning—one's own, I mean. . . . Me, thirty-eight, a literary man, a Brooklyn toughguy, a confident, even bold, professor, and so on, in fact dissolvable, liquidy . . . a perfect subject for the next brilliant chemist who traipses along. . . .

An author whom I admire greatly, in commenting on Character, referred to Heraclitus' wisdom: a man's character is his fate. Yes, I thought then, what a fine notion! But now . . . what happens if the very essence of that character is suddenly thrown into question? If the foundation, once thought to be firmly understood and secure, wobbles, shifts, changes unexpectedly? Touched by the right catalyst, concrete begins to dissolve. . . . Isn't it a curious situation, in which we act out our roles in life—teacher, father, writer, whatever—with a dull confidence that they represent approximate embodiments of our wishes and innermost selves? Yet what a naïve and oversimple assumption! What a quicksand premise provided by the age of specialization! One serious shove from a subtle intruder and whoosh! we slip away from our self-images and roles as if we were passengers playing shuffleboard who are suddenly pitched from the deck of their ship out onto the open sea! One moment a man is a writer with a shuffleboard life—cozy routine, lovely girlfriend, novel-in-progress, and the next he is a chaotic swimmer without routine, loved one, or novel, fighting for survival! (Which serves him right too, by the way, for trying to hide within his secure titles, his comfortable ship!) No, no, I find character and fate, mine at least, as firm as mercury, shooting up and floating down depending on the tricks and whims of climate. But, if this is so, as I believe it is—at least for the modern Nervous Man—what are we to make of it all? *How can one take oneself seriously? Anchor any act to any solid interpretation? Why, one's "character" is no more than a playacting mask, a self-deceiving disguise!*

But where is the real man, you ask? Who knows? I answer. Here there and everywhere, *if he allows himself to be. . . .*

And do you know, it's bracing to see one's life as humorous not grave, one's condition as one of contingency and flow, not certainty and permanence. So what if the body must be beaten about somewhat in order for the spirit to be liberated? Hasn't *that* been man's fate since history began?

Character, hogwash!

Coherence, mythical!

The comedy of the self, yes! The fluidity of man, yes! The condition of liquid, a reality. Yes.

And you know what? I don't mind it anymore. I understand it. As a man of liquid, I applaud it! Right now, I'd even venture to say that I've come to dislike ladies and gentlemen who have remained solid!

(Easy does it, Lionel. Take it easy now. Come back, and make some sense now.)

# 2.

# Her First Visit

LIGHTS, CAMERA, ACTION.

Late March, 197-. The amber hues of late afternoon sun. A man jogging around the Harvard track, in blue sweatpants and yellow sweatshirt bearing the imprint University of Wyoming, a gift from several students when he gave a talk there a year ago. He runs now with his entire foot planted, not simply on the balls of his feet, and his arms pump slightly. It is his first week out after the long Cambridge winter, and he will go around five times, or a mile and a quarter. The dirt is still soggy, the wind is brisk, several tennis games are in session in the oblong of concrete around which the 440 track runs. He loves this time of day, especially on the backstretch where he can watch the sun hitting the aging Harvard Stadium and making bands of amber around the top. That old sandstone structure, decaying slowly, always reminds him of the ancient Roman Colosseum, and that of James's great tale, with its macabre ending. He runs on, breathing steadily, having run through his tiredness on this his third time around, his head cleared by the fresh wind coming off the river and by his own warming body heat. He will run this way three times a week now, throughout the spring, summer, and autumn, here and in the country, as regular as the seasons themselves, and the knowledge of this cheers him as much as

29

anything. A man who enjoys his solitariness, who loves it, needs it, and mocks and abhors it, he is grateful to his body for its steady performance here in his late thirties.

He runs easily, the body coordinated, no jerkiness of arms or hips, an athletic man's stride. Full-bearded, wearing gold-rimmed glasses. Running now on this clear Thursday, he feels good, extremely good. It has been a fine day of writing, and he is high with a writer's satisfaction. He has done his three or four pages, he will know tomorrow for sure how many, and the new book keeps on coming, keeps on flowing. A long, steady, slow, sure passion. Now, after the previous year, when the only thing that came was false starts, isolated scenes that never made stories, beginnings and endings of things, life was bearable again, even pleasurable. Immensely so, after the horrible twelve or fourteen months of struggling nowhere and waking, knowing he was going to go nowhere for six hours that day—so much so that all he desired now was a future of routine, that horrible and necessary prison of dull routine, to go on and on until his present sentence was finished. Writing a novel, especially at crucial points, was like carrying an eel to market, your attention was everything and even then it could slip away and be off.

He heads in now for his finish line, a dog barking in the nearby grass (winter stubble turning green). He slips on his windbreaker, and walks the two hundred yards to his car, in the Harvard parking lot. The car is an old blue Mercedes, eccentric with age, in Lionel's grand tradition of used cars, dating back to his high, rat-colored, brakeless Nash, his first. He started it up now, handling the temperamental pedals and choke with affectionate familiarity, and pulled it out from the lot, past the Business School toward the river. Like an old horse knowing its rider, the Mercedes seemed to respond to his touch with more pep and drive than when others took over. Prideful mirage? If so, just one of many.

Across, on Memorial Drive, he noted several spring crews already out, one with a female coxswain. He rolled down his window, hoping to hear her call, but she was blocked out by a crazy honking behind him, as if he had stopped for a drink on the highway. Ah, civility. He pulled forward, not caring, having done his running, his writing, and now about to close the cozy circle at Sheyna's apartment. Let the gentleman blow his brains out.

Several blocks from the house he found a parking spot, and walked back to the huge complex of apartment buildings along the river. Sheyna's building contained a charming circular courtyard, set above ground level, and whenever Solomon climbed the steps to it, he half expected to see, looming above, the Hunchback of Notre Dame. The 1930's apartment houses had the effect, for Lionel, of a Gothic church with its peculiar arches, elaborate overhangs, and secret sudden wings. Lionel preferred its furtive intricacies to the blunt boxes of functionalism found in modern housing; it was why he had helped her get in there, three years ago. In the wood-paneled elevator, he got a warm hello from Mr. Bream, the small Polish refugee who worked in the foreign bookstore near the Square. "Your picture is ready, Mr. Solomon," said Bream proudly. "Will Sheyna pick it up?"

"No, it's a surprise for her, I'll get it myself."

"Who is the boy?"

"Heifetz at age eight."

Bream raised one eyebrow and nodded. They chatted and Lionel got off at three, tapping the older man's arm a good-bye. From a concentration camp to framing pictures was a lot to take in in one's lifetime, Lionel mused; better not to take it all in, actually.

In her apartment he ran a bath, put on Mozart, undressed, and took his day's writing to look through, in the bathroom. "Last Letters" was made up of letters written to good friends from one period or another, composed at the point of saying goodbye. They were based on real letters he had written during his low point at Swerdlow's two years ago, when he had wished to leave life for good; he had gone back over those letters and had begun to shape and chisel them for fiction. Invention had come to mean not merely the investigation of the real, but breaking through rhetoric and the appeal of the fantastic to the real. Just the opposite of what he had imagined when he first started writing; the real was so far from the naturalistic. The problem was tone, detail; here and there he had to make sure the sharply personal was enlarged for general understanding. On the other hand, the last thing he wanted to do was to dilute the despair or lessen the pain with artful rhetoric. The caverns of despair, the feeling for the friends, these had to be kept intact. And while he had to be on the lookout for repetition, he discovered that the actual letters and bits of letters varied greatly with each friend; some were not even focused on his despair, but on theirs; others had more to do with gratitude than with lament. They were composed first in his head, like soliloquies, and later typed out. And they were usually precipitated by actual reminders—a photograph here, a ticket stub there, a friend's

31

handwriting, or whatever. Sitting on the chair in the large bathroom, tub filling, he read the present letter; stimulated by a sports piece on an Olympic prizefighter, he remembered another fighter, of years ago, by the name of Green.

Dear Harold:

A smart Jewish boy you were not, but a Jewish brute with a staggering left hook you were. Where are you now, alive or dead? If alive, how mangled? Can you hear anything but bells ringing with those cauliflower ears? Breathe anything but resin through that flattened nose and splayed nostrils? Count anything but one to ten after taking or delivering how many counts on the deck? Not that you were a loser, Harold, not at all. Most of the time, in fact, you were a winner by KO or TKO. (By the way, can one be relieved of punishment in life by that merciful route? Solomon, defeated by technical knockout at age thirty-seven? But who will throw in the towel for me?)

Why remember you now? Because you lived across from me on Ralph Avenue, and happened to be a bona fide contender for the middleweight crown? Because I, at age eight, could read a *New York Post* article about you, or see a boxing poster with you in your gorilla stance, and then see you on the street that evening and have you wink at me? No, those were joys pure and simple, which any lucky boy could and should have in his childhood. I remember you for a deeper reason, a more personal one. For you and your odd occupation represented the one point in America where Papa Solomon and son Lionel were united, where they enjoyed themselves together like an ordinary father and son at a baseball game or out fishing. That filial unity gave your bouts, which we attended religiously, an extra healing edge. Of course you knew Papa and respected him, and knew that he loved your fights. But did you know further that knowing you gave him native pride for the first time? and that it enabled him to be a plain old native fan? For someone like my father, Harold, that was a great deal.

Of course boxing then, in the forties and fifties, was different in every respect, from audiences to competitive quality to social meaning. Marches were not the high parodies of the sport that the recent sparring clowns have made of it. In those days there was still an exciting resonance to pugilism, and a dazzling democratic pomp (akin to racing perhaps), so that, years later, when I read William Hazlitt on the sport, he made perfect, beautiful sense. All over the city then, especially in that borough unto itself, Brooklyn, boxing flourished, in small arenas, local clubs, youthful dreams. Competition was serious, accomplishment admirable. If you wanted to climb the ladder fast to fame and fortune, then boxing was your sport; hence the excellent fighters who were Negroes or immigrants' sons. The sport of self-defense, not unbridled violence, boasted in those days of *artists* at the top, not goons: Willie Pep, Kid Gavilan, Sugar Ray Robinson, Joe Louis. The names alone stir me even now. They were thoroughbreds, not mongrels, or muggers. Pep, for example, the magnificent featherweight, might go an entire bout, some thirty to forty-five minutes of actual fighting, and hardly be touched by a real punch, so swift and Houdini-like were his reflexes in moving, ducking, feinting. To hit him was like trying to punch a swallow in flight. A violent sport? Not compared to football or street fighting. Furthermore, the arena itself was a kind of town meetinghouse where immigrant laborers and small merchants mingled with flashy nouveau riche and high society; Packards and pinky diamonds and Havana cigars alongside greenhorn fedoras and grease-faced mechanics and candy-store owners in windbreakers, or like Papa, in double-breasted suits. Boxing dramatized democracy through the spectators as much as the boxers.

We attended most of your fights, Harold, from neighborhood Eastern Parkway Arena to St. Nicholas Arena to the big one, Madison Square Garden. (To a young boy growing up in Brooklyn, the Garden in Manhattan was like the Garden of Versailles, the Eighth (Avenue) Wonder.) Your bouts were the only sporting events that Dad and I ever went to regularly, though every three years or so he dragged me to Ebbets Field to see not the Dodgers but a European soccer match! On a boxing evening, he meticulously prepared us for the event, him with fresh shave and blue serge suit and tie and white shirt, me in my one sport jacket, and new slacks. Next came that ritual half-hour walk through Brownsville to the Arena, up Ralph Avenue, right at East New York for three blocks, then uphill two streets to Eastern Parkway. Our Brooklyn Champs Elysées was shaded by huge elms and oaks, with citizens strolling or lounging on the wooden benches, reading newspapers and chatting in three or four languages, and the breeze blowing through the leaves; oh, it was magical walking along there, hand in hand, heading for the fights! (Secretly hoping that I'd run into a friend along the way, to name my destination *casually*.) At the Arena, the noise was a din, the cigar smoke thick, the world mostly male (with several stunning front-row exceptions), and as palpable as a movie set. Fact and fantasy mingling. Dad always knew at least a half-dozen persons, so the strangeness was mixed with neighborhood coziness. We sat some fifteen rows away from the ring, with the cone of light focusing down on the rectangle of white canvas roped by thick hemp: that square gathering everyone's attention, and also their hopes and dreams for the next two hours, like a human heart removed, set out there on an operating table and beating beneath the surgeon's light, arrestingly alive.

Right there, for perhaps the only moments in his adulthood, Papa was human and relaxed, his rigid prejudices and biases softened, his predetermined formulas for censuring everything American dissolved. Elitist and Communist in his life, there at Eastern Parkway he was fan, all fan, caught up in the sport, the excitement, the unpredictability; and spurred on by the boy-pugilist he knew, the main attraction. I exulted in watching him root and cheer as much as I enjoyed seeing the fights themselves. Those moments when he would cup his hand and yell out encouragement, or brandish his fist to urge a preliminary fighter on! Calculating, programmatic, ideological in life, there at the fights he was warm, spontaneous, passionate; with boxing as therapy, he was a temporarily changed man, a new father.

After the warmups you'd come down that aisle, Harold, in the seedy bathrobe belying your talent (not your wealth), weaving from side to side like a human ape; and when Dad would catch your eye or touch your arm and you winked or gave a big smile, and he'd say something encouraging in Yiddish and call you "Heshy," I'd almost cry with joy and pride! I was seeing him easy and *recognized,* so different from his everyday life, where he was displaced, anonymous, frustrated. Into white fish and pink belly lox instead of White Russia and the Red Army . . . Do you remember the Morris Rief fight, Harold? That fine Jewish boxer with the quick hands and smart footwork? I recall how he stung you those first few rounds with sharp left jabs and short hooks, making you look clumsy, slow. But you were deceptive, with that thick upper torso and short but powerful arms that could spring out so rapidly. Around the fourth, however, you began to make him wince aloud in the infighting, with shots to the ribs, kidneys. (The painful sounds of wincing and gasping beyond the realm of the television world.) The fifth opened quietly enough, with his jabbing as you came in, circling and clinching, when suddenly out of nowhere it seemed his head was lifted back and up, and his entire body was hoisted in the air as if by a crane, and then with a thud set down on the canvas! The swiftness of the punch was mostly invisible; the force, characteristic Green; it made the crowd gasp together for a long long second, before they knew what was happening. A left hook thrown maybe eight inches in the air, landing flush on the jaw, is a thing of beauty, *if* you can see it. In retrospect, one does, I think. Rief was lying flat out, the bowtied ref was counting loudly, you stood in the far corner, maroon gloves tapping each other, mouthpiece hanging loose while you gulped air, your Everlast shorts absurdly overlong. My father was on his feet, red-faced with excite-

ment, swinging his fist in the air, having hit Rie...
*your left!* It was a lovely moment, expanding indelib...,
my memory, a poignant snapshot in the midst of that ongoing show, and blurring past. The simian Semite had
charmed the sophisticated Communist with a democratic
hook.

And the whole march home, accompanied by acquaintances across the Parkway, was a slow glide down
from a heady height; birds, stars, trees seemed everywhere;
the world glistened with justice, chirped with beauty. Somehow, *we* had won!

You see, Harold, the man you knew from Dave's Blue
Room under the El, who occasionally pinched your cheeks
after a victory as if you were six, he was not big on relaxing, or comforting. Or on taking anything American too
easily. Like Lenin when he was thrilled by a red fox in the
woods, my father was excited by your brute work—physical
beauty and sport a wonderful therapy for overpurposeful
men. Dad never understood or *felt* America; there really
are people who, like certain organs, don't take transplanting
well. But when you were in the ring, snorting, grunting,
taking leather in the hunt for an opening, he was suddenly
at ease with nation and son, with himself. Was there any
better, or odder, medicine than your matches?

Anyway, we followed you faithfully, through the Riefs
upward to Fritzie Zivic (the dirtiest fighter then in the
game), Rocky Graziano (you split two fights, and in the
third you took a dive, suspended a year for that little incident), and finally to your big chance, in the Garden,
against the French champ, Marcel Cerdan. With the winner
getting a shot at the king, Tony Zale. I recall sitting in a
high balcony of the Garden, using Dad's binoculars, my
blood pumping wildly over the glamorous surroundings and
your performance in the first round, belting Cerdan hard in
the gut in the infighting, when he chose to mix it up with
you that way. And so, in the second, as you hammered
away at the body again and again, we were hardly prepared
for the sudden shot to the head, the series of well-placed
shots, the slow-motion fall to the canvas, and the long
count to ten as you just failed to rise in time. The easy
Frenchie mark turned out to be for real—later on, beating
Zale too—and there you were, just missing getting up by a
fraction of a second. (The difference in destinies, too frequently.) You might have weathered the storm, might have
come back, *might*—anyway, after it was over, the whole
Brownsville rooting corps were deflated by that final upper-
cut and straight right. Dad was especially upset, and
couldn't forgive you. Shook his head and uttered derisively,
*"Gesuntah ferd!"* And all the way home in the rickety IRT,
all he could do was continue to deride you, your manager,
your strategy; an hour of calumny and anger. You had

failed our tribe, our neighborhood, and him personally; disgraced him, as I did when I failed to get a gold star in elementary school. And forever after, no matter how many smaller club victories, the disappointment stayed. Did you ever know that? Probably not, for he probably loaned you a sawbuck when you came around a few weeks later, after you had blown your wad on the nags at Belmont or at gambling. Well, at least you didn't go out with a bullet in your brain, like Bummy Davis. Or did you, Harold, later on?

But now, old hero, for the rounds of fervent excitement and filial warmth that your force in the ring brought Papa and me, I remember you fondly. I like to think that if you had had a little more luck that night in the Garden, or learned to duck a bit earlier in your career, you might indeed have had your shot at the top, and maybe even convinced Papa Solomon that America wasn't too bad after all, or that it didn't corrupt young Jewish boys without rewarding them in return.

Lionel lingered with the pages as if they were his old baby teeth, unwrapped and set on the table. They charmed him. Saddened him. . . . He made a note to say something more about Harold's wife, who led a loose life, and Ely, the younger red-haired brother, who befriended young Solly for some reason, but who always lived in his brother's shadow.

Lionel, moved by this second reading, set the pages back into the manila envelope, stood up and disrobed, settled into his tub of water. He lay back, letting the warm water drip steadily, immersing himself in moisture and memory. Did he mind this servitude to routine at the tender age of thirty-eight? He smiled. You could take all the talent, stamina, luck in the work, and watch it go down the drain without regular beloved routine. Working at work you liked made your thirties the best time of your life. Otherwise you wound up writing advertisements for your work rather than doing the work itself.

Afterwards, he was about to trim his beard at the mirror when Sheyna showed up. "Hi, kid," he said, and when he went to kiss her cheek, she took his lips instead.

"Oh I have a nice tale for my boy," she beamed as if he were thirty years younger.

"All right, I'll try to imagine it," he responded, trying to nudge her out. "C'mon, now," he edged her to the door, wanting back his privacy. She laughed, and left. He removed his English Dubl-Duck scissors from their plastic holder, thinking how the girls he knew, lived with, loved, seemed to get better and better. Of course what he meant in part was difference; each one brought her own background, fragrance, childhood name and passion. His routine here seemed to be for four- or five-year marriages with his beloved girlfriends; was this one, with the saintly soul, in the fourth year? He snipped at the edges of his full beard, noticing how, in the last few years, his face had come to interest him more and more. Never having given two glances at it before, he now periodically stopped and stared at it. (Was it earning its way by now?) The eyes were a mixture of light blue and green, at times suggesting mirth and mischief, and at other times a skepticism and sternness. The forehead was high, and the cheeks full, with the exposed skin remarkably smooth for one in his late thirties. The nose was prominent, with a bumpy bridge (childhood fights); and its prominence, with the surrounding beard, seemed in place. A Frenchman's nose, say. The eyeglasses, which in grad school were hornrims, were now golden and wire, adding judiciousness. Finally there was the beard, black flecked with gray, scraggly, very full, though not drooping prophetlike. He liked to keep it reasonably short, with Charlie at LaFlamme's doing a serious trimming job every three months or so. So what do we have then? he assessed. A face indicating openness, reasonableness, prudence, but not without its measure of justice, even if this included the burden of judgment. Not a Russian revolutionary, its first appearance, if you observed closely, but that of an enlightened judge, say. One willing to temper sternness with compassion, to see individual imperfection as part of a larger evolution; a man more interested in revelation than retribution. Stroking his beard, he mused, with a certain ironic narcissism, that it was not an unworthy self-estimate or face to live with. (You see, he could be playful indeed about his self-love.) A *feeling* judge, a just man, a gentleman with a direction.

With the satisfaction of small details one grows to cultivate, he took pleasure in trimming his beard for the next half hour. He cut it rather close and aimed for evenness, though it still stuck out curly and scraggly and uneven. For a man who had once thought himself quite homely, had he come around to allowing himself to be a trifle spoiled by others, in the last five, ten years? He permitted himself this small vanity without publicizing it, or acting on it. Admissible vanity, yes? Especially considering that he remained, by native standards, average-looking at best.

In the kitchen, he sat dutifully at the table and shelled

37

peanuts, a huge bagful. Sheyna worked at the sink and counter, preparing too, and Mendelssohn serenaded. The peanuts were for chicken and peanuts Szechuan style, and the other ingredients were being laid out and prepared for hot and sour soup: Chinese mushrooms, tiger lily shoots, tree fungus (or, as she preferred to say, Cloud Ears). Sheyna worked slowly at her cutting and chopping, and he admired from afar as she ordered things for the wok. She had her own time clock, and it was slow, baseball slow. In everything—violin practice, writing her occasional short stories or articles about Israel, talking and thinking, coping with new developments—she had her own slow clock, and like a purple martin, couldn't break her routine. At times it would drive the nervous or urgent Lionel wild, her slowness next to his nervous quirkiness about small things. Everything of course came out beautifully, but it took her time, slow time. Too many people or even sudden change hammered her with an immediate headache, driving her to Tylenol and tears. Renaissance in looks, a north Italian beauty, she was Old World in feelings and ways too, Judaic at heart. She had a built-in instinct against the contemporary: airplanes or discotheques, new theories or fashions, motorcycles or flashy writers. Against speed, anywhere, anyhow. Half the time it irritated the hell out of Lionel—though it reflected his instinct too—who sought out the heathen, the contemporary, the revved-up because of their New World ways, and biological mystery. The new persons seemed a new species, just as technology developed new machines. She was Dvořák (on now), and he, admiring and knowing that harmonious music, sought out the more dissonant Stones.

While she cooked, Lionel thought how Japanese, too, his Jewish beauty was. The neck was swanlike, the figure slender and curved, the hair dark and very long, swept upward now. But it was in her style of serving Solomon that the Oriental appeared. The effect was much more complicated than he, or outsiders, imagined. For example, at times she would take his hand and bring the palm to her lips out of a need to express her love spontaneously; this might occur while they were reading, or in a public place; she barely noticed what she was doing. At first, naturally enough, the gesture and the form of attachment embarrassed Lionel, who sought to avoid it. But gradually, the master here became as much a part of the ritual, and hence emotion, as the indentured. This was because of the grace and depth with which Sheyna believed in and practiced the ritual; serving served her emotion for him, which flowed from and through it. To put it simply, her love was religious. Again, at the beginning, this had offended Lionel sharply, used as he was to the age of secular relations, and to native women. The lack of ego-rivalry, or the channeling of ego into a conduit of devotion, was something he didn't quite understand; an engineering of emotion that he found hard to accept. It was only gradually, and through her natural persistence despite his criticism and rejection, that he began to sense how she loved. Began to accept the cultural difference. Where had she been brought up after all, outside Worcester or inside Kyoto?

In his gradual realization of her foreign quality, he also came to see why music appealed to her so strongly. Inherently, he felt, Sheyna expressed herself through beauty, the higher beauty of music and literature, meaning that her deepest stirrings of soul and spirit were realized through sonatas, quartets, novels, stories. (Interestingly enough, and for Lionel finely enough, not through poetry.) The humdrum trappings of dress, cosmetics, cars, money, meant little to her, which was why she remained so basically impractical. Literature and music were her media, as water is to a fish. (These genes or instincts, it should be said, had little to do with her more imperfect sides, those neurotic slashes of behavior created by upbringing, family, circumstances.) It was Solomon, with his periodic withholding of love for one or another reason, who added sadness to the situation. Yet, paradoxically, the sadness brought out her beauty all the more, only enhancing Lionel's affection. Sometimes alone, just thinking about her and the pure arc of her aspiration and passion, brought tears to his eyes. Privately, perfectly, he appreciated and loved her. Which made him wonder: was this the only way he could love another, by himself, alone, in private? (As if she were a literary character, perhaps?)

In the living room, he turned over the record on the stereo, made himself a Scotch, and for Sheyna, still in the kitchen, a dry vermouth, and reposed on the couch for an hour of reading. It felt especially civilized to get it in at this time of day, before dinner and the current news.

His story in the literature class for that week was Melville's "Bartleby the Scrivener." The characters were now like old friends, the better for not changing, not getting any more battered by life, except insofar as he perceived in them something new. Now, once again, Lionel was thrust back into that lean tale and mysterious figure, and was enthralled. And the famous five words, signifying everything, came back to haunt him: "I would prefer not to." Five words worth five thousand pictures. This gentle scrivener, this powerful dissenter, this colossal cripple, who surfaces briefly in the world, to reveal his odd exquisite plumage, only to end up huddled against a wall in the Tombs, knees drawn up and on his side, dead. At this "wasted Bartleby," Lionel felt his heart pound and his eyes well up. He tried to stop the tears, but couldn't. He stood up and walked around the living room seeing the nice rugs, the lamps, the bookcases, the river below. But his heart stayed with the forlorn Bartleby. No other story affected Lionel this way; it was Chekhov darkened by an unmitigated pessimism, a protagonist whose No, and style of acting it out, made all the later so-called existential heroes—Sartre, Camus, Hemingway—look like flies on flypaper. Revolt and independence at any cost, darkest pessimism and a will to die on the other hand, all real, really felt, and effected in thirty-four pages! (Lionel, with his four-hundred-page monsters, marveled!) He searched the bookcase, thinking now of that darker Melville of a hundred years ago who, like Bartleby, was dropped into a thirty-year pit of obscurity and indifference by the critics and readers of America. An exile in his native land. (While old friend, cool Nat Hawthorne, stayed aloof, buoyed by praise.) He found the Arvin biography of Melville now, and stared at the photograph of the novelist. With the high forehead and straight gloomy stare and rectangular beard, he reminded Lionel of his own grandfather, Zeyde Moishe.

Thirty years. Why, Lionel had another twenty-eight more years to go. He felt a chill and dropped down on the sofa. He drank. (Yes, he was affected that strongly, he took it to heart personally, he believed that one man's history was often repeated in another's, especially with artists; and no comparison shamed him anymore. With his growing isolation had come a somber liberation.)

When human beings wrote that way, Lionel thought, couldn't the dead be resurrected for an hour of literary talk, and life-counsel? Need death be so perfectly and foolishly democratic in its sentencing? Couldn't Herman return now, for a chat?

At the high window, Solomon saw the Charles wend its way, like some blue-black winding sheet, and he wondered momentarily about his own sentencing . . . when and what that would be like?

"It's for you," called out Sheyna from the step-up kitchen, looking spiffy in her blue Israeli apron. "Are the students

40

calling you now here, at your 'girlfriend's' apartment?" She smiled, amused. Closing the door considerately, she returned to dinner preparation.

He appreciated the privacy. Lionel picked up the telephone on the wooden desk, eyeing Sheyna's square plastic box of photographs of them together in New Hampshire.

"Yes?" he asked formally, and heard the extension click off.

"Mr. Solomon, this is Tippy Matthews. You probably don't remember me, I'm sure, but I wrote you a fan letter after *Rosen at Fifty* and you sent me a postcard, thanking me. You also said if I was ever in town, to have a drink with you. Mr. Solomon, I'm in town now."

His stomach fluttered, and he stared at the receiver as if it were a snake just entered the living room. Postcard; yes, he did answer that way. He'd have remembered that name, that letter, wouldn't he? Or would he? He needed time to check his envelopes and drawers. Hundreds of them that would fill a coffin easily.

"Where did you get this number, miss?"

"Matthews. We have a mutual friend on the Coast, and when I told him your number was unlisted, he suggested this one."

The voice was cool, Sherlock Solomon detected—his daughter sometimes referred to him that way, with medium derision—arched here and there by the trace of boarding school.

"Which mutual friend?"

"Stan Arnow."

That professor of history at Santa Cruz? Were Solomon's affairs now known publicly across the continent? Should he change continents then?

"Well, what is it you want to see me about?" The familiarity of the Chinese aroma wafting his way settled his fears, and reminded him of what a child he was.

"Mr. Solomon, your books speak to me in a special way, as I wrote to you. Now I want to meet you and speak to you in *my* special way. I want to make you happy, exhilarated, the way I get after *reading you*. Mr. Solomon, I want to wrap my legs around you and feel you locked inside me. I want to put your penis in my mouth and *just give you pleasure*. Mr. Solomon, I want you to do whatever you want, or fantasize doing, to me."

She paused, giving his heart time to feel the words and pound accordingly. *Reluctantly, sir, stomach pounding from*

*the words, Mr. Solomon put the receiver back onto the hook.
Fact. You see, Doctor, he was not a thoroughly stupid man;
when his heart beat very fast, he handled it with prudence, or
tried to.*

He stared out at that winding river, breathed deeply and
poured himself more Scotch.

The snake returned however.

She rang again.

"It's for me," he called out to the kitchen.

He might have taken it off the hook, yes. But she in turn
could have showed up at the door, right? Also, he was afraid
by now, shaking even. And further, he was always on the
lookout for creeping conventionalism. . . . Writers, like ex-
plorers, could die that way he knew.

So he lifted it.

"Please forgive me for putting it that way, Mr. Solomon,"
she said immediately. "I don't usually come on like that, and
I knew you wouldn't like it. Or take it too easily. But it's all
true, it's all honest. Like Pamela, in *Self-Portrait*. I've been
thinking this way ever since I began to read your books. How
to repay you for what you've given me, I mean. And now
I've flown here from Albuquerque, to tell you."

His head dizzied. Too many things going on at once. From
reading his books, to talk this way? From following those
lonely tortured intellectuals, she wanted to stick his prick
places? He'd better reread them himself.

It wasn't fair, he thought. Nothing ever came in the right
package. In fiction she'd be terrific! But here, in life? Repay
him all right. A nut, a neurotic. A dangerous reader!

Reaching him here in his sanctuary, in Sheyna's living
room, while she cooked no less.

"You're not talking," she took up quietly, "but I know
what you're thinking."

He waited still, heady, but also with a sliver of aesthetic
calm breaking through, he perceived that she had spoken a
very contemporary paragraph. Graffiti for a new Norton anthology perhaps?

"Mr. Solomon, I want you to know that I'm not *crude*.
Weak sometimes, but not crude. I generally keep my urges to
myself, like everyone. Like Miss Grunbaum in *Rosen at
Fifty*. And I'm not looney either, sir. My shrink will vouch
for that. It's just that I'd like very much to see you, and make
you happy. Tonight. I can, too, if you'll give me the chance.
It's . . . it's difficult over the telephone to express myself
well."

"You're not doing badly, Miss Tippy," he replied, trying to remember Miss Grunbaum now. But who could keep track of one's characters, or after a while separate them from the real-life models. Did it matter?

That letter from a shrink was not a bad idea, actually. Or from his own shrink. He needed time! "Who are you? Where did you go to college? Grow up?"

To his humorous defensive queries, she replied slowly and clearly. "Twenty-four. Two years at Bennington, then I finished up at Stanford. Made an M.A. in anthropology at Yale, too. And I grew up everywhere—Arizona, Connecticut, San Francisco, New York."

Her lucidity and ease mocked his own ambivalence. *But he knew it was* meshugah, *and he imagined you, sir, his whitehaired Ariel—whispering, "Dangerous."*

She had waited before speaking, letting him have his thoughts, the timing just right again.

"Mr. Solomon, I'm good. Like you, only in *my* thing. Oh, yes, one other point. It's easy to *do* me well. It really is. You don't have to worry about that at all. I mean I get satisfaction very fast and *keep* getting it. I mean . . . not just in a physical way but . . . on a subtle level, if you see what I mean. I do so want to please you, *tonight."*

"I'm good" stayed in his craw, and "do" induced perspiration along the neck. He sought relief in Sheyna's beautiful violin on the shelf, taken out for practice later, and in the shelves of her books.

"Please come. I so want you to. I'll be at the Chez Dreyfus. At nine-thirty."

*"I would prefer not to," he wanted to say.*

"You must be crazy," he did say.

But it was too late, she had already hung up.

He stood there with the telephone in hand, the dial tone murmuring, the perspiration crawling. He set the phone down for the second time, feeling as if some place like Monrovia or Dallas were beckoning. Would he ever be able to explain this new tropical climate to anyone, except doctors? To readers, for example? But when he had tried in small part, they had lacerated and mocked him!

He sat back on the love seat, thinking how, at thirty-eight, he still found it impossible to resist confusion, chaos, childish whims. Something new, an evening of adventure, when would it stop? In the grave, in an iron lung?

He looked at Melville, in his hands, who stared back somberly. "A man who had lived among the cannibals," went his reputation; and Solomon's? "A man who lived among the comforts?" Or, as one kindly reviewer put it, "A man who would like to live among the savages perhaps?" *So is that what I need, Herman, some cannibals?* If one came to Pittsfield and said, "Hi Herman, remember me, from *Typee?*" Would you invite her inside for a vermouth? Put her up for a few nights in the barn loft?

Dear Sheyna was saying, "Would you like me to refill it? It'll be another ten minutes or so before dinner."

And while she did, her small breasts accentuated in profile, she asked, "A student?"

"Uh . . . that Kuper girl. Wanted to know if I'd give a talk on the future of the novel. I was polite, as you advised."

"Why the second call?"

"Cut off. The place is getting like New York." He smiled confusedly at the trival lie, while his heart drummed with a guilty beat.

She brought his drink and leaned forward, kissing his scalp tenderly. "Poor Lev," using one of her Hebrew names of endearment, "always forced to perform!" Pushing his nose into her breasts, she uttered, "Mmmmm, my sweet."

Usually he didn't take the display of warmth too easily, but now he did. Balm for betrayal. Where else was he going to get this, all this? From Tippy with her dirty mouth? No. No! His heart, beleaguered, suddenly flowed with gratitude for his Sheyna, who had brought him companionship, comfort, order, warm intimacy. Three years plus of order without hysteria, politics, bitchiness, shenanigans. (He'd surprise her tomorrow with half a dozen yellow roses.)

And now Tippy, this Tippy from Albuquerque (?), wants to put his member in her mouth. To reward him. He put aside Melville, who had only whales and cannibals to contend with, not Tippy and paperback celebrityhood. Near forty, and the surprises continued to come in. Or traps, lures. What was he here in middle age, a responsible adult or a helpless cub?

Dinner was first class. During their three and a half years, Sheyna had become a real cook. Her only problem was serving too much, from zeal and heritage. First the soup, beautiful to look at, taste; then the chicken and peanuts, hot, pungent, heavenly; it was the real thing. The wine was a white muscadet. (He had forgotten to buy beer.) Last girlfriend, Elizabeth, from an upper-crust Boston family, had educated him to drinking wine, though he never knew the

44

names or became a connoisseur. Still, he admired the connoisseurs, and connoisseurs of all sorts.

At the round oak table, Sheyna shone radiant in the candlelight, her small-featured face a warm brown, creased by a lovely smile. Her full brown hair was coiled high on her head, revealing more fully the animate brown eyes and the extraordinary dark lashes, butterfly wings. The lips were delicate and mobile, showing her fine even teeth. A soft, olive-brown beauty. In her low, limpid voice, she told Lionel about the day at the Rehabilitation Center while he poured more wine. The Braille class had found its true saint in her, and she in turn found there a receptacle for her deep and fine feelings for helping others. She was one of those persons who feel best when warming other lives first, a result of old-fashioned upbringing, certain genes, and a dedicated idealism. It was little wonder perhaps that George Eliot was her favorite writer, since Sheyna was an updated version of that author's heroines. (Was he, Solomon, her Casaubon?) Though, it should be added, saints these days, male or female, were as noted for their neurotic symptoms as were devils. But didn't this make them more human? their selflessness more real, even charming?

"Oh, that little story I have for you!" she went on, in that limpid voice, sharing with him her tales of the newly blinded. "Her name is Sandy Zenith, and she's from a town on the South Shore. She's twenty-four or -five, and *very* pretty. About six months ago, she discovered that she was going blind, from her diabetes, and was crushed. She was afraid of telling her husband and put it off and off, until she couldn't help herself. Well, she was right—it upset him terrifically, it seemed. He started staying out nights and drinking, and a few weeks later told her he was leaving. Know what she did? Swallowed a handful of sleeping pills, went upstairs to her closet, and hanged herself with a strap attached to the light. Her little girl found her later when she came home from school, at lunchtime. Nice surprise? They got her to the hospital and somehow she lived. Next, her husband started coming round to see her. Slowly she got the will to live again. She's in my class now and doing fine."

"Nice fellow," Lionel observed, sipping wine.

"And she claims that she understood how he felt, all the while."

"Understanding girl. Any other cheerful tales?"

And as Sheyna began to relate another horror story from the Rehab Center, where she taught the Braille class, and

Lionel wondered how he'd ever want more in a woman, a curious thing happened. *More.* As he took a bite of chicken on his knife and fork, *a blond girl appeared in the doorway. Unsmiling, she slowly opened her denim shirt, revealing crisscrossing bandoliers of bullets over bare breasts and protruding nipples. She said, "Mr. Solomon, I've come from Albuquerque and would like to speak to you in my special way."*

"Too many hot peppers?" Sheyna was asking.

"Uh, a trifle, a trifle perhaps," Lionel noted, slipping the suspended forkful into his mouth, and remembering the photograph of the female guerrilla that he had seen in the *Times* that morning.

(A movie script? Yes, yes, I agree. I know what you mean.)

And a bit later, over tea, Sheyna was saying, "I've a new letter from Gila if you want to read it. A few nice incidents with those new Russian immigrant boys that have just come to a nearby Moshav. Boy, they are something!"

And as Lionel took the aerogram and started reading the letter from Sheyna's pal, teaching there, it happened again. *This girl was a brown-haired coed, in Radcliffe T-shirt and brief white shorts. She walked over to the coffee table and placed one sneakered foot onto it, saying with just a slight pout, "Mr. Solomon, I'm good. Like you, only in MY thing."*

"Do you want to say something?"

Lionel closed his mouth and said assertively, "I think Gila might do more real teaching in the South End than over there. Those kids need more *discipline* than teaching."

"What do you mean? The letter is all about the surprises this term." She eyed him oddly. "Remember that Pavel who used to throw things at her? Look at what she says now. . . ." She went on.

Oh, he was worried by then, obviously. That girl's voice had tracked him like an old radio voice, prompting his imagination to work overtime. And he realized with dismay how much imagery from everyday movies and television news and magazines he had absorbed, without knowing it; an imagery of melodrama and trashy banality.

"Yes, I see what you mean," he said when he saw it was his turn to talk. "If I were younger, or not a writer, I'd settle there. Life is *meaningful* there. Where is that map again? Does it have her kibbutz on it?"

With quiet joy she got out the long detailed map of Israel that she had brought back from her last trip there, and spread it out on the floor. "There, see, on the road between Tiberias and Beit Shean."

"Yeah, I have to get there soon. As soon as this book is done. Maybe this summer."

"Do you know how long you've been saying that?" she teased him.

He thought. "Four years?"

"At least," she half-smiled. Then, serious, "If I catch you going *without* me . . ."

She went on about Israel; he helped her clear the table.

Presently, he was back reading on the couch, with Paganini and Bach violin concerti soothing the room. Bach and Mozart to cool down by, Schubert and Beethoven to get moved by, later at night. He saw the perfect spot for the photograph of little Heifetz, and couldn't wait for the surprise.

The slim Sony digital, which he had bought to further Sheyna's education in the modern, flapped 9:17. Lionel looked up, annoyed. *Before him, bending over in a squaw's dress was a young woman who was fixing her stocking. Her dress was lifted slightly by her position, flashing the outline of her beautiful full bottom. Through long braided hair, the girl said, "One other thing, Mr. Solomon. It's easy to do me well. I come fast and—"*

Solomon stood up and headed for the kitchen. "Jesus," he called out over his shoulder, "can't you ever have any fruit around?"

Sheyna got up from her armchair and followed Lionel to the refrigerator, and tapped him on the arm. He followed her back in the living room where she pointed to a wooden bowl of fresh fruit on the dining table.

He grabbed a pear, mumbled an apology, and bit into it zealously. And went back to the sofa.

"Is that girl still on your mind? That Miss K.?" She tried to understand his irrational annoyance and to calm it. "Were you rude to her? Or did you just have second thoughts about preparing a speech? It would be very good for the students, you know, if you gave a little talk. Especially the grad students."

He nodded, feigning consideration of the idea.

(Our friend was in a fever, true. But while the three appearances by the young woman were strikingly melodramatic and embarrassing, he was still helpless before the visions. Although he was over and beyond his helpless polygamous days, this seemed different. He knew you didn't get such fans often. He repeated to himself that he wasn't being asked to drive a getaway car in a heist. He knew that in a short enough time he'd be on his deathbed, regretting all of possible interest that he had passed up. This last appeal, of the skull and bones (his?), of time and dust (his, too), overcame his suspiciousness, fear, guilt. Fake fear masking real impulse?)

He replied to Sheyna, "Well, maybe you're right after all. Maybe I could use a public appearance. Maybe I am unnecessarily standoffish and reclusive. Besides, maybe then I'd behave more civilly toward you." Relieved slightly of his guilt, he leaned toward her with sudden affection and kissed her cheek. "I am sorry about that outburst, pal."

She hugged him back tightly and kissed his cheek.

"So you think you can get by me, huh?"

"No sweat," she said, catching the game and with an imaginary basketball, she went into her dribbling act, protecting the ball with her body, ass out humorously, while he guarded her. A good shot, she had needed dribbling skill to complement her game, and so he worked on this aspect with her. Now, she faked one way, spun the other, and suddenly went up in the air, crying out, "Swish!"

Oh, he loved that!

Down again after her successful shot, she held out her hands for him, crying out, "A-l-l r-i-g-h-t!"

And he slapped her waiting palms, in mock approbation and real love.

Then he went into the bathroom, and rinsed his hot face with cold water. He was delighted with the play, developed over the last year; and glad for the turtleneck he happened to be wearing, casual bohemian. From his childhood days when he came home with the brine of half-sour pickles on his hands, he washed his hands vigorously with soap.

In the living room he gathered his folder and paperbacks into his briefcase, and said, "Call me tomorrow and maybe we can get a swim in before dinner, okay?"

"Sure, but didn't you want to see that chair for the country?"

"Good point. We'll do both. And maybe get in a little Shanghai ham at the Hunan, maybe with the Schindlers? Call me about three, okay?"

"Come here a minute."

He didn't want to, late already, but already guilty, he did. And she squeezed him to her hard and kissed his face, just the sort of devotion *he* used to lavish on his last girlfriend. God, how the merry world spun round in coupling irony!

48

He commented, "I fouled you, going up. Owe you a foul shot."

"My sweet!"

He winked, in exaggeration, and walked out quickly, through that room of seventeenth-century Dutch order and human dimension, and even some celestial music stayed in his head. With a Vermeer Sheyna at the center.

Outside the air was crisp, abetted by a wind up from the river, and he huddled in his sheepskin. Characteristically, he felt frantic, having planned on an evening of reading and class preparation, only to find himself outside here, in the howling night, in the midst of an unforeseen action! Once again he felt pressed by ambivalence, and by his adolescent fear of overregularity and organization in his life, especially at night. After all, what was the point of being regular by day if you couldn't be irregular at night? So his heart cried out, ah, ambivalence! ah, improvisation!—if only for a night.

A Yellow Cab, a Checker model, curved around Memorial Drive, and his voice cried out, "Hey taxi!" and he ran toward it, where it stopped up ahead. He could get his car later, or tomorrow, he was already late.

Getting in, he said to the young driver, "Chez Dreyfus, please." And sat back in the shadowy comfort, grateful for anonymity.

The cab took off and sped along the dark Charles, going the wrong way until it could turn around and come back again toward the Square. That was fine with Lionel, actually. His heart beat with slow excitement as if he were a young man out on his first blind date. There was something special and inimitable about going out this way, on your own to a secret assignation in the night; and with someone you didn't even know! Like dating a radio voice you loved. Oh, it was magical indeed to be an author and to receive, as he had, letters from strangers all over America, or to get sudden telephone calls. (Not all were like this; none, to be exact.) Here in this wide patchwork-quilt continent of chain drugstores and paperbacks, of daily bombings of information, and confused ideas and lunatic proposals, of fake priests and incoherent philosophers, from all this the people yearned for clarity, for belief and help, for salvation; and the right author became a kind of authentic priest, a mass shaman, a public (though private) shrink. Was such counsel all that the girl wanted from him?

The old Checker now had turned and was headed back the

49

right way along the Charles, clean and swimmable thirty years ago but now scummish and polluted.

The best thing about the job at the university was the way it offered excuses for going out suddenly—student papers, faculty meetings, talk invitations—if you needed a night out, away from the coop. It helped to balance the atmosphere of petty politics and epicene gentility that too often dominated the academy, once you left the classroom. Here school was for real, for learning, with several good or superb students each year. (This year it was the young Faulkner from Brookings, South Dakota, the son of a womanizing Methodist minister father; and a rangy Jewish girl from Allentown, Pennsylvania, with a meticulous prose style and wild personal life.) It always surprised him to see how naïve he was and continued to be about student lives; how they swarmed with experience on the one hand, and how it was all taken so innocently and casually, all in a day's work, on the other; they could murder and not take a deep breath.

He relaxed with the river charms—the pale yellow beams from the darting cars, the little red-brick Harvard buildings, the childlike Coca-Cola neon in the distance reflecting off the Charles, and the faraway glimmers from the new Boston skyscrapers—all this transported him back to childhood, and various games.

Curious, as the flesh moved in one direction, toward dissolution, the mind moved in the other, toward beginnings. The pleasures from remembered childhood in Brooklyn, with summers by the ocean or in the Catskills, were enormous. Partly, he knew, because he was able, through time and loss and disposition, to transform even the most hated hours—like those spent in Papa's appetizing store—into poignant moments. He remembered Dr. Lirič's half-amused definition of an artist: "One-third God, one-third man, one-third child. Or three-thirds narcissist." Oh, he was only about one-third off, figured Lionel, with that middle third.

"Excuse me, sir," intruded the young blond-haired driver, glancing back at the light by Boylston Street (Lars Andersen Bridge), "aren't you Lionel Solomon?"

Flattered immediately, but quickly prudent (or terrified?), the narcissist hesitated before saying, "Yes. What of it?"

"I've read *Posthumous Thrills* and *Journey to Manhattan*, sir, and I want you to know I'm a great admirer. Also, we've just done a short story of yours in my writing class."

Lionel breathed easy. "Where's that?" Where am I being remembered now, Bridgewater State? "Which story?"

50

"At Boston University. The story was 'Broo...
We did it last week and spent a whole hour discussing ,
use of subways and delicatessens. My professor is kind of a
nut about details. I was impressed."

A warm glow bathed Lionel. Admiration was a cushion of
down, and he couldn't resist lying there momentarily when it
was offered him.

"Gosh, you look much younger in person. That beard, in a
photo of you, makes you seem . . . *older.*"

*Oww! But Jiri told me it was a beautiful picture!*

Sobered, and half smiling, he remembered the short story,
with a kind of dry pride. His past work made him feel
slightly uncomfortable; was it the permanence of it, while he
himself changed? Or was it that that story, of seeing his father again, was a tale of retribution, and prejudice; it lacked
tolerance, real judgment. And art without judgment dripped
with indulgence.

(Oh God, why does one always pay for one's words? Eat
them, as it were, as one goes on? Why?)

"Who's the professor?" wondered Lionel.

"Mr. Silverman. Know him?"

A young professor, professing to be a writer, whom Lionel
had met once or twice and didn't like much. So much for
your judgment, Lionel.

His vanity was a stallion, dragging him around at will, as
he queried, "How'd the class like it?"

The boy, German or Scotch-Irish in looks, smiled, and
spoke of their enthusiasm.

Lionel's face burned at his own vulnerability.

"Are you working on another book, sir?"

The "sir" made the dreaded question bearable. "Sort of,"
he mumbled. Solomon now saw where the old-fashioned politeness came from: the South.

The taxi was inching through the traffic at the Square,
ready to turn down Brattle, and curve up Church. Lionel's
stomach began to quaver as a double-parked car honked crazily.

"Where are you from?"

"North Carolina."

"Where?"

"I'm sure you never heard of it, a town called Henderson-
ville. It's down by the South Carolina border."

From the Carolina border and he had read *Posthumous
Thrills* and knew Solomon by sight—the power of paper-

51

backs! When we landed on Mars, would we find a Signet or Bantam stand already there?

"What's the population?"

"Oh, five thousand maybe? Maybe less."

While his stomach multiplied with butterflies, his tongue roamed with questions. "Why'd you come up here?"

The boy, christened Luke (Lockridge) but going by his nickname Lucky, started explaining about a university scholarship and Boston being a cultural center, when Lionel, seeing a policeman, imagined assassination. His. By this Tippy. He shuddered. She had a gun, which she had hidden in her purse, or boots, and would pump him full of bullets. And at that precise moment, of course, when he'd be wanting her! The motive? *No* motive. Who knew *why* they killed these days. The so-called ' motive was a lie, nowadays, a quaint, nineteenth-century Scotland Yard notion. In our splendid century and country, killing was in the air, in the implements and appliances, in books and newspapers and television tubes, in movies and Movements and million-dollar schemes. Maybe she thought he was a male chauvinist pig and had just had a fight with her boyfriend over whose turn it was to boil the eggs this morning? Or over who had had the last orgasm last night? Maybe his books figured in it somehow. (Had she thought he approved of the one killing in the five novels?) Should the author enter, in the margin, his personal disapproval and initial it when a character did something wrong or offensive? Who knew? Was any of this crazier than her talk?

And while Luke here spieled on, *his own father's bony face turned to him from the other corner of the cab, and Papa said reprovingly in Yiddish, the way he used to say in the store when Lionel was some place he wasn't supposed to be,* "Vu krichstu?"

"Uh, we're here, Mr. Solomon."

Solomon leaned closer, perspiring as he saw the red canopy, just ahead. "Can you do me a small favor, Luke? There's a girl waiting inside the restaurant and I'd like you to tell her that I couldn't make it tonight after all. Something's come up, and I won't be available for . . . for a *few months.* All right?"

Bewildered, the boy shrugged, relented. "Sure, I suppose so. What's her name?"

"Her name? Oh, she has many probably. She'll be there alone, you'll recognize her I think." (Or she you.)

Luke shook his head, and smiled. "I will? Okay. moved the keys from the ignition, and alighted from the cab.

"Can I ask you something?"

Lionel stared at him.

"Do you really think somebody can *write* under the name Luke?"

The boy was serious, but Lionel couldn't help laughing. "Would you prefer Fyodor?"

Luke got it, nodded, and went to perform his errand.

From his dark corner, Lionel congratulated himself on his prudent move.

But just as the boy entered the canopy area for the door, "Lockridge! Hey, Lucky, come back!" Maybe Lionel was right about "Luke"?

When he arrived, out of breath, Lionel said, "Forget what I just told you. Sshh, I know, I know. Look . . ." he forced the words out, "just tell me what she looks like instead. Size her up, you know?" He drew a girl's figure with his hands. "Make sure she's not carrying any firearms," he said, as a joke.

Lockridge from near the border was thoroughly puzzled.

That made two of them, as Lionel saluted him.

Lockridge smiled, showing bad teeth, and marched back.

Cool air rushed in upon warm Lionel. He closed the window, hid in the corner of the seat, wondered if all this meant he should go into therapy and not come out. Could you play football without shoulder pads or helmet? Or live today without a doctor?

A tapping at the window brought a youngish bearded face and a single earring. (In the country it would signal a chickadee.) Mesmerized, he rolled it down.

"Peace, man. Can you spare some change?"

Lionel, who usually couldn't for these jejune Jesuses, found one now.

Behind the boy, a girl with beads glowed confidently. "You must be a Sagittarius."

Lionel, an entrenched Virgo, nodded.

He wound up the window, and settled back with a cigarette.

*In the front seat a stunning black girl now turned around, wearing a driver's cap. She put out her hand and said, "That'll be five G's, Daddy."*

*Lionel blanched. "I . . . I don't have that kind of cash here . . . please . . ." And he slowly searched for his checkbook, his neck and arms weary.*

"Sorry, Mr. Solomon, we don't take any checks you know."

Lionel was surprised to see Luke settling back into his seat.

"Oh . . . sure." He gazed at his blue checkbook. "Thought I dropped it."

The boy smiled with his yellow teeth and nodded.

"If it's the right one," he shrugged, "she's a knockout."

"Really?" Then he remembered that these southern Christian gentlemen sometimes had their own Miss Semite Contest. "Short, dark, on the plump side?"

"No, no. She's not like that at all. She's—"

Lionel, embarrassed, handed the boy some bills, getting out of the cab. "Is that enough?"

"More than enough, sir. Thanks."

"You never get that much," Lionel said, beginning to walk off.

Luke called out, "Can I show you something of mine sometime? A story?"

Lionel looked at the choirboy face.

"Sorry, Mr. Solomon, that was pretty silly," and he started the motor.

"Send it to me, at the college. Sure. And maybe we can talk about it." He waved and turned, gearing himself up. Luke pulled away in the darkness.

The maitre d' nodded and smiled at Lionel, and came toward him.

So did a familiar voice. "Hey, so this is where you hang out!"

Steve Schindler, a bouncy colleague from the social sciences. "How the hell are you? Are you out of hibernation? Where've you been, New Hampshire?"

Lionel, flustered, looked around. A group of three middle-aged people were waiting to be seated. And tucked between them, seated, was a light brown-haired (or blond) young woman, wearing glasses, who sat with her hands in her lap. Her legs were crossed demurely, and boots reached her long skirt. When she caught Lionel's eye, she nodded, once.

So much for fantasy.

"Where have you been? Joyce has been calling and calling you to come over for a dinner. You and Sheyna. How is she?"

"Fine, just fine," Lionel said.

Drink in hand, the enthusiastic Schindler continued on, while the young woman, a refined librarian perhaps, observed. "I guess you've heard the news about the new layoffs and eight percent, across-the-board cutbacks. What do you think of it all?"

Lionel restrained himself, hesitated. "Can we talk about it some other time?" He liked Leon, but not just now.

"Oh, sure." Uncertain Leon. "Did you—hey, *sorry*—" He smiled broadly, with admiration for Lionel. "Didn't realize you . . . were *waiting* for someone." He looked at the strange girl with eagerness.

Pressured, Lionel walked over to the seated girl, who stood up when he reached her. It was like an old-fashioned minuet, the male asking the female to dance. She was Lionel's height, or a bit taller.

"This is Miss Matthews."

Tall and slim in a suede skirt and dark ribbed sweater beneath her open coat. She reminded Lionel of that nice blond reporter on the NBC news.

"This is Professor Schindler."

"Oh come off it, Lionel. Call me Leon, won't you?"

"I'm Tippy Matthews," the girl said, shaking his hand. "Mr. Solomon was kind enough to say he would do an interview with me."

"An interview?" Leon's face lit up. "I didn't know you gave them anymore!"

"I don't," smiled Lionel, nervous.

"For where?" Schindler continued with good-natured enthusiasm.

"*The Atlantic, Esquire,* maybe *The New Yorker.* It depends on the material I get." She paused and looked at her wristwatch. "But I am overdue on a phone call. You wouldn't have change, Leon, would you?"

Delighted, Schindler fished in his pockets, and came up with photographs, bills, and change.

She steadied his excited hand, and removed a dime. "Thank you." She glided away.

"Christ, does this happen all the time? Why didn't I become a novelist?" His long sideburns were humorously at odds with his button-down-collared shirt hanging slightly askew from his trousers. He took Lionel's arm, and urged him backward. "Come on, let's have a drink, tell me about it. Her!" He paused, asking the famous conjugal question, "Does Sheyna know?"

"What, the interview?" Casual. "Let it surprise her, if it comes out. You know what those things are like. But look, pal, you're a dear friend, but three's a crowd during interviews. I really wouldn't feel loose. Couldn't talk easy."

"Oh come on man, you don't have to worry about *me*. I'm small fry. Besides, it's going to be public anyway, isn't it?" He jerked his thumb toward the telephone booths. "That's a dish! I won't say a word, cross my Boy Scout heart!" This sweet Belgian transplant, who knew about Boy Scout hearts, and "behavior-typology models." The wrong hearts, the wrong models.

"Two Scotches please!" Leon called out.

"One cognac," the crestfallen Solomon corrected.

And there he was, on a barstool like a sitting duck, listening to Leon's queries about writing stories. The bar was darkened, the discreet lighting promising the indiscreet.

But the young lady was back presently, and they made room for her.

"Thank you," placing her leather shoulder bag down.

"Where are you from?" Schindler began, "Up from New York? Have you been in Cambridge before? Provincial isn't it?"

Tippy smiled and removed her square glasses, attending to her questioner.

"May I say something personal to you, Professor Schindler?" she said, after a moment of looking at him.

"Leon. By all means."

"Those sideburns are very very sexy."

"Really?" He ran two fingers up and down one sideburn. "And Joyce keeps telling me—I mean I've been vaguely thinking of cutting them back, too long. God, that's nice to hear! You know about men's fashions obviously!"

Lionel, furious, thoroughly confused, on the edge of leaving, felt something brush his leg. He looked down to catch a white hand running his thigh like a rabbit testing the ground. Before he could remove it, however, it was gone. An accident?

The bartender set down the drinks.

"What'll you have, Miss Matthews?" asked Leon. "Scotch? Gin?"

"Ginger ale, please."

Schindler, taken aback but delighted anyway, said, "With nothing in it?"

"Ice cubes, thank you."

Lionel couldn't help smiling to himself. The bartender shrugged and went for the drink.

"Where were we?" put in Schindler. "Oh yes, where you were from. And what've you written before this—anything on Lionel's work?"

Just then: "Mr. Schindler, Professor Leon Schindler? . . . Telephone please!" A form of a hatcheck girl.

Leon was amazed, but excited. "Who the hell can that be? God, Lionel, I have to hang around you more often—things happen! Be right back, don't start without me!" And he hurried toward the doorway.

Now, for the first time, Tippy turned toward Lionel. "Your hair is much finer in person than in those pictures" (she ran her hand through his hair) "and you look so much younger."

Lionel, not a dummy, just yet, set the hand down.

"I could use some sexy sideburns, don't you think?"

"Oh, come now," she chided him slightly.

The bartender set the drink down by Tippy. She sipped through the straw, then, with her forefinger and thumb, scooped an ice cube, and sucked upon it.

To which Lionel said, "Can't you make a more adult sound?"

"That's what Mummy used to say, the dear." She removed the ice and returned it to its fizzing glass-funnel home. "And slap my wrist." She held up the wrist, between them—for viewing, for slapping?

Nervous, Lionel resorted to, "Well you better do your interviewing before Leon gets back. It'll be a bit crowded then."

"Oh, I don't think Professor Schindler will be back after all, as he had planned. I have a hunch that at any moment now . . . he'll be forced to leave, called away suddenly."

"What?"

"Can I take a raincheck on the evening, Miss Matthews?" called out Leon Schindler, on cue. "Uh, an old friend has just flown in from out of town and I should get home." He waved.

"We'll miss you," Tippy responded, waving back, "both of us."

As he ran off, Tippy noted, "It's too bad. He's infectious."

And as they presently made their way to the dining room, and settled into a far booth, Lionel marveled at the B-movie trick that he had just witnessed, there in real life. Must humankind, or academic kind, be so bumpkinlike? (And would you believe that out of a beginning so silly and amateurish there would issue scenes of deadly seriousness?)

They sat opposite each other in the candlelit leather booth, in the long rectangle of dining room, comfortable with carpet, chandelier, and dark lacquered woods.

Lionel sipped his cognac, and the young lady handled the

menu. The tasteful elegance lent an approving air to the tryst, civilizing it, mocking Lionel's past anxiety. The girl's long hair, now more dark blond than light brown, was parted in the middle and bunched up at her shoulders in blanket thickness. The face was a mixture of the demure and the sensual. The cheekbones were prominent, the skin was pale, the eyes were smallish and green with an odd blue-violet tint to the iris. The lips were thick, the underlip too thick for perfect good looks?

"So you're a sleight-of-hand artist, how nice." Thus did "Mr. Solomon" begin, feeling his business-oats. "What was your trapdoor for Professor Schindler?"

Looking up from her glasses, which hung on the edge of her nose like a quizzical student's, she said, "Coq au vin. How is it?"

Solomon made a facial gesture of wonder, "It may be a little simple for you."

She continued, reading the menu. "Oh, it seems that Mrs. Schindler heard that her husband was in the dark bar of a restaurant in the company of a young woman with loose morals. Who knows, maybe even a working girl. And all the time she thought he was hard at work on his Colloquium paper in his office. Some women get jealous easily, don't you think?"

The words were not that interesting, though he was sad for his pal. But what struck him, as he sat there, was the growing sense of her presence, her beauty. It gave off an aroma all its own. Was it because the beauty was of the blondish sort that he was so quickly immersed in it (especially with his own Sheyna so utterly different)? No, there was more than that; the thickness of underlip, for example. (Mustn't overestimate the sexual object, he cautioned himself; mustn't underestimate natural beauty, he retorted.)

A waiter in a red jacket appeared, bowed slightly. *"Bon soir, mon professeur. Et mademoiselle."*

The girl's neck craned the slightest at that. Lionel asked, "What do you recommend tonight, Edward?"

*"La spécialité, aujourd'hui, est . . . une bouillabaisse."* Small mustache, and slim torso; Eddie Carlyle from Cedar Rapids was not bad as dandies went.

"Another cognac for me," Lionel advised. "But the lady will have something to eat." And to Tippy, "Which is it, coq au vin or bouillabaisse?"

Forefinger went to mouth, in thought. "Hamburger. Well-done, please." Closed the menu. "With some olives."

Edward's eyebrows arched perceptibly, and he glanced at Lionel momentarily.

As he moved two steps off, however, she added, poised, "May I have some celery stalks first? Plain, on a plate. Thank you." Dismissing him, she turned back to her subject, removing her glasses now.

"They speak French and charge you double for the celery."

"It's you who chose this place as I recall."

"It's you who write about such places, as *I* recall. Of course I could have taken the Parthenon or the Welles, but this seemed the stuffiest—although you didn't put it that way. And if I had said the Welles, you wouldn't have come. You would have read me as too," she rolled her shoulders in crude parody, "freakish."

Lionel took out his cigarettes and offered one to Tippy. She took out her own cigarillo instead.

He gave her a light and asked, "That mother of yours. Where is she now?"

She looked odd smoking. "Phoenix. His French is lousy too. He'd get murdered in Paris."

"And Daddy?" (Was someone asking *his* daughter the same question?)

She jerked her head slightly, like a fine horse startled momentarily, strands of wheat hair falling over her right eye. "Ever hear of Jeremy? Colonel Jeremy Matthews? Jeremy Vance Matthews?"

He stared. "What are you talking about?" Almost derisive.

She looked at him as if he were a slow pupil. "Eighteen hundred seventy-six, the battles of Rosebud and Goose Creeks. On the way to Bighorn. Remember? It was Colonel Matthews who happened to hold his own against the fiercest Sioux and Cheyenne attacks, earning their respect as well. He lost one hundred fifty-two men and his right eye at Rosebud, and saved the lives of maybe five hundred more. In my opinion, he was the greatest Indian fighter who ever lived." She used her shoulders to relent. "Well, in Sherman's opinion, one of the two greatest. He could never make up his mind between General Crook and Granddaddy. I thought Granddaddy because he was not only a superb military man, but also—oh this gets to Mummy," and her face lit up with a child's delight—"because he was a great Indian *admirer*. And he was trusted by them too. You know, Lionel, it was only because of Gran Gran that Crazy Horse came in peacefully in '76, and it was old Gran Gran who allowed him to ride in like *a man and great chief,* riding in full procession with his eight hundred warriors in paint and feathers and carrying their shields and weapons, singing war songs. It was President Grant himself who pinned on his chest the Congressional Medal of Honor."

Lionel nodded slowly, and said, "I think your celery is here."

Tippy, slightly miffed, lifted a gold locket out of her blouse, just as the waiter set down the plate of stalks.

She opened the locket to reveal a daguerreotype of a blue-coated army man, with a patch over one eye and a long beard in two strands. In the showing there was also the revelation of her unusually full breasts, which were loose and white and lovely, unfettered by a brassiere beneath the ribbed sweater.

Lionel was disconcerted. But he said, "Moshe Dayan?"

Tippy's eyes flared, and she retorted, "Colonel Matthews. Jeremy Vance Matthews. West Point, 1852, check it out. And Jeremy Matthews the third, my father, crashed in an airplane in the Sierras on assignment for *National Geographic*. I was twelve then, and six months later, Mummy took Daddy number two, Randolph." She shut the locket, and held it in her long fingers. "This is one thing the dear couldn't swindle from me."

She bit off a piece of celery, loudly.

At this point Lionel took the locket into his hand, and held it up, evaluating it. After a moment, he assessed, "Vermont thrift shop, when you were in boarding school."

Tippy took back the locket, and returned it to her swelling chest, color coming to her cheeks. "Where was your great-granddaddy then?"

Lionel put his forefinger on his chin, and he gazed at the high ceiling, trying to recall something. "I think I remember the whole story now, yes." He looked back at her, "If Colonel Matthews had had his way, there would have been no Little Bighorn, and no massacre of General Custer. Or, if he had been in charge, the soldiers would have won a great victory. But in any case, when Colonel Matthews died, they bore his body down the mighty Colorado, and warriors and soldiers stood on the banks, watching the passing of the great leader. It was the first and only time in our national history that white man and red man joined hands in common unity, and passed the peace pipe. And he was not only awarded the medal by the President, but also Sitting Bull—or was it Geronimo?—made him an honorary Navaho. And at a

60

special ceremony, this locket was passed on to Grandmummy, for Gran Gran. Along with some beads." He looked at her sideways, and said, "Too much Faulkner, undigested? Or . . . Fenimore Cooper? Eat your celery." And he handed her another stalk.

She smiled, not wildly, but warmly. "You don't believe me, do you? And you know very little about American history, don't you?" She nibbled at her vegetable. "There is nothing more difficult to believe than the truth, is there?" She stared at her green stalk, making a decision. "And I suppose you wouldn't believe it either if I told you that one June morning when Mummy was visiting her younger sister in Presbyterian Hospital in Atlanta, Randolph came into my room and . . . did things to me. I was thirteen then."

"Randolph, who's Randolph?"

"Daddy number two. The one you asked me about." She bit again into the celery, and chewed it with loud satisfaction. "Anything else you want to know about 'family history'?"

Lionel looked at her slightly puzzled. "I'll tell you when I do."

*You see, while he had the upper hand, she puzzled him right there, too, from the start. How many people, sir, puzzle you in life? Make you unsure of what you think about them? Come unpegged whenever you think you have them "pegged"? Furthermore, Lionel always read people rather well, rather easily; most people in fact are so interested in "making an impression," in "acting straightforward" and "honest," in being "there," and "themselves," that when one comes along who tells you a fabulous tale and pulls off simple tricks right in front of your eyes, and scorns your disbelief, well, if you allow it to flow, the provocation is sharp, the confusion real. Especially if certain obviously actressy gestures are added as topping to the words.*

A gesture. As the waiter approached, Lionel felt a climbing pressure tickling his leg and then thigh, just like that. But her hands were right there, above the table.

"Your hamburger, *mademoiselle,*" said Edward, who had waited a moment. "Well-done."

Lionel, gently feverish, moved back slightly as the plate was set down.

It was clear now that a stockinged foot was inching toward his crotch.

Tippy said, "I think you forgot the olives."

Did he linger a moment, in perverse delight? "Pardon me."

61

He bowed then, and face flushed, departed. Flushed from what?

Tippy spoke slowly now. "Oh I think for the money you should get better service."

*Is this what the Chinese adored for centuries, he thought? And for just a few extra seconds, sweet seconds, he understood the foot's voluptuousness.* (Yes, he allowed his thoughts full license, and buttressed them with international support where possible.)

His heat came forth in fury, of course. "Is your foot quite through by now?"

And since it didn't seem to be, since it seemed to have a veteran endurance and cool poise, he took the foot in hand and set it back down in its normal home. "Enjoy your burger," he added.

Erotic ambushes in public, accompanied by tall Indian stories. It hurt Lionel as much as excited him, the way he was vulnerable here, and used this way. By some stranger off the street no less.

She ate, with renewed enjoyment, the three-and-a-half dollar hamburger.

Where was her interview? Well, why not have one of his own, before letting this beautiful kook take the long ride home, *alone?* He loved interviews, conducting them that is. Inquisitiveness was second nature to him.

Leaning back now, he took out a cigarette and lit it. Exhaled. Remembered a question that was most dear to Master Babel (Isaac). "Tell me about the first time."

She looked up at him, the green eyes going icy.

"Go ahead, I'd like to hear about it. Your loss of virginity." The old words sounded nice, coming up from the mothballs.

"I don't have to stand for this," she replied.

"No," he said, smiling, "you don't. You can leave at any time." He paused. "So can I."

The eyes seemed to edge toward blue, and the cheeks warmed. She half-smiled, in derisive appreciation. "Sure," she finally said, shifting gears. "It was actually cute. Or should I begin farther back, with that Daddy number two and some . . . preplay?" Her upper teeth edged forward, in a kind of gleaming greed.

She was like some wonderful colt, and so he let her have her head. As she began to talk, however, he edged to the corner of the booth, away from foot sieges. "Don't worry, I'm

62

not running away," he consoled her injured look. And offered a fatherly smile, "I just want to concentrate better."

Suddenly curling her legs underneath her girlishly—to Solomon, ravishingly—she spoke of her new father, Randolph, nearing fifty, silver gray, polished; and as she spoke here, her voice curled lower, into a curious nasal tone, like the old actress Jean Arthur's? During Saturday jaunts to shopping or to riding lessons, he always happened "to cop a feel on my thirteen-year-old buttock or thigh, always half kiddingly of course." And he made a habit of barging into her room to catch her in the midst of dressing, by "perfect chance" in her nightie in the bathroom brushing her teeth. And as Tippy proceeded—Lionel leaving her on her own, no cues about narrative or point—she was all adult poise, except perhaps for her hand going to her hair every so often, or those teeth scraping the bottom lip. Just a few minor cracks in that otherwise cool inanimate mask. Of course her mother sensed what "Randy" was up to and attracted by, and let Tippy know full well that she blamed her for the problem. Always managing to get into her "undies" (Mummy's term) when he was about. "The lying cunt," observed Daughter now about Mother.

For an ambiguous moment Lionel did his own remembering, or wondering, about Rachel's new daddy? . . .

"Are you all right?" Tippy was asking, hand on his face, concerned. "You seem anxious."

"This place is always overheated," he retorted.

Restaurant or heart, he asked himself?

He drank his cold water, disliking the ice.

He remembered a phrase she had used in the discussion, like some passed pawn. "What did you mean back there, 'and other things'?"

She cast him a sidelong glance, filled with cold fury, the kind that Lionel imagined she reserved for her rough moments with tough shrinks. A splendid winter fury in redden hues because she couldn't transform it into power, hers, through sex. Not just now, anyway.

"All right," she decided, with her gift of turning the vulnerable into the powerful, " 'other things.' One day, I was about eight or nine, I'm awakened out of sleep by something tickling my bottom. I turn around and discover Daddy Randolph down there, smiling at me mischievously. An experiment he tried several more times before I swore I'd tell mother if he did it again. So he would satisfy himself with dropping his trousers and, looking at me *half* jokingly, playing with himself in front of me. That was the scene from then on." As she went through this, the voice dropped into a teenage toughness, the tone a delinquent defensiveness.

Lionel persisted slowly. "Did he force you to touch him then?"

She shook her head. "No, he just played with it, hoping I couldn't resist and would make the first move. The *drudge*. I had a better time with *True Confessions*."

"Did he ever try to sleep with you?"

She laughed, good-naturedly, at his innocence. "You're really neat. If you mean fuck me, sure, many times. What he'd do is to climb into bed with me and dry-hump me until I'd wake up and push him away. Of course then he'd pretend it was my 'fantasy,' and if I ever told mother, as I threatened, he said he'd have me thrown into one of those looney bins for wayward girls." She nodded in agreement. "I guess I was kind of stuck. We both knew that Mum would have gone along with him, charged it all up to me—her little whore." She shrugged with those wide, expressive athletic shoulders, and exhaled.

She turned now to her suede pocketbook, and rummaged. "I always keep a favorite letter of hers around, in case I should ever feel like regarding her as a real mother." She smiled and handed him an envelope. "My graduation present, Lionel."

Lionel, who loved mail, his or others, took out the sheet of paper.

Dear Tippy,

Now that you're graduating from college, I want naturally to congratulate you. But I think that I had better write to you here as a friend as well and speak frankly. Pooh, you are fooling no one with that degree. That piece of paper will do you more harm than good if it succeeds in making you believe that you are a success. Though I wish, with all my heart, that I could tell you so, *we both know* that this is not the case.

I am not very fond of criticizing you this way, but if I don't, Pooh, who will? Certainly not those ridiculous chiropractors or whatever you call them that you've allowed to dominate your life since you were thirteen. I *never* should have allowed you to transfer to that Commie prep school in New England. It seems to me that, apart from putting you into hopeless debt, they consistently bring out the worst in you—your arrogance, your obstinacy, your self-concern, your promiscuity. Remember, I've lived with you, Pooh, and seen you in everyday roles, unlike those QUACK JEW

64

DOCTORS who cater to you for forty dollars an hour. Wouldn't you be better off buying yourself some decent underwear with that money? And wearing it! (You may be allowed to go elsewhere with nothing on, dear, like into those doctor's offices, but you will not be allowed to set foot in this house again like the last time.)

It is "those" roles that will be the end of you, my dear, if you don't discard them. This latest fantasy, of graduate school in art or English, is as much rubbish as any of the others. You know damned well, Pooh, that you have neither the constitution nor patience nor sheer intelligence for those sorts of things. As for being a lawyer, which was my early hope and with which I could have helped you considerably, you know that's all finished now. You're still like the little girl in junior high who would say that she was going to be an Artist when she grew up. Ha! It was nonsense then, and nonsense now. I know you don't like to face this, dear, but if not now, when will you?

I think I know why you continue on this way, however. I'm afraid to say that all your roles in one way or another have to do with your confused and dangerous desires toward men. (Look at what you put Billy through, Pooh. Surely the Quacks have gotten you to see that for what it was?) I accept my share of responsibility here, having been forced to shift fathers on you several times. But the rest is on your shoulders, Pooh. And I am afraid that the problem is not simply your sleeping around with every creature who wears pants; God knows I'm not a puritan. It's that you carry around with you an awful lot of the bitch. (If that's what your new Movement is about, then I'm against it, young lady.) Where you got that from I honestly don't know. Maybe it's a protest against me, my own success in life, possibly. You've always been terribly unfair toward me in your emotions, obviously. But your coldness is another matter. What I wish to impress upon you now is that if you don't rid yourself very soon of this pervasive bitchiness, this unremitting selfishness, you will wind up doing all sorts of harmful and even degrading deeds. I shouldn't be surprised to see you hauled into my own courtroom one day. A nymphomaniac is one thing, I suppose that's your private business, Pooh; but a criminal or doped-up degenerate is a menace to society, something more serious. And society *will cop*e with such wrongdoing, young lady, believe me.

Again I say to you, as I've said before, the only thing that can keep your life from ending in disaster is a Solid Marriage. For goodness sake, won't any of those studs of yours put a ring on your finger? You may think this is rather rude, Pooh, but if it takes this kind of bluntness to knock some sense into you, then I'm willing to try it.

Pooh, at my stage of life you earn the right to put aside politeness for honesty if the matter is important. That is

why I have written to you in this manner. And I honestly
feel that a letter in this vein will do you more ultimate
good than any silly wristwatch or money I could give you
for a graduation present. There are times for sentimentality
and emotion, surely, but there is also a time for hard truth.
I think that time is now.

Yours,
C.C.L.
The Honorable Constance Cecelia Logan
Third District Court
Pima County, Arizona

Solomon looked up slowly. Humbled, quizzical, moved; not
knowing what to make of it all. If she made it up, the writing
was equal to the projection; was she an Artist after all?

(He also promised himself to transcribe it if possible, later
on, for future fiction reference. Even if not a word was true,
it was a cunning invention, especially "The Honorable" Cecelia Logan.)

He asked, "Did you take your mother's advice and buy
that underwear?"

At first skeptical, she then smiled. "Yes, for my M.A. If I
ever get my Ph.D., I'll start to wear it."

He smiled himself, but then, taking it literally, found himself swallowing emphatically. "Who's Billy?"

"Younger brother. C.C. did everything but take him to bed
with her. Maybe she did that too, who knows. When I saw
his swishing friends at age fourteen however, I got him on
the sly to see my old shrink. A cardinal sin. C.C. found out
and stopped that soon enough, adding that I wasn't going to
drag him down with *my* dirt. He's now nineteen and shacked
up in Greenwich Village with a fifty-year-old TV actor. Poor
kid, I think he got a shitty deal, though he seems happy
enough. Mummy never forgave me for trying to keep him
from being a fairy." She sipped her ginger ale through the
straw.

"Anyone else in the happy family?"

"Oh, there's a half sister around somewhere, I suppose. But
she barely exists, poor thing."

So where were you better off in this world, trying to leave
your immigrant father's barrel of half-sour pickles, or trying
to escape your native mummy's hard-core courtroom? Where
were the Dagwoods and Blondies to bring you up?

The girl's disturbed past, lying explosive beneath the casual
crust of the present, moved Solomon poignantly. Should he

press forward, or just leave it all be—that deep mine of anguish, raw and Christian?

"Your loss of virginity. You were saying?"

She threw her shoulders as if in rock dancing. "Can't we . . . go back to your place and . . . talk there?"

Her foot had started to journey again but this time he caught it early and set it down, like a fork.

"Do you need more ginger ale?" he asked pleasantly, smoking.

For a split second she reverted to tantrum and pierced his wrist with her fingernails. Eyes narrowed and nostrils flaring, she looked spectacular in scorn, thrilling and scaring Lionel.

She said she needed coffee, and he had it brought, waiting patiently, considering the late diners eating and talking, the glasses tinkling, the restaurant proceeding in fine civilized fashion all about them.

Her sturdy posture slipped to teenage slouch over her cup as she began. The boarding school in the Vermont hills was coed, progressive, expensive, with about a hundred and fifty kids mostly from broken homes in New York, D.C., Phoenix, Beverly Hills. The idol of the school was a young handsome English teacher, one Todd Emerson, who taught (and wrote) poetry. The girls especially jock-eyed to "get a place" in his creative writing class. (Lionel wondered whether they'd soon be teaching creative writing in nursery schools.) Tippy, a freshman contributor to the literary magazine, had no trouble making it in as a sophomore. Todd was a very serious, very literary young man who worshipped Robert Frost; when he recited from the master, he stammered badly. In private counsels with Tippy he advised her that she had a "literary gift," and must "cultivate it at a topflight college." Never once did he look at her legs (though she always wore her skimpiest dresses to those meetings, or let slip an erotic hint). Instead they talked solemnly about "poetic traditions" and "sonnet sequences" and "the examined life."

Lionel noted aloud that Mr. Emerson sounded like a good prep-school teacher.

"I think we should shave that beard one day," she said in her strange low nasal voice, then went on. "It was all so *boring* that I'm sure nothing would have happened at all if one day I hadn't seen this tall thin chick, wearing freckles and hornrims and *plaid wool pants*"—she said it the way you would say wearing a swastika—"take his arm after class and lead him away, in her possession. *In*-credible. That turned out to be wife Nellie, Nellie Rockingham Emerson, from an old

Vermont family. Oh, I *dug* that." She rubbed out her cigarillo neatly. "And then one other time, when I had to drop off this late paper at his house on campus, I knocked on the door and there she was, up close, and I *knew* I had to do *something*. I mean she had on that horrible New England uniform of tweeds and wools and kneelength socks, and she had that manner and accent which was so fucking *proper* and *square*, and to top it all off she had no tits or ass, absolutely nothing except the uniform and the name and title, *Nellie, the wife*. And that's what my Todd, my boring hero, was married to. Shit. No wonder he couldn't read Frost without stammering! Poor guy. So," she shrugged like finishing off a soda, "I did it."

"Did what?"

She shook her head and gazed queerly. *"Made it interesting*. Made it hot. That's what we're talking about."

"How?"

"How?"

"The details."

Impatience switched to derision. "I'm not sure I came for this," she repeated.

He repeated slowly, "You're free to leave, Tippy."

"The *com-plete voyeur*, aren't you?"

Lionel waited patiently, reminded of *The Compleat Angler*. (To put her through all that. To watch her pain. Hard. To accept the scorn she had kept in reserve through the years. Hard. No wonder they loved their shrinks deeply, everlastingly; the patience it took, to pull the hurt from them. It hurt him almost as much!)

The magazine-cover face tightened for a moment or two, before relaxing. And breaking out with a spring smile. "You really mean that, don't you? Throw me out, *for not talking*? That's a change! Oh God, *you are special*," she reached out and squeezed his hand, "I knew you'd be. I knew it! I like you, I really do!"

Lionel was astonished at this new flip in personality. It was a thing to see; Lionel stayed, and saw.

"Just take your time," he comforted, freeing his hand. "The seduction. How? Where? Was it all . . . planned?"

(One set of unusual drives for another? Were art and perversity perfectly matched?)

She considered matters and continued with poise. "I came for an afternoon conference, and asked him if he would look at some poetry of mine. Only I didn't feel like sitting there, cooped up, could we walk outside and talk about it? Oh, I didn't mention that I had written the stuff the night before, stealing and changing bits from Frost, and then touched it up the hour before in trig, adding math metaphors. He called them "from the metaphysical school," I remember, and asked if I knew Donne, Marvell? He looked at his watch, said he could take a half-hour walk but had to be home by four-thirty, and got up. Oh, I recall something cute. He had this red-and-black hunting jacket hanging there, and I asked him if I could wear it, I was a bit chilly. It was like this, late March or so, and up north that's still winter. He didn't go for that idea, I could see, but I put on Appeal Face, and when he didn't budge, I took it from the hook and got into it. Saying to myself. *Move over, Nellie!* Soon we were walking on a woody path at the edge of the campus. Dear Todd, he really did believe that the woods and nature were the proper place to discuss poetry. Let's see . . . I stopped by this big tree, and let him go on about a particular poem, line by line. Some variation on 'Some say the world will end in fire/Some say in ice./From what I've tasted of desire/I hold with those who favor fire.' " She laughed. "Did I get it right?" Lionel, who knew little Frost, nodded. Beaming, she went on, "So I started things." Shrug.

Solomon, on coffee now, waited. For people who are used to talking, to shooting off their city-tensions in conversations, waiting quietly had its peculiar cumulative force.

It rankled her, the small nose twisting with the mouth. No, she wasn't liking it all as much as she had anticipated.

She reshrugged, and started again, as if each physical gesture recharged her confidence. "Well, I suppose I said something profound, like about the poem really being about him, what I felt for him, and I was sorry, really sorry to subject him to it, but since he had urged us so often to be *honest* in our writing, to seek *sincerity*, that I just *had to,* and so . . ."

"So?"

"Jesus. So, he took it very seriously, said something more about the poem, the grand fucking poem, and I kissed him." She drank her coffee down, and looked up refreshed in her cheeks, as if she had been out there right now, strolling in the fresh air. "I guess I did this little guilt number then, all boo-hoo Nancy Drew, until he began to soothe me. Something like that. And when he did, I raised my poetic preppie face into his neck so that he had to kiss me or fall over. By that time, however, he was into it, so it was no problem." She played with her knife.

Solomon, dear Solomon, stayed meticulous. "What were you saying?"

She put her finger to her chin, an adolescent pose. "I think I said something about *really respecting him, besides 'liking' him.*" The face lit up. "And respecting *Mrs.* Emerson, too, she was such a *super* woman."

"And?"

"And? And then I took his hand and put it to my heart. Well, tittie. Talking about respect and how I wouldn't hurt Mrs. Emerson for the world, but how my feelings were so deep that they *just had to come out,* somehow, or I'd just be going against myself, and his own class counsel!"

Solomon disregarded the mockery. "His hand on your . . . heart."

She frowned. "He pulled it away, frightened. I put it back, determined. Only this time under my sweater. Oh yeah, I had forgotten the bra, already." The early wild smile now was flushed out, and Solomon thought that it was not so much of lust, as of greed, victory. They had their beauty, too.

Softly he pushed. "What were you *thinking?* Do you remember?"

Curiously Tippy slowed down, and gazed, beyond Lionel, to the past. "You're smart. Yes, I was thinking something. Which I haven't remembered for years and years. I was thinking, 'Now how do you like a pair of real but illegal boobs, Todd dear? Go ahead and feel and squeeze your proper brains out, and then go home to your legal ironing board! How's that?' Whew, what a trip. I was one bad preppie, I guess. Oh, I didn't say that, though. I just pressed his hand against my free boob—yeah, I was almost as big at fourteen as I am now—and rubbed around on it until he went sort of nuts and made no resistance when I switched him over to the other track. Poor Emmie, I think of all his hours in bed with no tittie to hold—anyway, the rest was *all downhill.*"

Re-creating her youth-power had animated her face wonderfully. A perverse bloom appeared, which relieved Lionel of whatever guilt he felt in pushing his questions.

"Go on, continue."

The question suddenly thrust reverie from her face, leaving a dissonant anger.

"Is this the way you get your kicks? Maybe you'd like to look on with a Polaroid while I make it with someone?"

Lionel paused, knowing he was more Lionel than Babel or Melville.

"Surely," he advised, "you've gone through all this before, with your psychiatrists?"

Those thick lips quivered slightly, and she poured more coffee. "Some of it."

"Why not all of it?"

"Is it really that important how I got my first prick?"

He leaned his head sideways, a habit, and looked at her kindly. "It seems important to you now," he said. Then played a hunch: "Or were you taking your shrink's prick too?"

The face slowly lost color, indicating direct hit. "You think you know everything, don't you!"

That lovely mask, blanched and twisted, caused Lionel remorse, for guessing right and punishing her. But he fought down his desire to return to easy cordiality, believing that questions were the best way of befriending this girl. And immersed himself for better or worse in his exacting task.

He thought of the psychiatrists, young and older, who fell prey to their power and the new calls of liberation. He recalled Dr. Lirič's word for that type, *chazers*. Pigs. (Was he a "quack Jew" after all?)

Two furrows, thin and distinct, creased the smooth forehead.

Real fear or another disguise? wondered Lionel.

"Please take me back with you," she pleaded suddenly, from nowhere. "I don't mean necessarily now, but later. Please." Her hair had grown wilder, a mess of gleaming straw; he had an impulse to bury his face in its lusciousness. "I want that, I really do. Most men are . . . so easy. So into macho play. You're interested in me. You frighten me, but I think you're kind too, I really do. So I won't mind being frightened by you, *honest*."

The words and furrows appealed to Lionel, urged him to reach for a hand, hers. Long, white and cold, unexpectedly cold. A piano hand?

"My blood's not too good," she smiled. "Not leukemia, that's been used already. Just a tiny case of anemia."

Did she have a good doctor, Solomon worried aloud? "Sahlins at 51 Brattle is a fine internist."

The girl laughed wonderfully, head thrown back, and she squeezed Lionel's hand. He saw the humor, and released himself.

Her face narrowed with determination, and she said, "You'll see, I'll be loyal to you, in the deepest way, beyond words. I'll make you hungry and I'll feed you."

The non sequiturs were noncomprehensible, yet his heart beat faster. He retorted coldly, "You were saying."

She smiled. And as she continued on, he wondered, Was she telling the truth right now, or making it up? Inventing for Lionel's sake *unbeknownst to her?* He couldn't tell. But he could tell that she was thrilling herself now, back there by that tree at fourteen, using coitus early for political purposes, power at the heart of pleasure.

"Oh yes, Toddy had just discovered boobs, mine. Let me think . . . I think I took his hand down on me, then, and slid my own hand along his crotch. By then we're on the ground, his jacket spread conveniently, and he was going at me pretty heavy. I think by the time I got his baby out he was almost crying, from pleasure and from guilt, if you can imagine, and I kept thinking of how Mrs. Ironing Board had 'deprived' my English teacher."

(Is that the way Rachel does it? Lionel wondered. Tells it?)

". . . and then he was saying he loved me, loved me and it was all over." She paused and recalled, "And all over me, too."

"And you felt what?"

High school shrug. "Not much really. Some pain, and then not much of anything. There was some blood, that was scary for a minute. But not even much of that, I had ridden horses you know."

No, the power then, and now, was what counted. A certain controlling power, and fantasy? We're all artists in our way, aren't we? concluded Lionel, not without satisfaction in the idea.

"Oh it got better, the sex I mean. He was really a pretty good lover, once we got it on in the next few months. You know, after his fear faded, and the passions came on. Boy, did it come on." The voice trailed off, and she took another cigarillo.

"What do you mean?"

She shifted positions, this time raising her foot onto the leather seat, her long skirt making a suede tent. "Well, he got so upset that he finally split from Nellie and the school and had a kind of breakdown. At one point he was very hot on running off with me, using Keats as a role-model; I split too for a couple of weeks. It was pretty heavy there for a while."

Solomon appreciated the modern adjective to describe Mr. Emerson's dilemma and the sociological lenses with which she looked back.

The waiter came by to say they were closing, it was near midnight.

Tippy's face was disturbed, exhausted. The furrows were still there, the strands of hair mobbed the lonely face chaotically; it seemed to Lionel both saddening and yet heartening. There seemed to be flickerings of character there, somewhere; would it be ruined forever by the Personality? The struggle was fierce, but real. But he was not in the healing business.

They made ready to leave, getting their coats on and Lionel paying the bill, by credit card.

Lionel felt exhausted too. It had been quite a session on his side as well.

*Yes, Doctor, he appreciated your profession all the more. To himself he momentarily envisioned the splendor of this young gazelle with underpants on (or off), loping around the apartment! But better in movies, he figured, where blackmail and assassination were most pleasant to observe. His own head was buzzing too. He had listened to two hours of motives, plot, character and disaster all tangled and detailed, and the young woman was right there before him, to be remembered and possibly reconstructed. You see, he felt a certain pride, in that he had chosen, from the alternatives, the right sort of evening with this sort of fan, and there was no doubt in his mind as to how it should and would end. The part of Lionel Gullible was not for this evening, or for this woman.*

The sudden rush of cool air beneath the canopy was refreshing as they waited for a taxi. Also, it had begun to rain and he looked upon that as a sign, a good sign.

"Here's one now," she said, clutching his arm securely.

The Yellow Cab pulled up, the driver this time an older man.

Solomon opened the door for Tippy, and as she lowered herself in, a flank of thigh flashing, he was grateful that his decision had already been made an hour ago.

He closed the door and leaned down through the open window: "Good night, Miss Matthews. Thank you for the interview, it's been pleasant."

(Ah, what a marvelous close right there. Polite, charming, shrewd, self-protective. Having your cake and then saving it to savor in memory, or fiction, perhaps. Taking no chances while you've made it out free.)

Tippy lunged closer. "You can't do this to me. Please, it's not fair!"

Solomon replied, "You'll like the Sheraton Commander. It's old-fashioned. A bit of the Old West."

73

"Are you folks going or what?"

"Throw the meter for godsakes!" she said. And to Lionel, "I have no money."

Solomon reached in his pocket, swore he'd never say another word against his paperback firm, for making it easy to take out some bills now. "Here, this should cover it." Pleased at his efficiency.

"I don't want your bribery!" the girl screamed, pounding her fists on his wrists.

He opened her delicate hand and forced a twenty and a ten in it.

"No, no, no!" She took the bills to her mouth, tore them with her teeth, and threw them outside the taxi.

And before he could bend over for them, she had grabbed his hand and held it and was covering it with kisses, and looked at him with wild passion, like a Grushenka. "Please don't leave me this way. Don't send me away, it's not *fair!* I've come all this way to see you, please!"

Her face of swollen anguish made her a frightened doe in a field, eyes large and helpless. Was this character here? And was it character to shoot her down just now, out here in the open?

Another taxi had pulled up behind Lionel's and was honking. Others were waiting, obviously.

"I wanted someone I could trust . . . someone I could talk to . . . A man who was an adult. . . ." The torment deepened, along with her physical beauty. "You should see what my old man was like, what they're *all like* . . . it gets degrading after a while not to be able to respect a man!"

Rain dropping down his forehead, unprepared for this assault of feeling, Solomon leaned there, riveted.

He was poked from behind suddenly, and a matron said, "Can't you rob your cradle inside the cab so we can get going?"

Did she look *that* young? Or he *that* old? *My* God.

Tippy picked up the cue and slowly opened the door, "Please?"

The woman mocked, low, "Please?"

Lionel, his head swimming, bent down to the wet gutter, and retrieved the crumpled, torn wet money. Straightening it out, he held the bills up to the angry woman, "For my Geritol," he proclaimed, and got into the cab.

"Are we ready now?" the driver put in.

Tippy, through tears, said, "Are *you* coming with us?"

Solomon hid in his corner. A short ride he told himself.

74

"To the Sheraton Commander." He had no idea of what to make of the little scene of soap opera.

The cab took off down Church heading for Brattle, the streets glittering with red and yellow reflections.

Every now and then Lionel glanced sideways at the girl, but, surprisingly, Tippy sat quietly, composed. Sitting on the edge of her seat in the center, she peered ahead of her, frankly. The two-way radio of the taxi was chattering on and on.

The taxi pulled up for a red light.

Tippy leaned forward and said, "Driver, forget the hotel. Take me," she paused, "to the airport."

"Airport?"

"Yes." She sat back.

Lionel said, "I thought you didn't have any money?"

Without looking at him, she answered, "I have a return ticket."

He didn't want to speak, but he asked, "Where will you go—back to Albuquerque? At this time of night?"

"You don't have to worry." Marble.

The light changed and the cab groaned forward.

The driver checked back, "To the airport, you're sure now?" and received a sure yes.

Then she said, "If I told you, you wouldn't believe me."

Lionel, wary, but curious, challenged, asked, "Where?"

"Zuñi."

Okay, she was nuts. "Oh come on, Africa at this time of night? You can do better than that."

She shot him a look of enormous disdain. "You've never heard of it, have you?"

Lionel was startled by the look, and taken aback. "What do you mean?"

She looked straight ahead of her, sitting upright sternly. "And I suppose you've never heard of one of the oldest civilizations in the hemisphere existing right here in your own country? Or heard of the battles going on right now to rob the Pueblo Indians of their thousand-year-old traditions and culture? What's the difference, you wouldn't care anyhow."

Was she mad? Out of her mind? Was it real what she was saying? That is, it sounded real, but . . . "What are you talking about?"

"You were in the West last year, weren't you?"

He nodded, surprised, dumb. "Yes, but how did you know?"

"Take Wyoming. How did you like it?"

Without thinking he spoke up, "Some of the greatest country I've ever seen! The plains were incredible. And the animals . . . the elk, moose, and even the buffalo herds running loose and—"

She shook her head, cutting him off. "You don't really care any more, Lionel, do you? You used to care, you know. You used to."

"What do you mean? I—"

"Shoshone. Arapahoe. Sioux. Did you visit any of their reservations?"

Reservations? You mean had he made any? "It wasn't like that at all," he protested. "Not that kind of trip. You see, I gave a lecture the first day, and then there was a week of culture panels and . . ."

"Culture panels? Shit. That herd you saw is a white man's herd now, Lionel. And do you know, while you were on those 'culture panels,' what they were trying to do to a people perhaps *older than your own?*" She waited.

Confused, he retorted that "Jewish history goes back several thousand—"

"Break it up, destroy it." She took hold of his hands and faced him. "Do you know how the government buys off the tribes to punish its own rebel warriors?"

Solomon, bumping along, had no idea what she was talking about. Or how she then got there. "Look," he pleaded, faintly alert to the content, "I'm *for them,* I'm against the injustice and the past atrocity and—"

"What did you do about it when you were there?" She left his hands to plead on his upper leg and thigh, and spoke slowly, "Do you remember *Journey to Manhattan*?"

Flabbergasted, his throat went dry, "Yes, but—do people still read that?"

By accident her hand seemed to be searching him out, and when she found something to hold onto there, she held on. "In jail six months ago there was an old paperback copy lying around. Do you have any idea of its youthful energy and ideals? It kept me up when things were down, down."

He shrugged desperately to concentrate on her words, to remember that ancient novel of his, to pay attention to her anger, while she somehow was gripping him in that confusing place. Feebly he said, "What energy? . . . no, don't . . . what ideals? . . . a paperback in prison, how . . . how? . . ."

By then his clothes had been invaded subtly, and his mind was distracted too sweetly as he checked the driver, wondering how much he could see through his mirror.

"Do you know what your Joshua would have done had *he* gone to Wyoming? Have you forgotten, Lionel? He would have gone out on his own, and *explored.*" She was staring ahead of her, only now and then glancing his way. "He would have turned those panels of culture into panels of *challenge, disruption, attack.*" She gazed at him, icy. "You know that, don't you?"

Did Lionel know that? Was she right? *Explore?* Head hot, and below, mounting indescribable pleasure, so much so that he barely perceived that the girl had taken a hand to her mouth and returned to him with hot saliva; barely perceived that she had gotten him to move for her, to her hand's will, underneath and around squirming like a man dipped in a vat of honey. What he did know, somewhere beneath perception, was that he was in the hands of a master, a thoroughgoing professional, and that he himself was an amateur in the field, a boy from Brooklyn again.

Nearby, her attack continued in a nasal whisper, "And Joshua's still in you, Lionel. Only you've forgotten about him, you've lost track of what he *fought for.* You need to be *reminded.* Joshua and his ideals are *deep down* inside of you, and they need to be brought out, resurrected. *Let him come,* Lionel, *let him come.*"

His rising Fahrenheit and the careening cab made him pass over the crude punning, and he wondered instead, Was Joshua in him still? Had he lost "ideals"? Would *he,* the younger Solomon, have acted differently in Laramie? And now?

What he knew was that he was being brought out now, Joshua slowly but surely, in a spurt of adolescent ease and sporting dissolution reminiscent of Joshua days, only made all the more sensual here by the public exposure and public risk. What he had forgotten for sure was the amazing power in a woman's hand, oh it was a supple limb which you knew about in car-adolescence and had forgotten about in bed-adulthood, but he was reminded now, reminded for sure, reminded once and for all.

The taxi pulled up short for a red signal, and Lionel thought he'd shoot right through the partition before she held him back.

"Sorry about that," the driver apologized, and shifted tone: "Good time for the airport, I'll tell you that."

A pause.

Tippy, licking fingers casually, leaned forward, hair cascading. She said to the driver, "Uh, Eighteen Chatham, please."

The driver did a double take, and looked to Lionel. Lionel, however, was slumped against the back, blitzed, not caring. He was no match for machines like this.

"Eighteen Chatham," she reaffirmed; and to Lionel, "Correct, isn't it?"

He nodded at his address.

The taxi now jerked forward, driver in anger, and Tippy kissed Lionel on the cheek tenderly.

She took her forefinger and put it into his mouth, wiping the sperm on his lips and tongue. She smiled widely. Her eyes glinted. Lionel, taken aback, blushed, a bit afraid. It tasted sticky a touch salty. Him? Hmm. She observed him with great interest, wiping her finger back and forth, and watching him as if he were a child. She shifted tone, "Share and share alike." Sweet and teenage. A cover he knew. But for what—these new customs?

Did he have a handkerchief?

He got it out and gave it to her, and she cleaned up like a green-eyed cat in the night, all the while explaining to him about something called the allotment system and its consequences for the Indians.

(Now obviously you can ask many questions here, and tear apart Solomon's behavior. Ask him to call himself names, label his folly—which he will do, gladly, later on. But just now, he didn't. Just now he sat back there, being cleaned up as if a striking whore in Rome had picked him up in her Fiat after a lovely pasta dinner, and given him an extra treat; or, to go back in time, as if Antony had just run into the first of many numbers by an unusual woman named Cleopatra. No one of this particular genre had crossed Lionel's way before, hence his bewildered excitement. Was he tricked into it by the crazy talk? Yes and no. Let's say that the talk didn't decrease his vulnerability, that he had just pummeled the girl with questions for two solid hours, that her own vulnerability had slowly grown apparent, and finally, that she was thrown off balance by his decision to depart from her; all these factors added to the lowering of his resistance to such childish play.)

When they pulled up on narrow Chatham, a tall black fellow stood by the hedges in front of Number 18. To Lionel, he looked menacing.

"Keep the change," Lionel told the driver.

Tippy, observing the fellow, said, "They're beautiful too, aren't they?"

"Yes. Here, let me go first."

78

"Oh no. Black people don't frighten me. They're the future of the world."

She stepped gracefully onto the dark sidewalk, followed by Lionel. As they passed the tall young man, resplendent in white fishnet sweater, Tippy smiled at him amiably, and he nodded to her while lighting a cigarette. At Lionel he simply stared—or was it glared?—the whites around the eyes swimming in the chocolate face. Were they beautiful, he wondered, his knees weak?

Walking through the path on the oval lawn in front of the huge red clapboard house, Lionel observed, "This place has been burgled twice in the last year. Do you think he's . . . casing the joint?"

She turned and threw him a look which was more scary than the crooks.

Lionel shut up and proceeded. On the porch he opened the outside door, walked inside, and just beyond a deacon's bench piled high with the landlady's newspapers from the thirties, he unlocked the door to his apartment.

Immediately he noticed a light in the apartment which he hadn't left on, in his study. With one hand he held back Tippy, and very quietly edged toward the lighted room. Then he realized that if there was a thief there, did he want to sneak up on him? He coughed, loudly!

From the study, a girl on a wooden step ladder near high bookcases called back, without looking around. "Hi! I was just looking for that Chekhov biography. Who's the author again?"

Lionel, his heart pounding still, contained his anger. Curtly: "Magarshack, David Magarshack. Here." Feeling fatigued suddenly, he walked over and found the book on a lower shelf.

The blue-jeaned girl climbed down the ladder, which reminded him of his used-bookstore days—and took the paperback from him.

"Do you know what time it is?" he said in a clipped voice.

"*Sorry, really.* We did try Paperback Booksmith and the Coop and the Lamont, and couldn't come up with anything decent. And Richard needed it badly for this week." Presently seeing Lionel's friend in the hallway, she climbed down the last two rungs of the ladder, and shifted into high cheer. "Oh hi, I'm Rachel Solomon."

Tippy came forward to meet her, taking Rachel's hand. "I'm Tippy."

A pause in the action, the two young ladies observing each

other like boxers meeting in the center of the ring. The one medium-built, dark, frizzy-haired, in Radcliffe sweatshirt and jeans; the second taller, blonder, attired in soft suedes.

Should Lionel referee? Sell reefers? Set up trust funds?

Tippy nodded toward the biography and offered casually, "Wasn't it awful the way that actress ran Chekhov's life? Imagine that beautiful writer being led by that melodramatic woman."

"You mean Olga Knipper?" Rachel said, lighting a cigarette and offering one to Tippy, who declined in favor of her cigarillo. "According to Richard, Chekhov was ill by then and needed her. Or something. Richard's in drama and very into Chekhov right now."

Lionel, nervous, put his hand to his brow and recited, "'It's been almost a year now since father died, and I still haven't gotten over it.'"

Tippy took two steps to Lionel, and removing a thread from his corduroy lapel, said, "May I?" Walking around him as if he were a maypole, she recited, "It's exactly a year ago that father died, isn't it? This very day, the fifth of May—" She pulled up in front of Lionel. "Don't you find that opening awfully sentimental?"

Lionel said, "Do you prefer Peter Pan?"

"You *are* touchy, aren't you?" she smiled.

Rachel spoke up, "Are you a student of his?"

"No."

"Good. But make sure he doesn't treat you like one. *Lecturing*, that's his thing. He's terrible if you let him get away with it." Seventy-five percent in fun? "Beneath it all, he's a moralist I think." Her cheerful smile revealed a crooked tooth, a result of a twelve-year-old roller-skating accident. She was tapping Daddy on his turtleneck chest. "Show him quickly who's boss, that's the thing."

Tippy, interested, nodded. "I'll have to remember that."

"Maybe I should just leave you two alone?" Lionel asked tartly.

"No," Rachel said, "I think I'll leave *you* two alone. I don't want to keep Richard waiting, he hates that. You two enjoy yourselves now." She smiled brightly.

(Dearest daughter, what are you up to? Lionel wonders. He immediately wants to phone Dr. Pearlman, in New York City, her old shrink, and ask, "Could you please tell me what I received for my seven grand and change?")

At the door, Rachel stopped and said, "Good night, Dad."

Solomon, who had followed her, said, "Do you remember my phone number?

"354-6762."

"Good. Try it next time."

Rachel reddened, took a key from her change pocket, and flipped it the short distance to her father. "I will. Maybe I'll even forget it." And left.

Lionel locked the door behind her and put on the latch. Tilt, guilt. Dumb remark. His heart grieved as he walked back through the long vestibule toward the study. How could you have a college-age daughter when you haven't even hit forty yourself? It was so *odd*. No Tippy, however. He took off his jacket, set the key on the desk with a mental note to return it to Rachel, and went to find his guest. Why did tiny actions lie on him so heavily? "Tippy?"

Music was coming from the living room, and Lionel walked there. Rolling Stones? (Through Rachel he had gotten to be a sophomore in his rock education.) No girl, still. "Tippy!"

Nothing.

Was she hiding after all? Nice trick, Reality!

From the bathroom, a voice.

"What'd you say?" he called out.

"Your daughter is neat, and really likes you too. How unusual. Any more kids?"

"None with my name," he said, moving to the foyer to hang up his coat. What should he do with hers? Ambushed in his own woods, he felt, leaning against the wall and waiting for the girl to emerge. What was he going to do with her? How long was she going to stay around? A bachelor and writer, he was no more than a stone upon which his habits clung like barnacles.

"How'd you get her to like you?"

*Stayed away from her for years.* "Big allowance," he replied, walking back and forth, wondering what the hell she was doing inside. "What's your fee for all this?"

"You'll be billed," she observed.

Finally the door opened, and she appeared. She wore a satisfied smile—so different from the polite civilized one she had put on for Rachel—and Lionel's teenage club jacket, reversible wool and satin; on the back was written "Iroquois, SAC," and on the front, "Solly." Snug on him, it hung loosely on her.

"Come on, get that off," he cracked, shocked at his work talisman in foreign hands. "Where'd you get it from?"

Tippy, pausing to take something from her eye, noted dumbly, "But it's satiny on the skin, and besides, I have nothing on underneath."

Indeed, the jacket just managed to shield her pubic area, Lionel saw. He saw also the extra length of her legs, and their sloping curves, hidden previously; the purple wool went well with her wheat and honey colors. No, he wouldn't stare, wouldn't tempt himself unbearably, wouldn't let her get the upper hand with all this . . . lower stuff!

And besides, why should his adolescence now be turned against him?

In the living room she said, "Really, is it so important, Solly?" She walked by him to the fireplace, where she languorously picked up a poker. Handling it tentatively in two hands, she asked pleasantly, "What did Iroquois mean? And SAC?"

She seemed serious, and Lionel responded. "It was the name of our club, when we were, oh, thirteen and fourteen." He relaxed, reflecting. "We were quite organized really, for little animals. Paid dues monthly, and rigorously, for maybe three or four years in order to buy those jackets. And if you didn't get them *reversible*, with wool *and* satin, you might as well forget it." He looked adoringly at his thirteen-year-old self, and pal cubbies. "Here, a club photo—" and he showed her a snapshot of the club on his bulletin board, in their Iroquois jackets, sent to him by a boyhood friend years later, from San Francisco. One of the nice rewards of newspaper fame, hearing from old schoolmates, and receiving trinkets and photographs without having to see the adults and be disappointed. Boyishly, he asked, "Can you pick me out?"

"Mmmm . . . skinny, weren't you? And your hair was so thick and blond!"

He was flabbergasted at her perceptiveness.

"Did you ever braid it?"

"Yeah, when we went on a war party. Anyway, SAC stood for Social and Athletic Club, although I doubt that half the kids knew that. It was like IRT or USA. There were twelve of us, mostly kids from East Flatbush and Crown Heights, with myself the 'outsider' from Brownsville. It began in public school and went through junior high, 'hanging out' together, playing ball at Lincoln Terrace or the schoolyard, and fooling around in the clubroom." She made a face and he realized she probably had never heard of that. "Ah, the clubroom . . . it was sort of like the Cherry Orchard, sacred property to our thirteen-year-old hearts. A large basement

82

room, rented for about thirty-five bucks a month, where on weekends there were the 'social gatherings'—and the place would stink to high heaven with the latest hair grease or lanolin discovery, and the light bulbs were changed to blue and red, for serious petting, and then for after school, there were free-for-alls and lights-out surprises, and maybe even some puberty rituals revolving around masturbation, as I recall. The clubroom, where the little good-natured toughies came to gouge, fight, scream, scold, play cards, even hold kangaroo courts where members were fined and kicked out—oh, Schlossy, I'll never forgive you for giving in to the masses and suspending me for a week!" He smiled, shamelessly, impassioned by his youth. "That's *who* the Iroquois were."

"I see," she said, walking a track at the edge of the rug like a child following a line. Then, raising a poker as if it were a teacher's pointer, said, "Lionel, do you know anything about the real Iroquois?"

What? He admitted, "No, not really."

"Did you then?"

"Only what we saw in a Saturday matinee at the Sutter, when they attacked a wagon train and gave us the name. Pretty vicious, weren't they?"

The smile was narrow now. "Fierce. Strong. Proud. *Not* vicious. One of the great tribes. Lionel, you do know the names of the Six Nations?

Surely he knew one, at least? "Not offhand, actually."

"Hmm . . . Mohawk, Seneca, Onondaga, Oneida, Cayuga, Tuscarora," and for each title tapping an object—lamp, table, typewriter, book, photograph, telephone. "If you were *once* an Iroquois, you ought to know a little bit about them, don't you think? They were great fighters, and great hunters, but they were also a rather sophisticated people, Lionel. Do you know how or where they lived, for example?"

He pondered. "Tepee?"

She shook her head slowly. "In apartment houses, Lionel, perhaps the first ones. Lengthy dwellings called longhouses. Lionel, they were great individualists, the Iroquois, great hunters, fighters, but they *shared* property. To them there was no such thing as *private property*. They were not possessed by *things*." She came closer, and widened the smile. "Of course they were deeply religious, like all Indians. They still have Souls." And while he stood there in a trance, she did this thing with the poker, she ran it slowly across his cheek. "Lionel, I think you would make a fine adult Iroquois, maybe even a chief. It's in you, I can see."

83

For a full moment he realized the paltriness of words next to stunning beauty. She could say and do anything, couldn't she? And yet, consciously, she was innocent, he believed.

He took the dangerous poker from her white hand, and said, "Shall I do my Iroquois war whoop for you?" He cupped his palm to his mouth, clapped it several times while emitting little yells. Along with hopping on his right foot and then his left, until he was slightly out of breath.

Tippy, however, did not smile.

She said, "Oh, you're a warrior in your novels, but here . . . in life, you're *too white*. You live too easy. Too comfortably. It's not healthy, Solly."

His heart pounded when she spoke with that sort of lunatic authority.

"Should I get a tepee? A tomahawk? And wear a headress when I teach?"

She smiled, without humor.

"You certainly have a talent," he noted, "for acting. Have you done any amateur work?"

"Oh, I act, when I have to. But mostly I speak, Mr. Solomon."

"Speak? You mean on the telephone?"

Once again, she did that circle number around him. "Yes, on the telephone. And at council meetings. In courtrooms and jails. Sometimes on college campuses. You see, I *care* for people, Mr. Solomon. *Actively* care. I have two Czech friends in California whom you ought to meet sometime. One was a writer and they crushed his two middle fingers. The other, a doctor, tried to hang himself on the central heating. And they have terribly low radiators in Prague."

The thing about the writer terrified him. Surprised by her shift in topics, he was frightened by her sudden move to his side, onto her knees. "Do you know what a death-wish is needed to hang yourself this way?" And somehow or other she took hold of his belt to show him. "You don't *care* anymore, do you?" On her bare knees, on the Mexican rug given to him by Sheyna. "You did once, Lionel, but not anymore. Why? You mustn't give up."

She stared at him with green eyes wide with curiosity, and hope.

For a moment or two Lionel wasn't sure how to take it all, or what exactly was happening. Radiators, hangings, crushed fingers, a girl on her knees looking up at him? . . . Above her he glanced at the bookshelves, and seeing *Journey to Manhattan*, recalled that novel of social conditions and life of privation leading to fierce psychic struggle. Was it any different now, the result? And recalled that later novel *Each According to His Needs*, a document of passionate radicalism involving Puerto Ricans, blacks, Jews, against the government—

"Cut out the theatrics," he said dryly, bitterly, trying to maintain control.

"I'm telling you the truth, and you know it. And that hurts. Well, I won't let it be, I won't cut it out, I won't let you grow *old*. Do you hear me?" She paused, letting it sink in. Then: "You were a Jewish boy once, and I won't let you turn into a cold unfeeling Wasp!"

Lionel flinched at the words . . . at this . . . creature, on her knees, imploring and charging him.

The creature knew it too. "You want to hit me, don't you? . . . You do, don't you?" Her gaze was that of adoring passion, and resolution. "Go ahead, do it."

The words sounded like a foreign or new language. Their strangeness was eerie, exciting.

He stood there, terrified, furious, the girl there, there.

And when he still didn't move, she on her knees took his hand from his side and dragged the back of it across her smooth cheek, as if showing a slave free territory.

She pronounced, slowly, "Stop trying to be the virtuous professor, the good father."

That provoked and freed him, and he slapped her.

Yet when she looked back up at him, the face was gleeful, radiant, stung with bliss.

He slapped her again, this time with the back of his hand.

She recovered, her cheeks rosy, and said, "Good, isn't it? It's what you wanted."

*What* you *wanted*, he protested privately, *you devil*!

Suddenly she lifted his trouser leg and, like a cobra, bit into his soft calf.

"Cheesus!" he cried out, and dove to pull her from his leg, grabbing the long hair and yanking it hard. To his amazement she held on, and jerked, and finally managed to topple him down over her. Oh, it was comical and operatic all right except for Solomon, who was still getting hurt! At last he pried her loose, got one arm in a hammerlock and spun her forward over his leg and, out of availability, not habit, began to spank her bottom. (It turned out that she had fibbed, and wore a pair of bikini underpants.) He hit her hard, furious at his stinging leg and her unfair provocation.

She resisted, but not all that ferociously, and also moaned.

And, more surprisingly, after several minutes that might have been hours, and more gasps and groans, she turned to him through fallen hair and said, distinctly, breathlessly, "Will you put this in your next novel?"

Lionel's hand, in midair, was stilled.

Her eyes narrowed with leisure and the black pupils grew vertical. The skin everywhere was wonderfully smooth and gave off the incredible scent of youth. The lips too had thickened in grievance—or in pleasure? As he had loosened his grip, so now she clung to his leg, rubbing her soft cheek against that assaulted calf; and he had to fight with himself to hold on, to remain somehow civilized or sane with this strong crazy primitive. And he would have, too, he believed later, until she said, knowing her man well by now, said it with the same (nasal) slowness and power that Bartleby earlier had said his five ultimate words, said, slowly to his face as if she were spitting, "I won't be taken."

Whereupon Solomon proceeded to take her.

And yet it was true that while it was happening, while he fell prey to her cunning provocation, with the wool of Iroquois beneath them, it was true that he felt stronger and bolder in his intercourse than he had in a long while. Those four words were repeated, "I won't be taken," and his orgasm turned wild and freewheeling and fuller, and the experience which has become more or less routine and domesticated, had opened out to the new and exhilarating and the frightening. Like swooping down suddenly in a childhood rocket-ride at the carnival, with your throat dropping to your stomach, and your stomach blown away completely, and you are flying between terror and glee and gasping for oxygen. And when it was over and he lay there, taken again, his chest pouring sweat and his heart thundering, and she faced him sated and green-eyed, he was even more frightened, surprising as that may be. Cars whispered in the distance.

She spoke low, up close to him: "The body is true, isn't it? Words lie, spoken words, but not the body. In the middle of this cruddy society, with its killing and cheating and lying, *it's* still religious. And all the shit words they lay on you everyday and you're forced to pretend, I understand. But the body isn't a lie. Not yet anyway. One day it will be, they'll get to it too, with chemicals, more ads. Lionel, you must learn to trust it, to give in to it, everything else is shit, mechanical shit. You will, won't you?" She cupped his neck determinedly.

Lionel, exhausted, satisfied, and not wanting to rev up the

lunatic again, nodded in agreement. Think of a cat being stroked; this is Tippy purring, that's all.

"Will you *trust me*? Let me make you religious again?"

So he nodded, not bothering about words, but savoring the wonderful wide shoulders, the smooth skin, the body aroma (vanilla? musk? orgasm?). And if, he reflected dreamily, in order to have that scent and that skin up close for an evening or a few hours, he had to don a *yarmulke* and *tefillin* or a headdress and feathers, or put his face up there on a public totem of sorts, why it would be a fair enough bargain. He nodded.

They slept.

But later on, maybe at 1:30 A.M., Lionel found himself famished and did the unlikely thing of cooking in the kitchen. He was panbroiling a steak when Tippy entered, barefoot and Iroquois-clad, and sat down behind him, on the long oak table. Surprised, he nodded welcome.

"What's it like in Brooklyn now?" she asked, swinging her legs as if she were sitting on a wall. "Do you go back a lot?"

"No, not too often."

"No more trips to Coney Island either?"

He glanced at her. "What do you know about Coney Island?"

Impatient: "I've read *Journey to Manhattan*, have you forgotten?"

"I hope you like pepper and herbs," he said, sprinkling liberally. "Actually, it wasn't that glamorous. That's the difference between youthful fiction and actual reality." He reflected. "See this cut?" He turned his face upward, to show her a mark just above the eye.

"Where? . . . Oh, that nick?"

Lionel, pricked slightly, explained. "It used to be bigger. A long-term token from three Syndicate Midgets . . . six-feet-high midgets at age fourteen . . . who caught up with me at . . . Beach Fifty-two? They held me against the rock reef and took thirteen dollars and change, my grand earnings for twelve hours of trudging the sands selling popsicles and fudgicles and chocolate sundaes. My Saturday Good Humor. Having smart alecks trip you, or children run up and grab your trousers . . . in either case, hitting the sand at least once or twice. Oh, it wasn't much of a beating . . . enough, however, to make Nina cry out when she saw me."

"Nina who?"

"Nina . . . Marchetti? Marchelli? A good Jewish name." Going back to that memorable incident over twenty years back in time, a card flipped in his memory. "She wouldn't let me move until she put iodine on the cut, and a bandage, and for my bloody nose, a wet compress." Lionel warmed, shaking the pain and memory. "And she held me in her arms, as I recall, calling me her little bambino. Fellini in Brooklyn, huh?" He attended to the steak now, cutting to test it. "She was one of twelve or thirteen brothers and sisters. The parents came from Syracuse—the one in Sicily." Glancing back she saw that she was making a little home right there on the table, chin on knees, bare feet up on oak; *a little girl's tepee.*

He removed the sizzling steak from the pan, and went for a serving dish.

"Use the cutting board," she said, and inquired, "Did you make love to her?"

A cutting board? Okay, he took it. "Me to her? Do you know what eight Italian brothers would do to a sheeny seducer of their nineteen-year-old sister?"

She laughed. "Sheeny? What's that? How old were you?"

He sliced a tomato in long thin slices, and smiled, in reverie. A reverie so gossamer-beguiling that he didn't realize how their positions had reversed. "Not very long after my Bar Mitzvah, I think." He laughed. "She couldn't stop giggling when she noticed in her hands a circumcised penis. And with those people walking over us, I very nearly shit in my pants."

He brought the steak to the table.

Moving over to make room, but staying on top of the table, she said, "People? How do you mean?"

"Under the boardwalk. That's where it happened. Ever been there?" She shook her head, enjoying it. "You're missing something."

He set the cutting board down and got two steak knives and forks. He went for plates, but she waved him to sit down. (Where was the wet sand?)

Why, were they cavemen? But, following her tendency for simplicity—was it that?—he obliged. For an evening, why not? And sat down himself in his curved padded armchair.

Tippy, at home on oak, stretched lengthwise, on the long table, and cut pieces of steak. She offered the first bite to Lionel, who reached forward for it, playing the children's game. By the light of the overhead bamboo hanging lamp, she looked like some cozy blond crocodile, resting on the banks before slipping into the water for prey.

It all seemed so unreal and breathtaking, like scuba diving

the first time and discovering that whole new world of slow-motion blue. Young women didn't stay overnight here. None had eaten with him at this private hour, and in this unusual fashion. And he himself was usually fast asleep by now, not up, hungry, catering, eating.

When she took her first bite, she made a child's frown. "What did you *put* in it?"

Solomon, chewing with great appetite, said, "On it. Horseradish. My father's style. Or, as he would say, *chrein.*"

Tippy, face beet-red, repeated the word. "Krane?"

"*Ch.* Harsh, guttural, a Hebrew CHrein."

"Ch, ch, *chrein!*" She did her best and with watery eyes, said, "Does it always make you tear this way?"

"Just the first few years."

A point. Sitting in the kitchen there, in the early morning, eating steak by this strange girl, watching her range of expressions from little girl's giggling to frowning to food faces to mature understanding, and more, *more,* Lionel felt the undeniable power of newness. And exotic strangeness, not simply the presence of yet another girl. The attraction of a strange species in life, who happened by chance to have the same chromosomes and use the same language for communication, was enormous. It brought out new sides to one as well. Remember too that in the midst of taxing his intelligence, tolerance, and imagination to the breaking point every day in fiction, a writer grew extremely guarded, frightened, narrow in life. At least it worked that way for Lionel, this seesaw of the emotions. A balancing that conspired, with his approval, to keep him innocent, profoundly and embarassingly *innocent,* beneath the sophisticated skin. And although this innocence mocked and mirthed him continually, it also enabled him to trust anew, see anew, start over perennially with fresh faith. To stare with a child's eye at the adult world. Did anyone but an artist know about this task, this pleasure, this sacrifice?

Suddenly a harmonica, a guitar, and raucous singing began, and Lionel started.

"Easy, ssshh," she put her finger to his lips. "Easy. It's my traveling companion, I always have it with me." She beamed with pride at a small black tape recorder, no bigger than an address book, lying on the far chair. "Just some early Dylan, sweetheart. Nothing dangerous. Makes me feel at home, I'm on the go so much. Does it disturb you? Tell me more about your 'ch-rane' father."

He restrained his nervousness, told her to turn it down

(which she did), and tasted the father's strong recipe. Raised his eyebrows, said, "Not bad." Remembering when it could blow him out of the room as a young boy. Eased by food, urged by curiosity, coddled by memory (even the bitter sort), Lionel opened up (to eat) and out (to talk), and began to tell of Papa Solomon, that stocky bushy-browed immigrant who had provided Lionel's childhood with trials and judgments. And who even now, in Lionel's adulthood, would awaken him during occasional nights, in dreams of unquenchable yearning, to remind him of an earlier father who had indeed loved him, and been loved. "He was fine until I hit six. Then he took to heart the fact that I was a young male, growing; and that I was going to be a native boy, not a Russian. Not so much the politics, but the sentiments. Also, the fear of my turning into a species called *goy*. Know it?" She made a disparaging, mocking face. "Okay, okay. His greatest curse was '*Du goy*,' meaning not only 'You Gentile,' but 'You vulgar, crude, *ordinary* creature!' And for synonyms, he'd try, 'You'll grow up to be a truck driver.'" Lionel smiled, "I don't think he ever knew a truck driver, actually." Chewed on steak, shook his head in disbelief, remembering further. (Not around certain corners, however, or he'd cry in yearning to see him again! Papa, Papa.) "And those foods he ate. *Plate flanken*, ever hear of it?" She shook her head. "Boiled meat on the bone, with lots of salt, came our way twice a week or so. Try that with black bread and a potato, and you have Minsk in Brownsville. He loved it, it gave him a chance to load on the *chrein* and mock the family." Solomon hooked his arms behind his head. (Odd, all the stories that Sheyna yearned for, here were slipping out; here, where there was no routine of talk established, and where this strange creature stared at him intently, hand on chin, in the kitchen light.) "He ran an appetizing section in a small supermarket, and I had to work there. It was like prison."

"What's 'appetizing'?"

Lionel smiled, realizing provincialism, his. He began: "White fish, a freshwater fish with golden skin; lox, unsalted smoked salmon from Nova Scotia; fresh bagels, those you know; cream cheese, of course, and something called farmer's cheese, my father's favorite, like a chunk of marble which he ate with salt and a hunk of bread; and pickles in barrels— you name it, Yerna's on Sutter Avenue, had it. Actually, it was mostly sours and half-sours, period."

"Kosher dills like?"

"No such animals existed in those days." He looked at this

one, lying propped on her elbow on his dining-room table, waiting for more. She was having her interview, wasn't she? He went on, talking about his father. "He was a pretty violent fellow when he lost his temper—which took a split second or two, and occurred no more than once or twice a day with my mother or me." He thought. "What's called 'Jewish family feeling' may have been there but after I entered the first grade, it came out by way of fierceness, punishments, slaps, mild beatings. Sometimes not so mild."

She said, "CHrein beatings?"

Lionel smiled, nodded. "You got it."

She asked, "Like what?"

He saw her innocent green eyes and fair untroubled curiosity, and vaguely remembered—for to remember precisely was too painful here—those punishments and stronger beatings. Why bring them up, here in public? It was family chrein, you might say, too strong for public consumption. And why load others with your terrible baggage? Carry it yourself, with your doctor, with your fiction. He said politely, "He was a one-man judge, jury and warden at the same time. And one Jew who happened to be a terrible businessman. Trusting no one, or the wrong one, and always winding up in debt, or bankrupt." He scratched his hair. "We all have our fathers, don't we?"

Undeterred, she eyed him, nibbling a tomato slice. "And did you fight him back then?"

"At six, it was difficult; at twelve, when I did, it was worse. Fighting back was not a shrewd strategy, unless you could win. At twelve or thirteen I had little chance. He was strong."

"Are those the choices," she noted evenly, "getting beaten or getting raped?"

He considered. "There are other habits, I suppose—indifference, brainwashing, subtle bullying. I guess there's love too between fathers and sons, buried there somewhere; of course I'm exaggerating. But maybe fathers should be banned, and uncles or grandfathers brought in from the bullpen to play with the sons."

"Like the Zuñis, you mean."

"Sure, if you say so, like the Zuñis. You might send me their address sometime."

"Zuñi Pueblo, Zuñi, New Mexico—I forget the zip."

Lionel broke into a laugh—

"You don't do that very often, do you?"

Lionel disregarded that. "Should they need an extra uncle,"

he thumbed his chest, "Solomon Pueblo, Jerusalem, New Hampshire 03741."

She reached forward—frightening him!—and ran her finger down his nose.

"Oh yes, just for the record—"

"What record?"

"I did avoid both, beatings and rapes, in my tenure as father." He added, *"My* record."

He ate and talked, about his mother, still living, while Tippy fed him with her hands now, pieces of meat between words and sips of red wine.

At the end of another half hour or so—the tape had apparently ended—she smiled warmly, and said, "You're still so *young*, still *fighting*, just as I *knew* you'd be."

For a moment he took it seriously and inquired like a boy, "Do you think so?"

"You've CHrein on your chin," she responded, placing her left foot to his mouth.

"Hey—"

She used her toes to wipe his chin, and he sat there, transfixed.

Her smile grew wider as she moved her bare foot deliberately, subtly teasing a cheek. He found himself kissing the instep, and next the bottom of the foot, which was surprisingly rough, with only babysmooth spots remaining, and it made the girl make a noise, a small swoon. (Did he have ancient Chinese blood in his modern American veins? Was this a clear sign of the famous fetishism?)

She inched forward to curl the long leg around his neck, he instinctively put his hand on the leg, hooking it securely, caressing it in wonder.

Moved by the leg's attraction and driven by her knowing, straight sensual look, he put his face against the perfect calf, rubbing it, exulting in its smoothness and sensuality.

Slowly hooked, he raised himself awkwardly, but powerfully, and pushed his cheek all the way up the leg, finding the thigh supreme with scent and flesh.

He caught sight of her green eyes closing and the mouth opening and, fighting himself as well as Tippy, backed off, down. Resisted, out of the fear of the huge attraction. He knew for sure he was afraid of the girl, her beauty, its power over him.

He took a sane hold of the leg. "Good foot, ever try soccer?"

It took her a moment to shift gears, then she said low,

"Hey you, come here!" and when he moved nearer, hesitant, she sat up to take him in her arms and hug him tightly, with great affection, and plant little kisses on his cheek, forehead, scalp.

"What's all this about?"

"It's my way of showing hostility, Uncle," she whispered, nipping his ear.

He escaped her child's hug, appreciating it, and realized how sleepy he was, once he had conquered the erotic pull.

Walked into the bathroom, removed his robe and shorts, called out to forget everything till morning, heard a refrigerator door slam and water run while he got into his pajamas and bed. He left a bedside lamp on, on her side, but barely felt her slip in beside him, several moments later, so drowsy was he, and approaching sleep. Which was very unusual for an insomniac.

*He was walking about in an art gallery, at an apparent opening, filled with onlookers, mirrors, doors, paintings, when someone was laughing at him. He turned his head away, trying to escape, but the laughter followed him.* He opened one eye, and to his dismay and surprise, saw the light on and the girl Tippy sitting up in bed, reading. He closed the eye, heard the laughter, and turned around, trying to bury his head under the pillow.

A hand found the back of his neck, however, and from afar came words, "God, this is *funny.* You are close to animals, aren't you?"

What was she jabbering about? he thought asleep.

He mumbled sleepily, "Funny? At this time of night? No one's funny, not even me."

She kept her fingers there, gently, and began to read aloud, in a matter-of-fact voice:

"Dear Sabre,

"Tell me first, what happened to you? Did you run off because I kept leaving you alone? Were you stolen? Shot? You knew you were my steady pal, didn't you?

"Oh, Sabes, don't think for a moment I didn't know how you suffered from tail-envy." (Slight giggling.) "I know what it must have been like, growing up into a big beautiful powerful dog, with your subtle taupe color and intelligent quasi-human look, and suddenly to look around you and see—see nothing! No long bush of furry hair wagging behind you! When practically everyone else in the neighborhood had one of those things to wag and exhibit. Poor Sabes, when I used

93

to see you wiggle your minuscular taupe stump, the size of a small thumb, with Hank over there brandishing his bushy collie-shepherd tail, my heart broke for you, pal. It really did.

"And no matter how angry I'd get at you for your neurotic habits, I forgave you in the next minute or so. . . . Remember how you'd sit there, upright, like a stone gargoyle, with the gravity of a Prudential vice-president, until the dish was full—and then bang, you'd be uncontrollable! And if I'd try to say a civilizing word to you about dog manners, why you'd just barely keep yourself from growling at me. At me, Sabes! Was that fair, or reasonable?

"I realize that Hank was an enormous trial for you, Sabes, but we all have to put up with trials in this life of ours. And with enemies; but with some restraint. I face the same trials, pal, but you don't see me going around brawling constantly with the *same guy over and over?* Is that sensible? I realize it was hard for you, having another male dog in the immediate vicinity, but that was the way things were. That was Reality. Do you have any idea of how you'd look after one of those titanic battles? A vigorous fellow like you, bruised and laid out for forty-eight hours, lying curled up, upstairs, outside my room, with huge gaping holes and wounds in your side? Can you imagine how *I* felt, Sabes, seeing you that way? Knowing that taking you to the vet would be yet another trauma? But for me to face your helplessness and injury-riddled body was a painful sight. Oh, those battles were impressive ones, I admit. I recall one when Blynn had to take a small tree and bang his own dog, Hank, over the head as hard as he could to separate you two, otherwise you might have killed one another for real. A tree, Sabes! And the curious thing was, with your Weimaraner jaws, you could have broken his neck easily; yet you never did. Was it because you were not out to kill, after all? Or was it that you could never get a sufficient grip through his long hair? I like to think the former, that you restrained your huge strength. But it was always you who came away looking worse, as if you had been machine-gunned or had tried to run through barbed wire. It hurt me Sabes: I felt responsible somehow.

"I'll tell you the habit of yours that was most endearing to me. I hope it doesn't embarrass you, and prompt you to put your paws in front of your eyes, another quaint habit. Evenings, I'd be reading in the living room in the maroon chair, and you'd be asleep in the den. Suddenly you'd awake, not fully, you understand, but enough to take your ritual night stroll. Come into the living room, yawning away, raise your heavy eyelids and gaze at me, then walk around the coffee table and squeeze beside the couch, and finally walk to the end of the room, always around the platform rocker, and back down the homestretch where you'd face me again. And yawn. Three or four times this cycle went on, with you farting all the way (no, I cannot forgive those, pal—sorry, the whiff was too too strong). And seeing all was in order, you returned to the red couch in the den and went back to sleep. Without hurting your feelings, I want you to know that I was frequently tempted to buy you a fedora, a cigar, and maybe even a leash with a poodle, for that evening constitutional. For you looked a solid old fifty then, a sleepy old bourgeois fifty.

"And when I lost you, Sabes, not only did I feel your absence for six months, but I could never bring myself to replace you, or your private blanket. How's that for human fidelity, Sabre? For without such loyalty, where would we all be?"

Tippy said, "Didn't Gogol take care of the subject?"

Solomon in his sleepiness, felt stabbed. But then he felt a kiss on the back of his neck, and momentarily she was reciting again. He wanted to stop it, but didn't have the energy to move. Besides, wasn't it a good run-through, to hear it this way? Her sandy voice mouthing his fond memories?

"Dear *Chaver* Goichberg, although you are dead in body, dear old teacher, I want you to know that your spirit lives on with me, that you are a powerful and real *lehrer,* and that I remember you with overwhelming fondness. As you know, I was not a well-behaved boy, in the least." ("I'll have to remember that," she said, running her finger along his arm.) "But if it is any consolation, please understand that I had much more joy in being wild in *cheder* than in misbehaving in grammar school. What I mean is that it was a sense of joy which motivated my shenanigans in your one-room basement school, and not the boredom which provoked my doings in the public school. Believe it or not, I think, looking back, that I even enjoyed your physical discipline when I grew too disturbing to the small class. There was a sense in which your rough handling of me, which might sound like 'teacher brutality' if written up in a modern 'education' text, was a demonstration of real care for me and for the class. At those moments, when you'd be forced to leave the old wooden desk up front and come to my cockpit schoolboy desk and grab my arms and shake me, shake me hard, at those moments there was a look of puzzlement and even failure in your fiery eyes, an expression of confusion as to my motive and even a hope that I didn't take your handling of it in the wrong way. *Chaver* Goichberg, I didn't.

"I always thought your face and skin remarkable. I associated the color and the posture and expression of the face with an Indian penny, the color of red-brown that looked as if it had been burned onto the skin with a blowtorch. The face, with strong features, had its share of hatchet-crosses and rivulets, and when you'd get excited, the perspiration would run down, glistening, in mosaical patterns. You were like Chief Crazy Horse, whom I once saw in a Saturday matinee at the Sutter Theater. And your hands too were unusual, apart from the little blue numbers on your arm, signifying a history I knew little about. They were hard, callused, enormously powerful; the grip was that of a claw on a logging truck. When you grabbed me, you never seemed to use forearms or biceps, just those hands for power. Did I have an eight-year-old's intuition that those hands were raised in fury against the world, or Europe of the thirties, which had torn up your life and sent you here, from Poland? Possibly. In any case, there was about you a mystery, a force, a suspected rage, so that if I had to pick a Jew to play Ahab, it would have been you, *Chaver*."

She coughed and scratched on: "Can you imagine my dumbfounderment years later, when in my surprise visit to your Upper West Side apartment, I found out a little bit about who you really were? That while you lived in Manhattan, and taught science in a public school uptown, and afterwards took the IRT for an hour's ride to teach four more hours of Yiddish to us in Brooklyn, that besides all that you wrote poetry in Yiddish and also translated major works of Tolstoy and Dostoyevsky into Yiddish? And how incredibly touched I was when you gave me three slim volumes of poetry, with your warm inscription (in Yiddish), tracing the impact of New York upon your Polish refugee sensibility. (*Verticals* was one title, I recall.) Or to hear how you had turned down, later on, a college teaching post somewhere in Oklahoma (?), resulting from an old college friendship with a Gentile gentleman who had become president out there, because you believed that educating the young in Jewish culture was your prime responsibility? Otherwise the culture would not get passed along, and would die. Do you know how many professional Jews there are around who give great lip-service sermons on Jewish culture, but who have never taught a Jewish child? Or lent a serious helping hand to Jews? But who have pursued rigorously their own careers while moralizing about 'Responsibility'? Ah, many, too many, Mr. Goichberg. (Or *Chaver*, Friend, as you taught us to call you the first day, at age seven or eight.) No, friend, you were right there, editing *Kinder Journal* when I saw you that last time, after reading it for some six years in your school. The admiration I have for you, teaching Sholem Aleichem, Peretz, Singer, Jewish history, to that pack of twelve wild little Indian Jews like myself, is limitless. Remember, not one of us knew your real interests or capabilities during all those years. (As if Mr. Eliot had finished up the day teaching church history to a group of twelve-year-olds, before going home to work on his own poetry.) Not that it would have made any difference, of course.

"And then the abuse you suffered, from the respectable as well as the budding street hoodlums. Oh I remember so well how, after endless vandalisms and harassments at the basement window (including rocks thrown and faces made) by the *goyische* (Italian) kids there on Topscott Street, how your face would do that slow frustration and fury burn, and, cursing in Yiddish, you'd run out of the room and jump up the stairs and down the alley and into the streets to try to catch them. Every now and then grabbing one, and shaking him hard! But mostly not catching anyone, but scaring them off for a time, maybe for a week or two of relief. But the saddest thing, that etched itself in my heart, was when you'd chase them, miss them, return to the class and take up your text in hand, only to see them reappear at the window and thumb their noses! Your face of futility, restraining tears, inspired my own crying. (And the one time I ran out with you, you sent me back, knowing that they wouldn't hesitate to rip into me.) Then there was the pressure of the Respectable; not the Gentiles but the Jews. The respectable crowd of merchants, furriers, jewelers, and jobbers, the entire corps of petite bourgeoisie from the neighborhood. Who referred to the Sholem Aleichem School as 'that Red school,' and condemned you, *Chaver*, as that 'Commie teacher.' Misguided immigrants, poor patriots. It may have been true, so far as your political sympathies were concerned; there was no way of my telling. For through all of my six years there, I never heard you utter a political, let alone proselytizing, word. All you did was teach hard, very hard, for incredibly little money, to students who were mostly coerced there by their parents; teach us *geschichte*, Yiddish literature, speaking and writing, and the last two years, Hebrew and the Bible. (And have us give spoken book reports in Yiddish on a Sholem Aleichem or Peretz short story.) Were you a Red because you wore no *yarmulke* in class, and forced no one else to? Because instead of a long black coat and huge black hat and somber beard, you wore a suit with a tie, and loosened your collar as soon as you could? Because, in other words, you abandoned that horrible *shtetl* dress and the rituals of the *rebbes* who taught in the Talmud Torah school, which most of my friends went to and hated with a passion and learned not a single Jewish or Hebrew item? Surely the scorn of the respectable had to do with your sacrilegious style, and not the fact that the Sholem Aleichem School was a Bund school, deriving from European socialist traditions. For what did the small, brainwashed burghers-to-be of Brownsville know, or care, about serious political traditions?

"*Chaver*, I don't mean to flatter you needlessly here, I don't have to at all. But I think you were more of a *man* than most men. I gathered that there was even a kind of family resentment against your sticking it out in those shoddy conditions when you could have traveled upward, socially, leaving shabby Brownsville and even Manhattan for the Respectability of a college professorship. Now, who was around then to honor your stubborn devotion and ideals-in-action? If not the family, if not the Jews, if not the community, if not the world at large, *who*? Did we, in our eight-year-old hearts, if not brains, honor you? Time softens, memory lies, but I would like to think so. At least I have the evidence of my twenty-year-old self, who wrote a short story in which you turned out to be the wronged hero, and my father the villain. Certainly down there, in the heart of conviction called fiction, you had a strong and favored place.

"By the way, did you know that it took me into my twenties to appreciate the meaning of the word *chaver*, though I knew its literal translation years before? And that your spirit appeals to me now, deeply, dear dead Friend and Comrade?"

The voice shifted now. "A little too long perhaps. And some ideas buried. Did I pronounce *chaver* right?"

Solomon, who barely heard those words, was being whispered to, right down under the pillow in his ear. "But you *do care*, don't you? In *cheder* you were an Iroquois, and did know a *real* chief, didn't you?" She licked at his ear. Was that a tear dropping from her eye? "Oh my wild little Indian-Jew."

At the crazy words and tickling tongue he stirred, against his will, came out from under his pillow of protection, and glanced again with one eye at the girl above him, trying his best not to wake up. (A single night's loss of sleep, which meant a weakened concentration the next day, sent him into a forty-eight-hour fit of temper at his stupidity.)

In her hands were pages of manuscript. His.

"Where've you been creeping?" he asked groggily. "Give it over," he said, and took the pages and placed them on his bedside table. He wouldn't allow his fury to come out, or rise up, and so didn't want to get into it now.

"Sshh . . ." she urged, "don't wake up, don't get angry. It's so strong. Full of feeling. Real. Like you."

Solomon, who didn't feel real, or strong, turned away for a few hours of shut-eye.

"Oh God, it's *moving*, that last letter," she cajoled, moving herself now, in the bed, upon him, toward his pajamas, as if she wanted to tuck herself in there, with him. But there wasn't any room!

"Come on," he protested meekly, already feeling betrayed by his insistent thoughtless member, who couldn't care less about his WORK and ORDER. "I have two classes to teach . . . four hours of writing to get in . . . an accountant to see and two writing students . . . I need some sleep . . . have a heart . . ."

He was being nudged again, however, and sought to brush her hand or whatever away!

But the whatever turned out to be her heart, in a way: a large white breast, with a shrewd reddish eye, and it was beckoning to his face. He tried to turn away, but it was there, in the darkness, teasing. He could do little finally, except open his mouth then, and use his lips and tongue in an effort to placate her somewhat. It. Foolish idea. For he began to be taken and tantalized by that beautiful breast, its full pliancy and special aroma, and by the girl above him; this succubus who yawled loudly, and scratched his shoulders and neck in her wanting. (So different from his Sheyna's lovemaking.) In his somnolence however, he took to the sucking in a way that he had never done before, finding in the act here—in which the girl used her breast not only in his mouth but also upon his face, using it for her need and pleasuring power—finding in the act a climbing consuming passion removing time and space and transporting him back to billowing moments of be-ginning need and gratification. In truth at any such moment he fully expected, and yearned for, a spurt of milk to come forth from Tippy's large, growing nipple, so plugged in was he to the element of pristine power in the pleasure. This ex-

99

traordinary sucking went on for a long slow sweet time, with the girl shifting breasts at one point, somehow taking each breast from what felt like a nightgown.

The experience was so sensual, and redolent of ancient pleasure, that Lionel barely realized—or didn't bother to care?—that the young woman had then positioned herself like a smooth rider upon a helpless horse. And he only thought he heard her above him, in the midst of his savoring and succoring still, saying or singing, "Of course you must sleep . . . two whole classes to teach . . . accountant to see . . . four whole hours of writing . . . students to see . . . poor poor Solly . . ." The mockery pierced his drowsy pleasure and drove him to try to buck her, but he saw then that the smile on her face had widened fantastically in its greed and she glued onto him more firmly, even reaching down somewhere in behind to teasehurt him, and crazily, too, in the midst of this exquisitely controlled sweetness of honeyed rotations and ongoing breastsuccoring he heard her talking, reciting, a litany from a far-off dream: "It's exactly a year ago . . . that father died . . . isn't it? . . . . This very day, the fifth of May . . . I remember . . . it was very cold and it was snowing . . . I felt then . . . as if as if . . . as if I should never survive his death . . . oh no Lionel his death . . . and you had fainted . . . and were lying as if you were dead. . . . And now . . . a year has gone by, and we talk about it *so easily*. . . . You're wearing white . . . and your face is positively radiant . . . oh, the snow, the snow, the fucking, fucking snow! . . ."

And Solomon was pleasured as he had never known, had come through with more strength and potency than he had imagined possible for this time of night, or than he had allowed *himself* for this time of life.

And then she was lying, curled half on him, half on her side, out fast asleep just like that, with her face glowing like a convent girl who has just seen God.

Lionel, not sleepy, lay there, eyeing the ceiling. Content, but anxious, too. A patient in his own bedroom, every muscle in his body feeling whacked at, honed to the edge, overfatigued. A trout that had been baited, hooked, brought home and cleaned out swiftly and thoroughly, now ready for cooking . . . *was this satisfaction?*

His Polynesian from Albuquerque lay there, hand entwined in his, peaceful. A happy girl when she was able to move her limbs, prime the anatomy. Could a gazelle be happy in restaurant booths, secure, easy? No; she needed room to roam, to lope, to—

*Slowly the figure of a bearded man, the face gloomy, thoughtful, metaphysical, appeared.*

*"Herman,"* Lionel wondered, *"now I see why you wound up back in Pittsfield, chained in a marriage to the very proper daughter of the Chief Justice of the Commonwealth. You can't write books if you're in the eye of the hurricane, whether the hurricane is blond or brown-haired, North American or Polynesian."*

*When the man came closer, however, the figure was not the great novelist, but the immigrant father: from Herman to Papa. No metaphysics here; no deep understanding in the eyes beneath the bushy brows. Rather judgment, stern judgment. Papa Solomon said, "Vu krichstu? Enough is not enough for you?"*

*And when he raised his hand to slap Lionel,* Lionel jumped.

Tippy turned over hard, like a child.

Releasing his hand, Lionel then eased out of bed, sneaked quietly to the bathroom, threw cold water on his face and neck. Dried himself vigorously with the thicker of the hand towels. Caught himself standing there in the buff, uncharacteristically. Gently, with curiosity, he held up his penis, and looked at it; perplexed, affectionate. Tiny in detumescence. Poor fellow, forced to perform more than his share of work that night. Where was the overtime pay? At least for your feet you could provide Adidas or Wallabees, but for this fellow? Punish with a prophylactic? Harness with a codpiece? He patted it with a forefinger, a loyal pal, and let him down. (Not a long trip.) Just then he saw what girls were missing, with sympathy.

And then realized what a betrayer this little prick was! The blind alleys it led him down, holes it trapped him into, ups and downs of mental life it provoked! Here he was, off sex you might say in the last few years, off pickups and one-night stands and multiple girls—delicious as those were—off all of that and modestly satisfied (or modestly dead?) and here was a girl who showed up, and bang! his existence was on fire again! Reminded of his salad-days tricks, returned to his vulnerability to a . . . foot, a buttock, all in the guise of Ideals, Idealism, Political Nobility? Was this fair; this irony healthy? Oh, if he could have, he would have sold that penis off right then and there to any decent bidder, or traded it in for a good steel tool like a saw or a drill, and be through with the whole silly business! He thought of Sophocles saying somewhere how happy he was, at age eighty, to be through once and for all with the bondage of sex! Counting on his hands, Lionel figured he had only forty-two years to go.

Finding a pair of undershorts in the darkness, he put them on and got back into bed. He had slept naked once, and felt like an adventurer, a savage. Lying on his pillow, he tried to console himself with the thought that all this was for one night and one night only, this present bondage. And he'd have days, years, to rest up. You didn't run into a Tippy every other day, he knew. A year in the Marquesas and then you had a lifetime to rest up from it, miss it, yearn for it, be afraid of it, and compose *Moby Dick* in an attempt to savor and recover it. *(What did you experience there Herman, that you had to keep secret? Or that you could only write about it unbeknownst even to yourself, through giant and oblique metaphors? One white whale for how many dark truths?)* He lay on his side, away from the girl, cheek on hands, nose squashed into the pillow. (Did others with smaller noses experience squashing?) His body felt weightless, an astronaut . . . a skeleton. He touched his temples to feel the skull. Prominently there. Could he take it off and gaze at it, unadorned? What are you thinking, dear skull?

But it was Tippy who responded, turning into him and turning him over, where she curled like a fetus in the womb of his body. In this tent of protectiveness, she was sleeping fast again. And Lionel now had the excuse of his own awkward position of arm and body for his sleeplessness, and excessive worry. Meanwhile, the scent of her sex remained on his groin, and he couldn't resist scooping in that secret moisture of ardor and sniffing it, like perfume or opium.

(Doctor, literary people were like the subclass Cirripedia, not changing much through the centuries. Eternally, human creatures who spent their freshest hours locked away in a room, isolated from species company, pushing their imaginations into virgin territories, searching desperately for truth and originality, pushing their probe to points of despair and mental exhaustion; no wonder that when they left the room they'd come right over to you on the outside, and eat straight from your hand. Trusting souls! Perfect innocents! Grand suckers when it came to real life; the bigger the writer, the bigger the sucker, sir. Just as their characters were playthings in their hands, albeit autonomous and obsessive playthings, so the creators in turn were no more than playthings, albeit with tiny wills, in the hands of real people. Thus a nice exchange occurred; during the evenings the artist was paid back, in spades you might say, for his daytime conquests.)

The yellow light of morning peeking in at the edge of the shades. Eight-thirty, about an hour before young Mr. Solomon's usual awakening hour, and he's up, wide awake, like a tired alarm clock. The Tippy still ticks asleep, limbs curled. He eases out of bed, slips into dungarees and railroad shirt, carefully gathers his manuscript papers, and quietly leaves the bedroom. In the bathroom, legs weak, he pees; then brushes his teeth and washes his face. Checks for . . . markings on his face? Nothing. Beard a little grayer, perhaps. He puts on his shoes and goes to the kitchen, where he proceeds to squeeze oranges on the electric juicer. He loves the scent and the taste, even the orange pulp on his hand. Senses that he will have to stock up on soul-and-strength foods for the next few days. The perfect hypochondriac, after not sleeping. Taking Tippy's glass of juice, he sneaks back into the bedroom to surprise her. (*Like being a* "schön kind" *in the Ralph Avenue apartment, and surprising Mama that way?*) But the girl is still far away, in dreams. Ah, he envied her! The blanket had come off, and he set the juice down in order to correct it. Instead he edged it off more, revealing that she had worn Sheyna's short nightie(!), and revealing also her lengthy form of natural nubile beauty. Like waking up in a mountain camp and seeing a doe in your bed. Here, doe, some o.j.?

He gazed and adored.

On impulse, knowing it would hurt no one and be seen by no one, he knelt down by the side of the bed and, heart pounding, kissed the perfect babysmooth bottom! Lightly, so as not to disturb. As if she were Rachel, at three or four. *Ziss*. His head swirled with shame and fear! The doe didn't budge.

He stood up, aflame, and covered her—rather dramatically, in case there were witnesses about. Glancing, he saw no one. Under the bed? A smile. On the floor, however, lay the Iroquois jacket, in a bundle. He retrieved it, folded it neatly, and set it on the back of the upholstered chair. On the seat lay the young woman's suede bag. He had another impulse, and the springs creaked as Tippy turned over sharply. Asleep. He waited a moment, then, with his back to the girl, he opened the bag, and rummaged. A blue checkbook, traveler's checks, green bills. So we have a little liar in our midst! At first angry, then he smiles. Couldn't he, a professional liar—in the service of truth, of course—appreciate a colleague, in the service of . . . ? He smiles, admires, adores, closes the purse, and leaves the room.

In the kitchen he puts on the kettle for coffee, runs water into his green watering pitcher, and taking his pages, walks into his study. He sets down the pages, in place, he crouches down and waters the four-foot-tall avocado plant, Sheyna's baby, which he has watched over tenderly. A shaft of yellow sun hits the big tobaccolike leaves, several with holes; a small illness? The sun splashes the telephone too. Before dialing, he remembers something. From his low bookcase he takes out Volume 14 of the *Britannica*, "Lighting–Maximilian." As he flips toward Matthews, the book turns open to a group of photographs of the Malay Archipelago. Didn't Wallace once write a book on it, which Conrad read? Enchanted by: photographs of a Balinese farm, with cattle grazing under coconut trees and terraced rice paddies in the background; a street scene in Medan, Sumatra, men bicyling down a promenade in the cool beauty of shade trees; a young Balinese dancer, with a tiara on her dark head; a young body hanging sheets of rubber to dry in a processing plant in Medan; the elegant white palace of the president of Indonesia, in Jakarta—four pages of photographs of these lovely exotic islands. Should he go there? Live? Become a geese farmer? Write for the Balinese? With a postal address like R.F.D. 2, Malay Archipelago? Exoticism had always been his opiate. Was that a Balinese girl at the other end of his apartment? Under Matthews, he found Charles, an English actor; Shailer, a U.S. educator and theologian; no more. Matthewson, Christy, next. Lionel, a baseball fan, learns that the old master of the screwball was a righthander after all. About Jeremy Vance Matthews, Indian fighter, he learns nothing. He tries to recall that other name . . . and gets down Volumn 6, "Cocker–Dais." The photographs of cosmogony and those of Crete arrest his attention, and finally he moves on to . . . Crook and Willington, and Sir William Crookes. No "Crook," Indian fighter. Liar, liar, liar. Okay. He sets down the maroon volumes, in a small pile. (The piles piling up.) Telephone spangled with sun. Sitting on the floor he dials. Heart guilty, he prays.

"Hi kid, how are you? I just called to say good morning."

"Hi! You just got me, I was going out."

When she's delighted to hear from him, he loves her all the more! On his haunches, he speaks low. "I'm sorry I rushed out like that last night. You're right, I shouldn't let students take up my time that way. Or give talks. Anyway, pal, you have a good day now and I'll see you at seven. Maybe I ought to take you out for a change? I—" was that a sound in the hallway, a movement? He cocks an ear . . . nothing. A siren splits the morning, spiraling to its piercing decibel height, tails off. "No, no, I'm here. Just an ambulance having some fun. Maybe we can buy a siren for New Hampshire, instead of the rooster, to feel at home, instead of cockle-doodle-doo. Whooooooo!" he sirens.

"How'd you sleep, my sweet?"

Sweet responds, carefully, "Actually, not that well. Maybe I'm straining too hard in the jogging, too early on? We'll see. Hey, you know what? *The avocado lives.* Knock 'em dead at Louis Braille's place! No kidding, don't trip anyone. Well, maybe just a new one. 'Bye for now."

"'Bye."

He feels like a man home safe again, after a forty-eight-hour stay in the caboose for illicit behavior. Home free and clear.

From his sitting position, he finishes the watering, adoring his beautiful Sheyna. Creaking upright, he walks the long walk to give his visitor a nice goodbye. A short farewell for a long goodbye.

Except that when he gets to the bedroom, there is no girl sleeping fast. No sleeping Tippy. The bed is made, the orange juice drunk, the Tippy missing. Not a sign or note, or mark of last night's chaos.

What goes on in this world?

In the kitchen no Tippy or note, or in the other rooms. Disappeared. *She* had said goodbye first. Like an Indian leaving no trace. He touches his scalp; it's still there.

And suddenly, he feels his knees rubbery, his chest heavy, his brain fuzzy. Is he supposed to write in this condition? His thirty-eight years on this globe seize his body suddenly—a reasonably long time, right, friend?—and he wobbles to the refrigerator. Trusty GE with the bad handle. He removes the pitcher of apple juice and the head of fresh lettuce, and carries them to his bedside. He lies down and observes the pale head of green, veined white and leafy. Where are the ears, the noticeable nose? the beard? He tears off a leaf, and grazes. Replenishes you quickly, they say. His eye catches sight of the club chair, and something missing. Fatigued, he bolts up, nevertheless. Liar is also a thief! His Iroquois jacket!

Tears flow, he lies back down. A little boy who has had a toy stolen. The morning's shot, probably the day. He has to recoup, rest up, remove the girl from his head. There's a book to write, of a different content and tone. He can't deal with this woman from Porlock or Albuquerque; he's exhausted. Was it three or four times he was asked for last night? (And did that include her performance in going down on him, moaning and raving like a drunken samurai attacking someone?) Four is geometry to this arithmetic Solomon, this guarder of his semen. For *Beowulf*, of course you could have your orgasms and run off immediately after your breakfast to chase monsters. But he? He couldn't chase even little harmless characters!

The muscle in his eye jumps, subsides. Tension. Should he call his GP and have a room reserved in Mt. Auburn Hospital? Or go straight to Swerdlow's? Hire bodyguards?

*"Come on, body, I promise this won't happen again, I promise. Just come through for me this one time, recover in twenty-four hours—or twelve?—and I'll be your bodyguard for the rest of my ten or twenty years!"*

With such self-dialogue, such mocking vows, he tries to lullaby himself back to sleep for an hour or two.

Succeeds.

*A short man with a curling mustache, deep-set eyes and wild wavy hair, marched in. He made no attempt to hide the little clicks made by his high patent-leather shoes. No smiles, all business, with a fixed grimace at the mouth. The suit was black and old-fashioned, Europe of the nineteenth century, with a short, stiff white collar at the neck. He fixed his stare on Solomon, and it was like a hand accusing. "What do you know of misery suffered at the hands of a woman?" he said, in his Scandinavian accent, "Nothing. This is no more than child's play next to the real thing. And what is that real thing, my young comrade? Ten years of this sort of shenanigans, up close, and then, later on, for dessert, exposure to the world. Grist for your enemies, shock for your friends. Do you receive me?"*

*He smiled derisively and lifted up a photograph of Rachel, at twelve, with Solomon. "Not only will they torment you privately in their special way, using the power of their sex with a cunning that no man knows of, but then they will sink their teeth, their other teeth, into your bone and not let go. They'll drive you so you won't be able to tell truth from lying, common sense from nonsense, love from fear. First your writing will go, my friend, and while they laugh and mock you, your life will break into pieces. Wives, daughters,*

106

mistresses—sometimes even mothers—they're all cut from the same cloth, believe me. I don't have to show you the actual scars do I?"

He set down the photograph. "At the beginning there's the torment of their beauty and its temptations, as they learn what they can make you do, or want; then, my amateur friend, there's the torment of the lies they invent to make sure that you don't even get credit for the courage of your instincts. Ten years of that baiting, and biting, and you'll be through—a wasted man, a scarecrow. Hardly worth bothering over. All done nice and legal too, under the laws of the land. Listen, you've got it easy my friend, easy, getting to know the viper before you've signed your life away in a prison sentence called the marriage contract. And produced those little hostages to fortune known as children." Here he began laughing strangely. "Oh God, you don't know what torment is until you have those little creatures, and invest in them all your strongest energy and love, and money too, and then watch them turn against you and side with their mother! Why? Because there's prejudice in biology too!" His laughing was now shaking him violently, his face turning crimson. "Oh yes, try living when your own flesh and blood sides against you, and with her, with your enemies, with the critics, and they all declare that you're not fit to have dinner with! That you're a monster, an animal, not a civilized human being! And that the only place safe for you, and for those associated with you, is in the asylum!" A paroxysm of emotion gripped him like a fist, and he doubled over, his mouth muttering syllables, but no coherent words.

And the fierce Strindberg could speak sensibly no more.

Lionel shuddered.

Was Solomon to grow that mad, that paranoid? Was the whole world of women to be traded away because of this one experience? Would his daughter eventually give it to him too? Lionel felt sympathy for the great playwright, seeing him so crippled. Soon, however, the sympathy flowed back, inward . . . toward himself-to-be?

Dr. Lirič, it was just ludicrous the way he couldn't handle one night of chaos, one girl of powerful sensual ways, and thought immediately of hospitals, illness, death. Ludicrous, except that all those quick paranoid instincts turned out, alas, to have their measure of truth, even if it was self-fulfilling truth.

And will you note, too, the connection between Mr. Solomon's extreme pleasure and the turn toward morbidity. Were the two wired up early on in his instincts? Did they ride side by side toward a finishing line, which itself was pushed closer by the riders? Is this Mr. Solomon's case alone, or is this a general rule among artists? Or even, is it simply the fact that such extraordinary pleasure was difficult to assess or to compartmentalize in one's ordinary life?

Did sudden sharp unexpected and adventurous potency, issuing not only in number of orgasms but more significant, in quality of orgasm, really stand for something more significant than semen, more potentially powerful than physical potency? And perhaps more poignant than pleasure itself? Didn't it, in other words, whisper to him, in his subconscious, that what he had been calling living had not been quite living, but something like holding on, motioning through; that one avoided great pleasure just as one avoided great pain; that aging was a trick of mind as much as fact of time; and finally, that art killed you as much as primed you, not merely by taking its exhausting toll but also by forcing you to hoard your energy for her, and her alone? And if you stopped, She, unattended, would disappear, and then where were you? Begging like a pauper for Her to return, to punish and whip you if that's what it took to acquire the presence of the vain muse again? Did Tippy, Doctor, this very young fan, experienced in one way and innocent in another, teach something simple by means of her sensual attractiveness: that Mr. Solomon was in something of a bind, and that he had been suffering from a most subtle illness, his life?

And was he getting paid back in the most elemental fashion for his recent five-year addiction to languorous self-love? Did I mention that he had grown extremely lazy and subtly indolent over others' attention? That he had been rewarded by the opposite sex with adoring, succulent sexuality and warm massages? That he had grown vastly spoiled? And that this Tippy, of course, was not going to have it! In fact, if anything, was going to have it the other way? So that along with whatever destructive force she may have brought with her, or represented, he also knew that she represented, in his context, something possibly healthy?

In truth, I didn't really know what I was into with that girl. All that powerful sex made me naïve about her real power. That was the trouble, looking back. I thought I had a simple (sex) machine on hand, a panzer division attacking an exposed flank, and that that was her true potency; well, it was a smoke screen. A fleshy smoke screen. Why shouldn't I have *fallen for it, who wouldn't, if that screen yielded so much pleasure in so short a time, and then was gone, to be remembered? If gratification is potent in itself, do you know how much potency is sweetened by means of such memory and recollection?*

*Is there an equation to express lewd talk plus potent body and hidden literary cunning, to issue in disarray and disaster?*

# 3.

# Teaching

WORDS. WORDS WOULD SOLVE EVERYTHING—literary person's instinct. What better place than the classroom to demonstrate that? Spoken language—that fabulous civilized symbolism used for understanding and for subtle destruction, for clarity and for obfuscation, for truths and for lies; to impress the young with, defeat them with, to impress yourself with, and defeat yourself with. Through the years, Lionel's suspicions had grown concerning words and classroom glibness. At the same time, he enjoyed teaching more and more, though he did it less and less.

As you went on teaching you had to make a decision, to teach for the students or to teach for yourself. Two years after Solomon had started teaching, about 1965 or so—from places like Stanford to Dartmouth to this good small university outside Boston—he realized that the only way he could enjoy it was to instruct himself first. If he taught for the students, he found that his ideas became necessarily simple and simplified, and his standards came to include, with subtle deviousness, the views of the students. Hardly knowing it, you played to and for them. The intellectual act became a theater performance; truth was frequently diluted into theatrical shallowness, clever formula. In teaching for himself, Lionel inevitably raised the level of the best students to his level, instead of falling to theirs; and as a bonus, they could at times surprise him with their quality. What the best lacked was mainly experience, and a literary language (sometimes a healthy disadvantage); they made up for their lacks with lively imagination, curiosity, and great energy. The energy to learn; the energy and capacity of a select few, not the majority. Lionel knew that certain texts were much more accessible to students than others—Hemingway and Dreiser, even Joyce and Faulkner, easier than Proust or James. (Students might *academically* understand those two complex writers, but *experiencing* them was another matter.) In this vein, *Billy Budd*, with its simple dualism, or *Moby Dick*, with its giant reputation, were more accessible than the small, lesser-known "Bartleby the Scrivener." Which is why he reserved this story for a special class, one he knew well and respected. English 101b that spring term, a continuation of the fall term, was such a class.

On Tuesday at 2 P.M., a few days after his Tippy-venture, Solomon walks up and down in his classroom like a caged animal, working up his adrenalin and the right questions. The ones to inspire the right talk, literary and experiential. (The classroom itself supports the image of a cage, with one half of its hallway wall made of ceiling-to-floor glass, an invitation for visitors to stop and gawk at will. A desk in front, a blackboard with white chalk, rows of chairs with wide armrests for taking notes—or, as now, an oblong table with chairs around it for a seminar—all the poignant furniture of childhood still here, intact. On the walls reproductions of literary greats—Dr. Johnson, Dickens, Shakespeare—though hardly with their true madnesses showing. The light buzz of fluorescent bulbs, the chirping of students passing in the hallways. In this teaching zoo, they see the present descendant of the apes in corduroy jacket and with paperback in hand pacing in front of that seminar table with fifteen students sitting around it, listening.) He has spent a good part of the last term stripping off their layers of academic varnish and dirt, before starting in on the refinishing process. Solomon no longer lectures per se; his ammunition is the text and his notations, his method is questioning, so that when he does discourse it arises spontaneously out of the discussion at hand. The repetition and remoteness of his lectures in the old days put him off standard lecturing, and put him onto student perception to provoke thinking. He relies also on his day-in day-out experience behind the typewriter to separate real accomplishment from literary phoniness and glibness. The Fake in modern novels—ah, but that is another obsession.)

"All right, boys and girls," this thirty-eight-year-old boy of indignation begins to his beloved class of twelve plus the three newcomers this term, plus an auditor, daughter Rachel, "now begin with the obstacles created by the writer himself, if you wish, or consider the basic impulses behind the story—anger, resignation, whathaveyou. Or, consider the function of the narrator, what and why? And how does 'Bartleby' compare with other Melville works—*Billy Budd, Moby Dick?* The 'Encantadas.' '" Assuming the reading here, he realizes that, as usual, he has begun by putting too many lines out. So he returns by chiding himself, "I think you better answer the professor's questions *one* at a time, or we'll be in trouble." Students smile at the teacher.

Two of the newcomers shoot up their hands, high school habit. The first, a serape girl taken to displaying her summer in Mexico, says sullenly she doesn't think there *are* obstacles in the story—that part good enough for Solomon, who welcomes opposition—and proceeds to demonstrate as proof a summary of the plot. Lionel, a traffic cop for runaway undergrads, puts up his hand to halt the nonsense. (Later the girl will come to him and complain that he didn't "like her"; true enough, but he resents her literary stupidity more.) The next fellow, a toughie from the lawns of Long Island, uses a different approach: "Well, like there's no other guy like Bartleby in the literature. Man, he's a loner, he's far out, he's in his head!" Lionel stares at the suburban aborigine, nods instead of mocks, says briefly, "Bartleby is not 'a guy,' '" and out of desperation turns to an old standby favorite to get the discussion going reasonably. Eileen Randolph is a tall shy girl from a small town in Pennsylvania, who writes stories of mixed generations and values that are powered by Bellovian emotion. "What do you think, Eileen?"

She laughs shyly, "Nothing really."

"That I know," he responds, smiling. "But do it for your teacher's sake, you know, before he gets old here."

She plays with her doodle pencil. "Well," she begins at the far end of the oblong table, her lovely embarrassed smile emerging, "he works with the barest minimum of materials. Five words are not much of a . . . a rhetoric. Or refrain. And the character himself, Bartleby, is rather limited. There's no background, family, or too much information—what he reads, where he goes, all that stuff. Just those five words, and his sticking by them. Betting his life on them." She paused. "That's all we have. We really know so little about Bartleby!"

"Too little?"

She considered, doodling.

"No, not too little at all. Just so little for . . . so much. That's the point, I suppose." The voice slightly gravelly, reminding him for a moment of The Gravelly One herself.

"One point, yes." He adjusts.

Jim Rayburn, a freshman, asks in his roughhouse way, "Don't you think he kinda cops out at the end there, when he dies I mean? Does Melville have to take the story that far?"

"If he were writing today," Lionel acknowledges, strolling, "he might not die there at the end. Yes."

Tough but sweet Dru from Indiana came through, however, in her sharp twang. "But his end is very, very moving. That's the final test, isn't it? Also, it's not really a *realistic* story, but rather a sort of . . . fable. Or parable." Dru is happy at finding the right word. "Yeah, a parable!"

The teacher wonders if the moral of the Parable is, Don't Say No.

Rick Rankin has now brought up the matter of the narrator and his ironic function. "He's a necessary foil to Bartleby. Apparently solid, secure, safe . . . everything Bartleby isn't." Lionel lights up a cigarette and observes the animated faces of his young students. At one point, however, the reticent Eileen looks up at him, *and turns into the long-haired blond girl, who slowly sticks out her tongue at Lionel.* Solomon immediately turns away, toward a prettified engraving of Dr. Sam Johnson. Privately Lionel says to the Doctor, *"Nu,* Sam, what's new with you?"

The talk about the narrator continues, and Lionel is grateful for its competence. His tie is orange wool, and he has an impulse to flap it at the impudent girl!

So he acts on his aggressiveness, and intrudes. Speaking to himself as much as the class. "Now first of all what's the difference between characters like the Captain of the *Pequod* and this strange scrivener? What drives these two different men? Do you remember the crazy Captain, and his forceful or . . . *mad* pursuit? Here, let me refresh you." He picks up his *Moby Dick,* and finds a typical underlined Ahab passage; beginning slowly, he reads:

> "Drive, drive in your nails, oh ye waves! to their uttermost heads drive them in! Ye but strike a thing without a lid; and no coffin and no hearse can be mine:—and hemp only can kill me! Ha! Ha!"

Or this:

> "Here's food for thought, had Ahab time to think; but Ahab never thinks; he only feels, feels, feels; *that's* tingling enough for mortal man! to think's audacity. God only has that right and privilege. Thinking is, or ought to be, a

112

coolness and a calmness; and our poor hearts throb, and our poor brains beat too much for that. And yet, I've sometimes thought my brain was very calm—frozen calm, this old skull cracks so, like a glass in which the contents turned to ice, and shiver it."

Now Lionel is more than warmed up, he is getting within Ahab's skin, his anger in his determined, obsessed will. For as he drives into yet another section (this one following the Captain's actual chase of his enemy), Lionel observes a framed photograph of a sailing ship, *and for a moment sees on the prow of the 1850 whaling boat in a raging sea, himself, Solomon, in Norwegian turtleneck and dungarees and captain's cap, screaming out, "Come on, Tashtego! Pull to, Queequeg! Yank, you lazy Daggoo! I'll whip the hides off of ye if ye make me lose her now! Thar she blows, ye loggerheads, ye dregs, ye jealous daughters! you moron critics! ye good mistresses! you fucking lawyers and accountants! Students, fans, daughters, doctors—come on pull to! If ye keep me from her, I'll carve your civilized hearts out! I'll cut your runt erections off! I'll blow your timid Freudian bodies down! Come on, climb to, beat on, shove that oar, get me to her! If I lose this Tippy because of you good little sailors and proper little laws, I'll take you all down to the filthy Charles and drown you! Parasites! Dullards! Magpies! Cowards! Jailors!*

In a hot maze he looks up and sees bewildered faces staring open-eyed and openmouthed at him. Not all; one young man is smiling derisively, and another student is writing away (oblivious?). What has he said *aloud*?

His temples beating wildly, he excuses himself and walks out of the room into the hall. At the water cooler, he sips water, dreams of his New Hampshire hills, and how nice it will be to be up there, outside in the cold dry air!

He wipes his mouth with jacket sleeve, wondering if he should just call it a day for now?

But, back in the classroom he asks, while praying privately, "Well, what do you boys and girls think?"

*"Are you sure you want to know, Uncle?"* a voice asks.

Glen Thompson, a Dorchester black, speaks up. "Man, Ahab has all that energy. That dude is right there with it, laying it on *aloud*. Put the Scrivener up there against him and like you got *one wasted hero*, from the start."

Lionel breathes easier, his congested chest rising and falling in relief. Reminds himself to speak to Glen about that lingo, in private.

113

"Yes, that's true," rejoins Paul Cohen, "but even though he's wasted—or enervated—he still stands up, doesn't he? Like Eileen said. Stands up for his principles. It so happens his principle is No. Not a chase."

Good for you, Paul.

Eileen speaks up, "Paul's right. Abstention is his . . . style. Or faith. And the story is built on that. On the principle of No. Except that that 'No' is really 'Yes' for Bartleby. And for Melville, I suppose. Do you see what I mean? It's their way of . . . surviving."

Ah, how simple. *No.* Why didn't Lionel pay heed to his masters, or his students? And himself *prefer not to.*

Philip DeSantis, newcomer and radical, was speaking. "I can't get over the way you all refuse to recognize the social conditions of the world of Bartleby. Isn't it clear that this No is also a politics of Rejection, and that it applies to the world of New York, of finance, of mercantile capitalism in nineteenth-century America? Have you forgotten too that Ahab was originally a member of the working class who was then bought off and corrupted by the managers in order to exploit his own crew for them?"

As Philip continued, Lionel searched his Rinehart text for a curious poem he remembered. "Interesting," he said to DeSantis, "and the whale?"

"An outlet for his pent-up frustrations. A revenge object for his class ambivalences. The man's sold out and he knows it in his unconscious."

The old Marxist in Solomon admits that that was at least as good as an allegory of Oriental gods, a recent scholarly explanation. "Pretty good outlet," observed Lionel. Then, addressing this (smiling) class, he went on, "Here, let me read you a section from a late poem of Melville's. It's called 'After the Pleasure Party.' See what you make of it." He reads slowly and matter-of-factly:

> Now first I feel, what all may ween?
> That soon or late, if faded e'en,
> One's sex asserts itself. Desire,
> The dear desire through love to sway,
> Is like the Geysers that aspire—
> Through cold obstruction win their fervid way.
> But baffled here—to take disdain,
> To feel rule's instinct, yet now reign;
> To dote, to come to this drear shame—
> Hence the winged blaze that sweeps my soul

> *Like prairie fires that spurn control,*
> *Where withering weeds incense the flame.*

"Are you able to get that?" he asked, and when they nodded he tried another section.

> *Could I remake me! or set free*
> *This sexless bound in sex, then plunge*
> *Deeper than Sappho, in a lunge*
> *Piercing Pan's paramount mystery!*
> *For, Nature, in no shallow surge*
> *Against thee either sex may urge,*
> *Why hast thou made us but in halves—*
> *Co-relatives? This makes us slaves.*
> *If these co-relatives never meet*
> *Self-hood itself seems incomplete.*
> *And such the dicing of blind fate*
> *Few matching halves here meet and mate.*
> *What Cosmic jest or Anarch blunder*
> *The human integral clove asunder*
> *And shied the fractions through life's gate?*

"Now what do you think about all that? Rather frank, don't you think? 'That soon or late . . ./One's sex asserts itself,' 'or set free/This sexless bound in sex, then plunge/Deeper than Sappho.' Or, 'Why hast thou made us but in halves/Co-relatives? This makes us slaves.' "

A pause and Susan E. said, figuring it out as she went along, "Are you speaking of the connection between the sensual urge and the author and his work?"

Lionel had asked for it that way—the old saw—hadn't he? And where in the hell has he taken this conversation? He chides himself and nods to Paul Cohen.

"A frustrated man, that's for sure. But maybe that's where Ahab comes from? Not to mention Bartleby?"

"Man, I been livin' the wrong kind of life!" laughs Glen, his gleaming white smile spreading to his peers.

Dru, meanwhile, has worked up a fine private anger. "Christ, I just think it's so obvious that Melville is terrified of women. Why the hell are so many writers like that, Professor Solomon? Conrad, Hardy, now Melville." Trailing into a little girl's voice, she plays with him. ". . . Do we bite?"

Laughter.

Lionel considers that, holding his lectern as if he were a pastor.

115

"Some of you do, yes," he replies steadily, causing a chorus of mock hisses, and a few cheers.

"By the way," DeSantis with the flowery mustache comes back, "what do *you* think Ahab is after? How do *you* read him, or Melville?"

Lionel walks up and back, trying to translate oceans into visions, whales into impulses. And integrate those metaphysics with the facts about the whale industry in the nineteenth century.

The bell rings, and Lionel raises a finger. "Saved."

"Next time, okay?"

He considers and adjusts. "Oh, before the term is over. First I'll try to stick to Mr. Bartleby's case a little more. Meanwhile get out your old whale novel and have another go at it yourselves."

"Don't cop out on us now," advised DeSantis, who could flush out a petit bourgeois writer like a hunter with a fat partridge.

Solomon packs up, answers several questions about papers, and heads for the exit. Embarrassed privately by the looseness of the discussion, and his private roaming—some of it aloud.

Outside the door, Rachel catches up with him. "Shit, Daddy, when you got going there, whoosh! Where were you, in your head, I mean, when you were reading that stuff? Want to cut a disk of *Moby Dick?*"

"Sure, Rachel," keeping quiet about the "shit." "Why don't you ring up Decca and tell them about it?"

Walking along the corridor, brushed by students, father in corduroy jacket and daughter in bell-bottoms and sweater. "You know," she takes up, "I *really* liked your friend the other night. I'm impressed. how do you . . . do it?"

*I have a telephone and it rings,* he muses.

Scared, annoyed, he recalls, "Geritol. Regularly." He smiles nervously. "Actually, I wouldn't take her too seriously." Foolishly, however, he adds excessive information, "It was just an interview."

Eyes twinkling, "Oh." Rachel takes his arm and pulls him up. "Dad, I'd like you to meet a friend. Over here." She veers him to the wall opposite his office. "This is Richard Muffalo. My father, Lionel Solomon."

Richard reaches out a large brown hand toward Solomon, who takes it. Tall, he is made huge by the heady Afro cut of his hair. A basketball forward?

"Pleased to meet you," the young man says easily, "I saw

116

you the other night, but it was rather late, and you looked occupied. I thought I'd wait for a more appropriate occasion." The accent is a perfect Oxbridgian, and he is wearing a very fashionable suede Levi's jacket with a big flowery collar, revealing his fine chest.

Lionel realizes that Muffalo is the "prowler" of the other night, and also, the Daggoo of his *Pequod* fantasy.

"Well that's thoughtful," he says, referring to the timing. He releases his hand from the gentlemanly British grip.

"Thanks so much for the Chekhov biography, it was very useful indeed. I'm playing Vanya, I hope you'll come and see it. I was at Christ's College about four years ago when you gave a small talk there, if I remember correctly. I'm sorry to say I missed it."

Lionel smiles, slightly touched. "You didn't miss much." About ten or fifteen students had shown up, for the impromptu talk set up by a friend there.

"I'm hoping to get to one of your novels this summer, at last. Which one would you recommend for a beginning?"

"Rachel can recommend one to you, I think, better than me." His old error in pronouns stings him now, with this perfect brown gentleman from White Oxford. He looks at his watch, uneasy. "Are you studying here, by the way?"

"I'm visiting in the Philosophy Department at Harvard for the year," he replies.

"Philosophy?"

"Logic, specifically."

"I better get going," Lionel waves slightly and walks off.

Rachel runs alongside. "I'll call you this week, okay? For dinner, or whatever."

"Whatever," Lionel nods.

"How do you like him, Dad?"

Lionel paused, always trying to remember to think twice when it came to this area of paternity. Three times now, perhaps. "As a friend of mine says, 'They're beautiful. The future of the world.' "

"Oh come on, don't be a racist pig. Be serious."

Lionel grows red, then calm. "Or as another friend says, 'I'm impressed. How do you do it?' "

She pinches the skin on his wrist, moving from momentary pique into good humor. "You're hopeless." Kisses him suddenly, laughing, and runs back to Oxford logic. Runs the same way she ran at age three, arms pumping and body rocking sideways. Lionel misses her in jumpsuit at three!

After teaching this Tuesday, he sat at the old Royal stan-

117

dard that he had picked up at Stanford for twenty-five bucks, years ago; his old reliable pal. Lionel at the typewriter felt at home with the boredom, the routine, the long-term project. It took him some forty-five minutes of calisthenics to get into the mood of introspection; this warming up was done with the radio on (a folk station), and with various pages of trivia for him to concentrate on. Just now he read thoroughly the sports pages of the *Globe* and the *Times,* focusing on upcoming NCAA basketball playoffs and spring training in baseball; and in a little while moving on to *The Want Advertiser,* and things for sale, everything from captain's chairs to chainsaws to fine audio components. The flow of fact and incredible lists of trivia cleared his mind of students, classes, books, the university. Only after this warmup period and erasure of what happened today, was he ready to take the plunge into the deeper hole of his own life, with another one of his Last Letters.

Next to writing, teaching was a sport, human relationships an interesting hobby, daughters merely difficult. Writing was, in a word, hell, a no-escape hell, after the first book or two. It was fatiguing, relentless, punishing; it grew more difficult as you went on, and the early great enthusiasm was tempered by constant work; the outward rewards meant less and less (*if* they came); the larger habit and illness induced a variety of offshoot illnesses, for which there was no cure except extinction. Or cease writing, which was impossible because of the overwhelming guilt that the absence was filled with immediately. The only *real* guilt, Lionel knew, that afflicted him. So, a novelist had to have the patience and endurance and psychic armor of a Galápagos tortoise, who sometimes went a whole year without sustenance. Earlier on, there was the youthful energy to match the compulsive drive. On the second novel, *Each According to His Needs,* which took four years to complete, he worked every day, Sundays and holidays included, with the exception of one vacation break of ten days, during which he worked only half days. Thus he spent some 1,450 days working on a book which took, ideally, four or five days to read; let alone the reader who finished it off in one or two nights, or the reviewer who had two thousand words in which to evaluate its two hundred thousand. The effort to make book after book added up anatomically in pressure, it seemed. Each book inspired a new disability: chronic back trouble, serious sleeplessness, stiffening leg muscles and knees, neurasthenia; and worse, each small infirmity was looked upon as earned, deserved, and therefore as a permanent possession, like a new barnacle. Of course this perverse accumulation and insidious acceptance occurred in the subconscious, mostly. But as you can see, we are describing a very special species, a most aberrant (and weak) strain.

(And that was why, when certain friends didn't bother to respond at all to the books, he didn't bother to take *them* seriously anymore. He couldn't. He wasn't strong enough to face people who called themselves friends but wouldn't acknowledge four years of work, or who would give it three to five minutes on the telephone. Or was it really better to hear an opinion of a friend which exposed his literary ignorance and his unacknowledged biases? A toss-up. Did doctors have their tests and operations reviewed by friends? Or lawyers their briefs and cases? Why was it only the writer whose work left him exposed to every amateur's opinion or jackanape's joke? What sort of unpleasant occupation was this, that your work of three years could lose you a friend of thirteen?

An occupation which he had chosen, or had chosen him.

A resentment which was deep, somewhat paranoid, and hopefully at some point, useful.

And friends? Come now, Lionel, did they necessarily have to be literary critics? Why?)

Each novel brought with it, too, a new set of literary strains and questions as Solomon struggled to find the appropriate form to house the content. Would it be third or first person speaker (or both); was the form to be narrative, epistolary or . . .? Was the action better carried forward by character perception or by incident; was the emphasis on the moral or psychological life? Clearly the possibilities for serious literature had been narrowed considerably in the last seventy-five years of accomplishment. The "stuff" of great novels of the past century now could be taken care of by newspaper and magazine writers on the one hand (American action legacy of Hemingway and London, say), or by the social scientists on the other (studies of social injustice like those of Steinbeck, Dos Passos, Sinclair). What was left—Solomon figured—was what had always been there for the greatest novelists, the anatomy of intimacy. The father of this sort of operation was Proust; Proust whose book was too long, too minute, too overblown, too personal to be taken by a publisher then, or now, if he were to submit his two thousand pages. And yet how easily one could spend the whole of one's life on one book, namely the story of your life, if the sensibility, the patience and the stamina were sufficient. The irksome difficulty was merely the high cost of recording one's life, having to face it day-in day-out in a serious fashion; how much nicer, neater, more polite to write about some faraway character, out there in the purely fabricated world. How much pleasanter for the self!

Lionel circled a fine Grundig Majestic radio for sixty bucks in Watertown, and put a sheet of paper in the roller, though he probably would just stare at it now. A difficult letter to an old difficult friend, now dead, the memory would open up barely closed wounds. Teaching and these thoughts had reminded him of his old friend, a teacher too, and a well-known critic. Lionel found the photograph of them together during their close years, the brash young novelist and the older man whose work Lionel admired greatly. Sidney in his good days: the thin hair combed neatly, the cheeks boyishly puffy, the embarrassed smile before the camera, the thick eyebrows, the mirthful sense in the older man's skeptical face. The humorous tint in the animate brown eyes. Yes, he could be very funny, though hardly ever on the page. Lionel felt close to him now, and, for the fifth or sixth time in the past few weeks, began talking to him. These letters-to-be were polished verbally in his mind, over and over compulsively, until it seemed as if they almost forced themselves out, as it were, from head to typed page. Sometimes he barely knew the line between the two, so worked up did he become, so intertwined were the two ways of imagining.

*(No doubt, Doctor, these soliloquies need more polishing, later on).*

"Dear Sidney.

"I remember the good days well, the early kindness and warmth you showed me when I first showed up in the East, on the campus. I recall that first time I met you, at the Roberts's party, when you took my arm, in your Russian way, and asked me my opinion about the contemporary novelist you happened to be reviewing. Your odd way of approaching strangers—either they possessed a literary sensibility or not, either you had a serious dialogue with them, or you shifted topics abruptly and monologued. Yes, your swarthy face lightened, your forbidding presence softened, as I criticized the fablelike narrowness and limitation of the novelist in question. Our literary wavelengths were similar. And after that evening, you befriended me generously, inviting me to dinners on the Hill, where the good talk matched the gourmet cooking (yours), from literature to politics to society and sex. Even when you gossiped in those days, it was more with charm than malice; and I can still hear that famous raspy voice, incomprehensible to many—yet curiously clear to me from the beginning. Talk, as much as print, excited you. And in that luxurious house, where I felt in awe of surroundings and persons, you and Margaret made me feel at home; having a kind of family fun with my ignorance of drinking, eating, high living. And Margaret, your fine Brahmin wife, was super too. I like to think that had she not died so prematurely (and tragically), your own ending might have been delayed. Certainly your last years would have been different, easier. To enter your tough literary—and personal—world, and to try to learn about it, was no small feat of courage for that refined lady. . . . Imagine her sitting in on my freshman humanities class, sitting in the back row, in elegant black dress, behind the kids in jeans, and venturing forth, slowly and timidly, about Kierkegaard's interpretation of the Abraham and Isaac caper. Oh, that was poignant, amusing. . . . Sidney, you were wonderful about reading anything I wrote in those days, and giving me your frank opinion, in private. Now only a writer can appreciate what that means. For to have such . . . consultations with someone like yourself, whose literary judgment was often so superior, so shrewd, was the ideal sort of literary criticism, especially for a younger writer. Moreover, you did it out of friendship and interest—nice motives indeed. I have little doubt that *Each According to His Needs*, that bulky triple-decker of a novel, was a much better book for your criticism, not to mention a dozen stories.

"That I became close to you, in turn, was obvious enough. But wasn't that perhaps part of the problem, that deep closeness? More like a son to you than a friend, frequently. Looking back, I'm sure you felt somehow 'betrayed' by my growing independence, and by my success outside your realm. Sidney, believe me, I felt hurt at your getting hurt, I knew what emotion was for you, and how you avoided it wherever possible; but you know what? *I also felt betrayed at your sense of betrayal.* Perhaps you were too close to me too, in a certain sense; too similar, both of us, a pair of Russian peasant boys who came to look at the world through literary eyes, . . . excitable temperaments . . . stubborn wills. (How does one put all of this, Sidney, short of a story?) But what I did forget in those days, made too little of perhaps, was your permanent sense of exile; it was something you never really got over in America, did you? Your heart, beneath the mask

121

of authority and vulnerability, may have been more truly vulnerable than I knew. Or than you knew. . . .

"That closeness, that filial intimacy, was perhaps never clearer than that eerie morning when you rang me up at 10 A.M. and said, in a broken voice, 'Lionel, I've just returned from out of town to find my house destroyed by fire, my library and manuscripts ruined, and Margaret dead. She's dead, Lionel, dead! And everything I have has been *ruined*. Will you come over and help me?' Was there ever a more potent appeal, in life or literature? Doubtful. Or, to see you fifteen minutes later at your sister-in-law's, a Lear of a man reduced to a Loman of helplessness. And when we drove over to the charred shell of a house in Boston to see its condition, I realized your shock . . . your perfect madness, as you began to unload the refrigerator of perishable items. My job was beginning, in earnest. Removing the jars of jelly and mayonnaise from your arms, I explained they were of little use just then. After bearing the badly smoked clothing to the dry cleaner's, I found you a temporary hotel room. And for the next three or four months, I was at your every beck and call, finding you permanent lodging, buying you paper, pencils, books, helping you arrange substitute professors and make other practical decisions, and of course having dinners with you four or five times a week—not to mention the endless afternoon and evening hours at your side. Trying to soothe and settle your depressed state . . . your elevating hostilities . . . your growing fears and moods of negativism—a task harder than treating the actual shock itself. But what else are friends for, if not to play secretary, confidante, shrink, practical guide in crises? Besides, I was more than a friend, I was that (adopted) son. Fair enough. For fathers, one drops one's life and work if the call comes, yes?"

Lionel stood up here, took two steps to the window, looked out at the distant church steeple and the near black telephone wires. A row of pigeons sat on the church roof, waiting, watching. Lionel, terribly moved by the memory, was upset by what was coming next, the recounting of growing hostility. How did one make sense out of family relations, sibling graftings? And finally what portion of all this would go into the novel's letter, how much of the whole truth? What if the real was much more dramatic than the imagined? Did you have a right to keep it in? For now, all he had to do was remember. He stared at the fat city birds and began speaking again.

"Skip four or five years, the friendship had hit some rocky

waters, the magazine you had started and we had coedited had gone under from lack of funds, you had married again and that too was going downhill fast; also, you weren't really working anymore, another blow. So, with old friends, you had grown unpleasant, sometimes rude; by then I had gotten used to your misanthropy, and even, some cruelty. (I won't go into the instances of cruelty that I had seen in you earlier, with friends and wives; no, not here, not for future print.)" (Censoring even here! Lionel smiled, and shook his head.) "Still, I was much too close to you, to the experience, to view it with sympathetic objectivity; to pass over it with the understanding that you had grown old and afraid very swiftly, lost your writing powers and married the wrong woman at exactly the wrong time in your life, and that anything but strict obedience on my part was considered a breach of loyalty; too close, I admit, to feel anything but sharp loss and stinging betrayal. And at last, after an especially rude note from you in August (1972), happy riddance to the present friendship. I would remember the good times, the literary and political education, and let it go at that.

"But then it happened again, the telephone. During that very same August of rudeness, out of the blue one midnight you called me again, as if nothing had happened in the past two years, and bemoaned, 'Lionel, I'm in real trouble, Helen's killing me, she's driving me crazy. Can you help me? Can you come down and give me some help, some advice? I'd really appreciate it, Lionel.' You had done it again! Rationally, I knew my answer. 'Oh, I don't think so, Sidney, not this time, not anymore.' I waited for the words, I even tried for them, but they didn't come. Instead I nodded, nodded dumbly, and was still nodding dumbly the next day on the two-and-a-half-hour drive down, refusing or trying not to think. I was a son locked into an emotion, a man, and beyond my reason. And no sooner had I come to your table at Joseph's—with you no longer criticizing my recent beard—when you said, 'You were right two years ago, Lionel, you were right! I never should have married her. She's killing me. We've got to do something.' Ah, I loved that *plural* responsibility. Your voice was raspier than ever, and your face ghost-white from domestic battle fatigue, fear and confusion. For the first time, you, a Leninist in human relations as well as politics, you seemed *truly baffled* by human relations, truly battered by a real woman—not a literary heroine. All your previous mockings of people trapped in that ancient trap of Unhappy Marriage had now come home to roost. Yes, you

123

had grown old, frightened, slightly senile, and all the alcohol and sedatives and barbiturates you imbibed to escape your life did nothing to mitigate the misanthropy, cynicism and fear. Yet, what had I said two years before? Why, nothing more than that you and Helen had come from very different lives—one life from Russian and High Literature and the Great Depression and High Society Ladies, the other life from Oklahoma and personal depression and Dust Bowl Society, with a teenage child thrown in—and were you sure that you, at your age, could tolerate such drastic difference? Or she?

"So there I was again, the prodigal son returned home, trying to comfort and aid. And there you were, the vulnerable father, in great need. But how long did it take—a few weeks?—before you changed back to Sidney Karamazov? Certainly the cycle was accomplished in a time fit for the Guinness Records for Threatened-and-Vengeful Fathers.

"Dear Sidney, you were a better man than the one who would half-lie to my face, or slander me behind my back. . . . Or were you?

"Old friend, I know that behind that mask of Bolshevik antibourgeoisdom, behind the fixed postures of stern autocracy and self-sufficiency, behind all that lurked a corner of loneliness, great loneliness, and embers of human feeling that flickered on, embarrassing you till the end. Curiously, I don't think you ever realized that by suppressing such feeling with political slogan and dogma, you frequently edged sentiment into sentimentality, so that when you did 'feel,' it often came out maudlin? (When you weren't using your burst of tears for political purposes, that is.) You were a lonely man, more lonely than you could ever admit, to others or to yourself; therein was a major flaw. And more—your fear of admitting your own impulses, or discovering them, and your immediate closing of doors once you peeked into new rooms of feeling, was actually tragic for you—it affected your later critical work, as well as impaired your later life and equilibrium. (Without feeling, or friends there at the end, when work grew impossible, you desired death more strongly than anyone I had ever seen. Death for you, and death for others. At the end you were the first in-the-flesh nihilist I had ever met.) Oh you were a master at putting up complicated camouflages and disguises to yourself, let alone the world. Consider your obituaries, see how they all missed out on you? How they described you as if you were an intellectual well, pumping away continuously, instead of a man whose emotional life was buried like an old mine shaft, in disuse, draining your life. Clearly, the discrepancies between feeling and mind, feeling and performing roles, were enormous in you, and painful. It accounts for your relentless ambivalence toward so many things—Jewishness, intimacy, friends, and family. Spending your life, for example, mocking bourgeois manners, in the name of High Trotskyism, while marrying High Society Episcopalian ladies and living the life of a perfect bourgeois gentleman. Or again and again mocking professional Jews and Judaism but boiling in rage privately and delivering living-room lectures on anti-Semitism at every single incident involving Israel. A non-Jewish Jew in public salons and print, a heated Jew in private; the vise of contradictions gripped you more than most.

"Now why would a man of great literary insight never acknowledge such obvious life-tensions? Because, to my mind, you were a man constantly in flight, in exile: from Russia, from near-peasant origins, from Jewishness, from family life, from the life of feeling, from America, from yourself. To me it's rather astonishing how a self-proclaimed Realist could be such an Escapist; how a Bolshevik could be such a steady Bourgeois, an Internationalist such a strong Zionist; and how a Rationalist could be such a clearcut Intuitionist. Why were you so strong upfront, and so fearful underneath? That someone along the way would discover that one of America's great literary critics and prose stylists first learned Russian at age eight by means of a kindly Czarist army lieutenant who was bivouacked in the house? That your first language was Yiddish and your second Russian, your third Hebrew—before you got around to English? That you knew more than a little about things like stocks, bonds, banks, investments? That your mother still lived on, in an Israeli old-age home, and that you had a brother with a good Jewish name, your real one, and that he was a fine solid citizen? Was there anything so terrible about all this, or did all Personal Items belong to that realm of the Bourgeois in the Cause of Political Revolution? How much of Kralisch, the real man, was lost when you took on the new name, Sykes?

"Was it this combination of contradictions, the constant shifting of masks, that drove you to meanness? to a penchant for destroying weak souls in particular? to small cruelties to your wife, which embarrassed me deeply, or revelations about an old friend, through his letters, along with sex gossip, as a kind of blackmail on him? There is no point here, Sidney, in recounting all the details of the meanness, the late-life cruelties which, when added up, may indeed add up to a will of evil. But I will say that it is one thing to conjure up images or Lucifer or Hitler, or other embodiments of the Metaphysical Absolute called Evil, and quite another to view it up close, as a daily round of behavior of deceitful intentions and conscious malevolences which impaired people's lives and hurt them deeply. You may be surprised to know, actually, that yours was not an evil of Tolstoyan magnitude, but rather of the Jamesian variety. How ironic."

Lionel paused, smiled at himself here; if he didn't remove this sort of truth-telling, surely his publisher, an old friend of Sid's, would try to. Oh well.

"You see, the irony was fantastic: to read one of your literary essays in which you elevated and eulogized the power of morality in literature, and then to see you act out a life guided by principles of pragmatism and convenience. Or even, later on, in print and talk, to see you excoriate this or that writer for his lack of morals, only to act in the most immoral manner with regard to an enemy, a friend, or a writer submitting a manuscript for our *Review*. Hypocritical, Dispiriting. Especially when I'd pick up one of the old essays, on Chekhov, on Dostoyevsky, on James or Melville, and observe a small classic of literary judgment, intelligence with sympathy, morality with flexibility. . . . But I'm being naïve, Sidney. I'm underestimating what it must have been like for you *to lose your power to work;* work, not people or feeling, was your life force. I remember seeing that wooden shelf in your apartment, the shelf which you had installed in every place you ever lived, on which you composed, while standing, in longhand; always with the same notebook of useful quotations from famous critics that served as literary touchstones. Usually that shelf was filled with manuscripts, notebooks, books, the paraphernalia of your industry; the last time I saw it, it was clean and bare. Just a wooden plank. I cried to myself, friend.

"Yes, in those last tortuous years you could have used a psychiatrist badly, it would have helped—but since you had banned psychiatry in the 1930's as 'a bourgeois deception,' and since the thought of submitting troubles to someone else signified Weakness and Humility, the whole thing was out of the question. The intelligent Sidney was but a prisoner in the hands of the various superego wardens, political, personal. If your heroes Lenin and Trotsky managed to live without shrinks, you would too. Besides, no matter how much you might be suffering, it was no more than 'subjectivist' in nature; in other words, sinful. For that you needed a political confessor, not a medical doctor. Those inhibitions helped to bring you down in the end, swifter and surer than you ever knew.

"It also helped to impair your criticism of contemporary writing, I think. You came to this writing with a sort of fear and loathing, quite unlike your balanced response to the older works, no matter how strong the irrationalist or nihilistic impulse. It was as if everything post-1960 was a mistake, an insult, a torment. Why? Perhaps because the best of the modern novels are a literature of the self, not of society, which was your forte; a literature of ego-honesty and truth and stripping down of the self in ways that went deeper than nineteenth-century literature, though it was no more than a continuation of the Tradition of Baudelaire and Dostoyevsky, Chekhov and Proust. In other words, the revelations of the private individual or the exposures of the self, at once self-conscious and painfully enlightened, helplessly chaotic and anti-ideological, or a literature of personal life that included the impact of twentieth-century psychiatry and personal breakdown, without recourse to a philosophy of hope or a religion of salvation—all this was a long long way from the old ideas of the novel which you helped design and develop; and a long long way from the sorts of categories and imprisonments that you yourself, and perhaps many others of your generation, were at home with. How could a man so enormously restricted and blinded (deliberately so), so Old World patriarchal and neoclassical, so much a believer in authority and order, swim easily or intelligently in the chaotic, transitional sea of contemporary letters?"

Solomon left off, weak. He had wanted to get into the whole breakdown in their relationship, but hadn't. It would take a whole other conversation, if that; perhaps a short novel. From the present talk his arms and upper chest felt tired, and he stretched, stretched upward and out. But he couldn't quite stretch away from the grief in his chest at the memory and sight of the older man. The pigeons had been joined by others, waiting too.

"The most surprising thing of all perhaps is that when you did die, and I thought I was through with you, I wasn't. Despite the bad times, I wasn't. On the contrary, I found myself returning to the old days, and fonder times; your classical sanity, insight with the older books; your true curiosity about all sorts of things, behind the print-mask of the indifference, from marijuana to sex to the Beatles to student mores; your humorous fears and ignorances (about directions, driving, practical things around the house); the small pompadour in your hair, a hint of you at twelve perhaps; the great early stories about growing up in Russia, journeying to Palestine, falling in love in Oregon (and being shocked to discover that the young Gentile lady didn't care at all that you were Jewish!) but deciding you had to go to New York to try for a literary career; your first published review, in this new language, and in-person praise from a respected New York magazine editor named Chamberlain; the softness in your abrasive voice when telling about your salad days, and your embarrassed smile at that innocent youth; the smart shirts and fine suits and flashy ties and the meticulous gourmet cooking, which you handled with consummate ease; and memories of Margaret, dark-haired and slow-voiced and darkly lovely, who cared for you and was sustained by that caring, and who fought her limitations to understand your intellectual directions; I returned to those days of fondness, and *realized how much you meant to me, dear Sidney*. Which made me feel irritated at my later indifference, understanding its logic and inevitability, but *wishing that I too was better than myself*, better than a bundle of injured responses and hurt feelings, though one is not better than oneself or not more cunning than one's emotions. The sadness was the deterioration of the relationship; it springs up so rarely as one proceeds in life, especially it seems between literary creatures, that the breakdowns are all the more disappointing.

"Now, several years later, I've returned to love for the younger man who took my arm in Bob's living room where we discussed my origins, you taking a growing quiet pride in my being the son of a poor Russian immigrant, imitating your own childhood, odd origins indeed for one who became one of the two or three foremost critics in the *English*-speaking world."

As if on cue, the pigeons fluttered off, away. The pounding chest and brain told Lionel enough, enough. He scribbled down some notes, three or four basic ideas, that he had just obtained from his torture rack. The last years of Sidney's life would have to be protected, of course; the painful later details, many of which he even now had censored. Did readers ever sense the censorship necessary when trying to turn the real into the fictional, when it touched home somehow? More censorship for a friend, of course, than for oneself. His back and neck ached from stiffness of that truth rack; he hated the solitariness of these explorations, and the addiction of the occupation. He got on his jacket, hurting; and looked forward with delight to a yoga session that would wash his mind clean of the task of memory and interpretation; release from an addiction that more and more seemed to produce truth in inverse ratio to the man's pleasures. Like a wounded animal he reeled out of the apartment and house, across the cool lawn and shadowy twilight toward his old blue Mercedes. That was a far safer machine, he thought, than the small one in his study. Though before getting in, he noted, with irritation, that the silver emblem on the hood had once again been tweaked by some casual passerby so that it drooped like a wilted metallic flower. A good emblem for Royal standard? . . .

(As you can see, his recovery proceeded nicely after the Tippy virus had swept through. He taught decently, if wildly; he would write from his heart's memory and gut's need in the letter to Sidney; it would seem that he had absorbed the strange microbe rather well into his bloodstream and routine. And if you had X-rayed him, peered inside the shell of motion and functioning, you would have gotten a notation like this, from Stendhal's Paris diary of 1810:

> Nevertheless, and in connection with vacuous creatures, they must be possessed, because a given woman who's very insignificant provides delightful pleasure in a good mahogany bed; . . . because the whole comedy is transformed the moment they are possessed. They're Tancredi's flames.

In other words, what he remembered deep down was that this was one of those creatures, not really vacuous or insignificant, but rather disjointed and neurotic, not nineteenth-century but twentieth, whose value was to be seen and felt, in the bed, mahogany or Harvard-frame. If it was not a very original interpretation of the woman, at least it had solid "historical precedence"—Valium for the intellectual. The only twist here, however, concerned the comedy, when it started and how serious it was; and also, at whose expense?)

"I don't think you're getting the right arch in your back . . . you want to bend all the way, as far as possible, your chin touching the ground, remember—*that's better*—can you feel the curve in your upper back that way?"

Chin crushed against workout pad, Solomon croaked out a muffled "Yes" and then raised his head off the ground to face back toward his heels, up on his fingertips. The Sun exercise

129

was supposed to be a warm-up, yet it was extremely trying for the neck and back; lay-ups before a game were not that way, Lionel compared. But *ah*, when you came up and rolled your neck all the way back and felt the massaging effect spread, it was all right, it was splendid, it was yoga-perfect again. With graduating pleasure, he next proceeded through the bow, half-lotus, delicious cobra (his best), then the murderous pelvic stretches (worst). All in preparation for one of the two high spots, the headstand. Having been doing it figuratively for years, he had learned, after four years of practice here, to arrive there literally, with his body. Surprisingly, once you made it there, the position and perspective were most soothing. And you knew, too, that working the earlier exercises carefully, you loosened your neck and back muscles sufficiently for the headstand; just as five exercises later your work will have prepared you for the shoulder stand and plow.

The surroundings of the private living room where the weekly workout took place also relaxed him: the cello on the wall with its sensuous curves, the row of tall potted plants with giant green leaves, the four or five regular girls; and mainly Kate Rogers's routine high spirits and most agile body. In her forties, with three daughters and a basketball-playing, math-professor husband, Kate looked like the old actress Jane Wyman in face, but in athletic grace, in her skyblue leotards, she reminded Lionel of a legendary figure from his childhood, Gertrude Ederle. (He recalled from his *Sport Magazine* and *Jr. Scholastic* the 2 × 3 photo of the great swimmer emerging from the English Channel in her white cap, and covered with oil slick. What did she do during all those hours in the Channel besides swim—sing, read, play with fish?—Lionel had wondered.) So he loved putting himself in this Ederle's hands every week for two hours; yoga massaged his fragile body and kept away the old plagues of upper-back and neck stiffness, and Kate soothed his nerves with her easy confidence and great skill. It was a treat to give himself over entirely that way, abandoning all thinking observing, deciding, and *just follow Kate's orders and directions* for the particular exercise. In truth, he loved being a pupil again. It had been so long, and he had always adored it. And a pupil of the body with a gentle skillful master was most special when you were in your thirties.

Something else. Even if he did adore Madge Coburn's blooming tushy-in-tights when that slim kindergarten teacher scrunched herself up for the lotus, or admired the strong full thighs of dancer-computeress Gerda Mueller—even, in other words, if he did for a second catch assorted female limbs and points of interest with a gaze of lust and hope, *mostly* Lionel didn't look upon the bodies with a sexual eye at all. Rather, with a fellow sportsman's aesthetic regard. Yes, mostly it was the *de*emphasis of sexuality, and the emphasis on treating the body as one treated a paragraph of prose, to be worked on and limbered up and improved, that pleased Solomon. Just the way that Kate now was standing above him, saying, "Now don't let the shoulders sag, keep the back straight and arched, yes, *now* you've got it. And unravel slowly, slowly— wait!" But it was too late, the unraveling had gone too quickly, and there was Lionel tumbling over on his back, just missing the planter but rolling easily with the fall, avoiding any damage or pain. Sat up, smiling, in his sweatpants and gray T-shirt, a man practiced in the art of falling by now, a thousand falls later. Kate inquired, "Did it feel any better when you were up there?" "Sure, for those three seconds it was great. Really." Kate mocked him pleasantly, and suggested that he try to get back farther on his head, his forehead seemed to be touching the mat.

But it was fine, this small failing. After all, you worked on the same posture the first day out that you did five years later; that was the beauty of the art. And at the last position, the twist, in which your torso faced one way and your head and neck the opposite, like a pretzel, he was soothed totally, his mind blank save for the music along with the perfect silence. There was some two or three minutes of this silence there at the end, just as there were intervals of quiet after every strenuous movement, when you bent your head between your knees in a counterposition, known as the baby posture. At one side he faced the baby-grand piano, at the other the couch on one wall; both objects gradually vanished in the quiet of his concentration, and he felt the full relaxation of the room merge with his body. He had never felt his muscles so entirely at ease, and he barely had the will to leave the position. . . . Afterwards, tugging his trousers over his sweatpants, he accepted a private thanks from his body for giving it time this way. Sanity had come to include cooperating with the anatomy, among other things. "Are you going to come to the Bach Oratorio?" Kate asked him, putting on a shirt over her tights. "I get it here." "Oh come on Lionel," she kidded him, "it'll do you good to get some culture!" "I'm going to the Celtics game, what more do you want?" "That's not culture," interceded Marcy, the sexy middle daughter, reminding him of the usual outside temptation again. "It's the only kind I can take, *kid*," he kidded his gum-chewing critic. She glanced up at him briefly, while teasing her cat on the bannister. A slender fourteen-year-old in a wraparound skirt, covering womanly hips. He said, "Do you know that in New Hampshire you can marry at thirteen and not have to hang around stairways?" Mother groaned. Daughter smiled, teeth-braces of a year ago gone. "It's an idea." Did either of them mean marriage?

Standing in the bath, he soaped his chest and neck, and then moved down to his legs, thigh, buttocks and ass, genital area. Taking special care with his water-shriveled pouch, hiding testicles somewhere. He sat down and lay back in the warm tub, gazing at the yellow tiles. Could use some grout, he thought. The running water and subsequent steam closed the workout period with a perfect liquid peace. Through the slightly ajar door, he heard Sheyna practicing; a Beethoven *Romanze*. Scratch, squeak, then a burst of liquid melody; the uneven product of only five or six years' work. Sometimes he stole in the room to watch and listen, though he wouldn't tell her anymore, since that one time when, knowing he was there she shook terribly, nervous. So now he'd spy, to watch her stand there, rather stiff, her grandfather's beautiful old violin on her shoulder, chin tucked in determinedly; he cherished the labor, the aspiration. Particularly Jewish? Perhaps. (But then didn't Elizabeth, his old Gentile friend, play the cello for years while growing up?) He recalled the Babel story about playing the violin in that famous Russian village that had produced many of the great ones. *There,* a perfect sensuous sound; like when she played him the piece she was working on, as done by Oistrakh or Grimiaud, and he would hear the note she was aiming for. . . . He closed his eyes. He had always wanted Rachel to play, for some reason, which turned out, naturally enough, to come from his father's own wish for him to play. Which he had resisted successfully, having given in to attending *cheder* for five years. Then there was Sam Gold in San Francisco, and his love of the instrument; what was the name of his great teacher in Chicago, Misshikoff? Was it in the Russian blood? Or in the Semitic? . . .

*In his mind's stage now, Papa Solomon drifted in . . . the brown eyes fierce beneath the tufted brows, the thick fingers and strong hands, the embarrassed laugh that camouflaged his arrogance, anger. . . . Working at the appetizing counter all his American life, handling belly lox, white fish, herrings, half-sours, instead of being back in the homeland handling horses, Marx and Lenin, an engineering project. . . . Leading the life of a near nobleman, the son of a rich timber merchant and beloved youngest son of a large family, entered in the Gymnasium, no small feat then for a Jew, when all of a sudden it was shattered: a marauding Czarist band, on a pogrom, had come to the small village of Turov, outside Minsk, but his own father, Alexander, refused to leave the house he had built, and so, while the family huddled in the woods behind, they heard a shot, and saw the house go up in flames. . . . Then a year of wandering through Europe working, at a coal mine in Belgium, assorted jobs in Germany, before coming to America with the aid of a distant cousin. . . . At night high school, learning English, while working by day in an appetizing store, and then later studying to be a pharmacist, giving it up finally for business . . . and later, marrying Belle, Lionel's mother, when she was sixteen and he twenty-nine . . . a life of hardship and poverty, in East New York and then Brownsville, aided by his poor judgment in business and of people. He had gone into partnership with another immigrant, whom he didn't know well, against Belle's advice, and one day the partner was gone, with the business's savings, never to be seen again . . . leaving Morris holding the bag. . . .* Seeing his father now, in the dirty white apron and same pair of baggy brown trousers and black shoes, his prisoner's outfit of twenty years, dragging a heavy barrel of half-sours moved Lionel terribly.

"Will you be ready soon?" Sheyna was calling out. "I'm nearly done."

Stuck fast in his heart's journey, he couldn't respond for a moment. Then called back, "Another ten minutes or so?"

She peeked in. "I wish you shaved, so I could give you a shaving brush. My grandfather still uses one."

He nodded. "Close the door, okay sweetie?"

He felt possessive about his privacy here because it was a hot-house for memory, idea, story plan. His writing antennae were benefactors of the steam.

Shaving brush . . . Her own family life, especially with grandfathers, always touched bases that his own father had stepped on. . . . *There was his older sister Ruth, sitting in her Lindenhurst chrome kitchen several years ago, saying, "Love you? Oh Lionel, don't be silly, don't you remember how he treated you? Come on. He was partial to me from the beginning. Don't worry," she added jauntily, "Momma never cared for me, so we're even."* But it wasn't true, Momma did love you! . . .

133

*Shaving brush. Papa used one, with a lather bowl, when he shaved. Twice a day, before breakfast and before supper, without fail. For the evening shave, Lionel came in, and sat on the porcelain tub, to watch—avidly. Was it a barber's long razor he used in the beginning? Long sharp strokes down the cheek, shorter ones under the neck, and, near the end, he would dab some shaving lather on Lionel's six-year-old cheek, and shave it off for him. Oh, Lionel adored those moments. Or the times he would take Lionel to see a sporting event, either boxing matches at Eastern Parkway Arena, to see Harold Green, the middleweight who lived on the block; or else, once every year, to Ebbets Field, not to see the Dodgers—for he hated baseball, it was American—but a European soccer team on tour. At those times Lionel went along to please his father, not caring for the sport because he didn't really know the rules or any of the ballplayers. So he sat in those grandstand seats above third base, imagining it was Reese and Cox and Hermanski he was observing, until there was an attack on the goal and his father would stand up and lift Lionel onto the wooden seat to see that shot. And—*

*Father shaving again. This time, Lionel and his mother have just come back from the doctor's. After years of taking hormone injections to bring down the testicle undescended from birth, Lionel at thirteen has gone to the specialist, a kindly man who talks like Jean Hersholt. An operation is imperative, says the older doctor; the displaced testicle, if left in the stomach region, can cause cancer later on, among other problems. There's also the question of reproductive power; two testes are safer than one. His mother explains all this, softly, to the father shaving; carefully she keeps Lionel away, but he listens in, pretending to study.*

"An operation?" His father looks warily at his mother. "How much will it cost?"

His mother shrugs, reducing the figure automatically. "A few hundred probably. Maybe less."

He shakes his head, shaving cream on cheek, looking out of the bathroom door. "BIST DU MESHUGGAH? Two hundred dollars." Sheepish laugh. "Where am I going to get that?"

She persists, quietly. "It's important. He has to have it. Period."

The father turns again, holding the razor, saying, "You want to break me, don't you. Put me in the poorhouse, you and your son. You won't do it, believe me. You won't. I'll take him to a different doctor."

And then, there, in slow motion somehow, Lionel is on his

*feet, enraged, saying, "I need that operation, the doctor said so. And I'm going to have it."*

*The father enters the living room as if on cue, and says slowly to his son, "Don't* YOU *open your mouth, you hear?"*

*His mother pulls Lionel away. "Ssshh, Lev, go do your homework, go ahead. Please, for* MY *sake."*

*Father doesn't budge but stares at the boy, eyes aflame, shaving cream still on face, razor in hand. Lionel, trembling, backs off, and moves into the kitchen. After a few minutes, his mother appears and, opening the cupboards, takes out pots and pans. She silences him with her finger, saying, "You let me handle it, okay? Don't mention it over dinner, or again. Remember."*

*So presently, in stony silence, he is eating his* FLANKEN, *watching his father salt it mercilessly, and eat with gusto. . . .*

*In the hospital, nine months later, the testicle has been restored to its rightful home, and the scrotum has been attached by stitches to the thigh. The first few days are pain, but then okay, as streams of visitors come and go. Papa visits once, spruced up in suit, tie, fedora, charms the tough brown nurse, and cheerfully jokes with Lionel, "Well, sonnyboy, how are you?" . . . Lionel in the bath adjusts the hot water, wants to stop the memory, but is helplessly locked into it. A few weeks later, recovering at home, Lionel sits on the toilet seat, for this terrible ordeal. Sweating wildly to drop a tiny turd, Lionel notices that the discolored scrotum has suddenly swung free of the thigh! He's strained too much! Shaking in terror, his mother out shopping, he instinctively calls his father. He tells him what's happened. "Very nice, you fool," says knowing Papa, "now you'll probably have to have it all over again.* OY, BIST DU A NAR!" *Somehow, Lionel gets the receiver back to the hook, crying. Remembers his sister, a legal secretary in Manhattan. Calls, and overcoming his timidity about the intimate details, tells the story again. Ruth says, "Oh don't worry, Lionel, if all you were doing was going to the bathroom and the doctor never warned you about it, it's probably nothing. Call the doctor, and see what he says before you start worrying. Really, Lionel, I'm sure it's nothing." He will thank her all his life for this calming, he promises privately—and indeed sinks ten grand into her husband's failing business twenty years later, for this kindness in adolescence. He has a chance, perhaps he's not a total fool, a criminal. And indeed, in a minute or two, the doctor apologizes for the slipup; he thought the nurse had explained, those*

135

*stitches are dissolvable. Did he think he would go through life with the scrotum attached to his thigh? the doctor asks kindly. Come in on Friday for the regular visit, and he apologizes again for frightening him. It takes Lionel a few hours to quiet down, to stop shaking. And when his mother hears about Papa's response, she says bitterly, "The bastard, the dirty bastard."*

The music shifts, from the violin practice to a lovely trio. Brahms?

How could a two-minute reflection hit so deep? lie stuck so fast in one's life? The water has gotten chilly, he turns on the hot faucet; and, as if turning over in a long dream, he sinks back again, the water dripping in the overflow drain.

In his thirteenth year? *A Friday night, with Momma away for the weekend, a not uncommon occurrence in the past few years. Alone with his father; they've had dinner, and a good Hebrew lesson for his Bar Mitzvah? he forgets. His singing has improved to the tolerable level. Lionel explains casually that he's going out later, to East Ninety-second Street, to Boodie's house, to kid around with the guys. Momma knows about it. Somehow or other he's put it wrong, or said something else wrong, for Papa says, "No, you'll stay in tonight." His father is washing the dishes in the narrow kitchen, Lionel dries, and puts them away in the cupboard; the smell of horseradish in the air. The boy says that he has been waiting for it all week, and Momma knows all about it. The wrong authority cited, he realizes immediately. His father turns and faces Lionel, eyes dilating; dish towel, like a waiter's, is over his shoulder, and he's wearing his old-fashioned vest undershirt. Lionel, sensing danger, claims nothing more, puts away a plate, backs off. "So your mother said you could go out, eh?" The father, medium-built, sturdy, black hair protruding above his undershirt, goes to the cupboard drawer, and takes out a long bread knife, used to cut challah. Why? Lionel wonders, moving back, heart pounding, past the wooden kitchen table, past the black and white porcelain stove. His father takes a step forward, and another, slowly, determinedly. "What she says counts here, eh? And what I say means nothing, eh?" Lionel still steps back, until there's the window at his back, closed, with the fire escape beyond; the noises of busy Sutter Avenue recede. His father approaches, and Lionel raises his arms to shield himself, to show defense without trying to provoke his father. His father clamps the boy's hands by the wrists, and forces them down. Then, controlling his own ferocity, his father stands there, maybe eighteen inches away, blocking escape. Papa's ears look extra large, the nose more bulbous, the eyes wild; as if his racing blood has pumped out his features grotesquely. He holds the long wooden-handled knife between Lionel and himself, lips trembling with anger, just on the verge of a momentous act. He holds the knife there steadily, for a long time, a minute like an hour, the blade facing Lionel's stomach. Finally he says, "You hate me, don't you?" Lionel, limp from fear and terror, shakes his head, whispering, "No, no." Without speaking, the father judges (correctly) that statement to be false, unpacifying, and shakes his head. Then says, "You'd love to use this on me, wouldn't you?" Lionel can barely shake his head. The father then takes Lionel's hand and urges the knife into it. Shrewdly. "Go ahead, go—" The knife is dropped to the floor. Papa's brown wild eyes face his son, and he bends and retrieves it; his patience in all of this is steady. Lionel makes a fist at his side, squeezing it tightly, swearing not to open it! But Papa, stronger, pries open the fist and clamps the knife back into the grip, and raises the boy's unwilling hand. "You'd love to, wouldn't you? Your* MOTHER *said you could go out, eh? Use it, go ahead." The boy almost topples over from this unusual terror; he might even stick the blade into his father, so* STRANGE *and so long is the moment. But there is no willpower in him, no hatred now, just a limp* UNREALITY *and exhausted fear. Tears are coursing down his cheeks, at last, as if they've been paralyzed too. A horn on Sutter Avenue sounds and somehow Lionel manages to release the knife once again; does he kick it a few feet away?* Doesn't remember. *The father shakes his head now, facing him; Lionel, expecting, wanting a slap, receives nothing. The father just shakes his head in mad disappointment? . . . in triumph? With a very slight nodding and small condescending noise, Papa at last turns away, picks up the long knife and returns it to the cupboard; goes back then to the sink, and goes back to washing the dishes. Slowly, the outside comes back to life; cars whisper by, shoppers outside talk again. Presently, with the water running, Lionel thaws slightly from fear, and like a man who's been out too long in bitter cold, tests his unused legs, moving out of the kitchen, slowly, very slowly, not wanting to panic here. In the living room a sobbing begins, and by the time he makes it to the bathroom, a shaking of his body begins; he turns on the faucet, for camouflage. He rinses his face and forehead, and sinks to the linoleum floor to shake and sob . . . he leans over the tub, and rinses his face again, and falls back to the linoleum in an uncontrollable paroxysm of shock. . . .*

*After his father has gone to bed that night, the shaking starts again, in his bed, and lasts into the night.*

Lionel's neck is crooked into a stiff position in the bath, his heart is excited, he moves his head and neck. The yellow tiles are there, and this floor has a bathrug. He pulls the plug from the drain and sinks back to Brownsville.

*The next morning his father makes a casual reference to the night before, treating it as an unpleasant argument. Lionel goes along with the casualness, pretending it's forgotten and saying the hot Ralston tastes good. When his father talks to him, he shakes privately; and when he thinks about the incident, while playing left field in the schoolyard that morning, he starts crying, right there, and wipes his face with his mitt. The rest of the weekend Lionel keeps up the charade of being good-tempered, casual, polite. Occasionally, the unusual terror machine grips him and tosses him uncontrollably, in private minutes; he crumples over, like a sick man; the two days and night pass like a century of history before Sunday night comes, and Momma returns, and time, as he knows it returns. She isn't in the house fifteen minutes before Lionel breaks down, sobs, shakes, and stuttering—which he never does—tells her about the incident as well as he can. Even then, JUST FORTY-EIGHT HOURS LATER, it's hard for him to remember all the pieces, or to speak of them aloud. Stuttering, shaking, he finally gets the story out. His mother, calm, replies, "Don't worry, it won't last much longer, Lev. And I won't leave you alone with him again." And in a few weeks or so, a locksmith comes and inserts a new lock into the steel door of the apartment; Lionel brings a bundle of his father's clothes to a mutual friend on Union Street. His mother calls Papa at the store and tells him that if he tries to come home, he won't get in, the lock's been changed, and she will call the police if he tries. The mention of "police" frightens him, as it always did, because he had entered America on a dubious passport; he doesn't try, though he telephones again and again. Wants to talk to Lionel, who won't talk to him. . . .*

Solomon got out of the bath and began drying himself off briskly, feeling as if he had just taken a long walk in the New Hampshire cold, and overworked his body. It had been like writing, this peculiar helpless exhaustion. At the bathroom mirror he trimmed the mustache of his beard, snipping carefully. Then, to shake himself out of the nightmare memory, he dabbed some shaving cream on his nose and cheeks, put a

138

stroke of lipstick on his forehead and lips, stole into the living room where he got two peacock feathers and his jogging headband, and keeping on his robe and shorts and nothing else, hotfooted it into the kitchen, where he began an old war dance from his adolescent days, whooping and hollering and chanting so that Sheyna thought he must have had the best writing day in quite a while! Not a bad guess, actually, one that he could tell himself as well.

And over dinner, a lovely light quiche with green salad and white wine, he asked Sheyna about the history of Zionism she was reading, which he had brushed over before. "What was Herzl like actually?" he asked, wanting to be cleansed of all intimate memory. "What brought on this interest?" she asked, surprised. In candlelight, her beautiful soft-brown color was highlighted, and her clear full-bodied voice soothed him. "He wasn't an intellectual, you know. Not really. And his main ambition in life was to be a great literary man, a playwright; but his plays were supposed to be pretty awful. He was a journalist mainly, and wrote for a well-known Austrian newspaper. He was a dandy, a dilettante—just the right sort to start a Zionist movement. Anyway, he went to Paris in 1891 or so, had a bad time in his marriage, and got very interested in the Dreyfus affair, and then began to think seriously about the Jews. And in 1896, his pamphlet *Der Judenstaat* got the attention of Jews around the world, and a year later, he was creating the First Zionist Congress."

"Was that the first pamphlet about the Jews and a homeland?"

"No, not really; there were men like Pinsker before him, and even Moses Hess before that. But Herzl, well, he came at the right time in a way, and also was a great propagandist. From nowhere he became one of the most famous Jews. He then spent the rest of his life trying to convince Jews and the rest of the world to give the Jews a homeland, at first either in Argentina or Palestine, and later on, possibly in Uganda. He traveled to Constantinople and tried to negotiate with the sultan, Palestine being under the Ottoman Empire at the time; later he went to Egypt and negotiated with Lord Cromer of Britain, and near the end, went to Russia trying to get help there from the Czarist government. He was a man suddenly possessed, and the Jewish masses greeted him in places like Sofia as if he were the new Moses. He was a kind of one-man operation, with all sorts of theatrical ideas as well. When someone claimed that all the 'noise' he was making would ricochet against the Jews, he said, 'What do you think

139

world history is except Noise?' Or when the first Congress opened, he made his associates like Nordau dress in swallow tails and white tie." She poured and drank wine. "He put Zionism on the map really, and gave up his adult life to the cause. And all the while you know, most rich and influential Jews looked down their noses at him, scorned him, mocked him. He died at forty-four."

Lionel listened carefully to this lovely girl with the fine excited interest, and was slightly jealous of Mr. Herzl and his Cause. Couldn't he, Solomon, lose himself in one? And give over his foolish private life for such a grand scheme and idea? Did Herzl sit in the bathtub, hounded by a bizarre past; and even, sometime later, feel impelled to write it down? To stick his face in the mud and pain of his life, when you could go to Constantinople?

Lionel observed, "Sounds like a great movie, with those meetings with the Sultan and Lord Cromer, and then that first Congress."

"Oh yes. And he was a momma's boy all the way. His wife never really counted in his life."

Solomon took that in, slowly. Was he, Solomon, the same sort of boy? What Movement would he start? "What happened after him?"

And as she spoke about the idealists and martyrs and brave men to come, Lionel was pacified. Felt sane again, safe again. So, while she made tea, he got out the framed portrait of Heifetz, and set it at her place setting, ready for her.

"Hey, what's this?" her face glowing with delight. And when she opened it, she kissed him and hugged him, and asked who the young violinist was, a relative? "He looks like a real beginner, the way he's holding the bow."

At nine-fifteen he was walking through Harvard Square, on the way to the Orson Welles Restaurant to meet Rachel. Peace had returned to the sixties' war zone around the MBTA island, the Coop, Holyoke Center. No more klieg lights, snarling shepherd dogs, bands of visored police, curfew hours, angry students. The revolutionary stirrings and radical energies of the past decade had been swept up, vacuumed away into poster-humor, pop tunes. Prague had left Cambridge and returned to Eastern Europe. And after the exile of the petty tricky Tyrant, the mood here was one of Babbitt tranquillity and Main Street conformism; wasn't that old chaotic energy far preferable? Or was it? For an old radical like Lionel, it was sad, pathetic. Students with a passion for social justice were now would be doctors or lawyers, worrying about

140

careers at a premature age. "Lionel, you don't *care* anymore," spun in his head as he passed the Harvard Book Store. Each to his own complacency, right, Mr. Solomon? Mr. Flaubert? he asked himself. Or, as he noted in the window the book about the old slave's narrative, was it that caring had its own evolutions? (And revolutions?)

The darkened Welles was alive with music (taped), picture slides, customers. *Au pair* girls and foreign students and local undergraduates and "freaky" professionals huddled around butcher-block tables, lit by candles. If you closed your eyes and were asked where you were, you'd say the entrance to a lumberyard. Rachel waved to him from a corner table, between a hanging vine and huge rubber plant. She hugged him in greeting and sat down. He sensed the looks around them, knowing how often they were taken for a budding couple, not old family.

"I ordered, you were late, okay? I'm having an orange-chocolate something, wanna taste?" She wore a black turtleneck, and the old Mexican pin he had given her for high school graduation.

Lionel tasted the drink, found it too sweet.

"Hi."

The waitress was an old friend, a slender blond from Utah who had escaped the Mormons for Cambridge Jews. "Hey," he said, and kissed her on the cheek, having forgotten she worked here. There didn't seem to be enough room or time for everyone he knew. This tender Jenny, wounded in life, stirred him. "How are you?"

"Okay, okay. You've been well?"

"Uh, yeah. Pretty well." He introduced his daughter, ordered a beer, and Jenny left.

Rachel sipped her drink, eyeing him, not saying a word. He was most grateful.

They waited.

She said, then, in her thin voice, "You were really revved up in class the other day. It was something to see."

He was surprised at the size of the beer Jenny brought. "Thanks."

"Are you after a bigger allowance?" he asked. A year ago, when she had complained that he had stopped her allowance at thirteen, he had started it up again, two bucks then, now three. They both enjoyed that. (Or did she?) "Tell me a bit about your friend," he said. "Does your mother know about it yet?"

"No," she answered, smiling. "I want something to look

forward to. I'll wait till Grandma Jackson comes up for a holiday." Lionel smiled at the thought of Evelyn Lou Jackson of Baton Rouge meeting Mr. Richard Muffalo. His daughter began to explain about the gentleman, a West Indian educated at British schools, then Oxford, and now teaching at Harvard. With a side interest in drama. "You know what, Dad? He once acted with the Burtons in Oxford, and could have played Othello there if he wanted. Found it an insulting role."

Lionel considered. "He's got a point. Not a very credible citizen, was he?" He adjusted the vine, to see his daughter better.

As she spoke, in her staccato New York way, he was appealed to in ways deeper than her high forehead, fine skin, crooked tooth. By genes he knew: the quick humor, the irony, the sudden sensitivity; then there was the other side, not genes but . . . resentment? (earned) distrust?

"I didn't realize he teaches at Harvard," Lionel observed, caring little about her beaux, really. A pact he made with himself when he saw her first one. About her relationship to him, to Solomon-blood, he was fascinated.

Rachel lit up a cigarette. "That's how I met him. He's my section leader."

The line hit him oddly; as did the way she smoked out of the corner of her mouth, or the slight makeup she wore on the lips and cheeks. His sensitive, ironic Radcliffe girl had for a moment turned into a cunning sporting girl, out on the make. (Making *whom?*)

Immediately he wondered how much of this was Solomon projection?

The face had changed and he was grateful. What had she asked him?

"I said, now what about Tippy? Of course you couldn't talk the other day, and I shouldn't have brought it up there. But what's happening with her and you?"

And when he gazed at her sipping her tall drink and chatting as if he were her roomie, not father, and he didn't speak, she said, "Now don't go silent on me, or tell me you've given her up, it's all over. I know you better than that. Besides," she sipped it to the end, the straw making a rasping sound, "I think she'll make it interesting for you."

"You're seeing too many movies," he said casually.

"Just so long as Sheyna doesn't find out! You don't want to lose *her*, you know. Who else would take care of you? Live with you? You've grown rather impossible . . . into yourself,

142

your moods. You know that." She fingered the vine to her hair, almost absentmindedly.

Lionel burned. Is this what he got for his monthly checks to Dr. Mirsky, this neurotic provocation, teasing? Was she to speak her thoughts, no matter how whimsical or injurious?

Her tone lightened. "Look Dad, don't get so uptight, it's none of my business. It's just that I liked her . . . style. Sense of cool. And she's really a *looker*." She shrugged. "Look, I'm all for it, okay? Why not? You've worked hard, you've earned your good times, you're going to be immortal . . . why not? Even if it's a little trouble. As you've always told me, that's not the worst thing, right?" (Taking his language.) "Let me know about it now and then, that's all. I'm *interested*." Exhaled smoke.

Lionel savored the bitterness of the beer. "I'll try to keep you up to date. Post the details outside my office." He forced a smile.

"Now you're talking. That's better. You're so *touchy* sometimes, honest." Persistent had turned breezy. "Hey, did I tell you that Mom and Ken are buying a new house? Yeah, in Park Slope. You ought to come and visit sometime. Ken's published some new poems, did you know?"

Lionel shook his head, and began to listen to the light rock music.

"Hey Dad, look there, isn't that super?"

Lionel turned around, and saw on the huge wall a color slide of great steep hills shooting out of red desert.

"Monument Valley! Mickey and I went there two summers ago, coming back from California. You have to go there sometime, no kidding. Shake some of the old Northeast out of your system!"

"It does look spectacular," he responded. "Maybe when I finish this book I'll take a trip."

She waved her hand. "Oh come on, do you know how many trips you *haven't* taken between books? I mean, Dad, it's . . . it's . . ." fighting for the right term to express the obvious, "it's *sick* not to be able to take off from writing. Or from *anything*. God, you'd write in your grave if they threw a typewriter down there with you!" Half mirth, half something else.

For a moment Lionel took the thought very seriously, seriously afraid.

"Okay, where's my three bucks?" she asked cheerfully, at last. "Or are you copping out? And oh yeah, you don't have to listen to those kids about what Ahab is after, Papa. You

do your thing, it's better than anything they get, believe me."
She leaned over, pecked him on the cheek, her scent his. "I
better run, can I drop you off? Hey, did I tell you about
those great wool booties that Grandma sent up to me?
They're the cat's really. When are you going to go in and see
her? She is your *only* mother, you know."

He handed her the three (play) bills, thinking of another
hand and request a few weeks ago, and answered, "The cat's,
eh? I'll walk out with you."

"But hurry, huh? I'm supposed to pick up Richard at ten-
fifteen sharp!"

She had got on her pea jacket, and Lionel walked to the
register. He patted Jenny Lynd on her bony hip, gave her a
few dollars, told her to keep the change. She protested, blushing. He kissed her cheek. "I'll call you one day, okay?"

"That'd be nice."

Outside the Welles, Rachel took his arm. "Brrr! Only in
Boston do you get weather like this the first week of April.
My car's over there."

They walked across the street, toward a long low sleek tan
car, she hugging his arm. She unlocked the door and kissed
him with a flourish. "Mmm, that's good."

"What's the name of this again?"

"Jav-e-lin. That's three times now!"

He nodded, still surprised that he couldn't remember the
name of his own gift. "What happened to Pontiac and Chev-
rolet?" he asked aloud.

"Went out with the steam engine. Bye, sweets."

And she gunned out.

(A word about such talk: At the time naturally it was hard
for him to take such accusations, "Impossible, Moody . . ."
But of course that's all true, he was rather impossible. He
was subject to moods. Fits of irritability, or great excitement.
Why? The writing did that to him. If he did well during the
day, he was playful by twilight, honey at night; if he did
badly by day, especially if he had been interrupted, he was irritable at 5:30, and, by the evening, near-unbearable. Which
he would take out on Sheyna, naturally; jump at her at the
slightest provocation, and turn it into a mountainous disturbance. But such moodiness is nothing new for a writer, to be
sure. A hostage to his work, through and through; simple
enough bondage. As for the Impossible, that included his
growing penchant for absorbing each and every one of his
habits as if they were new and fascinating data in a research
experiment, to be observed with clinical care and interest.

Hence, minor abominable habits—overlong finger- and toe-nails, scratching his scalp and ears, hypochondria during common colds (a favorite; he had written a long story about his getting a cold, adoring the details, and when an editor found it "too personal," Lionel, hurt, understood with some gratification)—all these and much more he looked upon with interest, not disdain, as he went on; he wouldn't dream of altering a single item for the sake of *adjustment*. In other words, the petty foibles and eccentricities of his personal life were not merely valuable data concerning an endlessly fascinating subject, himself, but also, they were part of his life, like children.

Yes, Impossible from a practical point of view, yes. But no more than the whims, aims and aromas of the artist. Or the societally useful narcissist, whichever.)

Walking back, toward Sheyna's, he stopped at the used-book stalls in front of the Harvard Book Store. Browsed among the paperbacks on the wooden rack. Portable Veblen, popular novels, Beginner's Chess, all half price. He picked up a copy of *The Long Death*, a description of the last days of the Plains Indians. A present for his friend? Leafed through it: photographs of Indians, maps of the Little Big Horn, names like Custer, Crazy Horse, Little Wolf, Captain Fetterman, General Crook. Lionel stopped at that; said the name aloud. Crook. *General Crook.* It came back to him now. . . . Tippy's restaurant tale. What he took to be her "tall tale." Was it? He read about Crook a bit, discovering him admirable and very competent. In the index he searched for Matthews . . . Jeremy something Matthews. Nothing. Was there one? If Crook was for real, was Colonel Matthews for real too? He felt confused, penitential. He went inside, and purchased the book, thinking it might come in handy at some point—to learn a bit about his country's history.

Leaving the store, he decided to walk back by way of the river, by Memorial Drive, along the august Harvard dormitories with their high black gates. Cars hushed by, hugging curves; trees swayed; the river flowed imperceptibly. Despite the risk of mugging, there was the special reward of solitary locomotion at night, here: the imagination was most alert. It acted like an amazing minesweeper, sweeping over the terrain of facts, and subverting it, enlarging it, changing it. Just so long as you didn't break your ankle on the factual hunchback brick of the sidewalks.

*"You've worked hard, you've earned your good times,*

*you're going to be immortal. . . .*" The crazy, humorous, capricious words came back, stayed.

The sensuous black river brought on thoughts of Melville, that odd dark life. From sailing and tropics and exotic novels and cannibals and early soaring fame to New England puritanism and joyless marriage to the Chief Justice's prudish daughter and conventional domesticity and then *Moby Dick* and critical ambivalence, to be followed by censure, growing isolation. And finally a breakdown, resulting in great part from the exhausting struggle with the great book and its indifferent reception; and then *Pierre*, and wholesale total abuse. No, he was not allowed to write a bad book, nor to deviate from happy adventure stories. For *Pierre*, he was treated like a criminal. Gradually, the will to write in the greatest native talent of the century was stifled, dried up, with the aid of native critics and the featherheaded public. Ah, there was real crime! Even old Nathaniel H. didn't—or *couldn't*, constitutionally—stick by his friend, after a time. The temperament of Herman was too gloomy, the imagination too feverish, the experience too foreign, for remote restrained properly trained Nat. Lionel remembered Herman's anticipated meeting with Hawthorne in England when he, Melville, was depressed and then Nat's cool reception, complicated betrayal. How was it that Hawthorne had put it, that Melville had "pretty much made up his mind to be annihilated." The word sent a shiver up Lionel's spine.

The air had turned warmer, the breeze seemed almost sirocco, and the trees swayed softly.

Lionel allowed the sympathy to shift to himself; to his abuse, his isolation. Of his pain he had a precise memory, helped out by a few lines he had saved from the reviews in *Time*. He knew one by heart, keeping it near his heart, on paper.

> *Rosen at Fifty* and *Pamela: Self Portrait* both exhibit a sick imagination pondering pathological ideas and pandering obscene scenes, and the results are nothing less than degrading for a once interesting and insightful author.

The words, even now, a few years later made his heart drop. The substitution of moralistic judgment for literary criteria burned him. The shallow reading of complicated scenes hurt him. The middlebrow prudery distorting even the bare surface of the novels, let alone their meaning, scalded him. Must you be a Good Boy and Top-notch Citizen in your literature?

Couldn't scrupulous realism touch all aspects of life without resorting to literary tricks or adolescent euphemism? Was there any writer more obscene than war ministers, shyster lawyers, indifferent doctors? Come now, we're over twenty-one, one's private urges and ego-tricks are mostly humerous and harmless, save perhaps to oneself. . . . On top of this "literary criticism" had come personal innuendo, slander, gossip: charges of arrogance, elitism, perversity, dislike of women. Would impotence and homosexuality come next? Oh, he had hurt, hurt! (He leaned against a tree.) You spent years building a reputation, and, in a week or two, saw it hacked to bits with a print-cleaver. . . . Couldn't the narrator of a novel be separated from its author? and if not, why *pretend* then? why not just write LIONEL SOLOMON instead of a protagonist's name? Because if you did, you were dead—accused of Unconscionable Vanity and Self-indulgent Art. His work vilified, his reputation blackened, what could he do but take it, take it? Break down in private? Not write for months? And seriously contemplate ending that rack called living? . . .

A car pulled over to the curb, followed Lionel slowly, and a young man asked directions. Lionel, gripped in his resentment, pointed out Winthrop Street, and the car drove off.

He crossed over to the dirt path of the river side of the Drive, and walked there. The river flowed rather rapidly now, and gleamed with light-reflections.

The consequences. Near breakdown, depression, dejection. A horror known only to those who have been down there, that way. Not understood by the healthy, the active, the functioning. By the moral doctors who would read about such grit, and then perhaps write an essay of jeweled wit concerning it; by the physical doctors who went home and had fine wine and the comfort of family, and didn't have to lie in your soiled clothes or dirty pajamas, knowing you wouldn't sleep, and knowing that morning would bring nothing new; and knowing too that you were in an asylum, called a sanitarium. Shouldn't the doctors be forced to lie down with you, to feel your despair in their bones? to lose their appetite for food, sex? the will to deal with the world? Did Lirič, a good man, a wise doctor, sense that his purely clinical questioning was missing the point of Lionel's deep spiritual gloom in those days? It seemed so. He had a touch of the philosopher, the artist, which made him more than a head doctor; he was not a determinist machine. Having a soul, he recognized it in others, and recognized when *it*, and not the ego, was troubled. Most terrible about the depression was that you knew it could come back; put that in your memory and try to live optimistically. How had he made it? With the talks with Lirič; with the great affection and devotion of Sheyna; and of course, with those letters he had started writing—the real pain giving impetus to the artistic work, which renewed his will. The paradox of hurting and writing.

Yes, paranoid too. But why not? Wasn't it reasonable and inevitable to suspect everyone *after* people had gotten on you? Oh, he knew well enough that it was an "inconvenient emotion," as a country friend had put it; but which emotion of his wasn't? His anger, passion, jealousy, anguish, why even his highs were "inconvenient." So feeling himself in a corner wasn't something totally new, then, even looking over his shoulder occasionally. (Once he had had a bankrobber student, for example, whom he had lectured sternly, and then he had worried for weeks, months, that the young man would come back and get him. And wasn't this new crazy girl, this misguided fan, following him everywhere, somehow?) But Solomon didn't need these shadowy presences for his fear and resentment; there were critics, colleagues, old friends, academic acquaintances. (And literary oblivion.) Room enough for everyone to look in and laugh, mock, vilify, put down, shame. Paranoid. In retrospect, it wasn't so bad, the state; he even rather liked it; it was as modern a perspective as any. Better than other styles these days—violent schizophrenia, macho narcissism, pussy-whipped manhood, whathaveyou. Only during that month at Swerdlow's, and the parenthesis of months before and afterwards, paranoia—and they!—had all but killed him, brought him to his knees in hopeless crying and shaking.

Solomon apostrophized:

*"O Herman, I sympathize, I sympathize. Ten years ago I accepted my life as a confusion, voted for it, gave in to it. The repetitions, barnacle habits, friends who wanted me to stay the same as I was at twenty-seven and resented any change. And losing them, just when I needed them the most! The mistakes, the accidents, bad judgments, unwilling sacrifices—all for the sake of the work, the "immortal" work! It was this which would offset the shoddy life of error and confusion. The author Solomon was the god, the man Lionel was his circus clown. But when the parasites and the lice got to work on the man, how could I play God, distant and amused? I was too weak, Herman, too weak! Pouring pain with every breath. Herman, in your time they did it with*

*public abuse and isolation alone; now there's* MOCKERY *added
to it. The mockery of cheap fame, salt on the wounds. And
now, sir, this new book of suicide letters—is this pathological
too? silly? But can't we use our lives, our pain, for
"material"? Must it all be Let's Pretend, fantasy, "fabula-
tion"? All we abuse is ourselves (maybe our loved ones).
And doesn't the real question concern the book, not the life?
Herman, am I headed for another deeper bottom because
those letters were* REAL *at one time? How does one know,
judge? All I remember is how difficult it was to* MUSTER THE
WILL TO BEGIN AGAIN. *Should I become a customs inspector
for the next twenty years and check out student papers the
way you checked out shipping crates? in silence, in exile, in
oblivion, on one's native soil? . . .*

*And what would you do, my spiritual friend, if someone
named Tippy arrived in Pittsfield, on her way back to the
Marquesas? Would you have turned her away? Stashed her in
the barn with the cow? Told Hawthorne about her? her and
you?*

*Austere Herman, standing there, spoke solemnly, "I lacked
the will, Lionel. At least on native soil I did. Don't you."*

Lionel, intensely interested, walked closer to the water. He
asked, *"Did you mean, sir, 'Don't you,' or 'Don't you?' "*

*"Don't I what, mister?"* asked the hooded nightjogger, easing to a halt a few paces beyond where Lionel stood.

Solomon was taken aback by the strange face.

"Who are you?" Clipped authoritative voice. "You okay?"

"Sure . . . just walking . . ." Solomon gave a little nervous laugh, explained who he was, and still dazed, offered his
faculty card.

The jogger threw his hood off, revealed a strong face with
prematurely gray hair. ". . . Well, Professor, if I were you I
wouldn't talk out loud, or walk around here, at this time.
Lots of queer, dangerous characters wander here at night."
Citizen's warning.

Was the river's edge only for the healthy, then? Joggers
only? Maybe, maybe. . . . Yes; even this stranger could see
that Lionel wasn't safe out on the streets, out in the world.
"You're right. I slipped up. Foolish. Glad you came by." To
remind Solomon.

The man tugged at the drawstring waist of his sweatpants,
and walked Solomon up from the grassy bank to the lighted
path, explaining he was a part-time guard at Harvard.

"English literature, eh? The stories I could tell you, buddy.

The *characters* you meet." He laughed. "If only I could write!"

*Characters like me?* "Thanks. See you around."

"Good night, professor. Let me know if you ever want to hear some *real* stories." He shook his head. "And watch where you walk these nights."

The message stayed with Solomon as he walked the last few blocks to Sheyna's place.

It was much later, after a late cognac (with Sheyna making her child's face of distaste for the strong liquor) and late reading (Tanizaki's stories; a far more interesting writer than the better-known Kawabata), and Solomon lay there, in bed. Next to him nestled Sheyna, her lovely head in the crook of his arm. Content after sex, both of them. On a late-night talk show the other night, Dr. Christiaan Barnard had said yes, sex was a risk factor for men and their hearts. Solomon listened to his, pumping regularly. Nothing crazy, like after a session with the girl from the Southwest. Here the intercourse had been strong but reasonable, no screams, obscenities, scratches, dirty fingers or dirtier taunts; he had flowed into the gracious woman with contoured satisfaction and easy pleasure. A fine sane orgasm. (Suitable for a man nearing forty, Dr. Barnard?)

Light from the streetlamp had edged shadows upon the ceiling, oppositions of odd shape. Here too sex had been peace, not war. The act shaped by many past runs and performances; sculpted and more finished by familiarity; controlled too, subtly and gradually, by days of companionship and friendship. An act of motion and spontaneity fixed after a while by repetitions, sexual and nonsexual. So that the very thing which brought it a comfortable pleasurable structure was also at work inhibiting certain variations and wildness. The paradox of repetition. His beauty moved, and he saw her in profile: a fine firm nose, full chin, brown skin like a high yellow's or a sabra's, the fine distribution of features, the dark flowing masses of hair. A Jewish Madonna. A Rembrandt Sheyna. There had been moments in their relation when he could have had her do many naughty sexy things; he hadn't wanted that route for her, for them. Felt too much tenderness for her; love. Of course his own inhibitions were showing. Inhibition with the one you felt intimate with, an old story. Desire modulated, tamed. Desire made tender; like dressing up an anarchist in a three-piece business suit.

It was such an odd thing, desire (and its fulfillments). It

150

had as many shapes as women you met. (He didn't like making comparisons between women, particularly with that Tippy, particularly here, in his good woman's bed. In fellatio, for example, he remembered his early wife, who really had little feel for it; a later girlfriend, who came to it kindly and refined, as if she were bending down to aid a welfare child; Sheyna, whose aim it was to give him pleasure, and who did; and the Creature, for whom it was a weapon, a powerful weapon that she used expertly. . . . ) And what may have been a full head of desire to begin with, in the beginning of an affair, evolved into something else, something domesticated by time and familiarity. And changed ultimately to something else, some other things. You spent most of your time out of bed, not in it; and if you were going to spend time with someone over a period of time, then it was those qualities outside of bed that gradually interested you. Good talk, intelligence, humor, common sense, practicality, kindliness, fidelity, comradeship, competence; on and on the list went; then what about desire? What happened to it after the initial stage of fulfilling it?

If it atrophied with your long-standing companion, then why did it reflower and open up with a new woman? Was this fair? No, but what *was* in sexual selection? Was it that the new woman, by means of her different style or emotions, different way of valuing or speaking, different moments of silence even, challenged you in some way? Scared you, opened you, and educated you—about yourself especially? If that were the case, then the charge of promiscuity for promiscuity's sake was not merely a crude one (at best) but actually missed the subtler strands of desire. You could learn from desire the same way perhaps that you might learn by a pursuit of other emotions, if there were an outlet for it. The point was, to take desire seriously, *and* ambitiously; and not back off from it because of fear, but rather be spurred on because of that. Ah, easier said than done! Sheyna curled into him from her backside, her habit.

Enough. He got out of bed and went to the kitchen. He opened the refrigerator, saw those gleaming Temple oranges sent up from Florida by Sheyna's grandfather, but decided upon a banana instead. Easier peeling. He ate it while marching around the darkened living room, checking on her various plants: rhododendron, coleus, flowering begonias, a potted avocado. She loved growing these from tiny shoots. (Like her favorite, the avocado, now four feet tall.) Lionel had never believed in the theory about tenderness aiding plants, until

151

these past years with Sheyna. A green thumb meant endless touching, fussing, frequent praise. The plants seemed to listen, and everywhere sprouted. He proceeded to the bathroom, brushed his teeth, paid special attention to the gums, in danger of gingivitis since the age of thirty. His gums, his feet, his hair, suddenly they all needed nursing, watchfulness. What the hell happened to you at thirty-five? The body was making its nonnegotiable demands, suddenly. Pay attention, or pay up! Okay; he massaged the gum with the special brush. *At his side Tippy sat on the bathtub edge. She wore his pajama top, looking up at him as if she were eight. Her upper teeth were biting her lower lip and chin, and then he noticed too—while trying not to look—that she had raised her knee to her chin, and placed her hand there. Solomon felt himself getting stiff, and he had an irresistible urge to touch himself, right here!* . . . In a flushed muddle he fled from the bathroom and returned to his bed.

Saved. Sheyna's back was to him still as he slipped beside her. But his presence brushed her; in her sleep she turned toward him, nestling. Lionel, usually a protector, became an attacker. To their mutual surprise, he was there upon her, slipping under her nightgown and then inside her. And as he began to move, he was paying back that illicit teenage fiend for her lewd defiance! for showing up on the porcelain that way, in his pajama top, flashing those teeth and raising her leg!—all the while his good friend lay sleeping in here, trusting him faithfully! He'd show that tempting twat who was boss here as he worked deliberately and with concerted strength, more than he usually used, more than he usually had, so much into his vision of the harlot in the bathroom that he barely heard the woman beneath him moaning aloud, unusual too, and saying aloud his name in Hebrew, lullabying, "Lev, my Lev," in her own mounting passion and passionate surprise. . . . And afterwards she held him tightly in sleepy gratification and was saying, "Dodi, my Dodi," her affectionate Hebrew (for "my love"), and groggily whispering that he hadn't done that in so long, waking her up to make love this way!

She kissed him tenderly on the cheek and neck, and Lionel, his fury partially fulfilled held her back firmly, solidly; and in a moment or two, he was delighted to see his Sheyna's face, like peeking at your hole card and discovering an ace.

Was it so unhealthy then, to have Tippy-in-fantasy this way? he wonders, seeing his ace's warm smile.

New Hampshire is everything it's supposed to be, only a little better when it's turning spring, and when you've come up from a winter in Cambridge. (Otherwise, of course, spring can be more brown with mud than green with buds.) Especially when you have a built-in family right there, waiting for you. The Robinsons lived in their own apartment at the end of the house; seventy-five years ago it used to be the attached barn. A family of three, with two dogs, a cat (excellent mouser), and the little girl who had become like Solomon's own. She had been one year old when he first knew her, and her daddy was in Vietnam at the time. (Her first whole sentence was, "Sabre muti-lated Snoopy's ear," in reference to Lionel's dog and her doll.) She knew Lionel worked in his study and was not to be disturbed, but in the late afternoon, after her nap, she walked the length of the house and knocked. And offered, "Li-o-nel, would you like me to draw a picture for you now?" At that point, the interruption was like ice cream. "First give me a big hug," he'd say. And get it.

Now there is nothing quite like having a family relation with a family that's *not yours;* affection without twenty-four-hour responsibility seemed to enhance his affection.

The big thing about the north country is of course the retreat from city noises, teaching duties and the routine rudeness of everyday life nowadays. A respite from the nonstop vortex of telephone calls, visitors, distractions, theories, newspapers, insults, endless talk. Out there it was green and dull and birds chirped and roofs, not magazines, leaked, and back yonder in the woods on his dirt road raccoons and partridge passed, not trucks and cycles. Cities had fulfilled their teleological function, they had become Frankenstein machines, crudely efficient, grimly mechanical, breaking down and missing parts. People, who built them, were now helpless before their monsters, day in, day out. A comic horror show. Solomon sat in his study and faced Mount Tug and Smarts Mountain, and had only the typewriter and paper to fight. (Yes, it was true, he admitted, that he frequently played records and radio in the midst of that silence, a reflexive habit developed in Cambridge noise and not dropped easily. Yet, what appears to be an idyllic situation, a house in the country, and room to work in, is, for a writer, not quite that. It's the same hell and heaven as a room in Hoboken or Paris would be. The dream of a country house is quickly transformed by authorial reality into a room of ordinary Olivetti slavery. Only after five o'clock did the landscape become real, and then only if it had been a decent day.)

Retreat. At first his home was a place to go to write and to enjoy himself in the country, as a kind of squire and writer. But gradually, retreat came to mean something else, something darker and less pleasant and *much more necessary;* it moved from desire to pressing need. Not merely a country house, but a foxhole, a fortress (a hole?). Somewhere away from Cambridge, where that mighty native triumvirate had come to reign in the universities—success, career, power. Where the reign of terror was spread through the courtrooms of tenure in a travesty of justice. The academy had come to draw out the pleasure from the literary climate as industry and autos had sucked the fragrance from the air. (Easy now, Lionel, simmer down.) He was like a sergeant whose platoon was losing a battle, and now *had* to retreat. Leave the world he knew. Inwardly he felt this sense of "must," much as he wanted to stay, and battle. You see, sir, most of his colleagues had so come to *despise* him because of his books that he had become a *caste* figure walking amidst the Brahmins. Solomon felt unwanted, unclean. . . . This three-year term at the university, he sensed, would be his last. Colleagues had even dropped small remarks about him to students, small venal darts which he would later hear about, bleed from. . . . All this, sir, because of his work (this "dirty" work . . . ) So he drew closer to what was outcast, himself and that work. Retreat then was a sort of rest home for Solomon, a paramedical abode where he could be alone with himself (and Sheyna on weekends), his thoughts, his reading, the slow drifting snow and the squeaking winter trees, the thick forest, and the *alive* work. Lionel seemed at home there, in exile from the literary and academic worlds, in the friendship of his characters, his writing, his memories. It suited him if not with great pleasure, at least with a modicum of pain, like a rheumatic ache. An ache other writers certainly had known. Besides, thirty-eight was a fine time to retire from the world and reflect upon one's past, one's immersions, one's sad comedy, wasn't it?

On that Saturday morning, the slave, before sitting down at his Olivetti oars, took a freeman's walk outside. The dirt road was dappled by morning sun falling through the old pines and maples, and as he walked down it, he began to compose a letter in his head to his students, remembering their stories, their personal lives. With the writing students, he was a doctor, father, shrink, as much as a writing teacher, all in the service of getting them to keep up the impulse, the crazy nonutilitarian impulse that would drive them unnaturally, toward depths and heights. He ambled amidst the birds chirping and spoke:

"My dear students, I want you to know how I miss you when you leave, more than daughters or wives. You writing creatures, special to me, because I know what it's like to want to do what you want to do, with the rest of the world, society, in one way or another seeking to squelch it. Tamar, dark, diminutive, with your wonderful olive complexion and your deeply depressive life, you were always a gem to me, helping me edit those unwieldy manuscripts of mine, always on hand if I needed you, visiting me at Swerdlow's and taking care of practical details. All the time in the midst of your own complicated intrigue with your British psychiatrist, who first treated you, and then fell for you; and there you were, bravely trying to be a good undergraduate and a writer at the same time as you took the special cure. Oh, it was interesting to read those harrowing seventy-five page autobiographical tales of yours, which you tried ardently to turn into fiction, but which remained most effective as autobiography. What could I tell you, live less and invent more? Live less intensely? All that's up to you, my friend. But the story of that affair was strong stuff, and while you may not have had the experience or distance to control it just yet, to manipulate it for the purposes of self-understanding and truth, the content will remain with you, just stick with it. That scene in which Doctor R. stayed over at your parents' Philadelphia home, and ate lox and bagels in the morning with your concentration-camp survivor mother and father, while chatting with them in Oxonian English—a cultural mix I'd like to have seen. The tough Philly furrier questioning the English ego-defense chap, with innocent Tamar passing the cream cheese to her lover, nice details those. Don't worry, you'll write it someday; and if not, why worry anyway? By that time, you may be living in Oxford with the gentleman, writing a different version; the desire and talent are there. So you take it easy now, over there in London, and thank you, pal, for those visits to Swerdlow's, at twenty-one taking care of my helplessness with adult order and responsibility. When you left, there was your old professor crying, helpless, nearly incoherent!

"And you, dear Diana, with your odd combination of Iowa twang and Russian-Jewish brains and peasant braids, you had great lyrical powers as a short story writer. Yes, you too couldn't wait to grow up, to be in the 'real world,' as you called it. But weren't you already there? Consider that half sister, who tormented you for being 'bohemian' and 'putting on airs' in the East; the mother who always wanted to write, but who, as the wife of an Iowa farmer, lived through you instead; the ex-father, actor, who still cared for you madly, too madly, calling you from provincial theaters around the country; and how many boyfriends strewn about? My God, college was kindergarten next to *that* life! And you, torn between wanting to settle down and play mother and wife, and wanting desperately to write, to make movies, to tell stories, to be an 'artist.' A serious conflict, Diana, but a fine ambition—just don't leave writing for movies; your prose style was too sure of itself, your everyday observations too perfect, to abandon all that for a director's medium. Oh, you'll be tortured all your life, and the writing will doubtless intensify all those ambivalences, but what can you do, toss away your gift? Nah. Make do with it. Make it work for you. I know you're capable with cameras and brownies (like the batch you brought to the sanitarium years ago), but with words you're a dream. So let the experience come, and flow with it, accept it."

Lionel stopped to see the neighbor's collie-shepherd walking with him, bushy tail wagging in delight at the walk, and thought what a good lesson that was for Lionel too, about accepting that flow. But supposing it took you down, down? . . . How grown-up these students were, how adult their range of experience—too adult? Their youthful aspirations moved him!

"Matt, you were probably the best pure writer, good enough for Sidney and me to publish you in our *Review* when you were a junior. Not bad company—Chomsky, McCarthy, Lowell, and so on. But then again, you were from the South, and did anyone ever come from that peculiar region who tried writing and couldn't write up a storm? Who couldn't weave a spell of imagery and rhetoric like a Brooklyn boy could talk?" Yes, about fifty thousand, Lionel figured. "Well, you had it all when it came to prose style and literary sensibility; will you have the necessary stamina to carry it through?

"Or the necessary life-stability to concentrate on work? My classic memory of you occurs while passing through Harvard Square late, and seeing you in the taxi you drove, a midnight driver working on his honors thesis, for me. Right there, on page 12—always on page 12—on *Death in Venice*. An excellent twelve pages too; but that's all that ever came. It was as if Tadzio were at the center of the tale, not Mr. von Ashenbach; what Mann was imagining, you were living. No wonder it was difficult, punishing—messy life mocks finished art with its tricks and racks! I would love to see you write a version someday, and see the real pulls between the illicit passion and artistic impulse. Will you ever do it, Matt, there in Fantasy City, L.A.? Or is all that in the past now, with Mozart and Beethoven on the piano to distract you pleasantly from an art which demands a little too much life-reporting? Stick to chords, they're prettier than verbs. Hurt less. Whatever, it was a pleasure to read you that year, and afterwards; and a delight to see you, in your shy manner, offer up literary judgments in the classroom that were always on target. My little profligate minister's son, don't let your steamy life of boys-and-girls sexuality suffocate you prematurely, confuse you irrevocably, so that the thought of quiet reclusive work becomes out of the question. . . . And one day, my little Mr. Faulkner, will you kindly complete that thesis so that the grade I gave you can be written off the ledger in good conscience?

"Nahum, you were a different kettle of fish altogether—hardly a writer at all, for fiction. No, you were a literary critic par excellence; your head packed so tightly with Joyce, Mann, Kafka, Dostoyevsky, that you couldn't sit at the typewriter without the ghosts of those giants hovering above you. And look at you now, as far from Matt's Southern California as this universe will allow, wandering around the concentration-camp sites of Europe these past two years searching out every vestige and clue about the Holocaust, to find a Jewish past, a family past, out of the ashes and soap. How purposeful, how noble, how masochistic! But there you are, educating yourself in the history of misery, in German and Yiddish, making yourself at twenty-three into a kind of survivor of sixty-three; a curious task for an American young man. But who can predict motives, or needs, let alone discipline them? You made me realize that critics could be 'possessed' too—your Viennese family history possessed you, Europe and the Holocaust possessed you, literature possessed you; in the new world you moved about like the alien wandering Jew in *goyishe* nativeland. Not a novelist or a secular historian would you be, but a Talmudic boy, a Judaica scholar, perhaps a Chief Rabbi somewhere. All this was seething in that five-foot frame, and a Great Religious Title

157

of some sort would be your ambition. Do you know that yet, Nahum?

"To me, too, you represented well this university of B. You were a kind of spirit from the Old Country, more at home with dybbuks and rubles than with Chevys and heists, your body having been dumped here by circumstance; a grim joke. Here at B., amidst *yarmulke*'d boys and kosher food plates and Sabbath services and *kaddish* prayers, here you breathed easily, here you didn't have to run, here you studied and glittered and came out like some Semitic diamond. Perhaps you could come back someday and teach at the school, in Judaica or Mediterranean studies, and have a statue erected in your likeness on one of the hills, a small young man with a sensitive mustache and fine small features and an iron will, carrying The Book and wearing a white silk *tallis*.

"And I want to thank you, Nahum, for your most kind notes—your formal and solemn note of gratitude for the year of work, and your most poignant one, to wish me a quick recovery from my 'untimely illness.' What a phrase! While everyone else was learning 'it sucks,' you were still using 'untimely.' How appropriate, I thought, reading your note, postmarked Austria."

Lionel stopped himself, moved by that talented band of misfits who had passed through his classrooms this past decade of teaching. Had his gratitude toward them arisen partly out of his narcissistic impulse? Perhaps. And had he overestimated them? Perhaps. But only time would tell, of course. Their common denominator, however, was clear enough: hurting. There was as much neurosis as inspiration there, wild chaotic conflict as single-minded purpose. It came back to that, really; and to their desperate courage and honesty in trying to deal with it. Lionel's sense of that—with this solemn Jew, Indiana bohemian, minister's son, furrier's daughter—his sense of these talented students as confirmed premature patients at eighteen and nineteen made him feel all the more attached and paternal.

"One final point, concerning the act of teaching itself, in the classroom or on paper. I've come to believe, innocently and foolishly, that there is a purity to the act of teaching that is to be found nowhere else in *our* adult society. A purity of relation between student and teacher which is akin to that between child and parent, in which outside motives and corrupting influences are for the most part suspended. An exaggeration? Perhaps; but it does strike me that when we discuss a book, an idea, a feeling, there is no ulterior motive involved, no subtle 'sell' working, no profit motive lurking. I'm speaking of the situation where the real student meets the real teacher, in which one's own prejudices and biases are taken into account, as well as the content of the subject. There is a beauty in the search for truth for its own sake, in argument as argument, that is most appreciated *only after* one has left the classroom for the marketplace, the Book for the Sell, reflection for promotion and propaganda. A most idealistic view on my part? For sure. But in the best situations, which seem to occur every year, such idealism and affective purity have been demonstrated, powerfully felt."

The spring air of New Hampshire filled his senses with its pungent pine and spruce fragrance, and he breathed in deeply.

In his study he jotted down crucial, pertinent notes, wondered whether that last paragraph would make sense to outsiders, seem sentimental. Exhausted but refreshed, he got up again, looked for Sheyna inside, then went out again.

She was on her knees in the garden, in threadbare jeans and vest jersey. Her olive body was turning coffee tan from the sun, and save for Lionel's baseball cap on her head, she resembled the kibbutznik she had been once, after college. The plot of earth she worked on was like a postage stamp set amid the green fields. Indeed the eighty acres of fields and woods could probably house a nice kibbutz or moshav as an Israeli friend had suggested; it was larger than his own moshav of childhood, just outside Tel Aviv. Should Lionel deed it to a group of friends (including Yitzhak) in his will? Make it over into a Degania of New Hampshire? He could have his fifty years of privacy and solitude, his half century of sanctuary, and then hand it over to the communal idealists, who could re-create a farm from the grown-up woods. The old socialist in him stirred at the prospect; the writer smiled, sighed. (But at least Tippy should know that he had had the idea!) Meanwhile, Sheyna, carefully using her hands and trowel, was pulling up rocks and witch grass, and preparing the ground for early planting of peas, Chinese cabbage, flowers. (He had yelled at her for thinking of putting the flowers in between the rows, just as the year before he had yelled at her for planting the corn wrong, just as he had yelled at her for so many other small things—most of which turned out to be perfectly unfounded accusations. The bursts of temper in perfect inverse ratio to the success of the writing day.) She labored there with knowledge, ardor and care, her ample behind propped in the sun; she loved gardening, watching

159

things grow, and he loved coming out of his cage to watch *her*, quietly.

So he crouched on his haunches like a baseball catcher, and observed her from the slightly hidden slope by the house. There was hardly a wind, the air was astonishingly warm (for mid-April)—at least a month away from blackflies to bite at her. Time to put back up the purple martin house. The flies that pursued strangers mostly, in alliance with the granite natives; after the first year here, some five years ago, they swarmed around him but didn't bite. (Were they afraid of his short fuse?) Sheyna loved the earth like a Tolstoyan, loved working it, feeling it; only a garter snake slithering by would turn her into a bourgeoise! As she worked, Lionel drifted momentarily back to that *week in a Worcester hospital, when, visiting her parents, she had been afflicted with a mysterious blood disorder. For several days she lay helpless in the hospital, bruising at any real touch, doctors mystified, and Lionel hurting, hurting for her. She had just enough strength to hold his hand and squeeze it lightly, as a child would, her innocent slim body cadaverous, assaulted. He knew then not merely how much she meant to him, or what it would be to lose or hurt her, but how unfair it all was. . . . And how unfair to go through someone's near-death; it bound you to them too strongly; that is, too strongly for Solomon, the unbound sort. I:: the hospital bathroom, in the stall, he cursed the stupid chaos and vengeance of living, let tears fall on the small squares of bathroom tile, and contemplated the sham defenses put up by men against death! The illusory powers boasted of or implied by those structures of comfort: religion, language, morals, art. Medicine was more truly powerful, and yet there it was in that hospital, helpless too; but arrogantly helpless. Lionel had wanted desperately to punch the tall mustached doctor who barely deigned to talk to him, while Sheyna lay there. . . .* But now, platelets long since restored, his slender gardener was healthy and vigorous, up to her old basketball tricks just that week, and he *valued* her enormously. Unlike those you *overvalued* because of sex, because of habit, because of convenience, and in whom you therefore overlooked trivial pursuits, petty emotions, Sheyna was *worth one's affection.* You wouldn't wake up ten years later and perceive that your companion really was a venal soul, an ordinary creature, and you were stuck.

"Well look what our little Burpee-serf is up to," he called out, approaching. "Seen any friendly snakes pass by?" She smiled her full smile, brushed hair from her forehead, said,

160

"You know I heard a brushing sound before and my heart *jumped so.* I was all set to run, but it turned out to be the cat." He crouched by her side, saying, "Okay, the little piggie writer is ready to help—now that everything is done. Anything left to do?" She indicated a section to be hoed and cleaned up. "Are you kidding? What have you been doing? I thought the rows would be ready, and I'd simply go along and drop in the seeds." With good cheer, having had a decent day, he got to work with the hoe and spading fork on the turned-over soil. After about twenty minutes he was perspiring freely from bending, hoeing, pulling up roots, witch grass. And the sun was warm out there.

He stopped momentarily and wiped his brow with his shirtsleeve. Drops of perspiration burned his eyes, and when he cleared them, he saw a curious sight.

*Tippy was dragging a chaise longue with one hand, while with the other holding a glass of ginger ale. She was attired in a canary-yellow halter and skimpy shorts, which squeezed ridiculously her large breasts and showed off the full length of her long legs. She moved the chair to get the late-afternoon sun, which, there on the slope of lawn, also faced the garden. Lying out on the chaise, she took a plastic tube and squeezed suntan lotion onto her skin; as she rubbed it in, she acknowledged Lionel with a cursory nod. She massaged the lotion onto her shoulders, neck, exposed chest. Solomon stood and looked transfixed.*

"Hey, what're you doing? Quit already?"

His heart beat fast, heaved. Glad for his dungarees, which kept down and hid his desire. Turning away from chesty Tippy to valuable Sheyna, he exclaimed, "Look at these rocks you've left, and the grass! Jesus, this all has to be done over! What the hell have you been doing?" Sheyna's face blanched with the accusation, and she murmured, "Okay, it's no big deal," her usual protestation when he got irritable and crazy suddenly, and blamed her.

He began bending and tossing away rocks with exaggerated emphasis, knowing that in fifteen minutes he'd be ashamed and a bit later, guilty. But he couldn't help himself. Somewhere in him he promised to play a game of tennis with her, and later to make love with her for sure. Despising himself for his weakness, and for taking it out on her, he also noted with derision her chest, slender by comparison. Why did voluptuousness have to show up in the wrong person? Cheap, he knew while thinking it. Unfair and stinking, as he hoed harder.

161

And in ten minutes or so he surprised her with a kiss, his sanity returning earlier than expected. "Sorry for being so rotten back there. You're really doing a bang-up job, pal." She shook him away. But after a few minutes, she said, "God, you are a loon." He could be that too, on other occasions.

Afterwards in the kitchen he was surprised by the wafting odor. She opened the oven door of the huge black restaurant stove, a leftover from when the house had been a country inn. Sitting on the rack were one, two, three twisted breads, *challahs*, baking wondrously. The smells brought back the bakery on Sutter Avenue, where he had shopped . . . as he leaned over, *he saw out the window the girl in the chaise, stretched languorously, baked by the sun . . .*

Where was *honor* in one's emotions?

At the oblong kitchen table, Lionel berated himself, in a mild rage. At the nature of things intimate. He peeled an apple while Sheyna washed up. It wasn't he who had invited the girl there. The vision was as unfair to him as it was to anyone else. Did anyone think that he *liked* having her there, prancing about like a sexy colt on his lawn while he tried to get work done and help out Sheyna? Did he *want* to feel like a rat, a heel? Suffer from vile comparisons as well as from the fantasy-desire? "Adjust the ledger," he told Dr. Lirič privately, so the bad feeling of debt is balanced with the perverse pleasure of the desire.

*Was the taste of the Tippy so strong that it lingered in his consciousness that way, sir? or was the routine of his life so boring and familiar that it brought on that girl so temptingly? . . . And was the fact of Tippy more powerful than the fantasy? Certainly if you asked him then which was the more dangerous, he'd have said, the fantasy. So would you, I would imagine. In retrospect now, I for one would beg to differ.*

In a sweat, not knowing what or where, he retreated to a path in the woods. Instead of sensual graitification, there would be imagination, memory, headtalk. A soliloquy of the heart amid the dappled sunlight and the pine-covered logging road. Spoken to his old friend Abie Z., who had told him, in their visit of a year or so ago, about his kibbutz on the western shore of Galilee. Lionel walked on the soft path, heard the birds twittering, felt easier, and began seeing before him the sturdy-chested youth from college days, with the head of thick blond curls that reminded one of Harpo Marx.

"Abie, I admire what you did and what you are doing. I know, old chum, how broken up you think your life is. Don't.

At least it's a real life. *Realer* than what you had left in the States. And more than what many people have, it seems. Maybe too real is the only problem.

"Anyway, I wouldn't have thought that the young man who cut out from Brooklyn College to be with the woman he had knocked up would eventually have wound up one of the heads of a citrus orchard on an Israeli kibbutz—planting by day and, by night, listening to the *katushas* explode a few hundred yards away. Always on the alert for the guerrillas coming down from Lebanon, to greet the children perhaps. Yet why shouldn't I think all that? You were already then among the most widely read and most idealistic of students; you were thoroughly bored with student life in the 1950's; you yearned to be out there, in the flux of living. So why not go to Denver as you did, marry the girl, and take a job in a furniture store? Yes, that was understandable. Yet when you wound up in Los Angeles, as I came to hear, managing another furniture store, and earning twenty-five grand a year, one would have thought that the course of your life—native, capitalistic, family-oriented—was firmly charted. How wrong we can be when we try to chart human beings!

"Then, to see you years later, in Cambridge, the blond curls vanished forever, except in fond memory, and a roly-poly paunch in place of a firm stomach, and thick glasses to boot—that took me back a bit. Yet less so than your story. How you suddenly decided one day that your life had little of its old meaning or ambition, and that you had to make a radical change, and so decided upon the complete change—a kibbutz life in Israel, period. With or without wife, children! My God, Abie, that's change, in Jewish spades. So look what happens. The wife reluctantly decides to come along; after a year or two of culture shock, she sees the virtues of Western Galilee alongside Santa Monica, and you, meanwhile, apart from learning agronomy in the special school, you get an education in *katushas* and guerrillas and blood spilled; yet, after making peace with all that new change, an old problem crops up—the marriage starts falling to pieces. Amidst the orange and lemon groves, amidst the new good rich life, ancient irony creeps in. And when I see you in Cambridge, on American holiday from dilemma, you're broken up, bewildered, hurting. Well, how are you now, any better? Is living tolerable on that same piece of ground with the family now divided? Or, in this situation, are you much better off in some faceless city and apartment house, where anonymity can be a protector during such times?"

163

Lionel paused at a clearing where the light fell beautifully on a clump of white birch. In such startling yellow and green clarity, it was easy to push difficult questions, probe dark human moves. When gripped by conundrums, one should always walk into clearings to think things through, he mused, to get cleaned up. He ambled among the tall white trees, his ballerinas of the north woods.

"Abie, what is it like to kill? Does it affect you somewhere inside? Change the blood count, shake up the chromosomes, blacken the bile? Or, if you do it for the 'right reasons,' does it become no more than a necessary duty, like clearing some trees for the sake of practicality? Or, in your case, a duty for survival? I didn't want to ask you about it, on our last visit, when you casually cited the battles with the guerrillas coming down from Lebanon, who deposited some souvenir shrapnel in your side, or showed me a picture of your buddies and you bearing semi-automatics as if they were tennis rackets. Had you bargained on killing when you came to plant and cultivate and lead a more purposeful life? Naturally it's difficult for us here to understand survival as a fact, not a metaphor. We live by metaphors so frequently here that we sometimes say foolish things, or by chance, get people killed. . . . I can see how having a son or daughter shot at while they're in school can drive one to animal fury and primitive vengeance very easily. Is killing not quite killing then? . . . Does it have its pleasing variety as well?

"Now I want to suggest some emendation of our talks concerning the state of Israel and its future. I'm afraid I was a bit naïve and arrogant, par for the course, during those few days. In the last year or two, I have come around a bit in my thinking. After having looked in on those routine guerrilla murders on CBS; seen some fascinating UN decisions; witnessed democratic countries like France and England line up, like good little former imperialists, with the Arabs; heard the so-called 'arguments' of some PLO leaders and spokesmen (for example, the tirade against Zionist racism and the exclusivist nature of the Jewish state)—all of which had convinced me until I remembered my old freshman English teacher, Stet, who believed nothing unless he saw it with his own eyes; and so I went to the trouble, great trouble too, to search out the two constitutions, the Israeli and the Syrian—and also examined the actual PLO charter—and what I discovered was the interesting fact, so conveniently glossed over, that the Arab constitutions are abundantly more racist and exclusivist in character than the Israeli document; and so on.

Furthermore, because of my own dear girlfriend of the past four years, I have learned a little bit about Israel, its settlers, philosophers, parachutists, its raison d'être; just a bit, you understand. I'm still not 'a man possessed.' (Would that take another Dreyfus trial?)

"Now, Abe, to amend my opinions of a few years ago; perhaps it will be of interest to you when you argue policy at the Histadrut councils. I think that un-Jewlike Jew Jabotinsky was more right and more prophetic than is fortunate when he suggested that anti-Semitism is a permanent illness, and that a strong, select military cadre (cf. Judeans) should always be a part of the new state and its policy. With the 'respectable' Arabs pushing their oil and money, and the PLO peddling murder and terror, the turn toward anti-Semitism is now established in the world. Who can tell what will happen in America as the propaganda and money increase? I believe the terrorists must be countered, *not* with the tactics of enlightened liberals, but with those of the terrorists themselves. So, bands of bold Jews should begin operations around the world to act in retaliation against PLO acts, against those countries that, by their support of the PLO, help to shed Jewish blood—shed it with impunity.

"Of course, dear Abie, these tactics are deplorable, uncivilized, savage, retrogressive; my fear is that this is the direction the world is taking. The majority of the nations of the world in any case. It is most unpleasant. While suggesting it, I deplore it, and myself. Where will it end? I don't know. But I do know, or feel, that if the present situation continues unabated—squeezing Israel, blackmailing America and its weaker allies, drawing blood from innocent Jews as a matter of everyday course—the state of anti-Semitism will slowly creep back into public acceptance, as it already has in many nations, and in the United Nations. To try to act civilized in a savage world is suicide; read natural history (Darwin) or human history (World War II) if you doubt this. The Jews obtained their state, please remember, not merely by fifty years of propagandizing and a piece of paper authorizing it; that is a pleasant myth. They won their state by first losing six million bodies, by realpolitik on the part of Stalinist Russia, and by losing more lives in 1948 and afterwards. In other words, they *made their state*. And kept making it through each and every war.

"Abie, the Jews have always stood for something a little superior in the way of civilization, and once again what we have to pay for it is a rise in worldwide persecution and

165

anti-Semitism. If the history of the human animal teaches us anything about this barbarism, it is that it will not go away with words or be won over with conciliation, but rather fought against directly and brutally.

"Yes, you might say I've become less dovish and less optimistic in the last few years. I worry for friends like you who went to start a new life, learned agronomy and citrus management, fought guerrillas for your children, and now have to fight big money and oil, and the hostile democratic world. Once again the question of survival for people of your blood and mine is in question. Abie, have you been surviving?"

Lionel, blood pumping, saw the long white house and beyond, the garden. He went to his study and dialed the operator for the right number and called 1-505-555-1212. Jotting down notes from his soliloquy, he asked for Albuquerque information, and when he got it, he asked for *her*. (Was he going to tell her about this letter? this sudden political militancy? No. Besides, that new Jabotinsky rage would have to be deleted or thought through more carefully for the actual letter. Too right-wing, prejudiced, JDL-crazy. And what did he think of his friend as a killer? He'd have to work on that too, he noted. Some of these sections had been worked through endlessly in his head, while others popped in freshly, but too crudely—awaiting refinement in the writing.) The operator paused, cited Terry, Tim, Tom Matthews, and several others, but got no Tippy. "Would you like to try the Santa Fe area, sir?"

"Sure."

A male voice was saying, "I'm telling you, Jimmy boy, this Reserve Oil and Mineral looks *real hot*. I've been down there, looking at the actual mine, it's not exactly—"

"Hello, hello?" Lionel interrupted. "Operator, are you out there?"

"Who the hell is on this line?" asked another voice.

"Look, sorry," Solomon said, "I've been left in the lurch here. Mixed lines."

"What?"

"Operator? Hey, op—"

"Where are you calling from?" asked the second voice, calmly.

Lionel, fully perplexed, said, "New Hampshire."

"Really? Whaddya know, I have a summer place up there. Near Winnipesaukee. Hell of a spot."

"Uh, yeah, it's nice. Operator?" He was about to hang up

166

when she came back on and said she was still trying to contact the Santa Fe operator.

"I'm up here in Santa Fe myself," said the second man. "Is that where you're calling from?"

Lionel couldn't help asking how come he summered in New Hampshire.

"No, no, that's *me,* I'm down here in Philly."

"By the way, you wouldn't happen to know if they've decided yet on that nuclear reactor down by Portsmouth, would you?"

Lionel shook his head.

"What'd you say? Couldn't hear you."

Lionel remembered something and said, "Well I think the governor was for it, but that's about all."

"See what I mean, Frank? It's happening all over right now. Another six months and it'll be too late. Hey, what's your name, anyway?" The voice was now friendly. "I'm Jim Thayers and my friend there is Frank Edwards. You don't have any *uranium* by any chance?"

Why did he hang on, why didn't he get off? "No. But I'm on here with the operator, or trying to get back to her. Operator, are you there?"

"Well, *I am* sir, I've been trying to reach your Santa Fe information operator and I am—"

*"But you have the lines crossed,"* he controlled himself.

"Who do you want out here by the way? Maybe I know them. It's a small community really."

Lionel, baffled, told the man the girl's name.

The fellow made a sound with his mouth. "What's your name anyway?"

For some reason Lionel told them his name.

"Like the king, huh?" Philly said.

"Yeah."

Philly continued, "You know, I believe in coincidences like this. Have you ever heard of something called Reserve Oil and Mineral on Over the Counter?"

Lionel felt trapped by the instrument in his hand.

"Sir, did you get your number? Would you like me to put the call through for you?"

"I'm over in Wolfeboro, near the lake. Come on over—"

Lionel gave up and bailed out.

Exhausted, he was delighted to see Sheyna in the reading room, and noted once again how Oriental her looks could be in repose, when she was reading that way, framed by the large wine-colored chair. A Bathsheba?

She looked up. "You must have been inspired. That typewriter didn't stop for a while back there."

"Inspired? You know me better than that. Just note-taking. Any news?"

She shook her head, and he was glad there had been no exciting guerrilla ambush on the screen while he was trying to chase down his own guerrilla on the telephone.

*He sat bewildered. You can see how crossed his wires were getting. Turning from the fantasy of the bikinied girl to praise for the mad ideologue Jabotinsky. What is perhaps most interesting and most frightening is that the passion for the girl didn't stop him from his composing; in a way the passion, emerging here (or stifled, whichever) in a frustrating fantasy, propelled him into a certain compositional frenzy. Missing the one gratification, he moved on to the second and fulfilled himself. In fact, as I recall now, when he finished the writing just then, he looked upon that New Mexico telephone call as a kind of reward for the doing of a duty. And down deep somewhere there seemed to exist a connection between the sudden political passion for that fiery spokesman of Jewish militarism and the "guerrilla girl" sporting in her halter on the lawn of his imagination. Already, Doctor, she had made him crazier than usual—inwardly, and in his work too. To use a phrase from another realm, his situation was already one of double jeopardy. Was there an insurance you could take out on this sort of predicament?*

Two nights after returning from the country, Sheyna and Lionel went to see a local basketball game between his little college and big-time Harvard. Usually they went to the Celtic games, but Solomon had heard that baby B. had an interesting team that year, with an exciting fast-break game. Originally scheduled for a month earlier, the game had been put off because Harvard's ancient gym blew some fuses. Actually that failure was a nice gesture to college sports, just as you knew you were back in *school* sports when you entered that old hippo gymnasium not in Pauley Pavilion or the Bloomington Auditorium, where the pro farm teams went thinly disguised under the name of UCLA or Indiana. An old wooden bandbox with fold-up stands on either side of the court, it held maybe eight or nine hundred, not eighteen or nineteen thousand. Yet because of the acoustics and closeness, the crowd roars echoed and resounded as if you were in a sound chamber with the decibels ricocheting and climbing. The announcer was a young student who spoke with a staccato imitation of sports announcers and an amusing partisan appeal. The Harvard team, dressed in laundered whites, was bolstered by several tall ghetto imports, from D.C. and Harlem, and was coached by a cool ex-Celtic who resembled Malcolm X. Baby B. was shorter, whiter, scrappier, with most of the kids from local areas, its star an Irish backcourt boy from Somerville, a basketball midget at 5'10". Their uniforms looked as if they were hand-me-downs from big brothers, and their coach was a hefty red-faced Irishman with wavy hair and a fast temper, also an ex-Celtic. The audience was fitted around the court like a glove on a hand, just as in high school days—when fans were much more a part of the game, in noise and gesture, than in more professional games, in which the team was some formal object down there.

The game, instead of being a one-sided affair in favor of heavily favored Gulliverian Harvard, was a close one through the first half, with B. leading all the way. They passed nicely, scrapped and stole on defense, fast-breaked, classically, and moved shrewdly inside for lay-ups, like clever Lilliputians. The leader, that tough little guard, continually hit with a southpaw jumper, like an accurate slingshot. During the half, the stands filled up as busloads of students piled in from Waltham, including a seven-girl cheerleading squad for B. Underdog B. continued to play smart basketball and steal the game away from the taller Harvards, and the crowd pounded and roared and steadily deafened the place in approval. And the cheerleaders did their thing, too, with charming "locomotives," T-E-A-M cheers, splits, and nearly successful cartwheels.

The whole thing began to work upon his memory. And as the game got closer in the second half, he was moved strangely, beyond the immediate game, place. The wild cheering—though here, most of the kids were spectacled, premedlooking kids, little doctors and scientists, and they yelled out strange advice, "Horseshoe, horseshoe!" and "Crab, crab!" to indicate defense patterns—the hard-fought game of give and go's and fast breaks by B.; the great *fun* of amateur competition; the heated closeness of the game drawing oohs and aahs and bated-breath moments. So perhaps he wasn't too startled when a young cheerleader ran off the floor, and not six feet from him, while pulling up her white kneesocks, looking up at him, and, very *knowingly, her eyes turning ochre, the lips getting thicker, was saying, "Have you forgotten your youth, Brownsville? Shame on you, Lionel, shame!"* And he shook

from confusion, accusation, those teeth edging forward. . . .
In the last minute, the crowd went ecstatic as the little guard
dribbled around in a broken figure eight. . . .

*Getting off the bus at Marcy Avenue, with three white
friends, and walking the streets of Bedford-Stuyvesant toward
that prison-building called Boys High . . . through the alleys
of peeling corridors where blacks bebopped in peaked caps
. . . into the bandbox gymnasium filled with one white face
for every ten brown or black . . . the frightening warm-ups
of the Boys squad, every member living up to their nickname,
"Kangaroos," by dunking the ball, to the famous rhythm
which would dominate the game, B-O-Y-S, B-O-Y-S, B-O-Y-S
. . . and the game itself, Jefferson vs. Boys, the best in city
basketball, spectacular rebounding and leaping, lightning
Boys fast breaks, beautiful disciplined Jefferson offense,
jumpers by Salz, ball handling by Tarrant, set shooting and
passing by Tiebout . . . a Boys streak of several baskets accompanied by the systematic stomping of feet on boards and
the B-O-Y-S cheers climbing the walls and ricocheting like
howitzers firing and the Boys male cheerleaders in white V-
neck sweaters leaping as high as forwards . . . a bad referee
call in the second half causing wild jeering and stomping and
cursing, and then the amazing sight, almost religious, of the
little white coach of Boys walking slowly onto the hardwood
floor, like an understanding father settling down some of his
naughty boys, and like Moses speaking to the masses, only
the black masses here, quieting them into an awesome silence,
the basketball court of Mickey Fisher a quais-religious arena
. . . and by the game's end limp from emotion and exhausted by yelling, and exhilarated by victory in that Bedford-
Stuyvesant hothouse of emotion and athletic grace and
sporting pride . . . wandering out, careful to look straight
ahead, in those corridors famous around Brooklyn for robbery and mugging and knifing . . . cn the bus back, like
leaving the front line for everyday reality. . . .*

. . . dribbling around and around as the crowd clapped
and whistled and shouted until the buzzer came and little B.
had knocked off big Harvard. Suddenly, the throngs of people
rushing forward. Solomon and Sheyna moved with them, the
excitement of the game mixing with the older excitement and
wrapping Solomon in the warmth of youth and fever of
memory. Sheyna talked to him as they wended their way
slowly, amid the crowd, still high. That peculiar cheerleader
haunted him too. He nodded to Sheyna and, in the corridor
at last, asked the burly policeman for a telephone. The po-

liceman pointed downstairs and around the corner and Lionel headed there, saying he had to make a call before they had their espresso.

The corridor below was a colorless hollow, darkly lit, resembling his high school's.

At the wall phone a short man in a business suit was speaking, back toward Lionel. The man wore a soft felt hat with a tricolored band, neat.

Lionel waited, hot with expectation. Wanting to hear that *strange voice* somewhere out there.

The man went on talking, and after a minute or two, Lionel, fidgety, tapped him on the shoulder. "Excuse me, will you be very long?"

The caller turned around. Middle-aged and brisk, his face was a terrier's, and it tightened up. With his forefinger he poked Lionel in the chest with surprising force. "I'll be as long as I damn please, buster!" And he squinted at Lionel through his glasses for another ten seconds before turning his back again.

The vicious poke and stare astonished Lionel, all the more so because the gentleman was not a Hell's Angel, but a very respectable citizen!

Lionel, furious, knew he should walk away and forget the whole thing.

Was he getting warned by someone above to stay away from this cheerleader?

But he stood there, unable to break away, irrationally fixed.

The gentleman turned around again and, directly facing Lionel, continued his chitchat on the phone. A small ruddy face, with little blotches of red birthmark by the neck and clean-shaven cheeks.

Was he a madman? But he looked so ordinary!

Lionel scratched his scalp, his heart pounding.

He'd turn the whole misunderstanding into a joke. "Look, she'll kill me if I don't get through—"

"Hold on a sec, dearie," the terrier said politely in a thick Boston accent. Letting the receiver dangle, he suddenly took hold of Lionel's lapels near the neck and shoved him back up against the wall. "Do you want two fists in your face? Then bug off, quick, hear me!" And he punched Lionel in the ribs, taking his wind away.

Lionel slumped by the wall, gasping, while the gentleman went back to his conversation.

"Some wiseacre, leaning on me," he began, straightening

171

his tie. Cheerily he continued, "Now what were you saying about Gracie's on Friday . . ."

Lionel, his wind back, was near tears from fury and shock. *Take it easy,* he cautioned himself, *leave it alone.*

The man, totally confident, had turned round again, so that Lionel's lunge caught him around the neck. Gripping him with one hand, Lionel, with the other, grabbed the telephone and belted the guy across the head two or three times, taking pleasure in crumpling that hat! The fellow then wrestled them both down to the ground. Saying in his own amazed voice, "A character, a real character!" as if it were Lionel who had started the entire incident! From the dangling telephone came the surprised voice of the speaker.

They fought on the ground like two clumsy bears, rolling over each other harmlessly, missing blows and grabbing wrists and forearms, and suddenly they were being lifted as if by a crane, and separated.

"Oh come on boys," said the black policeman, half-smiling, "it can't be all that important."

A circle of students and fans had gathered around, watching, smiling.

"Hey, whoa there! The round's over, killer!" laughed the cop at the little terrier, who continued to flay away. The policeman picked him up and set him down in the arms of the onlookers several feet away.

Solomon too found his arms pinned.

The rest was a kind of humiliating fog to Lionel: the exchange of names and addresses for an assault charge (Mr. Jack Keenan, a vice-president of Prudential, and Harvard '47, demanded to press charges), and the policeman's genial paternal view of the whole matter. ("Fighting on a dirty floor like street toughs, and in front of all these kids? Now come on fellas, shake and make up, huh?" But the terrier said, "If ya didn't have that badge on, I'd show ya something to remember too!" The policeman shook his head.)

And then the humiliating walk through the crowd.

As Lionel began to walk away: "Are you all right, Professor Solomon?" asked Lauri Sherman, from English 87a. "Your lip's cut slightly."

Lionel put his hand to his lip, and saw the blood on his fingertips. He felt prideful, and foolish. "So you're a basketball fan," he said to the very quiet young lady.

The girl smiled. "If you can't beat 'em, join 'em. Actually, I cover it for the newspaper. Weren't they wonderful? But what happened . . . over there?"

"A . . . Harvard fan," Lionel observed, as if that explained matters; and when two more students came their way, he turned away, saying goodbye to Lauri.

"Your wallet, sir!"

And he had to turn back for that too, with the three faintly familiar students standing there, looking on.

Burning with embarrassment, he walked away, upstairs, as embarrassed as during the walk up the aisle for his Bar Mitzvah.

"My God, what happened to you?" asked Sheyna, shocked. "Look at your lip—and your jacket's ripped! What were you doing? Oh, Lev!"

And alongside stood colleague Leon, who said enthusiastically, "Why didn't you tell me you were going to have a boxing match, was it a *real street fight?*" Smiling with pride.

Lionel tried to smile. Sheyna took his arm and squeezed it for support, but he pulled away, too upset. They walked out of the building, Lionel thinking, Was it so funny encountering madmen these days? Madmen wearing porkpie hats? . . . Or so funny trying to get through on the telephone.

He had no heart now for espresso and chitchat, and begged off.

Later, in the apartment, Lionel sat in the spare bedroom, trying to get Arnow in Santa Cruz. Sheyna was in the bathroom, getting ready for bed.

"How are you, what are you up to?" said his old grad-student friend. "When are you coming this way, it's been a long time."

Lionel went through the polite exchanges, remembering fondly his pal, who taught at Santa Cruz. He then asked him about Miss Matthews, and Arnow said, "Who?" Lionel repeated the name. "Never heard of her. Are you sure you got the right name?" Lionel answered, "Well, I'm not sure she has." Promising a visit in the next six months, he hung up.

He was in the midst of dialing New Mexico again, when Sheyna came in, in a clinging yellow nightgown. "Who are you talking to at this time of night?"

"Marty Green, if I can get him. Lawyers are never around when you need them."

She shook her head, in disbelief. "You can't be serious. At this time of night?"

"Why not? Let him start on this thing first thing in the morning!"

She leaned down to her helpless boy, sitting on the floor in his undershorts. "You should be grateful he wasn't in. You know what this phone call would cost you, besides money? You wouldn't sleep."

True. He considered matters, gazing at the huge bookcase in front of him. All those books, all that wisdom imparted, and he was a fool. A complete fool. Where was the Guide to Practical Living for Men Who Read Books? He remembered once seeing Mike Harrington, the democratic socialist, on the New Hampshire PBS station, suddenly giving a sophisticated analysis of the country's economic ills. In the midst of the Granite State's primeval granite politics, Harrington sounded like Plato. And it made Lionel realize all over again that the gap between the intellectual and the ordinary citizen in America equaled the Grand Canyon in width. Why did intellectuals forget this? Lionel, sitting on the floor, felt like a fool.

"Do you like this smell? What is it?"

Lionel smelled her wrist. "Nut of some sort?"

"Mmm . . ."

"I give up."

"Smells almondy. It's cocoa, cocoa butter." She lifted her head, and offered her long neck, to digest further. It was lovely.

"Come to bed," she said, "it's been a long day."

And in bed, through his pajamas, she ran her hand on his stomach, knowingly. And then her hand crept beneath his top.

"Yes, my Solly's had a *long* day," she cooed, now rubbing the cool cocoa lotion upon him, sensuously.

And in a minute Lionel mounted her, throwing up her nightie. Except something curious happened: Out of the corner of his eyes, he noticed something in the shadowy darkness.

*His old friend, whom he had been seeking around the country, was now sitting on the edge of their bed, chewing gum and looking on.*

Lionel couldn't quite believe it, and stared.

Sheyna, surprised, ran her hand along his thigh.

*Tippy took the pink gum from her mouth, and stretched it forward like a strand of spaghetti. She sat, lotuslike, wearing his jacket.*

Lionel perspired, hated the girl, kept glancing at her.

"Is there something wrong, sweetie?" Sheyna asked kindly. "Should we try another night?"

174

Lionel grew fiercely determined, but his mind had distracted his member.

*Tippy cracked gum.*

"Come on, go to sleep, it's all right, Lev."

In a daze he got off her, and sagged by her side.

Sheyna, dismissing it, rubbed his scalp and offered, "Maybe you're exercising too much."

Lionel, near tears, nodded and let Sheyna nurse him.

*"Be a big boy,"* commanded Papa Solomon in the next seat at the Stanley Theater, in Manhattan, as Lionel slumped down clutching his paper program for a telescope to look through. *"Sit up!"*

At that Lionel did sit up, kissed the cheek of Sheyna, and said, "Well, Sharky, looks like your old man is getting to be an old man. Wanna trade me in?"

She grabbed and hugged him, not knowing the truth that the statement hid, or disclosed, but full of faith, splendid faith, in him; the faith and fidelity, without which, he figured just then, we were all animals.

*Poignant, isn't it, to see how desire in one area can lead to frustration and failure in another. Now I'm not sure that Lionel actually saw that girl there, although he felt her presence. And I'm not sure that the failure was as dramatic as it is pictured here. But it is true, as I've suggested, that familiarity tends to still and muffle excitement. And this instance may have been no more than a rather dramatic evidencing of the rather routine dilemma of domesticity. But the irony here is not merely that the lack of potency flared with the woman he held dear, and not with the strange fan. More ironic is that the failure here led to nothing more than renewed, stronger fidelity—nursing added to passion, maternity to sensuality—while the fully felt potency and performance with Tippy led to nothing less than stronger disaster. Why be potent, only to be a helpless fool in the end?*

*Obviously too, there are potencies and there are potencies, there are impotences and there are impotences: they should not be discriminated against, or for, simply because of their general category.*

*Or was this small scene something else, something in its way more painful in itself, and more painful to admit; namely, the lack of desire itself? Was it Tippy, the name and body of urgent desire, who called forth the most aching of the emotions, the lack of desire where one most ardently wished for it? Was the extreme Tippy merely raising one of the tragedies of intimacy, so very ordinary and so very sting-*

*ing? In other words, was intercourse with dear Sheyna no more than the performance of duty, of payment even—for her loyalty, devotion, her years with him—rather than an act of sharp desire and lustful pleasure? Your Honor, was Solomon too weak to admit this himself? Did he feel shameful for experiencing this most sad emotion? Was the girl sitting there, chewing and pulling at her pink gum, like a mischievous adolescent, really a healthy spirit—despite and beyond herself?*

# 4.

# Sonnyboy

"EXCUSE ME, PROFESSOR SOLOMON, COULD I see you for a moment?" whispered Jean, the English Department secretary. "To be continued," he told the class, leaving.

He knew it concerned his mother since in ten years of teaching no emergency had been grave enough to warrant breaking in upon the classroom. "She just said it was 'very important,'" Jean continued, following Lionel as he walked hesitantly to the English office to learn the news, from his sister probably. He knew his mother would go one day, she was seventy; but now that it was happening, it stabbed at his chest. Her face from its youth floated toward him: the soft auburn hair and alert hazel eyes, the sharp nose and smooth complexion, the infectious smile with the perfect teeth. A face of great gaiety, or stoical despair.

She was both realist and stoic through the years; she also had enjoyed herself tremendously. He remembered that, and would remember it. Was it better to see her one last time, or should he pray for the shortest road to restful peace? Involuntarily the tears welled up, and over, as he recalled the bruised mask of tears and broken blood vessels on his stepfather before he died in Memorial Hospital.

"Yes, speaking," he answered the long-distance operator, his knees weak. The two secretaries had thoughtfully slipped out.

"Hi, dynamite! How are you?"

Pent-up, confused, startled. He managed, "Tippy?"

"Of course. Did you think I had forgotten you?"

176

He looked for a chair, settled for a piece of desk to sit on.

A little laugh. "Silly."

"What?" Several deep breaths, a clearing of eyes. "What do you mean getting me out of class this way? You had me frightened. What the—"

"Can't you speak louder? I can *barely* hear you, sweetie."

"What the hell—"

"Oh you know how things are these days. No one ever gets messages straight. Besides, we're both waiting for you."

"Both?" Visions of an orgy tingled Lionel, stopping his protest. He looked around to check the emptiness of the office. He hoped the telephone wasn't bugged!

"Where are you now—New Mexico? Manhattan? Cambridge?"

"In the Rockaways. With Belle."

It was a long moment.

"Belle?" The name rang a bell all right, but he was so confused!

"Have you forgotten your mother's first name?"

He swallowed.

"Is this another joke?"

"Sshh. Settle down, tiger. I'm with your mother, would you like to speak to her?"

He got off the desk, nervous. He stared around the placid office, something like a hospital room with typewriters and files. All he needed was a bed, and perhaps a Zenith up there on the wall. Yes. Out the huge picture window he gazed down upon the pleasant little campus, asleep with its pulse regular, undisturbed. He wished he were just another little building like them.

"Give her my regards. I better get back to my class."

Cheerily she continued, "We'll see you for dinner, won't we?" A little private giggle, and then, "We're making something *special*."

Lionel nodded, glanced at the door, tried to figure things out.

He said, "You get around. Like a private eye. How'd you find out—forget it."

"Now don't be so—stuffy! Come soon, won't you? We can have a walk on the beach first."

*"I'm in a different city, have you forgotten?"* He whispered angrily.

"Uh, Professor Solomon, could we . . ."

"Sure, Jean, right with you."

*"There are a lot of jet planes, have you tried them?"* The hard shot returned with equal intensity.

He started to protest, she cut in with, "Is it really true that you haven't seen her in almost a year? Lionel, you ought to be *ashamed.*" And lower, "I mean she's a great woman—not just your old lady. Seriously."

He paused, as Jean pleaded silently at the door. "I'll try to make it," he forced out, but before he could hang up he heard the dial tone.

A bit aged for sure, he lifted himself. Walking out of the office, Jean offered, "I hope it wasn't too bad?"

"Bad enough," he acknowledged, and asked gently if she could book a flight to Kennedy, if the shuttle didn't go there. Jean said of course, and clearly sympathized with his grave, mournful look.

He disliked airplanes, the bore of airports and unnecessary travel. Upsetting his day on the spur of the moment was particularly irksome. He promised himself, walking aboard and being greeted by the hostess, that he'd be home that night, after dinner. When the magazines came around, he tried *Time* for a while; found the *schlock* rough, the flight smooth. He picked up a sporting magazine, but stared over it, at the hills of white clouds floating in the air. Thoughts drifted to him of his destination, of beaches of adolescence. Coney Island and Good Humor Saturdays; that big whorish Nina, huge buttocks and breasts, whom he had innocently thought adored *only* him, until he found out from Marty about all the guys. He smiled now, thinking of her ice cream smells and chocolate and strawberry stains smearing her white uniform. Yet, she had given him a taste for big women that he still retained. He recalled the Rockaways, and their huge waves. And taking Rachel out there, to visit Grandma.

*Rachel at eight. In pigtails, blue swimsuit, with pail and shovel, slender little body with a child's pronounced belly. A meticulous architect-builder of castles and forts by the edge of the sea, with her daddy: Lionel, younger, slimmer, full thick hair and smooth cheeks, enjoying her mirth and mischief. She played the princess, looking out her castle window, and he was a shepherd, in theatrical delight. Interrupted when M. came along, his female friend for the day. And immediately, subtly, Rachel grows jealous, distrustful, goes inward. At eight she will pay him back for the female interloper. Her small face scrunches up in stubborn withdrawal. God, she could be stubborn! And when he tries to build a special wing for her, she picks up her pail and shovel*

*and claims that she has to play with Josie now, at the next
sand castle. His little darling walks off, while M. puts her
hand on his shoulder, and begins to rub on sun lotion. It
burns! A half hour later Rachel allows him a "makeup," allows him to carry his pumpkin into the ocean and piggyback
her through the waves, while he goes under and she remains
aloft, on his back, squealing and holding on to his mane! . . .*

The airplane jolts upward momentarily, and Lionel feels
the pressure on his back. Then they are landing peacefully.

In the cab from Kennedy, Solomon stared out the window
at the breaking water of Broad Channel, and the distant
banks of piled rubble, neglect. More of the past flooded him
. . . taking the rusty black IND downtown and changing at
Fourteenth (or Fourth) for the AA Mott Avenue to Far
Rockaway . . . discovering he's the only Caucasian on the
subway platform in Third World New York . . . Spanish
chattered rapid-fire and pleasingly, shiny chocolate faces and
limbs flashing, wide-brimmed Panama hats and tight yellow
and red dresses hugging delectable off-limits flesh, . . . he
leaned furtively by a filthy pillar, feeling like Meredith at Ole
Miss. . . . Did prosperous New Yorkers, his friends now,
know what it was like Down Below, here in the Underbelly?
. . . How odd, too, to be an outsider and potential victim at
the turf of his youth. History had turned the tables, paying
you back for pale skin, good English; making Manhattan
over into La Paz.

The cab veered on a turn, headed toward the darkness of
evening and the long jagged island called the Rockaways,
snaking out into the Atlantic like an elongated curving fork.

Back in the dark underground: would they hold their own
Master Auctions one day? Solomon in T-shirt and sandals at
the typewriter, hoisted onto the Fourteenth Street platform,
with the brown auctioneer saying, "Now what can I get for
this writer-professor here? with his high ambitions and these
five books, his big library and hot emotions? C'mon don't be
shy folks, dig in—this paleface here can help the kids with
the writin' 'n readin', sweet-talk the bank manager and read
the *fine* print, bring home the *New York Times* and write
some funnies for the kids." His chin was held up by the auctioneer: "Now don't be fooled by all these whiskers, shave
'em off and you got a bargain here! There's some *fine* ancient
Jew-ish blood flowin' for years down here in these veins."
The subway fantasy was interrupted by a question from the
cabbie about the address again. Instead of Charon taking him
across by boat, it was Alfonso Díaz in a Yellow Cab.

They passed more piles of rubble, pyramids of neglect, waiting to be transformed. Past streets of shabby one- and two-story clapboard houses. From his Gladstone bag, Solomon took out a small notebook and jotted down a note to his guerrilla in Hades:

All right, I've given up radicalism, grudgingly, inch by inch. To be an experience-watcher. My own, my country's. Not that I've turned against the philosophical idea embedded in socialism or whathaveyou. The idea is most admirable. But the idea of individual liberty is not bad either, like some other "old-fashioned" ideas in our constitution. (Nothing there about the necessity for capitalism, Tip.) Certainly the carrying out of the ideas here has been sloppy, slow, even retarded at times, but in a way, isn't it better than the devastating implementation of those other fine ideas? Yes, we have vulgarity and mediocrity smearing our society, but there's cost everywhere, isn't there? For example, for the sake of wheat, shelter, and health, consider the consequences to freedom and honest thinking in Russia. Or, in China, suppose you're not a peasant, but an intellectual, why should hoeing, raking and planting be the be-all and end-all of society? Or why create, like China, the World's Most Perfect Boarding School, where only proper manners and proper thinking will be tolerated? Oh, we've come close to 1984, maybe a dozen years earlier in fact, this last time around; a black janitor and a piece of tape on a door stopped it. Changed history, short-changed fascism. So yes, I've become a patriot of sorts; a private one. Unless it's to dissent out loud.

Admitted: we live by odd equations. The cost of personal freedom, highways with billboards and television commercials; the price of democracy, the dollar sign a national value, the trailers, snowmobiles, broken autos and junk next door. An exchange; something ugly for something worthwhile. Yet look at what Pure Idealism has produced, a society of lookalikes and conformity beyond one's (democratic) imagination, or perfect political logic crushing imperfect human beings and human differences, of Friends to the State rather than friends to each other; or Perverted Idealism, a society of Secret Eyes and Ears Everywhere, forced labor camps, strict hierarchy and bureaucratic privilege, of Vast Hypocrisy and Public Lying. So, who wins, vulgarity or political prisons, a society of informer-friends or that of political Babbittry? Depends on what you need or want for survival: rice or free thinking? Personally, I'd like both; if you can't have both, then you choose. Now, why couldn't we be a little more like Scandinavia and show some public civility? Sure. But remember, lend them two hundred million more persons, and see what happens to public manners. The problem is people, masses; too often they mean social injustice and chaos, or strict regimentation. . . . I care plenty, care too much perhaps, Ms. T. But what shall I do, ape Steinbeck, play Solzhenitsyn, repeat the obvious? Become a novelist fit for high school reading, small-town literary shelves, Pulitzer prizes?

He smiled, and began to cross out those last few lines, amused once again at this infirmity of resentment, like having a club foot. At least with the foot, you could kick it once in a while, for fun. And feel yourself strong, with reason. The cab meanwhile pulled up at 314 Beach Fifty-sixth Street, a four-story building owned by the city; Lionel paid the twelve bucks, thanked Alfonso. Then, as he stepped outside into the late afternoon and saw up close a group of teenagers eyeing him, he wished Díaz could accompany him. Four or five kids, black, a boy bouncing a basketball, two girls wrestling a third. Like Lionel, when he was in high school. Now, walking the few steps toward the curb and their kidding, he felt foolish, afraid. One fellow of fifteen caught his eye, seemed to search him out, peer beneath the corduroy jacket to the heart. Measuring him, on the Solomon scale of fear? Lionel, stomach loose, wanted to offer him his credentials: basketball, Brownsville, Jefferson High. He kept up his stride, evenly. No looking back. Another ten steps and he passed a wooden bench filled with old people; there's an absence every few months because of mugging, or the death of one of the gang. A guttural voice called. "Hey, is that you, Lionel? It's Frieda Josephs, your mother's friend, you remember?" "Sure," Lionel said, trying to. He stopped by the thin lady, maybe seventy, wearing a pretty choker under a white cardigan. The faces perked up, Lionel shook hands; old, weak, limbs lifeless, life only in the eyes now. "How's your daughter, Mrs. Josephs?" now remembering, "still designing those great bathing suits?" She broke into a wide smile, "So you remember! You know where she is now? On a cruise off Florida! Her company's paying for it." "Mazel tov," he said, remembering that too. Those old faces staying with him. Lined up like geriatric pigeons, waiting, waiting, as if this were death row, and not a block from the ocean.

He excused himself and entered the apartment house, and stood by the elevator. The mailboxes nearby were scrawled with graffiti; half of them were broken and the flaps hung loose like steel tongues. As Solomon stepped inside, a couple entered, and he held the elevator door for them. They didn't nod. The girl was very pretty, ebony, wearing hoop earrings and heels with jeans; she looked faintly familiar. The prostitute-daughter of his mother's friends, the Johnsons? The boy is wearing a wide-lapeled yellow shirt and wide-brimmed hat. Solomon stares dutifully at the black buttons indicating floors. "Don't jive me, you oaf!" "I ain't *jivin'* you chick, I'm *tellin' you what is.* That ain't no man to run with if you want to keep them ears for earrings." *"Shut your mouth, oaf."* Lionel holds his ground, listens to the lingo, smells the Woolworth perfume. The colors are dazzling—ebony, canary yellow, silver. He recalls Mr. Johnson, a large broad-shouldered man with a mustache and a gentle manner, a postman; Ella J. was a nurse. The car rides upward shaking sideways, and the boy's trousers remind Lionel of his prized possession in Winthrop Junior High, a pair of purple pants, with a thirteen-inch "peg" at the bottom, and chartreuse pistol pockets in back. In the schoolyard, Lionel is told to be careful wearing those, the "boys" don't like it. Frightened then, he yearns now; yearning has replaced fear by the time the compartment stops, and the door opens, and releases everyone.

For a moment in front of 6E he wants to be that boy again, and race downstairs and spend the evening with the teenagers. Hanging around, playing with the girls, wearing the costumes.

A Spanish couple with a child passes him toward the elevator and Lionel is reminded of how odd all these migrations and immigrations are; his father died in a building in Green Point, where he was the only white man among Puerto Ricans and blacks; and here his mother is in a building coming close to that proportion. 6E. He rings. Twenty-five years ago he lived in 1E.

"Who's there?" comes the skeptical voice.

"It's me, Mom," repeating the ritual.

"I thought so," the voice says, and there's a snapping of steel, and the door opens. A red-haired lady with cracked skin and lively face: "Well, well, it's about time." His mother grabs his face forcefully, and kisses him loudly on the lips, wetly on the cheek, smearing him with lipstick. "I have to wait a whole year before my son visits me," she shakes her head, "it's a shame."

"I invite you to Boston practically every month," the son at thirty-eight offers back. Still, the accusation stays.

"I know, sweetheart, I know. So come in already, yeah!" She locked the door, again, put on the safety catch and asked, "So how's Sheyna? Rachel? Rachel just called me the other night out of the blue."

"They're both fine, Mom."

Nodding toward the kitchen, she whispered, "Oy, *is this* a maidele. Can she get things done! And warm!"

His mother always had such good instincts for people, how had she gone wrong now? He glanced at her sideways; her badly wrinkled skin didn't keep the mischievous glint from her eyes, nor did her age keep the alertness from her brain. She remained a great rebounder in life, receiving hardship and bouncing up from it.

On the side he tried to speak privately. "Look, Mom, this girl . . . when did . . ."

This girl, however, appeared at the edge of the vestibule, her cheeks flushed with heat, his mother's flowery apron over her blue denim skirt. "Oh, hello, Mr. Solomon. Belle, would you taste the strudel?"

Lionel swallowed hard. There was some crazy insidious thing going on, he felt up his spine: what was it?

And then Tippy ducked back to the kitchen, Belle looked up at her son, and put out her hands. The gesture read: "Nu, what more could you want in a girl, she bakes too!" She said, "Where do you find these girls, tell me!" And he laughed in appreciation. To Tippy she said, "Sure, darling, sure. Coming." Adding on the way, "She won't let me touch a pot since she's been here, can you imagine?"

"How considerate. How long's that been?"

She laughed her throaty laugh, less wicked since her polyp operation of a year ago. "You know, I've lost track myself! Three, four days? Tippele, when did you arrive?"

*Tippele? Oh, boy.*

Tippy, kneeling by the oven, looking up through disheveled hair—Zola's *Nana*—said, "Monday, at four. Here, would you try this?" Businesslike in her position, she thrust out a baking sheet of apple strudel squares, toward Lionel. The absence of a brassiere was again emphatic.

Lionel, a strudel lover since the age of six, a breast lover since way before that, hesitated; he had forgotten the sheer sensual appeal of this Tippele. The lush waves of hair upon the shoulders, the tongue emerging to lick the full lips, the cheekbones—He lifted a piece of strudel with his fingers, and tasted. Good. Very good. He made a face, puckering out the lower lip, indicating quality.

"I know you don't like to taste the cinnamon." She slid the pan back into the oven, adding, "Please, Belle, you go into the living room and I'll get the coffee ready and bring everything in."

Her command of the situation was startling. So different from Sheyna's respectful diffidence here.

"Don't be silly," Belle protested. "We'll stay here and talk until—"

"No, *you* don't be silly. Your son has flown in to see *you*, not me. Now go inside and see *him*." Properly impatient with Belle, and properly busy with the next chore in the refrigerator. "I'll be in in a few minutes."

Belle, shaking her head, edged her son into the living room, heeding the affectionate martial law of the apartment. You could have picked out mother and son in a crowd of fifty: long sharp noses, hazel eyes, lightness and patience in the face; except that her hair was bleached and her face was painted. Who knows maybe it would happen to him? (he mused)

"Where do you find girls like her?" She shook her head in amazement. "Ruth's been a daughter for what, forty years? This girl has done more work for me in four days than Ruth in forty. And do you know what else, she's so *warm. Oy.* A shiksa yet. So go figure it out, right?"

*Yes, that's what I'm trying to do, Mom.*

She bent over to retrieve a particle of lint from the red shag rug, a particle visible to her and a microscope. She straightened with a groan.

Lionel, sitting on a familiar green vinyl recliner—which cost more than any chair he had ever bought—spoke low, and asked, "Mom, what does she want here?" He shook his head slowly. "What is she doing here?"

"Oh don't you know?" She shook her own head, and put a hand to her back. At seventy, she was still picking up lint in spite of her chronic back trouble; yet she had outlived two husbands and a lover (her true love), and was still pursued for marriage. But she was "through with responsibility," she had explained to him, and had rejected the proposal.

"She's doing a story on you," his mother explained, cheerfully, "for one of the big magazines. Which one now . . . *Saturday Evening Post?*" She shrugged. *"Ver veis* she'll tell you. *Oy*, this back of mine."

"You've not been well?" he asked.

"Not bad, not too bad. I don't complain, you know that." Not knowing what to do without a task, she began dusting the clean coffee table. "I had a little trouble with my leg, I think I told you. But you know, darling, we have the most

184

wonderful doctor that you can imagine. On the Medicaid, but it makes no difference to him. I went to see him and expected he'd take a minute or two and brush me off like that other *schmegegge*, but this Dr. Rudnick was *so patient, so gentle*. You wouldn't believe it. And you know who he is, Lionel? He's Ida's nephew's cousin. How do you like that?" She laughed.

Now all Lionel had to do was to remember who this Ida was, and he'd get it too. He gazed at the reproduction of a formal Victorian parlor scene bordered in a thick gilt frame, a nice contrast to the vinyl, shag, and knickknacks about the room. He asked about Ida, his mind elsewhere; she upbraided him for not remembering Ida Greenburg from the third floor. She continued tidying up the tidy room, talking about her leg, Dr. Rudnick, Ida, and her position on the waiting list for the new apartment house in Far Rockaway.

Finally he asked, low, "Well, what has she wanted from you?"

His mother looked at him as if he were crazy. *"Who?"*

He motioned with his thumb. "The girl."

"Tippele? Wants to know about *you*, what else? For a magazine, I already told you. *Oy Gott*, does she know stories by now"—sung in her Yiddish singsong inflection. "You know, some of them I didn't even know I remembered myself." She beamed. "And photographs, Lionel—she got such a kick you wouldn't believe!"

Lionel was getting used to surprises, though each one numbed him a little more.

"What *photographs?*"

"Are you nuts, please! Dirty pictures of my son I don't have, I assure you. And if I did I wouldn't give them out, yeah?" She made a face of annoyance at his skepticism of her. Feisty, stubborn, and sharp; her own woman to the end.

"Old pictures I've had around for years. What's the matter, I can't keep my own collection of photos now?"

"But who gave you—her—the right to—"

"The ones I like best," interrupted Tippy, appearing in the doorway carrying a loaded tray, "are you at four in the soldier suit, marching in the parade alongside your father." (His mother made room on the coffee table for the tray, and Tippy set it down.) "And that other one of you sitting on what looks like the potty, with your pants down around your ankles. God, you really looked like a *shaygets* in those days."

"Nu, do you hear that Yiddish, Lionel?" She squeezed Tippy's arm in joy. *"Oy, es iss ziss!"*

185

"Belle, why—"

"Enough Belle, call me Momma you hear!" In effusive delight.

"Isn't that carrying it a bit far?" Lionel wondered.

"What?" his mother stared. "Go on, will you! Why not?"

"Momma," Tippy relented, "why don't we open Lionel's bottle now?"

"Why not? I don't get a bottle of schnapps that often." And she shifted into sardonic gear. "Of course I don't see my sonnyboy that often!"

Lionel felt very hot in his light turtleneck, and craned his neck. Helpless and somehow revealed, he started to protest . . .

"I'm just joking honeybunch, she knows what I think of you, don't worry." She pecked his temple before he could turn away. And when he edged her off, she laughed at his childishness. "Even though he is my own son, he is cute isn't he, Tippele?" Laughing, having a great time.

At thirty-eight, Cute was not having a great time.

"Especially when he's embarrassed," Tippy nodded, pouring the coffee, "or furious."

Lionel wanted to hit her now, for real. The twat! This shiksa with her chutzpah!

He proceeded to pour out three shots of peppermint schnapps in glasses brought by his mother.

For some reason—to change the subject?—Lionel asked, "Should you be drinking this, Mom?"

Shaking her head, she slapped her leg. "He wants to put me in the old people's home! C'mon, will you! In the old days I'd have three or four straight Scotches, have you forgotten? This is a child's drink, come on! Besides it'll do me more good than harm."

Quietly, the single adult of the three had gotten up and brought her own drink in. The ginger ale fizzed from the cubes.

"Won't drink or smoke. *Klug.*" Nodded. "Smarter than we are."

Lionel, inhaling his own cigarette and remembering the cigarillo at the restaurant, agreed.

Belle raised her drink. "A toast, yeah? To Tippele."

"No, Belle, no—to Lionel's new book!"

Lionel, in a gesture of sudden enjoyment, his first, toasted, "To Tippele."

Tippy said, "You two are ganging up on me, no fair."

186

Lionel and his mother tipped their heads back and gulped; Tippy sipped.

"It's like a crème de menthe," observed Belle. "It's not too bad," being polite about the difference between it and a real drink.

Lionel, warming now, said, "So tell me some of the stories you've heard about me? I'd like to hear them myself. Who knows, my mother may be making up a few for your 'magazine piece.' "

"And why not? Can't I? Only you have the right to make things up?"

"Touché," said Tippy, patting Belle's knee.

"Come on, a story or two, to satisfy my appetite."

"Whatsamatta, the strudel's not enough?" Belle rolled her eyes and laughed at the corny line.

"Okay, one story," Tippy said, holding up one long slender white finger to the little serious student. "And then a walk before it gets dark, a deal?"

Lionel remembered an old line, and said it aloud: "The best deals are the ones you don't make."

She made a prep school face of puzzlement. Pleased, he poured more schnapps, and revealed, "Branch Rickey."

Tippy looked at Belle, who made her own face. "He's in his own world, don't listen to him."

"Your story?"

Tippy began to narrate the accident that befell Lionel when he was six. "I understand Steven Werter accidentally—"

"You got the names too, huh?"

"Accidentally hit you with a rusted pipe while digging, on that vacant lot in Ralph Avenue, and suddenly blood was running down your forehead and T-shirt. And she first heard about it when a neighbor came running upstairs and said, 'Please, Mrs. Solomon, your Lionel is bleeding from the head, hurry! He's in . . .' uh what's that name Belle?"

Belle laughed, loving this. "Dorfman's! Remember, Lionel?"

Tippy continued, "And there you were, standing in the drugstore having the wound washed out, not crying. And later on at the doctor's—Weinberg, wasn't it, Belle?—you stood like a perfect little patient, not panicking or screaming, barely crying while he stitched you up, thirteen stitches in your scalp!" She seemed to revel in the numbers, the details, and suddenly hovered above Solomon. "See? Right here, what most people take for baldness is the old wound from where the hair never grew back!" She smiled with pride, showing

187

those sharp gleaming teeth. "How everyone marveled at how grown up you were! How brave!"

"Weren't we all that way at six? I never did repay Werter for that little knock. Actually, I could use that pipe nowadays in Cambridge instead of my muggers' whistle."

"Oh go on," Belle said, biting into the strudel, and then holding it up. "I couldn't do better myself." She laughed. "And I'm the mother!"

But Lionel was already back there on that vacant lot—of punchball, and sledding, of cowboys and Indians and World War II wars, that beloved Ralph Avenue of his youth, with Shlossy, Dizzy, Katzie, Kamphorballs, Bully, Boodie—back there in a bliss of memory and wanting.

"Hey, one story is all you get now."

"So go already, yeah? She's been waiting for a walk all day." She imitated an Important Manner, *"To interview you,* I suppose."

"Go on, tell me another," he said, as they walked on the wooden boardwalk, before twilight. A boardwalk that stretched far into the gray distance, wide, deserted, poignant.

She smiled with a curious enjoyment. Her hair blew loose in the windy air, and she seemed looser out here, in the open. A broad-shouldered bird no longer cooped up. Or was that Lionel?

"Which do you want: almost losing the right eye or a battle of wills between father and son?"

"You have a whole menu, I see," scratching at his beard. "I'll take the father story." She pulled his hand with two hands, saying, "Someday we'll take this disguise off."

He fingered his beard, protectively.

"Come let's walk on the beach!"

"What's wrong with the boardwalk?"

"Oh come on, don't be so fuddy-duddy. You want your story don't you?"

"But . . . I've got these shoes on?"

"Poor baby." She tapped his nose. "Take 'em off, see?" showing him, by removing her sneakers. "Or get some sand in your socks, it won't kill you." Clasping her sneakers in one hand, she began tugging Lionel down the wooden steps, toward the expanse of beach.

He plopped down on the wooden steps and pulled off his shoes, remembering concrete-stoop days and Coney Island mornings.

Shoes and socks off, he tested the sand with his toes and realized he had better roll up his cuffs.

"Mr. Gerontion." She shook her head, in dismay. "It was the time you wanted to go upstairs to Joey's apartment, and he said no."

He raised himself up, seeing her denim leg and stretch of beach, the name Joey transporting him. In an instant of stretching time: Joey Zeitlin, dark, slender, and a great older athlete in the neighborhood, was scribbling in Lionel's j.h.s. autograph book, 'May you be a fine straight shooter!' It took Lionel weeks to figure out that the cryptic line meant pool, straight pool. Joey Zeitlin later "sponsored" him in Barney's Poolroom, that special male sanctuary where Brooklyn boys passed through their puberty rites.

"And you just wouldn't do it; you *wouldn't* say, Yes, you *would* stay in the apartment; you said, *No, No,* you were going to go upstairs to Joey's, you *always* did on Friday night, *always.*" Dramatized in her best creaking voice, as they walked in wind and sand. "And every time you said no, he slapped you. And when your mother tried to intervene he pushed her away, which only made you *more* stubborn. And him *more* angry. But you simply wouldn't give in, *would* you? While he kept slapping you!"

Lionel's cheeks burned now—from those slaps or Tippy's excited *woulds?*

He tried to make light of it. "Yes, they were worse than stitches, I suppose. See where the hair stopped growing?" He pointed to the clear half of his cheek.

Tippy, grave, innocent, blooming here by the sea, inquired, "Who was Joey?"

"Oh he was older, and a kind of hero I guess," he began, recalling. And went on about pool ("he never hit the cue ball hard except for the break, or follow for position; he never took a shot that didn't include table position for the next two shots"); baseball ("he was a great long-ball hitter in softball, although he was really slender and had these slumping shoulders; sort of like Ernie Banks of the old Cubs, who had a string-bean body but great wrists, and hit the long ball"); ladies ("he looked like a young Montgomery Clift, remember him? Didn't think you would. A kind of wounded handsomeness, an introspective spirit; inward and injured, but handsome on the outside"). Lionel paused and reflected, remembering something curious that he didn't even know he knew, or remembered, and the words flowed. "We once had this . . . strange conversation. I must have been ten and he

189

about fifteen or sixteen, and he took me for this walk around the block, up Ralph and right on East New York Avenue and down Union Street and back on Sutter, a whole square block you see, and you know what he wanted to talk about? How difficult it was, *having no father. Missing one.* And being *jealous* of those who did—like me, like everyone else on the block. Well, it stunned me. Of course it didn't help that his mother was nutty, and had all sorts of boyfriends coming and going. But you see, here was this Jack Armstrong of the neighborhood," Lionel nodded at Tippy, "and his older hero suddenly revealing uncertainty, weakness, fear. It scared me. And I seem to recall a line like 'Until you don't have a father you won't know how hard life is, *you've* got it made in life, kid." And there I was, not only feeling badly for him, but also suddenly feeling guilty for hating my own father! Do you see?" he appealed, innocent himself.

And Tippy replied, "And there was your father, not letting you go upstairs to visit him."

They trudged on, closer to the ocean, their faces sprayed lightly. "I remember seeing him years later, by chance, when I was visiting New York from California and was down on Fourth Avenue by the secondhand bookstores. I stopped into that department store on Fourteenth Street, Klein's? And there he was, a floor manager or section manager, speaking a fluent Spanish to the Puerto Rican customers. Turns out he had married a Puerto Rican girl. He looked very very thin, his color had become that of nicotine stain, and his old ironic bite seemed to have gone. He was delighted to see me, claimed he had followed my career by means of my mother and then the *New York Post*. He made some nice joke about my beard, a reminder of his old self. There was something . . . odd about him, however. Painful. Unfortunately we didn't have the time for a real talk. Too bad." Lionel paused, pulling a cigarette stub from between his toes, said, "Fossil, in the year 2020?" walked on. "I guess you should have made time, because the chance doesn't come around again. Anyway, about six months after that I got this letter from my mother. She was coming upstairs one afternoon in the old apartment house when out from the stairway emerged this shadowy figure, who said, 'Please, Mrs. Solomon, don't be afraid, it's me—Joey!' And it was, at least a shadow of the old Joey. And in an embarrassed wobbly voice he asked if she could spare some money? My mother, completely unnerved and sympathetic, gave him a few dollars that she had in her purse, and then begged him not to ask her again; you

190

see, they both knew what it was for. Hard dope. Despite his condition he apologized to her; they had known each other since he was a baby and he felt humiliated, she hurt. And he never did ask her again. It turned out that he had become a serious addict, had been away in withdrawal centers several times, but couldn't kick it. Poor creature." Lionel found himself choking up, and turned his face away. Said nothing for another minute, remembering. "He died about a year later, and I remember getting that letter, and remembering the first conversation, and this curious pride in me. It was as if he had been an older brother, now suddenly defeated and feeling guilty and ashamed for his behavior with me! . . . Not unlike my father in his last years. More irony. Poor Joey, he was an orphaned soul."

And with the right intuition she took him around maternally, just as he felt fears from the memory of that lean dark face and the old boyish irony, all eaten away by those needles. The salt from the sea mixed with his wetness; he was unaccountably moved.

Tippy whispered, "That's what I always loved about your books, and knew I would love about you, *the deep feelings.* You must write about him sometime, won't you?"

Lionel was in pain, dazed, embarrassed. He held on as if for dear life; but if he had such feelings when could they come out, without embarrassing him? And come out in life, not in fiction?

Finally he released himself and got his head clear. It was wonderful out here, in the space. He trudged on, she surged, and he called, "So you like the ocean, eh? Play with the fish? Bite them back when they bite you? Where're your gills, young lady?"

She didn't seem to pay attention, but after several more steps she suddenly put her hand on his shoulder, stopping him. And peered at him with a gaze of fixed intensity.

*Here it comes,* he knew, heart racing, *this is it. A punch or knife or bullet, just when I'm off guard! Or toss me into the ocean and drown me! She knows I'm a weak swimmer!*

"Ayy-ashi!" she cried out, doing a swift, high pirouette and coming down in a fixed position, torso crouched on right-angled knees, ass perched, hands flat out like knives.

The sea roared and Lionel blinked.

She stared for a *long* minute, then, moving her hands slowly in a rotating position, she began to circle him.

Scared, he began to circle too, even getting into his old-fashioned boxing position, left hand out for the jab, right hand tucked up against his chin. Expecting anything.

With a "Hyaoo!" screech she went after him with her left foot, kicked high, and he just ducked back in time!

"Like Rocca," he mumbled.

She didn't speak, in fact she didn't even face him anymore, she was in a new position facing the sea, in profile, one palm high over her head and the other a knife in front of her eyes. She didn't budge, and he realized she was back in her own thing, and he gradually let his guard down, and observed. It was too fascinating to be humorous.

In a flash she removed her denim shirt, an encumbrance. However she wore nothing underneath, and, while she looked splendid, it frightened him terribly! He glanced around: long white beach and breaking waves . . . were those boardwalk watchers?

And for the next ten minutes or so she proceeded to move through this peculiar set of rituals, which he had occasionally seen performed by persons in white judo jackets at Fresh Pond reservoir. But where was her judo jacket (or any jacket)? Hands rotated and palms sliced the air, arriving at sudden halts; positions changed every few moments with little leaps and bold cries, whereupon she'd plant herself on those right-angled knees; the body glistened with salt spray, and the face was frozen in a mask of granite beauty, fitting the stylized poses very well. Speed and stillness, anger controlled and force channeled, grace and force alternating in every movement; thus she performed. And he, with his yoga years, admired; especially there by the sea all these stylized formations seemed elegant. So much so that the force of the exercise competed favorably with the sheer sensuality of the splendid young animal, reveling and revealing.

The performance went on and on, hypnotic and adventurous. A blond dolphin playing freely, sleek, strong, . . . a Christian shark out for Jewish lamb-blood perhaps? Should he dump her back in the sea and hold her head under for . . . baptism? evolution? Would she drive him to do that? Drive him crazy?

"Hey, what are you doing?" he forced to plead as she pulled a lower trick by slipping out of her skirt, suddenly, revealing only a narrow strip of flowered loincloth. Except that she was already racing past the beach edge and running into the first low waves and finally in a headlong dive into the ocean. Hers, it seemed. Some were made for sea and sun and she was one. She disappeared in the white foam and waves and Lionel admired. She swam straight out, turned abruptly about and swam a hundred yards easily and then cut back in a pretty hypotenuse to complete the triangle. Except that now she was gone, underwater for an unusual length of time, which made him wonder if he, the weaker swimmer, should dive in after her? . . . But she bobbed up just then, at the edge of the reflected amber path, the dying sun on her back, and motored by those lovely long legs kicking steadily, she floated Solomonward.

The spell of the samurai had disappeared in the strength of the swimmer as she ran toward him, and throwing off water, human again, she announced gleefully, "God I've been wanting to do that since the first minute I came!"

The salt water ran down her body as he held out her shirt, and as she got into it—"Brrr!" she whispered—he couldn't help nuzzling her neck and cheeks; she shivered and leaned into him for warmth.

"You do have gills, don't you? And fins. Plus guts." *Plus spectacular body and sea smells and animal capacity, Lionel.*

"There's no sea in the Southwest," she explained, "so when I get near one I can't resist." Half giggling, half shivering.

Oh she was very young right there, very innocent, needy, foolish, powerfully natural and he felt special for having her.

*(And he loved her then too; was hopelessly in love with her the way you loved a wild mustang or colt, who, for all its vitality was also vulnerable. And who had permitted you, picked you, to be her protection.)*

"Here, take this, it's warmer," handing her his jacket. She huddled into it, a corduroy nest; and into him.

"Are you a black belt?"

"Are you kidding? Do you know how many years of practice it takes to get that? And how many people make that?" She got her skirt and shirt on. "No, no. I just like to keep in shape. Stay trim. The forms are fun and challenging."

"For self-defense."

She looked up at him, the resplendent young skin approaching holy. "And offense." She shifted tone and asked, "Rub my back a bit, my pussycat?"

His mother's name for him. Oh, he liked doing things for her like this—having done it for his own daughter for years—and he held her and rubbed and massaged her long back until he felt warmth return to her skin. And curiously, as the sea and wind howled, Lionel had this intuition that it was indeed a roar of intentionality, of approval, of jealousy, of symbiotic attraction. A mating howl even.

Warmed and succored, they walked on, bumping each other and holding hands in understanding.

(Now do you see, Doctor, he had by now completely lost that feeling of awkwardness and suspicion and fear that had cramped him in the small apartment. It had been Tippy there with his mother, the profane with the sacred perhaps, Tippy there for two or three days with his past life and baby youth, sacred youth, that terrified him. Why? As if there were deep dark secrets in his past life that she could uncover? But what were those? Where? Was he criminal? Homosexual? Incestuous? Back there without knowing it? Did his mother *know* certain things? . . . But out there by the ocean, on this little beach promenade, the air seemed clearer in more ways than one, and there seemed to be more clarity and space and cause for cheer. That the girl had also performed her dazzling little number here was quite nice, despite the initial shock; much nicer than the usual running along the beach or holding-hands scenes, reserved for celluloid and advertisements. But it was mainly the fact of their being out there together alone, without the presence of his old and beloved mother, that made the Tippy creature more beloved, and her *act*, the acting Tippy, easier to take.)

After the razzle-dazzle and the sudden shark spectacle they walked on quietly. At one point he tried to say something, but she put her hand over his mouth and shook her head, and that was fine. With the steady intrusiveness of the sea he was able to observe her on the sly, and she looked happy here. A splendid amphibian, arching forward, smart, strong, at home. . .

On and on along the moist sand-castly edge of the ocean, whipped by wind and spray—

"Hey, look—come on, let's climb up!" she pulled him.

Just there to the right loomed the high lifeguard's chair, and with no one around, Lionel allowed himself to climb the chipped wooden rungs after Tippy. Up maybe twenty feet, she squeezed onto his lap, and they had before them the Atlantic to observe. Up close the waves broke in a kind of greenish foam, while further out the sea rippled midnight blue far onto the horizon.

"That *smell* is heaven, isn't it," said sweet hell. Lamb nodded. A rude noise whirred, and overhead a police helicopter dipped down briefly like a dragonfly to skim above the water low, as if on a bombing raid.

"They used to have patrol boats for that," Lionel said preferring the easy putter to the splashing whirl.

After a pause, Tippy, face thrust forward, announced, "We'll live by the sea one day."

The calm authority which always startled him.

*By the sea or by my mother, my youth? Solomon muses . . . Why do women keep turning up in my life who discover new intimate addictions for me? And exploit them? Well let her babble. Sticks and stones will break my bones, but babble will never break me.*

"God, is that *a whale?*" she pointed.

He peered. "More like a freighter."

She was delighted. "How could you tell so quickly?"

"I used to sail on them."

She looked at him. "Are you kidding me? When?"

"Sixteen. Seventeen. . . . Eighteen."

"In high school! When other kids were dragging cars—I knew it! I knew it! I knew the sea was in you somewhere." She squeezed him and steamed into him and looked at him with glowing green eyes. "Tell me about a trip." He tried to beg off, but she persisted, cajoled, demanded, and perched that way, up high in this baby crow's nest, she got her way. He recalled his first sailing. At sixteen, a high school senior, he took the IRT subway from Sutter Avenue one early June morning up to Atlantic Avenue station, and walked the few blocks to the Scandinavian Seaman's Institute. ("Why there?" "Unless you had fifty bucks for the bribe, American seaman's papers were impossible. All you needed at the institute was your passport, and the desire, and you were on.") And from a bulletin board of 3 × 5 cards, which advertised for various members of the crew, he took one to the teller and the man said in his singsong English, "She sails at 3 P.M. today. Pier 52, Manhattan. Goot luck." Fantasy into reality by means of an index card. And so after rushing home and packing the navy duffel bag bought for the occasion in the Army-Navy store, and kissing his mother goodbye, he took the subway uptown, looked on with delicious envy by those would-be sailors and dreamy girls who noted, in the bag and dungarees, a rider to real adventure. "I think it was worth the effort for that subway ride alone." And when the indescribable thrill of walking up the gangplank of the S.S. *Ferngold*, and reporting to the Bosun in smeared blues, and later that day to the Captain, in spotted whites, who shook your hand and eyed you narrowly and said, "This ship is your home. You take care of it the same way." And at 3 P.M. the 6,200-ton freighter creaked up its huge anchor along with giant seaweed, and was off for a two-week tour of the East Coast—Philadelphia,

Boston, Baltimore—picking up supplies of flour, barley, some automobiles and also twelve passengers—three missionaries and their families—and lo and behold there he was, out on the Atlantic. Watching the hypnotic wake of the ship from the stern, the dream sprayed by real salt water.

Now with her own wide-boned Scandinavian face right there, asking and prodding—she looked something like the Norwegian pen pal from Bergen, whom he had gotten out of a pen-pal booklet sent to Norwegian merchant seamen—Lionel found himself dredging up precise details of that magical journey, that fairy-tale dream of youth hardened by duty and tasks, but remaining at center, a voyage of virginal excitement. Did he really perform at sixteen what he now recalled at thirty-eight? he himself wondered. Chipping paint by day, taking the wheel of the ship at night, the graveyard watch; awakened for Sunday morning chess by the First Mate, and every evening playing *whist* with the Bosun and two AB's, for a case of beer; the night landing off the coast of Monrovia, with fifty black young Africans boarding the ship like surreal phantoms in the still air, their gold-filled teeth gleaming in the pitch-black night; and later that week, Lionel standing at the head at the ship's prow and turning around to face three young Africans, coal black and smiling, and being terrified, only to find them filled with curiosity about the single American worker aboard; they lived in a tent above the front hold, ate gruel, did the dirty hard work of unloading, and at twilight, played self-made musical instruments made with rubber bands and wooden crates, and danced together in their pajamas like children out of a fairytale, while from above, the towheaded missionaries and the crew looked on. And then Lionel remembered an embarrassing incident. "One night I'm reading in my cabin and there's a knock at the door, and it's the Captain, whom I hadn't seen since meeting him that first day out. There he is, in perfect white shorts and laundered white shirt with epaulets and captain's cap, asking if I had cleaned midships that day? I said yes, I had, and he asked very politely if I would come with him? Trembling with nervousness I followed him, and I realized as we walked back toward midships that we had a large audience observing us too. You didn't often see the captain of a ship leading a young deck boy across ship, after dinner especially. Presently we were in the large shower room, which contained several shower stalls and urinals, and he asked if I had cleaned there that afternoon? I nodded, scared, but confident that I had indeed cleaned it. He then crouched down on his haunches at the very corner of the indented shower area, and using his index finger wiped up thick grease and held it up in the air, as if it were a handkerchief of evidence in a murder trial; the prosecutor knew I was guilty and simply waited for my sentencing. Evidence continued to pile up as he hopped like a prosecuting frog around the edges and corners, and I was ready to walk the plank by trial's end. He pronounced, "Remember what I said to you that first day?" No. "This ship is your home, you have to treat it the same way. With care and attention." A firm pronouncement softened by a kindly pat on my shoulder, "It's all right, it's your first voyage, Lionel, you'll learn, you'll do fine. Always do your job thoroughly, we all depend on that, on each other here, you remember, yes?" Oh, I would, I would, grateful for his mercy! And afterward on deck I was the center of the crew's attention. When they heard the story, they shook their heads and made their own pronouncement about their captain: "He's crazy! Aaahh, a real nut!" But I disagreed, privately. I thought he made sense. And I cleaned every nook and cranny, scrubbed the walls, washed the latrines, as if I lived in every spot. That early warning took hold, I'll tell you."

"Is that why you keep such a spotless apartment?" Her eyes glinting and then a peck. "Was that your greatest sea-error, my Ahab?"

Her Ahab considered the question, and remembered something else. "No, actually there was a more serious error." And he went on to tell of how he had left his watch too early at the fo'c'sle head to go for coffee, and missing an approaching tanker in the night. Hence instead of the early two-gong warning signal to the wheelhouse above, it was up to the fellow at the wheel to spot the ship, maybe three to five minutes later, and tell the Second Mate. That was indeed a criminal neglect of duty, truly dangerous; and he burned with shame as the Second Mate, his trusted friend, gave him a serious lecture. "Oh it was pretty rough, I can tell you. It's one thing to miss some shower grease, but another to have abandoned your post, not done your job and endangered lives."

"Did you make amends?" she wondered.

"How could I? I just did the job more efficiently afterwards, with no slipups. That's the thing about being out on the sea with freight, property and a crew; there's not too much room for slipups."

She felt his thinning hair. "You mean like Lord Jim?"

He nodded, interested. "You get the idea." And he recalled quickly the futility of trying to teach Conrad to children of the suburbs, whose "ships" are Sunfish and Chris-Crafts, and whose mistakes were abandoning the tunafish sandwiches, not eight hundred pilgrims.

She curled herself into him more securely and they stared at the sea and slow freighter. Cirrus clouds had begun to line up in the sky, strands of gray brushed lazily in the blue.

It took Lionel several minutes to bolt the door on his perfect, powerful, dangerous memory, and to reestablish the steel distance of time. No more memory morphine just now; just cool sober distance from that overheated undefined hope! From that wild-haired T-shirted boy of sixteen who was wild, anarchic, driven, and revved up for adventure.

Tippy's sea-green eyes stayed on him, *What did she want, what could she bring him? All that back again? He knew better.*

"You've stopped traveling," she interrupted, "haven't you?"

"Of course not. I was just in—"

She laughed the little laugh. "I don't mean *places*. In your *head*, your *heart*—that was an adventure of the heart just now. Your S.S. *Ferngold was you*. Years and years later, and you're still *shaking* telling about it." Her look was narrow and tutorial. "And that's why I want you. I'll take you places again. I'm your . . . S.S. *Tippy*. I knew it from the beginning, back there in . . . Arizona, Albuquerque, back there with *Journey to Manhattan*."

Lionel tried to shift his leg, falling asleep. She moved with him, permitting it, smiling confidently. The wind and the sea whirled and for a long green sea-moment he loved her desperately, as if *she* were sixteen!

Then, remembering his daughter's LP album, said, "Well, Miss Suzannah, I think it's time to get back to the boardwalk."

The reference showed in her face, but her manner indicated that while she took the song humorously, she took her own will and desire much more solemnly. "Do you always get this serious by the sea?" he asked, climbing down.

At the last few rungs he reached out for her, and noted, "By the way, young lady, where's my jacket?"

Ran her finger down his nose. "I love it, long and unashamed." And laughed. "I've sent it on to Cooperstown, for safekeeping. Do you want it back, silly? Come on, Indian giver!" And she pulled him into a run.

He jogged at a fair pace, picturing the Iroquois jacket next to Ruth's bat and Cobb's spikes . . . next to Chekhov's medicine bag and Tolstoy's writing table. . . . .

"Sure I want it back," he called.

They ran. She ran fairly well, though she rocked too much from side to side; her behind was robust and larger than he had remembered. It was a fitting close to the day, running free this way. Panting, at the boardwalk's steps, she had an idea. "Hey, let's walk underneath. See if it's still the same?"

Huh? What had he told her again? Besides, it was a different beach.

You crouched down slightly when you first entered beneath the boardwalk, but then the cavernous darkness hollowed out somewhat, and you could barely walk in it upright, though carefully. He stopped and scooped a fingerful of the old familiar sand, wonderfully moist, hard, brown, the way he had remembered it. Like clay, or the ocean edge. Bending their heads periodically, occasionally bumping each other, they tramped on; it was like walking in caves in Provence perhaps, except here the caves were scrawled with chalked graffiti and puppy-love memorials on the wooden posts. Still, it was mysterious, odd, serene. The smell was ocean and wet sand; though soon enough, as they proceeded, smells from above floated down too. Just as footsteps began to clack overhead, and they smiled, realizing that they had arrived at a pedestrian boardwalk area.

Suddenly she was not at his side, and he, annoyed, turned to look for her. He had to wander over a section to the left, and there she was, and he could see she had turned strange again. Transformed herself once more. Leaning up against the corner wooden post, hip cocked out to the side, belly (deliberately) dropped down and thrust forward, torso flaunting and face defiant. The sheer exhibitionism of the pose struck him dumb.

Not the sweet listener anymore, not the vulnerable girl needing protection, not the athletic colt, no: with her sudden beret, she was like a Paris streetwalker, on exhibition.

*Doctor, right here I shall try my best to get it straight, the pose, the setting, the language. Because it was unusually rude and embarrassing. And because you'll wonder how much is my projection. Doctor, not much. Believe me, not much. She was a chameleon, changing her colors with a violent brillance.*

"Come on, toughguy, let's see your stuff," she said, sullen, smoking, challenging.

*Where* the hell, and *how* did she get that way so swiftly?

199

*Why?* Why did *he* go helpless there in life at her sudden crude transformation? Why didn't he slap her for her impudence, for her playacting? Or walk away? Leave it? She was all cheap thrills, honky-tonk stuff, country-music tough, and he knew it, or sensed it; is that what he desired? She said, "You're *scared*, aren't you?"

A transistor radio passed overhead, blaring with guitars and drums.

"Your momma won't show up, don't worry." Her smile was derisive, her slouching style teenage, her thrust-out hip and dropped belly sensual. "C'mon sonnyboy." She stared at him coldly. And, edging the role to its hilt, she said slowly, with the determination of a witness pleading the First Amendment and emphasizing the word "freedom," she said, *"Shit."*

And he? He was caught between Lionel the old and Lionel the client she was looking for now; between the young boy and youth he had just been reliving warmly to and for her, and the crazed animal she was demanding now. His life, which he had always thought too complex, was now mocked for its naïve simplicity; his emotions, which he had perceived as wild, were now revealed for their ordinary predictability; what could he rely on? act from?

In slow motion she moved out her bare foot, and kicked sand on him.

He didn't move.

She reached down and tossed a handful of sand upon him, underhand and casually.

He didn't move. She did it again, with derisive glee.

Sand trickling down his neck, he took the three steps and grabbed her by her shirt lapel, his heart beating crazily. Except she lowered the hand to her breast and dug her nails into it.

Now by this time she had driven him to a point of intensity that later was to remind him of a son's joy for his mother, which erupts in the young boy of six taking a bite out of his mother's thigh in sheer joy and cannibal love.

She began to claw at his chest and back, and got her knees in his groin, and began to cling to him like a prisoner-of-war wife who has not seen her husband for years, and goes after him with accumulated need and an angry lust.

He took her down to the sand and turned her about and flung up her denim wraparound fig leaf—isn't that what they were for, Doctor?—a kind of maniac now, admittedly. Her mania sure. Up, up, up his hand along the long white flank; and finally that narrow strip of bathing suit panty.

Looking back at him, she said, "Use your teeth."

Huh? How, for what? Nervous and unnerved, he bent upon her like the Hunchback of Far Rockaway, and tried to yank it away! The cotton material hung on like bikini floss in his gums.

In his madness he didn't mind, kissing and licking that sensational buttock along with yanking.

She pressed his scalp toward her with her hand.

In passion, he yanked it away with his hand finally, and mounted her from behind. Steps clattered above as he sought her underneath; but when he had found what he wanted she moved, anticipating, and maneuvered so that she put him tightly elsewhere, in a more difficult region, she gasping and he hurting, temporarily; "use spit," she urged, and he followed orders and finally settled in like a tight nut and bolt; and she grabbed one ear hard with her hand, and placed his other hand around on her vagina. Between her that way, he got to the point of locking in there, rider and steed, though Solomon for one wasn't quite sure which he was, or she; so hot with fear and fury was he.

Turning, she mocked low, "Come on sonnyboy," and pulled at his hair. His head rushed with pleasure, and he drove her hard but slow. The wooden boards above his head rattled and for a moment he half expected strangers and tourists to drop down on his intercourse. Slants of light peeked in between the planks, voyeuristically. He hated her, loved *it*.

The girl rotated slowly, and, between groans of labor, asked, "As good as the first time?"

In his bliss he didn't answer, but worked upon her, controlling himself as carefully as he could; powered by his fury, her body.

*"Es is ziss, huh?"* she mocked, she fucked.

Presently her sex smell rose up like the sharp aroma of bacon fat, and somehow took him back, transported him briefly to fourteen and the Italian girl . . . the powerful odor, the large breasts, the sensual grin. . . . "Bambino, . . . that's it, my bambino . . . my sweet fucking bambino!" Were those her words?

The shocking words aloud jolted him back to the present, and he fucked uncontrolled, furious at her for timing his memory clock so perfectly, and bringing him here, into this honeycomb of moist clay and childhood sea-smell, this nest of his premature addiction . . . and as he thrust into her with that memory and this fury in a longloosespasm of pleasure, he knew too that she had won again, somehow, that deep down this girl had his number when it came to pleasure, and that whichever way he turned or tossed to escape, in the end, the deep end, he only arrived.

Presently tautness gone, he lay on her, over her, her pure green eye gazing at his, like a pure marble, sated, he thought; and he closed his, to hear the sea, and above, two voices, coming in clearly now:

"Are you sure you didn't hear something? Like a scream?"

Quiet; his heart pounding, stomach empty.

"You're watching too much television. Look, your candy is getting all over you . . . There, is that what you mean?"

A scream of a teenager and a jet in the sky.

Footsteps clacking away.

She opened his eye for him, and stared and stared, making her point with her postcoital pleasure. Her face, light and wide in repose, filled him with satisfaction. It was like lying with a beautiful doe, big-eyed, furry, smelly; unbelievably animal-tender. As special and powerful as the intercourse, this beauty.

During dressing, sneaking out from under, or walking home on the boardwalk, she didn't talk. (She walked barefoot, he wore his shoes.) He left the hollow of the boardwalk like a cat fearful of witnesses to his coitus. (The only trouble here was that the other cat could talk, squeal.) All the way to his mother's house, he cast furtive glances at his taut curving bait, and realized that it, she, was just too strong for him, and he couldn't chance any serious temptations. (Which were?) It was like offering a brook trout to a shark. Except that he was confused here too: who was the trout and who the big fish. The positions seemed to shift all the time. Right now, in late twilight, she had changed back to trout, golden, wearing blue denim.

*(It's difficult, isn't it, not to overestimate the sexual object when it comes framed within a background of ocean, sand, boardwalk, and sweet adolescent memory?)*

After dinner of Tippy's roast chicken and *knedel* soup, his mother asked him in the living room about Sheyna and Rachel, and then nodded toward Tippy cleaning up in the kitchen.

"She's a good girl, yeah?" checking up on her own opinion. *"So* kind. *Giving.* You don't see that too often in young people

202

these days, you know, Lionel? Am I wrong? Take Mrs. Wolfson's Nancy and Maury . . ."

And when she was finished with her examples, Lionel observed, "Yes, this girl seems to have her kind side. But I don't exactly know her too well. Nor, do you, come to think of it."

"Yeah, it's true," fixing a doily, "but you know when you spend a few days with a person, living and sleeping in the same house, you learn certain things." She made a face of reflection, "I think she's a trifle lonely." But another thought provoked merriment; "I think she has her eye on you too, if I'm not mistaken!"

"Just what I need, right, Mom?" passing on daughter's advice to mother.

"Ho ho!" she cried out. "Just what you need! My *chochem* here. Go on, will you! Are you *meshugah*? You have a lovely girl already, *if* you don't mind. You need another one like you need a hole in the head. Here, have a little more strudel? *Oy*, it's good, I can't put it down!" She took a bite, drank her coffee, and suddenly spoke gravely, "You've been well, Lionel? It's been a good year?"

"Pretty good, Mom," he replied, admiring the continued vitality within the wrinkled limp flesh. The auburn hair was thinned out, but kept up well, neatly, short this season. How odd, it struck him, that with all her great virtues, common sense, open affections, good sense of humor, and his old emotion for her, still he was not able to spend too much time in her company. What a great irony, that now, when he appreciated her, clearly, when their love was firmly felt and understood rather than in those years of upheaval in his late teens, now, the gaps between them were bridgeless. The vases of artificial flowers and gilt-edged fake Victoriana and vinyl chairs always bothered him after a while, when combined with her endless useless chatter about this or that irrelevant person or other trivia. And yet, at certain moments, an hour or two for every twenty-four perhaps, she would recount an experience that would be impressive for its richness and keenness of observation. As when she had told him, on the last visit, about being forced to see her own dead mother lying in the coffin when she was a girl of thirteen, and fainting; and for years afterward, waking up with the nightmare of the mother's face in the coffin, done up with wax by the undertaker. After an hour like that, Lionel would lacerate himself for not spending more time with her before it was too late.

"You're not working too much, yeah?" she was asking now, sipping coffee. "You take some time off, to relax?" With the same concern that she had shown thirty-five years ago, unvaried in its focus or authenticity.

Her future absence in the green chair made him turn away for a moment. Then he said, "Mom, I have it easy, believe me. Easier than most. I play tennis, swim, cross-country ski and—"

"Go on will you! I've seen you work, remember? And when you're not in your study it's on your mind. You're a nervous hyena most of the time, it drains you so. That's not relaxing in my book."

The water ran in the kitchen from Tippy's washing up.

"You're doing another book, yeah? So what's this one about?" She laughed robustly. "I'm still reading the last, you should know. You write . . . epos, so that I can't read too much at one time. Some of the words," she shrugged.

"—too *earthy?*"

"Too earthy for me? Are you crazy? I'm not a child, or one of these timid sorts, as you know. I've lived close to seventy years, I've had my share of good times. Too earthy for me? Ha, that's a good one! Life's earthy, whatsamatter with you! Nah, I mean the words are too . . . deep or big sometimes, and I suddenly need a dictionary to read it. It gets me *epos* frustrated . . . but I'll get through it, after my fashion. You don't mind my telling you?"

"I enjoy it. One of these days I'll write a . . . simpler story, with simpler words. Okay?"

"This present one's not so simple, is that it?" She laughed.

"Well . . . it's not finished yet. We'll see. If I can make it simple, Mom, I will." But maybe it was simple? "When can I expect you this summer, by the way?"

They discussed possible dates for her journey to New Hampshire. She had her own life of friends here in Rockaway, and this included trips to the Poconos in the summer, and Lakewood, New Jersey, in the winter. So in truth she had to fit her son in, as much as he fitted her in. "You're too busy, Mom."

"*Oy*, Lionel if you only knew the *tummel!*"

"She's right, Lionel, I've watched it." Observed Tippy the Dutch maid, with hair up and braided in back, bringing more coffee. "She hardly has a minute to herself."

"Except for reporters, huh?"

Tippy smiled thinly, refilled the cups, and picked some crumbs off Mrs. Solomon's lap, casually.

And when Tippy walked out, Lionel said to his mother, "How is it to be near seventy, Mom, to get older?"

She blinked her eyes as if to get something out of them, a recent tic. "You know, Lionel, I was never one to look back too much. What's happened happened. You have to go on. I think that helps a lot. You know what I went through with your father for twenty-five years, and then later on with Sol. I never thought I'd live through *that*." She shrugged; a response to living through two years of nursing a simple man who didn't know he was dying of lymphoma, and who would wake up in the night sometimes and fall unconscious in the bathroom, where she'd find him, not knowing if he was dead or alive. "But I had my seven good years with Sam; I can look back on that if I want. But you have to live for today. And I do! Having the Community Center here is just wonderful. It's saved me. The friends I have, *uhh*. So who has time *to think about* getting old. Oh you have more aches and pains, I can tell you that." She smiled broadly. "But you know since I cut out the smoking three years ago, and had my polyps taken care of, I've been in pretty good health, considering. The rest is keeping busy and having friends and the right attitude. You know Lionel I'm not a complainer. If things break good, good; if not, not. You have to face reality, and take the good with the bad. Otherwise you don't sleep, you worry all the time, and you become a *kvetch*. To yourself as well. That Edna Farbstein from 5A, everytime you go near her," slap of leg, "she has another complaint. Who can take her? Being sick is one thing; but being a complainer? *Feh!*"

Lionel said, "So I don't need a second head, huh?"

His mother looked at him oddly. "What are you talking about?" Then she remembered, laughed. She asked, "Why, do *you* think you do?"

Lionel considered. "It would look funny, but it might come in handy."

She half broke up. "Oy, is this a *meshuggener!* What you would do with two heads, work twice as hard? Is that what you want?"

At that point his second head, radiant and golden and long, entered the room, and his mother asked the girl if she knew what a *meshuggener* her son was! Solomon got very uptight at the inclusion of Tippy in their intimacy, and asked about the Community Center.

And the next morning, when they went downstairs for their taxi, Mrs. Solomon said to the girl, "You call me, hear? I want to hear how you are, Tippele! And don't forget to send me the article or whatever when it comes out. I want to see what you say about my sonnyboy here!"

Whom she kissed loudly on the lips again in a show of pride. And for Tippele, the kisses were equally loud, in a display of affection. To her credit, Tippy hugged and kissed her back with equal ardor.

Lionel was not ashamed here, but admiring, believing in his innocence that his mother could indeed have helped this forlorn girl with her heart's greatest need.

"I can see why you love her so," Tippy said to him, her legs crossed in the TWA lounge, waiting for Flight 164 passengers to board. "She has an awful lot of guts and common sense combined. And God, her warmth! You're lucky to have a mother like that, Lionel."

The son said, "You didn't do badly as a daughter. Or daughter-in-law."

She wore her square glasses and looked like a pretty elementary schoolteacher from Grand Island, Nebraska. One whom the producer might find and turn into a "star." The denims had been exchanged for suedes.

The ticket announcer called out, "Mr. and Mrs. Healy, Adam Koosman, Mr. and Mrs. Solomon, please."

She didn't have to give that name, did she?

They came forward.

"Mr. and Mrs. Healy?"

"Solomon," she said.

"Oh yes. Congratulations, you're on. 57G, 57H—not the best movie seats but at least you're aboard."

Handing them tickets, he asked, "Vacation?"

Tippy held up her portfolio. "Homework."

The agent smiled, "What school?"

"A professional assignment," she said, taking Lionel's arm and walking off. His fears receded when she commandeered that way, like Rommel—he still burned at that small lie. Why?

Aboard the dinosaur tail of the 747, she busied herself with printed pamphlets and handwritten loose-leaf pages. She looked studenty—darling with her version of hornrims. "Have Hornrims and Tits, Will Travel," he mottoed privately.

"What's that?" he asked, indicating a large pamphlet that read, *Hopi-Navajo Land Dispute*. "I didn't know they had a dispute. What's it about?"

She looked over her glasses at him, "It'd bore you. You'll see."

"Will you give a speech? In . . . Hopi? Or Spanish?"

"Cool your jets," she said, arranging her pages. "I'll tell you all about it over some Colombian on 'A' mountain."

"Oh good, thanks." Colombian? "A" Mountain? Actually he was more nervous than curious, just now. He was terrified to think what he was actually doing here, on this jet, *with her*. All this for . . . for what?

"God, I just *love* jet planes, don't you?"

"No. Actually they frighten me a bit. The thought of their falling down."

"Don't be *silly!* Stats show that cars are deadlier—though I like those too. God, I could live my life up there, in the sky, on a jet. Once I get up I don't ever want to come down. Especially on these jumbos; I'd like to pay rent and *stay*. It's the only place I can really relax." She turned to his face. " 'Cept maybe underwater, or *playing with you*."

"Oh?" he emitted, to the innocent teenage fact (now).

He looked up to see a man peering at him furtively over a *New Yorker*.

Speaking loud enough for the man to hear, Lionel said, "CIA keeping an eye out on you? Or is it Mission Impossible?"

Tippy, her eye on a sheet of neat handwriting, replied without looking up, "Not quite. But the lady to his left, knitting, is. An old friend."

Lionel smiled, did a private double take, and looked around. There sat a lady dressed in conservative skirt and blouse, knitting.

Lionel smiled. "You mean that librarian from Iowa?"

"Close," she replied, shifting pages. "From Topeka, Kansas, to be precise. Claudia Sue Colbert, used to be a psychiatric social worker at Menninger's. Before the government invited her on over. We had a very nice conversation once, in the waiting room of O'Hare."

Lionel couldn't help glancing back again, and noted the earnest face and pulled-back hair and busy hands, and stared, unbelieving. So they did look like that after all?! Or was he being put on? The woman finally lifted her own eyes, and Lionel winked broadly. Very calmly she returned to her knitting.

The hostess said, "We're about to taxi, cigarettes out, please."

Tippy asked the hostess, "Will you see Ursula, in Miami, by any chance?"

"Uh-uh, not on this trip. I think she's staying over in Lima."

The giant engines rumbled seriously now, and Lionel put out his cigarette. Above, golden print flashed, "Fasten your seat belts please."

That struck home somehow, and he unbuckled his, and stood. He asked the hostess, "Which way to the men's restroom?"

"There's one at midplane sir and one back there, but you really ought to hurry."

Lionel leaned over busy Tippy and said, "Do your homework, I'll test you when I return."

He hastened toward the midplane bathroom on the giant 747, opened it, and began to pee, a good way to think. The cubicle of chrome, mirrors and fluorescent light engulfed him, and he wished he could stay here, and not emerge. Not to fly to Phoenix and from there . . . desert towns and rebel Indian meetings? Or who knew what? He thought of his book, his teaching. The metal bird trembled beneath him, and turned slowly like a prehistoric animal hesitating. He shut off his flow in the middle, tried to open the door and found it stuck and grew panicky and then realized the lock was still engaged; then he was flying out of the restroom and up the circular stairway leading to the second-floor lounge. From there he sighted an exit up ahead, raced there and down more steps, like running through the carcass of a whale. Out of breath he said to the hostess at the closed steel door, "I must get off, it's an emergency."

"Sorry, sir, it's a little too late."

"My wife. She's on the operating table right now. I never should have listened to her and taken off. Please, I *must* be there. It's a mastectomy."

The hostess's implacable mask winced at the name, and situation, and the male aide, her assistant, looked dumbfounded. She nodded and the aide ran off toward the cockpit.

The embarrassed stewardess said, "Where is she?"

"Memorial. Know it?"

The hostess nodded immediately. "My mother died there."

He grew slightly terrified at what he had started now, gave the woman his name and seat number, hoping the list wouldn't be checked right there.

"You do look out of sorts," she put in sympathetically. "Take it easy."

The aide had returned out of breath, and nodded. "They're pulling up the sleeve right now." A moment of confusion, a sudden stop, a long silent moment and then a face in the porthole window. Slowly the giant door slid aside.

"Thanks a lot," Lionel confided to both of them, and alighted. He broke into a run up the gray sleeve.

He had run maybe two hundred feet, out into the corridor, when he pulled up, and for no reason began tossing a quarter in the air and catching it, even whistling. ("I Got Rhythm," which he now remembered.) He walked carefree and whistling for another hundred yards or so, telling himself that sometimes you just ran with the luck!

The quarter dropped through his hands, he bent to retrieve it, instead he began to jog again, then to move from jog to run, but now in the opposite direction. Back to the airplane he had left. When he arrived at the end of the sleeve, there was wide blue sky and the giant silver plane was rolling forward into the distance.

The roaring of engines was near-deafening but he stood, transfixed, observing.

The same black man with a TWA jacket came up, removing his ear protectors. "You okay?"

He felt at the tip of the lousy globe. His eyes grew wet, and he nodded. The sweetest thing in the world was leaving him, or he, it. Her. That *sweetness*. His eyes grew wet, and he nodded.

He tried to concentrate on her in there, in the seat, like a point of concentration in his fish-exercise in yoga.

"No flight again till tomorrow at this time," the middle-aged man offered.

Tears rolled down Lionel's cheeks. He tried to turn away, but couldn't budge. *At thirty-eight, out of control like this over losing a piece of chocolate; his supply of chocolate.*

Big silver planes moved around clumsily like steel reptiles, and he tried to figure out which one held her. Was it that one standing at attention out there, waiting, waiting? He was crying. He tried to turn away, hurt, stupid, embarrassed, self-lacerating; but couldn't budge from the edge of the sleeve.

"Hey, want the rest of this ham sandwich?"

Lionel wondered . . . he held out his hand dumbly.

The older man had a thick mustache and baseball cap and graying hair. "Miss out on something? She usually comes round again."

Lionel took a bite out of the sandwich, remembered strudel and his mother's high opinion, held it up in gratitude. Turning slowly, he walked off, feeling heavy. His heart, trained in dormancy out of concern for his fictional characters and their passions, now heaved in life confusion. In remorse and self-anger. Crushing loss, mocking cowardice. He felt three hundred pounds as he walked, and was sure that jogging was a thing of the past now, a vague memory from youthful middle age. Breathing was difficult; he had turned a corner.

Wearily he wandered through white corridors, passengers scurrying by with packages, timetables, anticipations. Amid the ubiquitous fluorescent maze, Muzak haze, snaking corridors, he felt like a Pavlovian dog let out of the control cage, confused by new territory and a strange efficiency.

*Doctor, a hotel room for a night when you don't really want it, is an exercise in anguish. It seems the perfect place for amnesia, for dejection; for suicide; paying twenty-six bucks for your bed of dejection and insomnia doesn't help matters. Especially when you're shaken out of near sleep by low jets, jolted awake by the toilet flushing, or kept awake by an all-night chatter-show just the other side of the wall. Oh, the true-blue banality and fulsome trash of everyday native life is overwhelming here in Motel-land, USA. But stop: for all this Lionel knew that the presence of his buffy Tippy would pick the whole thing up, lift it from a graveyard of chrome pornography into a garden of banal delights, were she here! The environment needed Tippy to bring out the contradictory feeling of freedom here, he knew; surrounded by elephantine lamps and Mediterranean-style furniture and drapes of Aztec design. Here he'd be free, delightfully free of responsibility, teaching, friends, writing. Free, to be childish, perverse, a stranger unto himself, not Lionel Solomon.*

But the fact that his briefcase was gone (along with the girl), that he had no familiar book or pajamas, that his (beloved) student papers were on their way to the Southwest (who would give them their A's and B's, Doctor, like milk and cookies in the afternoon?), that he had some T-bone stuck in his gums painfully and no floss with which to remove it at night, made him feel like an orphan dropped onto a foreign doorstep; and so he cried as he covered himself in bed. Then he remembered that bikini floss of yesterday, and his heart pounded and loins tingled with that sensual memory.

What do you do then, sir, at the age of thirty-eight on a motel limb outside Kennedy? Follow your memory and your member, or search for your brain and recover reason?

You barely sleep, in any case.

And you remember odd bits of conversation with the shark, which you replay:

"You know, Lionel, the trouble with most intellectual men? They're either too refined, and act like prissies; or else they're so filled with *ego,* and themselves, that they become tough little bullies. Well, I won't put up with either. Why should I? I want boldness, not a bully, in my man. Boldness, courage, honor. No bullies or prissies or dickheads. I forgot to mention them too. The kind that think you can cure everything by flashing that little stick of theirs. Now you know where they can stick that stick don't you? If you're rude or dumb or crude, I mean? In a fence, in some mud, in sheep. That's why you *wreck me so*—you're gentle, Mr. Solomon. Even when you're a tiger, you're *gentle.* Sometimes too gentle, actually. Like you are sometimes with *these*" (holding her breasts; gentle with those when? he thought). "But that's all right, I'd rather have you on the side of the gentles than the bullies. And you have courage too, I know that." She squeezed his arm and whispered, "When I'm with you, I like myself a lot, *a whole lot.*"

She talked that way; it wasn't meant for return conversation, really. But he returned anyway, in her vein of self-monologue, with *the other* present. "Bold? I'm not so sure. But why'd you *pick on me?* Why, on a writer who's a . . . a *failure?* You know you could get Mr.—"

"Ssshh." She covered his mouth with her fingers. "You're not a *failure.* You're . . . you're a hero. *A man.* My hero. You write the *best* books, and they treat you like dirt, and *you keep on doing it.*" Her face shone with pride. "You hold your ground in the face of all that *shit.* Don't you see, it only makes you bigger, *bigger!*" And she looked at him admiringly, expectantly. "You mustn't lose your courage, and I won't let you."

Impressive, until he wondered, courage for what?

He got on the plane like an old chief driven back out to the hunt. A smaller plane, maybe a 707, and he wondered if he would catch yesterday's jumbo? Strapped in, he felt nervous as the plane lifted off and up, up, and began curving over the channel water and soaring toward the clouds. "It's the only place I really relax . . . or underwater." Well, Lionel thought best on the ground, by the typewriter. And here he was, in the air, and for what purpose? Charted by what (irrational) cause? To prove to himself he was still up for adventure with middle age closing in? To . . . ? Oh come on, pal, you're simply chasing down a young woman to find out what she's up to. Who she is. Is there anything so dreadful about that? (And to recover your briefcase, papers, jacket . . . penis?) He shook his head, dumbly, never having been driven this way before.

"Did you say something?" asked the clean-shaven long-faced gentleman next to him.

Lionel looked at him, reminded of one of his colleagues. "I wondered if you knew the names of those clouds?"

The man peered outside. "Cumulus is my level."

Lionel nodded.

"On business in Arizona?"

"Oh," Lionel reflected. "A kind of scouting mission."

The man smiled. "How interesting. No pressure that way." And returned to his papers.

The jet soared and leveled out, and settled into its smooth arc through the lovely azure. Yes, he could stay up here perhaps; suspended between East and West, between Cambridge and Tucson, between girlfriend and wild goose. Suspended here, he was free of credibility, passion, ties. Writing and bills and daughters and telephones and classes. It wasn't all that bad, was it? He gazed out at the long silver wing, and the slowly passing clouds below. Visibility seemed endless on the verdigris horizon; indeed, the heavens had a therapeutic effect upon the earthly dilemmas of man. A Magic Mountain in the sky perhaps.

He pulled down the adjustable tray from the seat in front of him, opened his spiral note pad (for notes at the airport) and saw before him the beautiful face of his old Slovenian love. Longing nudged him. Then another face, also European, also beautiful, edged into view. Sitting there peacefully, his heart revved up.

"My dearest Maja and Milena,

"Why does flying now remind me of you two, my European loves? of your two special cities, the one I know personally, Ljubljana, and the other only through letters, Budapest? Why reminded here, at this heavenly altitude, of the small absurdities of human relations? Why reminded by that apt absurd phrase 'Due to circumstances beyond our control this plane will be forced to land,' that our relationships were forced to land. What is perhaps the most curious is not our separate lives, but rather the way you, Milena, followed Maja in my life, and stunned me as she did some ten years ago, with your East European style of feeling, passion. Plus of course the repeated impossibility of our lives together.

"Maja, did you know that I actually had spotted you inside the Reading Room of the British Museum *before* I stopped you outside, in front by the august pillars, and asked you for coffee? Spotted you in your black turtleneck, scribbling away furiously on index cards with your fountain pen, a luminous model of scholarly passion bent there at the writing desk in that huge mahogany womb; with your pale face illuminated by the desk fluorescent, you looked more like a Bergman heroine than a serious English lit scholar and professor. And though I sensed your literary passion, then and later over coffee, I didn't think that it carried over into your life—not with your particular situation: a woman of serious purpose with two days left in London after a six-month stay, married faithfully for over a decade (with no affairs) and with a five-year-old daughter. Oh I was *impressed* with your knowledge and passion over I. A. Richards and modern poetic criticism, but who dreamed that you, a most determined woman, a convinced Communist, a married woman, and a professor, could also become like a virgin *possessed?*

"And by whom? A twenty-five-year-old American graduate student, used to common American romances of ease, divorced without noticing it anymore, almost oblivious to his own passions, over in gentle England for a grant year to write his dissertation? An idler, no more.

"You startled me from the very beginning. The next afternoon, in that High Serious Reading Room, you had me sit with you on your chair while you showed me your Richards text, and casually your arm went around my shoulder; to keep me from falling? I wondered, hoped! But why every once in a while run your hand through my hair and look at me that way, so up close? . . . And later, after an Italian meal in Tottenham Court Road, we were telephoning from Senate House, I recall, when suddenly you took hold of my ear with your mouth and half swallowed it! I was an *American* young man by then, thoroughly dehydrated by a good graduate school, learning proper manners and behavior, and whoosh! a Communist professor from the University of Ljubljana was biting my ear! . . . And you bit more that night and the next, remember? (As I did, my dear.) And why the *ferocity?* Because in part you hadn't loved anyone since the age of fourteen, when the young man you had loved was killed by the Nazis and the man you met and married was a much older man, a partisan. And although you had a child and stayed together, on your part there was only emotional deadness, sexual stasis; in my FitzJohns Avenue room, that long beautiful, beige room looking out to the garden, talking and making love and you telling me that you hadn't

213

had orgasms in years, and I not quite believing it because you had them so quickly and plentifully that night. And my surprise that you, so serious-minded would even think of such things! And telling me stories that were hard for a poor American boy-innocent to *experience*, if not to believe: walking over dead bodies in the streets to get to school when you were eight; at seventeen marrying an older man who had been tortured by Nazis and himself had tortured others, and subsequently had little human feeling left; coming from an aristocratic family from the Hapsburg monarchy—history come alive!—which had been broken up during the Communist rule; naming places like Trieste, Zagreb, Venice, Istria, Rome, as regularly as I might talk about going to New York, Boston, Washington. Oh, when I left you the next day, Sunday, getting out of your train at the last possible minute and crying like a deserted child on the platform, the huge Victoria Station seeming like a Piranesian Erector set, blown up and ridiculous and mysterious, with thousands of foreigners and foreign languages crisscrossing the platforms, trying to make sense of timetables and relationships, among those fabulous steel girders and grids.

"Still, three-day romances usually end three days later, I knew. Therefore I was only half prepared for the series of letters that started coming my way immediately; letters which I still have, on onion-thin sheets of white paper, your small legible handwriting squeezed onto both sides and all available space, filled with sublime thoughts, harrowing stories, literary descriptions (child, work, teaching, writing, Ljubljana, friends, history, literature, books to get, what else?), here and there missing a phrase or distorting the idiom; and mostly putting down feelings, an incredible avalanche of *feelings*, which, in truth, drove the affair into my heart like a needle of passion. No talk of 'commitment' there, of 'relationships' or 'involvements,' none of the double-talk and triple-think blurring thinking here, but simply how and what you felt, and had felt in the past. For suddenly you were *feeling* again after a womanhood of absence and nothingness. . . . And those feelings were so overwhelming that I was drawn into their vortex, drawn into their language, and found myself responding in kind, in huge letters seven to ten pages, two or three a week; we became a regular letter-writing Factory and Laboratory, testing our stamina! stability! ink supply! . . . and producing, producing!

"Until finally I was on the same railroad, choochooing across France and Italy just as when I was four and went to a tiny hamlet in Ohio to visit my grandfather, except that now the traveler was half mad; and finally, after Graz and sipping vodka into Belgrade, I saw my first *real* peasant—after years of reading about them in Russian novels, history books, or using them as metaphors. Poor souls! thousands of them, huddling by the station, with sacks of food or clothing; bantering, exchanging, looking around before returning to the countryside. So different from Ljubljana, the next day, small, perfect, charming, a well-off Western city, compared to that impoverished Eastern capital. Into Ljubljana, with your warning ringing in my head that your husband, already a bit psychotic, was furious over our affair (you had told him), and if I ever dared to come over, it would be seriously dangerous for me. No idle threat coming from an ex-partisan who had done his share of violence in his lifetime. Hence your astonishment when I showed up there, outside your office at the university, with you arriving from class followed by students; and there, despite students, practicality, colleagues, you impulsively flung yourself into my arms and kissed me wildly! I, who had prided myself on 'being emotional,' once more learned what a self-deluded novice I was next to the real thing. And all during the next hour or so, in which you had to take care of teaching responsibilities, you couldn't leave your hands off my neck, chest, face, while colleagues in your office pretended not to notice and to continue their academic work. A nice scene.

"It is difficult here to go through that astonishing week in Ljubljana, it would make a good short novel by itself. But take that bizarre evening with your husband, at my suggestion; if I was going to be terrified every time I heard a door open in my hotel, I wanted to meet the source of the terror. Somehow or other, I believe, in my naïveté, that a man who has killed and tortured and has been tortured will somehow wear that *visibly;* the signs of brutality will be upon him. No. Instead I met a man twice my age, medium-built, stocky, taciturn, with thick eyeglasses that constantly reflected the light; and while you Maja bathed Meta and put her to bed, he and I sat in the living room, well furnished, and observed each other. Forty-five minutes between two odd strangers who spoke no common language, and could only sit and stare, listening to Bach; he drank whiskey, offered me some, I took milk. The American lover of twenty-five and the Slavic husband of forty-eight; the dissertation boy, and the Philosophy Professor; the innocent with his heart beating fast, in amazement, and the older man, thinking what? waiting for the boy

215

to break somehow, under the strain of the silence and the sitting? And with my knowledge of his capacity to turn violent, suddenly without gun or knife range, he had a point. And a good reason, may I add.

"Later at a restaurant, he had asked through you why I had come to Ljubljana? I replied, to see you. He drank his coffee, not reacting. When I asked about his work, he asked derisively if I had 'read much Aristotle?' and I answered, not really, not seriously, but I'd like to hear anyway; in Slovenian he discoursed, peremptorily. But still, he took my ignorance rather well. What he took less well was a different detail, one that I can't help thinking was *intentional* beneath its casual look; you touched my arm at one point, briefly, and he took his fork and threw it violently on the floor! Diners at the next table in the fine restaurant turned in amazement; I was sure he was going to turn over the table and go for me, or you. Probably you, at that point. Later when I asked you why you did it, you said you couldn't control yourself when with me, couldn't control touching me; was that all? Or was it also touching me in front of him, flauntingly, after fifteen years of a loveless and dominating marriage?

"And what could I imagine later on in the night when suddenly, at one or three in the morning there was a knock at the door? I had been there a day and a half, remember, in a hotel where the languages spoken were Slovenian, Italian and Serbo-Croatian, with some German *(hatred)*, and now there's a knock; I shake, think of hiding. A stranger? A hired killer? Him? You? Which was worse? For when it turned out to be you, I was as afraid as if it had been he; better on my nerves in some ways if that had been the case. And it showed too, when you got undressed and came to my bed, and we began to make love; at the slightest creaking or door opening I was on my guard, not with sex but with survival, defense! For I had already heard, from you, that he had been showing around to his friends his old partisan pistol, on my behalf; I was sure that was the way he would get me, us, right there in the saddle! What a perfectly fitting moment for murder, don't you think? . . . Or are such endings for fiction only?

"Actually, there was a reason why he didn't come or shoot. It turns out that you promised him that after that week, it would be all off between us. (And also that you would be back home by dawn, every night, which you fulfilled.) Your 'American Prince Charming' (his phrase) would be gone, once and for all. He was right in this sense: I was gone from Yugoslavia, never to see you again, *there*.

"Oddly, Ohio was next, and not for a week or two nights, but for a year. From London and Ljubljana to Oxford, Ohio—what better location to spend a year of adulterous bliss? You on a special Fulbright Fellowship to do a year of graduate work (though a professor back home) at an American University, that wonderful high school called Miami University, while I lived in a basement apartment of a vacant house three miles out, where you would join me four or five nights a week. What an *odd* year. I would write my dissertation at night, from 11 to 4 A.M., say, and if you weren't there, read Evelyn Waugh to forget seriousness! and to sleep. In that hamlet of German churches, amusement consisted of foreign movies twice a week, and good college basketball games a night or two; and then back underground, to write and be with you. And you, a make-believe graduate student taking courses with provincial professors and living in a dormitory with girls whose concern was to pad their bras and obtain an engagement ring along with their B.A.'s. The only persons we knew were a rich older couple in Cincinnati, whom we visited once a month in their Mitchell Avenue mansion; a nice introduction to America, that house containing great art works from Matisse to Picasso to Calder, having been bought with money taken in from *Underwear*. Not in Ljubljana would you get a Picasso by beating out Fruit-of-the-Loom. So there you were, writing dutiful letters home to parents and husband; dutifully interpreting American literature in papers and thesis for your professors; passionately involved with this stranger you had known for two days and one night in London, a year ago. Senator Fulbright, how many illicit international affairs has your generosity sponsored through the years? Do you give an extra stipend for such Complete Fellowship?

"Yes, your passions were powerful and strange there, and in the bedroom too. I shall not go into that area of intimacy here, except to ask a question and make a note or two. Is it in the bedrooms, my dearest, where the effects of the full repression of the East European regimes are most keenly felt? Where the urgings that erupt there are the best evidence we have, or at least the most serious private evidence, of the strain and pressure of life in a totalitarian country? Or does this mainly apply to those who first had to live through Nazi occupation and Jewish/European massacre, and then, afterwards, the grimness of native totalitarian regimes? Was this double dose of repression the breaking point, so that only bizarre gestures of release, in sexual affairs, could emerge? A

217

speculation. Certainly in the novels I have read from Eastern Europe, there is little serious realism about the matter. But I will say this, Maja: I understood then, and I understand now, the passion, the need, the love behind the extreme acts themselves. And certainly I was swept up into them myself, with as much passion, if more fear. (And now, of course, myself having lived through an extreme passion with a native woman, I know that intricacy is not confined to your side of the curtain, or born from politics alone.) Someday, I am sure, there will emerge a writer from Eastern Europe who will speak the truth about human intimacy there, if he has not already done so; about the visible iceberg of totalitarianism, we have been glutted by now.

"Maja, you were such a mixture of strong passion and analytic intelligence, scholarly knowledge (do you still speak and read easily six languages?) and childish wonder. On the one hand we could discuss your deep guilt, repressed anger, unresolved Oedipal complex and masochistic tendencies—the scorecard of ailments with which most of us normal folk limp through life, give or take a variable. But you had a healthy sense of the *fatigue* of these categories, or words. Yet, on the other hand, put you in New York City, and you were the best walking advertisement any city mayor ever had. You adored wandering amid skyscrapers, jumping on buses and riding subways, being faced with ingenious advertisements *everywhere;* you were Ms. Kafka come to Amerika, your gloom relieved by our giddy toyland. You couldn't get enough of it, on our week's visit there, and said it was the most exciting city in the world. And writing it all down in your letters to Meta, six, back in Ljubljana, with you about the same age over here; there was the added irony of taking around Jackie, the seven-year-old black son of my friend's white girlfriend, and having natives ask if you were from Sweden, and if your husband was an American GI?

"The next year was less fun when you returned home, with the intention of divorcing Stefan and then joining me, either there or here. . . . The shock of discovering that your husband, in conjunction with his sister (supposedly your friend), had taken legal custody of your daughter, possible because of your extended stays in foreign countries and Yugoslavia's fear of losing its young. . . . The supreme torture of trying to make friends again with Meta, who had felt deserted . . . the wearying divorce battle and your husband's vengeance . . . the snail's progress on your critical book . . . the aloof scorn of your parents for messing up your life so dreadfully

218

. . . the constant teaching . . . The punishing labyrinth became too intricate, internalized, and so you broke down, stopped everything, retreated into silence . . . your letters ceased. . . . Just as I was on the verge of coming over, a note arrived saying you couldn't handle it . . . finally the letter stating that you had lost all your emotions by now, you had been washed clean through, what a fitting irony, the woman of the deepest feelings now dispossessed of them totally . . . and a year or two later, a note mentioning in passing your recent marriage to a colleague at the university. . . . If I had to picture an end to the romance, I would have thought, naïvely again, an explosion of rage, not a slow draining erosion. . . . No, my dearest, there is little need to arrange your complicated life into neat tired categories . . . no, I'd rather remember images: your luminous face looking at me in the British Museum Reading Room chair; your stomach pains in the middle of the night in Ohio and the narrative of your nightmares about World War II, and your fears for your daughter, as you stood there by the glass sliding door staring at the black woods . . . your ferocious love-hunger, urging on those special acts of passionate devotion which, out of context, seem no more than sensational . . . your fine literary intelligence, and discussions of Richards, Eliot, Pound, Hardy, Twain, James. . . . (Oh Maja, you spoke for my suppressed life in those days, you said we were two bodies who shared the same soul (quoting Ovid's line), I remember you with enormous tenderness, and good will, may you be cared for well, my dear old friend. . . .

"It took me a while to move back to American affairs . . . the differences were so emphatic . . . the blandness and the neurosis, the bitchiness and the gentility, the local color and the studied narcissism, the therapy-scars and the programmed confusions, the lack of natural sympathy and selflessness and the new creeds of Self and selfishness . . . oh yes, one got used to it, like returning to tough city streets after a sojourn in the beautiful wilderness. . . ."

Solomon turned his neck round in a circle, very slowly, as in yoga. He jotted down notes furiously. His seat companion noted, "You must have a lot of dope on that mission." Lionel took a few seconds to understand the reference. The gentleman continued, "I've never seen a pen move so fast."

Lionel considered the matter: "Legwork, you need a lot these days. And these Bics, they go on their own after a while." The man smiled and Solomon got up and ambled the lengthy aisle for the bathroom.

After his earned pee, face-wash and drink, he returned to his seat and started in again, reflecting, staring at the lines of pastel pink and blue in the sky; settling back with his second memory.

"Dearest Milena, then you, several years later showing up on the stage of my life, Act Two from Eastern Europe. By providence, by instinct, by chance? Not that the same Yugoslav romance was repeated in Hungarian fashion, not at all. Here, only the *promise* was offered; *desire* was at the center, *not* fulfillment. Desire supported by the same extraordinary letter writing, as if flower buds appeared and then reluctantly, on their own, decided not to bloom. A reluctance on both sides, intentional, thoughtful, necessary.

"Not that your two styles were the same either; Anna K. was a very different sort of woman from Emma B., although their predicaments may have had similar aspects.

"With you, Milena, there was an older husband, too, but this gentleman I knew, and liked; he was my friend. Therein lay the thing that made the whole thing so powerful and so impossible. But there is more irony to come. For Anton also turned out to be a collaborator of mine, working with me on a film script based on a story of mine centering on an older man's passion for a younger girl. Life as a Chinese box of ironies existed in New Hampshire that summer, as we co-wrote that story, in that house and summer where I first met you, M. In any case, despite arguments and sharp differences, Anton and I understood each other well, and admired one another. Now A., after his 'full' life of nine lives, was a rather controversial figure, thought to be authoritarian, demanding, egotistic—all of which he was, but so what? Who of serious talent isn't, in his way? But in the work, in our working together, he was open, instructive, intelligent. (I had a complete course in film-scripting in four weeks, and was delighted to discover how unsuitable it was for me; a sport for novelists, a hard occupation for directors.) And Anton's talent as a director was authentic, his movies were witty, pointed and truly interesting, and how often can you say that in cinema? And he had been 'around' in life, seriously around; not simply with New York and Hollywood celebrities fashioned by media, but around experiences and people fashioned by history. Places in his life included London in the Nazi blitz, Buchenwald at its first liberation, Budapest at its democratic high and Stalinist low, Moscow during the purges in the 1930's, the figures he had seen up close included Stalin, Patton, Nagy, Virginia Woolf, as well as the Oliviers and Fellinis. Happily, too, his stories were neither idolatries nor predictable hates and loves, but rather humorous and ironic angles on grave happenings. He had become a Life-ironist, a worldly skeptic; the content of his life may have been Dostoyevsky, but the tone was a mixture of Gogol and Montaigne. He had been through too much to ever again take it *too* seriously: it was all part of a great comedy. And this all-out *experience* showed up in every centimeter of his vividly expressive face, with the sharp nose and red-faced laugh, as did his fortitude, in his European conditioning and athletic vigor. He walked, swam and skied with a Prussian's diligence, which made his sixty-five look like forty-five.

"And if he hadn't weathered it all perfectly, or at moments too nicely—three marriages, several legitimate children, political betrayals and prison, official lies and friends liquidated, two dozen movies and Venice prizes, and recently, a painful decade of exile and decline and near-obscurity—well who had? who could? After all, the less burned by life, the more energy you had for tolerance, reason, all the nice calm states. But wasn't he more intelligent and interesting and heartful than the majority who sat down with you at the dinner table? And isn't that partly why you, Milena, chose to be with him in the first place?

"Dear M., I didn't really want you to turn up in the country, in my house, hang around with the flowers, be beautiful. I *didn't want* to see up close those incredible lips and buttocks, that chestnut filly's mane; or see you in your wide-brimmed hats or nineteenth-century dresses or European bikini. *Didn't want* to watch you work hard at making things beautiful, a bouquet of wild flowers, a plot of ground, an un-pruned bush or vine, a simple lunch—after all, dear Milena, my own Sheyna was there on those weekends, and she was most dear to me; after all, your own stepson of seventeen, a Hungarian Proust, was on hand, looking for affection; after all, my student Diana, on hand to type and cook and correct manuscript, also happened to turn out to be a real woman, not a kid, I discovered; and after all, Anton himself, working with and befriending me, demanding with his rigid ways but vulnerable too because of his age and hard times; . . . no, no, no, the last thing needed was the planting of yet another passion, a passion illicit in the sense of hurting friends! against one's will!

"It happened. Mostly through glances and jokes and mistakes and . . . it grew on the side, as it were, and flourished by the closeness and the impossibility, and the comic absurdity . . . it didn't need any hand-touchings (which it received, by chance mostly), or any gesture approaching the sexual, although there were moments alone, in upstairs bedrooms . . . or in fields at the edge of the woods, while throwing away brush or collecting wild strawberries, moments when I'd have to remember my friend up there, resting or waiting . . . with the small jokes and playful kidding between us increasing as attraction grew, mirroring it, intensifying in intimacy; it would make a perfect subject for the good Dr. Chekhov, that chronicler of unfulfilled dreams and passing lovers . . . and afterwards, plenty of water and sunshine provided through the mails. Enough nourishment for three ordinary romances. Letters about Budapest and the past and you, the walks, the gardens, the flowers, the churches, the music, the streets, the buildings, your family; about habits and cats and drawing, about wild strawberries and wild mushrooms and lake swimming, everything small and nothing missed, and everything beautiful. Oh, I was back again with a European woman. . . . Once again the force of the affair was being stamped emphatically by the U.S. Post Office, once again pages and pages of legible blue-ink handwriting, squeezed everywhere on white sheets—Do you see, my dear Milena, that I got crazy all over again, whipped by an emotion I thought had passed and died, and all the same time, of course, there I had my own lovely woman, and—I ask you, *how many sorts of affairs can a man be involved in? How many strong affections can an emotion-system juggle? Please, tell me?* And how many small frustrating obstacles must there be? . . . It seems to be the actual history of life, doesn't it? . . . No, one didn't betray a friend, especially an older friend; or at least I couldn't, *couldn't;* friends had become too important in life to lose them over affairs; . . . only what happens if in the process you *lose the affair? Please, tell me!* Lose *that* friend? Oh, I felt often enough your sense of things, namely, what was wrong with simply being in love, did you need the shallow certification of the flesh? Need a flight of the heart be so fragile, uncertain, needy? You implied: wasn't the body's connection anticlimactic and even crude next to that exquisite special flight itself? . . . Yes, yes, I understood you, I agreed! . . . And yet, I've often wished . . . You see, Milena, I'm *weak* . . . I'm probably *crude.* . . and one needs to be martyr-strong to be content with the soul alone! I'm weak, my dear Milena, and therefore I've often wished . . . So what if he'd shoot me, and pay me back for that first partisan who didn't shoot! So what if I turned out to be *not* a good friend, if I had you in my arms! Don't we live in modern times, where everyone marries but no one takes it seriously when it comes to love affairs on the side? So what if—"

The sky had turned into geometrical lines of violet, and amber, with azure below. Exhausted, Lionel wrote a few notes down, the main theme, and then set down his ballpoint, having gotten his nineteen cents worth; closed the spiral pad, put up the square tray on the back of the seat in front of him, shut down his imagination-jets. As if he had just come from a long swim, he now breathed and gazed out at the lengthy sliver of silver wing, bearing him through the heavens to another sort of woman. A certification type, you might say. He closed his eyes, a single tear floating downward for his Milena in her old-world dress and necklace and straw hat with red ribbon. He sought the jet's steady hum to soothe his whirring heart, overheated brain. Wondered, tapping painted steel, whether it was not too much of a burden, a piece of still-uncorrected evolution, to have both of those organs, heart and brain, housed in the same body trying to mesh gears harmoniously, glide naturally, to be like this big steel bird flying effortlessly with a computer brain and a jet engine for a heart? Bearing baggage, not desire, in its belly.

(Did the chasing of the crass native goose remind him of his exquisite European pair, who flew in rotation like the Canadian geese? He had never before composed on an airplane, and now had written up a storm, so to speak, effortlessly and swiftly and abundantly. Maybe jets were best after all, and the only way to think?)

# 5

# Searching the Southwest;
# Back in Brooklyn

> No, facts are precisely what there is not, only interpretations. . . .

> It is our needs that interpret the world; our drives and their For and Against. Every drive is a kind of lust to rule; each one has its perspective that it would like to compel all other drives to accept as a norm.
> —Nietzsche, *Principles of a New Foundation*

PHOENIX. A BLAZE OF WHITE LIGHT and gleaming porcupine-skyscrapers protruding up from the desert. Sharp angles, glinting reflections. Inside the airport, Muzak and air conditioning tried to ease Solomon into the strange land. He walked through pastel corridors, somewhat startled at the passing species in flowered shirts and ice cream-colored slacks; fascinated at the way the species bore their golf clubs and tennis rackets as if they were extra limbs. After Cambridge and Kennedy Airport, this place had the touch of a Rousseau painting, childlike, unreal, primitive. He had an impulse to telephone an old friend who taught at the university at Tempe, an Oxford-trained medievalist with a passion for *The Pearl* and *Sir Gawain and the Green Knight*. (Who also, having a native side, as he wrote, could appreciate the ASU Sun Devils and their halfback knights.) But as he was dialing, he thought better of it; the ground at the Dorans' was too safe, too social, and he was on quite another mission. Walking outside for a moment, Lionel was hit by the blast of warm air, a half minute of furnace-blower heat. It seemed as bizarre as the conditioning inside. And the light, the blinding light. His dark prescription glasses felt like a paper shield in the path of a laser beam. Who could see anything straight or true in this brilliant but discomforting, unnatural dazzle?

At the car rental he ordered an auto ("Glad to have you

aboard, Professor," smiled the Avis girl; in conspiracy? wondered Lionel; aboard what?); and while waiting, got back to the telephone booth to seek clues, begin his search. He was grateful suddenly that he had a self-imposed time limit of a week—his colleague would take over his classes for that time—otherwise he might be searching out here till doomsday. (His?) He had also called Sheyna and said something about the sudden need to get away for a week, to think a section through. Implausible stories were always justified by fictional intention, he knew. As he dialed information now, a sticker on the window asked, "What is it you're really looking for? Have you tried TM?" Yes, Lionel responded softly, she works.

Information for Phoenix and Tucson turned up nothing. Next, the Bureau of Indian Affairs. Here he quickly learned that in this area there were hundreds of tribes, all separate and distinct from one another. And no one at the BIA had ever heard of the girl. Dumb, bewildered, he tried the tribes themselves, Papago, Salt River, MacDowell; it turned out they knew little about each other, and cared less. Furthermore, the telephone was not the redman's thing. They spoke in monosyllables, at best. Better by far to poke around in person, as usual. And so he found himself at that unreal institution called Chamber of Commerce, obtaining maps, brochures, a complete reservation map. Beforehand, standing on the sidewalk of hygienic downtown Phoenix, he had what he took to be a typical Tippy feeling: the sense of no connection with a city, no responsibility for its habits or people; and this spurred him on with a sense of careless freedom, anarchic independence. As when he came in from sea to a foreign port when he was sixteen, and knowing that he was moving on soon, felt that he could do anything! How different Cambridge and the bondage of home ground, family, friends; he was married to the city, wasn't he? To be a footloose sailor again, a loose traveler, was a pleasure, a slight terror.

At that same Chamber of Commerce he asked the young trim woman if by chance she had ever heard of something called "A" mountain? She removed her glasses, smiled brightly, semiwhispered, "Anyone who is *alive* in this state has heard of 'A,' but especially if you went to the U of A or ASU. If you've never gotten high on A, or made love up there, you're nowhere." She leaned closer over the counter. "It's the best grass anywhere down here. *Pure* Colombian." Coffee? The Chamber of Commerce was changing, Lionel felt, its information growing more diverse. He bid goodbye to the expectant young woman, and decided to try down there first, at Tempe. Once again a casual sentence of Tippy's, which Lionel had distrusted as nonsense gibbering, had turned out to have a referent in the real world. From General Crook to A mountain. His heart thumped. Should he believe in her more than his reason had allowed?

But wasn't he believing in her already, he mused, driving south on the four-lane highway? Otherwise, what was he doing out here, looking for? And who *was* she? Was it just the 125-pound package of dirty blond hair and dark female power that had driven him out here, crazily? Taking him on this curious—and for Solomon, *unbelievable*—leave-taking from his teaching and writing routine? It was as if she had bitten into Lionel and left her teethmarks, or he had bitten her, and the animal taste had lingered, spread. (Doctor, have you ever had a taste of another human in your blood, and yet craved more? A cannibal need?) And as he drove through that landscape turning slowly strange with the first hints of desert, he wondered if the taste might not *mean that too*, that strange new space passing slowly? . . . One thing he began to feel, it was a relief, almost a sensual relief, to be out of his study, out of Cambridge, out of cramped quarters and gray weather and that constant taskmaster, work. Courtesy of Mustang and Tippy, he was delivered from unremitting duty and inescapable memory into the free and easy world of tangible things and palpable sites, the world of carefree, everyday native illusion.

At the campus of Arizona State he didn't know exactly where to begin, so he strolled. A campus very different from the campuses back East, gray, old, European-tired and tradition-laden. Blooming here were green lawns and palm trees and sandstone buildings with red-tiled roofs; the entire landscape was bathed and splashed by a scorching white sun; and, astonishingly, on every other lawn was a grove of orange trees, the trunks painted white against disease, the blossoms perfuming the air wondrously. And while he had spent graduate years at Stanford, this was a sweeter, hotter league altogether. Here at ASU—the initials struck him as adorable little nubiles—there were the sun, the green, the oranges, and pubescent movie stars, called student body, passing in a pageant, like a Hollywood set. Was it *real*? He leaned by a tree and stared. Included on this set was a string of tall stringbean blacks, colored lovely chocolate and brown, whose struts and caps signaled Roxbury, Bedford-Stuyvesant, Watts, Detroit inner city, Chicago South Side; imported fauna to shoot baskets, run sixty-yard sprints and pole-vault, leap for the football in end zones. They mingled with the pink students and orange trees, adding beautiful color and exotic locomotion.

He sat in a square by the Student Union, dazed by this powerful adolescent Via Veneto, this southwestern painting done by an American primitive. At least half a dozen Tippys passed, showing more curves and skin on campus than strippers onstage, and he couldn't resist stopping the seventh. Margo Manners from Cleveland. Did she know his friend? No. What was Margo doing out here, why had she come? (Oh Doctor, if you only could have seen this lovely number she did then, making like a high-stepping camel walking silently through the desert, peeking around all the sleeping creatures.) "You can do your own thing here, and no one cares!" she whispered in the sun. "You just ride *easy*, see? Smoke, study, draw, swim, you just do it easy. See?" Did he? He saw a beautiful young camel with a tiny skirt and svelte limbs. "Did you come here to goof off then?" She shook her head, and responded, in campus code, "I'm a 3.8 you know." All she lacked in contrast with his special friend was height and a certain gleam of purpose, that deviant promise in the eyes. "By the way, did you ever visit the reservations around here?" he asked. "Huh?" Her look read, Are you one of those weirdos? "Okay, I'll see you around now." She smiled, and just for him, high-stepped away, winking. A nice civilized camel, with a 3.8 hump, no less. But *civilized* meant no relation to Tippy.

Driving out and looking for the highway, he was given a direction which included the nearby MacDowell Reservation. He drove there, and after a mile in, there appeared a small greasy-spoon restaurant. While eating fried popovers sprinkled with sugar, he asked the stubby Indian who ran the place about his friend, but the fellow just shook his head. In a strange grunting lingo he asked the woman cooking, who shook her head too. The two Indians who were present looked at Lionel momentarily, and then went back to their meals. Not too loose in here. Depressed, he paid and left.

Driving south on Interstate 10, Lionel turned on the local RKO, and for the first time observed closely that desert terrain. A treeless brown stubble with dried-up riverbeds came into view, with vegetation nowhere and the land eroded, burnt out. Instead of landscape invitation, there was rejection. Different. Several miles beyond Tucson, he turned into the Papago Reservation. The houses were few and far between,

227

either squalid trailers or cement-block dwellings resembling ranch houses; an occasional Indian sat on the porch, or drove toward him in a pickup truck. Lionel pulled up at one house and asked the Indian sitting on the wooden railing his sleuth question; the man shook his head slowly, as if he had been sitting there for many years. Blue-tip match in his mouth, white stetson on head, dark-brown skin, shaking of head in response to an inquiry. No words. The small drama of obstinacy in his gesture, in the sultry air. More and more he felt the foreigner.

Driving back out, he saw a huge white bird of a building perched on the desert horizon, and headed there. On the banks of the dried-up Santa Cruz River, a Spanish mission sat upright, all white steeples, domes and cupolas rising in the middle of the brown stubble desert. Above it, on a rise, when he got there, Lionel found two bronze Spanish lions, set on stone pedestals, peering out over the wild terrain; Castille and León guarding this white outpost of civilization. It was stunning, incongruous, another movie-set mission; except there were real automobiles parked there, like a drive-in, and tourists with cameras strolled by. He went inside the ornate building and thought it the proper place to say a prayer: that he wasn't at the beginning of a long, crazy goose chase, or, in some way, at the beginning of his own ending. He walked on, and through, surrounded by heavy dark woods, blond and tan vacationers, and many Jesuses. Founded some two hundred fifty years ago by a Father Kino, the mission contained a huge vaulted center three stories high, with Catholic saints way up there, peering down; they had been painted by Indian converts tied to the ceiling with ropes. The torture pouring out of those multiple Jesuses on the walls—rich, psychotic imagery. With the curious skirts draped around their lower bodies it was queer, queer! . . . Walking through that mass of thick woods and white stone set out to symbolize His suffering and white man's civilization, Solomon, a pagan innocent, was astonished by the religious savagery, the primitive sensuality, commingling.

Did Tippy pray here? Convert heathen friends?

Outside again, it was like leaving a Turkish bath. The sun was dying slowly upon that empty landscape, devoid of anything white, religious, civilized. He walked around to the back to relieve himself behind the mission, his hiking boots crunching on the hard arid ground; and when he was done, he had an impulse to walk out farther. It took only five or ten minutes to be far away from tourists and smack in the

228

middle of the desert. Without his quite realizing it, the land-scape had grown stranger; was it the time of day that added to it, or his state of mind? The ground itself was a kind of faded brown crust, baked and flaky, like a stale pecan pie; as if it hadn't been watered in a hundred years. And the plants that grew from that arid surface—they were *hardly plants*, or vegetation that looked growing, living. One was stuck up straight in thick porcupine bulks with quills; another had huge pear-shaped leaves with stingers; a third seemed to jump out at your hand when you touched it or attached itself to your shoe when you got near it. *(Doctor, have you ever heard of plants with such names—organ pipe, yucca, prickly pear, hedgehog, devil's fingers, pin cushion?)* And when he sought to disengage a quill, it stung him sharply, as if by in-tent. In fact they all had stinging apparatus, all possessed that barren stare of ulterior motive, as if they had survived the abusive aridity by means of open combat against all things, vegetable, mineral, and human, a kind of physical anger held in store for survival and revenge, and ready to let loose at any given moment. The unsightly shapes of the barks and the leaves, the bareness of the colors, the severity of the touch, the extreme unevenness of the collection, as if they were sharply unrelated and even antagonistic to each other, and the unearthly parched dryness everywhere gave off a sense of bare survival, of Darwinian struggle, of negative life and earned perversity, that made Solomon shiver.

He backed off, dazed. But to where?

For he seemed to be drawn out there, fascinated and hexed somehow. And presently, he was wandering among the strangest plants of all. For suddenly there sprang up, all around him—in desert conspiracy against his eastern self—an arcane assemblage of huge green monsters ranging in height from ten to thirty feet. He had never experienced anything like it, in natural life; in nightmare or bad dreams, perhaps. It was like walking on a crust of pale moon only to be am-bushed by sets of huge green fingers in various combinations, protruding straight up from the ground. This plant, the saguaro, had a central green stalk that thrust straight up, out of which climbed other limbs, straight out and stiff—not one curving or languorous like familiar limbs. No give or yield there, just frozen growth. Robots in the desert. The bark was pale green, fitted with striations, and covered with intermina-ble small stingers to keep visitors away. And if you had told him then that the roots of these huge tree-plants reached down six or eight inches, he wouldn't have believed you; or dreamed that you could walk over, and possibly push over with the force of your hand that giant cactus rising two stories in the air. He stared unbelieving at the strange symbiosis of devious heartiness and fragility, revenge and vulnerability, green clarity and black mystery. . . . Moved back slightly as if nudged by a current. When suddenly something moved and his heart leaped up! Was he at sea again, on the graveyard watch? Black men with spears surrounded him. Figures with pitchforks and giant shovels! . . . Shadows. Huge black shadows that seemed *alive* engulfed and imprisoned Solomon. He couldn't budge. . . . The surreal environment held and compelled him as if he were in Matadi, waiting for that late ferry to return to his ship, at a tiny docking in the jungle where two Norwegian merchant sailors had been murdered on the last run. . . . A Stonehenge of the Sonoran Desert, bizarre, obstinate, deathly.

And yet, despite Solomon's terror, their pull attracted him. Fascinated him. Drew him deeper into their labyrinth of shadow edifices. He rambled amidst the giant plants and their shadow selves for a timeless while, at least till the sun was gone, immersed in their grim shapes and seeking to understand them, him. At one moment he heard a slight sound, a rattle, his body stiffened with numbness, and he waited to see it slither by . . . a cellophane wrapper scraped past instead. He wiped his brow and sat, seeing the spectacular sunset through the green stalks and black shadows. . . . Was all this Tippy? her ambiguous appeal, her ambiguous deception, her ambiguous malignancy? . . . Was his own search out there as cockeyed and melodramatic as his present ruminations and imaginings? Had he come this far, some two thousand miles, to sit in the desert and be afraid and amazed? Lionel, a city boy and a rationalist, suddenly longed for a candystore, a librarian, an automobile, anything to turn this nightmare landscape into a territory of familiarity. But it was not to be. Large black birds, vultures or buzzards, flew lazily overhead, and the lack of sun made him huddle into himself for warmth. Is this where she wanted to take him? show him? . . . Why? For what purpose? What did he have, after all, that she could want?

He ran all the way back to the car, saguaro pursuing.

The campus at the University of Arizona becalmed his jangled nerves. It struck him as a more comprehensible one than its northern neighbor; here the Mexican and Spanish flavors were more pronounced, and there was more evidence of age and tradition with the lovely stone wall surrounding the old part of the campus. Again here were the luxuriant palm trees and heavenly clusters of orange, plus the strong cultural mix of student body, shades of tan, caramel, red, coffee, coal black. A little Pan-American alliance, a melting pot Eden of smells, faces, flora. As he ambled, he thought it wouldn't be bad at all to try the spirit here; hadn't he already been introduced to it by one of its bodies? The sun beat down strongly, and Lionel walked along the shaded walks and beneath the tile roofs. After visiting the bookstore (reasonable, with an impressive collection of southwestern lore), and asking around, he got directions for the anthropology building, the home of the state museum. Housed on the ground floor of the forty-story sandstone building, the museum was a tasteful, large, rectangular hall filled with exhibits, most in glass cases. Harmonious Zuñi pottery, colorful, varying Navajo rugs, Apache clothing including a chief's long headdress, woven Papago baskets and Hopi silver, an impressive historical map tracing Indian origins back to the ancient Basket Maker culture, some two thousand years ago; that was a bit older than the Nuclear Makers' Bicentennial age, approaching. At the front desk, Lionel purchased some postcards, and a bone necklace for Sheyna from a tribe called Menomini. Who were they? A tribe back east, up by Lake Michigan, answered the pleasant hefty girl wrapping the package. Lionel then asked her his perennial question, almost by rote. "I don't know if it's the same one or not," the girl replied with her midwestern trace, "but a girl named Tippy helped the museum acquire some Indian masks just a few months ago. For years the museum had been trying to get hold of Yaqui masks, but no luck." Lionel restrained his voice, but his heart beat fast at the discovery, the reality! "I don't know too much about it," the saleswoman replied to his further questions, handing him his purchase in a brown paper bag, "but it seems that some Yaqui women who trusted Tippy came to her and offered to sell their husbands' ceremonial masks; the men had gotten very hard up for money. So this girl Tippy acted as the middleman for the museum."

"Do you know her personally?" Lionel asked gently, feeling the detective excitement.

The girl shook her head. "Professor Coppard dealt with her privately."

"Is he around just now?"

The girl smiled, and brightened an otherwise plain face. "Sorry. He's in Brazil for the semester."

"Oh . . . by the way, what did she look like?"

Leaning her elbows on the counter, the girl described her as best as she could. A reasonable facsimile of Tippy, without the full sensuality. "Is she in trouble?" the girl asked. "Do you want to leave a message in case she turns up?"

"Sure." Lionel took a pad, considered, wrote, "I was a little slow in getting back on the plane. Good for you for helping out the museum. LS." He put the note in an envelope with her name.

"Are you interested in seeing the masks?"

"Sure."

And from the wall behind her she lifted one down, saying, "It's used in ceremonies, even today. Except that the Yaqui dance is at Eastertime now, in honor of their Christianity. These are really a kind of minor coup for the museum, a first."

The mask was wooden, painted black, with white and red slashes on the face; a white dotted line down the nose; the eyes were black holes; from the chin hung strands of white hair; the mouth was fixed in a sharp red grimace. The effect was frightening.

"What's that stuff?" touching it.

"Goat's hair, I believe. Either that or Yaqui wool."

"Is it for sale?"

"I'm not sure," she said, and set the face down on the glass counter while she looked in a loose-leaf notebook. Lionel gazed at the mask with interest. It stared back with its dumb rage. Objects old, objects that signified, appealed to him; and this particular mask had of course an extra appeal. *It was proof of the existence of the girl in his head, somehow.* "Yes, it is. Forty dollars."

Lionel said yes, he'd take it, and she put it in a box carefully, using his Master Charge plastic for this ancient wood and wool. Thanking her, he left the museum, intrigued by a Yaqui rattle on the way out.

But once outside, facing the campus again, he wondered *where?* He lay on a patch of lawn, within the shade of a tree, package and bag at his side. Pubescents of the sun, wearing their A of U T-shirts, swung by. Bronzed starlets and sports stars and chickadees in yellow halters and tall blackbirds with goatees. They carried sports equipment like students in the East carried ballpoints. When a breeze came up, the scent of oranges blew his way as on some South Seas island. This must be Tippyland, he thought; but where is she to complete this aromatic paradise? *Or is she all around, in the orange fragrance and the sunshine air and the mask at my side?*

232

A grassy thud, he was startled, a textbook had slipped to the ground. He reached over and lifted it to the student, who smiled a thank you. Of course, why hadn't he recalled the simplest of things? *That green paperbound book she had in her portfolio.* He jumped to his feet, excited again, and loped with purpose. Began to jog, lightly over the lawn, easily through orange grove and palmy path, feeling younger and looser than in years, on the way to his Mustang, his maps, the reservations! On the way to surprising her for a change! Why, running out here made you think that you could run all the way, easily, to wherever—and whatever—your destination was. So perfect and smooth was this Tucson air! this campus oasis!

Jogging, smelling, exhilarating. It was becoming an ordinary detective chase, ABC style, say, and he was delighted. From metaphysics to the physics of sleuth's work was more fun, more native. Didn't it fit the particular place appropriately? And the girl: after all, *who she was* was as significant as what she did to him, right? Maybe he could live here for six months a year and feel eternally athletic and youthful, a Solomon de León? he mused, leaving the paradise of oranges demarcated by the stone wall for the ordinary street, and his car. Looking at his maps, he thought how nice it was to have this lighter project in the midst of his graver ambiguities.

The thing about Arizona, however, is that it is a very large state, larger than many nations, and a chase was not as easy as it was in smaller places (like France or England). Nor was the scenery familiar, or inviting. You drove, and you drove, and instead of ripe valleys, blue lakes, spectacular color ridges, all you saw for miles and miles were shades of pale brown, uninhabited desert land, dried-up riverbeds; only on the far horizon sighting a change, snow-tipped mountains. You drove and you drove, following that slashing, receding white line, our native insignia—while you passed through the low Sonoran Desert, high-plateau deserts, good-sized foothills and finally mountain ranges themselves, high and spectacular with Rockies glamour. (His poor New England mountains were baby hills by comparison.) Gradually, the breeze changed from siroccan soft to mountain cool, and you had to stop to put on a sweatshirt (U of A)—after using the air conditioner the night before and seeing the coeds in their T-shirts that morning. And by the time he hit Flagstaff three and a half hours later and got out to have a bite to eat and check out the Indian museum, it was time to purchase a lined lumber jacket and wide-brimmed felt hat, and don both.

Flagstaff sprouted the first real trees and running blue water he had seen in the state; otherwise it was a dinky town of gasoline stations and chintzy stores and a small college, except for the museum, which the girl at the U of A museum had touted to him. A flagstone residence on the banks of the full-bodied river, the museum contained an extensive collection of Navajo and Pueblo Indian artifacts, including a very graphic map of Pueblo history, and a simulated kiva, the religious center of Indian life that was once off limits to whites.

At the sales counter, he spoke with the part-time curator, a tall regal Swedish woman of forty-five. Maren B. had high cheekbones and a fine complexion, and her young daughter look-alike also worked in the museum. Maren explained, in strongly accented English, that the Hopi Reservation, Lionel's destination, actually had a new motel and restaurant, which stayed open till eight or nine, and he should be able to make it there by then. Her story was memorable. After the death of her American husband in Germany, where they had lived for some years, she had decided to come to America with her daughter, who was entering college here; so she put her finger down on the map on two or three places where she would live. Flagstaff, of all places, was one of them, though she had never seen it before, or knew anyone there. By now she had been in residence some two years, and had loved every minute; the luck of the topography had turned out well. Daughter Holly, on leave of absence from Bennington ("so-so"), was now here in Flagstaff, working at the museum and living "with her man." Maren's melodic voice, European charm, and American daughter made Lionel wish he had come to Arizona a free man, on vacation. He might have stayed on in Flagstaff for longer than an afternoon, and switched from transience to permanence. Is that what unexpected trips did, led you into new alleyways of interest? (And of course, Doctor, I knew very well that older ladies were much more *interesting* than the young chickadees; they had more stories, experiences, deeper lives; *and* had daughters too. (So did I, right?) Everyone knows this, *I* know this; so why was I hungering after one of the daughters? Another point: here in America, there seemed to be all sorts of unusual dropouts and refugees from straight life, lying low out there in windswept offbeat towns like Flagstaff. Unpretentious and isolated towns which lent themselves as hideouts for interesting lives. These were emphatically *not* the familiar magazine spots like Carmel, Santa Fe, Sausalito, but rather the also-rans—a Flagstaff, a Troy (New York), a Portland

(Maine). All one needed was wheels, curiosity, time, looseness, some personal freedom. And a light grip.)

As he was leaving and dropped the magic name, Maren's face lighted up. "Oh so you know Tippy? You are one of the lucky ones then. I would call her . . . one of the truly civilized young women I've met in this country." She continued on, in that awkward vein of a reference letter. "Whatever she does is done with a care and a *conscience* that you mostly don't see anymore in young people, here or in Europe. Believe me, I know. I have two of my own. And she is one of the most knowledgeable persons I know about Indians. She's not 'into' Indians, as so many seem to be; she has a professional interest and sincere commitment to the people themselves. Very unlike my own daughter, I'm afraid to say, who whatdoyousay *flits* (?) from interest to interest like a bumblebee. Holly *worships* her too; for once she has chosen an excellent model. You must give her my best when you see her, and tell her to come and have dinner with me, it's been too long. She might be up at one of the reservations, right now she's there quite a lot." Solomon, amazed, asked where she worked, or lived, but Maren shook her head and smiled. "Tippy's very, very private about such things. Actually, very European. The American way is simply to shove the beans, you know? But with her, no. She discourages that sort of interest; which I personally find a delight. She hates being labeled an 'anthropologist,' or anything. And have you met Alan, her boyfriend?" Oh that hurt, that stabbed and turned in Lionel!

"No I haven't."

"Oh perhaps I shouldn't speak. And I don't know how steady he is, or serious. But he's like her, quiet, committed, serious. Very impressive." (The "serious" prick! and *in* her, too! Lionel thought.)

He thanked Maren and left the museum, taken aback, dumbfounded. What was going on? In the car he upbraided himself for his arrogance, skepticism, accusations, near tears from remorse! . . . But do you see how incredibly different a public side of someone could be? How differently she appealed to these people, or at least to this Maren? a woman of judgment and common sense who wouldn't easily be taken in by a charlatan? But then again . . . What Lionel saw was the blanket of soft hair, the wide sensual breasts, the daring teeth, the special teasing and play; and Maren was simply telling him about another side of her uniqueness. They both agreed that she *was* unique. Through those tall trees and cool

235

air he drove, thinking; still, who would have dreamed of such privacy and determination and real social commitment, not simply talk, in her? Certainly not Solomon. *That* was impressive. It made his heart pulse with delight, realizing that there was a healthy citizen on the other side of the dark bedroom girl; that instead of digging up dirt on her, dirt which would have made him terrified to see her again, or else finding nothing, a complete blank proving her a complete liar, he was finding *good;* finding corroboration and evidence; finding that there was a *real woman* there. And as for the boyfriend, let her have her boys, he saw; what did he care? In fact all the better; that way she wouldn't come to *depend* on him in any way. Wouldn't want to stay around, become permanent, *domestic* (the end to all allure!). He already had his own steady companion, his lovely steady friend, how many did one need, or want? *One,* thank you. Just one. Tippy as a sometime visitor *was* the right arrangement, along with the domesticity; the stranger *along* with the familiar one, a certain fear and crazy temptation—even *some* lying, sure! —along with the comfortable routine and reliable equilibrium; to keep him alive three times a year and asleep, in dull routine and work, for the rest of the year. It struck him as a proper arrangement after all; now all he had to do was to cement it somehow, *make it an arrangement.*

Immediately Solomon stopped at the nearest Gulf station and telephoned the real glue, Sheyna. Camouflaging his detective work, he explained how the "work" was proceeding nicely and he was about to try his first stay on the reservation. "I still don't see why you had to skip out on a school week," she said. He responded, with some exasperation—for his quick guilt didn't keep him from having a short fuse, on the contrary!—that before he could go on to the next section he had to check some things out for himself. And added, finishing up, "Look, if it's at all interesting, next year we'll come back together, okay? On the way to Jerusalem, say." She tried her best to restrain her skepticism, and even anger, and changed to cheeriness. And you know what? Lionel did love her just then, as he told her, he did miss her! Why shouldn't he? He kissed her goodbye and returned to the road.

*Doctor, on the highway east he moves, in his Mustang, and if he is caught in the midst of an ever-increasing web, he shouldn't be blamed; rather, blame the wonderful gossamer tricks of reality, native reality especially. America is such a mysterious place, at bottom; looking to be one thing, giving solid evidence of one thing, and proving to be quite another*

236

*in the end. The irony is, in this case, what apparently fits the detective puzzle only adds to the psychological trouble; what satisfies one level of pursuit, will only, because of that very solution, dig the emotional trap a little deeper. So don't hold it against the fellow in his red car, speeding along with some satisfaction and cheer; I don't. And if I don't, why should anyone else? Let him have his moments of resolution, his sense of accomplishment; even his passionate desire, kept intact; before all fact turns to illusion, or to scalding betrayal, why not?*

With anticipation Solomon left Flagstaff and sped on his way east, along Route 66 through strings of gasoline stations and sleazy Indian curio ships and cut-rate tourist towns, called Winona, Two Guns, and the big one, Winslow. Before changing direction due north, and following that solid black line of Route 87, curving up and up into reservation land. *Doctor, after all this is over, please do me a favor and take your nice interesting wife and enthusiastic children up into that land; and when you do it, sir, please make the trip at twilight time. I know that your Yugoslavia is special, with the mountains up north in Slovenia and the drive along Istria down through spectacular Montenegro; but I'd like you to try the reservation land. At sunset, or dawn. I don't imagine too many natives have ventured there, so why shouldn't you, a transplanted Croat with a keen eye for Americana?*

On the reservation, you drive and you drive and you drive, and you see nothing but vast space, vast sky, vast land. The endless space of deserted landscape save for an occasional pickup throttling down toward you on the two-lane blacktop, with bunched brown faces peering at you from the packed cab in the closing instant. The land was that same faded brown, though not quite as crusty, and the sky a gray blue and violet with lines of burnt amber beginning to spread out and diffuse. In the bluish distance, the upside-down V's of mountains loom against the horizon. And slowly, after a half hour of driving at fifty-five miles an hour, the landscape shifts as these V's thrust into dominance. Like skyscrapers shooting suddenly up, and up, the mountains turn into buttes, rising vertically from the flat terrain. Odd groups of buttes shooting up from nowhere, nature's freaks, saguaros of stone, their sandstone color reddened by the dropping sun, and Saturn rings of blue vapor mysteriously curving around them. They rise and pass in no more than a few minutes of time, so sharply have they sprung up from nowhere, like sleeping soldiers bolting upright in their beds from a sudden noise; and then you have to crane your neck backward to catch the effects of that slowly dying sun upon these ancient hills, sharp, bare, harsh. Hills and buttes that were, deservedly, gods, to people who passed them daily, or looked down upon them every morning from their mesas ten miles off. Only very gradually, after you have passed beyond the mountains and their vapors do fragmented herds of their horses and cattle grazing, or godknowswhat, come into view; by this time they have been dwarfed into miniature by the enormous elements of nature. And one wonders, can humans live out here somewhere, and have they been, for thousands of years? Blessed and cursed with this harsh desolate beauty!

"I want you to see *my* country one day," she had said, "it'll make you see things differently. Feel differently." Is this what she meant, this newfound fear and awesome uncertainty that spread through his bones at the sights before him?

So that when Solomon came to Route 264 and turned left for Second Mesa, he was glad for the darkness, for the natural shield against any more visible landscape. The next twenty minutes of snaking darkness gave him time to pinch himself, to realize that this was the real thing, Indian land, that site in his mind which had been stored there since he was eight, from his first *Last of the Mohicans* comic book, Lone Ranger on the radio, and his first cowboy movie at the Saturday matinee. It's real, for real, he told himself now. The Hopi Cultural Center, another contrast. The lengthy winding center gleams white in the electric-lit darkness, and sleek compacts and shiny pickups are parked neatly outside, by its retaining wall. Most have Arizona license plates, but not all. The center is a series of adobelike buildings, low and interconnecting, surrounded by the high wall and opening out on a courtyard; it houses a motel, restaurant, museum and shops in one site. The air is crisp, busy with crickets, and the whole place, modeled on the traditional pueblo, has the air of secrecy about it that seems so emphatically Indian. The mixture, however, was surprising: the carpeted restaurant with the modern television area and the traditional Navajo rugs folded over wooden partitions; southern fried chicken and french fries sold alongside the stiff pancakes of Indian bread served by young Hopi girls in peasant blouses and skirts; white tourists and dark-brown Hopis, both wearing the same combination of sporting jeans and Stetsons and long-sleeved white shirts and checked lumberjack shirts. And after dinner, when paying his bill at the cash register, Lionel asked the short somber Indian, "This place . . . did the Hopi build it?"

Placing the Master Charge in his machine, the fellow eyed Lionel cautiously. "This is not real Hopi, sir, or the way the Hopi live. If you go around the reservation tomorrow, you'll see what I mean." A faint smile in a penny-brown face. "An architect from Phoenix designed this motel, based upon what *he thought* Hopi wanted." He returned the card to Solomon and handed him a room key, stone-faced, with the hint of accusation in his manner; as if somehow Lionel were responsible for this spanking new motel, this credit-card machine, his presence there. Was he? "It's back to the right, sir," he said, indicating the room. That "sir" uttered like a cunning peasant serving his colonial master, scorning him perfectly by using the nominal terms of the contract with exacting repetition. And in answer to Lionel's foolish question about noise, he explained that this is Hopi land, there was no noise here, "sir."

Oddly, Solomon felt refreshed by the gentleman's quiet abrasiveness as he walked in that thin mountain air back to his room. And the room turned out to be not unlike him, in certain aspects: somber heavy wood, thick dark carpet, big unadorned furniture, no television, no radio, and, indeed, no trace of noise. Trying to ward off the cold scratching at his throat, Lionel sat in a comfortable chair and sipped Jack Daniels, and took some brief notes on the evening's journey . . .

And for a moment as I sat in that comfortable vinyl armchair, *that girl appeared, in headband and painted cheeks and squaw dress, and she said in her gravelly voice, "I'm ashamed of you, exploiting the Hopi this way."* I protested immediately, *"But it's fifteen dollars and change to stay here! And I'm getting a cold! Where else shall I sleep?"* Her face turned to slow scorn, as she stood with hands on hips, delicious hips. *"Outside. On the* LAND." All right, I'd show her, cold or no cold!

Possessed, hot, he went to the door, and walked outside, through the archway to the paved road and the edge of the empty land, covered with darkness and small bushes. The air had grown even colder, and he shivered slightly—

"Sir, is everything okay?" said his Hopi pal, this time sympathetically.

Oh, Lionel was grateful, grateful! "Yeah, thanks. I was just wondering what'd it be like to . . . sleep out."

"On the *ground*, you mean?"

Well yes, that was the same as *land*. Solomon nodded.

"Oh I wouldn't do that. It can still get pretty cold at this time of year. Is there something the matter with your room?"

It was fine, Lionel explained, and thanked him. He waved and Lionel waved and they went their separate ways.

Lying in his hot bath in the new bathroom, Solomon was glad for the chance meeting outside.

He slept well, except that his throat was parched and burning the next morning and he was in the grip of a real cold, for sure.

The morning was sunny, clear, windswept. After breakfast, he tried the small museum but it turned out to be closed. So he wandered around the three Hopi shops before starting his day's hunt. They contained the various arts and crafts, silver jewelry, woven baskets, kachina dolls, Navajo rugs. Lionel remembered his mother's birthday coming up, and purchased a pair of silver earrings set with an inlaid rattlesnake design. Rattlers are impressive that way. One of the two Indian shopgirls noted his address on the plastic credit card, and commented, "My husband was in New Hampshire. At school." Surprised at that, and at the fact that this teenage-looking girl was married, he asked where and she said Dartmouth. It turned out that the husband had spent nearly a year at the college, after going through an ABC program at Woodstock, Vermont, but had dropped out before the year was up. When Lionel asked why, she giggled with her friend. And where was he now? "He works at the Head Start program on First Mesa." It was just the sort of innocuous lead that Solomon wanted, to move beyond the tourist barrier. She wrote her husband's name down, at Lionel's request, and gave him directions to the school. Her husband was available after three-thirty or so. Did they know Lionel's friend? More giggling, though not without sympathy he thought, and curious shaking of heads.

On the winding mesa road, Lionel drove out to Third Mesa for old Oraibi, supposedly the oldest inhabited site in America. Also, the fact that it was off limits to whites challenged him. Hard to believe, as he drove along, that the Hopi had been out here for some six or eight hundred years, uninterrupted; wasn't *everyone interrupted?* Civilizations and individuals? Against his own liberal sentiments, he realized that this was not merely a longevity record, but a privileged one too. This was corroborated when, at the entrance to old Oraibi, he saw a hand-lettered sign reading, "This village is off limits to whites because you have broken our rules. You are no longer welcome here." However, such signs were to Solomon the strongest invitations. Why? Because he's curious, curious to the hilt about things, especially secrets. Also, to admit the truth, because he's rude. Impolite. Impious. Whatever you call it, when it comes to *wanting to know*. And he certainly felt no responsibility, or guilt, for *being white*. Luck of the chromosome draw, no more.

The village was situated about a quarter of a mile down the road from the sign, at the very edge of the flat-topped mountain. He left his car at the sign and headed there, walking into a stiff wind. Wearing dark glasses, a wide-brimmed hat (to keep the sun out), and with his beard and lumber jacket, he looked like some badman cowboy moving in on the town. Half of him was subject to his own sense of humor; the other half was frightened and fascinated. The rutted dirt road led through half-crumbled houses and piles of brick rubble, lying on the side of the road, tokens of the past; ahead were spread the clumps of one-story stone dwellings with ladders stuck up to the roofs, to climb into the kivas; and beyond the village edge, the incredible spread of valley desert, where the crops were somehow tilled. An outlaw from Brooklyn wandering amid the ancient ruins of his own country which was soon to celebrate its bicentennial year; how odd. He felt as if he were walking into the deep, deep past—until a rumbling noise rose behind him and he instinctively moved aside to let a red pickup roar by. Fords if not whites were welcome at least. The wind whipped up the dust into clouds through which Solomon walked, and walked.

He drove back on those slender roads, which wound at the carved edge of the mesas like razor cuts, overlooking six-hundred-foot drops and acres and acres of desert vista. Once again, here were cliffs of geological harshness, valleys of desolate beauty, landscape that indicated an unyieldingly stubborn denial of time, man, and conciliation. Giving in only so much, an inch or two a year if that, as if it knew its destiny was dissolution, but fighting it all the way. At one point he parked and walked to the edge, and holding on to his hat in the fierce wind, contemplated it. Trying to fathom how they had survived and sustained themselves on agriculture in a climate and terrain of such arid severity. Were the Hopi brothers to the saguaro? Better, were they the Galápagos turtles of this America, possibly even to the point of looking fierce but actually ready to eat from your hand in innocence? And did that go for Tippy too?

Climb and wind now to Second Mesa—First, Second and Third Mesas, Hopi villages—to a road leading like an arrow straight up the center of a mountain into a hillside clump of stone houses. Turn in a sharp U a quarter mile on a dirt road, a stone schoolhouse. He got out of his car and went inside and asked the group of female schoolteachers sitting around a table in a deserted classroom if Raymond Lokadema happened to be around? Once again a question of Solomon's provoked giggling laughter, and a simple answer, the back room.

Seated at a low children's table, writing in a child's seat, in a room that reminded Solomon of his Brooklyn kindergarten in P.S. 189, was a young Hopi of about twenty-two. His face was red brown, smallish, weasel-like, but nice-looking. Lionel walked over, introduced himself, sat down, his legs extending far. It was a new perspective on the adult world to be so low to the ground. He explained how he taught at B. University, but lived up north, near Dartmouth, and wondered why Raymond had dropped out? The casual routine to get a deeper clue. At first Raymond thought Solomon was from the college, and had come to retrieve him, or perhaps to punish him! Lionel explained again, more slowly, and offered to help. The young man doodled, listened, mumbled a monosyllable, gradually spoke up. The hair and eyes were jet black, so that when he smiled it was an impressive white crescent sneaking into view. Wearing a wool lumber jacket and dungarees, he looked too young to be married, let alone to have fathered two. "I was the only Hopi there," he said slowly, "and, uh, it got pretty lonely after a while. There were other *Indians*, but no Hopi. And, uh, though I had a full scholarship, I had to pay my way back and forth, and the tribe couldn't afford that. So I decided to leave." I asked him how he had done there, and he claimed that in anthropology courses he had done very well. Coincidentally, a foremost scholar of Hopi lore and mythology taught at Dartmouth, and Raymond used to talk with him regularly. He had also taken a few incompletes. "Anthropology and child development are what I'd like to study now. I'm an assistant teacher now, and, uh, with a degree I could become a regular." He smiled. "With two children you need that." Impressed with his quiet intelligence, Solomon mentioned friends at the Arizona universities, and Ray's face lighted at the prospect. He proceeded to show Lionel several projects for the elementary school, cardboard paste-ups of Indian artifacts for arithmetic, instead of the usual consumer products. While he did this, a bulky young teacher came over, lodged herself down, and began in gushing tones to praise Raymond. Then pumped Solomon with questions about where he was from, and what he taught, and did he know her friends in the Northeast? The lonely, wound-up creature embarrassed both of them.

At some point Raymond, loosening up, growing confident, asked if Lionel would like to see his village? "By all means," he responded. Monica Jane Houten from Fort Wayne immediately put in, "May I come along, Ray?" Raymond shrugged and said sure. Though she had been teaching there for two years, she had not yet been invited, it seemed. Partly because she was a woman, and mostly, Lionel surmised, this woman.

In Ray's pickup driving out, Solomon put forward his question, carefully, about Miss Matthews.

"Oh my God do you know Tippy!" blurted out the girl. "Are you *really* a friend of *hers?*"

"Sort of," he hesitated. "Yes."

"Tippy is a good friend of the Hopi," Raymond acknowledged, more soberly.

"You mean she's a kind of legend!" pounced Fort Wayne.

His chest heaving, Lionel asked casually, "Do you know her well?"

"Oh *I've* seen her only once, but the way she's *talked about* hereabouts you'd think she was the original Joan of Arc come back to life!"

"Monica exaggerates," observed Raymond, churning up the sharp hill in low gear, enjoying the shifting.

*So it is really true, dear Solomon? Was everything that she had uttered, considered by you to be a downright lie or crazy fabrication,* TRUE? *How do you like that, Mr. Wise Man?*

"Does she live here on the reservation?" And when Raymond shook his head, Lionel pursued, "Do you expect her to come through here soon?"

Ray smiled, boyishly handsome, and even somewhat embarrassed. "Oh you never know when Tippy will come through. She just comes and goes, like the wind."

Lionel took the poetry in stride, foreign territory speaking. They bumped along in the Dodge, Lionel quiet, not wishing to push things. Names came back to him . . . Jeremy Vance Matthews . . . General Crook . . . what else? . . . where else? . . .

"How exactly does she help by the way?"

They turned up a gutted road, like the one leading to old Oraibi, save that this time Solomon was driving in the truck, the town was Shongopovi, and he was on the inside now.

"She does many things for the Hopi," the young man said, peering through his glasses at the road, and pushing the pickup forward as if the road were a smooth macadam. Enjoying his skill, its power. "She found us our lawyer and helped draft legislation in the fight to reclaim our land from the Navajos. Right now she's trying to raise money for a Hopi high school. . . . Would you like to see my father's kiva?"

"That'd be nice," Lionel offered, his excitement for the other pursuit emerging here. "Where do you go now for high school?"

"Border schools, uh, all outside the Reservation," he explained, and named places like Phoenix, Fort Defiance, and sites in Oklahoma and California.

The approach to Shongopovi was a dirt road leading to a village at the edge of a mesa, with fewer ruins than Oraibi and more livable and newer stone dwellings here. Lionel observed that he hadn't realized that Ray had to travel *out of state* just to go to high school.

His smile was one of understanding, and now again he was not a boy having fun with a pickup. The split in him was emphatic. "The Hopi only got their own elementary school not so long ago. That's why if we can get a high school . . . we would prefer our own rather than sharing one with the Navajo." The last part of the sentence spoken with derisiveness. In fact he came most alive in the looks, the emphasis; the voice itself was flat, monotonous.

Lionel thought of Tippy's efforts, and felt arrogant . . . guilty . . . shallow . . . uselessly *self*-oriented. . . . Words like selfish and elitist crossed his mind! . . .

In her style, Monica brandished her inside knowledge once more, saying, "She's been officially adopted into the tribe, hasn't she Raymond?"

Raymond acknowledged, "She's a member of the Bear Clan now. Her name is Running Water, for her good luck. . . . We'll park right here."

To Lionel's left was a spread of mesa terrace leading down to sheer cliff, a few hundred feet out and down. And to his right a mound of stone fifteen to twenty feet high, with a ladder leaning up against it.

Raymond suggested to Monica a side door, but motioned to Lionel to follow him.

Slowly Solomon was climbing the wooden rungs behind him, holding on tightly because of the wind. It reminded him fleetingly of the tall narrow ladders he used to climb at midships, to change flags; climbs of palpitating danger and, at the top, exhilaration! Cautioning Lionel to be careful at the top where you descended, Ray showed him how, and Lionel followed. It was immensely strange and memorable, like descending to a hole in the ground as you left the light for the darkness below. A sacred darkness here. So was this where his Running Water hung out?

The kiva was a rectangular underground room, the size of a modest classroom, made from cement and mud. A potbellied stove heated the room on the near side, with a stovepipe leading through the roof; there were stone benches built along the sides, into the walls. An old man was working on a weaving on one wall, assisted by a young boy. They didn't look up as the new group climbed down, in.

Raymond walked over the ten steps to the bench, saying, "This is my father. He's hard of hearing. From the war."

In the Hopi language he spoke to the old man, who still didn't hear his son, and continued to weave the wool. Raymond touched his arm, leaned down and repeated his words louder into his ear, and finally the old man got the message and craned his head around, slowly, slowly. The sound of iron creaking would not have surprised Lionel. It was a remarkable head, maybe seventy or eighty years of flesh turned to near stone, with a red bandana tied about his forehead. He nodded his hello, a movement of perhaps an eighth of an inch. The face was a terrain of dried-up rivulets and tiny crosshatches, and the nose was long and prominent; it reminded Solomon of his grandfather's face, which he hadn't seen in thirty years. The stillness of his gaze resembled a photograph that now and then moved, ever so slightly. Very slowly he had turned back to his wall weaving.

"This is my brother Dan," put in Raymond, and the young fellow on the bench gave a slow nod too. *Slow*, that was the key here. For several minutes Lionel watched as the old man's hands went up and down on the wool strands, while his son helped out on the lower strands. "A robe for a friend's son, who's about to be married," explained Raymond. Lionel glanced around at the bare stone room, the chunk stove fired with wood for heat, and the benches affixed to the wall . . . a rectangle of maybe thirty feet by twenty . . . for a moment he was back in a familiar place. . . .

*In the dank basement of my father's store, after school . . . the night after Father has scolded me for not knowing my lines for the upcoming Yiddish play, in which I play the father. I read the lines now with a burning avenging heart . . . the smells of fresh fish mingle with sawdust from the wooden floor . . . my father comes downstairs in black shoes and stained smelly apron, looks about for me in vain, and begins to take upon himself the burden of carrying upstairs the monstrous pickle barrel, turning it round and round toward the stairway. . . . My pleasure is mixed with guilt as he lifts it in his arms to the first step with a loud groan, and the tears fall from me with spiteful delight! . . . Twelve years old, I sit on my wooden crate trying to concentrate on the Yiddish lines and to imagine myself talking loud and clear through the beard I'm to don for the part, but I have to fight myself to keep from running to Papa and crying sorry, sorry, here let me help! let me! . . .*

"World War II," said Raymond, in reply to Lionel's involuntary query, as he kept himself from shaking. He went on to explain how his father had been a code man for Allied Intelligence; the Germans could never break or decipher the code because the Indian dialects were not written languages. After the war the old man had come back home, with several medals, to Shongopovi, his clan's home for maybe six hundred years, and returned to his weaving. He was one of the last weavers remaining in Second Mesa, mostly everyone else had turned to the silversmithing craft. In his soft voice Raymond narrated that all the religious ceremonies of the clan as well as various work activities took place down here. He half-smiled. "I was initiated into my manhood here." The word stayed with Lionel as he was shown something else. *And the boy of thirteen, in a blue serge suit and knit tie, with* tallis *around his shoulders and* yarmulke *on crewcut head, was bending over to kiss the velvet* Torah *in that small synagogue in Brownsville, with his father looking on a belt length away. . . .*

Outside again, through the side door, he asked if Lionel had something in his eye, and he admitted that he did, momentarily. Raymond acknowledged that the wind up there took a while to get used to.

The wind was refreshing, though; Lionel's head was spinning with this new world of kivas and clans and strange lingo (One Horn kiva and Bear and Corn society) and that old world of tribal patriarchs and victuals; of these strange poignant Hopi and those strange powerful Jews. Solomon was seeing his own tribe, and its customs, in a kind of fresh anthropological light. Then he and Raymond walked out the few hundred feet down the terraced ledge of the mesa to its broad point. The view looked out upon fantastic endless desert and valley, and elaborate erosions of mesas and cliffs. Abstract art, done naturally by time. The next mesa over formed the U of a horseshoe a few miles away, where the next village existed. Raymond pointed to a spot down below, at the bottom of the mountain. "Down there was the old village, those ruins there, see? That was the original village of Shongopovi, uh, maybe a thousand years old. I don't know why they call old Oraibi the oldest village, it's not. Shongopovi is. It started there and then moved up here after the Spanish attacked it, but it's never stopped existing." The wind almost blew Lionel's hat off as he tried to make out the ancient ruins, a crumble of discernible rocks across and down the sheer drop. Raymond went on to recount the old scourge of the Hopi, smallpox, which had reduced them from a tribe of twenty-four thousand at one time to a mere two hundred in the last century. But they had survived, had managed to make it through once again, and now were back up to four thousand citizens. "Now all we have to worry about is the Navajo," he said with a smile. Yet the smallpox was not really a surprise to the tribe; the disease—and its cure—had been foreseen in Hopi religious prophecy. As he cited the prophecy and also included a story about a great Serpent God of Earth, Lionel began to see how living in the midst of this enormous, unique and hostile landscape would give rise to rather exotic myths and religious beliefs. If you went back thousands of years in the same spot on the globe, why not stay there in religious time as well? (And beneath thought, Lionel brimmed with confusion—double confusion of past memory and present purpose.)

Walking back from that edge, that double edge, he felt somewhat easier. On the way Ray casually pointed out—so casually that Lionel barely realized what he was saying in his low baritone voice—various spots of bush or stone decorated with tall feathers. Mostly eagle feathers, he explained. "Those are sacred places of prayer for Hopi," he said. The ignorant eye never would have recognized them, however, since the spots were not marked off at all, and the ground nearby was littered with beer cans and coke bottles and wrappers. In fact if the civilization were to fold up the next day, Lionel realized, the archaeologists of the next century might very well consider Coors and Cokes as sacred Indian talismens.

In fifteen minutes they were on Raymond's private turf, several miles away on another part of the mountain. His house was a small ranch-style, needing paint, and containing only three rooms. Inside, it looked like an unkempt trailer: chrome kitchen set, food and dishes lying about, a TV set dominating the living-bedroom area, with a lead-in for the huge antenna on the roof. Only kachina dolls on the wall showed signs of Hopi. Out back, to Solomon's surprise, a wooden backboard and net had been set up, and a patch of ground smoothed out from obvious play. When he went to pick up the basketball lying at the edge of the bushes, Raymond said he had a better ball inside; presently he was dribbling a snappy orange ball onto the mowed court area, asking Lionel what sort of fan he was, and putting up a proper jump shot. It was immediately apparent then, and for the next half hour, that Raymond knew the game and played it well. His jump shots arched high and were thrown off the top of his jump; he used the backboard on side angles; on lay-ups he leaped impressively high, and stayed up there for an extra second. He seemed surprised too that *Lionel* could play the game, not saying it, but passing and shooting with more vigor as they proceeded. As they traded shots in schoolyard fashion, he explained how the Hopi loved sports and did very well at them. "Some of the best runners in the state are Hopi, at ASU. The Navajo are no match for Hopi runners," he added, dribbling smoothly. Moreover, in the summertime, there were long-distance races up and down the mesa roads, and marathons from one mesa to another.

"You're like the ancient Greeks," Lionel said.

Ray grabbed Lionel's miss off the boards and laid it back up and in with one hand, saying, "Or like the ancient Hopi." Nice point; in school why did Lionel learn about the one and not the other, closer to him?

"Is that your field?" Lionel pointed to the planted field alongside his house.

"No, my father-in-law's. Mine is out there," and he indicated a far-off point in the valley.

"Why so far?"

"That's my family's plot of ground, and always has been. It's handed down from generation to generation. Where did you learn set shots that way?" he asked. "I didn't know anyone shot them anymore."

"P.S. 189 and Lincoln Terrace Park," Solomon replied, hitting one. "In Brooklyn. Ever hear of Sid Tannenbaum? Don Foreman?" Ray shook his head. "Max Zoslofsky?" Ray shook his head. Lionel expounded about those old two-handed set-shot artists of the fifties, who used to play in Lincoln Terrace on weekend mornings, on occasion, and for the local colleges during the week. "When do you work in the fields?"

"After Head Start. For three or four hours through the early evening. It's not like Vermont, where you put some seeds in the ground and come back in a few months and have vegetables. Here you have to watch *each plant* very carefully, or it'll never make it." His attempt at a set shot jumped wildly off the top of the round backboard, and he laughed. He went back to the jump shot, and told Lionel about growing maize, beans, squash, peas. Agriculture out there was not a friendly occupation, but a necessary ordeal; and all the effort in the world was nil if you didn't get the magic stuff called rain. He shifted hands on the dribble, stopped on a dime, and threw up a sidelines jumper that went in. As Solomon took the ball out Raymond asked which pro team he rooted for?

"Used to be the Knicks, now the Celtics," Lionel answered.

Ray beamed warmly. "Good. They're my team too, ever since my New England days."

Gentlemen of the Celtics, did you know you had such a devoted Hopi fan out there? Lionel pondered. He had come for one education and was getting another. Or were they the same, somehow?

Ray invited him to see a Hopi ceremony in the early evening, and with keen pleasure Lionel accepted.

"Have you seen any other villages?" Ray asked.

"No."

"Walpi?" Lionel shook his head. "You should." Ray smiled. "It's Tippy's favorite village, though she won't admit it to me."

They parted and he gave Lionel directions to the ceremony site later on.

Walpi. Overwhelming Walpi. Perched out at the narrowing wedge of sheer cliff in the sky, a wedge that at its widest point was the width of a narrow city street, and that at its tip resembled the prow of a ship, Walpi existed. Had existed up here, for nearly four hundred years or since the Spaniard Coronado attacked the village in the valley below, in the 1590's. Would exist. Harshly and emphatically *there* with its sixty or seventy citizens. You drove on a winding dirt road up and around a sharp mountain, driving first through the two lower villages of First Mesa, where TV antennas and electric wires had been recently acquired; and just before the bottleneck leading to the farthest village, Walpi, you had to park your car, and go on foot the rest of the way. And walking out there was like walking out to a bottle lying on its side in the sky, with a village set out in it, the neck at the far end. The village consisted of tiny one- or two-room stone houses or huts, fitted together like compacted teeth, with pickup trucks or shiny sedans parked vertically up against the houses, ugly molars set on blocks to allow room for the path. Toilets were outhouses constructed at the edges of the two parallel cliffs, urine and feces dropping down the sheer sides like a new natural element. Unlike the two lower villages that had adopted the wires and pipes and spigots of comfort, Walpi would have none of it. Nothing. Just stuck to its old stone ways. Tippy had her unique taste, yes.

Walking along the dirt path Lionel was stopped by a heavy lady, who mumbled. "You see my kachina doll?" Out of politeness, he traversed the stone steps up to her place, when a wind blew, and nearly blew him off the mountain! Literally, a stairway in the sky, without a banister or railing, and the wind increased in velocity incredibly as you moved up it. This large woman obviously climbed it daily. Her abode was a squalid room, fetid in odor, where she and her crippled husband lived. Toothless and wild-haired and foul-smelling, she showed Lionel the doll and smiled weirdly; was he in a witch's den, was hell up high not low? He lost track of everything, managing to shake his head no to her offering, and stumbling out, getting back down not by walking but by half-sliding on his haunches the way you got down an icy slope. Absurd. Terrifying. Out of breath, nervous, dazed, he walked on. Just then two pretty teenagers, one Anglo, the other Indian, sauntered toward him; in jeans, tie-dyed T-shirts and bead necklaces, laughing to themselves, hip; they passed with flirting eyes and flaunting laughter, and might have been walking in Harvard Square, not Walpi. Thirty more feet and a young man asked if Solomon wanted to see his grandmother's pots? A come-on? Mexican hustle? He followed him inside. Theresa George was about seventy, she sat on a worn sofa, one arm bandaged, the other around her little granddaughter at her side; the lady's pots were quite lovely. Lionel purchased a small clay bowl, ornamented with traditional Hopi swirls in black designs. The little girl Sally, gypsy beautiful at three, prattled on about her kachinas and rattles on the walls, and what Grandma was going to make for her, in good English (unlike Grandma). "What are you doing in Walpi?" this little Hopi beauty queried him, rather shrewdly. "Buying a pot from your Grandma," he said. "Oh, I have lots of pots, don't I, Grandma?" Who nodded, eyebrows rising. On the walls were World War II photos of Hopi Indians in army uniform, while a solid-state tape recorder sat near an ancient chunk stove. And unlike the poor creature's room in the sky above, this room was neat and orderly and had a warm smell of piki bread being made. The poverty was bearable here. The young grandson was by now reading a letter by the window, and in the back room Sally's father lay on the bed. Did Theresa's craft support them, how? What would happen to Sally's precocious charm and intelligence without schools? Lionel walked outside, carrying his bowl, and ambled along the road past those oval ovens where the bread (and bowls) were made. A few hundred feet beyond, at the prow of Walpi, you looked down with great care, the drop being so sheer and so enormous. The ocean here was one vast valley of desert space, and you felt as if the mountain could move straight ahead, either on wings or by rudder and sails; the illusion of living in the heavens, high above mortal earth, was effortlessly real. Tippy and Walpi, Solomon murmured to himself, Tippy and Walpi; how perfect, perched there, incredible, long-lasting, a dark horse of survival, surviving on its own terms of geographic heroism. Was all this *her* as well? . . .

Raymond's ceremony was held at Second Mesa, and by the time Lionel returned and drove up past the Head Start school into the higher ridges of the mountain, cars and trucks were already lined up in a dusty Detroit phalanx. Getting out of his car, Lionel perceived that what he took to be the top of the mountain was no more than a plateau on the way up; above him lay a steep peak resembling an arrowhead. Upon its sheer side, climbing like red ants, were Hopi and their children, and he followed suit. It was as much a rock climb as it was a stairway: You had to hold on to a jutting ledge or rock for balance before you could lift a foot at many points. Up and up and up you went, breathing rapidly from your effort in the thinner air, on one of those ingenious stairways built into the sides of the mountains that the Hopi were so skilled at. The wind blew fiercer as you climbed higher; and finally there, high alone was a cliff-top enclosure of stone houses and walls, and from within lots of football cheering and yelling. Through a natural entranceway in the rocks one entered, looking in on yet another extraordinary setting, and scene: an enclosed courtyard, created by the attached stone houses with women and children huddled together on benches and steps and peering through the windows. Save for the absence of a second-floor tier, it resembled an Elizabethan set for a Shakespeare play. The courtyard itself was an oval of earth the length perhaps of a basketball court, the width a bit narrower; at the near end, where Solomon stood in a noisy cheerful crowd of male onlookers (and would-be racers), was

251

the starting line. He peered around for Raymond, couldn't find him, and stayed put. At the corners the houses were not attached, he realized, and you could peek through to see another endless view of sky, drop-off, and desert. A wonderful setting for Greek tragedy, too, he thought.

But the present races seemed on the surface more comic. They went like this. A kachina racer, a living representative of a Hopi god, ran against a regular male from one of the villages; at the signal of Go (in Hopi), the racer took off, with a step handicap over the kachina running after him. The sprint was perhaps forty yards or so, lasting ten to fifteen seconds, to the far end of the courtyard; the object was for the kachina to catch the racer and anoint him with a smear of mud or chili. The kachina god, representing rain and fertility, was elaborately costumed; silver bracelets on his wrists and ankles, turquoise and coral medallions on his neck; naked chest and legs painted with black, white and yellow stripes; eagle and buzzard feathers glued to his shoulders; face an explosion of black and white stripes and slashes. This *live* adult kachina served as the model for the dolls made by fathers and elders for the children, so that they could learn and absorb the religion. The same dolls which little Sally owned and showed off and which Raymond made for his children. All the actors here were male, by the way, with the exception of a creature called the Shalako, a solitary figure camouflaged in black, gender unknown until—

The Shalako got Solomon. Yes, Solomon. For sure enough, Lionel Solomon of Brooklyn, Palo Alto, Oxford (Ohio), London, Cambridge (Mass.), New Hampshire, suddenly found himself in the clutches of the Shalako. It started like this: Out of dancers, they urged Lionel—grabbing him goodnaturedly by the arms—to participate, and against his growing misery of the cold in his head and chest, he got caught up and was suddenly at the starting line, hearing the exciting cry of Go! You know what, the first time out he actually beat the kachina, running like crazy and never looking back, just hearing breathing and grunting a few steps behind him. And the crowd's delight at his victory! Having won, he then retraced his steps across the oval, where he picked up his spoils, little cakes and sweet rolls, which he put in his rolled-up jacket. He felt good! Not for long, however. For in a few minutes he was obliged to run again, with another kachina, and they were off! This time Lionel, heady Lionel, made the great mistake of glancing behind him about midway through to see how many steps the kachina had on him—a well-built kachina in his forties, jangling and breathing hard right be-hind him, a rattle in one hand and his face wild, part clown, part animal, part man!—and with a kind of glee he caught Solomons shoulder with one arm, his wheels spinning beneath him, and with the other smeared Solomon's forehead and cheek with his mud! The anointment so strange, Solomon hardly minded it; just checked the mud with his finger.

Now if the crowd cheered that move, the cheer turned into a raucous oohing and aahing of warning immediately after-ward; and as Lionel glanced around, there was the Shalako stalking him, a hungry leer across its face, at first frightening him terribly; moreover, Lionel simply had no breath or stam-ina left to escape; he moved slowly, she moved more swiftly, she cornered him, and then heaped upon him and began her act of rape and intercourse! (Yes, Doctor, right out there in the courtyard she commenced humping him, undressing him!) She toppled him to the ground, reaching under his shirt and scratching playfully at him, all the time screwing him with open obscene delight through the clothing! Solomon was too *scared* to be a comfortable sex object in front of a wide audience. Now, in this play there were supposed to be his "womenfolk" who would emerge from the crowd and pull her from him, keeping him from being *kidnapped* to the Shalako's world. But, whom did he know? He thought, *Ah Tippy, where are you now? And suddenly she was there, miracle of miracles, her strong hands jerking upward the dan-gerous black Shalako and then reaching down to lift up her fallen Solomon. Tippy, Tippy!* But you know what? She was no longer lengthy and blond but short and dark! Yes! And she giggled with another older woman! Giggled! In fact not fantasy Lionel had been rescued by Raymond's wife, and her mother! (Not fair, Doctor, not fair!) But the crowd loved it, loved every single moment of the Anglo's rescue and cheered him to his bench where the kindly women led him. Solomon sat there, exhausted, feverish, the wind refreshing on his hot face, his back patted by spectators in sympathy and apprecia-tion; he felt the mud on his face; all that was missing was the rain. When would that come? And the curious truth was, that sitting there and watching the next sprints and shouts and Shalako plays after every fourth or fifth male, he believed fully that he—they—had indeed helped speak to the God of Rain, aided him in his decision toward bringing it, and that the magic stuff would fall down on them, soon enough mak-ing them ally with the land. Fertile. So real and so exhila-rating had been the races! Can you imagine participating in those ceremonies steadily for *six months* every year, each different and each memorized precisely by the village medicine men. Do you see how you'd get to believe in anything—miracles, gods, ghosts, serpents, whales, prophecies, tall myths and tall stories, and Tippys too?

*I would, Doctor, I would. I did. I began to believe fervently. Wasn't it the Spirit of Tippy that I had been learning about out here, just as earlier, it was her body?*

The ceremony was officially closed when, after the sprints, all the captured racers like Lionel were brought individually before the oldest ladies of the village, and there anointed with a bucketful of icy water on the head, and a Hopi blessing. A *cold* experience! And then all the kachinas lined up, looking like a line of conga dancers at a spectacular carnival, and received from the two or three medicine men (or elders of the village) a handful of cornmeal seeds. The reverence for the Old People there at the end was striking. Just as the complete frankness and sexual humor in front of the children during the ceremony had been. No euphemism there; and no movie-star types to hand down benedictions. Just the Old People. The oldest. Yes, it was a community. And walking out, there was Raymond, smiling widely, saying, "You did very well. You can run." Lionel nodded, coughed, wondered if he was serious.

They began climbing down the sides of the mountain in the wind, Solomon stumbling and Raymond easy, while carrying his son. He asked, "Would you like to come back later this summer and witness our Snake Dance?"

Solomon felt touched. His head was buzzing feverishly with the cold, the scene, and his spinning thoughts and hopes! "Thank you. It's tempting." He took a new pride in his mud.

"Your friend was invited two years ago, but couldn't make it. Maybe you can come with her?"

Had he heard right in that swirling wind? To be here with his special friend and run races with her and—high from the event, the wind, Raymond's invitation, not caring whether he fell the few hundred feet or not, Lionel stumbled down; somehow easier than if he had observed cautiously the fierce incline and narrow steps. Raymond walked down casually as if it were a stairway in his house.

Lionel had dinner at Ray's place (beef hash with beans), and retired early to his motel room. By that time the cold had exploded fully, nose running, eyes teary, head wobbly. Whereas he used to enjoy colds as a boy, now, in his late thirties, he perceived them as personal attacks. He hardly

254

slept, was visited by no apparitions (despite the fever), felt miserable physically. And yet, on the inside, he was warmed with a curious satisfaction. Stirred by this very different people. From the Hopi *and* Tippy Lionel felt a spiritual upsurge, a new fragrance. As if the exhilarating air had entered his spirit as well as lungs, cleansing him with hope and new wonder.

At the parting with Raymond the next day, he gave Solomon an eagle kachina, red and yellow with eagle feathers, a gift. Coughing, Lionel thanked him, and said he'd try to do something about getting him back into college. Ray, red-brown and reticent, nodded once his gratitude. And Lionel realized that the young man's realest personality was somewhere out there, connected to the land, the history, the tribe rather than to himself alone. He asked if Lionel had "been to Zuñi yet?" Taken aback, Lionel shook his head. "Uh, Tippy is a good friend of theirs too," he observed with a quiet smile. And so Lionel took off, head and heart pulsating with feelings, impressions, sights. An education at several "levels," as she might have put it. Driving this time, however, it was hardly with the same precise and simple destination—or notion—that he had started out with, of finding the girl herself; now Lionel looked upon the journey as more ambitious, though more ambiguous. It was not so much the girl's corporal self he was pursuing now, perhaps; it was rather the experience of her presence, the imprint of her soul as it was felt in this place, by these friends. Oh, he wanted her, of course; but wasn't he getting a realer Tippy than even he had imagined? Didn't the special fragrant air and those magical cones and mesas express the truest shape of her desires?

The simple detective mission was turning metaphysical, he reflected; Lionel was investigating more deeply who Tippy was, and what her native talents included.

Yes, Zuñi was really a place too—check his Checker Cab ignorance—not merely a people. It also dated back more than a thousand years, uninterrupted. Life lived in the freedom of private space and ancestral land, of tribal hills and spirits, of a long chain of the dead and the living. History there seemed at one with the land, continuous, engulfing, dynamic, visible. Forbidding and awesome too. It was hard to keep in mind that the actual peaks of these pueblo civilizations rose way back in the twelfth and thirteenth centuries, as he learned in Zuñi, way before they were attacked by Spanish armies looking for gold, or by Navajo and Apache searching for new hunting and grazing land. Without the stone evidence of those cliff dwellings in places like Canyon de Chelly, or the ruins of the semicircular cities as in Acoma, the fact of ancient pueblo civilization would have been harder to believe, and less impressive. Houses and planned cities of the desert that were the product of architectural genius and madness; why settle in this barren land? Why pick a desert? But even while he formed the question to ask Bernard, the Zuñi tribal historian, he recalled his own tribe and their piece of desert land by the Mediterranean. You chose or got what no one else wanted; and then when the others wanted it, you fought with your lives to keep it. The land became mixed with your blood, and private property included ancestor bones. You were fighting for your fathers and grandfathers in the end. Their right to rest in peace seemed to rest in your hands.

He had met Bernard Derawitha, a small old man of coffee color wearing a large stetson, in a low modern building that housed the administrative offices of Zuñi government and culture. "Call me Bernard," he said, smiling, "we Zuñi are informal." It was Bernard who, after regaling him with religious myths and secular stories for hours, took him to see the old Zuñi mission and a painter named Alex B.; and it was through them that Lionel came to feel that the Zuñi were *unlike* any people he had ever met. Short, richly dark, seventy, with a nose of character, Bernard had recently been appointed "tribal cultural historian," and was very proud of the position. (The Library of Congress, Yale and Harvard had taken to flying him East to record orally his knowledge of Zuñi life.) That large beige stetson framed his small head, and a fine turquoise pin was set in a bolo tie; the voice was a low bass. His slow stories, where men changed into animals and back again, where violence and murder took place when social codes of the tribe were violated, demonstrated the force of their beliefs and the validity of the psychology. That an embattled people will construct a tight religious system to unite them in their jeopardy is not surprising. What was, perhaps, was the way the Zuñi had managed to keep their beliefs intact—like the Hopi—while adopting office buildings, pickups and televisions, "turquoise dealing." It was this last, a new passion and social disease—which had led to the setting up of a branch bank to handle the flow of big money from the "Anglo" dealers and traders coming through daily—that frightened Derawitha. He shook his wizened head and said, "Every family does it now, and makes a lot of money. It worries me." One thousand years of inviolate tradition was in danger of going the American way: for the green stuff.

Yes, he certainly knew Tippy, but why not let Alex tell Solomon about her? Lionel was coming to accept casually such startling news. They walked out in the streets of Zuñi, where the wind was whipping up the sand fiercely, whipping it into Lionel's eyes and mouth and hair, making him stagger, stall, turn sideways, while Derawitha, slender and fit, ambled easily, talking all the while, as if sand were oxygen. The Zuñi mission was striking, but very different from the traditional Spanish church. This one, dating back four hundred years but refurbished maybe twenty years ago, blended the new with the old. But blending the *Zuñi new* with the Catholic old, to form a most incongruous mixture: ascetic Jesuses hung alongside Navajo rugs, small pictures of the Ascension mingled with large stuffed moose and buffalo heads, the pale imagery of the Church was dwarfed and overwhelmed by the fantastic murals being painted by Alex B. This mural, covering both long walls of the church, depicted the kachina gods during their annual evolution through the different seasons; it was being painted with exacting realism, nature taken seriously down to the thinnest blade of grass, and the most spectacular colors—canary yellow, cobalt blue, fire red. The agony of Christian suffering and dying was confronted with the joy of Zuñi living. Old Agony was losing badly in the race.

Alex B. was a large heavy fellow about Lionel's age, with a contagious gold-toothed smile and huge drooping earlobes. He was sitting on his scaffolding high up against the wall when the pair entered, and after finishing a few strokes, came and sat down in a pew, and talked. Chain-smoking, he spoke at first about the mural itself, the way he worked at it ("Oh you know I'll work for six weeks or several months, and then just get tired of it and leave off and not come around at all, or even take off, take a trip to New York City and walk around there for a few days."). He inhaled and smiled. "I've been at it four years now, and I don't know how much longer. It doesn't matter to me, I'm in no rush. I don't get paid for it. I just do it for myself, and for my people." He laughed. "I don't even know if it'll ever get finished. Maybe. We'll see." Bernard mentioned that Lionel was a friend of Tippy's, and Alex's face brightened. "Yeah, she *sure is* an unusual girl. It was she you know who first suggested that the Zuñi do this, and after we made up our mind, she who proposed it to Father Hopkins. Oh, he went along with it right away, thought it a good idea." He gazed up at it, and gave his self-mocking laugh. "Sometimes I think he's sorry, and I don't blame him. Mess up a nice old church like this!" He laughed again.

The kachinas, twice the size of humans, were three or four times the size of the sacred Christian paintings hung in gilt frames along the walls. Towering above the smaller Crucifixion studies, the Zuñi kachinas practically obliterated them, with their robust sensuosity and polytheistic play.

"Yes, I've known her for many many years," chipped in Bernard in his low sonorous voice. "Since she was a teenager, really. She's kind of Zuñi by now, in her ways and thinking. Peaceful and easy and generous, you know. Always helping out on her own, without being asked. Do you remember, Alex, what she did with John Derawitha's eldest boy when he got in trouble over in Gallup? She personally got the principal there to give him a probationary term instead of throwing him out of school, saying she would tutor him herself, which she did." He shook his head. "She's always doing things like that. Just showing up when someone's in trouble, or when she can be of help; she seems to have an instinct of sixth sense for that sort of thing."

Alex beamed, "Don't I know it. She spent a whole week practically every night teaching my Lewis fractions. He'd sooner listen to her than to me!"

"And she does everything so quietly, you don't even know she's around half the time," Bernard concluded, the face leathery beneath the cowboy hat. "She's not the flashy type, but just *gets things done.* I wish she were here now, you'd see!"

"Where *is* she now, by the way? Does anyone know?"

"Nah," said Alex, laughing. "You can't ever tell with Tippy. She's too Indian, right Bernard?" Another laugh. "She won't show up for six months, and then'll come around and spend a month here, snooping around, figuring out what the Zuñi needs that she can help with. All quiet, like Bernard says, ssshh!"

There it was again, a view of his friend so very different from his knowledge and expectation. Did anyone know anyone? Was everyone in modern life in camouflage, in drag? A guerrilla in private, an angel in public?

They asked Lionel if he had visited Hopi and he said yes. Should he try Navajo? "Nah, she doesn't bother with them." Alex smiled good-naturedly. "Did you try the universities? She might be there you know." He explained that he had tried those in Arizona, and would try the University of New Mexico at Albuquerque. "Yeah, maybe she's there. But if you can stay around here, in Zuñi, she'll show up, she always does, right, Bernard?"

It was hard to push for further leads, and why? There she was, swimming gracefully in her own exotic waters, and doing so well—what was Solomon going to get out of hunting her down now anyway? A trophy? If she turned up for and at Zuñi, she'd turn up for and at Solomon, right? If she really wanted to. He not only had his own teaching to do, but out here he had gotten his own lessons.

He absentmindedly asked whether the local Bureau of Indian Affairs would know her; they laughed heartily. "The BIA? That's the last place. She dislikes them worse than Zuñi does. Yeah, try the college at UNM, or maybe Flagstaff. And once she mentioned Berkeley, didn't she, Bernard?"

"And Yale and Harvard too." Bernard smiled, running his hand through his thin white hair. "Oh she gets around, but is hard to get to. She telephones sometimes. Do you want to leave your number?" He took a pencil out.

"Yes, but it's unlisted actually," Lionel said, before realizing the humor. "Actually, she knows it. Just tell her I came around, to say hello. That'll be good enough. Solomon's the name."

"Like King Solomon?" smiled Alex.

"Like him, yes. Only it's Lionel, not King."

Alex inhaled, "Isn't he the one who had all those virgins at the end?"

"King David, I think," Lionel said. "His father."

His eyes glinted with mischief. "Who knows, maybe it helps at the end?"

More laughter. "Do you do anything besides teaching?" inquired Bernard.

He told them that he wrote.

"You mean journalism? For magazines?"

"Novels, actually. Stories."

Alex nodded, dreaming. "That's what I'd love to do, if I were able. All the stories you can tell, and they'd be set down there, *permanent*. Tell what people are thinking and all. The Zuñi didn't ever write things down, at least until recently. Our tradition is to pass a story down by mouth from generation to generation. We're great talkers—talk your ears off!" He loved his phrase. "I really admire someone who does what you do. What sorts of things do you write about?"

That notorious question, endlessly asked and increasingly nonanswerable. "Murals for my tribe."

They stared and then roared.

"I think I need more scaffolding though. I bet it'd be *fun to write high up* like that, in the air. If you had the right sort of story to tell."

"You ought to listen to Tippy sometime," counseled Bernard. "She has some *great* stories. For children too. You should hear her, or *record* her. They should have her at the Library of Congress instead of me. I sometimes think she knows *all* the Zuñi stories."

Lionel listened carefully. Nodded.

After another ten minutes he shook their hands and told them how much he had enjoyed it.

"Hey, look for us on television," Alex said. "Sometime in the next year or two. NBC did a little show on the mission, and my mural, for the Bicentennial." He beamed at the word and its meaning. "See ya in church now. Do you go to church?"

Seeing he was serious, Solomon explained that his was a synagogue, if and when he went. At this Alex made a clicking sound with his tongue and smiled widely. "You know, I thought there was something a little different about you. You didn't seem . . . shy or afraid of being . . . contaminated by an Indian!" He laughed at his verb. "So you're a *Jew*. Well whaddyaknow. That means you're . . . like us, I think. Some people think we're even from the same 'tribe' way back." He laughed again and smoked with new interest. "I've thought sometimes of looking into that connection. It just goes to show ya. I've never known a Jew before." He stared at Lionel, in reassessment. "Yeah, if ya got some more sun on ya, I bet you could pass for Indian." He inhaled with pleasure. "Maybe we should make him an honorary Zuñi, Bernard. What do you think?"

The old man nodded, half-seriously giving it some thought.

Solomon, bewildered, flattered, said, "See ya in church."

"Synagogue!" admonished Alex, with interest and merriment.

Lionel smiled.

Outside, in the world again, he felt odd, odd. Were they brothers beneath the skin? he wondered, wandering, taking a new pride in the length and unevenness of his nose. Now called prominence. The Zuñi twilight settling upon the chipped-away mesas reminded Lionel of the banks of pink and amber on his own Harvard Stadium. This, in turn, made him miss his jogging, his routine, his own tribal Sheyna.

A last walk around old Zuñi, he figured, heart astir. Keeping his face down, half protected by the badman's hat, Lionel worked his way around the windswept streets, narrow alleys, and open squares where the ceremonial dances were often performed. It looked like a South American town, except when one got a glimpse inside a pueblo house, and saw a re-modeled kitchen fitted out with new white appliances. The power of turquoise paid off in its way.

*My heart beat quickly and suddenly as I saw her.* The power of fate, he *knew*—hadn't he in fact lingered on for those extra few hours just in case of this? this providential accident?! Getting down from the cab of a pickup, *she* wore jeans, Wellingtons and western jacket, her blond hair tied in back and hanging beneath her cowboy hat; a special creature, clearly. Lionel knew her from the back, and then from her walk, the confident walk of an animal back on home ground and exulting in each step. She was helping an old Zuñi woman, he saw, carrying several packages; oh she was splendid, splendid! His heart went out to this southwestern heroine, unknown to the world, but here, a legend. Forget the private shenanigans, here was a woman doing serious things; forget the heroes and heroines created on the front pages and television, here was an authentic one. He followed her at a reasonable distance, if and until she was alone; sure enough, she deposited the old lady at her house, gave her the packages, and hugged her. He stealthily followed her back to the red pickup, enjoying her lengthy beauty from the back, anticipating her front, her surprise. She climbed up to the driver's seat and Lionel raced around and called through the passenger's window, "Hey, can I get a ride?" He had already opened the door and jumped up to the seat when *he* said, "Sure." He had a ruddy face, clear blue eyes, and wore a friendly smile. "Where you headin'? Don't believe I've met you, name's Ron Corbett." He put out his hand. Lionel shook it limply, limply, and told him the culture center; he barely heard what was said on the way back, bumping and nearly hitting his head and not caring. Dejected, foolish!

Checked in with Bernard for a final goodbye, and as they shook hands, Solomon noticed a small faintly familiar object on the shelf behind him, and asked what it was? He took it down and showed it to Lionel, explaining that it was a sacred Zuñi fetish, a bear. Lionel smiled, recalling his own fetish— the early gift of the girl, which he had taken casually, and skeptically. He tried now in this office to recall where it was? He was going to tell Bernard about it, but thought better of it. Thanked him and left. If Tippy had turned into one of these sacred animals, or supposedly had her spirit deposited there, he would have conceded it now, understood it, believed it. As for her turning into a young man, a trick of the culture and Solomon's longing, no more. . . .

Flying back in the jet through the limpid blue skies . . . eagle kachina packed carefully overhead . . . alongside Yaqui mask, regards from Tippy. . . . Lionel brimmed with new feeling about the girl's *authenticity,* her sincerity, upbraiding himself, but still wondering who was who in our native land during these decades of charade and play in everyday life. . . . The plane flew with a sensuous ease through the endless azure dome, and he saw what Tippy admired in the journey. His own, he felt, had proved a surprising success in ways that he wouldn't have imagined. He opened a *New Yorker,* and, seeing all the sophisticated commodities and expensive deceptions, he sensed more than ever what she meant about natural beauty and Indian strength. You had to come out there, travel around, touch down on reservations in the mountains, *to feel* what she meant. Oh, she was a special species, he knew now for sure, as if he had just *proved it,* mathematically. Just then, the woman next to him, handsome and fragrant, tapped him on the arm, and, apologizing for intruding, asked if he knew what *hebetude* meant? Lost in thought, Solomon asked her to repeat it, and to read the context. She read a few sentences, which were quite lovely. He shook his head, pleaded ignorance, but asked the title. " 'The Secret Agent' by Conrad," she explained, a touch of the Midwest in her accent. "I'm a great fan of Conrad, ever since undergraduate days in English lit," and she smiled. Oh, there were a bundle of questions he would have ordinarily asked her, but since he already had one fan, one secret agent in his life—and in his longings—he simply nodded and turned away. Contemplating hebetude, however, Lionel thought how nice it was to be ignorant when such a lovely sound came your way. You could hear its beauty again and again, without the distraction of meaning.

In the clouds one minute, in a dark tunnel the next. Brooklyn not Boston had beckoned. And memory alone didn't seem to satisfy the wanting here. Poor hostage to his impulses for a week now, Lionel played the prisoner once again. Flooding reason with impulse, he followed his heart's unforeseen signal.

The IRT Seventh Avenue Express hadn't changed that much through the years, it still bumped along crazily (unlike the smoother BMT), the sounds were harsh and raucous, the strapholders read their *Posts* and *Newses*—except now the long benches were vinyl-covered and you didn't have to worry about splinters of loose straw piercing your buttocks as you sat. There was fresh orange and green paint, but also, fresh and plentiful graffiti. What was clearly different were the faces in the advertisements and subway cars: the complexions now were ebony, olive, caramel, chocolate; and the language now was broken English and Spanish, in word and print. A Caribbean Brooklyn. Yet when you left the darkness of the tunnel at Utica Avenue and emerged into the late afternoon sunlight of Sutter Avenue, you still got the old lift of an El, replacing the subway. The rooftops sprouted silver and black antennae through lines of wash, but this time they moved him; even the rooftops themselves, uneven, rude, multicovered, now had a touch of the poetic for him. In the distance of Brownsville, there appeared huge gaps here and there, like bombed-out areas or missing teeth. Strange, Lionel had spent the first twenty years here, and the next twenty or so away, yet as he stepped out on the platform of Sutter Avenue, he felt back on home ground, on those wooden planks of his youth.

On the streets, these new and yet familiar streets, he walked and walked and walked, and stared and stared. It was like seeing an old friend who has been in an accident and has had plastic surgery. You know him by the old gestures, old movements, genetic signs, but can't quite get used to his new skin, scars. Here and there existed a store that he knew, the new paint and Spanish sign a weak disguise. Many of the streets had the same width and asphalt slant, where he had played punchball; and the sewers were still the same distance apart. Okay. Also, in that square of blocks that Lionel knew like the palm of his hand, from Ralph to Howard, from East New York Avenue to Sutter, many of the old buildings still existed. Like his own three-floor tenement at Ralph and Sutter. But if the old face was that of a neighborhood, this new one struck him as a battle zone; or an occupied territory. *Struck him, I say, Doctor, because who but someone living there knew if it was a neighborhood or a battle zone?*

At least half the stores in this old shopping area had signs in Spanish, and more than half had placed steel gates or iron fences in front of the windows. And how many stores were empty, up for rent? A multitude of For Rents where, in the old days, there was never a single vacancy. He walked out past Howard Avenue, to Grafton, Amboy, Strauss, Saratoga, and was confronted up close with those "missing teeth." He was stunned. On the street where Solomon had been Bar Mitzvahed in a small synagogue, where a movie house had existed, nothing remained; the entire city block had vanished. More precisely, the entire vertical block now lay horizontal, curled into piles of brick rubble as if smashed by tons and tons of TNT bombing. Ancient ruins of ten years; would they last a thousand? Mangy cats and dogs roamed, skinny dark children played, just as he would have; a razed building was a great toy of childhood. But what about an entire block? *I don't know, Doctor, I don't know.* How long will it take Strauss Street, after the riots? Move a couple of streets, to the site of the old YMHA where downstairs you played basketball and upstairs, if you wished, you could hear lectures on socialism versus anarchism; or down the street (around the corner?) there was that peculiar barbershop where, while you had a haircut or shave, Mr. Bugsy Siegel and other Jewish gentlemen known as Murder, Inc., blew your (or their) brains out or sliced your throat by artful design; if had all vanished into those piles of rubble. All that cultural mix and history demolished, transformed. A cavity of brick and mortar and smashed glass and decayed beams—was this history? Whose? What did it commemorate or mean?

Lionel wavered, staring. In reasonable shock. His knees went weak at the sights of his old mesas and deserts and prayer places and kivas smashed to the ground; there had been no chance to put up Off Limits signs; would the Hopi have moved out or protected their temples with bow, arrow, hand, gut? Didn't they fight off the Navajo for encroaching?

At his old bagel-and-lox haunt on Sutter, Lionel had a glass of milk and a glazed doughnut and found himself the only white person in the busy greasy spoon. For the second time in a fortnight in his own country Solomon felt like an *outsider.* His bones and nerves were strange here, on his own growing-up turf. Slowly the milk and strangeness swirled to his head like liquor and he half-reeled out, dizzy with unfocused fear. Across the street he suddenly found himself back in his old dome of dreams, that familiar rotunda of darkness that stirred his Saturday afternoons with celluloid fantasy and MGM lion-roars. In those rows of seats of the old movie house, those true pews, Solly had sat glued to the screen, or taunted the matron, or sneaked an arm around a pubescent shoulder in the slow-motion art of movie-petting. Casual, casual, adjusting the hand exploration to the movie-moment. But now, now he was wandering in a huge darkened hall, lit by a hole in the roof letting daylight in, a hall scraped clean of movie seats and appurtenances, its walls and floors looking as if giant crabs had gone wild sharpening their claws. And into the slashed space had been tossed anything and everything: tires, cartons, wrappers, rinds, bloodied bedsheets and charred clothes, rusted chains and punctured candy machines, smashed speakers and part of a porch railing, fenders, gaping teeth of strange machines, stacks of soaked Bibles, a porcelain toilet, fetid garbage, rummage, rubble, bricks, rotting plaster, cement blocks, a newly laundered white shirt, a pack of protest proclamations and notices of real estate auctions, elementary school textbooks half burned, partial posters of Black Power and California Surfers, a sideboard on three legs stuffed with broken records, a yearbook from the University of Minnesota 1928, sections of pool tables, dog shit and mice droppings in drawers, a birdcage holding a crystal snowball, an overstuffed chair with an arm pulled loose, two sawed-off trees (horizontal), pieces of children's toys, and on and on, including the rancid odors of decay; were there rotting human bodies? And up front, there was the old stage, battered and garbage-filled, and his old pal, the movie screen, now useless, slashed and ripped; Lionel sat on a rubber tire pile, and stared up at his old faithful servant, only this time it stared back gaping, wounded . . . waiting for Lionel, it seemed, to perform for it now. To pay her back for all her shows and performances. . . .

Presently a train rumbled overhead, shaking this Ruin the way it used to shake the old Sutter Theater. . . . Snapshots from the past passed before him, from him. . . .

One. *After the customary Saturday morning baseball game in Lincoln Terrace, a Saturday matinee at the Sutter. After ten wild little Iroquois occupy a row of seats; the movie dull, we trick the huge matron in white uniform and absurd sailboat white cap to search for a "lost wallet" under the seats, and as she's bending over and down, we begin a mock fight with the matron getting squeezed and felt and pinched like a Mother Bear fondled by her pack of cubs. Why does she fall for it week after week? And then, of course, playing self-righteous and injured, marching the pack of us out of the theater, a line of twelve-year-old Saturday sinners.*

Leaning back, seeing the next sequence move into frame:

*A late summer night, in the early morning hours, in steamy Brownsville. The bedrooms are airless and air-conditionless, and so the occupants ooze into the streets, turning night into day. Mothers in loose, print dresses, fanning them-*

265

*selves on folding chairs, gossiping; and fathers in vest under-*
*shirts or naked to their baggy trousers, sitting on orange*
*crates, kibitzing. The bunch of us, maybe eight or ten teen-*
*agers, hang out by the corner mailbox, while the Sutter mar-*
*quee gets changed; or else playing Johnny-on-the-Pony*
*against the brick walls. The streets are still glistening red and*
*green beneath the stoplights, from the earlier hydrant splash-*
*ing and sprishing they've received, to cool their inhaled heat.*
*The blazing night has brought out most of the block, turning*
*it into a family of a few hundred, tribal in their repetitions.*
*Mr. Werter, barechested, is taking on his son Steven in a box-*
*ing match, consisting mostly of body punches. I look on, with*
*envy; my own father is at Dave's Blue Room, a few blocks*
*away, in his shirt and tie, not deigning to nakedness, or to*
*mix with the block's fathers, or its sons.*

Solomon rolls his neck and adjusts his spectacles.

*I'm walking up the long flight of stairs with Joey ahead of*
*me, to Barney's Pool Room. At twelve I'm two years under-*
*age, and will lie, with Joey vouching for me. Inside, it is like*
*walking into a sacred temple that you've heard about for*
*years and years, until you don't quite believe it's real. A long*
*rectangular room, filled busily with young men holding cue*
*sticks, playing or not, the smell of chalk, the sounds of balls*
*clicking, resonating. A small bespectacled man, sitting on a*
*high throne chair, asks me how old I am, I say fourteen, he*
*eyes me and says I don't look it, and Joey says he's sure of it.*
*Abie goes back to his newspaper, like a warden or overseer.*
*All the young men are wearing either dungarees or green fa-*
*tigues with huge patch pockets, souvenirs from the army. The*
*room is lit by those overhead cones of light which fall on the*
*green carpets of the table, and highlight their greenness.*
*"Look who's arrived, the hustler himself." Good-humored*
*banter back and forth, then:*

*"C'mon, hotshit, spot me ten in straight pool and I'll take*
*ya on. That way you won't have to hustle the kid." Meaning*
*me. The offer is made affectionately by a hugely built curly-*
*headed fellow named Hootch. Joey, slender, freckled, hand-*
*some, plays him, hitting the colored and striped ceramic balls*
*with great care, almost delicacy, shooting very slowly, and*
*putting some sort of English on every shot; also, before*
*shooting, he walks around the table like a scientist checking*
*his apparatus, measuring angles, chalking his cue. At every*
*missed shot, Hootch says, "Cocksucker." "Well fuck me."*
*"Mother-fucker." And if Joey makes a difficult shot, Hootch*
*stamps his cue on the floor three or four times. It is this same*

*Hootch who will, in a year or two, take that cue and wrap it around a stranger's head, whom he's caught hustling on strange territory, leaving the blood on the floor. He has spotted Hootch the ten and beaten him by six, in a game of fifty, the points registered by means of a rack above with small wooden chips on a string, one moved over from one side to the other for each shot made; usually he flicked seven or eight at a time. At a quarter a point, he has made one-fifty. Hootch pays him, saying "Here, jerkoff." And afterwards, Joey gives me my first pool lesson, lasting maybe an hour: the grip (thumb and forefinger bridge making a circle), chalking up the cue tip, rolling the cue to check its straightness. Next come the shots: the opening break shot (on an angle), the bank shot, the straight long shot. "What's 'draw'?" I want to know. He takes the white cue ball, puts it in a line with another ball and hits the cue ball at a low point, withdrawing the cue quickly, so when the cue hits its target, it returns sharply like a boomerang. "Ya ready to go out on your own now, and hustle?" he asks. "Almost," I say, my heart much too excited from the two hours to understand anything, or know anything. "You work on that grip now, and when you have it down, I'll show you another. Okay?" I nod. Before accompanying me down, he goes over and huddles with Abie's partner, a man in rolled-up shirtsleeves, and they look at a sheet together. The man nods. Going downstairs, Joey explains he's made a little bet "on the ponies. You stay away from that, stick to pool." Downstairs, the El had just deposited hundreds of passengers who calmly leave the station to walk home, and I'm half amazed that no one has run up to me to touch me, congratulate me! I realize that we're standing outside Dave's, where my father will be that night. And I think, If he ever finds out where I've just been, I've had it! For the poolroom, to him, is a sure sign of American degeneracy! I feel delicious, having cheated secretly.*

Lionel changed his position in the tires, trying to prop his neck more firmly. In the new position he sights an old boxing poster from Eastern Parkway Arena, with two boxers posed in their fighting stances and big red and black letters announcing the match.

Lionel scribbles down a few notes in his pad, then leans back, allowing memory to transport him again. . . .

*Sundays. The day of the week spent with my father. (The market is closed.) Chess day at the club, maybe Russian movies uptown at the Stanley. While Momma sleeps Papa* makes breakfast for the two of us, while I go downstairs to fetch the giant Times for him, the Mirror for my mother and me. I couldn't believe anyone could read such fine print, or such a bulky paper as the Times. Upstairs, there is hot Ralston, his specialty. Black hair escapes his vest undershirt, a dishcloth is over his shoulder as he serves it up, saying, "Salt it, don't be afraid silly boy, saltz!" And against my will he is raining the cereal with excessive salt. Afterwards, I eat two soft-boiled eggs, one at a time from the egg cup, and enjoy my favorite breakfast taste, my favorite taste from childhood, thickly slicked challah dipped in dark coffee. The thick curst of the twisted challah becomes aromatically soggy, and the yellow dough is like wet sponge cake. For this taste, I forgive him everything! Privately he jokes with me, and I accept with complicity, about my mother still sleeping, at 10 in the morning. He reads the Times pages, folding them in quarters carefully, while I read the Mirror's sports. If he's in a good mood, he'll ask, "So, how did your Brooklyn Dodgers do yesterday, the gonifs, a victory?" His peculiar language betraying his baseball ignorance. (For which later in life I'll punish him, when he wants to learn the game, and I won't help him.) At the age of eight, I wrap myself in this Sunday morning ritual like a moth in its cocoon.

Trouble starts when I have to fly out, later, and dress. I'm forced to wear long woolen socks and a tweed knicker-suit, as he did in White Russia in 1910. Downstairs, in front of the apartment house, my friend's mother holds me up to her son, for Sunday dress, and half-smiles privately at the absurd costume! And while Steven goes off to play softball, I have to stand there, a wooden Jewish-Indian boy, stiff with embarrassment in front of 701 Ralph, until my father emerges, in his large-lapeled, single-breasted suit and shiny tie and wide-brimmed gray fedora. With kindly condescension he nods to the neighbors, and with formality marches me, hand in hand, down Ralph and up Sutter, toward Union Street and the club. We pass all those shops of protection, my beloved ports of weekday shelter, which are closed today. These merchants have become my extended family: ever since I was four, each of them has given me a penny or a licorice or a charlotte russe for mispronouncing the English language—"lambztops," "fi'-nenjin." "'ouse and 'ome." ("Where'd you buy him, Mrs. Solomon, in a London department store?") Short crazy Rosie, and the variety store, where I buy pink spaldenes: Hymie the jeweler and his fair Scottish sister who drink tea in the afternoon from a silver service: Phil from the furniture store, who takes me for rides in a real truck; Saul from the fish store, who holds up and flaps the fish for me to see their last life; and of course Sally and Walter from drygoods, who shield me from bullies. (We pass the one store that is open, Maury's Delicatessen, and wave to Maury; if we don't go uptown, we will probably eat "deli" at six-thirty.) This street of merchants that harbors me, and that brings in goods from all over the world: diamonds from Johannesburg, and jade from China; salmon from Nova Scotia and white fish from the Great Lakes; teak and mahogany from the Philippines; silks from India and England, beef from Wyoming, leather from Italy and alligator leather from Florida—these riches and their sources signal in my head like beacons in a dream world. I want to go to each and every country. My father pulls me along the street toward the club.

Brownsville Air Raid Wardens. . . . A good-sized storefront . . . evenings and weekends, men gossip over pinochle and poker and gin rummy, and of course chess; . . . heavy cigar smoke and cigarette butts, folding chairs and card tables and benches along walls. . . . My father joins a pinochle game, while I take my seat, propped by a Brooklyn telephone directory, opposite Sol Goldstein for our regular game. . . . Sol wears glasses and is pushed around by his wife, by my father, and relaxes with chess, while he's the best in the club . . . above his shoulder a framed letter from President Roosevelt to my father, thanking him for his service during the war. . . . The kibitzers gather as the game proceeds, the smoke circles following suit. . . . After a cautious opening game, I take a chance on a bold exchange, which leaves me a pawn down, but in a strong position . . . in nervous excitement I scratch at my woolly itchy calves as I harass his floating queen, caught surprised like a battleship without cruisers . . . news of my impending success brings more observers, including my father, my original instructor two years ago. . . . Outside the first circle of gossip concerning the game comes another circle of comments, in Yiddish for disguise . . . I understand the sense, if not every word. . . . "Herschel, er spielt cortn, und mit der weiber, er is ech nicht shlecht . . . split mit roita Perela a bisl too. . . ." My father was playing with red-haired Pearl, my mother's friend? My heart leaps. The robust green-eyed woman I like so much, who in the Catskills, puts her hand down inside my shorts and asks, "Now what do we have here"? "Geschmect shein, Herschel?" "Es is a shanda far di kinder . . ." "Nah. For Herschel, a gute kleine fress,

269

moishekapoyer." *My father blushing, at the edge of the circle, whispers,* "GENUG, yeah? Genug *with that* PISK *of yours, Irving." A swirl of smoke lassoes me perfectly and I scratch at that calf with renewed vigor. . . .*

*In heated confusion, my heart pounding in fury, I commit my own queen precipitously. And in a few moments Goldstein cries out, sadly,* "Ah Levele, how could you . . . back there?" *Amid sighs of disappointment my queen is suddenly trapped by his knight and a bishop pin. Will my father think it is a* MISTAKE *on my part? He says venomously, dissociating himself from the move,* "Ah, bist du klug." *I feel hot with guilt, but satisfied. My chest pounds perversely, but with joy. I stare intensely at the pawns and pieces, at the series of squares and files and ranks where surprise is pleasurable, combinations fascinating; where my father and I have played regularly for two years, not without moments of great intimacy. At last, with great relief, I resign. My shoulders and back are patted affectionately by the adults. Goldstein takes me around and says,* "Lev, you did VERY well—if it wasn't for that queen error, I think you had me this time." *He pinches my cheek as I hold back tears.*

*The walk home, a funeral march. When I lag a step at the light, my father pulls me hard.* "DU GOY," *he lets out derisively.* "Losing to that schnorrer. You've LEARNED NOTHING. You'll drive a truck when you get older. Or wind up in jail." *The adult consequences for chess loss are something I accept, if need be. I picture my cell. Across Sutter, the view of our kitchen fire escape, chipped and peeling orange bars, calms me somewhat. And upstairs, my mother, having a bite of pickled herring while reading the newspaper, lifts my gloom. My father notes,* "You should have seen your son this morning. Ah, a first-class PISHER you're raising!" *My mother, familiar with his bullying, a scholar on its reasonable and unreasonable levels, retorts,* "Oh you mean he embarrassed you? Too, too bad. You know what, you're meshuggah, truly." *And to me, in a tender voice,* "So how did you do, pussycat? Was it a good game? Look, you're perspiring, did you run home in this suit?" *And as I hug her tightly, feeling her smooth, cheek and strand of hair, she is somewhat surprised, saying she didn't realize the game meant that much to me.*

My upper back pains me, and I realize I've been sitting in this one awkward position for too long on the tires. I get up, and wary of the stiffness lingering in my neck, I bend over and let my head dangle loosely between my legs. My shoulders, neck, head relax totally in that position.

I want to leave. Instead, I find a loose front seat from an old automobile and it fits my back snugly, wonderfully. Expensive leather, cracked nicely; I fold my arms, and lean back. When it gets very quiet again, I hear a slight movement maybe a hundred feet away; a rat, mice? remembering their past too?

*Frames come, pass by quickly . . . a scene at the appetizing counter in the market, my father using the long thin knife to cut thin slivers of lox from the magnificent pink smoked salmon, while I stand by, fascinated, wearing my apron . . . my father corners my sister, sixteen, asking her about her two months of hooky-playing from Tilden High School and slaps her hard two or three times before my mother restrains him. . . . The next scene refuses to come into focus . . . remains shadowy. . . . I find myself struggling there in the dark as if resisting a bad dream . . . Click.*

The theater walls shake familiarly, like the old days. Lionel, exhausted, lifts himself up. The old theater's crazy shapes and hodgepodge objects feel less scary and more familiar now, after the private reels. He doesn't want to leave now, but wants to remember everything, to dig the trenches and the holes necessary in order *to understand more, see more clearly* . . . what happened then, who he is now. . . . Outside, the light, pale as it may be, surprises him, makes him squint. Can it still be day? Hard to believe, after his unusual transport, and vehicle. Like an animal he moves with an ancient instinct he doesn't even recognize toward the red-brick tenement across the street, that housed him for the first fifteen years. No trolleys now, or even trolley tracks; vanished. But 701 Ralph is still there, stolidly. The air is sultry, Brownsville floats back, and he sees the folly of his earlier judgment. No, it wasn't a battle zone out here, he perceives, two black kids racing past him rudely into the building (just as he would have). It was rather a different set of people acting out and building *their* way of life. *Different.* Like the *shtetl* Jews who came here years ago, and probably looked absurd with their thick babushkas and shawls and wooden pushcarts. (They were back again, actually, right there where Sally's haberdashery used to be, on Sutter.) In fact *outside* here was easy and carefree next to back there, locked up, *inside.* Next to *back then.* . . . Back then, and within Solomon, were the real wars, the deep wounds, the permanent scars. . . . Near forty, and he couldn't shake them. And when he remembered them, they shook him. Still. Still. When would they cease?

A hand on his shoulder. "Hi there buddy, you visitin' someone?"

A black policeman, with a mustardy complexion, smiled. By the curb was a squad car, one door opened, from the old Seventy-third Precinct.

"No. Just revisiting. I used to live here."

"Right heah?" the fellow said, looking up, admiring. "No kiddin'. When?"

"Oh . . . fifteen, twenty years ago."

A fine gleaming smile, and understanding nod. "Things are a bit different now, ain't they? I grew up in these parts myself. C'mon we'll give you a lift to the subway. Or wherever you goin'. After dark it gets a little touchy for a white man. Where'd you say you went to high school now?"

And Lionel, like a hospital patient, was gently escorted to the police car. Inside, Officer Gilliam and he discovered they had been at Thomas Jefferson High just a few years apart, and that they even had an old mutual friend, a basketball player from Rockaway Avenue, where Earl Gilliam had lived as a young boy.

While Earl told Lionel about their old friend Tee, "married with kids in Chicago—you know, middle-aged and settled down like the rest of us" (winking), he also took him for a quick spin around the old territory. And as they drove in the near-darkness, lit by new leaning fluorescents up and down Pitkin Avenue, and then down Hopkinson to Sutter and back toward the El on Sutter, Lionel recalled the cozy richness and excitement of the old streets. Even the gangs that roamed— the Jewish gangs (Black Hats, Syndicate Midgets and Juniors), the Italian and black gangs—provided a kind of rich Elizabethan texture to the scene. Gangs of six or seven kids, fourteen to eighteen, wearing pegged pants or bell-bottom dungarees, garrison belts and studs and hugh buckles (for slashing), hair slicked back in DA's and shoes pointed and black (with taps turned outward for kicking), cased the avenue, or headed for Lincoln Terrace or Eastern Parkway, in search of territory, and a place to shine, to preen. While his friends and he roamed in search of girls, here and there nodding to a tough they knew in one of the gangs, or avoiding their turf. And Lionel began to have this odd sense sitting in the squad car, of what Brownsville had meant to him: passion. The passion of family, sports, adventure, sexual adventure. While now they were, he and Earl, riding safely in the vehicle of the law, in the car named sublimation: middle age. He was struck urgently, pungently, by all that hot youth on

272

the prowl, by all that endless energy in pursuit of pleasure, active immediate pleasure, and realized why for his part he had never as a boy really dreamed of leaving Brooklyn permanently. For trips to see the rest of the world, sure: Manhattan, San Francisco, New Orleans, Africa, Europe; but to leave youth and boyhood adventure? Never! What was the need?

By the Sutter Avenue El, Lionel shook hands with Earl, said to look him up if he ever came through Boston, and headed up the rickety wooden stairs and through the new turnstile, racing at the last moment when he heard the train lumbering into the station above. He just made it as the door was sliding shut, out of breath but prideful as in the old days, only with the heart pounding faster longer. As the IRT lurched and floundered forward, he felt his past as a mixture of oats and wounds, wild oats and wild wounds, and his heart overflowed with hot flowing emotions and new excitements. And as the snaking train left the El of open sky to descend toward the tunnel, he wondered if there ever had been boys (and girls) who were sent down through the narrow chute of childhood with the help of reasonable loving fathers? Dreams. Ah, dreams!

In the tunnel, he remembered two old friends.

"Dear Jackie R. and Burt B.,

"A dual letter because in my fondest memories you two appear intertwined, my earliest heroes. You, Burt, in your leather air-force jacket and fur-lined cap and silk scarf, when I was five, and you, Jackie, in your loose baggy Dodger flannels walking pigeon-toed to home plate, when I was ten; the perfect ages for having heroes. Both of you then in the prime of youth, energy, drive; but now, Jackie, you out of your misery for good, and you, Burt adrift somewhere in America, your life torn apart irrevocably. And what a curious coincidence, that both of you were shattered early on by the same blow—the death of teenage sons. Was there a circuit of fate wiring your two lives, dating back to those first days when I used to sit with you, Burt, in the first-base grandstand in Ebbets Field and watch Jackie play? With one of you trying to recover from those endless post-World War II operations to remove shattered glass from your body, and the other suffering endless abuse because of his ebony color; one, a twenty-five-year-old war veteran, watching the other, a rookie; both involved in the boy's game. A particularly native story?

"Burt, you were so arrogant and smart-alecky with everyone, including your family, but so kindly with me, your five-

273

year-old neighbor on the first floor. With your apartment on the third floor and your family's dry-goods store below us, at street level, I was sandwiched between Berkowitz affections. Downstairs your mother, Sally, fierce and stubborn with others but grandmotherly to me, and upstairs your father, Walter, davening every morning with his *tefillin* and *yarmulke*, and on occasional Saturdays taking me to *shul*. Sally, that tough Polish refugee, that brunette Napoleon of Sutter Avenue, who would lullaby me to sleep in one arm while selling linen and cotton bargains with the other. This diminutive woman trusted no one, dominated everyone, from her own family to mine (except my father) to customers—working fourteen hours a day, believing in Palestine, green salads and family mementos. (Her tiny apartment was cluttered like a thrift shop in Warsaw.) All through my shortpants and knickers youth, Sally was a haven of warmth and protection when I banged up my knee or eye, or was chased by this or that bully—me, a skinny towhead who looked like some kraut-kid and spoke with an unaccountably British accent. So it was not surprising that you, Burt, should take me on as a younger brother when I was three or four, building for me that miniature railroad made from odd pieces of small wood from the carpenter's shop you worked in after college hours. Twice a week in my living room—who had a room of his own?—we would spread out those lathe-smooth odds and ends for the Ralph Avenue Depot, with the pitched roof, the platform, the wooden cars. And we would have gotten it done for sure if Mr. Hitler hadn't come along, and suddenly you were in the air force—a patriot to your country, a traitor to me!

"I recall even now, some thirty years later, the letter written by that five-year-old-boy to his best pal, snatched away by the silly presumptuous world, imploring Burt to get the air force to *promise* to hold the next empty bed for me! How I used to wait for a letter to arrive saying I could join you! But when one did arrive, all you could say was that, as yet, there was still no bed available. (Oh, the intense power of childhood wishes, as if *wishing* would influence the world for sure!) By that time I even had my own complete soldier's suit, just in case I had to depart at a moment's notice. And then the spring afternoon when my mother, picking me up from P.S. 189, informed me that you were "missing in action." Was it the first time that I couldn't control my tears? I cried for hours. . . . But months later, we were elated to discover that you were in fact alive, in a German prisoner-of-war camp, your B-17 having been shot down. Wounded, but alive. Only in 1945, when you returned home, did the full story of your injuries emerge, namely, that you had tried to escape from the camp and had been shot with glass bullets. Who had ever heard of such a thing, except perhaps from the Lone Ranger? So that for the next years you were in and out of hospitals as they tried in vain to remove the endless shards of glass lodged in your body by Nazi engineering. Enter Ebbets Field. It became your retreat from pain, your oasis for relaxation; and there was I, your private tail, benefiting from that hard turn of events.

"And while they were working to repair your scarred anatomy, Burt, arriving on the scene, at the same green oasis, was Jackie; and instead of the continuation of the Ralph Avenue Railroad, there was the beginning of the 'Robinson Express.' (Burt's phrase for your careening around the bases at Ebbets Field as if you had an engine and wheels.) Once or twice a week I'd manage to get out of school early, and Burt and I would IRT uptown three or four stops to Franklin Avenue and walk the half-dozen blocks to the ball park. We would generally arrive in the third or fourth inning, obtaining seats in the first-base grandstand on Burt's veteran's pass. From there we'd sneak down openly to the empty box seat by the field, greeted familiarly by the ushers. The thrill of it! During that rookie year you played first base, Jackie, so we were up close to you. In the midst of that sun-splashed green park, with the square of infield dirt, and the endless whiteness of ballplayer and fan alike, what stood out strikingly was your ebony color; emphasized all the more, it seemed, by the soft white flannel of the Dodger uniform. A blackness that was exaggerated and made a colossal fact by the cries of 'Nigger,' 'Blackie,' 'Porter,' 'Boy,' and assorted other nicknames that came from the visiting dugout, or from the visiting infielders, or from the stands. Emphasized by the black cats that were tossed on the field by the visiting Cardinals, say. By the crazy way opposing ballplayers, at least once a game, went after you, not the sack, in crossing first base. (And the following year, when you shifted to second, how many times were you spiked gratuitously?) All the time you never said a word, never uttered a complaint; you just hit more shrewdly, ran harder, stole more bases, made yourself a better ballplayer, and the Brooklyn team a pennant winner.

"Though you did everything well—ran, hit, fielded, threw—it was on the base paths where you played the hardest and jangled the nerves. Where you took your sweet

275

revenge. The fans knew it too, sensed it, as we rooted for you to get to *first base*, not more, so that we could see the whole show around the bases. A double or triple, you see, would have cheated us somewhat. Your leads at first were amazing, about double the ordinary base runner's and a third of the time, it seemed, you went to second or third on one of those endless errant pickoff throws by the pitcher. How could one count or measure the number of fat pitches that your dancing lead caused the pitcher to throw the next batter? And how to describe that baseball dance, once you reached the end of your long lead, arms out dangling, like a man alone on a high trapeze? You took leads and stole bases, to my mind, not simply on speed like Jethroe, or through science like Brock—though you possessed both—but on *vengeance*; out there, spreading your arms wide like a black hawk on a tree limb, you taunted the pitcher, tantalized him with your shim-mying, for a whole minute sometimes, shimmering pitch black in the dazzling sun, lips apart, daring him to throw over, daring him to stop you, flaunting your dominance now within the rules of the sport, expressing it in sweet function, getting back at every white slur and insult now, the way only you could do it in the fifteen years or so you played; teasing him with your intelligence, the power of your body and your baseball intuition, and revealing to him his (white) helpless-ness and stupidity. In those years I never remember you get-ting picked off, though it should have happened a dozen times each year for your boldness. But no, you knew your man, the pitcher or the catcher, too well; and they knew you knew, and the knowledge of their weakness and your strength created their ineptness, their impotent fury, their wild throws. Fifteen feet off first base, in baseball's no-man's land, you ruled the white man's roost like a black outlaw who was un-stoppable and uncatchable. You now made the laws.

"Then, in a flash, came the steal itself—moving in on sec-ond base with those subtle slides, a combination of basketball head feints and halfback hips, or the whole bag of UCLA tricks, hooking a piece of the bag the way a pitcher's curve caught a piece of the plate. No mistakes for you, Jackie; there was no room for mistakes from you in those days. No wonder the tag would come down hard, extra hard; you were not only speedy, cunning, and beating them, but you were that other color. You were Cobb with a black skin and racial spurs. And your intelligence threatened *more* than your talent alone. No, those extra-hard tags didn't matter much in those first years; with baseballs whizzing by your cranium, spikes slashing at your knees and groin, taunts filling your ears and blood, you could take an extra-hard tag coolly enough. You had done your humiliation job. . . . And remember, if Cobb matched you in anger, he was free to express it in words or with fists, whereas with you it had to be channeled into the skill, funneled into the run. . . . If the lead signified revolt, the steal easy victory, the coup of total dominance was the extra base that you picked up, that you never should have. Jackie, was there anyone in baseball history who went from first to third on an infield out as regularly as you did? Does anyone but a baseball player or fan know what this takes, in major league play? An ebony shadow in white flannels, moving into second easylike, and as soon as the shortstop or third baseman had gone through with the decision, in the instant before the gesture itself of throwing to first, there you were, shifting into high gear and heading for third and making it, beating the throw. Oh, you were a black Houdini there and in those endless rundowns, which you seemed to love to create, in order to show your powers of escape.

"'There he goes!' Burt would say. 'The Robinson Express!' And I'd shoot up to watch it pull into second with a burst of dust and as frequently as not push right up, and off again, toward third, if the baseball rolled away as little as ten feet. You made Burt forget the Nazi engineering, you made me forget the Hebrew lessons awaiting me back in Brownsville, you made believers, slowly and surely, out of the racists who came to see you get it. No, I never needed the romance of raft or river in my childhood, I had you on the bases at Ebbets Field.

"Skip years. Light years in meaning and event.

"I'm in graduate school in Palo Alto and hear that you, Burt, are living across the bay in a suburb south of Oakland. So I visit you there, and meet your beautiful Czech refugee wife, and lovely son and daughter. Seeing you again after a fifteen-year lapse is a shock. The last time I've seen you, that I recall, is just after you've returned from flying for the infant Israeli air force for a year or so, a rather gutsy act considering your World War II wounds and your great disappointment with the natives after you got to Israel. Once again I recall you in the pink flush of youth, with a mustache added for mature handsomeness. By now, however, time and circumstance have taken their toll, heavy toll. You're now shorter than I, with a bulging paunch, and the lovely waves of brown pompadour have vanished, leaving a bald pate. You wear eye-glasses. Your youth and beauty have now passed to your children; I feel a sinking feeling from having to see you this way. And though you're still flying, navigating part-time for Northwest Airlines, you're no longer the boy aviator in looks, but the chubby, substitute junior high teacher you've become. And your old (apparent) omnipotence has gone sour too; now you're just arrogant and cliché-ridden, bristling with a California conservatism. Sadder. The only thing I can admire is your obvious love for the children, especially the boy. The closeness reminds me of a past closeness, a past fineness of feeling. Otherwise, I can't wait to escape from that ordinary home and those ordinary people, and escape back to that sealed memory of my youth, permanently set in my mind.

"By about that time you, Jackie, had risen in status, no longer a guerrilla on the bases but a respectable citizen in government employ. Respectable and successful, at least on the outside. For within, diabetes was leading to growing blindness; and also, there was trouble with your son. The boy was having difficulty with you, the law, with being Jackie Robinson, Junior. You, who had pushed your way from survival to excellence, now watched this boy push his way downward, from ease to disorder and disaster; it was too much for you to deal with. Despair and cynicism came to replace anger in your system, as I sensed from your words on radio, in print. From social prejudice you had moved toward Melvillean despair.

"How much longer was it, Jackie, before your son, driven by dope, killed himself in an auto accident?

"How much longer, Burt, before your son developed a brain tumor, and died at eighteen?

"And then one evening there were Red Barber and Pee Wee Reese and a few other Dodger friends talking about you, Jackie, and showing reruns of you on the bases, the night of your sudden, premature death.

"And Burt, are you gone too? Or are you still out there somewhere, wandering in dejection, after your son's death, the breakup of your marriage? When I tried to phone or write, the line had been disconnected, the letter was returned unopened, with no forwarding address. Nothing.

"No matter. You both live on here, in transforming memory, the way you lifted my nine-year-old life, and provided the unadulterated joys and delights of boyhood heroes!

"I have made at least one error, thus far, Burt; I haven't yet had a son to take to the ball games, or one with whom to

278

build a Ralph Avenue Railroad Depot. The trouble is, Ralph Avenue means nothing now, and there are no more Robinson Expresses. And Rachel, my daughter, prefers basketball."

# 6.

# Sheyna; Rachel

HE STARED AT HIS FACE in the bathroom mirror and he couldn't quite believe it. It had been one thing to see the curious beardless face in the barber's mirror, it could have been a stranger; but there in his own apartment, the terms were for real. The skin was most smooth, remarkably smooth, in the cheeks and neck. Even the forehead seemed more wrinkle-free than ever before. He hadn't seen the exposed face in some five years or more now. He had forgotten the firmness of the chin, for example; the fullness of the cheeks; even the length of the nose (lengthier without beard all around). Cyrano Solomon? He seemed to look much younger, too; by five years or so? Or more? He couldn't keep from running his hand over his cheeks, as if he were massaging a girl's face or a baby's behind. What a remarkable difference! Youthful again! Not thirty-eight on the way to forty and fifty, but someone thirty-eight on his way to thirty-two, twenty-eight. On his way back. And the eyes too seemed now to stand out, more visible, the green gray of the eye was never more vivid and varied, filled with interesting combinations of amoeba shape and subtle color, perforated by a perfect black pupil. Undoubtedly the face now looked so much less judgmental and certain, and so much more open, light, youthful, cheery, untainted. No, not a judge now, just a new innocent in the face, a young student again, six years of beard was enough, enough; now he'd give six years of exposed face a chance. He wanted to stand there and peer and peer into this new face, study this new Solomon, so different it was and made him feel, but he had a class to teach, and so he had to depart from the mirror. Excited to be back teaching again, after his nine-day furlough that took in boyhood turf on the way back, on sudden impulse.

It took a few minutes for the change to sink in, in the

classroom. First there was indifference, as if he were *another* professor wandering into the room; then there were bewilderment and buzzing; finally came comments. "You're really one of us, beneath it all!" "Mr. Solomon, you do have a chin, after all!" "Why'd you do it? Did it happen while you were away?" Lionel answered Philip Spector, saying, "Time for a change, Phil. It's spring, can't you tell?" And when Rachel came in, late as usual, she just stared, unbelieving, and nodded toward him, as she sat down. He saluted her, in response—just as ambiguous?—and then called the attention of the class to the first story for the day, "Remembering Darkness." Wirtten by a quiet female freshman from Virginia, it evoked childhood and sense of place with a precocious resonance, and he listened to the students discuss it. Most did well, save for Jay Gould, unrepentant from "Modernist Thought and Literature," who wondered whether so "trivial a topic as childhood without symbolic meaning" could serve serious literary purpose. Fortunately, several students took care of that nicely, pointing out the work of Flannery O'Connor and Babel, among others, along the way. Next Paul Goldner described a few problems with the story he was working on and there was some pertinent questioning. "Where's the hero live, what's his room look like? And his face?" On this nice high note of workshop talk ended the section of the class devoted to student writing.

"All right, let's start on page 235," he began the final hour and a half, "or two pages into 'First Love.'" He began reading aloud from the great short story of Isaac Babel. Why should the poetry of a master go silent just because he wrote in prose (especially when that poetry was obvious even in translation)?

He tuned in at the point where a pogrom has intruded upon a small Russian village, and upon the ten-year-old protagonist's love for an older, Gentile woman. He read aloud what he had read privately a half-dozen times:

> "Captain," my father mumbled when the Cossacks came abreast of him; "captain," my father said, grasping his head in his hands and kneeling in the mud.
> "Do what I can," the officer answered, still looking straight ahead, and raising his hand in its lemon-colored chamois glove to the peak of his cap.
> Right in front of them, at the corner of Fish Street, the mob was looting and smashing up our shop, throwing out into the streets boxes filled with nails, machines and my new photo in school uniform.

280

"Look," my father said, still on his knees, "they are destroying everything dear to me. Captain, why is it?"

The officer murmured something, and again put the lemon glove to his cap.

Solomon read through the page, keeping his voice flat, letting the cruelties cut for themselves. But now they cut him too. Before Brownsville, in Russia. *His grandfather Alexander, refusing to leave his large house in Turov when a bank of Cossacks arrived, was murdered in his doorway when he wouldn't hand over his money. Papa Solomon, fifteen, hid in the woods behind the house, with the family, hearing the shots, the anti-Semitic curses, watching the looting and the house-burning.*

He turned to matters at hand. "All right, go down the page and distinguish the emotions. Just on the one page." It was not simply compactness that Babel was about, itself an achievement; but complexity, powerful complexity. That made him unique, Lionel felt, among the other major story-writers.

The students stared at him momentarily, then bent their heads to the texts, little Talmudic scholars. Groups of twos and threes shared single books, Babel being out of stock at the bookstore. ("He's not exactly Vonnegut, Professor," the clerk had answered in response to Solomon's query.)

"A little more than a page. Go ahead, name the emotions, it's not that difficult. In fact it's simple. Miriam?"

Without looking up, his old standby, the gangling girl with the superb prose style—better than Lionel's as he once told her blushing face—cited the *insult* of the father before the coolly indifferent Cossack captain.

Michael Frey, cherubic-faced, curly-haired, pointed to the ten-year-old narrator's *shame* as he is pushed to the window to witness the frightful scene.

Solomon next called on Josie Goodwin, a heavily acne'd sophomore who talked only when called upon. Josie's father was a well-known Miami psychologist who blamed his daughter for her physical condition; it came out in her autobiographical letter to him (the exercise based on the Kafka model). Now, in her slow uncertain voice, she referred to the father's plea to his boy—"Son, my little boy, . . ." a plea of bewildering *pain* and enormous *tenderness.*

*And, against his will, Solomon remembers his tyrant father during moments of powerful paternity, when Lionel was a beloved baby boy, not a growing young penis. His father holding the two-year-old in his arms by the clanging radiator pipes, saying "Sonnyboy, hot, hot," to caressing the scalp of the platinum-haired three-year-old in his lap, and rocking him, rocking him, while he sang a Russian lullaby in his native tongue with his fine baritone voice!*

Why teach if it all was so powerful and went against one's own wishes!

Bonner Johns, progeny of a Harvard professor, calmly took up the mother's shrieking *wifely frustration* and *hysteria* at her husband's pursuit of material comfort ("That cursed money!"). Did Bonner with her preppy voice ever hear such complaints in her Avon Hill house? Perhaps.

But Lionel did, now hearing that far-off plaintive voice which stabbed him. *"I have to beg for every single dollar, why, why?" she would say, his vibrant forty-year-old mother in her loose housedress wiping the table of crumbs in the steamy kitchen. The room for begging and slaps as well as roasts and* plate flanken. *In her bitter resigned voice, she pleaded, "If I have to buy a new pair of shoes once a year, why do I have to pull teeth every time?" And Papa, playing his special part, complained that they were wearing him down with their money needs! Confusing twelve-year-old Lionel, lying on the Hollywood bed in the living room, listening to every word.* Years later, he and his mother learned that during those supposedly lean years of the thirties and forties, fat money was made, and spent on girlfriends. Including Momma's friends.

The tall Blume boy, second-string forward on the basketball team, interpreted the young hero's hiccups in terms of overwhelming inarticulate *fear* and uncontrollable *humiliation* at the scene.

*The Italian kids tapping at his cheder's basement window, and Chaver Goichberg's face going red in frustration, and Lionel, seven, humiliated, his small fists pounding the desk. . . . The kids from East Flatbush, from the handsome one- and two-family brick houses, making jokes about his father's appetizing counter. . . .*

And finally the last paragraph—with Galina, the beautiful Gentile wife beloved by the hero, flipping her Chinese robe at her young adorer and telling him to stop hiccuping? ("You ought to be ashamed of yourself, my sweet boy," Galina said, smiling her mocking smile. . . . And the hero, stopping, admiring her bare arms and long braid, says, "I stared at her, in rapture.")

Lionel's own heart beat fast at the sensual mocking.

Two volunteers missed the point, circling and then missing.

282

"Sex," put forward Rachel, in her low voice from the end of the oblong table. "Sexual . . . enchantment. Fascination. In the midst of his family chaos and pain, he's turned on again by Galina. And it drives him nuts."

Solomon stared at her.

"Drives him toward illness, in fact," added Miriam demurely. She read the last sentence of the story, " 'And now, remembering those painful years, I recognize in them the seeds of the ills that torment me and the cause of my early decline.' "

*Early decline.* Lionel turned away, knowing you couldn't teach effectively this way. But in this hour for some reason he couldn't simply help himself; it was like a dream. (Wet?) He pulled himself together and posed, "Well, what do you want to say about it all? The page and a half?"

Sarah Barber said, "A frightening juxtaposition of feelings." She moved her head. "It's unbelievable, all together like that."

For the first time, Jesse Tarrant, from Roxbury via Vietnam and early marriage, spoke up. "Sex and violence, that's what I get out of it. That's what the man seems to be saying. Babel, I mean. The two seem connected. And he's right too," he added with a surprisingly embarrassed smile.

Solomon nodded. "Okay," he began, making sure to try to concentrate on useful observations for the student writers rather than his own private appreciation, or preoccupation. "Okay, there are several things to notice. One is the absence of psychological explanation. Babel avoids it. After that last paragraph, for example, he simply writes, 'Bookish small boy that I was, she seemed to me like some limelighted figure on a faraway stage.' Psychology, no. That speaks for itself, allows the reader to *feel* for himself, and works back to comment on the past confusion. That and that alone." He paused, making sure his own psychology didn't intrude, while starting up again. "Another point, a simple but important one. The number of actions taking place. Six or seven a page. Bang, bang, bang! they're thrown at us. That's what you want, as beginning writers—especially *actions*. They'll speak for themselves, don't worry. Forget about explaining, brooding, anguishing, at the beginning, and *get things done*. Let the gestures speak for themselves. It'll take a while before you can be a Babel, and *make it as rich and confusing as real life*. After all, you need a pogrom to help there: but you do have personal chaos, family madness, whathaveyou. Jesse, you with me? Tell us what life is like in Roxbury with a wife and family the hero doesn't want, while his mother works as a day laborer, while he's having affairs with blond college girls who talk to him about 'love' and he wonders what those chicks are 'rapping about' and so on?" Repeating the young man's own words about his confusing life in private conference, a life which never broke into print because of the young black's belief that he was supposed to write about racism and ideology and that his life was "boring stuff, man." "Do you see what I mean, Jess? Get it all in, pile it on!" The big gentle black boy, with the beautiful ebony skin and the expansive smile and the seething life, put his hands to his face and shook his head, in embarrassed wonderment.

"Now tell me," pursued Lionel, "what's the difference between this story of first love and Updike's say?"

Michelle Clark, from a French Canadian working-class family in Vermont, and the Catholic convent—oh how Solomon loved his students once he knew them; they were like calves and kids, lambs and colts in human dress—Michelle began speaking about the various worlds mixing in Babel's story, the pogrom, the family, the Jewish boy and "the older Christian woman." History, family, private passion . . . She used a favorite term of Solomon's, "What's at stake here . . ." This former convent girl was now a college bluestocking with a passion for Disraeli and Victorian literature.

Solomon, seeing that Michelle was on the right track and would stay there, drifted back to Babel's words. Veered off on his own track, private. With seeming spite certain phrases and words jumped out at him, as if italicized. "I see Galina, she smiles mockingly. . . . My head leaned against her lip, her hip that moved and breathed. . . ." (Lionel breathed.) "Under the lace of her deep-cut slip one could see the swelling of her white breasts squeezed downward, and the depression between them." Was Solomon reading Babel, the revolutionary Babel? Suddenly *his shrewd pal Tippy slipped in and with semi-mocking gesture, was lifting her full white breast out of Sheyna's nightgown, toward Lionel's sleepy face. "You don't know what that does to me," she whispered, exhorted, moaned, cajoled, begged, the live breast demanding. "Most men don't know. . . . But you do, I know, I've read you, you do, don't you, don't stop, don't stop, please don't stop, don't ever stop!"*

Overheated, Lionel glanced up furtively, criminally, not lifting his head just his eyes, sure they had perceived what he was up to! . . . But Michelle and Jessie were discussing fervently the various connections and emphases in the story, "violence and sex." And now Blume had entered the discussion, a marathon talker if let loose.

Solomon, safe, pressured, driven, let Blume loose, and eyed Babel again, sitting down now, His gaze this time fell on another curious paragraph, right there at the beginning of the tale, which he read, or thought he had read, a hundred times. But now, now—it concerned Galina again, that fickle beautiful irresistible "older" woman—in her late twenties, maybe?—whom the young boy Babel, is enchanted by, hooked on, addicted to:

> The whole day long she sauntered about with a meaningless smile on her moist lips, brushing against the trunks that had not yet been unpacked and the ladders for doing physical exercises strewn about the floor. Galina would bruise herself, pull her robe above her knee, and say to her husband: "Kiss baby better." The officer would bend his long legs in their narrow dragoon's trousers, in their smooth taut leather boots with spurs, and crawling across the littered floor on his knees, smile and kiss the bruised flesh, just where a little bulge rose above the garter.

Lionel stared at the paragraph, reread it slowly, his neck and cheeks burning. Babel . . . knowing this? That balding middle-aged man with the eyeglasses and sad eyes? . . . Lionel stood up, needing locomotion; he saw the framed likeness of his friend Dr. Sam Johnson askew, and went to straighten him out. Dr. Sam, why do you go askew sometimes? By design or accident? And in your dictionary, good sir, is there a proper definition of intimacy? Or perversion?

Standing there, viewing the photograph of the original engraving—pale plump cheeks and the eighteenth-century wig and black robe of this man who had his own private life—Lionel suddenly realized he was among friends here who understood: this Isaac, that Dr. Sam, that Will Shakespeare picture, his Herman. They knew, they felt, they themselves went through all this unwanted heartbreak and obsession.

He remembered words from a visit somewhere, those words in her shifted tone, a suddenly imperious tone. . . . *"Now you just come here, sweetie, just stay there. That's right now. I want you* LIKE THAT. . . . *Just do me up, my pretty baby, just the way your little sweetie has done for you. . . . Oh, that's very good, Mr. Solomon, that's* VERY NICE AND SWEET, *Mr. Solomon . . . go ahead, don't be shy now, use your good good nose there . . . yes, yes, yes. . . ."* And Solomon was returned to his new involvement in the erotic, his new definition of intimacy, in doing the girl's bold bidding. Her flaunting hints and body positions, her slightly dominating change and shifts to subservience, had driven him terribly until he couldn't distinguish fear from excitement, pleasure from fear, embarrassment from fascination, so that old emotions were scrambled and dissolved, and a whole new line of erotic circuitry had replaced it, which he still didn't understand. . . . Later, of course, his memory had haunted him, shamed him; the thought of a slave's life to that shrewd master had terrified him. Made him want to call it all off. Made him want her all the more. Want that new desire. . . . Having forgotten about it, having *warned* himself not to write about it, never to write about it, with his reputation black—and blue—already, and having succeeded in his New Literature Pledge, here was Babel, whom he thought he knew and understood, here was Babel, praised as a revolutionary, praised for his poetry, praised for his Jewish evocation—why, it wasn't fair! It wasn't! Why should Solomon be the one to read something in an author that was barely seen or publicly recognized or unconsciously suppressed? Why should he suppress what he knew to be true about sublimation, about desire? Just because he got crucified, and then ignored? Because colleagues, super sublimators, mocked him? And why should—

"Mr. Solomon? Professor Solomon?"

"Dad? Are you all right?"

Solomon looked to see the dozen faces staring. His Talmudists a jury of students now? Little Freuds and Jungs? He took a step away from the portraits.

It was very quiet and stiflingly hot.

"Your face sir, it . . . it's flushed! Are you all right?"

Lionel swallowed. "The heating in this room, it's incredible isn't it?" he stumbled. He took out cigarettes, lit one, saw all his pals and real jury on the wall—Johnson, Shakespeare, Donne. Comforts to English departments now, once upon a time provocateurs of discomfort, and souls of addiction. Sweet sweet addiction that only the heroin addicts, some gamblers and artists knew.

Solomon grinned at the huge doctor.

Finding his voice, he began, slowly at first, to talk about disparate elements in great stories, working up and off his excitement in words, rejoicing in words, realizing they were buoys in strange waters, even the crude-talking kind. "What you ought to do is to reread a story like Joyce's 'Araby,' a fine story, and compare it with Babel's 'First Love.' And I

286

think what you'll see, boys and girls, is the complex power of this rather untidy masterpiece, alongside the thinner effects of the tidier Joyce story. Beware of neat schemes, perfect endings, tight little short stories, symbolic strategies! Beware of surface tidiness, seamless form! *Look deeper.* Judge deeper. Look at underlying integrity, deeper feelings! Read stories at different ages in your life—at twenty, at thirty, at forty! Read stories again after your *life* and *experience* have in one way or another touched upon the content, and tested it out. Read—"

"Professor, excuse me, I have another class and the bell . . ." Sarah shrugged, embarrassed.

Lionel, more embarrassed, sought words. "Oh, did it? Sorry, sorry . . . What time is it, by the way?"

Five minutes after the hour, it turned out, as a mob of students burst into the classroom like a wall of water. The new professor, from French, muttered, "I do try to start my classes *on time.*"

Outside in the hall Miriam, freckle-faced and usually scooting away, came up to say, "I just wanted to say, sir, you were inspired today, or at least you inspired me, Doctor." And vanished.

*Doctor?* Lionel hadn't thought of himself as that in a long while. Or been called that. He had abandoned those titles a long time ago, to the psychologists and sociologists, who seemed to still use them. Was he one, or supposed to be one? Interesting. But where indeed had Lionel been for the past forty-five minutes? And what was happening to him? How seriously should he take this stuff? If you took it too seriously, as he had, inadvertently back there, against his will, look what it did, it embarrassed you and took you to God knows where. And in the classroom, among his students! But what did it mean then, when you tried to get students to take literature seriously? Ask them to take all that stuff to heart? . . . Take this man's elephantine lechery, that man's all-out obsession, this murderer's tortured involuted reasoning, that young boy's premature entrance into pathology? What were these young people supposed to do, emulate Humbert Humbert, Captain Ahab, Raskolnikov, Babel? Why? For what reason? To get ill and fall into early decline? He laughed and mocked the past away. Come, come.

The movements and steps of his automatic body memory had propelled him into the hallway. "Hey, Dad, where's your head today? Still out there on your trip?"

He grew alert. "On, I hope. How are you?"

"Did you have a good time? What'd you do," she smoked casually, walking with him. "Chase that girl down?"

Was she serious? He nodded. "Yeah. No luck though. But the Indians like her. I better see these students."

Rachel broke into a wide smile. "You're *kidding*. You're *laying* on it! Did you *really* do that? Oh my God, if that were *only* true. Oh, to have a man hunt me down! Seriously."

"Before you think too highly of me, not quite. Just got to a point in the book where I had to take a break, and check some things out." And her grandmother? "Actually I did run into our mutual friend for a time in Rockaway of all places. And then we parted company, on very nice terms."

She looked at him uncomprehending. "Hey, where's your briefcase?"

"What?" Taken aback, he held up his new one, for him to see as well. "Got tired of it. Needed a change. Temporarily." He turned to the three students sitting on the floor outside his office, waiting to inundate him with the aches and pains of baby stories. "I should have been a pediatrician, don't you think?"

She opened her mouth in surprise. "Is the word you're looking for gynecologist, Daddy?"

Lionel, angry, smiled.

Sweet corn is what Sheyna produced that evening, corn she had frozen from the summer before in New Hampshire and brought down here to gray Cambridgetown. Sweet corn that had never touched water and, some eight months later, was virginal fresh. And he Lionel, what had he brought? A bouquet of yellow and white chrysanthemums, and a special surprise: a wooden violin case dating back to colonial days. Which he had picked up at Hubley's, and kept for the right occasion. It resembled a child's coffin, probably because the colonial woodworker designed both. Her ginger-brown face opened into her lovely smile, and she hugged Solomon. A little girl receiving a surprise present! "I don't know if my violin will fit snugly into it, but it's *lovely*. We can put it in my study in the country. My sweet!"

As she fixed dinner, removing the corncobs from the freezer wrapping, he admired her. Admired how far she had come in their four years together. An excellent cook and Braille teacher, a fine young writer and violinist, a green-thumb gardener, and how many other small accomplishments? He loved her dearly, and even increasingly; but he felt guilty too, because he did not in the last year or so show

288

that increase as forcefully as he might have. Slept with her in fact with more of a sense of duty than from passion; and at times she sensed it, and was hurt, he knew. At first she thought it had to do with his affection, and its decline. But this was not so. If anything, the affection had increased; Sheyna was a gem. It was that he was no longer vitally interested, vitally aroused; the sense, much as he fought against it, was of a problem that had been solved—why go on solving it again and again? Not that desire or attraction were theoretical at all, no; it seemed to be the course of things. The problem seemed to be in couples, or coupling off permanently. After a year or two, pleasure, and that specially sharp stuff, lust, waned (that is, if lust, rather than a polite form of pleasure, was there in the first place). This was the hardest and saddest thing to acknowledge, this loss of desire for the one you felt great affection for. Who had orchestrated such an awful and stupid arrangement? Body adventure gone, you grew interested in other things of mutual interest—job, house, cooking, career, music, travel, children. In short, you sublimated. Couples, marriage, meant sublimation. What was there to do about it? And what was there to do about your urges, passions? Keep them in memory only, to dust off now and then? Drives in dry dock? Or forget them entirely? Pretend they never existed? Believe that age is settling in? Define aging by means of this change in usage? Or when younger, define adulthood so that it doesn't include passion?

For sharp pleasures, immediate gratification, outside of writing—which was hardly immediate, that long-range and delayed-prolonged gratification—he had on occasion gone elsewhere. Not with any regularity, the furious and chaotic regularity of his galloping twenties and early cowboy thirties. Just here and there for a night perhaps, or a few hours in the late afternoon, nothing that any ordinary (adult) soul didn't do, to get through. . . . Still, a week off like this, with strange desire alone (not consummation) made him feel somewhat guilty. (Briefly, he had told her that it had been a week of futility, so far as work was concerned. He had seen an old friend, and some sites, that was all.) Sheyna deserved the truth, but a truth which would hurt her? No. And why even bring it up, to make him feel more comfortable? Foolish. Better to make it up to her, be especially nice to her, rather than to hurt her, over *nothing*. Tippy was a wild freight train racing through, while Sheyna was his permanent comfortable home ground: was he going to leave one to hop on the runaway caboose? Not on your life. In fact didn't the one insure the permanence of the other? Didn't you want a freight of lust careening through every now and then, with you hooking on with one hand and holding on for dear life and coming in secret danger and then dropping back to land, exhausted, sated, grateful for home ground again?

He settled into his reading chair, listening to Sheyna's new record—a Dvořák quartet and his string quintet; rich beauty of the classical. Now, this guilt he felt was something he had gotten quite used to, as you got used to a low hum in your ear, or a twitching in your eyelid; you not only tolerated it, after a while you grew fond of it, it being *yours*. Moreover, he felt somehow that this guilt was the proper adult mode of behavior, at least in the West; it was a protective layer around the heart like the ozone layer in the atmosphere. This guilt was a *species guilt*, winding around and absorbed by the emotional system of new enlightened man, which kept intact his ferocity but restrained his promiscuity. Restrained, or modulated, not entirely suppressed or obliterated. Modern man had evolved this Guiltosphere, Solomon figured, listening to the charming spirit of the "American" quartet, as the best possible way of proceeding: it forced you to kindliness with your loved one and it forced you to stay on with her and at the same time it was not strong enough to strangle your basic desire to copulate with practically every strange animal of the female species. Even with happy paradox, it urged you toward this xenophobic attraction, for this desire kept alive, fed and sustained that useful nourishing guilt. Of course this scene is somewhat humorous, our good friend Solomon sitting there with his short-story collection and liquor in his lair, figuring out things in this language. But a gentleman has to make sense to himself, doesn't he? His brain has to be appeased, doesn't it? What better way then, than to take the enemy and seduce him into one's own camp—in this case, heart—instead of expending energy in useless battle? Lionel read, at home; and at home with his slight guilt-hum.

Sheyna lay on the sofa, long hair up, her dark beautiful face focused on her reading (Emma Goldman's autobiography), her music playing. In repose, a Semitic odalisque, drawn by Ingres. Ah, if there was any pain or discomfort in his guilt, it was a small price indeed for this grace and order, for his sweet corn and sweet quartets, for this peace of mind and peaceful living room. How small a price, this small hum, he reasoned then, for something of such high value, Sheyna reading, happy; a small price for not coming clean with her. No, no, he'd keep it in. No yelling or chattering while excellent music played, no crazy shenanigans while you read books, no feminist arguments while you read great women writers; in short, no stupid interruptions while you encountered the best minds and spirits of all those who had passed through and over the globe. As you got on in life, Solomon perceived, what a treat it was to enjoy the best of human life, by means of records and print, in quiet nights; while by day you enjoyed the natural life—black seeded Simpson lettuce, Burpee beefsteak tomatoes, the mustardy roquette for salads, which an eighteenth-century specialist had told him about. Lying there, Sheyna signified all this to the self-styled Oblomov. And why tangle up all this classical beauty and clarity with his confused, torturous desires? with modern chaos? Why tangle up Sheyna and Tippy?

The sound of the quartet came on, with its harmonic dissonance, and Lionel switched with satisfaction to his twenty pages of *Rebellion in the Backlands*. Reading a long book of serious value with its proportion of dullness had become as pleasurable to Solomon as writing one. Long projects pleased him more and more, especially as the fashion for brevity waxed.

And later on, in their bed, he showed his love actively, enjoying himself to be sure, but also feeling the comfort of a man who has done his duty, done it well, and feels adult and loyal because of it. He was something like a sea captain who has taken his ship, cargo and crew from home to foreign port and home again, with nothing arduous or spectacular about the journey, just the task fulfilled, on course. And in some ways this satisfactory performance was the most complete sort, Captain Solomon reflected on his pillow afterwards, the glue that held ordinary human relations together, and secured expectations. In other words, you were more of a responsible adult here in dutiful work than in those wild chases of adventure and orgasm; more societally manly here, say, than out on the wild trips of a youthful lust and selfish pleasures. Out there where you were that Brooklyn boy of fourteen and fifteen, easy with adventure, loose with impulse, hungry for fish—to catch, to fight, to win, to eat, and surely, along the way, to fuck in your fashion—a boy, a redblooded boy, a revved-up boy in T-shirt and dungarees all hunger and energy and spinning for flesh, where you were as much shark as sailorboy. Here, however, in yellow pajamas on a solid bed, you were an adult of duty and responsibility, a man of anxiety worrying about your heart pumping so furiously during an intercourse, pleased that all's well, that the prick still stands, the semen still spills, the satisfaction still comes. (Oh, you could dream, remember, fantasize!) Captain Solomon slept with his arms supporting his familiar catch, allowing Sheyna's hair to tickle his nose and her curved body to burden his hip, small infringements on his full sleep which, on most nights, he resisted. But now, it was fine, it was pleasing, so relieved was he with the return to safe port, adult harbor, civilized state.

And yet, there in the middle of a dream about a smooth swift jet landing, Lionel half-awoke with pressure from below. Sure enough, there was Sheyna—reading his earlier thoughts? sensing rigid classification? suspecting competition, perhaps?—working with her mouth to give him *more* pleasure, and fill her too. Now there was this curious aspect to the activity: Lionel *permitted* it to go on. Permitted her to please him greatly, after some months of abstaining in this precisely because he liked this too much from her, grew too attached to her because of it, attached and dependent, and hence felt guilty for not reciprocating with his own sensual ardor. Pleasing Solomon pleased Sheyna extremely; and Lionel had learned that the "safe" girl in intercourse—whereby *he* could leave off of it easily enough—was not safe at all in fellatio; *there* she was a powerhouse, and he, a weakling. With her moist loving mouth and child's delightful tongue and shrewd hands she knew his vulnerable area well, paying especial succulent attention to his testicles, his tender testicles, which she revered as if they were a bag of jewels, and she were a jewel thief, and Lionel knew, oh he had come to know it deeply and eversosweetly, that in controlled passivity this way a man was a slave, a willing slave, and there was nothing like the sheer sensual luxury it afforded; and when you trusted the other's capacity and ardor, she knowing how to play and to tease, and he how to control lengthily, why there in the bed in velvety semisleep you could think easy thoughts, pick up on odd floating details, allow your imagination to roam loosely and widely in sexual timelessness: so in this shrewd drive by his Sheyna, in which he knew he didn't have to aid or teach or ask because she knew it all so well, he could drift, and dream about what he wanted to write next (a story), about playing basketball as a teenager, about his mother when younger and his father in times of sympathy and love, about trips to Amsterdam and Jerusalem and New Orleans with this lovely girl, about the excellence of teaching and the luck of being able to do what you want. Thoughts drifted which were easy and avoided harshness and negativity: from childhood he felt his mother's fur jacket and smelled his father's special smoked salmon, and saw the fine line of his mother's young face and his father in his European handsomeness; there was the slap of a pink spaldene from punchball in the streets and Sally's singing to him in Yiddish *"Oyfen Pripetshok brent a fayerl, . . . und der rebbe lernet kleine kinderlach . . . ,* when she held him in her arms; and talcum powder mixed with vanilla, horseradish with gefilte fish; and he was a long distance from the here and now of this night when he felt an irresistible rush, as if he were being carried through a tight opening by a vast wave of water at an increasing speed; and he knew that in this soft trap of sensitivity, triggered in the midst of sweet deep sleep, there was a dependence created that was irrepressible and powerful, and yet dangerous; who was he to give up this exquisite dependence? this passive pleasure and power? This blissful cave of self-love, which she helped carve for him, and settle him within? To sleep he dove, kissing Sheyna's hair and face first, a helpless prisoner of his—and her—pleasure.

But as safe port kept him docked for the next few days, and he was not asked to go out hunting, there being no Tippy on the horizon, he felt alternately blessed and frustrated. And his ego felt injured; his ego, that nervous restless amoeba popping up and protesting at the slightest wrong word or gesture, the ego that he had developed in order to write his books and that now would wink at him mischievously like a dummy gone crazy, gone off on a life on its own, the ego that refused to be pinned down and committed like a middle-aged burgher, not satisfied with moving his life at a necessary tortoise pace, the ego that vanished wonderfully during certain books and allowed him to discover *the imaginary other,* be it male, female or monkey, the ego which he looked upon as bigger and more mysterious than the "I" of his personality because it included genes, temperament, month, climate, mood and energy—the ego was injured. So Solomon, growing sad, grew furious too. Why enter his life, stir it up, and then leave? . . . Yet, supreme self-regarder that he was, that was fine too, this stretch of boredom and safety. It was actually the perfect greenhouse for cultivating novels.

It was the third night of this boring stretch in this second week of May that a late-night telephone call came, which for the moment interrupted his boredom but which spurred him on to write a letter to the caller, in his novel.

The call came at 12:45, from Oregon, and the caller was Roberta Prossman, the ex-wife of his good friend Ben.

"Tell me Lionel the truth, were you and Ben lovers when you were together at Stanford? Come on, it's years later, you can come clean."

"No, Roberta, actually we weren't," Lionel responded.

"Well then what was wrong with him? Why wouldn't he make out with me? No one was that uptight! . . . He's a terrified guy you know."

Well, maybe he wasn't interested in you, Bobby, Lionel thought privately.

"He's pretty sick. I mean most of the guys are, who work in the academy. Uptight and sick as hell. Ben's definitely homosexual, and he ought to come out of the closet before he dies. And I think he'll make David that way too. Is he queer yet?"

"No, not that I see, Roberta," Solomon said to the tortured girl.

"He's a bad kid you know," she pointed out about her son, sixteen. "He's been fucked up for years now. God knows what he'll be like when he grows up; *if* he ever does."

Lionel wondered what the poor woman was high on this time, speed, liquor, cocaine?

"How's your last book doing, kid? I tried to get it at the local library here but they never heard of it. Maybe it's too dirty for Eugene?"

"Probably," said Lionel.

"Why do you write those books? Are you hung up that way? That's all right, we're all hung up in one way or another. You're not a bad guy though Solly. You were kind to me. I'll always remember that. You and Marie, you two were the kind ones when I was down and out. I'll never forget that. Not like my fucked-up husband. He fucked me over pretty good you know."

Twenty more minutes of stored-up resentment which Solomon put up with before he managed to get off. He left the telephone off the hook, for he knew from past experience that she might very well call him back again, at 3, 4, 5 A.M. Calls into the night, to whomever would listen, by this lonely ripped-up creature. He lay there, in his bed, and saw her years ago in her small unkempt kitchen, a dancer's leotard and ponytail, hustling to feed the family—and him, Lionel—before racing off to her modern dance class. Lionel smoked, felt a rush of sympathy for her, and began talking.

"Roberta, are you for real or are you mythological? Not fictional, but mythological? In this past decade of madness,

294

have you been for real, or have you come to me out of some Greek myth?

"Who or what could have saved you: a great psychiatrist? A movie of your life? The right man? A son who lived with you, not with the father? (Or a daughter who *didn't* live with you?) Flying around in jet planes possibly? Certainly what hasn't helped have been the psychiatrists, the Synanons, the mental hospitals, the halfway houses, the jails, the encounter groups, the relationships, the air, the West Coast, the liquor, the drugs, the men (and the women), the draw of luck over the past fifteen years or so. Would it have been the same in New York, where you grew up, or in some quiet New England town of a hundred years ago? Would you have been bombarded so ferociously and steadily?

"Do the phone calls heal you in some way, Bobbie? I know that once you get on a calling streak, you don't stop—calling ex-husband, ex-son, mother, brother, sister-in-law and brother-in-law, distant friend and close enemy, whomever else you know or knew, including me, whom you haven't seen for a dozen years. Mostly you call after you've left a depression and are on a high, a chemical high if you can get it. There you are, ringing up the world in the middle of the night to protest, to scream *to exist*; okay, that's fair enough. You're Roberta Prossman, and you're sick and wounded and you can't die but you can't get better either, and anybody who has a telephone or human ear in America, especially those who once knew you, had better take heed. You're a female Philoctetes, exiled on that island called Self, wounded and festering with guilt, with a telephone for a bow.

"Do you know what it's like to be called at 4 A.M. by a woman who was once a sane functioning person, a woman who was a reasonable mother and semiprofessional dancer, and now, at forty, she says, 'Hiya kid, remember me? Well I want you to know that I've just been balling five black guys and it's far out. Why didn't I do this before?' She laughs, adding, 'I think I've tired them out, they're all asleep now, on the floors and chairs around here. Why can't you white guys do as well? Like it would have saved my marriage if I had tried this earlier!' This, in the middle of the night, makes me wonder where I am, on what planet and what do the words mean? Instead I concentrate on the woman of my eye's memory: thirtyish Roberta, dark, slim, with a dancer's muscular legs and waist-length hair and a sense of humor, and a delight in her son three, blond and beautiful, and daughter eight, freckled and funny. Was that woman so *dead*? Is this one *alive*? Is gang-banging preferable to conjugal frustration? Perhaps. Is incest-talk better than love and connection? Perhaps. Does a madness like yours help matters any—lessen the guilt, soften the anger, make living more tolerable somehow? Perhaps.

"I don't quite know how to put this, Roberta, but why is it that what happens in life, when put into fiction, can sound 'in poor taste' and be near-impossible to write about? Or am I mistaken? Is it that the details of real pain are very hard to read about, most unpleasant, especially when they find a modern form? For example, the suicide of daughter Lotte at sixteen may be easier to take than the note she leaves behind, 'Fuck you, Mom.' And easier to take, in many respects, than the phone calls later on to a son three thousand miles away, in which you spend ten minutes making obscene suggestions to your own ten-year-old? Or a few years later, when he can understand more, asking him if the father has been obscene with him? (Why is it that even here I use euphemism, and don't use fellatio, or the real 'blowjob'? Why be polite when the REAL often is so impolite?) Those phone calls strike me as chillingly tragic as anything I've ever heard; as do the conversations with Lotte, in her last frantic year or so, that you told me about. You see, Roberta, if I match you up with some mythical figures like Niobe or Medea, or even heroines from literature, their stories seem old-fashioned polite.

"And if no one can heal you, can't society have a way of putting you out of your misery? Can't an advanced society be as kindly to persons as it is to horses and other wounded animals?

"Certainly your performance in pain and self-torture, not to mention your assaults on others, has been an inimitable act. It puts to shame most self-torturers in the history of that peculiar genre. After all, every time you've jumped beneath Anna's train, or taken Emma's poison—four, five times now?—you've come away merely wounded and bleeding, but *alive*, not dead, as you had wished. (Or didn't wish?) Was that fair of fate? Sometimes you seem to represent all the ways modern life can torture and maim, the end of calmness and sanity, perpetual excess and anger, no death or cure. Just codeine, speed, heroin and barbiturates to dull the pain, or gang-bangs and pluralistic obscenities to express it. And for respite, telephone calls around the world to anyone who'll listen; and for the first time or two, who won't? For those who have never experienced the fine line between the deeply troubled and the truly mad, can I give them your phone number?"

Lionel paused, drank apple juice.

"I want you to know that your son, Davie, seems like any other boy, playing basketball and baseball and excelling at swimming, dating girls, kidding around; actually, a little bit more sane and gentle than most, I'd say. And when he talks to you, he shows enormous patience and maturity, trying to calm you down, trying not to cut you off, trying to keep some sort of contact with you. He impresses me, moves me. Where are the full consequences of his relation with you? Will they emerge at some later date? What I see now are two people who have known each other a lifetime ago, and, like a couple lying in the sand and then getting up, they leave an unique impression. From the outside it may look grotesque, and unlivable; but you see, there it is, theirs, and it, they, survive somehow. (Of course it helps that Lotte was not particularly close to him, and grew up a continent away.) Life seems to hide within, to camouflage, many such strange impressions, odd souls.

"Roberta, sometimes I feel . . . heartbroken and want to do something for you, but can't, can't even let you know about it, out of fear that you won't let me alone, sensing sympathy, wanting it and not wanting it! What sort of life is this, please tell me . . . what sort of civilized savages are we? . . . are we better off with medicine men and sand paintings and animal totems? . . . A curse on trying to think for oneself! A curse on complicated life! A curse on useless sympathies!"

Lionel, suffocating now, rose up from his vision, hating it! He cracked the back of his head on the bedstead and accepted the pain with quiet approval. Massaged it, until it eased. Jotted down some notes. Would have to cut down on the Niobe and Medea analogy. Better save that for a short story. Thought of other, dirtier doings; save them too. Remembered freckled Lotte, at twelve or so, already frantic when he visited them briefly in Los Angeles. Saw Dave, who lived in the area, in his high school pool, doing his endless laps of butterfly and crawl stroke. Exhausted, Solomon tried to sleep. When it wouldn't come, he was on the verge of calling someone, maybe Ben, the ex-husband, when he realized the irony. He took a sleeping pill instead and was somewhat glad that it barely took, and he had to wait out the few hours before sleep came.

While shaving the next morning, which he did exultingly

now, after years of abstinence, he thought about the writing class. Perhaps he'd throw a change of pace today and use the *Times* article on the female movie star who had just had a hit in a recent detective movie, and was now being interviewed? (Couldn't he use Roberta's life? Play the tapes of her telephone calls, to broaden *perspective?* Show them a slice of real-life tragedy, not ancient literature's?) A contemporary story: a banal actress with interesting facts in her real life playing a banal girl in a movie which was itself a cheapened version of an interesting real-life Los Angeles case. If New Guinea primitives thought they were involved in magic mystery, and deception, what about citizens in media America? *Who was who* in America? He'd show the class the interesting biography of the real girl, measuring it against the puerility of her opinions on roles, and suggest how the authentic story was the real girl hidden behind the tinsel and mannequin clichés. What he wouldn't make mention of, he knew as he knotted his wool tie, was the powerful resemblance between the movie actress in her thirties garb and his own mother at the same time. It was this picture of her, this resemblance to the photo of his mother in his desk, which had held his attention: the haunting stark face, the fiercely accentuated lips and eyes, the sharp nose and cut hair of a Roman empress—a face of stylized black and white beauty. Anyway, he'd keep this to himself. In the classroom you gave only so much truth; more than that was confusing to undergraduates. For students you wanted clarity, simplicity, repetition; for literature you saved your originality, obsessions, paradoxes. Suddenly late, he realized (as always), he began collecting and stuffing student papers in the thin briefcase (that fucking thief Tippy!—except that it was *he* who had left the case on the plane; where was *she*?); finding his Melville texts and notes for the other class; swearing at his disorganization and pleading with himself to change, he rushed out. Hardly downstairs when he remembered a book he needed, raced up and galloped back down, and, sweating and nervous, sure he had forgotten *something*, he settled into his car.

There, driving, with his morning work done, a draft ready for tomorrow's rewrite (the real satisfaction), with his class material read, he felt uplifted. Turned his radio on, in business again within the dull routine that shielded him from the laser bolts of emotion-intensity and life-confusion-cycles, and at the same time provided the perfect tender cocoon for his imagined characters and *their* intense predicaments and temperaments. Those which he was most at home with.

And in the classroom, seeing the young faces around the room, talking about books and writers, he was in the right saddle, the intellectual and literary saddle, and he rode easily, breathed well, looked fine (he thought). When he was going good this way, teaching provided a sustained high that grew and grew as the hour went on. An innocent or silly question could set him going extemporaneously, a sport he did nicely. It was near the outset of the class on *Billy Budd,* an oversimple tale, when two things occurred to set his adrenalin flowing. The first was a question about Melville himself, which would lead into the author's use of actual facts and personal experiences in his novels. The second occurrence was the late entrance into the classroom of three students, one familiar, the other pair—girls—not. They arrived as the inquiry about biography was posed—awkwardly, as many authentic student questions are put—and what he remembered noticing was the attempt at a furtive, anonymous entrance. It was only as he talked on, got warmed up, that he noticed a resemblance in one of the newcomers to an old buddy, and somewhat later, that it was not a resemblance but the real thing, the buddy herself. His trim white whale had resurfaced, with a girlfriend it seemed, in his classroom. To spout what?

Curiously enough, instead of going rubbery and weak as he had *imagined,* he went determined and strong in her presence, gazing at first out at the hilly campus and then taking up a firm position behind the lectern at the table. Odd the way college classrooms were open to one and all, ex-wives, girlfriends, daughters, reporters, agents, unlike the offices and shops of the rest of the world. You were free to browse and look in on teachers, the way you couldn't at bank managers or army officers, tailors or coaches. Solomon, paranoid anyway, constructed barbed-wire doors, with guards, around his classrooms, as he answered Debbie Rogerson's query. "Yes, I think the question not at all irrelevant, but actually useful and interesting, if I may interpret it more fully. For I think it's precisely the pure *fantasy* element here in *Billy Budd,* alongside the strict *moral wish,* that impairs the story, while in other works, notably 'Bartleby the Scrivener' and *Moby Dick,* Melville forgets the desire for the millennium, the wish to be a *good* man, abandons morals altogether and instead turns to his experience and his life-facts, for his fiction. Ladies and gentlemen," he always used this opening when he wished to introduce strong or impious points, "do you realize what it was like after that real whaling ship, the S.S. *Essex*, after sailing from Nantucket in 1819 and being on the sea for a whole year, how, on a calm sunny day was suddenly and for no apparent reason struck twice head on by a bull whale, a spermaceti, then filled with water and sank, leaving her twenty sailors to fight for their lives aboard three open whaleboats in the broad Pacific? Reflect. Consider some of this, read the whole account here in Olson's book"—and he held up Charles Olson's paperback on Melville, with the fine opening account of the actual event, which Solomon would now paraphrase. "These twenty men had bread, water and several Galápagos turtles aboard their whaleboats and, ironically, were a short distance from Tahiti; but ignorant of the natives there, they were afraid of cannibalism, and so headed for South America, about two thousand miles away. An error, you might say. Now just listen my friends and judge which is a more unpleasant version, the actual facts of the case or Mr. Melville's fictional version. And as you do, consider if you would what would have happened had Melville been a more accurate historian and less of a fictioneer; if you had gotten the facts without any regard for . . . 'reader's feelings.' And remember too if you would that for what he *did* put in, soft as that was, he was looked upon by many of the reviewers as barbaric, primitive and sensational, fascinated with the grosser aspects of human life! To rephrase the author, 'Ah, novels! Ah, Herman!' "

A hand went up, but Solomon went on, not acknowledging it, not acknowledging the other girl's presence, not looking at his daughter, not—

"The sailors made their first mistake during the week when, in order to make their supply of bread last, they ate bread which had been soaked by salt-water brine, and then, to alleviate their incredible thirst, they slaughtered the turtles for their blood. But the sight of this revolted their stomachs. And soon, in the first weeks of December, their lips began to crack and swell, and a glutinous saliva began to collect in their mouths, intolerable to the taste." Pausing, he noted two girls making nauseated faces. "Presently, friends, their bodies began to waste away"—said slowly so the well-fed pink-cheeked faces got an inkling of hunger and hell—"so that they had to assist each other in performing the body's weaker functions. Please picture this scene in Melville's text appearing before a proper nineteenth-century American audience. Soon, barnacles collected on the boats' bottoms, and they ripped them off for food. Further, it is reported that flying

300

fish hit their sails, fell into their ships, and were swallowed raw. This was the way they ate . . . and wasted.

"Let me skip a bit. They came upon a small island, found some water there after a frantic search, and decided that all of them could not survive on the tiny island, so that seventeen of them put out to sea again. Now the three who remained discovered right off eight skeletons in one of the caves they took shelter in, as if they had lain down there to die together; these three survived this opening omen by eating the meat of a blackbird that roosted in the trees there, and a sort of peppergrass found in the crevices of the rocks, and survived to tell about it, amazingly enough.

"The voyagers at sea had a harder time of it, and a lower rate of survival. Of the seventeen who set out for land again, just six managed to survive; and their means of survival may have been a harsher sentence than death itself. For example, can you imagine what it was like to be one of four men on a raft at sea, exhausted and starving, and forced to draw straws to see who will be killed, and who will do the killing, so that the other two shall eat and live? Do you follow me friends? Which is what happened when Mr. Owen Coffin, a seventeen-year-old cabin boy serving on his first voyage out, lost, and it became the duty of Charles Ramsdale to *shoot him*. Stephanie, look at your two friends over there, go ahead, that's it, and picture either being shot by Jake Garber, or forced to shoot him." The girl moved her head in disbelief. "Anyway, Mr. Ramsdale shot the young man, and he, the captain and another sailor *lived* by eating him. This occurred on February 1, 1821, and on the eleventh, Ray did himself in, and he was eaten."

Susan Demery began to cough violently, and quickly left the room.

Lionel gripped the wooden lectern harder, and peered intently at the stunned faces, getting warmed up by this reality, his narrative, with the help of his Olson text. "On another boat it was not until February 8 or thereabouts when Isaac Cole died in convulsions that the First Mate, Owen Chase, proposed to his two men, Benjamin Lawrence and Thomas . . . Nickerson, that they eat of their own flesh. And they did it this way: they separated the limbs from the body, cut all the flesh from the bones, then opened the body and removed the heart"—a scream and a protest—"and closed the body as well as they could and dropped it in the sea.

"They then drank of the heart and ate it. They ate a few pieces of the flesh—"

"That's gross!" cried out Jeffrey Gold. "Why are you doing this?" He stood up, this lawyer-to-be, beckoning Debbie R., and commenting, "You're just vulgar, Professor Solomon. *Vulgar and irresponsible*. This is supposed to be a literature class, not biology or pornography!" He and his girlfriend left, joined by another coed.

Solomon, somewhat surprised, was also hurt that he hadn't taught them better during the term. Nevertheless, he proceeded full steam ahead with his story, his mission, disregarding (or spurred on by?) impediments to frank truth in the bodies of daughters, boyfriends, mysterious girlfriends and their sidekicks, shocked young boys and girls who were used to *comfortable* literature, *comfortable* lives, *pleasing* professors—

"Ate a few pieces of the flesh, and hung the rest, cut in thin strips, to dry in the sun. The next day they made a fire, as the captain had, and roasted some to serve the following day. Except that they found out the next morning that the flesh in the sun had spoiled, turned green—" two students made loud moaning sounds, approaching nausea, yet a few others had tuned out completely and seemed to be writing letters or finishing up homework. Florence Murphy, a lively Dorchester girl, suddenly interrupted, standing: "Why are you preaching at us like this, Professor Solomon?" Her pretty Catholic face was strained. "It's . . . it's like being in church on Sundays and listening to damnation stories! It's *awful!*" She burst into tears, standing there, lips drooping, and Solomon was moved; but he only stared at her, said nothing, and remained possessed—aware of his deeper debt, to Melville, to truth, *perhaps to this secret intruder come back to see him perform (and crushed? NO!)*—Father Solomon checked his text for facts, and pressed forward, to the remaining transfixed students, leaving Florence to sink back in her seat, trembling. "So they made another fire to prevent its being totally lost, and ate that flesh for the next five days, saving their bread. They ate it in small pieces with salt water, slowly regaining their strength, so that by the fourteenth they were able to take up their oars again, however feebly, and make some attempt at guiding their boat. By the fifteenth the flesh was all eaten and they had left only the last of the bread, and a few sea biscuits. Their limbs by this time had swelled during the last few days and began to pain them severely. They judged they had about three or four hundred miles to go yet. On about the eighteenth, Nickerson, who was seventeen, bailed the boat, lay down, drew up a piece of canvas over him, and said that he wished to die immediately. On the nineteenth at 7 A.M. Lawrence saw a sail seven miles off, and with fitting justice, all of these men, these survivors of the sea and of cannibalism, lived to very old ages: Nickerson, Ramsdale and Chase into their seventies, Lawrence till he was eighty, and the captain Pollard, thirty-one at the time, until the age of eighty-one."

Solomon paused and drank from his glass of water. Perspiration pouring down the back of his neck, he gazed at the frozen survivors—a dozen or so—who had come along with him. He realized his fingers were sore from his intense grip, and he relaxed his hold on the wooden podium when he took it up again.

"Now can you imagine, boys and girls, if Mr. Melville had had a scene in which Queequeg is forced to kill Mr. Starbuck and partake of his flesh? What his audience and critics would have said? Look what they had already said, about *Moby Dick*, from the *Athenaeum* in 1851," and Lionel, adjusting his spectacles, read:

> Our author must be henceforth numbered in the company of the incorrigibles who occasionally tantalize us with indications of genius, while they constantly summon us to endure monstrosities, carelessnesses, and other such harassing manifestations of bad taste as daring or disordered ingenuity can devise.

And this last sentence, boys and girls:

> Mr. Melville has to thank only himself if his horrors and his heroics are flung aside by the general reader, as so much trash belonging to the worst school of Bedlam literature,—since he seems not so much unable to learn as disdainful of learning the craft of an artist.

Far more devastating words than 'Bedlam literature' and 'bad taste' might have been used if Melville had put in the factual truth. Or supposing Ishmael had recorded a scene in which he had witnessed Captain Ahab and Stubbs killing Tashtego and Queequeg, and then eating their flesh—what they would have made of poor Melville those days? Or these days? Do you see how quickly cannibalism would have been transformed into colonialism? A barbaric writer then, for the nineteenth-century white civilized audience, a racist writer now for the ever alert politicized critics of today. No, no, Melville couldn't do it. All these unpleasant but true facts

303

had to be left out, boys and girls, just as he had to leave out most of the real but bizarre facts of his experiences in the South Pacific. For can you imagine what the reaction would have been of an enlightened civilized God-fearing audience to cannibalism, headshrinking, freer sexual mores, and whatever other sacred and profane rites of the primitives that he had witnessed? Or perhaps taken part in? No, no, no. Why so simple a thing as the open promiscuity encouraged by the Marquesans would have immediately made Melville's books Strictly Forbidden, Unpublishable, on the Index; not to mention Off Limits to all of his own family and friends." Solomon paused, perspiring, brushed his brow with his forearm, massaged his neck in a yoga roll. Smiled benevolently, with good wishes. "Friends, y-o-u c-a-n-'t d-o i-t t-o-d-a-y, o-n-e h-u-n-d-r-e-d y-e-a-r-s l-a-t-e-r," poor Lionel pounded lightly the slanted wooden top, "in our so called advanced society. You must save those deeper truths for anthropology texts, which are safely academic and unread, or you will be branded perverse, vulgar and a member of the Sensational School. Oh, how those schools change names through the years, but keep the same faculty and standards." He drank water, loving its coolness. "For the kind of human variety and cultural invention and daily habits of another society that went on before Melville's eyes or within his hearing, or even involving himself, all these were simply too awful, too impious, too 'vulgar' and 'irresponsible' for his audience—although it was real, ladies and gentlemen, *very* real. So that Melville was never again the same man after writing his self-proclaimed 'wicked' book. But no wonder he felt 'spotless as a lamb,' as he wrote Hawthorne, since the *real* wickedness and *real* horror and *real* blasphemy of what he saw he had *kept within him*, censored out of the text, removed from print, perhaps from his consciousness." Solomon looked around at the transfixed faces, these converted pupils and votaries, these surviving voyagers. In a softer voice he inquired, "But then what does an author do with his *deeper*, or 'impious' experiences? Where does the honest and serious writer put all that? I don't know, I'm afraid I don't know." He craned his neck, and slowly his vision brightened as he saw the hilly campus outside, and felt himself emerging from his own pit of empathy. That special girl back there stared fixedly, with devotion, belief? *Yes, yes, she understood, didn't she?!* And Rachel, she too was attentive, peaceful. But what did that mean? "I don't quite know, my friends, except that I'm sure that a good many authors take their most special and powerful experiences right down to their graves with them, and lie down with the experiences intact to put them to rest under wood and dirt. To be read by the worms, perhaps. Too bad. And that what you get in the fiction is more or less an approximation, a *polite* approximation of the horror, or what you might call a *literary* approximation, a special kind of euphemism. Instead of headshrinking, or a bizarre primitive ritual, perhaps an emaciated young man who wills his death by saying five words. Instead of a maddened desire for Marquesan orgy and a life of regular promiscuity, a metaphysical desire for something called Goodness. Instead of a powerful and perverse experience with real men and women, a furious perverse encounter with a whale. With the end always, please notice, destructiveness; not survival or triumph, but destructiveness. Strange, since Herman survived the real savages rather well, didn't he? The Manhattan and Massachusetts savages less well, it appears." Lionel shrugged, waiting for relief. "I don't quite know. But I think that is why it is essential to read writers like Rabelais, Baudelaire, Céline—interestingly enough, the French gave us the Enlightenment as well—to open one's perspective on the real and possible in this world." Another Frenchman came to mind, but he'd keep the Marquis de Sade to himself. "In fact it would have been wonderfully therapeutic for Mr. Melville himself to have read them, if that were possible, though I don't think their influence and example would have won out over publisher and reading audience and respectable criticism and literature of genteel virginal America of 1850; nor would European literature of intimacy and frankness have won out over persons like the author's wife, Miss Elizabeth Shaw, daughter of the Chief Justice, or Nathaniel Hawthorne, the author's eminently respectable friend, and devout superego. Mr. Hawthorne was not quite up to his friend's . . . wayward experiences, as we can see from his coolness to Melville in England a year or two later. No, no, the Marquesas, Tahiti and Hawaii, with their strange life of exotic passions and easy raptures were no match for New England proprieties and self-righteous conduct and family respectabilities. Boys and girls," the preacher leaned forward, leaving the man exhausted but wishing to sum up, to leave this pit of misery he had flung them all into, "the truth still is no match for the pressures of society, or the politeness of literature, or the burden of friends or family, or, alas, the final betrayer, the civilized ego of the writer himself. All these factors come together like a school of piranhas smelling out a prospective

305

client; and trying to swim free to safety, to a share of truth say, you are soon enough easy prey for being eaten alive and digested whole, perhaps while watching it."

At the end here he himself had weakened, and half-lay upon the lectern, stretched out, as exhausted as a cadaver.

Twenty, thirty, sixty seconds passed; one, two, three minutes—in which nothing happened, no one moved or talked, it was just still, with sounds of a secretary typing drifting in, a teacher speaking in a far-off room, a bell ringing. Then nothing again, but the silence in the class. What was happening, or, what had happened? The students and the teacher didn't seem to know. Odd. Odd.

At last, students from the next class suddenly began marching in, obviously annoyed, reminding everyone of the ordinary class routine, and dissolving that eerie hour of stunned belief (or disbelief) and unusual pedagogy.

Solomon himself was so out of it that by the time he looked up for his friend there was no sign of her. Gone. At another time he would have been crushed; now he paid little mind; his postoperative fog was so severe. Rachel said something to him about his new beardless state, but he paid it no mind either, nodding. He didn't remember packing up, talking with anyone, walking out, driving back to Cambridge; all he knew was that he was out on the street, with the bright shops and dressed-up pedestrians and students passing like theater people, and the whole thing was like playing ten hours of straight chess, and then emerging into the streets to see the citizens moving around jerkily like bishops, knights and queens gone wild. Only now they were not only breaking the rules of the game, they appeared to be looking at him strangely. Chin high, briefcase under arm, Solomon proceeded like a man with errands in mind, a guilty spy in professorial disguise.

*Now Doctor Lirič, why this performance? For whose benefit? Did it result from that innocent student query and Lionel's closer relationship with the text, or was it inspired by the presence of the cunning visitor? Apart from "excessive," was the performance humiliating and comic, or, rather, brilliant and incisive? "Vulgar and irresponsible," as Jeff Gold claimed, or truthful and responsible? Or both? Or, did the secret cunning appearance of the girl spur him on to where he realized that he had actually been toying with the students (that term and other terms) not really conveying to them the uncomfortable truths of literature? In short, did the test posed by the girl actually spur him on to an hour of teaching force, one of those rare lessons not to be forgotten, a kind of sustained literary orgasm which, in the past, he had been too inhibited to shoot for? Did this Tippy tempt him to be bigger than his usual routine, stronger than his usual teaching boundaries, and by means of anger or spite, seek extreme truth? Possible. Now as he walked in Cambridge, he felt most odd, knowing he had made a spectacle of himself, one that would be passed on and gossiped about, not the first time that Solomon's classes had verged on the obsessional side, but perhaps, the first time he had gone whole hog. Literature and life didn't balance all that well, like a child's seesaw. In fact, the more you took them seriously as a duo, the more difficult each became, the more of an adversary each became to the other. Perhaps the most disconcerting thing was that if it was a performance, it was both unrehearsed and unwanted, and it was another Solomon out there acting. A Solomon vulnerable, bruised, angry, vigorous, asocial, exposed, out of control. An Id at the controls. Was that literary too, the way Lionel had imagined it years ago? In any case he felt embarrassed, as if a mere paperback had been his cover, not only for nakedness, but also, for his pedagogic erection.*

Full alertness for Lionel started again with taste, lemony, as he emerged from the yogurt shop on Brattle Street, licking his yogurt cone. *She* was standing there, eyeing him, with a friend. The day was hazy.

He had forgotten what a spectacular creature she was. Like a great racehorse that has been set down on the city street. His heart beating fast, he asked, "What do you want?"

"Your bag." Between her long legs on the sidewalk was his small Gladstone. "You forgot it."

He reddened, took two steps toward it.

"Shall I help you?" She wore a suede skirt, longish, and a blouse and a leathery vest. Stood alongside Corcoran's window.

"I'll manage." But as he bent down to fit his slender teaching briefcase into the leather bag, it was necessary after all for her to hold the cone, which she did.

"This is Ursula," Tippy introduced.

Settling the one case into the bulky bag, and leaving it unzipped, Lionel gazed up at the shorter girl with jet-black hair and dark skin, lit up by a merry smile. She wore white bell-bottoms, a gay striped polo shirt, and carried an airlines bag.

"A friend from Peru." Tippy explained.

He stood up from his crouched position, embarrassed.

Took back the cone, and held it up in gratitude to Tippy. To the visitor, he said, "Enjoy the natives."

Tippy, tucking one booted leg up to the casement of the store window, asked, "Are all your classes like that one? As hot?"

Lionel felt easy, here on his own ground, the sun bright enough to keep his sunglasses on. As did the girls. "A special performance for you and your friend," he smiled good-naturedly. "Take her to see the Peabody, why don't you?" he flourished, remembering to enunciate clearly for the foreigner, "they have *authentic Indian artifacts*."

He tried a broken Spanish and the girl laughed, saying, "I speak English, thank you."

Lionel was slightly surprised that Tippy didn't pick up on his reference, and said, "I suppose you heard of my trip by now. Congratulations. I didn't know you were so well known. Or did so much."

She half-smiled. "I told you a long time ago, Lionel, that I don't lie—unless I have to."

Like me, he thought.

She reached forward and ran her hand across his cheek. "You see, you're *young* again."

He tipped his suede hat, from Arizona, and bid the girls good-day. God, it felt good to be in control that way! To leave off your addiction once and for all! Quickly he beat the traffic across the street, and inside the corner newspaper store, gazed at the magazines. This "liberal" one a conservative disgrace, that radical one a literary disgrace, the next, pure New York graffiti, and settled on a staid *Atlantic* and peppery *Crimson*. Ten feet away, however, at the nude magazines and pornographic pulp, his two friends were having a marvelous teenage time, turning pages and giggling. But why not, he had had a marvelous time there too, at times. (But all in fun? he wondered.)

He paid at the register, marched out, and sensed that they were following him. Yes, *following* him! He couldn't get over that. Like the movies. He thought, So you want to play children's games? Okay, have it your way.

He walked down the street, curving around Brattle. In the large Paperback Booksmith, he looked at the new titles, trying to remember if he wanted anything? On the sale table, he noted a Central American archaeology book, reduced to $3.95, with great photographs of Quetzalcoatl pyramids and totems. Nearby a remaindered copy of his own *Each According to His Needs,* selling for a buck. A reminder of its smashing failure at the book club. Lionel burned! He purchased the archaeology book and left.

On the street he sensed they were there too, this team of tall blond cool Quixote and her dark short sidekick Sancho Panza, from Peru via Braniff. A feeling of oddness, fear, and excitement mingled in him in the late spring afternoon.

At the record shop on Boylston he remembered the Kodály cello piece for Sheyna, and asked for it. A stocky assistant in Beethoven T-shirt checked the Schwann catalogue. Rock music poured from giant hanging speakers, and idols of rock stared down from wall posters, à la Orwell; come 1984, Big Brother will have sold a few million disks in America. Solomon, reading the dust jacket of the Archduke Trio, noted the two girls up the aisles, doing little rock steps. Ursula, in her tight bells moved a prominent backside, while lengthy zebra Tippy gyrated her shoulders and snapped her fingers with mocking exaggeration. Lionel gazed in furtive fascination, beneath record jacket, under the guise of classical admirer.

"I was going to say you lucked out," said the fellow, "but actually you lucked in. I have Starker doing the Kodály sonata in an incredible set of cellists. Look, it's seven bucks for three records, including the *only version* in print!"

Lionel, lucking in, thanked the young man, took the Great Cellists box with the two cellos on the cover, and walked straight ahead, vision restrained to the register.

Outside again in the refreshing air, he suddenly moved faster and crossed kitty-corner, skirting through the maze of honking cars like a halfback avoiding linemen—his image—and ducking quickly into the crowded Coop. He took the elevator up to the second floor, walked the length and back the down staircase. Out of breath, he glanced around, saw that he had shaken his tails, smiled, and thought, "Mr. Kojak, I underestimated your profession." And headed toward shoes.

He sat down in the small alcove, content, and waited for service.

After a few minutes, in which he had been passed over twice by a salesgirl, he grew impatient.

Finally the girl, wearing denim shirt and dungarees, slouched over. "Yeah?"

Lionel, slightly taken aback, mumbled, "Uh some boots please."

The girl was smoking. "What kind?"

Lionel didn't quite know. "I'm not sure. I thought you—"

"For hiking, riding or what, mister?"

"For walking, actually."

309

"Knee or calf length?" She turned away to call out to someone in shirts, leaving Solomon sitting.

He grew more irritable and nervous. Asked, "What happened to the old Italian fellow who used to work here, miss?"

It was the wrong thing to say, he saw immediately. The girl shot him a look of disdain and said, "Did ya make up yer mind yet?"

He pleaded with himself to stay calm. "May I see both?"

The girl picked up a steel foot measure—to whack him with?—and told Lionel to remove his right shoe. He did that, and winced as she squeezed his big toe while taking his measurement. Saying nothing she stood and walked to the back.

Lionel's heart pounded, and he cautioned himself. THE SURGEON GENERAL WARNS YOU, LIONEL SOLOMON, NEVER TO GO SHOPPING WHEN YOU ARE ALONE OR SUPPOSED TO BE WRITING. Choosing a pair of shoes, a hat or even a baseball glove for Lionel like figuring out a plumbing problem; it was hopeless. And with the new corps of dissidents who had entered the shops and services, offering disdain and ignorance instead of the old aid and knowledge, it made matters far worse. He tried to console himself with his clever childish escape from his tails, pretty tails.

The girl returned with two boxes, and told him to try them out.

He, who loved following orders, or giving them, labored into a pair by himself, and walked around the alcove. "Well, this pinches a little at the instep."

Attending to something else, she pointed to the other pair. He asked if it would always be this hard just to get into them? She looked at him, her look saying, "Are you for real, mister?"

He didn't push it. He got into the second boot, again by himself, and walked about on the carpet. Immediately he felt taller from the firm heel, and realized why Marlboro Men looked as if they were different from ordinary souls. Boldly he marched out all the way to the end of shirts, wishing he had a lasso and steer at hand! Oh if those friendly assassins could see him now!

Back with the salesgirl, he said, "They seem okay, except . . ." he was afraid to say it, *afraid*, but the boots cost over *forty-five* bucks, he was allowed a question for that price, right?—"except they seem awfully narrow down front, and I have trouble with my little toes. The pinky toes."

The girl blew out her smoke slowly. "The pinky toes, eh?"

She fixed him with a merciless sardonic look, and didn't move as the smoke challenged him.

Solomon swam with rage. He'd tell the head of the shoe department, the Coop president!

Helpless, he stared at the girl.

She let him stand that way for a full minute. Then she moved, saying, "Here, try these nines." And as if she were leaving a leper, she left him for a new customer, smiling brightly.

Lionel struggled into the new boot, exhausted, nerves frayed badly. (And absurd, of course, Doctor.) He walked, and of course the nines were too big.

When he returned the girl was writing out a slip for a new customer.

*But boots aren't slippers, ma'am! And is it my fault if I don't fit easily, ma'am? She'd crush your pinky toe for real for that!*

His rage bullied, he returned sheepishly to the original eights. They still pinched.

Could he try, just once more? When she turned to him, he asked humbly, "I just wonder . . . will they loosen up? . . . should I try the bigger pair, or the tighter pair? . . ."

*"It's all up to you,"* she shook her head, "I won't be wearing them."

He was on the verge of punching her cranky face and cursing her sullen manner ("You cunt, you fucking cunt!") as he felt his head bursting! Forty-five bucks, and you had to suffer insults along with ignorance—

Tippy leaned forward to kiss his temples, and said to the salesgirl, "Would you get the manager, please?"

The girl looked at her with surprise, then murder. The steady sarcasm had quickly vanished.

Tippy continued, "Or shall I get him?"

The girl stood up, reddening, staring from one to the other. Finally she acquiesced, and went to the back.

"I shouldn't get anything but Fryes, Lionel," Tippy said easily, "so *this* pair is out."

Lionel couldn't talk. He felt like a patient who has at last gotten hold of a doctor after a nurse's indifference to his pain. Grateful. *She was going to kill me, but here she is saving me!*

A mustached middle-aged man came up.

"Has there been some trouble?" he inquired, half polite, half insolent.

It was Dr. Tippy who responded, fortunately. In two sentences she explained that "Professor Solomon" had been treated with arrogance and incompetence, and repeated what he was looking for.

The title and the tone tipped the scales immediately, and Mr. Doyle said to the salesgirl, "I think you owe the professor an apology, Lanie."

In all his years of shopping wounds and clerk humiliations, Solomon had never received one. While handing out thousands.

The girl's nostrils flared her conflict, and she squashed out her cigarette while saying there had been a misunderstanding.

Before Lionel could toss it off, embarrassed, Tippy intervened, "I think we'd want the taller boot, but in the Fryes if you have them."

Mr. Doyle brightened, told Lanie to take a coffee break, and went himself for the boot. Returning with, "I'm personally very sorry for this, sir, we don't need this kind of behavior at the Coop. Now, if I may make a recommendation—"

"That's just what I've been waiting for," Lionel said, wanting to kiss him.

The manager, after checking Lionel's toes in the boots, advised taking the eights, saying that the leather would loosen up in a week, and they'd be fine. The whole thing took five minutes, and Solomon was handing him his plastic card for payment, willing to double the forty-five bucks for the quick satisfaction.

Dazed, but happy, he wandered out of the Coop, carrying his high cowboy boots, barely aware of the female escort on either arm. To him it seemed like kindly aid coming from an asylum.

Outside Tippy commented, "You'll have to model them for us sometime," and before Lionel could respond or think, she had moved off and away with her friend. Just like that.

He suddenly remembered that he had wanted to shake them! What were they up to, what was it all about? Who was this South American filly with the fancy tushy? A señorita from the Bronx who majored in Spanish?

The light changed and the crowd bore Solomon with it. Ah, if only he could stay with it, hidden in its bosom. And instead of empty-handed from the Coop, he had his armful of Fryes. Crackerjacks and literary critics and public school chums (Jeffrey Frye) criss-crossed his mind as he crossed over.

"Hey, easy!"

A huge bus driver held him from going over, after bumping him. He made it faintly to the sidewalk.

Climbed into a taxi right there at the Harvard Square island. "Broadway Supermarket," he said, but as they started off, he remembered something else. "Hold off a second—"

Out of the cab and around to the Out of Town Kiosk, where he bought a *Jerusalem Post*. When tension was on the horizon, Solomon became a Jew. Back in the cab, he said, "Sorry."

"Nah, that's nothing," replied the wizened Irishman. "You should see this *character* I picked up at Logan the other day, he . . ."

Lionel sank back, sighed, wanted to remove his shoes and socks and feel cool water on his overworked feet. He dreamed of jogging, of dinner with Sheyna, of safety from confusion. When would life not mean chaos? he perspired. An hour ago he had been intense about Melville; three or four hours ago intense about his own life in fiction; now he was fighting free from a pair of girls and shopping trials. Did medieval man have to confront all this?

And at the Broadway Supermarket, after picking up two Wines of the Week and steaks, he turned to see staring at him on the paperback stand a copy of his last novel, with the *cheap* cover. Did Herman ever have to go for lamb chops and find *Moby Dick* done over by Madison Avenue? Captain Ahab turned into a beautiful blond captain, torn between his beloved whale and his homosexuality? Would they invent an exotic woman, from a foreign port for Conventional Romance? In your customs work, dear Herman, there were just bills of lading and dull isolation and cowpers and crates, not huckster cosmetics and vulgar notoriety.

And when Lionel went for tea, there was again that little problem of variety, duplication, and deception. Tea bags or loose tea, Lapsang souchong or Earl Grey or Constant Comment, Twining's or Bigelow's or? Thankfully no girls around to witness this confusion. He settled on three different packets, an ice-milk package (healthier?), fresh vegetables, lemons and limes for drinks, oranges for scent. Ah, Arizona! He'd move there perhaps, as a tribe member, not a tourist. After having more trouble at the check-cashing counter because he had lost his ID card, he finally convinced them of who he was, and made it back to the apartment. The ordeal of shopping was over as he poured a drink.

When harried, busy work worked as therapy; and there was *always* correspondence of one sort or another to be taken care of. *Always.* He mailed out three bills and did a student recommendation. (How did he know if this shy Miriam was "good at leadership," "good at getting along with others," "of excellent moral character"? How could a university ask such kindergarten questions? Who gave two shits about leadership, morals, character, getting along? Did they want the next American President, or someone *intelligent*? Wasn't intelligence enough to get into graduate school? Schmucks! he cursed, writing out the recommendation, forgetting the endless grid of boxes of nursery questions. One day he'd write a formal request to banish every soul from higher education who had taken an education course or made up a grad school questionnaire.)

Next, he reread the letter from Mrs. Jane McElwaine, his old fan from Orleans, Massachusetts, who wrote him three times a year, and whom he answered once a year. A postcard for her two- and three-page letters. In America, you didn't have to belong to the CIA to find out about the natives, all you had to do was become a minor celebrity. The natives would write to you, and many, in the first or second letter, would spill forth their lives, with more detail than even their mates knew. Here in successland, the urge to talk with someone on the top was very strong indeed. But did they know he was on the bottom?

He searched back to find the first letter by this lady, and glanced through it. The desire to discover "who I am" and "be myself," no matter "where the chips may fall." They fell, unfortunately, upon her children, especially Suzy, sixteen, suffering greatly from her mother's need to take up with a lover, and her decision to "unplug from the family." The interest of the famous O'Reillys in her situation, and their desire to put her on their forthcoming TV show about open marriage. Her newfound "creative abilities" bursting out everywhere, all sorts of writing projects, and her "encouraging signs" from various publishing people. On and on the avalanche went, about "identity," "feedback," "good vibes," et cetera. Now what did Lionel, who knew so much about women from his *Pamela: Self-Portrait,* think about all this? And, by the way, was he a Scorpio? She was sure of it from his photograph! . . . Lionel had written a brief note, thanking her, telling her how little he knew about women—or men—as time went on, and wishing her well. She had found this "very supportive," she knew he would understand.

One day someone was going to hit his mid-September birth date. To this day Lionel still couldn't get over the jumbled confessions and confusing clichés, and it was only a bit later on, in the ensuing letters, that the full sadness and pain of the woman's life emerged. He looked through these last notes, ranging from euphoria to pure chaos and depression. From having left her husband's bed for a room of her own, and removing herself from her children for a month, the poor lady had then left the house and gone off to live with her lover. Life proceeded to be a series of encounters. Including one in New York City with the celebrity O'Reilly, author of a book on free marriages, in which the older liberated fellow seemed to be quite offended when Jane refused to disrobe and turn on upon meeting him in his hotel room. Alas, the hoped-for TV show had been put off. "Mr. Solomon, must one go that route in order to make it to money and fame? To think that a hero of mine could behave like that! My God, maybe *we* shouldn't meet after all!" Anyway, at the last writing, she had brought up the matter of her "co-counseling," now that she herself had been through so many "changes."

Lionel wrote out a postcard, now, thanking her for keeping him posted on her "progress," but wondering if she had enough "necessary training" to fulfill the position sufficiently? He also mentioned Jim Plunkett's conservatism on third-down plays, and asked Mrs. McElwaine if she thought he was a Virgo? He declined her offer of a drink. He put a stamp on, let his note rest till later, and turned to more serious letters, inquiries. From a small pile from old friends and students, he turned to his sister's troubles. A sister whom he hardly knew, and who came into real existence as an adult once he started writing books and earning money and becoming certified by society. What could he say to the stream of letters that had begun before the great misfortune of a year ago, and lasted right through now? Letters of confused ambitions, money troubles, unsolvable dilemmas, swift amnesia over past mistakes? Who was this stranger, called sister, whom he remembered as a young girl in her teens, dark and stubborn, who hated to babysit for him and fought with him, and yet was also extremely generous? A smoker, she had caught him smoking at the age of twelve, and bribed him to leave off with a printing press he had longed for; a legal secretary, she had purchased a television set for him when his father wouldn't hear of it, and he had to be a constant invited guest at friends' living rooms; she had calmed him over his hernia scare. So that, when, in another lifetime eons later, she had asked him to help her and her husband Frank buy a stationery business by loaning them ten thousand dollars, Solomon did it. Flush with a book advance, afraid of becoming "stingy" with money, astonished by the request, he did it; and to her question about what he thought about the venture, he responded, "One hundred fifty thousand is an awful lot of money, especially when you have very little." What else could he say about the enormous folly and patent recklessness of hocking your house, with a second mortgage, using every penny of your savings, and going into a business you knew nothing about? She would proceed, fixed, regardless. All that might have happened would have been a savings to him of ten grand, that's all. The business lasted almost eighteen months before the recession and gasoline hikes and lack of capital reserve dragged it down. Ruth, a youthful forty, grayed and wrinkled eighteen years in eighteen months while watching the business debts mount, the teenagers steal, the pressures build. Frank, a gentle soul, came up to Boston to see a Sinatra concert, and to tell Lionel how afraid he was that Ruth might go under, she was near it; the store was killing her, and she wouldn't leave off working there; suddenly there was Lionel, starting out with lending money, now asked to move into the emotions trade. So that it was almost a relief to hear the inevitable: Mrs. Goldstein, the elderly lady who had sold them the store, foreclosed on their note when they failed to meet it one month, period. A kindly guide and kind of aunt she *appeared* to be, to Ruth, until there was the question of skipping a month's note, and perhaps just paying the interest; she then became a rigid businesswoman, a petty tyrant, who dominated their lives. Ruth was dazed by the change; she pleaded and begged for more time; No. And when the end was approaching, just in time for the Jewish New Year, Ruth rediscovered her own Jewishness, and appealed to the High Holiday, their mutual God, and its sacred rest from business; No. The foreclosure came in fact right on Yom Kippur, and when Ruth, beside herself, cried out in panic, "You'll see Mrs. Goldstein, you'll be punished for this, God won't forget it!" Mrs. Goldstein was aghast, and asked if Ruth was threatening her with "this curse"? Ruth, dear sister, helpless, retracted; probably believing somewhere that this heartfelt religious curse was indeed too strong, could possibly be used against her in legal proceedings. In any case, losing the business and store was the best thing that could have happened: she began to sleep again at night, became human again with the family, lost her day-in, day-out depression. What could Lionel do but write a note, telling her to forget it all like a bad dream? Who would write a similar note to him, about the money lost? The careful planner and compulsive worker could live a whole lean year on that money; he couldn't believe he had just thrown it away, couldn't quite believe it. And currently, Ruth was describing Frank's three new jobs to meet the bills, and her son Arthur's need for a new car, the anguish of keeping up fronts with certain friends and members of the family, and, and, and. Lionel wrote three or four lines, realized they were too blunt and would need taming down, and put it off for later; sister memories had exhausted him. He gave it up.

Moved away from his correspondence desk, a standing slant-top desk built by a local carpenter on the old schoolmaster model, and got into his jogging outfit. Feeling revived by the wool stretch pants and hooded sweatshirt and the sneakers; hidden, with a narrow simple task to perform, as when he was twelve at P.S. 189 or Lincoln Terrace. Outside in the soft spring air, he peered around, just in case the girls were still at their game. Safe and sound on the quiet little street. He got into his Mercedes (the star crumbled), drove to Memorial Drive, parked by the stadium, and walked to the track; toward recovery from his day, his teaching, his thoughts, his tails.

*Doctor, the next small scene is embarrassing, even for me. If it were not so real and painful recalling it, I would laugh too. Is there a medical term for fear and obsession and overwrought nerves culminating in comedy? is this the Solomon Complex? . . . But what happens if that fear and obsession prove in the end to be right? and that the stop for comedy is no more than that, in a longer flight toward disaster? In other words, where projection produces the comic, but reality, mocking projection, moves something closer to the tragic?*

*Another word about this S. Complex, to include childhood, mothers, and fathers. Supposing you are not merely threatened by your father and wish to murder him, but your wish for his removal is conveniently fulfilled by reality, outside your will; supposing your anger, in retrospect, is perfectly defensible, since he has turned out to be, conveniently, a brute; and supposing your mother's love has been great, but not suffocating; so that, all told, what you are left with is a rather free road, fatherless at fourteen and ready to make your own image as a man? (and as a father, at twenty-one, to test the role out). In short, instead of a guilty cripple you become a guiltless survivor and even loved conqueror? A conqueror all the more as you go on, and look back at the path and the disturbing elements, and make use of the rem-*

*nants of guilt and threads of ambivalence in the new work you are weaving. Grateful for it all, as an artist. Am I speaking then of a most constructive narcissism, whereby guilt is etched and absolved, injury sketched and blessed, great love announced and earned; and the sinner, the neurotic, the mother's boy, the would-be murderer are all there visible, guiltless, and instructive? So that, in the end, even the so-called tragic has its most therapeutic side, its healthy relief? And even my own present ordeal, burning as it is, has its comic pleasures?*

Running around the track, slow and steady, eyeing the spring tennis players, he kept glancing around him, in back, along the hedges by the clay courts. In his memory's eye he saw a mesa, a long winding road; could he be a Hopi, one day? Was he being tailed? *In his mind the Crimson headlined: LIONEL SOLOMON, NOVELIST, WOUNDED WHILE JOGGING. The New York Times: AUTHOR FELLED ON HARVARD TRACK. The Lampoon: PROF SHOT IN ASS WHILE IN TRAINING! The Globe: GIRLS KILL WRITER, CITE HIS FICTION AS MOTIVE.* Around once, he smiled. Sweated. Ran slowly, raising his arms periodically. Late-afternoon light colored Harvard Stadium pink and copper. A jet plane was a shimmering white gleam in the mauve sky. His time of day, his pale light, his family of objects. Fueling memory. *At age twelve, pounding the pocket of his fielder's mitt by the (Flying A?) gasoline station on Bedford Avenue, opposite Ebbets Field. Waiting for the signal from Steven Werter, up by the right-field screen, to let him know when Shuba and Snider were going to take batting practice. The indescribable thrill of catching the real baseball on the fly (once!), or of fighting and winning it as it bounded in the streets, and handing it in at the gate in exchange for a bleacher seat.* Around again. *At night, doing homework in his Composition notebook, listening to the small Philco radio as Red Barber dramatized the ticker-tape version of the game with the Cardinals in St. Louis.* Around again. *Listening to Friday night boxing at ten o'clock . . . going to St. Nicholas Arena and Eastern Parkway Arena with Papa to watch main events, especially when Harold was boxing. Saw him left-hook Morris Reif, Graziano, Chalky Wright, but then, in his big chance at Madison Square Garden, saw Cerdan take him out in the second. Papa Solomon feeling kindly to his son and to America at those events.* Around again. *Making three long set shots at Betsy Head indoors, with that tinny rim in which you had to swish the ball straight through, or it bound-*

318

*ed a mile in the air. . . . Jogging to childhood soothed him
nicely, brought revelation. Remembering Rach at age three
coming into his study rubbing her eyes and wanting to sit in
his lap, or listening intently to a goodnight story about Ollie
Bumpo II the runaway circus elephant, and Captain Chippers, his mouse boss, and their adventures in the bear community in the Adirondacks—one mistake or slip of memory,
and Rach was there to correct him on the right details . . .*

A shot fired, Lionel ran three more steps, felt the sharp
pain in his kidney, and dropped to the ground. On his knees,
the pain seized him and, dizzy, he was afraid to look at the
blood. What was the point, his kidney was burning. He
stayed there, thinking lucidly of his folly, his stupidity, his
lust, his useless fiction; and to his surprise he had a rush of
sympathy for the poor deranged girl who, almost a murderer
now, had taken out her hatred and longing for a father, on
him. It would soon be all over. All over. The mystery would
end.

"Are you okay?"

Solomon nodded very slowly, holding his left side with
both hands. His vision was blurry. He observed the lengthy
clean face of a tennis player.

"Is it the heart?" the female partner asked, hair tied by yellow ribbon.

He shook his head. No longer able to sit up that way, he
flopped down on his side, with a groan. The earth of the
track was black.

"A seizure?"

He shook his head.

"Where is it?" the man asked. "Bleeding?"

Lionel nodded, and slowly indicated his hidden side, that
had been hit.

Gently, the woman lifted the shield of his hands, to investigate the wound. For the first time in his life Solomon took
note of the specks of black earth, feeling empathy.

For some reason, the woman bent him over, farther,
gently.

He had never fixed his gaze on this dirt before, or on so
many other things in this world! Oh, God, no!

The woman touched his arm.

"There doesn't seem to be any blood."

Lionel heard the words, and nodded slowly. What difference did it make now, anyway? Slowly he gazed down himself.

319

But all he saw was yellow sweatshirt and sweatpants and, when he peeked under the undershirt, unblemished pink skin.

He did a modest double take. Pushed his fingers into his side. The pain seemed to have eased up, too.

He shook his head, involuntarily asked, aloud, "The shot?"

The pair exchanged looks.

She remembered, "That backfiring a minute ago?"

Lionel's head hurt, his eyes narrowed. Kneaded his side again, pushing in and out.

The woman barely suppressed her laughter. Then standing by, she put her hands out toward the victim.

Lionel, dazed, sad, obliged.

Lifting him, she asked, "Were you expecting someone to shoot you?"

Lionel, who had expected it, imagined it, half-smiled. *Alive*. He thanked the kind tennis pair, and walked off, limping slightly from his foot having fallen asleep. Of course he had expected it, right from the beginning, a pistol from the purse or garter belt.

The sun was an orange disk half submerged on the other side of the horizon.


The narrow-faced historian ate his chicken with particular gusto, working over each bite as if it were a feast in itself, piling broccoli and rice upon the chicken, using knife upon fork European-style. "There's no *purpose* at all anywhere but in the Third World countries," Harvey Moates was saying to the dinner party of six in Sheyna's apartment, "no *national* purpose. No conscious set of ideals, civic, moral or political. No citizenry who thinks about anything but their lawns and coupons, or their dachas or country houses." Harvey sipped from his wine, the face long and the nose aquiline. "Certainly no one thinks that Americans count significantly anymore in terms of moral idealism or citizen integrity. We are an obsolete people already, don't you forget it. A comet that shines brightly for a few moments in history and then burns itself out. Oh, we'll go on making gadgets and weapons and deodorants for a while, and maybe even, with the help of the Soviet Union, blow up the world. But as a people of history, a civilization to be remembered, we are no longer very interesting. I'm afraid we have passed the point of our original experiment, and are now a demonstrable failure. Our leadership has been, at best, a complete mediocrity for the past few decades; and the worship of the dollar and the making of a millionaire are not very stimulating ideals for man. That's why we have to look elsewhere—to Africa, to China, to emerging South America—for new types of citizenry, ethics, and human community."

After a pause, Sheyna asked, "What about the *outsider* here, or in other nations. Not the typical citizen, the patriot, but your real citizen, the freethinking individual?"

Moates smiled understandingly, drank white wine. "A contradiction in terms here, I'm afraid. Freethinking, without the institutions to implement that thinking, means nothing. Affects nothing. Deceives instead of defines. Isolated individuals are politically powerless, unfortunately. However," he leaned forward, patient, extending his long forefinger, "if you refer to the *disenfranchised* in this nation, now that's something else. There's *hope* there. Revitalization. Possibility. In the black man, the red man, the Chicano and the Puerto Rican, all the Johnny-come-latelies to the melting pot who have never quite melted in—yes, there's *hope* there. In ethnic pride and tribal consciousness there's purpose, and that spirit may yet affect the nation as a whole. *May.* Yet to my mind their ideas, if not actual leadership, have to come from outside the nation. From Chairman Mao or Premier Castro or Williams of Trinidad, leaders who can serve as models of free men, citizens of liberated nations and liberated consciousness, whose ideas are not fettered by the dominating ideology of this monster America. I hope no one doubts that we are dealing with a monster here, one temporarily tamed and set back by events like Vietnam and Watergate." He smiled peacefully, took a second helping, revealing a small diamond on his pinky finger. This well-known visitor at Harvard, a thorn in everyone's side, pleased Lionel because of that thorniness, and his colorful life history.

"What Harvey is saying is quite obvious actually," asserted Betsy Greenberg, hair pulled back, pretty face untouched by makeup, a poignant academician, struggling now before the pressures of tenure, and poignant girl, struggling before the pressures of Marxism. "All you have to do is visit one of the 'new' countries to see what he means. The energy of the people in a place like Cuba is incredible. Or what it was in Allende's Chile. They have a new sense of history, of nationhood, of freedom, that's like watching a people being reborn again. A nation with a purpose is actually seen and felt in its ordinary citizens. Even the intellectuals seem *alive*." Making everyone smile.

And eat well, too, as the talk continued. Moe Kahn, a sturdy bespectacled critic and old Solomon acquaintance who had come to town to deliver a literary lecture, was also working on another helping. Despite their strong appetites both men looked pointedly trim and in good shape, a testimony to their digestion and health. Words seemed to do them good too, like food—reading everything, writing enormous amounts, talking voluminously.

". . . yes, you can see some of the reevaluations and eventual disgust with the nation in some of our best novelists these days," continued Moates, his hand-painted blue tie resplendent next to his tan summer suit. "This digging back into our history to turn over the estimates given us by patrician historians has at last and happily reached our artists. In a way they have become our *true revisionists*. That's the essential radical genius of Postman, for example, turning the novel into a forum for history. That was Tolstoy's mission, you know."

"But wasn't that the most boring part of Tolstoy?" Solomon wondered aloud, remembering those endless sermons that had impressed him when he was eighteen.

Kahn held up a finger. "Boring, but useful. Important." He smiled, his gold-rimmed glasses refracting light, almost elegantly, while he poured more wine. "So not boring at all in the intellectual, or philosophical sense."

*The last refuge of the errant critic—the intellectual sense.*

"And certainly the disgust is relevant in a writer like Scweezin," noted Harvey's lady friend, Sheila Wilson, "where the absurdity of the nation is the true subject again and again."

Solomon, burning from being discarded, his work casually obsolete and denied, felt his head swirl. "But is being *un*interested in human beings a strong point for a novelist? Isn't that turning a writer's inadequacy into a virtue, standing the defect on its head?"

"But you see the novel itself is in deep trouble," retorted Sheila, forty, British, prematurely gray in a handsome way. "Every writer feels this strongly in his heart of hearts," looking sympathetically at Lionel. "That's why aspects of the *old* novel, like character, story or plot, don't count that much anymore, for the avante-garde on our literary horizon— Scweezin, Postman, and the few other pioneers."

Lionel an also-ran, wanted to cry. *Do I have a heart of hearts?* he wondered. *Am I an artichoke along the path of the pioneers?*

Moates took up the thread of the discussion, rolling it into a perfect and understandable ball, while wiping his mouth neatly with the linen napkin. "The medium has lost its usefulness, yes, that's probably true. Outlived its stay, I'm afraid. Like Lukács talking about the obsolescence of the epic when the novel came along. So a new form, like the movies perhaps, replaces the novel. Representing the desires of the people, the impulse of the new age; in other words the death of the 'old novel' is the artistic analogue to the social reality. This nation is for all intents and purposes dead too. Why shouldn't the artistic expressions associated with it also die?"

Lionel scratched his thigh, as he had when he was a boy wearing knickers and feeling nervous. *Take it easy,* he told himself, remember, you're a country mole not used to people. You take this much too seriously. Easy now, easy. "But aren't you forgetting," he retorted at last, "that the novel has always been in *opposition* to the prevailing values, and dominant culture; always been a radical protest against what you call the worship of the dollar; hasn't it always held up a different sort of man as worthy of admiring, and a very different set of ethics from the ethics of profit? Then how can you call it the 'artistic analogue'?" Put so awkwardly, but he couldn't help it!

Moates laughed, not without sympathy. "As one of the 'old novelists,' you're quite right to be alarmed, and act in self-defense. And besides, our wine and food, as prepared by Sheyna of course, are old world too—thank God!"

The group enjoyed that, while Sheila chattered on, trying to make an inroad in Moates's thesis.

Lionel drank wine, and refilled his glass, his head swimming with discontent.

Somewhere along the line he tuned in again to culture generalizations.

Moe Kahn was saying, "There's a lot of forces operating to kill off the novel, but there's also strong competition, as you say, Harvey. Apart from movies, take a look at dancing, for example. Modern ballet, say. Is there a writer alive who's as exciting as Balanchine? *I* don't think so. And where would you rather spend an evening, with a contemporary novel or at the City Center?" He leaned back in his chair, fully fed now, his hands behind his head, and Lionel imagined him fifty years earlier, at sixteen in Brooklyn in the same position, arguing about social change. "And don't forget *money* either. Most novelists are corrupted by it, whether they realize it or not."

"They're *immoral* anyway," Moates concluded, smiling, "as Plato observed in *The Republic.*"

"True enough," continued Moe, argument and wine making him forget Lionel sitting there, and developing a theme favored by their old mutual friend, Sidney S. "Very few novelists have been *truly moral* creatures. Tolstoy, Chekhov, in our time Solzhenitsyn. Another handful, that's all." He went on amplifying his point, carefully avoiding the attention of Betsy, with whom he had had a painful affair while he was still married, an affair begun out of mutual politics and sympathies, and ending with the girl hurting desperately. "Lawrence, Céline, Dreiser, are three examples that come to mind immediately of totally disreputable characters, in one way or another," he went on, irrelevant moral thrust slipping easily to irrelevant moralistic lecture.

And when Moates asked whether this immorality did in fact affect the art, the example of Pound was taken up by Kahn.

At this point Solomon turned his attention to the second movement of Schubert's "Death and the Maiden," now on the record player. A beautifully haunting melody, which he had discovered through Sheyna and taped. He observed her now, long brown hair loose on orange sweater, face small, intent and lovely; soul seeking to protect him at any moment. Her style was *pianissimo*, he thought, in admiration. Knowing too how *determined* that style could become at times. To be a composer, he mused, and not be subject to the shallowness and hypocrisy of words. Composing movements for cello, violin, piano, horn, and not scenes for characters; then, when you were criticized, it would be by means of *technical* terms, not by extramusical categories. Your moral or immoral life rising and falling in fugues and sonatas! . . . Free from that classic critical sublimation—the critic's private life being deflected unconsciously onto his public criticism; a personal vengeance dsplayed onto a novel for complicated reasons, without any self-consciousness by the highly developed intellect. When would there emerge a psychoanalytic study of literary criticism, and of the critics, as there was of writers and their works?

Schubert soothed and haunted with fierce dissonant melodies.

"The expression of the pornographic is by the way a perfect last gasp of the old novel. It is the death-wish and death-admission rolled into one. A corollary I think to the pornographic war machine of the Pentagon. Yes," Moates leaned towards Lionel now, "I can see what you're getting at in your work."

Lional wanted to say, "Are you out of your mind? How can you be so indiscriminate here and discriminate in your own work?" He managed, "I think we read my work a bit differently." Sheyna tried to intercede angrily, but Solomon put in, "But forget me for a moment. Don't you think you're making all sorts of speculations which are rather easy? And rather oversimple? For example, pornography has been around for quite a long while, in Europe and, before that, in ancient China. Isn't there a very respectable history of pornography in the arts in China, at the same time that it was a high and respected civilization? Don't you think that creating an analogy out of the making of a rocket to kill and the writing of a book is farfetched? Missing some *distinctions?* In fact, if one didn't know you, but just heard some of your remarks, one might get the impression that it was a Soviet censor talking. Not a historian of the left."

Moates raised his glass. "Touché. However, there is one great difference between the censor and myself: I rather enjoy reading pornography at times, and even at my advanced age would not turn down a nice private orgy, if offered."

Everyone laughed, including the delighted speaker.

Solomon, feeling his bald spot with affection, tried to smile too.

Driving back to his apartment later, to settle down with two hours of reading, he thought back to the peculiar comedy of the twilight jogging. Thought about the propensity in his life for melodrama and exaggeration and paranoia, and how there was no leaving it for too long: he—and his life—were a joke, a serious joke, a self-centered scalding joke. No more than a helium narcissist who would float up and away one day, high on himself and his injuries, right?

But when he got to his parking spot on Chatham, he nevertheless wasn't taking any chances, and looked carefully when he got out of the car and locked it and crossed over, checking the hedges in case any filly guerrillas in bells were lurking. Oh he'd like to lurk for them sometime!

Climbing to his apartment, he heard rock music, and his stomach signaled fear! . . . With hesitation he opened the door quietly, and peeked inside, like a scared detective. And actually called out, there in his own hallway, "Hey. Hey, you, are you here? Anyone home?"

But no one answered, and when he closed the door, the music died out. He walked through the rooms, looking out for blond phantoms or Peruvian muggers; then bolted his door, and realized he should change his lock perhaps, just in case.

And although he fell off to sleep rather easily, he woke in a fright at 2:30 A.M., having melo-dreamed about being chased down by three women on Great Danes in a woods, and it took him a while to get to sleep again.

The next day, however, he got out of bed at nine-fifteen, and was at the typewriter by eleven o'clock, and through determined effort got things going really well for a change, after several false paragraphs. For lunch he stood by his white kitchen cabinet, spent five minutes spooning yogurt and cottage cheese from their containers, and went back to work. Maintaining the rhythm.

So that, at one-thirty, when he received a telephone call, he was not quite with it, and not quite delighted to be interrupted.

"I'm really sorry, Dad, I just thought we could get together a bit, before I took off for the weekend. Remember, we missed our last date, when *you* were out of town."

"Okay. Where are you going?"

"Montreal. On the three-thirty bus, if I can make it."

*Montreal.* "What's up there? I thought Expo was finished."

"Oh Dad, come on. I met someone, and he invited me, simple. I'm not going to rob any banks, I promise."

That might be better, dear daughter. "All right, give me a half hour, okay?"

"Mmmm! You're a good father sometimes. . . . Can I loan you out to some Cliffies?"

"No, just record it in the ledger, for future anger."

In forty minutes she was there, in camel-colored sweater and beige Wrangler jeans, looking casually lovely.

"Hey, you got the old Morris chair recovered, how terrif!" She curtsied in appreciation and sat down. "Put the cover on while you removed your beard. What's the symbolism?"

"Spring."

"Mind?" She lit a cigarette, and after saying how he should start combing his hair forward, like Caesar, she began talking about the excitement of yesterday's class. "As if you had been right there, Daddy, on the original *Essex!* And then on the open ocean, with Captain Pollard and Owen Chase, experiencing all those incredible . . . degradations. And survived! God, listening to you was a trip, believe me. And tripped out some others too." She laughed. "Daddy, you missed your calling—either a sea captain or an actor!" She paused for breath. "And Tippy there on top of it all—" She glowed, half-mocked. "Was it a *show* for her? Did you shave it for her? I looked for her afterwards, but she was gone."

Lionel nodded, and nodded. Then inquired, "Where'd you meet him?"

Her eyebrows clustered, and she shook her head at his hopelessness. "Except you'd have to give up your bourgeoisie-dom for the stage. Who, Jean-Claude?" She used the cover of the peanut jar for an ashtray. "In Boston, a few weeks ago."

Lionel, sitting too, asked, "What's he do?"

She smiled. "Inquisition time, huh? From actor to prosecutor, just like that!" She snapped her finger, got up, went to the record player, put on a female singer. Snapped her fingers, and made little rock moves too. "Oh, he sweeps floors, washes dishes, shoes horses. You know, Daddy, I always wanted a 'working-class man.' My Trotskyist past."

Solomon, stung, put a hand in the air, graciously withdrawing the query, the topic.

"He's a doctor. A single doctor." Miss Mitchell was singing about being a radio, turned on. "And he's a dish."

Lionel shifted position, wanting to tell her about a restaurant in the French quarter. "I thought you had a boyfriend."

She stared at him, this eighteen-year-old package: "I do."

Lionel couldn't help shaking his head, in bewilderment. "Then what's with Montreal? I don't get it, Rachel."

Speaking slowly for emphasis and for control, she said, "It's *another city*, and he's *another man*. Daddy, it's not the nineteen thirties but the seventies. Okay? No world depression, no world war. And the world's blowing apart. And there's *protection* for girls now. Anything else?"

Lionel understood the words clearly, took them rationally well enough, but his *instincts* stirred. *Protective* ones too!

"Look, Daddy," she said, resettling into the chair crosslegged, as she had at six. "You know the times have changed. *You've* changed. And I'm all for it, if it makes you happy. You've been *moving* too, right? There're such things nowadays as pills, diaphragms, IUD's, foam—"

"Thanks for the inventory. Which would you like me to purchase," he couldn't help saying, "any special brand?"

She pulled at her hair, his habit. "Trojans, Dad, a pack of Trojans, I'd say."

Lionel reddened, accepted it, recovered. He thought helplessly, *Is that what I raised her for—IUD's and diaphragms and vaginal creams—with vibrators next?*

She rotated her finger by her temple. "Buzz, buzz, buzz, 'Is

that what we raise them for?' You can do better than that,
Daddy, don't you see—you, your fiction, your classes, your
life—they *all challenge* those old assumptions in your head.
Don't go back on them with your daughter, that's not fair!"

Lionel got up, walked to the records, removed Mitchell,
and replaced it with the Goldberg Variations. He put it on,
and sat back down as the harpsichord and Bach braced the
room.

"Sure, Daddy, we grow up faster, hear about more things
to do, have more options, don't worry about the next ten
bucks. Sure. And something else—" her dark eyes firing up
(like his?) with argument and talk—"do you think it's apple
pie growing up as your daughter? A novelist's daughter?
Someone who is known, and read by one's peers? *Your*
daughter? Dad, it's not that easy all the time. In fact hard as
hell frequently, you know that. You're smart and have feeling
and are terrific, but you're also at times impatient, obstinate,
uptight, a pain in the ass—with me especially. And your
'role' lays a 'role' on me, whether I like it or not. And frankly
I don't, mostly. It's a heavy trip at times, believe me, a trip I
keep to myself. But it's there, and it gets me down." Having
laid it in, she now leaned forward. "Oh, Dad, look, I
wouldn't have you any other way, you know that too. But it's
just not all rosy or a ball being Rachel Beauregard Solomon—even though I know the 'Beauregard' was not of your
doing."

The extra humor didn't soften the attack any. *Was Lionel
asking for all this? Do I have to go through it every year, on
schedule, take a beating, like a birthday? When do I finish
the course in fatherhood, now that I know what a compost
pile I've made of it all?*

*And she's right, isn't she? Right, right, right. That's what
hurts the most, maybe. I'm in my own self-created mold, it's
frozen over, and there's not much I can do about it, except
write and live as decently as I can within it. God, daughter,
Tippy, world—I'm not Meister von Aschenbach. I'm Lionel
Solomon, can't you all remember that? I'm real-life-faulty,
not literary-perfect!*

Finally he said, "Okay, I understand. But I'm from a different time, I'm . . . old-fashioned, and that's that. I can't
change my biology at this point."

"Fine too, don't. But it's just that whenever I take a step
on my own, a sexual step, this buzzer rings in your head:
Buzz, my daughter's a whore! Buzz, she's promiscuous! Buzz,
she's fucking boys, trash, blacks—schwartzeh Princes! Buzz,

she's my daughter and she's shaming me! Buzz, I've ruined her. Buzz—"

"Enough, okay. Enough."

She pleaded. "Daddy, let up. *Leave it be.* Sex is sex. Sometimes it's good and sometimes it's not. Sometimes I'm with a man for that, and sometimes not."

"Fifty-fifty, huh?"

She smiled, most smashing when she shifted from anger to irony, like coming up from under water and glistening.

Laughed. "Sixty-forty. Fair split?"

"I'll ask my agent. Want a drink?"

She shook her head. Then said, "Sure, whatever you're having."

"Make yourself at home," he advised calmly, heart pounding. And walked the length of the flat, heading for Scotch quick. The energy it took, the terrific energy to carry this relationship on, who had it? Not he, anymore. Life had taken it from him. Writing took it from him. At thirty-eight, handling a grown-up daughter was too big a job, he couldn't do it anymore! Good, tell her that. He chose apple juice instead, and brought two glasses back into the living room.

Handed one to her and said, "As long as you know what you're doing."

"Oh, *shit.* Of course I don't know what I'm doing so what? Who does most of the time, who's honest? Shit. Isn't that what your books preach? Why can't you read them after you write them?"

"My books again, why do they always have to be used against me?"

Rachel smiled widely, trying to change moods, and jumped out of the chair and settled on his lap and began to kiss his cheeks and bury her nose in his hair, like she used to.

He wouldn't have it. "Come on, off. Save your 'shits' for your friends."

She looked at him suddenly, hurt. Unfair! her face read.

"I'll make a deal with you, Rachel. I'll remove your burden once and for all, okay?" Letting go for a change. "I won't be your father anymore. How's that? Let's call the deal off. A real divorce. I'll give you cash, and you can go and get a new name, and let's forget the whole thing, the whole thing—growing up, childhood, the relationship in toto. You go your way, I'll go mine, as your minstrel says. How's that? Be Rachel someone else. Okay, pal?"

The joy and hardness in her folded up, caved in, like a soft chaise longue.

Right there in front of him she was crying, slowly at first, then harder, crying desperately, crying hysterically and shaking. She sank to the carpet, as if punched in the stomach, and rolled into a kind of ball, reminiscent of her ulcer attacks at fourteen.

Lionel, in his chair, just having found his fury, found it slipping.

And in another ten seconds he was helpless too, on the rug with her, holding her in his arms and rocking her and crying himself and kissing her scalp, forehead and wet cheeks. Time dissolved, *ten years* meant zip. "Sssh, you know your father's just . . . stupid. Hot-tempered. *Dumb.* Doesn't know what he's saying half the time baby. Please, Rach, you know that don't you? . . . Don't you pumpkin?"

He held up her anguished face, and she looked at him with those watery dark eyes, just staring in fear, and he knew that in that look was embedded the black doubt of her adolescence, the ineradicable and monstrous doubt of the days when he had not given her love or attention or his presence and had left her alone with her mother, and it cut him sharply, this memory razor. He didn't seek to look away, as he wanted to, but let the wounded look scar him more, let himself bleed with memories of his abandonment and his own bereavement, when he no longer had her, and there was just cold absence and scorn from the flesh he had made and cared for. It was all too hard.

"Stop . . . okay?" He took out his handkerchief and wiped the tears.

She continued to shake, just shake in his arms as she had when she was four and terrified, and after several long minutes, she eased up.

He lifted her up, saying, "Come on, kid, I'll drive you to your bus. Tell you what, let's splurge a little and get you a plane ride up there. You can see Vermont on your way back down. How's that?"

She hugged him. "Papa."

Returning her hug, he bit his lips and squeezed his face to keep from crying again, at the use of the old name.

# 7.

## Some Serious Play

OF COURSE AFTER GETTING HER to the airport and driving
back himself, his concentration was shot, his day lost, writing
out of the question. So he went to the stationer's. Bob Slate's,
bought some felt-tip pens and pads and paper, and then to
Shea's, where he deposited laundry to be washed. At the bank
in Central Square, he thought about trout fishing in a brook
up north with his friend from down the road. Menial errands
to exorcise daughters, emotions, and characters too.

Should he take Sheyna to the Celtic play-offs that night?
See the flock of green-winged blackbirds race up and down
the yellow wood floor, and spring high into the air, stay
gracefully, and pump the ball into its nesting hoop?

Walking upstairs to his apartment, he heard the same sort
of music as the night before, but this time he smiled at his
paranoia, and walked in. Calmly closed the door, latched it,
and called out to no one.

Unlike last night, however, the music didn't fade away.

He removed his jacket, and hung it up.

Rachel? Miss the plane or, like her, change her mind at the
last second?

Sternly he walked toward the rock sound, having had
enough of fears and fantasies and female bullies.

In the living room Tippy was dancing slowly to the soft
rock, enveloped by late-afternoon amber light. Instead of
smiling a hello, she put her finger to her mouth, cautioning
silence. It was like walking in on a mountain lion in your living room, prancing slowly.

She was back, but not in the form or manner he expected.
His whole body bristled.

She danced to him, and, taking his arm gently, persuaded
him into the room, and down onto pillows taken from the
couch. Oriental style.

He started to speak, but she cupped his mouth with her
palm.

Amazed, he sat. While the music played, she unbuttoned

331

his shirt and, recalling his track aid, held out her hands, good-naturedly. Her strength showing she helped lift him up—and as he found himself easing out of shirt and undershirt, she worked lower on trousers. And to his protest of "Come on now," she said "Sshh, just take it easy, I'm just getting you more comfortable," patting his hair softly, but with some authority too. And to his surprise, she was moving him into his old dungarees, a white denim shirt (his?), and his new boots.

At another point during this hazy, strange undress and dress he laughed and shook his head. "Do you always . . . carry on like this?"

Tippy didn't smile back. "You don't take things seriously enough, Mr. Solomon."

"You mean these . . . games?"

"You don't take games seriously enough. You don't take me seriously enough. You don't take your love affairs with . . . any gravity. Actually, the only thing you take seriously is your writing, and your characters. I want you to learn to take me seriously, Mr. Solomon. To take me as a *character*, if you have to." Her tone now matched her words and her raspy voice in strangeness and foreign appeal.

The rock music ricocheted.

Finally he had had enough. After perceiving that he had allowed her to redress him, he began in his confusion to undress, saying, annoyed, "Now let's drop the posing. And either explain yourself, or get out." Sensing even then that he had uttered an absurdity, in reflexive self-defense.

Tippy merely eyed him, made a little O with her mouth in conjunction with the rock rhythm, and continued to move. Her hair was down loose, hanging like a massive blond blanket upon her wide shoulders. Had the hair grown longer since he had seen her?

Nevertheless, he was on the verge of breaking the spell, and would have, had not a curious thing happened. Like one of those odd circumstances that keep a man with excellent intentions from kicking his habit of cigarettes, or heroin. There he stood, shirt off and dungarees on, not knowing what was going on, what was the right attitude or emotion to feel, on what level he was being spoken to or demanded of, not knowing whether to removed his new cowboy costume or to throw her out first (or even to take her down right now, with that midriff showing and breasts loose in white halter)—when just then, to complicate matters further, another girl appeared. In the doorway leading from the study stood Ursula, smiling, only she had exchanged her bells and striped polo shirt for an airlines hostess outfit, aqua-blue short skirt, red jacket and white peaked cap, complete with silver wings on the breast pocket. Was she real, or a phantom of his fantasies? phantom-jet of this intimate rock opera? Smiling, as I said (very unlike her businesslike pal), she too danced then, danced in and closer to Lionel, so that momentarily the pair of girls brushed him like bumblebees attracted to a flower, cajoling him back into his teenage outfit. Around this point he began telling himself that it was all a dream somehow, or a nightmare, or a rare form of imaginative possession. That he was Prospero deported to a strange isle of magic and mystery. Afraid, anxious, he hoped his Miranda wasn't around.

In fact, so taken aback and surprised was Lionel by this dark Braniff apparition aiding her natural yogurt-looking radical in rock-stepping, that as they scented and lightly touched him into new ease, he could do little but oblige when they began to dress him again, oblige in the redressing, oblige by putting back on the shirt and the high boots, and wide-brimmed felt hat too. Tippy saying once, "Now you just listen to us for now, Lionel," and Ursula, beaming widely out of that olive Peruvian face, as he became their plaything, middle-aged cowboy, whatever. (*Why it was like age three or four, and having his sister and three girlfriends of fourteen dress him up in long dress, lipstick, heels and beret because of his platinum hair, so pretty was he then.*) And even his old friend, the living room, seemed to get the same message of strangeness, as Solomon gazed at the bookshelves, the framed pictures, the hi-fi set, and saw them rubbery and unreal too, here in the late afternoon, with his curious performance going on.

Once again, he had hardly noticed that they had set him (at first) on the arm of the Morris chair, where Ursula gave him a silver serrated pipe to puff on, which he resisted, making her laugh, and which she then tucked back into his mouth like a nurse giving a boy a thermometer. He glanced down to see a stack of Rachel's records pulled out (Chanukah gift), something called "Santana" out front, and he tried his best to take a "reading" on it all, like a teacher interpreting a tough line of modern poetry or a sea captain gauging ocean depth, trying in his way to negotiate between distance and immersion, between rhyme and reason, between flow and stop. Oh, in his lifetime he had fantasized this happening at times, even in one of his novels he had imagined it (and was blasted for it), but now that it was here and happening for real, he was in a sort of terror, heart and stomach fluttering as if the dancing of two girls in the late afternoon in his apartment was a bank robbery. He said to himself, "But you're a director, dear Solomon, a Fellini watching this clever performance and show, a Ziegfeld watching his Follies audition, sit back and enjoy! Would Federico be nervous as a choir boy in a brothel in his adult life? Or Ziggy tell the girls to stop dancing? Sit back, take it easy, enjoy, learn!"

He sat back, a big boy, forgetting he was on the arm of the chair and almost falling over!

Oh the girls giggled wildly, and grabbed him for support.

From resistance to the hash he gave in, a little at a time, the girls getting an enormous kick out of watching him trying to inhale the stuff properly! As things fogged and groggied up a bit, he tried to remember details, to distinguish surfaces. For they were such a contrasting pair, really, and once they had settled him down again into the pillows, they began to dance to and *at* each other, flaunting that contrast, in front of his long low bookshelves. Tippy the taller and blonder used smaller, less exaggerated gyrations in the pelvis, shoulders, arms; and of course, from his perspective she looked amazonian. Pal Ursala in sky blue made greater use of her greater rump, even at one point raising the short skirt so that it caught tight around the upper thigh and behind like a tight towel you wore around you after a shower, and, staying there, primed the pelvis and the rear with surprising energy—her face breaking with a passion for the dance. Tippy danced differently, more passionlessly, perhaps more dangerously; she bumped with small Protestant controls and Calvinist facial scorn; large upper teeth occasionally scraping the lower lip, with hunter's pearly greed: she hardly looked as if she were having a good time at all. But she moved with easy authority in the hips and shoulders, and her long svelte blond body was elegant and striking. For her, it seemed like an exercise in power and teasing; for Ursula, a dance of pleasure. A tall cool gazelle stalked by a small hot jaguar, perhaps. With the gazelle rather indifferent to it all, putting up with the hunt and her beauty and even her own superb limbs as understandable temptation, before the fiery wild cat. And for the first time Solomon saw and smelled the power of this dancing, the provocation of this music. And having two girls there, performing "in concert," one a mysterious *stranger*, added to the power. (Rachel had once said. "Dad, if you were my age you'd be a rock freak too, it's *alive!*") With every step and look, Tippy exuded this knowledge.

Should he pull out here? On what grounds—practical,

moral? But he was only watching a dance, remember, and
. . . Was she doing anything different from Salome, say? Or
from the magnificent Egyptian courtesan who danced with
her belly for Flaubert?

The record changed again (for the second or third time),
the girls slowed up and smoked some and Tippy ran her hand
down Lionel's smooth face ("I'm glad you listened to me,
Lionel," she whispered) and exposed chest, the telephone
rang and rang and when he tried to go for it Ursula danced
in front of him, urging him with those special moves to forget it, and objects in the room grew lighter and drifted apart,
at times off walls and off the edge of his consciousness—
which now struck him as round, not flat. And somehow now
that he was up, on his feet, they took him onto the rug of
dance floor, and had him moving slightly too. Ursula smiling
still her approval—she reminded him of a Hopi girl—and
showing him by gesture which and what to move more, while
Tippy didn't change her expression at all, just the slightest
pink flush breaking the imperious features; she just danced on
in her own self-contained orbit, regal, autonomous, self-sufficient, creamy in white halter and cutoff denim shorts. Lionel
moved the best he could—deft as a hippopotamus doing
nicely but *not caring much because it might well have been
the banks of the Congo right there anyway, with hyenas
screaming and zebras racing along the grassy banks,
freightering toward Matadi at age sixteen*—and it really was
cozy after the initial druggy nervousness. Intermittently he
self-instructed: "It's just rock dancing, Lionel. It's what
Rachel has always wanted me to do, for exercise if for nothing else."

Now the coziness ended somewhere along the way as the
girls shifted into a different area of play. Or rather as Ursula
aggressed, and shifted the tone, uplifted the play by moving it
into playful touch. As the amber light died away, a curious
mauve light appeared from the lampshade, and the red-
winged guerrilla lady had caught up with the blond efficient
administrator type, herself taunting in narcissistic oblivion.
And Lionel was there on the outside, really, not invited in—
did he try? no, he was bewildered and frightened and figured
he hadn't been asked, and also didn't mind his role—and it
was hazy and mysterious this passionate tropism of the one
girl for the other. A tropic of cancer was spreading through
the Solomon zone, the New England apartment (he thought
dazed), as the one girl knew just where and how to go, and
the other obliging now too, with her own shrewdness, as if

335

they both had been there before, to a private sensualand. And Lionel felt one minute terribly stiff and embarrassed, and the next outrageously wicked, a naughty voyeur. The excitement, fear and embarrassment of being there *looking on,* the exotic bland haze and the imbibed hashish, baffled him pleasantly, and made him a stranger to experience and to himself.

*I'm so middle-class . . . bourgeois . . . uptight . . . preju-diced . . . narrow . . . everything Rachel claims! . . . what Babel knows! . . . what Tippy teaches! . . . do my charac-ters know this territory? . . . know my own straightlaced lim-itations?*

At one point his Tippy, seated propped against the book-shelves (like a Brownsville adolescent playing pillow in Johnny-on-the-Pony), long legs spread apart and passion swelling her features, Tippy spotted him, smiled narrowly and beckoned her old pal, now the outsider, toward her; and when he did move there, on unsteady knees, she took hold of his fingers and slipped two inside her mouth, licking and smiling content, and put his hand down inside her blouse-hal-ter and then his head down upon the single exposed breast, and upon its fullness he swooned, and she scratched his back slowly, urging him on; in; deeper and deeper he found his need in her large nipple, an infant whose trousers had been slipped down and away (somehow) and suddenly underneath his shorts crept a different hand, hard, and next a tongue and then more hands it seemed, so that he began to squirm in the midst of his adult nursing, suck and squirm, get and take, suck and squirm.

(During these minutes, Solomon's mind spins, thinking. The thoughts of a man under the influence of pleasure; which may or may not be very different from the influence of war or pain, extreme forces which make strangers of our normal selves. Why is it that the influence of pleasure is so frequently inadmissible in the courtrooms of literary criticism? whereas the other influences are perfectly respectable and admissible as evidence of the human condition? Ah, Laws of Litera-ture—shameful things to be violated whenever possible!)

Solomon whirls inside his pleasure dome, brain lopped off from body below, not knowing which end is up, or down: *oh dig i'm lost and hot and wet, yet i feel strong and limber like a boy and all i want is for this to go on and on and to keep doing it is it so terrible? and then maybe i can control it and stay with it and not come too soon or else let me make me come again and again make me into a mancow go ahead de-licious girls blank filling spaces of honey and cream what was*

*i saying? superb gorgeous sensation these beasts offer and
these here, great succulent globes of tippy and these sudden
salty anglers of ursula is there anything more heavenly on
adult earth than this polymorphous child play? is this the new
sex like the new math, with giggling and the stones singing? o
friends and enemies too to be pleasured and succored at two
different ends giving and taking and having all those openings
fingered and tongued and slithered into simultaneously a double pleasure is four hundred times stronger please please believe me and swear to remember it lionel swear not to go
back on this experience like you swore in some other lifetime
not to forget taking sharp curves on the motorcycle swooping
toward mexico city or not to forget taking the wheel of the
ship in that atlantic storm and seeing the waves bob over the
wheelhouse with a surge of tidal force and not to forget that
pristine appeal of snorkling underwater amidst gliding golden
and vermilion fish making you feel liquidsplendid and
wanting gills and so later on when they go after you with
hooks the critics the colleagues the radicals the superego the
shrinks the friends the defenders of the public good to punish
ridicule mock curse ostracize and consume don't go back on
this easy swaying power here trust it lionel buddy keep the
pact intact with your eyes and ears and stomach brimming
with cunt and tits and sexsmells everywhere remember dear
friend you'll soon enough be fair game yourself for the worms
and dirt—oh i won't forget oh i won't i'll keep remembering
it and coming back to it and wanting it like eating lobster
with your fingers or smearing charlotte russes all over your
face or tasting fresh sweet corn buttery and salty just keep
coming with it and into it and staying on top and bottom at once if possible with strangers too . . . and coming in
every which way inside outside mouth or cunt or ear or nos-
tril or ass o fucking bastard shit hell motherfucker cuntlapper
pricks and cunts and tongues . . . o god they know what
they're doing they're smart all right they're animals don't you
forget it oh artists at least o tippy dear smart cruel powerful
tippy you're an artist a great motherfucking artist . . .*
Stop. Rest. End. Limbs limp. Would sex, he wonders, get him
in as much trouble as romance? as deep emotions? as crime?
as truthful fiction? If these wonder girls blackmail me for
pleasure, will it be more than alimony for misery? Peaceful,
blissful. Mauve light. Hashish smells. Perspiration. Female
beauty, variety. An hour's satisfaction to fill a lifetime's
memory.

Now, above Tippy's head, he saw his rows of books to

read, and he sits and looks at titles: *Three Ways of Thought in Ancient China,* Waley; *Mutual Air,* Kropotkin; *Breakdown and Bereavement,* Yosef Haim Brenner; *Varieties of Classical Classic Social Theory,* anthology; *Freud,* Reiff; *Flowers of Evil,* Baudelaire; *The Thin Man,* Hammett; *The Great Archaeologists; Three Case Histories,* Freud; *Bandits,* Hobsbawm; *Rosa Luxemburg,* Nettl; *Function of Orgasm,* Reich; *Two Cheers for Democracy,* E. M. Forster; *Collected Papers on Schizophrenia,* Searles, M.D. Below, a shelf of fiction (to reread): *The Idiot,* the *Odyssey, Dead Souls, The Red and the Black, Chéri, Henderson the Rain King, The Golden Bowl.* And to the right, a row of books bequeathed to him by Sheyna, beloved fine Sheyna: *The Kuzari; The Deed; History of Zionism; Israel Among the Nations,* Talmon; *Masada; The Pledge; While 6 Million Died; Judaism; Anti-Semite and Jew,* Sartre; *The End of the Jewish People?* Friedmann; *Three Jewish Philosophers; The Israelis; They Were All Jews; The Bunker; The Zionist Idea; Treasury of Yiddish Poetry; Israel Arabs and Middle East; Life of Spinoza—*

"Damas y Caballeros," Ursula was now saying, singsonging, cap on head, "en nombre del Capitán y de la tripulación quisiéramos darles la bienvenida a Braniff, vuelo 971 de Miami a Lima. Dentro de breves minutos decollaremos del aeropuerto internacional de Miami. La duración del vuelo será de aproximadamente cinco horas y aterrizaremos en el aeropuerto internacional Jorge Chávez en Lima. Estaremos volando a una altitud promedio de seis mil quinientos metros sobre el novel del mar.

"Mientras nos preparamos para partir quisiéramos darlas unas indicaciones sobre procedimientos a sequirse en case de emergencia. Sírvanse a justar sus cinturones de seguridad y colocar el espaldar de sus asientos en posición vertical. Por favor observen a la aeromoza quien les está indicando la posición de las puertas de emergencia. Estas salidas estan debidamente marcadas y se encuentran localizadas a ambos lados de las alas.

"Aunque esta aeronave está equipada con cabina altimática, es factible que por alguna razón haya oxígeno insuficiente. En tal caso caerán automaticamente las máscaras de oxígeno que se hallon sobre sus asientos. En case de que fallase, presione el botón indicado y proceda a colocarse las máscara, respirando normalmente.

"Ya que habremos de volar sobre agua, sírvanse prestar atención al uso del chaleco salva-vidas. Este se encuentra bajo su asiento. Colóquelo sobre su cabeza y tire de los cordones laterales para asegurarlo contra su cuerpo. Para inflarlo, basta tirar de la cuerda inferior. Por favor no inflar el chaleco hasta habe abandonado la nave.

"En la bolsa situada frente a su asiento hay un libreto con estas instrucciones y otras. Por favor tómense el tiempo de leerlo lo antes posible para familiarizarse más con esta nave. Entre tanto, por favor extingan sus cigarrillos hasta que el Capitán apague el letrero de No Fumar.

"Les deseamos un viaje cómodo y feliz. Estamos a su servicio si tienen más preguntas o deséan algo en particular."

At this, Tippy clapped, and Lionel followed suit, and Ursula laughed and bowed politely. And as he listens to this lovely talk in a language he doesn't understand, he feels happy; and ponders: will my book-spirits understand? forgive me, and laugh? keep my secrets? EMF, you had your queer secrets didn't you? Charles B., your great poetry rose up from the gutters, from your mulatto obsessions, yes? Dr. Freud, in front of you, I'm a bit *ashamed*—yet, this must be child's play next to what you've heard? And Mr. Waley, surely in fourth-century Ming they indulged in more bizarre acts? And Gogol, dear Gogol, isn't it absurd, lying here listening to this sweet incomprehensible Spanish chatter, and to Tippy here, singing now about her Cary in Paris . . . these two nice young ladies who, together sir, just about equal my near forty years on this merry-go-round globe? Ah, Nicolai, please don't forsake my soul over this . . . trifle absurdity . . . tiny malfeasance . . . this Minor Fantasy in B of Everyday Adult Life, . . . fantasy turned real, suddenly. . . . And Jews, dear dear Jewish people, who have suffered so much and been so wronged and come through so nobly, don't excommunicate me, sirs. Look what you did to Baruch S. over there, and see how you honor him now?

Spanish rattles on, Tippy sings "Oh Cary get out your card, I'll put on some silk, You're a mean old Daddy, but I like you," and Lionel, feeling high and easy himself, reached over and takes an old *Globe* sports section and joins this unusual Reading Aloud session:

"For Los Angeles, Calhoun, ten; Warner, four; Abdul-Jabbar, twenty-eight; Allen, twenty-eight; Goodrich, thirteen; Washington, zero; Freeman, two; Russell, four; total, eightynine; for the Celtics, Havlicek, sixteen; Silas, ten; Cowens, nineteen; White, thirteen; Scott, eighteen; Nelson, six; Stacom, four; Kuberski, six; McDonald, zero; Ard, two; total, ninetytwo. Other scores: Rockets, one thirteen, Portland, one ten, Buffalo, one twenty, New Orleans Jazz, one o five; Seattle Super Sonics, one hundred ten, Milwaukee, one hundred five; 76ers, one hundred twenty-five, Phoenix one hundred eight; the Knickerbockers, one ten, Cleveland Cavaliers, one o nine.

(During this poetic recitation, Ursula repeated the exotic names, "Chaazz! *Super*soniecs, *Neeker*bookers," while Tippy hummed her Cary song.)

And now his little Gentile guppies were disentangling, and Ursula was asking him "to pleese autograph thees Spanish edition" (of *Posthumous Thrills*) and he wrote, "To Ursula, a warm girl, who's improved Pan-American relations, Your gringo pal LS." And he lay there then still dazed sweetly, while the girls moved upward, settling a pillow under his head thoughtfully. Music came on, Villa-Lobos, and they came around with cherry sherbet and croissants and real strawberries! Eased him into his rayon bathrobe and new undershorts and he scooped at the bing cherry coolness. "You will visit my country sometime yes? You must, please!" Oh he'd visit anywhere just now, he thought, his limbs easy and light and massaged.

Yet he knew somewhere too that it was time to say adiós to his springtime Maypole treats, time for the girls to be on their way—to Albuquerque, Lima, or Manhattan? to the next client, or writer? . . . Should he give them an envelope with his check in it? or a letter of recommendation? Surely you had to pay for such mixed pleasures!

He was about to say something to Tippy when Ursula of the Great Rump bent down and whispered, "Now don't forget to come see me in Peru, yes?"

"Sure," he said, picturing a vacation down there, in the jungle. Her huge brown eyes and dark ebullience reminded him slightly of Rachel. "I'm on my way down. Don't forget to send me a copy of your great speech, now."

*Which she did, Doctor. Now, who will translate it?*

She laughed and kissed his cheek, wearing her peaked airlines cap.

He couldn't resist asking impishly, "Did you wear that to confession?"

At first she didn't get it, looked at Tippy, then burst into laughter. Wagging her finger at him, she retorted, "Eres un niñito malcriado!"

She moved away, and he lay there listening to the strong folk rhythms of *Bachianas Brasileiras*. At last there was someone to appreciate it personally.

He didn't know how long he lay that way, propped and pampered and peculiarly alert, a Chinese businessman having an afternoon at his favorite opium den in Cochin. The romantic rhythms mixed with classical Bach melodies were still sweeping him when a door closed in the distance, and Tippy was tapping him on the shoulder, leaning down.

"Hi," he raised his forefinger. "Yes, you'll be wanting to get along—"

"No," she said shaking her head, half-smiling, "it's time *for you* to come along now. I have a little surprise for our . . . mischievous young man."

Solomon almost looked around, for the young man in question. The tone and manner were so different. He was bemused and perplexed.

"You come on now; here, Mama'll help you up," she said, and did.

And as he raised himself, he wondered if "Mama" had for him next a platoon of camouflaged soldiers? A wooden machine gun, painted yellow? A Lionel Erector set? Whether she had somehow discovered his boyhood surprise toys too? along with other sweet weaknesses?

*Doctor, let me stop here and not follow Solomon through the long foyer, behind his Tippy, and into the bedroom; let me tell you simply that what went on inside there for that half hour or more was terrible, or two-thirds terrible, and one-third extraordinary; it is the fact of that last one-third which makes the matter so . . . unworthy of dramatization, actual details. Most embarrassing to say the least. Most humiliating to say the obvious. To relive it here instead of telling you about it in a private hour or week in your office, if there were time . . . you see, talk is cheap next to writing. Easy come, easy go. In print, the dirt stays; or better, it appears as dirt! Whereas in talk it's so easy to erase here, apologize there, modify now, pull back and remember, lie a little, soften with a laugh, a smile, mollify with the eyebrows—or do I have the whole process in reverse, Doctor? Is this what's done in fiction? I don't quite know anymore!*

*Dirt. Not to my mind, you understand, but to others. To the world at large.*

*And what is the point of going into the painful minutiae of one's vulnerability, one's confusions, if they're no more than the natural growths of one's biology, like birthmarks (which may turn into cancers)? Isn't it enough to say, to admit, that the human creature—this human creature—is weak, scandalously weak, regressively weak, weak to the point of pathology? A pathology which gains in ignominy, increases in*

341

blasphemy, by the unpleasant fact that there is a side to it that is secretly wished for; that the patient, or victim, has within his inner world of desire and upbringing the seeds of his own decline? Do you see then the garden of paradoxes he has cultivated unwittingly, fooling himself with beds of reason here, odd rows of instinct there? And do you see furthermore the strange nourishments taken by those pellets of illness, namely, the whims and cunning instincts of a random madwoman herself? The perverse water and sunshine of a woman who has no direct relation to his life, or purpose? My God! So that the illness itself is not even dignified—if this is the right word—by a causal logic to it, by a reasonable chain of human relations.

How does one live with the knowledge of unwanted wants, unnecessary necessities, sick pleasures? Do you become a double agent of the personal life—a secret soul unknown to friends, students, family, lovers; and a strange soul, unwanted within but living within, despite your wishes? And once there, within, mocking and tampering—mocking because it alone knows that in its perversity, in its black sheep stepbrother, lies satisfaction. Do you see that?! Can you imagine such a soul, such a worm of a brother, living within yourself? A self-conscious demented brother who feeds on your own consciousness, on your own conscience and sense of wrongdoing; who is sustained by its own brutal mockery, the more brutal the better the feed; and whose end is not to take charge completely, but rather to keep things as they are, to keep the various selves in a permanent position of pain, humiliation and jeering adversity. I know there are psychoanalytical categories to deal with this perverse brother and his powers; also on a lesser plane, theosophic and spiritualistic categories; and even on some further level economic and political analyses at hand ("that brother is the perfect expression of the sickness of modern man under a capitalist regime, which can only be exorcised by a complete overthrow of the existing system, . . ." et cetera.) All that may be fair enough; but, as I've indicated, words are just words; analyses, analyses. How would you, my friend, like to live with a sick self within, one that cannot be expunged by medicine, or cajoled by reason, and one, furthermore, that at times pleases you enormously with its sudden spurts of activity?

Look, other needs I had taken in, imbibed, lived with, even surreptitiously. You can see it here, earlier on in my bedroom with this Tippy, and her breasts; who dreamed that I could be hooked that way? Hadn't I known women before who had *ample breasts? Of course, who hasn't? But no one who knew and desired and manipulated the way this young woman did, who seemed purposeful about them. Do you see what I'm getting at, the lethal confluence of accident, design and personal history? Is it my fault that the first breasts I knew, loved and drank from were large and full? Am I supposed to rid myself of that buried memory, that early fact, and therefore wipe away this sudden addiction? (The addiction which itself is sudden, and delicious? Am I not allowed sudden pleasures to intrude upon monotonous middle age?) What shall I do, spend the rest of my life with small-breasted ladies in order to prove my adult controls, quell my infantile desires, erase forever voluptuous but dangerous memories? And what about the girl herself, couldn't she be as tyrannized by a desire as I, as much hooked by her own special desires as motivated by wanton design?*

*So, my dear Doctor, is there any need therefore to proceed into that bedroom of error, embarrassment, and downfall? No, I don't think so, sir. I think you get the point I am making here quite easily. Perhaps we can treat it with a therapeutic Victorianism—end the chapter and proceed to the public consequences in the next one. Don't pry into secret places, leave that for the psychiatrists (or "pornographers"?). For case histories, underground novels. For ladies and gentlemen of taste and culture, however, let us make do with clever summaries and elegant words with which to peek into the carnal life.*

*But what happens if we wish to pry instead of peek?*

*But what happens if the carnal life is also the sensual and psychological life, the moral and social life?*

*But Doctor, what happens if this is entirely for your ears, not for the guardians of the public good? the defenders of the moral health? the attorney generals of literary responsibility? Can't I, a writer who has already incurred the wrath of those good folk, I who have been chastized and punished for my slight, very slight transgressions in fiction, be allowed to talk freely here, to tell the truth to an open mind and tolerant intelligence? Why pass over the content of this lust here? Isn't it you who have always encouraged me to distinguish among the hours in my life, between those that have shaped daydreams and fears for years, and those that have come and gone, leaving no footprint anywhere? But you see, don't you, the difficulties of trying to describe the strangest private hours of my thirty-eight years? As we discussed, I have already been so tarred and feathered that I back off, afraid to speak out any-*

*more; and also, to speak frankly, even I am embarrassed and
hurt to relive the muck and obscenity and humor (black?
blue?) that went on in there. Do you blame me, sir, for moving on, to higher altitudes in my tale, to a responsible and elegant description of the long-term consequences of that half
hour of madness and degrading pleasure?*

*I sincerely hope not, sir.*

*Even here, with you alone privately, I remain weak! Cow-
ardly.* *

Actually, he didn't move at first. Smiling narrowly, the yellow in her eyes emerging like the weird ocher color of his
Weimaraner's eyes at night, she was close to him, above him,
and said again, "Now come along now, you." Ah, that leg
was long, long up to the cutoff jeans, and although he felt
frightened, he also felt curiously *secure*, in capable hands.
She had leaned down to him to nip his cheek affectionately—not letting him budge actually—and ran her fingernails down his bare chest, excited, hard. Then,
straightening up, she looked over her shoulder and through
her cascading hair, and advised, "Now come with me,
Lionel." No humor here, no nickname playfulness, no druggy
easiness. Just the five words of command. And a certain . . .
aging in the face?

Mesmerized, still slightly dizzy, Solomon stood up, jolted,
and began to follow that enviable behind as it jiggled down
his long foyer leading to his bedroom. Wearing only his
shorts and bathrobe now, he trudged behind his taller, sleek
visitor, admiring the broad shoulders and back leading to narrow waist, the high stately walk of mature authority. He felt
like a midwestern tourist led to his Japanese bath by a
veteran geisha. (All through this adventure he looked for a
context of identification, a frame of familiarity.) The whole

* The ambivalence of Solomon in presenting what follows is self-evi-
dent, and, as the reader shall see, with good reason. I do not believe
that he—or I—would have included the details of the next section if he
were not, as it were, forced into this position by the subsequent performance of the girl in print—like a poker player forced to spend his last
dollar to protect his hand and face up to what he takes to be a "bluff."
I believe the material should be looked upon as possible evidence, as
much as literature or autobiography. How much of this is fantasy, how
much truth, how much intentional distortion is for the reader to decide.
That the whole scene was not dreamed up by a feverish imagination,
however, is attested to by Miss Matthews's later commentary on it,
both here in the manuscript at hand and also in the outside world of
magazines. In this scene, as with the rest of this material, the present
editor's desire is an attempt to understand; my axiom in these matters is
that no genuine pathology is without its genuine interest.—Lirič

344

thing was done so . . . strangely, that he felt innocent and awed by it all. Do you see what I mean? A newcomer to this country, this apartment. Anyway, she led the way to the bedroom, not looking back, until she found the bedroom and there turned to Lionel and did another surprising thing: she told him to wait, she'd be right back. And departed!

*Doctor, this gentleman Solomon, whom I knew well, suddenly looked around his bedroom, where he had slept reasonably well for the last five years, where he had thought and read books at night—here, right by his bedside table, were a few books to read,* Byron, the Years of Fame *by Quennell and* Rebellion in the Backlands *by da Cunha, that strange Brazilian epic of which he read ten pages a night—yes, it was his bedroom all right. Also, in that curious minute he found himself checking out other items of friendly familiarity, the way a man looks over a room that a police officer has asked him to identify as the scene of the crime, or a psychoanalyst, to remember, while he sits in a cell, or asylum. On his dressing bureau, his leather toilet kit, with initials on it (from Elizabeth), and the two photographs of him and Sheyna in New Hampshire. There, on the old stuffed chair and on the wooden rack, a pile of shirts and trousers that he hadn't bothered to put away. Yes, it was his bedroom all right, down to the small note pads on the bedside tables, ready for ideas. (Oh, he could use a tape recorder now, and videotape machine!) When she came back, he would make some sort of joke, he thought, and sat down on the bed lighting a cigarette. (Smoking only at times of stress.) After all, it was humorous wasn't it? Or was it?*

When she returned and he saw her face, determined and glowing, he thought better of making that joke.

He stood up, and forced a smile. She was taller, much taller, and he saw why. She had gotten back into her high heels. And he realized something else, that his expectations had been deceived once again. Somewhere in the back of his mind, he perceived, he had half-expected her to show up in some exotic costume, in her sidekick's airlines outfit, or perhaps some special cutout underwear and negligee. But Tippy had returned with conventional formality: a simple black dress and stockings, formal, like her · first appearance. And curiously, here in the heart of his apartment, by the light of the foyer, she looked older too, not a kid or girl anymore. How she might look in the future sometime, at forty or forty-five perhaps (and remembering this little play); though now she was a stunning forty-five, practicing for that future.

She said, "Now you've been a naughty boy, Lionel, and you're to do as your mistress says. Do you understand that?"

His heart pumped wildly at the statement, at the demeanor. Who was this woman, with the girl's body and the older woman's comportment? And what did she mean?

He was staring in astonishment. A sharp crack, and Lionel saw that she had smacked the floor with what looked like a whip in her hand. A version of cat-o'-nine-tails?

"Now let's get that robe off, Lionel. Come on now, no stalling. We haven't that much time . . . come on. That's a good boy."

Lionel, dazed again, found himself taking off the robe.

Mollified, she said, "Now down on your knees, you *naughty boy*. Down on your knees before your mistress."

Solomon, frightened of the scene, of the strange girl, and at the same time excited, tremendously excited, did as he was told. His knees were pricked harshly by the rough sisal rug, and he promised himself to buy a new one. The mundane observation consoled him.

As she raised her dress slightly, he had an impulse to use Babel's line, and plead, "But I'm a bookish boy!"

Suddenly he couldn't resist hugging her around her full thighs, with her dress lifted that way, pulling her toward his face.

She let him linger that way, even dropping the dress as if by accident upon his head. *Underneath, in the dark, he remembered the Pitkin Avenue photographer with the box camera and tripod who took the family picture, and let little Lionel creep under the black curtain.* Now, he found it like a honeycomb of mystery, protective, sensual, aromatic. He nearly swooned down there.

From way above, she said, "I don't think I asked you to do that, did I?"

He shook his head, smelling her perfume, her body odor. She was right.

She ran the strap slowly along his shoulder, and he pulled back.

She told him then to unzip her dress on the side, and he did it, as she leaned down, grateful for the simple task. *Like the way he used to help his mother, he recalled.* He looked up to see her unusual length; she looked seven or eight feet tall from his position, like a great giraffe in black. Also, she wore a full slip, white and lacy; a complete change of pace yet again.

"Now, you bad boy, kiss your mistress's feet."

What? The sentence was extraordinary. Stranger than any he had ever heard. Moreover, she still had her heels on. He gazed upward, expecting at any moment a smile and laugh and great warm hug and high-school giggle! The face was unsmiling, however, the cheekbones and chin were firm, that *thing* was in her hand at her side, and she gazed at him imperiously. Her body was never more splendid than viewed from this position, he realized, and he wondered, *Is this what hashish brings? Such hallucinations?*

"Now stop fooling around, Lionel," she warned coolly. "I said to kiss your mistress's feet."

And she did the next amazing thing, she put forth one leg, long and perfect like a ballerina's, its pearliness encased in dark nylon, and ending in those high-heeled shoes.

The warning removed his (childish) doubt and urged him to his task. He took the leg in his hands and leaned to it as if it were a flute, kissing it at the calf and moving downward. She asked if he'd like to remove the shoe? and he did. And the nylon? Yes. With great affection and care he performed these small acts. Oh it was really a superb leg, unsheathed this way, and he realized the privations in his erotic life; concentrating on other parts of the female anatomy had forced him to miss out on this beauty. He caressed with hand, cheek, lips this sloping white length; and when he got to the foot, he was again surprised to find the pleasures to be found in the instep, the toes (long), the sole. Especially the sole, about the same size as his, though more callused, with wonderful tender spots that drew slight moans from her above. And when that sole closed at the ends of heel and toes over his face, in appreciation, he saw how well the Chinese knew what they were doing all those years. He adored the bottom of the foot the way he had lavished love on his baby daughter's foot, two decades ago.

"That's much better," came the directive. But after another minute she said, "Just be careful where you move. The feet and legs of your mistress, I said."

In truth the orders were marvelous to take, like yoga class.

Soon, the upper leg was heavenly too, and it was smart to be able to focus this way. Every now and then he hooked her around with both hands, the flute turning into a harp, and he even took small, greedy bites with his kisses.

Finally she said, with sardonic sternness, "You'd love to go higher, wouldn't you?"

He looked up at her, at the forceful mouth and dilating nostrils, and nodded languidly. She was already a firm ma-

347

tron in the mouth, the eyes, the calm during passion. And it was right, he knew.

"You may kiss your mistress's thigh," she allowed.

With devotion he raised higher on his knees, his neck craning freely, and he began to appreciate the two firm colt's thighs, with deep kisses and cheek brushings. The skin was babysmooth, and he was rewarded totally for his having *shaved*, and when she moved her hand to his hair momentarily it pleased and encouraged him. At one point he couldn't resist kissing a single strand of pubic hair, a stray from the underpant, and Tippy said. "Noooo," slowly, and slapped the ground with her instrument of warning.

For several long minutes he expended adoring attention and care on those fine thighs. The dress dangling above his head added strangely to the power of the ritual.

"Since you're enjoying yourself so much," she put, almost bored, but flaunting her boredom too, turning it erotic, "I suppose you'd like this removed too, wouldn't you?"

He nodded, lost and alert at the same time, and she gave him permission to remove her slip.

She helped out by pulling the leg back across his shoulder and running the foot across his face, an intriguing reminder of its everlasting power.

The old-fashioned slip slid down her wonderful body and legs, and he was enthralled by its soft silky quality. And the fact that it *hugged her* continuously.

Reading him well, she said, almost indifferent, "Go ahead, put your face in it, if you care to."

And Solomon did that, and felt too her toes rubbing the slip into his cheeks, nose, mouth. That too was new. That was strong. That too was old as well, from a past somewhere.

And then, like a horse amused by a small dog, she said casually, "You may," to his new greedy goal.

And with fear and care he rolled down the handsome lace (Chantilly?) underpant. With one hand she held the dress up at her hip, and with the other leaned on the mantelpiece, holding a cigarette.

Facing him, however, instead of a soft brown triangle of hair, was a soft exposure of skin. Hairless. Solomon was shocked. Looked up. She looked back down. His look read, "What is this?" Her look answered, "Tit for tat?" He looked back down, breathing sharply. *My chin for her genitals?* He touched her cusp with his forefinger, like feeling a new animal shyly. In the semilit darkness he moved closer to see; was this triangle of skin, with a slender opening that grew wider and developed lips, the cause of all the fuss, now, and down through the centuries? Bizarre. This pink space, and resting-place for the penis, the birthplace too of genius, madness, destruction, art, chaos? He saw it clearly, admitted its inesti-mable power, smelled a fragrance. Admitted *her* genius.

"What would you like now, you naughty boy? Go on, tell your mistress."

Ah, there was the real clue to the puzzle, the way in which the triangle was treated, thought of; the psychology behind the triangle; the psyche of that tumescent opening speaking and plotting, delighting and tormenting, catching men, pleasing men, (and at the same time) producing men.

"Go on, don't be shy. Speak up,"

*In the third grade tall bosomy Mrs. Langdon used to talk to him this way, pleading "Can't you be good?" or taunting "Why are you so bad?" jesting scorn disguising erotic play, eventually pressing him to her, against her bosom, her belly, and below. Before shutting him away in a narrow space between private closet and corner wall, closing the closet door on the space.*

"I would like to kiss it," he uttered, low.

"Kiss what?" Smoke curling downward, as in a bistro.

"Kiss your vagina."

"Your mistress has no *vagina*," she replied.

He was baffled, and his head swirled.

"Your cunt," Solomon said. "I'd like to kiss your cunt."

He sensed her nodding, this tall older lady. Wasn't he sup-posed to be the older one? but he felt like a boy. . . . He sensed her nodding, but waited for the words, frightened of those black straps in the midst of his play.

The words of permission were given, and he kissed her genital area.

But the buildup, the special odor (perfume?), the excite-ment of her pubic nudity, made him lose control and act pre-cipitously with hand and tongue. Enormously strange, enormously stimulating.

It didn't go on for too long.

"You've been naughty again, haven't you?" Tippy noted. "I've warned you about this. Now you'll have to pay for it. I'm sorry. Come on, get up against the bed. Now. With your backside showing."

Solomon looked at her and shook his head dumbly. Finally he managed, "Why?"

She laughed wildly for a moment. Stopped, and resumed order. Hers. "You were naughty, Lionel. You brought this on

349

yourself. You have no one to blame but yourself. You heard your mistress. Come on, don't make it worse by *lingering*."

*Worse, he thought? Lingering?*

Terrified of her firmness, bedazzled, and wanting too to get back to the pleasures of her body, he did as he was told. His knees cracking from being in one position so long.

"What are you going to do?" he asked, thinking he knew, but not knowing anything anymore. "I . . . don't want to be hurt," he found the courage to muster. Didn't he? In fact wondering what it would feel like, *swiftly calling for comparison the times his father had belted him with his strap*. He hadn't liked that, one bit. But was this different? . . . And had he been naughty? *Yes*, if *she* said so. *Yes*. Would he argue with his yoga teacher if she criticized his cobra?

"Owch!" he let out from the first lash, but not so much from hurt as from surprise. It was obvious that the lash was not a full-strength one.

As she did it again, he saw that he could take the light pain, but that there was hardly any pleasure in it. What interested him was the absolutely boyish position he was fixed in, like receiving an enema from his mother in the toilet.

"Just take it easy," he advised now, after the third flog.

"Oh, I'm barely hitting you, you crybaby," Tippy replied.

He knew for sure now that anyone who ever got pleasure out of such strokes was sicker than he. All it did was sting and hurt!

She stung him again.

*On my own bed. Did Melville ever subject himself to such indignity? No!*

One more!

"I . . . I won't be naughty again," he protested weakly.

"There's no need to talk back," she said, cracking him sharply now across his warmed-up behind.

He was about to turn now, in rage, having had enough, when she said to him—with that perfect sense of timing—"Now up on the bed, and lie on your back."

Whoosh! another sentence, another shift in scene!

Relieved to be freed from those painful strokes—not as bad now that they were finished, after the initial shock passed—he lay on his back on the bed; ready for what? (magic?)

In a jiffy she was climbing suddenly upon and over him, with her great attractive behind moving across and up toward his face. When it was near enough, she ordered, "Now lick your mistress's bottom. Go ahead, love it up."

Solomon was no longer stunned. On the contrary, he took the announcement with a measure of satisfaction, as if after a long arduous project he was now being rewarded with just deserts. And so, the words and the flesh—or the precise angle of the flesh—going to his head like strong alcohol, Lionel proceeded with a slow solid lust at the splendid alabaster bottom, flashing white and for him alone underneath that curtain of dress. (She had kept it on, at one with his deep wishes, not missing a trick.) Oh, it was fulfillment, reward, unusual gratification, prepared for by brilliant directing and rehearsal. (Beginning how far back?) And his excitement at getting there, here, reminded him crazily of the Greeks in the *Anabasis* who finally, finally reached their goal, embraced one another and cried out, "Thalassa, thalassa!" Only instead of the sea, the sea, Lionel cried out in his heart, "The bottom, the bottom!"

"Go ahead," she approved, moving, "lick that crack of your mistress. *That's it*, go right ahead, you naughty, naughty boy!"

*"I'm not crude, Mr. Solomon, I want you to know that,"* she had said, *"I want you to know me . . . on a subtle level."*

And Solomon did go ahead, never in his twenty-five years of sexual life having had a woman thrust such territory at him that way, and cherishing it. The aggressiveness of the act was as exciting as the anatomy. So he found himself a kind of avaricious creature, moving from buttock to buttock and between, from anus divider to exposed vagina, lapping, nipping, sniffing, nuzzling, stroking, hearing now childhood taunts of diving for muff and cuntlapper. Crossing over those twin tracks of pleasure like a boy who has locked up the switchman and is playing ferocious games. A willing adult slave as he obeyed his strong young mistress with all the abandoned ardor that his poor tools—just one mouth, one tongue and nose, two hands and a pair of open nostrils— knew, knowing that if she suggested he climb up and inside of her and stay in there, a round ball for her to keep and play with at her whim, he would gladly welcome the opportunity to try, gladly, foolishly, wildly, wetly.

And presently after he knew not how long the obedient servant was eliciting involuntary sighs and strange loud sounds from his mistress, and without fully understanding what was happening he felt below a sensation, a quivering aquatic sensation that was all-encompassing and too strong for words.

This pleasure sailed on through uncharted inlets of his energy, and he was most pleased perhaps at the sudden continuous excitements of that young smooth bottom (orgasmic life of which he adored with boyish pride), until she was saying that phrase, *"you naughty naughty boy,"* with a new sense, one of weakness herself now, the first sign of her own weakness or helpless pleasure, which drove him on deeper and deeper until he persuaded his mistrss silent, except for those strange loud sounds as if she were underwater, bobbing up now and then to gulp in and cry out.

Afterwards: two fish dropped on dry ground, limp, exhaused, looking dead. But, in truth, he never felt better or younger, his heart having pumped with a fifteen-year-old's blood, now resting with an adult's knowing satisfaction.

Solomon lay there drugged, and sensed the girl moving off quietly. He feigned sleep but observed with one eye the mysterious siren in his bedroom. He felt like Polyphemus, the classical one-eyed monster, and now had a whole new sympathy for that poor, tricked victim of Odysseus. This tricked victim, however, lay in his narcotic sense-cave as Tippy moved by the side of the bed, picking up here, bending there. She might have been planting seeds or laying booby traps, for all he knew. She could do anything, couldn't she? Transform any scene, this magician. Closing his eyes, he heard the neighbor's cat howling with a tom in the backyard; should he and Tippy howl too? Soon the cats aroused the watchdog across the way, and he joined in yelping. The barking and howling were rather pleasant, tonight; Solomon's mind was a swatch of velvet just now. Let the animals of the world scream out at night, it was safer than what their masters, the citizens, concocted on the inside.

(Solomon, half citizen, half animal this night, was terrified of what it had all meant, this evening; terrified at the thought of having to see others, tomorrow. How ill was he, how naïve, how stupid? He could worry about all this later on, for the next ten years and more.)

Minutes passed, a faucet ran, a bus groaned, streetpeople made a racket passing. No, the world was quite oblivious to what had gone on in his bedroom. No telephone call as yet from the university, from his daughter, from sometime therapist Dr. Lirič. The world had received no ESP vibes, or videotapes, as yet. Deftly his lithe companion slid back into bed, snuggling up close, and pecked him warmly on the cheek, in her sleep. Child Tippy again, she whispered sleepily that she'd have to tell him one day about her "Waldorf days with her Hungarian shrink," they were really "weird," and then the words ceased. A slow regular breathing took over. Sleeping peacefully again, bless her soul; her hand clutching his as if they had just made love on their wedding night. Her face, without passion, had grown smaller, younger, vulnerable again. And her sudden falling off to sleep struck Lionel as remarkable as any other trick she had performed that evening. How, he wondered, could any doctor analyze such a personality in the remoteness of his office? Surely you needed to be up close, under the bed like the old lovers, to watch the personality perform all its tricks, its twists and somersaults, its flying carnal leaps without the aid of shrinknets? O smart doctors of the head, won't you please *begin to live in with your patients for a few nights a week?*

Wearily he eased out of bed, struggling to free his hand from the girl's sleepstrong clutch. With the aid of the foyer light, he searched briefly for remnants of their debauchery, but there were none. How tidy she could be, this peculiar priestess. Smiling, he left the bedroom for the refrigerator, and peered inside. A cold breast of burnt chicken, week-old cole slaw, a half-used bottle of white wine. Opening the vegetable bin, he cursed the tattered iceberg lettuce, and tasteless tomatoes. Why hadn't he saved some of his Burpee hybrids from last summer? Or his baby cucumbers, heavily salted, skins on? Or even fresh grass to munch on? A cellophane bag of fresh oranges made his eye gleam. In the midst of squeezing a few, by the gooseneck light, he sensed that he was still nude, and grew embarrassed. Orange pulp on his fingers, he gazed down at the frail white body—actually, sturdy hairy chest and hairy legs (oddly, smooth white along the back) his torso growing thinner in his thirties; those tender tiny feet holding it all up—and he felt suddenly protective of it, newly fraternal. It would have to carry him the rest of the road, he knew, and he must be careful. Prudent. Mustn't subject it to the . . . whims or desires, his tireless curiosity. With determination he drank the orange potion, grateful for its thick sweetness. Was this how Raymond felt after the kachina race, holding his cornmeal? Were these oranges a prayer for renewed fertility and health? (*Mental* health?)

In the bathroom, he rinsed his face, neck, underarms. Everything was in order, porcelain, tile, mirror, yellow walls. Good. His penis, ignorant and insignificant in detumescence, filled him with quizzical wonder. With gentle skepticism. For the sake of those few inches of skin and muscle, a man could ruin his reputation, his work, his life. Absurd. He forgot about washing himself there, and looked at himself in the cabinet mirror. He looked for signs of disturbance there, for the ears of Pan, the eyes of de Sade. But the face was still only Solomon's. Intact. Smooth and boyish. Perhaps he had *imagined* it all? . . . Wait, there in and around the eyes, wasn't that unusual sadness, a hint of decadence? . . . Not really. They looked as spirited as ever. He put his fingers to his cheeks, and couldn't resist noting their taut smoothness, their boyish bloom. His mind roamed, recalled. "Boitchek!" his father would call him when he was in a good mood, and then fondle and pinch those cheeks. *Boitchek*. A habit he passed on with Rachel, and her cheeks. Would Papa pinch him now? Or belt him? Yes, he was lucky now. Intact. (Lucky too he didn't have to face his other cheeks, below!) No, the body had not been tarnished by the bizarre episode. It rarely was, was it? That was melodrama, Lionel concluded. Rather, the *spirit* and the *mind* were tarnished, punished. Unlike the flesh, they didn't heal so easily; and barely, if ever, forgot, forgave. All right, he thought, his fingertips massaging his chest, in partnership; all right. I'll have a lifetime to remember, and go over each excruciating detail. Many years ahead, many hours and fictions, to gauge my . . . eccentricities. (Three cheers for the British!) He pulled the light chain, and departed, a little older.

He lay back down by Tippy's side, adjusting her diagonal torso so that he had more room. She turned abruptly in her dreams, the way Rachel used to in sleep; and grabbed instinctively for his hand. A girl with needs as well as scars. Who else would become a mistress? Could the truly needy or dependent ever be trusted? Doctors not lovers they merited. In the dark well of a room, he drew up insights, thoughts. How huge the fantasy-life, next to the brief acts themselves. How strong the art of roles and serious role-playing, especially for those who had spent a lifetime at "sincerity," at being themselves. What naïveté, what folly! The eighteenth century, with its wigs, costumes, formal manners and hidden lives, knew better! How dangerous were certain human relations, which came and went and left their marks not on the flesh, but inward, on the spirit. Where they would lie and linger and fester. Solomon suddenly longed for the real wars and real injuries, the simple physical sort, where you took your blows, saw the marks, and healed with pride as well as pain.

Morbid musings, dyspeptic man. A single action, a thousand thoughts; who needed it? His life needed a Chinese master to make it simple. Seeking sleep, he shifted to New Hampshire in the summer approaching. Fields of wild strawberries out back, with wild daisies and Indian paintbrushes and buttercups fluttering; and afterwards, the raspberry patches. And of course the garden, which he and Sheyna planted, cared for, loved. Watching vegetables grow—even by binoculars in the morning at the kitchen window!—soothed him. Also the fragrance of lilac, syringa, lily of the valley—was that syringa now in the air? . . . His heart eased for the first time that night. The little girl Xana was playing with Duke, her large dog, collaring him with a rope and pretending he was a horse; and the tough shepherd-huskie who frightened everyone who came by, put up patiently with her shenanigans . . . she was the best daughter one could have, not merely because she was clever, and well brought up, but because she was *not his*. . . . Too bad his own father was not around, to see his country place; the fine mountains and deep forests and cold snowy winters were not unlike his childhood in the Ukraine. Papa Solomon, who seemed best when dead, yet who showed up at odd times during the year, mostly in dreams but not only there, causing all sorts of curious emotions . . . in New Hampshire, Lionel would have cleaner air, and be free of all this city madness and pollution. . . . Goats and sheep instead of fans. Maybe he'd get a couple of goats, for milking; the milk with the wonderful tart taste. . . . And maybe go all out and give his dearest Sheyna what she wanted more than anything, his child. Why not, at last? A girl violinist, or a boy cellist? Was it so bad to be serenaded on your deathbed by your own chamber group? The orange on his hands mingled with the aroma of syringa bush. . . .

Delivering flowers to Sheyna, in the garden, content, he was edged from the world of sleep and dream, getting stiff below; and he was being slowly turned, and the girl was upon him somehow, and as if she had turned over and smiled, she had put her mouth to his penis and glutted him fully and swiftly. And he, not awake actually, was grateful in that it was a return to *ordinary* doings, after the earlier madness. And she, why she was a girl charmer of sensuality all over again, that was all. After seduction, she was happy again, sleeping fast, holding him with her hand, small as he was, her possession now; let her, for the evening. . . . Rachel's words floated back, "is she too hot, Dad?" "Yes, dear daughter, I am afraid she is too rich and too wild for your poor father of thirty-eight, who has to work tomorrow, and the day after, and live the next year," and his mouth was dry once again, his head still scrambling from being cleaned out, baited, hooked and filleted before he knew what was happening, so that even there in good dreams he wasn't safe, with her. There she slept, peaceful, an angel; but who knew for how long before she became a succubus again? And which Tippy would wake next—child, sexpot, competent adult, mad mistress? Was this 3:45 A.M. bout a warm-up for more of the scary theater? An Inner Sanctum of adulthood, her raspy voice instead of the squeaking door?

Would you prefer a convivial marriage and reading student stories as your life, Lionel? Perhaps settle down to write your own charming stories for a *New Yorker* audience, full of polite craft and wise aperçus? . . . His extremes amused him, sadly, and he wondered whether morning would ever come, what it would mean, what the light of day would shed upon his long journey of Tippy-night?

Morning came with Lionel opening his eyes and feeling momentarily perturbed to see the strange companion to deal with. But he relented immediately, assuring himself that in an hour and a half at most, she'd be gone and he'd be at his typewriter. And a short while after that, secure again, on the road to recovery in his adult healing womb, the novel. (Except that this womb burned him as well!) He'd play it cool with the Tippy, send her away for the day, and in the evening, after a restaurant dinner, put her on another jet. Say he had to work on his lecture, and he'd see her in a few weeks, in New York or . . . the Southwest? With plans, unlike emotions, you could do anything, be in control. Clearheaded and cheered, he decided upon juice, coffee, cereal.

It was nine-thirty when he awoke her from a deep sleep, sitting by her drowsy side with a glass of freshly squeezed juice. Blanket up to her neck, she rubbed at her eyes excessively, he telling her gently not to, taking her wrist, though he adored the gesture. Oh she was lovely just then, tender with sleepiness, pouty with irritation, a Tippy-of-the-Valley with morning smell. All this little girlish posturing, this spoiled wakefulness, made Lionel feel so much better, as if the night before *hadn't* happened. *Couldn't* have. Not the way he *remembered* it. And, in twenty minutes or so, breakfast purred along so smoothly—she insisted upon making him a mushroom omelet and it was tasty and firm—that he slowly came around to believing that he had once again probably *exaggerated* the event; that the slightest aberration from a routine night produced paranoia; and wondered privately that if a certain amount of dissoluteness was not permitted at night, after work, when then? A wild night, period; or an interesting night, perhaps; and next to truly *wild* nights between people, between consenting and unconsenting citizens of this democracy, gone wild with choice, probably rather *tame*. Perspective, my friend; history; comparison. . . . In any case, as he watched her nibble her egg and sip her tea—with ginger ale and tea, Lionel, could she be all that dangerous?—he realized that things were under control again. By moonlight she might change into Tippy Mistress and he the sad little slave, but with the sun shining, Solomon was master again. And the marquee for Solomon's Follies, now read: No More Performances for This Year—Closed Down.

Relishing his classy omelet and coffee, Lionel talked easily about his trip to the West, to the reservations, and Tippy listened carefully, sipping her tea, blushing at Solomon's compliments. When she reddened that way, she looked supremely virginal, and vulnerable, and Lionel had to hold back from hugging her! So what if she is off her nut personally, he thought, look what she does out there, in public, for others? "If I can," he offered, "I'd like to try to help the Hopis get their high school. Maybe we can get something going." She seemed distracted, then responded, "Have you ever tried to get somewhere in Washington? Through red tape? Sometimes it exhausts *even me*." But she went on anyway, didn't she? Pushed through the bureaucracy regardless. He admired all over again her clarity, her natural modesty here. And when she took the dishes away and began to do them, he was surprised once more. His Tippy was a young lady of incongruities and paradoxes.

Descending the stairs for mail, Solomon reasoned further, *By day at least, she's all right. Lucid again. Stable, sane. So she becomes a wolf by night, maybe she had a Jungian skeleton in her closet of shrinks? Would Dr. Freud hold that against her? Doubtful.* In his mail he found bills from Fingerman, C.P.A., from Slavins, lawyer, and from Georges, his agent, who explained how his Italian publisher had decided not to publish *Rosen at Fifty* after all, despite the translation having been completed; Lionel wanted to cry. The advance had been paid almost a year ago, but what did that mean? He wanted the book! How could they do that, upset him fourteen months after the fact? He entered the apartment, heavy of heart, realizing how local the evening had been, how little his life meant to him next to the fate of his novels. As long as he had his hands for typing, his brain for thinking, his heart for feeling, what did he care what happened at night? . . . Let them torture the body for the sake of the

357

pages, if need be! . . . Oh the publishing bastards, the Indian givers!

"What's wrong?" Tippy asked, seeing his mood. And when, in his frustration and sadness he told her, she offered, "I think you ought to speak to your lawyer and agent immediately, about a lawsuit. It's terrible that they exploit you this way. You mustn't let them, Lionel. You mustn't be weak. . . ." A pause. "*I* won't let you."

The kryptonite of the publishing world and his sinking reputation were making him shake! Tippy kissed him on the cheek, and took his arm.

She left him in his study, where he telephoned his agent, who agreed with Solomon's anger, but said they'd get another publisher soon enough. "Don't worry, we'll make it up," Geörges said calmly, in his European accent, explaining how the firm had changed editors, and with Italy in a severe depression and the book being so fat, the new editor had decided against publication. "We'll make them pay double for the next one," he added. Lionel, dumbfounded, asked, "Do you think we ought to sue?" Georges replied, "I don't think we can, actually, unless they didn't pay. But they have. You probably could *try to sue*, but it'll cost you more in money and anguish than it's worth. And I don't think they'll pay in the end regardless. Let me worry about it, that's what you pay me for." True. "You're right, Georges. Sure. It's in your hands." "Just go back to your work, and don't let it distract you. I'm sure you have enough things on your mind, yes?" Solomon concurred, thanked his friend, and hung up. Just hearing Georges's calm voice was soothing.

His real master, Royal standard, sitting there, reminded him that the sooner he got to work, got his five to six hours in, the sooner he'd perk up, get cured. Feel strong and generous enough to try anything again. Even another night with that girl inside? Not quite, not quite. The anatomy needed some time between surgeries, at least his did.

In the bedroom Tippy was making up the bed, and he joined in. He explained what Georges had said.

She listened without saying anything, making hospital corners and then pulling the sheets up tightly, camp-style. From the opposite side of the bed she said, "I don't think I want to leave, Lionel. Cambridge and you, I mean." She held up the Moroccan spread as if it were a new idea. "Beginning this morning."

Lionel's heart pounded wildly.

He looked up at her face, to make sure he had heard

wrong. Tippy wasn't smiling, however, just folding the spread neatly.

He wanted to shout, "But it's *daytime*, don't you pull any shenanigans now. You can't, it's not fair. Come on, no madness now!"

Count to ten, he thought. Or turn it into a joke. "Sure," he tried, "I'll keep you on my lap while I type. Here, if you give me that, I'll fold it the right way."

"No, it's all right. I think I'll go out to Lincoln for the afternoon, and ride. They have some lovely trails." She continued to fold the spread, tucking it in at the end of the bed. "I'm not joking, Lionel. I don't want to leave all this. My life is . . . drab. I prefer it *with you*, I see that now. And you can use me." Her lips edged toward a smile, a slow intimate smile. "Besides, we get along, I think you see that."

The smile, holdover from last night, and the reference to last night, made him shudder. More, he lost his breath, like a blow to the solar plexus. The night, which was all done, was now being opened up and started again, with the sun out. His chest and head heaved with confusion and rage and fright. He sensed that this time he wouldn't be able to stick to stratagems, niceties, small tricks! Oh Georges, can't you agent my life outside of fiction?

"I already have a girlfriend," he observed.

"A very pretty one too," Tippy observed back.

"I think you'll leave, Tippy," he began quietly, "and this morning, too, now that you've brought it up."

Tippy didn't say anything, just took a bobby pin from her mouth to her hair.

While she pinned up her ravishing hair, she announced, "No, I don't think so. I want to be with you, and I will. Let's say . . . we have certain things in common that . . . bind us together. And," she fiddled with another pin, looking like a Swedish movie actress with her hair up, "I think we both know, too, that in certain areas, I'm the . . . *stronger* of the two."

Lionel was so shocked at the word that he found himself repeating aloud, "The stronger?" as if it were a noun in French to memorize. Or else news that his mother really was a secret agent. *"The stronger?"*

The wild yellow glint of the previous night entered her pupils, and the face grew taut. Smiling narrowly, she turned about, dreamlike—how swiftly the surreal took over with this woman, a phrase, a glance, an ocher color signaled the transformation. Into a woman possessed. It was real all right. And this one had a strap of three or four feet of leather attached to a wooden handle. Like a lion trainer she flipped it to the side, and cracked the air!

She took a step towards Lionel.

He backed up, not believing it, wanting to write it off to comic melodrama, but filled with terror approaching awe.

From the kitchen, the soothing voice of Robert J. Lurtsema was announcing an hour of Mozart on "Morning Pro Musica." A clarinet concerto commenced just as the first blow was flung, flicking the defenseless writer across the face. It stung!

Tears came to Solomon. The crazy girl stood there, in her red jeans with sewn decals, and Lionel had several seconds in which he felt this emotion for her, a kind of encompassing compassion. Christian. And love and compassion for himself. He kept his arms at his side.

Gently, he said, "Tippy, don't do this to yourself. It's . . . it's not good for you, believe me." His words came through tears of shock and pity. "Not good."

Yet he could see in her mad eyes that his message was having no effect whatsoever, and further, in her edging row of perfect teeth scraping the lower lip, that she was preparing to strike out again. Solomon, smart, was dumb; he didn't understand it, couldn't fathom it. And in the next few seconds, drawn out immeasurably like seconds before an operation or death, he said to himself in the shorthand knowledge of the interior life: *You will receive now what you want, what you deserve, what you've as yet escaped in this episode. This is the fulfillment of your desire to know all, experience everything, explore everywhere, in men and women. Here's your reward, Lionel. This pain is not merely the price of your knowledge, it IS your knowledge. You have come for it, now take it, take it.*

*(The level of the pathology, the depth of the masochism, hurts me deeply now. Can people sink this low? Civilized, intelligent citizens? In recalling these moments, I'd like to think—I'd prefer to think—that most of it is fiction, fantasy; sick fiction and ordinary fantasy to be sure. A sex fable of the crippled. The terrible trouble is, reality in that room was that bizarre and twisted, that fine May morning. And yet, even as I now set it down, from the distance of a not unsympathetic observer, I can only shudder at the pathetic folly and painful incredibility of it all.)*

"You've been thinking small in your life lately, Lionel, and I want you to think big. To grow stronger, be heroic. Like

360

your Rosen. It's in you, I know. Because I *know* you. You mustn't let your fiction outlive you in experience, Lionel, or *it* will die too. So, I'm doing this for you."

She lashed out and whipped his neck.

Lionel, amazed, remembered, *after a Saturday matinee of watching Zorro serials, James, the superintendent's son, and eleven-year-old Lionel, began to play at Zorro in the vacant lot, and suddenly James was hitting and lassoing him around the neck with a thick rope; the lasso burned Lionel again and again as James climbed out of control, in the exhilaration of his new powerful role of black Zorro, that lonely black boy in the neighborhood of whites.*

Tippy, nostrils widening with passion, lashed at him again, and he received it. Lionel, shocked, thought, *Were relationships best when the hitting was direct and literal, not in subtle glances and phrases? When wild feelings found deepest release?*

She hit him on the cheek and across the lip, and when he felt liquid, wiped his lip and saw blood, red blood, his, he grew very excited. *And suddenly he understood his other master, Babel, who, at the Polish front, is suddenly ambushed and shot at, feels delirious with the prospect of his own death! Yes, he'd have to survive to record this.*

Tippy too was intoxicated, and reached over in slow motion to the shaking, shocked Solomon and wiped fresh blood from his mouth to her forehead and cheek, with her fingers. She loomed more striking than ever as the sun slanted through the curtains.

*Would he be a new man for the experience, resurrected with a tougher, more realistic, hide? Leave off once and for all middle-class filigree, morals and manners? Be exorcised of his punishing emotions, his Jewish feelings, by this young medicine woman from the Dominant Tribe?*

She laced him around the back, and he accepted it.

*Weren't relationships based on camouflaged power and therefore all the more dangerous and confusing? This relationship was coming clean, aired freely in the open with no word-deception, discussed in a realm of frank clarity.*

She licked her dry lips and caught his neck sharply.

*The force of this sexual violence affected him like bullets whistling by his head on a road in the Oriente jungle, a territory of guerrilla terror and overwhelming excitement.*

She spoke for the first time, saying, "You were the aggressor early, Mr. Solomon, and now it's my turn." And she hit out at him, striking his forehead, which hurt him crazily!

Tears poured from the pain. *This is my Unsentimental Education. Take it manly, masochistically. Are the deepest intimacies revealed in the most humbling and shameful acts?*

The clock time for these strokes and reflections was no more than a minute or two, though the actual time passed like a large ship bogged down in a thick fog and trying to escape it, but slowly, interminably.

Glistening with her power-excitement, she whipped his face, all the way to the ear and beyond.

A familiar voice came back to him, *"Why not, Dad? You're not big on vices—you don't drink, you don't shoot morphine or sniff cocaine, she won't kill you, don't worry."*

It was in the middle of the next swing that the spell was (somehow) broken, and Solomon rose up and defended himself. (More and more he had huddled, over and in, turtlelike, not realizing it.)

"The stronger," he repeated to himself. Crying now because of his idiocy as well as his burning pain and blood, he circled about, his arms up like a wrestler (not her Tai-chi version) assessing her speed, sighting her left wrist (the firing hand). Boyhood matches had become adult games. She had cunningly blocked off the doorway, so that was out, and if he sought to hide in the closet—no, no, he'd never get out.

She lashed out at his side, he grabbed quickly at the whip, she pulled it back just as swiftly. Seeing her lion *fight back* now, her eyes lit up with a new lust and desire. The face took on a whole new glow, violent excitement raised to sensual bliss.

At that moment, he flung the bedside porcelain lamp at her, but she moved just in time and it glanced off her shoulder and into the wall, smashing to bits.

Gleefully, she recovered her balance in time to catch him around the neck with the leather, and he rubbed it briskly with his hand. Love had changed to venom, pure and full-bodied.

A gamble. He lunged for her legs, tackling a football dummy. He had her, too, for a moment, but when he went to bring her down the dummy showed sudden strength and spun free surprisingly. "Down, now!" she called, and bang, bang, bang, bang! she shot in for quick strokes upon his face, neck, back, and scalp. Not roundhouse shots, but shrewd short cuts of experience.

"Aaahh!" he moaned aloud, and heard other animal cries escape from his throat and lungs which he had never in his life uttered before, or known were possible outside the stage. And he saw more blood now, running freer than a trickle.

"Had enough?" she asked now, happy, moving in a step. "Don't make it too hard on yourself, you *bad* boy." Her hair was wildly disheveled and lovely, the chin seemed firmer than ever, and what looked like beads of real perspiration appeared on her face. A first. In the midst of her hurricane passion, she looked at peace. "Here, you naughty boy, would you like some of this for . . . consolation?" Slowly, with her free right hand, she worked the buttons loose on her jeans.

The trousers dropped to reveal that she wore no underpants for the occasion. The shift to sexuality was overwhelming, brilliant, and the bizarre power of last night threatened to engulf him all over.

But it was her mistake, and Solomon's break. Without changing his position of abject defeat and pain, he sprung out suddenly to grab her around the thighs and topple her down, over his shoulders. A wild spinning, and she tried desperately to struggle free, tried to whip at his back, but the angle was too short as he rolled himself into a ball and upon her, his knees pinning her shoulders. There he slapped her ONE TWO THREE times hard across the face, stunning her, and stunning him, with its sexual excitement! He was able then to take hold of her right arm; as he did, she lifted her head and caught hold of his ear with those piercing teeth. He shot his elbow into that prow of a chin and knocked her flat. It was no problem then to turn back the arm at the wrist, and force the release of the whip. With one arm holding the lock, he threw the whip into a far corner with the other. As he managed to turn her over onto her stomach, he noted that she was bleeding from the mouth (his elbow shot), and he had a great urge to tell her that he was going to kill her now. And then do it, with his fists.

He kept her on her stomach, face down, and held her arm in his hammerlock, a hold from youth. It really worked!

"Now just feel this, Tippy," Solomon whispered, alive with his own power, moving about three inches, causing the girl to break into panting tears. Satisfied, he continued, "Now you're going to get out of here, and if you budge once on the way down, I'm going to break the arm. *Break it.* And if you're not gone from the street by the time I'm back upstairs, I'll get the Cambridge police. Captain James Riley"—he had noticed a *Globe* picture of the captain at a picnic—"happens to be a friend of mine, and we'll have you in jail in an hour. And keep you there for more than a few days, on assault charges. In jail with the crooks, the junkies, the jailors. And if you haven't been there in your adventures, let me tell you it's not much fun." He urged the arm upward, far enough to elicit a sharp moan. "Got it?"

In her own tears and pain, she nodded, against her will.

Holding the lock, he carefully got off of her, telling her to raise her trousers, warning her that one wrong move and he'd break her arm. With her loose hand she did as she was told, whimpering, and then he was walking her out, like a prisoner. He began to sense his skin smarting terribly, all over.

As they neared the hallway door, he saw her high tote bag, and directed her to pick it up with her right hand. She did as she was told. Then he reached down and retrieved the Pan Am bag. He told her to open the door, after setting the bag down, and she followed his order.

They were on the wooden steps, descending.

"Please, Lionel," she murmured, crying lightly. "Please don't do this. Please. You really are the stronger, you don't need to. Please?"

The frightened little girl's pleas meant little to him now.

When they were at the front door, however, Solomon suddenly was chilled by the prospect of morning, and their appearance outside. *But he had to get her outside, off the property, and nothing short of that!* He told her to open the door, keeping his hands on her wrist. Drawing a deep breath he stepped out behind her.

It was sunny and cool as they descended the six steps of the old wooden house. She kept turning and protesting in a fearful voice, "No, I won't go. I won't. I won't. You can't make me. *I won't.*" She struggled and he twisted the arm, making her cry out, stumble, and fall loose into the hedged lawn. Her bag fell open on its side. A car passed on the street, not stopping.

"Now you get moving, go ahead," he announced from the steps, and suddenly abandoning all prudence, he stepped down onto the lawn and began pulling her off it. He felt like a policeman dragging away a sit-in student. He didn't dare look about, for fear, just concentrating on his task. Dumping her finally on the sidewalk beyond the hedges, he gazed about for the first time, perspiring but curiously beyond street fear, and saw that the tree-lined sidewalk was clear, empty. Fair enough. He walked back to the lawn, collected the Pan Am bag and the canvas tote, and brought them out to the sidewalk. Tippy was now sitting on the curb, by a large maple, someone's tossed-out daughter or a night crasher.

He threw the bags at her, not hard, but tossed like medicine balls. She caught one and the other fell over, spilling things. Sneakers, riding boots, paperbacks, brush.

"Go on, get!" he ordered the way you speak to a loitering bum. "Get those things together and get!" He pointed his finger at her and said loudly, to show her he could not be blackmailed, "Or Captain Riley will have you in his paddywagon in five minutes flat. Now get!"

When she didn't move, he moved toward her, and she backed away, frightened. "You were never better, don't you see?" she pleaded, crying. "But why are you doing this to me now, why? Why? You asked me to come up here, you know you did! Then why . . . this?"

A loon, a dangerous loon. Let her ruin him with the Hopi, with Bernard and Raymond, okay. "Go on, go on!"

He felt in his pocket and found two bills. Crumpling the twenty, he flung it at her. "Back to your city or you'll be in jail, young lady."

Chin defiant, she pouted, "Young lady . . . *shit*." And sat there, forlorn.

*Was Rachel being kicked out of some Montreal apartment this morning, uttering her generation's favorite all-purpose noun?*

He turned and walked back, through the hedged entrance and up the long lawn, scorning whatever neighbors might be looking from the large windows. But no one seemed to be looking.

Opening the door, however, he almost banged into Lily Carpenter, a thirty-five-year-old divorcee and graduate student in linguistics who already had her suspicions about his "vulgarity." Her mouth fell open, however, and she said in sympathy, "You're bleeding!"

He ran his hand to his cheek, looked at the blood, said, "Not used to shaving."

Upstairs he turned on the hot water in the bath, then went into the living room to peer out the window. The thought of seeing her there next to the tree made his heart fall. It had to be done, however. *She was still there.*

He went to the kitchen, poured himself a straight whiskey, and drank half. And returned to the living-room window, like a watchman.

She was climbing into a van truck, helped by a young bearded fellow, who was lifting the bags.

Fitting. Lionel thanked the young stranger privately and sat back in his couch, somewhat relieved.

Collapsing in the chair, he began crying and shaking hysterically.

After some ten minutes of this shock, he realized he was stinging with pain, bleeding still, and had to take care of himself. He got up, staggered to the bathroom, removed his clothes, turned on the water. The sight of the blood-stained shirt, however, caused him to tremble anew. Fresh red evidence of the morning madness.

*Doctor, do you see all the foolish things that a man has to go through after something serious has happened? That wrestling match, the hammerlock of youth, the curious lawn scene—these small comic events orbit around the main event and mock it in this galaxy of irony. And all the while, Solomon burned. Oh it's comic, comic; if only it didn't hurt so much!*

# 8.

# Therapy and Morbidity

> Men are never convinced of your reasons, of your sincerity, of the seriousness of your suffering, except by your death. So long as you are alive, your case is doubtful; you have a right only to their skepticism.
>
> —Albert Camus, *The Fall*

HE REELED TO THE TELEPHONE like a drunken man, shaking. You're in shock, he cautioned. Shot on the battlefield. Get a medic, friend, . . . Sheyna? Mt. Auburn Hospital? his regular M.D. (Milner)? Tried first his Yugoslav shrink. Answering service took his name and number.

He started to dial Milner, when his eye fell on a paperback on the shelf, *Childhood and Society*. For some reason, he changed numbers. He had little idea of what he was doing; the bath was running as the telephone rang on the other end.

*"Is Dr. Erikson there?"* he asked, wiping his eyes, trying to keep his voice steady. *"Would you tell him it's Lionel Solo-*

*mon, the writer? And that it's . . . rather important. An emergency, I think. Thank you."*

If the woman had been difficult, he would have hung up.

How to put it to the great doctor? Straightforwardly, matter-of-factly. But he was shaking! He had met Dr. Erikson once at a dinner party, and the doctor had said something like, "I've read one of your books. Your character Pollack interested me. A kind of Felix Krull with a nervous American appetite. Come and talk sometime, will you?"

When he heard the eminent doctor's voice now, he said, "I'm sorry to bother you, Doctor. But I've just been in a bad scrape, and my face and neck are cut. Also I think my back, sir." He felt his back, it was wet too. "I need help, very badly, and . . . and not only physically. Do you understand? Can you see me, sir? Now?"

A moment's pause, the doctor speaking privately.

"Yes, I think so," he said in a thick European accent. "I just must take care of one item, yes. Then, shall I come there?"

Solomon wanted to kiss him.

"Yes, that would be best. Thank you. Uh, I think you better bring bandages and . . ."

The doctor, puzzled but patient, explained that he didn't have too much in the way of medical supplies, how bad was it?

"I don't know," Lionel said, his eyes overflowing and voice breaking. "I don't know." Tears rolled down his cheeks and he warned himself.

Erikson put it delicately, "What exactly happened, Mr. Solomon, so I'll know what to bring?"

Solomon forced the words out, "I've . . . I've been whipped."

Erikson said he didn't hear it clearly, and asked Lionel to repeat it. He did.

"Oh, I see, I see," the doctor said, like a man informed of a slight change in the train schedule. "Yes, I'll be right along. Meanwhile perhaps you can take a shower? A cold shower?"

Lionel stammered. "I . . . I've just run a hot bath. Is that wrong?"

"A cold shower, with soap, would be better, I would think. Much better," advised the doctor, his voice a cello to Solomon's ear. "It burns?"

Solomon nodded. "Yes, it burns."

"A cold shower, then, perhaps you can do. Oh yes, your address again, please?"

*Solomon gave it to him, and thanked the doctor.*

*"By the way, how old are you, Lionel?"*

*Lionel, moved by the first name, embarrassed, told him. "Thirty-eight." The age embarrassed him, curiously, as if for some reason, sixty-eight, fifty-eight or even forty-eight would have made more sense.*

*"I see," said the doctor. "Nothing to worry about, I'm sure. The cold shower now, please."*

*Lionel thanked him and put the receiver down, grateful for it.*

Naked, his head swimming from the pain (and liquor?), the pain which seemed to be spreading everywhere like shooting darts in his body, he wobbled down his long hallway to the bathroom. He moved like a child taking his first steps, or a man just operated on, with the stitches still in, and at two points grabbed onto the wall for support. Then, in the bathroom, he shut off the hot water—leaving the water in the bath for fear of stretching in to get the plug—and then reached into the large shower stall to turn on the spray. It was a wonderful spray, a fine or thick waterfall, Sheyna's gift showerhead. Adjusting it to reasonably cold—did the doctor mean *very* cold? those excruciating details which he always got wrong—he dragged his smarting body into the tiled stall.

The water shocked but soon soothed; Solomon was grateful for it, for the wise doctor with his deep voice. For a moment he thought of his body in the hot bath, and trembled! The cold fine water sprayed upon him everywhere, upon all the parts that hurt, his neck, face, back, thighs, calves, head, kidneys. The only trouble was that as soon as he left off concentrating on one area of his body, another part embered and flamed. But turning round and round in the stall he felt relief to the spirit—knowing *she* was gone and help was on the way—and let the spray tingle and ease his hot punished flesh. *Would his body ever forgive him?*

He was nearly done when he heard the telephone ring. He didn't want to answer it, but what if it was the doctor for some reason? Closing down the water, holding his blue bath towel around him out of habit, he went to the telephone.

"Professor Solomon? This is Paul Goldner, sir, I'm sorry to bother you"—the language of politeness now seemed a societal mocking—"but you see this short story is kind of late and I was wondering if I should simply bring it by your place sometime today instead of leaving it in school for you?"

Solomon, dripping, said curtly, "Where'd you get this number?"

Goldner mentioned someone in the class.

"Leave the story in my school mailbox, Paul. Goodbye."

His hand still resting on the telephone, standing there, he felt the stinging mount again, slowly building up, and he patted himself gently. As he did that, the ringing escalated into a scalding flame of pain, hands or matches setting him on fire everywhere. Dizzy, frightened, he lay down right there, in the small dark guest room. Breathing deeply in the airless room, he wondered if there would be shock to the heart? Wondered how much pain he could take? Wondered if he could just close his eyes for good then?

Return to the shower? Another drink perhaps? Get up and look up contusions in his *Merck's Manual*? He lay and looked at the white rectangle of ceiling, seeing the uneven swellings and the need for paint, and promising to care for it. The tiny bedroom was not a bad tomb, a final resting-place.

He sought to doze . . .

*The downstairs buzzer shook him abruptly, and he sprang up, scraping his shin on the exposed bed corner and almost passing out. He limped to the hall buzzer, and pressed it to release the front door. In the bathroom he found a pair of undershorts and cotton bathrobe and made it to the top of the stairway as Dr. Erikson was halfway up. Gray-haired, mustached, he looked solid rather than elegant, older around the eyes, the hair still vital; he lifted his black bag in greeting, a gesture of casual cheer and even optimism; to Solomon at least a heartfelt signal that healing was on its way. Lionel waved a casual hello back.*

*The cleaning-up work was done in the large bathroom. The doctor, very matter-of-fact, helped Solomon out of his robe and shorts—a few lashes had caught him on the upper thigh, the doctor pointed out—and set him on a four-legged stool, painted white, like a little boy in his office. The doctor boiled water for sutures, ran cold water in the bathtub (next to Lionel), and then worked upon Lionel's body like an expert tailor making up a made-to-order suit. Cuts and abrasions were cleaned thoroughly with cold water, an antibiotic, and a washcloth; wherever possible Solomon placed a wounded part of his anatomy under the cold running water. ("Germs can collect in a basin," the doctor replied to Lionel's query.) Next came small applications of sterile vaseline jelly, which the doctor accompanied with a small joke about making him up for a television show, perhaps? For a cut by the mouth, and another by the right eye, sutures were made,* LIONEL REMEMBERING THOSE FOURTEEN STITCHES TAKEN IN HIS

SEVEN-YEAR-OLD SCALP BY DR. WIENARD IN HIS BROWNSVILLE OFFICE, ON SARATOGA AVENUE, WITHOUT HIS CRYING, WHILE HIS MOTHER SQUEEZED HIS HAND. *When the doctor took out curious-looking bandages, Lionel asked their names? "Butterfly closures," he answered, and together they examined briefly the resemblance of the cut adhesive tape to its namesake. Lionel wanted to say, "Tippy wore smaller butterflies on her jeans," but didn't. Band-Aids, butterfly closures, gauze bandages were applied to back, neck, face, arms. He had forgotten about all the lashes he had blocked with his arms, once he had started to defend himself. Terms like "capillary action, subcutaneous cuts, friction burns," trickled through as the busy therapeutic hands worked to restore Lionel's broken skin. Lionel admired the enormous dexterity of the doctor's strong hands; when had he appreciated hands before. And as the doctor explained that most of the burns were superficial ones, Solomon felt protected, his body anointed, his spirit calmed. Sitting on his white stool, in his strange moments of helplessness and fearlessness, of boyhood protection, he was reminded of his mother drying him after his baths, of drying Rachel after hers. Young life, beautiful tender skin, mothers' and fathers' hands caressing and shining it, oh it was magical. But then he saw Tippy in his mother's apartment, and he nearly burst out crying again!*

*In the living room, back in undershorts and robe, bandaged and burning, Solomon sat with the doctor and listened to him explain about welts, bruises, abrasions, and what to expect in the way of black-and-blue marks, ugly ridges, painful swelling. Somehow, coming from Erikson, they seemed to be talking about his inner life too.*

*Lionel asked, just above a whisper, "Will these . . . scars last? Can they be . . ." afraid to utter the word, "permanent?"*

*The blue-gray eyes of the doctor didn't avoid Lionel's, and he said, "It's possible, possible. Though unlikely."*

*Solomon understood, and nodded.*

*Dr. Erikson said, "When you're feeling better perhaps you'd like to come in and talk?"*

*"Yes," Lionel said, "yes, that would be very useful I think."*

*A pause.*

*"I have this lecture coming up later this week, and I was wondering if I should . . . should . . ." the voice trailed off and the eyes strained as Solomon caught sight of the Santana*

370

*record jacket over by the bookcase, and the area where the girls had rock-danced. He suddenly broke down, started crying uncontrollably, his body shaking.*

*"Are you all right just now?" asked the doctor from his chair.*

*Solomon heard him, tried to nod, but couldn't stop shaking.*

*The doctor said something rather odd then. "Come over here, Lionel, why don't you? Yes, come over, son. Don't be shy, come over." The doctor, sitting on the wide Morris chair, held his arms out.*

*What did he mean?*

*Solomon was moved and bewildered, and believed first that his shaking, which persisted, was playing tricks on his understanding. But when he looked clearly through the mist of tears he saw the hands outstretched, and found the energy to raise his trembling body to fulfill the command. As he moved forward, he still wasn't sure what the doctor meant, or wanted.*

*A few feet from the doctor, he stopped, afraid he was getting it wrong, and embarrassing both of them.*

*"Yes, yes, don't worry so, come, sit here, that's right." The cello voice beckoning Lionel.*

*So he took the few more steps to the doctor's chair, and Mr. Erikson settled him onto his lap. For half a minute or so he sat there stiffly, embarrassed, self-conscious; slowly and irresistibly his memory recalled age six or so, when he last sat in his own papa's lap, and had his "horsey-ride." But then another strange thing occurred: the doctor began to stroke Lionel's head, from the pate down to the neck, up and back, up and back, up and back. The gesture, the physical closeness, the instinctive resonance of childhood—all conspired to dissolve Lionel's hard-fought though tenuous control, and he leaned or swayed down onto the doctor's neck, and commenced crying and trembling! His face pressed tightly onto the neck and cheek, his shoulders quavering helplessly, Solomon let his full grief loose at last. And for a long time, maybe five or ten minutes, Lionel cried and shook in the doctor's arms, on his father's lap, feeling wool and hair and stubble cheek, while the doctor massaged his kepi and said words like "Yes, yes, it's all right Lionel. It's all be over soon, boitchek, don't worry." And "I'm here, Lionel, I'm here . . ."*

*When did it end, when did he leave the doctor's lap for the couch, or have the whiskey there before him? But he was tell-*

371

*ing the doctor the whole story, in broad outline, and the doc-
tor was asking questions. Why had he gone through with it,
did he know? What did he think of it now? "You asked for
the blows, you think?"*

*And Lionel began to answer in a flurry of semicoherence.
"Asked for them? Yes, I suppose so . . . but no, not really,
sir. I mean I don't know, I don't really know! . . . How
could someone SANE ask for them? Although perhaps I wasn't
sane, at those moments, yes, I see, not sane. . . . It's so hard
to describe, to myself even, like being in a storm at sea—it's
wild and chaotic and as thrilling as it is terrifying . . . something like that! As if the elements had gotten out of hand,
Doctor, and ordinary reality has been distorted, displaced! Do
you see what I mean? How . . . how surreal the atmosphere
gets? It turns one's reason or sanity topsy-turvy, and there's
just no such thing as bad or good, right or wrong, stupid or
smart! That's what's so truly scary, Dr. Erikson!"*

*The doctor waited, had Lionel sip whiskey, asked gently,
"Is there something in your past that would suggest or perhaps foreshadow this? Or perhaps prompted this?"*

*"Do you mean if it's ever happened before? No, of course
not, nothing like it, I assure you. Once, as a boy of twelve a
game got out of hand," and he related the Zorro incident,
and then paused. "Did anything else 'suggest' this? . . . I
don't know, you know, in terms of . . . indirect causality. Of
course there was my father, who provoked anger and guilt in
me, like most strong fathers—but no, doctor, I don't think
there's anything specifically related there in my history." Solomon shook his head, slowly, in ignorance. "But perhaps if
you . . . if you look closely at my books, if I do, we can see
a pattern or some clues at least to why this should occur?
That girl of course claimed this, in her maniacal way, but,
but . . . someone like yourself, you could read me more
deeply I believe, and we can talk?"*

*"Yes, that would be good," concurred Erikson. "And for
me, interesting too. Artists actually leave more visible evidence around than others, to complete the puzzle."*

*Lionel had never looked at his books that way, and it
pleased and frightened him that the evidence would be there,
and that his books, his years of putting scenes and characters
on paper, would constitute evidence. "Can it be my generation in some way, Doctor?" Lionel wondered, his face lighting up at the shift in responsibility. "I mean an older man, a
great writer like Bellow, would never be involved this way,
sir. It's . . . it's not in his upbringing or system to delve this*

*way. To* permit *it. But I, in between that generation of* luftmenschen *and Enlightenment souls and this current age of the Tippys, and a daughter only half understandable, an age of Youth Unlimited, of day-by-day hedonism, an age of putting-down, of dirt-and-shit, of fecal idealism—"*

*Erikson raised his thick eyebrows, smiled, and said, "You say you have a lecture coming up? You must save some of this perhaps?"*

*Solomon apologized. "Is erotic power so bad, Doctor? Does it have to mean . . . aberration, masochism or whatever? And are these categories useful without a whole context?"*

*Dr. Erikson, his long hands on the wooden armrests, leaned forward slightly, said, "Erotic power, if the phrase is taken literally, Lionel, may cause some injury. You are your own best example, I'm afraid, though extreme."*

*The attention to his words caught Lionel up, and embarrassed him. "Yes, I see. Doctor, do you know what? I feel so . . . so pushed always. I lose track of what's . . . off limits. No good for me. Do you understand? My daughter pushes me one way, my work pushes me (crazily) another, my curiosity propels me everywhere . . . my freedom, it pushes me, sir . . . even the atmosphere of sexual anarchy, pushes me . . . sometimes I can't distinguish . . . is this normal, is it fair? Has it always been this way, in history, men feeling this pushed?"*

*The doctor replied, "Perhaps you've gone too fast for thirty-eight? Taken too much in? But I believe men with ambition and strong egos have always been pushed unfairly, and pushed themselves unfairly, beyond others. Too hard at times, yes? Perhaps after a number of years of this pushing?" his head teetered, pointedly.*

*"Beyond their breaking point? Yes, I see. Pushed themselves unfairly too, why, of course! Why can't I remember that?"*

*The doctor half-smiled. "But if you don't push yourself, in all your ways, perhaps you wouldn't write your books?"*

*Lionel considered that; its implications were too sad, however, for the moment. "But, Doctor, she's interrupted my life, my work, my peace of mind. And she has my address and can come back and do it again, she's out there, free—I'm afraid. Terribly." He sobered then, to say, "I'm afraid I might kill her next time, I'm afraid of that too. If she doesn't kill me first."*

*Erikson took this in stride, saying, "Oh, I think we should*

*let the shock wear off first, and then you can figure out . . .
measures of protection. Less extreme measures than the ones
you've just enunciated."*

*The doctor paused. "What do you mean about this 'atmo-
sphere,' Mr. Solomon?"*

*"The extension of democracy in the sexual area, sir. The
careers made by means of sexual detective work and advertising. The air of sexual provocation. Where everyone is challenged to lead with their genitals first, brains and conduct
second. And I'm . . . I'm a sucker for all this. I feel . . .
caught in between, trying to loosen up from my Jewish puritanism, and yet living by old standards of propriety, achievement, decent conduct. So you see if someone comes along
showing genitals while warning me about my ethical decline,
how can I resist? And, why should I?"*

*Erikson stared at Lionel, and observed, "Perhaps after this
incident, you'll be able to proceed with more caution. Perhaps be able to discern the boundaries between sensual enjoyment and . . . more dangerous impulses. I'm not sure that
you knew much about this young woman, as I gather. Who
she was, where she was from? You said she came from the
Southwest, via the telephone, is this correct? Were you able
to verify this information?"*

*Solomon explained his verification in Arizona and Zuñi.
The doctor produced a tranquilizer, suggested a private nurse
he knew to come in for a day or two, and said he'd be in
touch at dinnertime. If something went wrong, of course
Lionel should "ring up." He took Lionel under the arm, like
Sidney used to, and aided him down the foyer to his bedroom. A glass of water for the tranquilizer (watching him
swallow it), a small bottle of Darvon just in case, a telephone
call to the nurse, Mrs. Kennedy. And then, back in Lionel's
bedroom, he went to the closet corner, and there picked up
the object. "An old-fashioned riding crop adapted for new
purposes," he observed casually. "Shall I dispose of this for
you?"*

*Solomon wanted to burn it, break it! He said, "Can you
put it in the closet for me, Doctor? Thank you."*

*Erikson deposited the instrument and came to Lionel's
bedside. He told his patient to get rest, plenty of rest, and not
to worry about anything. Mrs. Kennedy would arrive in a
short time, he'd get a key to her. He had turned down the
telephone too. And in six or eight hours, Solomon would feel
better, much better. Although, he added, "You might not*

*look better. Don't get frightened if you look in the mirror. In fact you don't have to look."*

*Solomon nodded, chin above the blanket. "I won't."*

*"Good. By tomorrow you'll be up and around, and the shock will be gone. You'll be fine. Good-day for now, Lionel, good-day. We'll speak soon, yes?"*

*"Yes, at six. Thank you, Doctor." Before the doctor moved off, Solomon asked, "I should call off that lecture, shouldn't I?"*

*"Oh, I wouldn't worry about anything, until at least twenty-four hours from now, Lionel. Just put yourself in Brigit Kennedy's hands, she's a true Irish fairy. Tomorrow, later on, when you're feeling better we can think about decisions. Good?"*

*"Good," repeated Lionel.*

*"And remember," Erikson smiled, waved, "you're in your thirties, you're a young man yet, you have a whole life ahead of you, many more books to write—no need to worry. It's I who had better get going!"*

*And so Dr. Erikson departed, giving a little wave.*

*Why the fantasy of Erikson, you wonder? Why not? To Solomon, the gentleman seemed, if not the Freud of his time—was Erikson even a real doctor?—perhaps the Father Zosima, with the same pure integrity and spiritual patience. Possessing a keen concern for special men, interesting cases. Had he studied an artist yet? Not that Lionel knew. Perhaps he could do a psychohistory of Solomon? the vulnerable patient must have half-wondered. The two had indeed met one evening, very briefly, although there is a real poignance in Solomon's imagining that clip of conversation about his novel. In any case, with you gone, Dr. Lirič, Erikson seemed the best man available, the only one perhaps who could understand that a novelist was not of quite the same species as an ordinary citizen. And perhaps thereby could forgive him more easily? Absolve him? Reduce somewhat his shame? Obviously, Solomon felt that the nature of the event, the illness in question, was too horrible, too bizarre in the context of his life for an ordinary narrow-minded shrink. Would you invite a Dr. Babbitt to try to cure a Bartleby? or a very sick Captain Ahab?*

*And isn't Solomon "entitled" to a comforting fantasy in the midst of an overbearing grim reality?*

In ten minutes, Lionel had dropped into sleep, but contrary to his hope that sleep would restore him with rest, or provide revelation, it did neither. It was rather an intermittent sleep filled with short violent episodes, familiar faces on odd bodies, overheated rooms, and stuffy settings. He awoke in feverish starts, sometimes bolting upright only to lie back again totally exhausted and burning; or to find a gray-haired lady in nurse's uniform and cardigan sweater, smiling at him and tucking the blanket in around his chest. And periodically, she would apply wonderful cold compresses to his forehead and face, give him cold water to drink and bouillon to sip, and all the while chatter on with a pronounced Irish accent as if he were a young Catholic nephew just come from Belfast, and now needed restraint. Hours floated by like lifetimes, faces streamed in and out from adolescence: round Willie Yellen with his Brooklyn Tech T square stubbornly accusing Lionel of acting as if he knew it all; gold-haired freckled Pesha Goldberg from *cheder* days turning away his advances for those of a shyer boy; black-haired toughguy Elliott, up from Bedford-Stuyvesant and bullying Lionel on a basketball court in the Catskills. There were desolate train stations with huge metal turtles lumbering after him terrifyingly; he saw Hamlet for the first time as a mad young murderer defending himself with a brilliant burst of rhetoric; and through it all he suffered from a sense of suffocating sunburn and heat, so stifling that at times he was *baked awake*, into shadows, white ceiling, and Mrs. Kennedy busying. And whenever he was on the verge of breaking into all-out panic, into a quicksand of fear and self-deserving shame, then the words and voice of Erikson came back to reassure and ease him.

It turned out that he had slept through the six o'clock check of Dr. Milner, his M.D., who had earlier visited him and patched him using the same techniques as Dr. Erikson, without the psychological inquiries. He did recommend a psychiatrist for Solomon, if Lionel needed one. (Lionel did not give the full story to Dr. M., just the fact that play had gotten out of hand. The doctor stared at him, and shook his head.) At eight-thirty, when he awoke, Mrs. Kennedy made him a small steak, baked potato (burnt), green salad. He got up for the bathroom—asking Mrs. K. to fix a curtain over the mirror there, which she did, using a pajama top—and for dinner, sitting on a pillow on the kitchen chair, his bottom tender, sore. The light was toned down too, in consideration for his burning eyes. Mrs. K. had mashed up the baked potato, furrowing it with a fork and adding butter, like his mother used to do in his childhood. And all the while she chattered on about her family nearby, a daughter now an

R.N. and a son studying at Northeastern, and Solomon wanted to recommend that she take *him* on too, as a kind of foster son. After she helped him back in bed, he insisted upon trying to read, managed a paragraph and gave it up, concentration impossible; his pain meanwhile forced him to take Darvon, and another muscle-relaxing pill. He fell asleep while watching "Mannix" on TV, though his crush on the pretty black secretary turned into a ridiculing nightmare in which she turned hard and sarcastic.

But after that, sleep was much better through the night, though he would awake at every turn from the sharp rubbing against his back, neck, arms (the forearms and biceps felt as if he had been on a ten-round slugfest). The violent episodes receded as the night stretched out and the chemicals worked their slow sweet pacification.

The next day—or the day after?—he felt *raw* but better, more normal, and spoke coherently to the doctor when he called at 10 A.M. Mrs. Kennedy, who had been sleeping in the small guest room, made him breakfast (white-bread toast, which he hadn't eaten in years; why, it didn't kill you!), told him he looked a "little beaten up, like a young Irish lad after some British soldiers had gotten hold of him"—making Solomon smile as he realized that the lady had more sides to her than he had given her credit for. "But yer eyes are clear, and yer appetite is better, I can take off, Mr. Solorman, don't you think." Since she lived but a few blocks away, near the Longfellow School, she could return easily if he needed her. He wrote her a check, shook her hand, hugged her gently, and she left. She had asked not a single embarrassing question, the dear. For several minutes he felt lost, abandoned, desperate.

With no doctors around, writing would have to do. He was just getting ready to enter his slave's quarters to try it again, writing like rowing, when Sheyna rang him, and asked what about dinner tonight? It seemed like two or three *years, not days,* since he had spoken to her. Three years of being down and out, very down and degradingly out. "I don't think so, for tonight, pal," he said softly. "I've still got a long way to go on this lecture, and maybe I just better sweat it out here. Why don't I call you later if I want to switch to On again, okay, sweetie?"

"Well, I'll probably go out myself then," she said, and he understood. Immediately she felt badly over her anger, and cheerfully said he was going to miss "great stories and a leg of lamb," but that she'd save both.

He kissed her privately, suggested she see Marianna, her funny Portuguese friend, and hung up. Dear dear Sheyna, his own full-time nurse, with her knowledge of his favorite everything, from lamb to gossip, begonias to basketball. To her credit she had remained a stalwart Knicks and Yankees fan, despite his Celtics and Red Sox bullying. Yes, she knew his weaknesses, his madnesses, his scars, except these latest. . . . Oh he yearned to be within the tent of her protectiveness and adoring routine tonight, amidst violin sounds and books and good food, but he couldn't, his flesh torn, his spirit mangled, his conscience searing, on fire.

Lionel sat down at his desk in the study, staring out the window at the familiar sights: the white steeples of the Lutheran church, two blocks over, with the fat gray pigeons homing along the rooftop; the ugly brick apartment house just across the street, replacing the charming 1700's clapboard house, which had mysteriously burned down, and where, supposedly, the Boston Strangler had found one of his victims (and would his house be remembered as one where the Albuquerque Assassin had gotten one of hers?); the rectangle of gray space alongside the apartment house; the little narrow street with the two impressive Victorian houses up the way a bit. Calming. He turned to the papers on his desk, the various piles of letters and notes, the chaotic stages of his manuscript; he chose the lecture notes. His eye, however, noted a curious sight: a narrow blue volume sitting on his mail desk. Odd. He reached over for it, a copy of the *Kabbalah*. Surprised he had such a copy, he was setting it down on the small white bookcase by the window when he noticed something tucked into it. A small manila envelope which held, folded neatly, a silk slip. That slip. His throat dropped and he jumped up furious. *That slip.* Stunned, he turned about, now knowing where to hide the book, throw the garment! Would she pursue him everywhere? What other signs of her lewdness had she deposited around the apartment for him to find, like a perverse treasure hunt? He spun around, feeling surrounded by whips, panties, dirty notes! Behind a row of books, on the high bookcase he set the lascivious *Kabbalah*, strangely powerless to throw out the strip of silk. He left it in the book. Yes, there would come the day when he would *use* all that dirt; *convert* it somehow into art. Dirt and art, he mused, abandoning the study, remembering Rembrandt and Vermeer by day in the Rijks Museum, and by night those storefront brothels and pornography shows. High and low in beautiful Amsterdam had seemed fine and appropriate; dirt and art here in Cambridge signaled menace, mockery and persecution.

Could he retire to that cozy Dutch city and *escape* there? What an idea!

He resisted liquor for coffee, which he took along with schoolwork into the living room. He drew the curtains and removed the rock records from the record changer, putting them into the jackets and out of sight. A Mozart clarinet quintet went on instead. He sat in his armchair with student stories, and with Mishima's short work. But he could read neither, really. The student stories, about a crazy divorced dad and a weak mom, and another about an unaware neurotic girl with her boyfriend, were too naïve for their material. And the Mishima stories, "Patriotism" and "Death in Midsummer," were too much about the attractions of the flesh for him to deal with just now. Seeing a photograph of the young Japanese gentleman as a young warrior, a man of utmost determination, Lionel wondered if suicide in fiction forced you toward the same in life? Did the one test your courage in the other realm—not merely to speak your ideas, but to live them out too? Oh God, why write—*in order to murder yourself at the end?* First, ritually; next, really. (No, you could get off with a mental asylum if you wished, like Brothers Maupaussant or Swift. The literary precedents are impressive there too, he was reminded.)

Somehow he made it through to two-fifteen, with the aid of Bach, Mozart, Telemann, when he realized that no matter what or how he looked he couldn't stay *inside* for another whole day. He had to return to life somehow. And the first road back, he knew, was the mirror. (Or was that the real reason for wanting to go out? so he could challenge that mirror?) The muscle in his eye began twitching as he left his reading and proceeded down the hallway. Once again, in a short space of time, a walk in his apartment had become a trial of nerves. He took a step into the bathroom, and, like a man testing the water and finding it icy, backed out, and moved into the kitchen instead. There, he poured himself a half a thimbleful of Jack Daniels, and drank some, feeling it spread warmly down. Heady and prepared, he returned to the bathroom, site of his first encounter with Tippy, site of his healing yesterday; from brothel to hospital to chamber of horrors?

Carefully, he removed the pajama curtain, which had been hung like a crucifix, bless Mrs. Kennedy's heart. Though daylight streamed in, Lionel put on the overhead light for detail.

He looked. His new face, which he had just recovered, was gone. Now as a small boy and youth, he had seen horrifying faces, mostly in the cinema: the bandaged head of the Invisible Man, the monstrous Hunchback of Notre Dame, the disguises of the Scarlet Pimpernel. And recently, in life, the painful face of the Hopi lady in Walpi. The mask he saw in the mirror now matched them, and surpassed them; so much so that he had to leave the room once again and walk to the end of the flat and stare out at the pigeons, the rooftops and the black wires, before turning about. An older man, he walked slowly back, knowing his sentence fully, this time without the aid of ignorance, whiskey, or even anger. No need now. In fact, he began to perceive the affection of the crippled for their infirmities; and even the affection-in-hate for the inflictor; Ahab secretly-in-love with his wooden leg (*and* his white whale). Experience, raw, was once again catching up with Professor Solomon's literary readings, adding to his appreciation. Three cheers for his Tippy Dick?

Simply put, his new face was a grotesque mask, a macabre parody. The immediate reflection showed a black-and-blue scarred mummy, wrapped in bandages from the neck upward, with only the eyes showing signs of life. As he stuck grimly to the reflection, however, the first impression dissolved in favor of a new one, that of a tortured or napalmed man. A Vietnam veteran perhaps. Fitting. Terms from the doctor filtered through his mind, and he pieced together some of the wounds and their sources, with the aid of his fingers. He saw and felt that there were quarter-inch welts from the whip-end action, and, as a result of the main portion of the leather (not the tips), ugly lacerations. His boyish cheeks were completely gone, in hiding. Instead there was Band-Aids and butterfly closures covering three bruises on the right cheek, two on the left. These alternated horribly with three ridges of swollen flesh already turned violet and black (one a particularly crazy diagonal slash). Across his pink forehead ran a lengthy, unholy purplish protrusion. To relieve the tension of his stare, Lionel turned his neck around and around, slowly; cried. His neck too was already violently discolored, yellow, purple, black, as if he had been strangled; even Tippy's ocher color was catching on there. His lips, usually mobile, were now clipped shut in one corner by stitches; the right eyebrow also had stitches. He smiled slightly; he understood; he had paid before. With an artist's care, he rubbed his fingertips along his strange swellings, and took a curious perverse pleasure in touching his new mask. If he had been blind, he would have found the topography unusual in its variety and interest. His hand moved to his scalp, and there, high in the back of his head (alongside the boyish bald scar on the crown), were two more welts. Oh, she had gotten to him. The girl from Albuquerque knew her business.

And gradually, imperceptibly, after many minutes of precise observation, as if he were looking over a war map of destruction, Solomon began to lean to yet another view of what he resembled, and *this* interpretation or reading yielded a certain admiration, though embarrassing admiration. For now he believed that the mask resembled the face of a Hopi tribesman, either an old painted warrior, ready for war, or else a modern kachina racer, ready for religious rites; the face decorated in accordance with the activity and the identity. (Was it any different from the way certain African tribesmen, Masai or Yoruba, slashed their faces with razors for *tribal identity*?) Should Lionel get a handful of cornmeal for healing, or was that only for fertility? And so what if his own skin was fair and pink—or used to be—not a dark brown-red? Now, in fact, his new colors created a rich mixture. An authentic Jewish Indian *now*? A role his Tippy had always desired for him? Or were these the markings of a Curious Explorer of the Spirit? Didn't dangerous inward explorations merit outward markings? Look at that ancient Jewish sufferer, who was no one until he had his appropriate markings as a Christian upon the Cross? From fear, loathing, and shame he had moved on to irony and homemade anthropology. The chemistry of his narcissism converting matters.

And in the living room, taking up a yellow pad for a list of things to do—now that he was going to fly the coop—he felt swept by another, curious feeling. Sitting on the couch, a certain satisfaction about his wounds touched him. A curious pride. It was what he *needed* perhaps, to join the world's wounded. The Vietnamese and the Indians, as noted. But the Jews too, those perennial sufferers from Europe, now struggling to stay alive as Israelis. Perhaps now he could lay claim to some of that heritage, farfetched as it seemed. (The girl's aim too for him?) Hadn't he really escaped the punishments of others, while sharing their experiences? His marriage had been lovely, his divorce, if not exactly painless, had not been painful. (Blossom had been an understanding chum about it all.) Money? Between his teaching and his writing he did well enough, thank you, made enough to be comfortable, and to be easy about losing twenty bucks on a wasted evening. Women? Well, in all honesty, once one gave him a hard time, created a neurotic—or reasonable—difficulty, it was over and out. Dropped, and left for the next fellow to struggle with. Sitting on the couch and staring at his friend Simone Best's marvelously complex collage-painting, in which the real and abstract blended almost imperceptibly, he realized he had taken his blows early on, with family; but who didn't, who was a reflective sort? And were his troubles with Rachel so terrible, relatively speaking? especially if now they were pretty good pals? And his novels: scorned and spit upon and ignored by critics, they were also admired and understood and attended to by other critics, other writers. So it was not a one-sided bleak-show. And they had made him a reputation, a seriously "controversial" one. (And enabled him to buy his homestead in the country, don't forget, in the midst of birds, mountains and rural peace.) Emotions? All right, he was ripped up there, at times. But still, he had recovered from his nerve-wracking periods, so that his breakdown had been more like a three-week stay in the country, in retrospect. But punishments?

Had he ever been marked up, cut up? (No.)

Had his mind ever gone *kaput*, flipped apart, crashed into fumbling pieces? (No.)

Had he lost a son or daughter through chance, or, worse, negligence? (No.)

Had he ever suffered deep and remorseless guilt, or shame, which drove him to exile in foreign lands? (Not yet.)

Or drove him to quixotic episodes of stupid danger? (Possibly, possibly.)

So how the hell could he talk about being through it? Through what? A sail on a lake where your twelve-foot sailfish suddenly tips over? And how the hell could he have boasted, perhaps unconsciously to himself—and subtly, indirectly, to his classes—that he had in fact experienced something of the trials and anguishes of those literary heroes and heroines they read and talked about? Do you see how it had all been a lie, an illusion, a pretense?

But did you have to get *wounded* like this in order to teach undergraduates literature? (Not quite.)

*"But to be a man, a full man,"* Tippy's voice said now, *"and to be a great writer, yes."*

Lionel, blinded by a tear, tried not to listen to the idiotic words.

Shifting seats, he got to work on his list. Postpone the lecture (through Jane, secretary). Make reservations for two weeks in Caribbean (through *Boston* agency). (Unless the

sun was the wrong healer just now, in which case perhaps
Rome, Montreal?) Call Sheyna, Rachel, and simply say that
the novel had suddenly taken a turn for the worse, and he's
going off, again, for a short time. (Like a section of
manuscript burned?) See the doctor before leaving, for a
check. Maybe even try London, where . . . no, no; nowhere
where he might run into someone he knew. Some truly foreign place . . . the Marquesas?

He sat back, feeling somewhat relieved by his escapes. . . . Chaotic on the inside, he took delight in external
order and organization all the more. He admired Sheyna's
lists, her order. If only he could use her now! No. The price
was too high in emotional complications, for the practical
aid. He needed time away, in a distant land. Remote skies,
strange shops and foreign faces would help him heal. To return him to himself, somehow. To find a reasonable excuse
for his markings while there. And best of all, should visitor
Tippy decide upon an encore performance, she'd find Solomon's Follies closed up, for the summer months at least.

His escape figured out, the South Pacific beckoning on the
horizon, he suddenly felt freer. Stretched his arms, slowly.
Why not have a quick look-see outside before taking off? He
felt like a mole in spring, dying to come up and have a look
round. Yes, of course. He stood, resolved, newly confirmed.
*To going out.* Is this how young men felt when they decided
to join the army during wartime and fight for their country—
at the edge of heroism? . . . (Before the frontline shits hit,
you mean?) A walk in his city before exiling himself for a
fortnight. Opened the window; May in Boston was typically
like March. Adolescent climate. Dressing, he found himself
putting on his red-checkered shirt and cashmere pullover, informal, and suede jacket. Trying a scarf, he found that the
wool irritated, and he shifted to something purchased fifteen
years ago, never worn, a silk foulard. And from his closet
(next to her instrument), he took up his (Hopi) walking
stick with the carved buffalo at the end. Checking out his
study, he covered his typewriter, and seeing his lecture pages,
stuffed them into the pocket of his jacket. On impulse he
reached over, and from his reference shelf pulled down
*Merck's Manual.* For reading. In the hallway, he checked his
hall mirror. What he needed was . . . there, he put on his
wide-brimmed hat from Tucson, to complete the picture.
Gazing, he fancied himself to be a kind of Wild West survivor, an Indian agent, scout, frontiersman, a Buffalo (or Kit)
Solomon who had been caught and tortured by savages and

then escaped; an escape which may not have been worth it, for reentering civilized society. A Kit Carson, or perhaps a General Crook, or Matthews? Only half amused by his personal theater, his historical cartooning, his self-aggrandizements, his back suddenly brushed the door and scraped with pain! He clenched his teeth to keep from crying out. All the way downstairs, the wounded writer and sad comic cowboy held on carefully to the wooden banister. Walking downstairs made him realize how *sore* he felt.

Outside the day was sultry and gray, the sun an intermittent gleaming. He searched for signs of green, for buds; where were they? He dreamed of New Hampshire, saying the state's name aloud again and again. He felt better out there, strolling through his private lawn and turning out to the public sidewalk. Until he noted the first pedestrian. A middle-aged lady carrying brown parcels approached. His heart beat, but he laughed off his nervousness. he poked a bark with his stick, testing it? When the lady came near, an anonymous neighbor from up the block, he nodded, his usual courtesy on this tree-lined street. She tried to smile, but then did a double take, her face tightening, her mouth opening, as if to scream. Solomon hurried on, shaken. So it would be this bad, he acknowledged. I must concentrate on the South Seas, white shores, coral reefs, he thought, walking in a direction opposite from his home ground. Every now and then his thighs burned, and he had to stop a moment. Wait a second. Up Broadway toward working-class sections of East Cambridge, Somerville. The sky was turning exotic, he measured, with the bands of steel gray and luminous edges of white clouds; what were its plans? He reached Inman Square, having gotten somewhat used to the strange stares, and began to feel and smell the Portuguese markets, the Italian restaurants, the Jewish tailor shop, the Irish bars. He was reminded of the Brownsville of his youth, with its melting-pot richness and human streets. The hot feel and hustle of democracy, not the cool tree-lined elegance of Brattle aristocracy. He stopped to buy some fresh pears, and the heavy Portuguese lady clicked her tongue in sympathy. "Take it mista, some good luck for you maybe!" Solomon, almost crying from the gesture, paid her nevertheless. And as he walked on, among bustling shops and stalls, he felt *back there*, on Sutter and Pitkin and Belmont, among those carts and shops and smells and heated bargaining. He was sorry now that he hadn't made better use of Somerville and East Cambridge.

But he could be *braver*, he surmised, more open, face the

present. Return here at another time. So just like that he turned around and began to retrace his steps, toward his native grounds of Cambridge. And gradually the streets grew familiar . . . Inman Street, Central Square . . . Putnam Avenue . . . toward the river. For a moment he stopped by the old clapboard house on Putnam, the pre-Revolution landmark owned by the elderly Italian couple he nodded to each spring when they were planting their magnificent flower and vegetable garden; strangely, they didn't seem to be around now. Nothing apparently growing either. He walked on, one out of two or three passersby stopping in their tracks, pointing from across the street. The sky held up, in indecision still. Down Flagg Street past the rickety wooden houses, past Elsa Kaufman's, his photographer friend who had taken his picture for the last book. Should he stop and ask Elsa to snap his mug now? For new publicity? Past Mather House and other Harvard buildings, where the young leaders of tomorrow, studying the past, were training to be civilized. Meanwhile the Charles loomed ahead for Solomon the Uncivilized, behind the great gaping holes and pyramids of dirt created by the new sewage system being laid down. The polluted Charles was going to be restored to health. What about polluted Lionel? Along the gravel path, he ambled toward the boathouse and the Weeks footbridge. Undergraduates bicycled, couples strolled, energetic teachers jogged by, turning in fear and disbelief. It was fitting, Lionel judged, using his walking stick, marching. He was *strange* on the inside anyway, wasn't he? *Weird*, Rachel would say. Why not come out of the closet and show it to them? Mocking his own lines, he crossed Boylston Street, and veered sharp left, toward the clumps of trees just below the concave bridge. Hidden there, by the riveredge, he observed in silence the blue-back water, flowing slowly, baring bits of wood and rubber. As he looked on, he felt something stir in him as the river beckoned, in revulsion. Along with fear, there was an irrepressible urge to accept that invitation to liquid peace, to black sleep, to feel the black molasses water submerge his face, neck, back, wipe the record clear of his bandages and wounds. For a moment he saw himself moving as if in a dream, a locked-in vision, setting down his stick, hat, *Merck's Manual*, foulard, lecture pages on the riverbank, removing his shoes and climbing down into the slow-moving dirty river. . . . He caught himself breathing hard, and craned his neck to break free from his dire self-prophecy. Was it such a horrible (or infrequent) act, among serious persons, artists? Any more horrible than your life when it went sour? The act took a few moments or minutes, while the life could drag on for weeks, months. So which was worse? If it wasn't work that forced you here, it was people, friends. Friends turning indifferent or cool, or friends turning traitor, were far worse than ordinary enemies. Now add *fans*. Once over there, however, would you meet up with the recent legion of the dejected, such as Schwartz, Mishima, Rothko, old friend Lichtheim? Not bad company, if that were so. His suicide would be another detail in the morning news, over coffee and eggs; an obit by that nice *Times* writer (who had once done an interview with Lionel, killed when the novel failed), and soon forgotten about. And yet, who would know *why? (Did he?)* Would Tippy talk, or be believed? Maybe by the *National Enquirer*. And yet her story would be true, if bizarre; *if* she gave it straight, that is. Could Solomon ever tell it straight? Without the cover of fiction? Or did it take that cover to bring out the full truth?

He breathed with relief, hearing horns blaring, perceiving he didn't have the energy to fulfill that wish, accept this river appeal. Too exhausted to make that plunge now; simpler to go on, easier to go on. At the end you needed energy, not inertia, to die. Something else stirred now too. For the first time in his adult life he was confronted with a new *condition* by means of his new face. Not since you were twelve and had to adjust to a changing voice, or at seventeen or eighteen, a new evolving face. Could he—or the artist-adventurer in him—throw away that "condition" so fast? Wasn't that partly why he was out here now—instead of locked up in his apartment, as reason dictated? Consider all those times when he *wished to be someone else, somewhere else,* and *not* Lionel Solomon! Not the man whom he had thought about, analyzed, spoken to and exploited endlessly in stories, novels, thoughts for years! (Talk about exploiting lives for fiction.) Consider: to approach forty years and take on a somewhat new front to the world—couldn't he try to have a new psyche, too?

Perhaps begin a new self-history?

He adjusted his hat and poked his stick into the hard ground, and perceived that right there, that patch of anonymous earth, was a perfect prayerground. So slowly he crouched to his haunches, broke a few branches and, lacking sacred feathers, used lecture pages instead, rubbing them with fresh earth and wrapping the branches. And by the side of a greening bush, he placed them, out of the way; and there on his knees, he made a silent prayer, "Dear God, let me be healed, let me work again, let the girl leave my life forever." He opened his eyes, moved suddenly by his uncontrollable need, by his need for prayer, and he wished he remembered appropriate words in Hebrew. *"Baruch atoi adonoi . . ."*

It made him feel better. He stood up and brushed his trousers. Then he walked the short distance up the grassy bank, and at the gravel path was almost knocked over by a serious sweatsuit runner, who was about to criticize him until he *looked*. "Good luck in the marathon," Lionel said to the gentleman. Proceeding back across Boylston, past the car bridge, and settling at the rotting wooden bench some twenty feet above the riveredge. Eliot House was at his back, Harvard Business School across the Charles. The holding clouds of the late afternoon had turned the sky bluish, mysterious; and in the distance, toward Boston, you could just make out the blinking lights of Coca-Cola, the neon sign overlooking the river. Still a strange immobile haze, no clear delineation between night and day. Lionel, a rationalist and a literary mind, wondered if the atmosphere was trying to signal to him, like a Greek chorus. What: to give up his kingdom and go into exile?

For a full minute he allowed his mind to drift, his eyes to close, and he was lying on a white beach, beneath a wide sky and Caribbean sun, with the scent of frangipani in the air, and spectacular budgies chirping. And slowly it was all washed from his mind, the girl, work, friends, reputation, lecture, daughter. Exile seemed sweet, restorative. Opening his eyes, the Coca-Cola signaled red and white native ground.

In his *Merck's Manual*, he turned to "Burns Physical and Chemical," and began to read:

> Tissue injuries caused by thermal, electrical, radioactive, or chemical agents.

No, and he skipped down.

> However, systemic effects resulting from severe burns generally offer a greater threat to life than do local effects.

Does the emotional system count, he wondered?

> Whenever epidermis is broken, invasion by bacteria may occur. Dead tissue, warmth and moisture provide ideal conditions for bacterial growth. The predominant type of pathogen found depends partly on the location of the burn;

nasopharyngeal inhabitants such as streptococci and staphylococci predominate in upper body burns while coliform bacteria and clostridia are often important in lower body burns.

Lionel grew fascinated with the terms, wishing he had a doctor in the family, as well as a nurse. A lawyer wouldn't hurt either . . . (And an accountant?) And what about a loyal sister who also happened to be a fine literary critic? And a shrink? Wouldn't the postnuclear literary family include all of these? How could one manage on one's own, with just a wife or girlfriend, when the world tugged and clawed and baited you?

Under "Symptoms and Signs," he read about the three types of burns, first- second- and third-degree, as well as primary and secondary shock. Embedded within was this detailed paragraph:

> It is frequently difficult to distinguish between second- and third-degree burns until areas of third-degree demarcate. However, the physician must make an immediate estimate of the degree and extent of the burn. Berkow's body surface scale is best but, if unavailable, a sufficiently accurate and easily remembered one is the "rule of 9," i.e., the head, 9% of body surface; each arm and hand including deltoid, 9%; each foot and leg as far up as the inferior gluteal fold, 18%; anterior and posterior trunk including buttocks, 18% each; neck 1%.

Ah, that's what he needed, facts and figures! But why did his neck, only 1%, make him feel as if it were 75%? And his buttocks surely felt like . . . like 18% *each buttock!* . . . And was Berkow's body surface scale known to the girl, or did she go by her own, Tippy's Body Surface Scale? He went on:

> The classic picture of shock (low blood pressure, weak thready pulse, cold clammy extremities, pale face with beads of cold perspiration, anxious expression, increased respiration, restlessness, confusion, and oliguria) is that of *advanced* shock.

Elements of this still lingered, for sure, and expressed themselves at different moments. For how long would they continue? In any case he pored over paragraphs, at home in this orgy of symptoms, signs, treatments, turning the tissue-paper pages in search of whip wounds. It was difficult to find those specifically.

But he did find "Wounds," and settled in as if it were E. A. Poe:

1. *Abrasions* . . . These lesions are easily infected by bacteria-laden foreign bodies ground into the abraded surface. . . . Abrasions on the face may be left exposed.

But why weren't his, then?

2. *Incised wounds* tend to bleed easily since the vessels have been cut cleanly by a sharp object such as a knife, razor or broken glass. These wounds are less likely to become infected because very little tissue is destroyed, usually little foreign material is carried into the wound, and the profuse flow of blood tends to wash out most of the infective material . . .

Couldn't she have used a piece of broken glass for a cleaner cut? Perhaps next time, dear Tippy?

3. *Lacerations* or tears usually are produced by blunt instruments, shell fragments, or falls against sharp objects. Such wounds have torn and uneven edges. Hemorrhage is seldom severe. . . . Foreign matter frequently present in the wound, sluggish bleeding, and damage to surrounding tissues causing necrosis are all characteristic of lacerated wounds and are conducive to infection. Following excision of all devitalized tissue, care of lacerated wounds is similar to that of contaminated incised wounds (*see* above).

Yes, he was open to infection, the doctor had suggested. She had not missed this base either.

4. *Puncture wounds* are made by penetrating instruments such as nails, needles, and knives. Such lesions are excellent sites of infection since . . .

Needles, Tippy—can you hear, my beautiful?

5. *Prophylactic and therapeutic measures.* Hemorrhage may be controlled in a minor wound by local pressure. This procedure may be supplemented by elevation of the involved extremity. . . .
Once a wound has become infected the patient should be given local and systemic treatment as described in the chapter on sepsis (q.v.).

Yes, he'd have to read up on sepsis, whatever that was. And the next large section was

Injury or state resulting from passage of electric current through the grounded body.

My God, she did miss out on a base, didn't she?

He kept searching for whips, but knives, needles and currents seemed to be much more in vogue. But real artists came across with unique messages, didn't they?

A young couple, the boy wearing a huge scarf resembling a striped lower intestine, was leaning toward him. "Anything we can do to help?" the boy inquired. (Lionel held up his thick blue book.) "No, thank you, just getting some reading in." But he was grateful, and promised no more prejudices against those scarf-bearers or preppie students as they walked off.

A wind blew off the water, and he longed for salt air. And remembered his salty years on the sea, as a boy; and before that his dreams.

In a small notebook he began to jot down notes and paragraphs for his lecture, which might or might not be relevant, he knew, to "thoughts on the novel."

When I was a boy of ten and eleven, I enjoyed two things very much. The first, sports, both playing and listening to them and even composing at age eleven a twelve-page history of hockey. My other great pleasure was daydreaming of exotic places. So that if you asked me what I wanted to be then, I'd have said an explorer, an adventurer. I remember sitting late into the night in my parents' bedroom, squeezed between double bed and chest of drawers, sitting in a webbed lawn chair which I folded up when I was through, using the small bedside night-table, my "desk." My homework lay in my lap, routinely dull and undone. And I'd be dreaming of those foreign, exotic places—Africa and Mexico, Venezuela and Cuba, Tierra del Fuego and Cape Horn. Where did those ideas or pictures come from, how were they nourished in a Brooklyn boy who had never been beyond Ohio, and that only once, to visit his grandfather's farm? First, from picture books and accounts of travel, some very watered-down, others the real thing taken from the Eastern Parkway Public Library: travels of Marco Polo, the story of Livingston and Stanley, the great Richard Burton going up the Nile, and later on at sixteen, the story of Rimbaud in Africa. It was the best reading a boy could have. Also, there were the radio shows and the movies, which took me and my imagination to faraway places, other continents. The idea which most excited me, I remember, was to try to go *where no man had been before, or at least no American!* I used to dream of making maps of previously uncharted areas and bringing them back home, like Magellan or Columbus, or, later, Rimbaud. And if you would have offered me a conventional career or conventional success, marriage or a professorship, as *goals* in life, I would have laughed. Or offered me Harvard or Yale in place of the Amazon Jungle or the Equator, or Lake Victoria, I'd have been furious! How could a university compare with the excitement of a tribe in New Guinea, a trip up the Amazon? What I wanted, as I said, was to be *where no one else would go*, that's what appealed to my curiosity, my hunger. Nothing less would do, as I sat in my lawnchair in that squeezed space, and dreamed, *wanted*.

Of course all this may strike many of you students as old-fashioned, when you have journeys to the moon or Mars to contemplate; but craters, rocks and new vegetation never excited my interest the way a strange people did, living in virtual isolation, out of the way, surviving intact . . . Now the impulse to write somehow came along with my interest in exploring, mainly to keep a journal, I suppose, about the new peoples. But both were born obviously from the same impulses—to see, to experience, to know—as much as I could, as much as there was, out there. And I have found that making literature keeps the writer hungry, keeps the man alive instead of just going through the motions of living, keeps one exploring without taking ships or charting maps. And furthermore—

He stopped. The irony of exploration now, the consequences of the adult hunger, need not be gone into there. No, let the illusion, the "high" or noble idea, stand. This was a talk for students and academics, not for Dr. Erikson.

On another sheet he wrote:

Advances in the novel, starting with Dostoyevsky, Stendhal, Chekhov, extending to Proust and Joyce and Beckett, have concerned *man's intimate* side. His boredom, his anxiety, his sensuality, his pressures, his degradations, his errors—these have been carefully, painstakingly investigated by the great writers. The *social* side of man, the novel of society, reached its apex in the nineteenth century, and clearly now belongs to the past; or else to the "factualists" (social scientists) the middling talents, the Third World or totalitarian-society novelists. What Dreiser did, Reisman and Oscar Lewis and Goffman now do—for better and for worse. For us, in the last quarter of the twentieth century, Society, once thought of as the most complex of organisms, has now proved itself to be a rather crude piece of machinery, predictable, finite, repetitious, extremely limited. No wonder it has continued to be run by dictators and boobs, manned by assembly lines of bureaucrats and censors of official and unofficial sorts. Those great ideals of Socialism and Communism now belong in the dustbin, after seventy-five years of actual practice. Malraux, the great adventurer, is now an administrator; the radical novelist now a conservative bureaucrat; instead of books, we get edicts and fellowships. The example serves as a paradigm for the modern world, perhaps . . . It is the solitary character, his antiheroic psyche, dreams, failures, fantasies, passions that alone remain interesting for the interesting mind; Grass's dwarf with a drum, Ellison's *Invisible Man*, Bellow's *Herzog*, among others. And looking back on writers like Dostoyevsky, one is no longer interested in his opinions on God, slavophilism, Christ and anti-Christ, but what has endured is his knowledge of man's secret motives, cunning defenses, primitive needs. . . .

Man's failures, not his successes; and interesting failures, not the mechanical white-collar Babbitts of today's novels. . . . Books that disturb, that provoke, that hurt; books that whip you with their power and insight, their terror and repulsion if need be, all in the service of making you feel more, think more, live more—that's an aim of the novelist, especially in a society dedicated to painkilling and numbing, to amnesia and anesthesia. But this power, this whipping energy, it should be understood, expresses itself in different shapes and different voices: the bone honesty of Chekhov, the intellectual paradoxes of Musil, the sensual elegies of Colette. What should be avoided are books that let you sleep at night, after you've read them. Valium, not a book, should do that.

A novel should be a needle or a knife puncturing the skin, causing a wound and a state of shock, to be followed, it is hoped, by a period of reflection.

The words could be changed later, the argument refined. A noise, the sense of someone nearby staring. He stood up, instinctively pulling up his collar. Tucked his useful notebook into his inside pocket. Starting to walk again was difficult, his thighs and buttocks burning, before he got going.

The first drops of rain fell just as he noticed that a couple, maybe a hundred feet away, was following him slyly while pretending to talk. A well-dressed fellow and a frizzy-haired girl in jeans. Self-conscious, paranoid, he looked away, and walked along the river toward Peabody Terrace.

He had taken maybe a dozen steps when up on the grassy bank, Rachel came along. She whispered to her friend, and the young man in smart pullover and beret walked off by himself.

Hesitantly, she moved closer, holding her books.

*"Dad?"* Not knowing, wondering, and knowing.

A strange inquiry, surprising the father. Did she not recognize him? Did she want permission before coming closer?

The water of the Charles slapped unevenly against the muddy sides, in the last light of day.

The small face of his daughter shifted from bewilderment and wonder to spreading anguish. As if she were asking permission for *that*, too. Lionel opened his mouth, wanting to say something. Nothing came. The mind wouldn't signal the tongue, or the tongue rebelled. So he stood there, dumb, numb, unable to soften her pain, or propel the situation of peculiar stasis into motion again. He stared at the paperback of *Tender Is the Night*.

The rain was a drizzle, making her face wet.

Then her face changed once again, panic appearing now, in the lips and eyes. He knew it immediately. Was there anger too, anger and accusation? But before she could rush to him, which she was about to do, he held up his hand, like a traffic cop.

"Stay, Rach. It's . . . just an accident. I'm all right, and under a doctor's care." He shifted tone. "Is that the friend from Canada?"

She nodded slowly up and down.

"He looks handsome all right. How was Montreal?"

Slowly she nodded, dumbstruck, unbelieving.

"I prefer *Gatsby* actually," he said, indicating her novel. "I never could believe that Dick Diver was a psychiatrist. Do you—"

She was crying now, it was clear enough, even in the drizzle.

"Daddy. Papa!"

Held his hand up, firmer. Keeping her away from him now was an effort of his will, and against his will. "Rachel, I'll be fine. Don't worry now, in a few days I'll be all . . . healed." The word resonated. "Why don't you join him, okay? Tell him I'd like to meet him, sometime. And I'll call you in a few days, all right, sweetie? Go ahead." Like telling her to take her nap in the afternoon, when she didn't want to.

She stood there, crying, wiping her eyes with her forearm sleeve, the dark hair separating into strands of ringlets. Not being able to stir herself, not wanting to, he saw—wanting

393

only to be with her father, in his arms, joined to his flesh in sympathetic attachment.

Just then direction came to her brown eyes, and she said, with a resentful clarity, "It was *her*, wasn't it? That girl. The one I . . ." she searched, "approved of. That Tippy did it, did something terrible to you, didn't she?"

Solomon didn't know how to answer her. He didn't know anything anymore, nothing. He wanted to tell her too, wanted the *truth* to be between them, but was as dumb as the black gate across the way, and the solid dormitory building. And she had sensed it, hadn't she? He shook his head, with a forced ease, said, "No, Rachel, not at all. Don't be silly. I'll tell you about it when I'm better. . . . It just hurts a little now, and I'd rather be . . . alone. For now, Rach. Go ahead, join your friend. For *my* sake."

He observed her fighting the urge to run to him; he wished she would too, though he couldn't have it.

Somehow, her body turned and ran in the opposite direction, with her little girl's anguished run of tucking the arms close in and swaying excessively from side to side.

His heart pounding desperately, he was grateful.

He wanted to sit somewhere, to drink something, to hit a baseball!

Instead there was just the gray isolation, the fine drizzle, her spirit here while her body flew away, that he had wanted with him! Very slowly now, he walked in the direction of home. Sensing somewhere down deep that he had gotten what he had come for, in spades—to be visible in his humiliation, to reveal his wounds to strangers, to one's blood. His eyes burned, the skin pulled. "Oh Rachel, Sheyna, I'll be better in a few days, I promise!" Hitting the ground with his stick.

But would he, he wondered? As he turned toward Mt. Auburn Street, he looked up at the unremitting dark sky, and felt the needle drizzle penetrate his skin. Would he?

He *longed* to be at Sheyna's, to eat her fine pasta, to read with her in the living room, to lie down with her.

On Massachusetts Avenue, passing Shea's laundry, he was lost in his head and oblivious to passing pedestrians. So now you know, he said to himself (aloud?). *Now you know*. But what? And what does it get you, this new knowledge of depravity, low adventure? He walked past the Orson Welles cinema, a hangout for the young and old hip; would they be any less conventional than their mothers and fathers in condemning Solomon the Sick? Lionel thought, What does it get you? And if she had told you the next night or the night afterward to eat her excrement off your white dinner plates, would you do that to satisfy your *curiosity?* your desires? *Why?* Will you know more about sacredness and the good by clawing into dirt? Or will you write better, write *deeper,* for what you do to yourself? Or even, will you learn more about your guilt and anger or the cost of your revolt against your father? And further along, by the Parthenon, his friend the Greek waiter was eating his dinner; he glanced up momentarily, then returned to his meal. Had he recognized Lionel? Why not go out and give away all your money, your clothes, your job, walk the streets naked and be a true Christian? Or be locked away in a lunatic asylum and wind up groveling in your own excrement on all fours like poor de Maupaussant? Will you *then* be satisfied? Or is all this seeking for *artistic* embellishment? The injured, the pauper, the madman, the freak, for the sake of your true master, Art? And supposing this gets you nothing? Can't you *imagine* sordidness and decadence without having to live through them? Yet, turning up Hancock toward Broadway, a new feeling stirred in him. A small reminder, a pocket of hope. It was *not* nothing, the experience; nor was it "mad." By itself, it was simply yet another act in chaos, another blind gesture; no more. What it really was, or truly meant, was unclear now. Like any other event of import in life. Only in *work* could he arrive at its meaning, in the novel find the true shape of the jigsaw puzzle. Not "nothing," in fact quite the contrary, a challenge to interpretation, a jolt to feeling. Like that crazy building right there, he held up his stick, a strange wooden house set down in a row of peaceful brick houses. "Hey, that's not an umbrella!" a passerby crowed. Would he have the courage to get at the truth, tell the truth, about himself, for himself, for others—not for Rachel and not for now, but for all time, all reasonable Gutenberg time? To place the facts so that they yielded *meaning,* clarity; and would not be scooped by a version of Cambridge gossip, or a Tippy version somewhere? In other words, to lay himself bare in the work for the sake of truth; spread out the unusual excitement and humiliation of his life into the larger tapestry of fiction? Where others (now or later)—critics, fools, natives, lunatics, fathers, realists— could view it and judge for themselves? Feel it privately? Consider it reflectively? after the battle, say?

Plunging into the Charles was one way, the way of the melodramatist and certain romantics; burying the incident totally was for cowards, liars, or simply, the ordinary; and forgetting it in Caribbean sun, no, that was for escapists.

Reopening it with a psychiatrist, yes, with an Erikson perhaps, or Lirič, but only after rehatching it in fiction under the special ultraray of the imagination. For Solomon, the aspiration—for good and for bad—was for the beauty of truth, and of truth-telling. That was his *thing*. And gradually, as he passed tall oaks and walked carefully on old, bending brick—on which in the past he had sprained an ankle sharply—there appeared to him this new hope, this old mission. To return to the cockpit: by the typewriter in his small study, to his art, where, slave that he was, he would face his challenge, his true master.

*Doctor, false optimism and noble illusion are the staples of the human creature, especially the wounded human creature. Look at Solomon here, trying his best to see a silver lining through his clouds of shame. Even if it means* imagining *one. This is not to say that what he claims doesn't have a certain validity, but rather to point to the pathos of the rationalization for comfort. What better ointment for open wounds than lofty thoughts, especially for the intellectual? Especially when the wounds are real, not metaphors?*

So, up Chatham he strode now, no longer the scout but the defeated chief, stoical, resolute, grimly responsible. Facing his fate as the underdog. He would cancel his escape plans and go on with everything, he knew; with the lecture, the students, with Sheyna, with Rachel. A series of small challenges next to his future work of truth, be it confession, autobiography, or "fiction." And even the she-devil herself; wasn't she but a minor mistress next to his mistress, Art? And how could you compare the demands and whipping of the one, corporeal, tactile, temporary, with those of the other, permanent, long-term, psychic and spiritual? What his novels took from him, nothing else could match in terms of exacting toll.

Everything was fine and clear until he came in sight of his walkway, and he noted a girl across the street, lounging by the hedges. Tallish, slim, in tan raincoat. His heart dropped.

But when she turned, to his surprise the face was dark, the smile was different. Not Tippy at all. *And yet for another moment she was Rachel, the face drawn in pain, anguish. Anger too.*

Solomon, crossing over, walked past the hedges, shaky; and on the other side, reeled downward, to the ground. It didn't matter that the girl was not his daughter, or the *other* girl, as he stumbled there on his wet spring lawn, like a doe shot and wandering out of survival instinct before falling over somewhere in the forest. Nor did he exactly fall down, or drop down, as much as sink down, onto his knees, out of sudden default, his grief spilling over, out, beyond words.

On all fours, he implored, "O Doctor, what is real and what is not? Warn me. What is permitted in sensual adventures, and what is prohibited? Inform me. What is perversity, and what is pleasure? Tell me. Why at thirty-eight do I feel like sixty-eight?"

Tears falling, sobbing, on his knees, he sensed two people by his side, trying to help him, asking what was wrong?

But he shook his head, inconsolable, within himself still, in prayer. "O Doctor, please heal me this time. I've gone too far, somehow, I'm hurt, inside, and I'm afraid, I'm deeply afraid. O Doctor, don't let me lose my precious Sheyna, my daughter, my teaching, writing. I feel as if it's all slipping away, sliding, and I can't get hold of it! Soothe my burning neck, heal this bizarre face, let me look naturally in the mirror again. Let me be out from the eye of the hurricane! Please Doctor, or Sheyna, or Rachel, or Babel, or you Momma, help me, before it's too late. Help me!"

They were helping him up. The woman was the middle-aged jewelry maker upstairs, the man was her friend; Solomon had no idea of whether or not they had heard him. He let them bear him up the steps, up the stairway, this kindly neurotic lady and her friend, and his head swam with emotion, and he felt his lungs needing air desperately, as if he were under water too long! He breathed in deeply, and felt his muscles taut and strained, but when he moved abruptly, it hurt, it hurt! At last they had him in the apartment, safe, and on his bed. He indicated the bottle of pills, and Helena gave him a glass of water and watched him take the tranquilizer. After promising that he'd call his doctor and thanking the dear lady—a forty-eight-year-old spinster survivor who had been through her own hells—he was left alone, in peace. In the living room he sat on the homemade sofa, and looked up at the paintings done by another friend. But as he tried to read, a strange sense enveloped him, namely, that these objects and pieces of furniture *knew* what had gone on: the low bookcase, the burlapped wall, the Morris chair, and these paintings, one large, two small; yes, his most intimate friends of ten years time had *witnessed* the performance. For once, he wished he lived in a modern high-rise apartment with spanking new furniture, anonymous steel and chrome curves, *made by no one he knew.* And his *books.* Those endless rows of books. Standing spines of conscience. Witnesses for the prosecution or defense?

He knew what he needed, a month in Swerdlow's. Where they cared for you like a little infant, where Dr. Lirič could come and talk regularly. A white house in the woods, therapeutic, kindly, safe. Where nervous types who had gotten in too deep could get a little rest.

To his great surprise he was relaxed and drowsy and it took him no time at all to fall into a fast sleep right there on the sofa.

Later, the ring of the downstairs doorbell startled him.

He didn't move, his eyes blinking.

It rang a second time, a third time, harshly.

For the umpteenth time in the last forty-eight hours, he worked on his body to move it, staggering up. (God, was it only two days long, this nightmare?) When he reached the hallway door, it rang again. And again.

"Who's there?" Angry. "Who is it?"

"Western Union for Sio-nel Lol-o-mons," came the muted reply.

He stood still, trying to get his head clear, figure this out. A Tippy trick? A hired assassin who had gotten his name wrong?

"If you ain't him, mista, could you grab it for him?"

"I'm coming," said Lionel, descending the stairs with enormous fatigue. Lolomons, huh? Not a bad alias in Peru sometime. But why hadn't he installed a peekhole like the rest of urban America?

Hands shaking, he opened the door, and the first thing he saw was a huge fedora hat, black, with an orange ribbon. There was also a naked chest, rat-colored, and a huge wooden cross hanging on it. The face was smallish, and mostly covered with sideburn whiskers which extended to below the chin.

Instead of knocking off Lionel right there, the fellow told him to sign the line in his yellow pad.

Lionel did as he was told, and he handed the telegram. The boy, looking him over now, left off his annoyance and said, "They sure can get mean sometimes."

Lionel raised his face from the yellow paper, and saw the slow head-shaking in sympathy.

"And scratch like alley cats." The messenger smiled, showing a row of teeth like overripe sweet corn. "*I* know."

398

My God, did everyone know?

The yellowing smile lingered on the mugger's face, and he was savoring Solomon, discovering a bond.

Lionel handed him two quarters, thought about being cheap, raised it to a buck. He observed, as if making a general statement, "You look pretty young to know about such things."

The crooked yellow smile, and the tipping back of the large fedora. "Never too young to know about women on your back, Daddy. Shit, Vietnam's nothing next to a baaad lady." He went on to tell about his stint in Vietnam, marriage and two kids, and a breakup. "I still run up to Springfield to see the kids when I can," the young man continued garrulously, "but it's heavy. The ole lady always has a new boyfriend around, and that ain't too cool." He shrugged.

"How old are you?"

"Me? Twenty-four man! Moving up there, ya know. Gotta make it soon or *forget it*." He put the hand down over his forehead, looking dangerous again. "Hey, thanks for this, an' I'll catch ya later. If it gets to hurtin', try some tequila, or some good grass." He winked and departed.

This brief encounter, this city-encounter, comforted Lionel curiously, and he was sorry to see the strange messenger leave.

Climbing the stairs, he thought about the sender. Mother dying? Why not a phone call? (Wouldn't that be an irony, the son turning off his telephone out of injury, the mother trying to get through because of one?) His heart shuddered at the prospect. But more likely, he knew, was a message from Miss Maniac, announcing what threat—his assassination? A fitting ending to the story perhaps. (Too melodramatic for a short novel?) Did you have to hire a bodyguard once your name hit print and your novels were both provocative and in paperback? He took the telegram to his drink in the living room and set it down next to his lecture, his list of cancellations, his *Merck's Manual*. His neck started burning again, and he was grateful, since it put him temporarily beyond fear, beyond real anxiety about what he was going to find in the telegram.

On the low table by his chair was a recent novel sent to him by a publisher. Written by a midwesterner with a *New York Times* reputation. He read the first paragraph, put the book down, took up a pad. Infuriated, he wrote a paragraph for his talk:

*Against petty writing.* A period of new gentility has taken hold, infected the literature, and the source is easy enough to discover: the rise of Creative Writing classes in the university. In the Creative Writing classroom, the student picks up habits of writing, and literary standards, from professors whose own novels are praised at writers' conferences and also in certain magazines for their "stylistic gift." (This phrase is used interchangeably with terms like "poetic gift," "lyrical magic," "artistic craftsmanship," etc.) The result has been a spate of persons who produce endless pretty sentences and godawful novels. You cannot read these books because they stimulate neither the brain nor the heart; their main appeal is to academic critics who, by chance, have created a body of criticism in which pretty sentences, called "language" (or psycholinguistics), or "style," are the uppermost criteria in judging fiction. It is not accurate to say that these books are about nothing; truer to say that behind the pretty writing are emotional clichés, insights thirty years old, characters that need wheelchairs. The pretty sentences are like some oak veneer which, when stripped away, reveal some soft second-rate wood beneath. Now you can take this whole crop of pretty writers, artistic craftsmen, Creative Writing teachers, and trade them all in for one solidly *bad* writer, like a Dreiser. There we have a writer who couldn't write a pretty sentence if he tried—who couldn't even write a good sentence most of the time—but who wrote some of the most powerful novels of this century. Now when I see a writer praised in certain journals, like the esteemed NYTBR, for his "beautiful writing," I want to shoot the critic. Instead, I use the review for kindling. Pretty writing is an enemy of literature and, for the novelist, immediate poison. And yet we go on turning out carbon copies of the original poison. I have a small alternative: is it not possible to return to older days and have the young writers become scribes for their apprenticeship? That is, have them copy out whole texts or great works during these Creative Writing hours. Wouldn't a young writer do far better copying the entire *Secret Agent* or *The Way of All Flesh*, experiencing the prose style as they copy it, stopping when they wish to recite it aloud, than trying to "create" their own pretty sentences, in the service of some pretty writing professor? . . .

What do I mean by this sort of writing? Here is the first paragraph of a novel of a few years ago, received splendidly by the popular press, whose author is an esteemed professor at a midwestern university and at various writers' conferences (although it was always my belief that a writer wrote, rather than conferred; and when he wished to impart wisdom, he preferred the essay form to the conference forum, the province of the businessman).

400

Lionel stopped. He could copy out the first paragraph later, and spend a page analyzing it. Yes, he was wide open to the charge that *he* taught one of those Creative Writing classes. Comically open. Fair enough. He knew he set dead aim on pretty writing, right from the start, in his classes. But would his audience believe him? Doubtful.

Putting the book aside, he saw the thin yellow envelope of sudden trouble. But he felt better now, work having relaxed him and Handel (concerti grossi) having healed him. He sensed now that of course it was from Tippy, in one way or another, but all right: bullets killed, not telegrams. This was . . . a more subtle, brilliant message than assassination. Something like, he imagined: YOUR MOTHER AND I ARE OFF TO SEE THE HOLY LAND TOGETHER STOP CAN YOU COME STOP WHY HAVEN'T YOU TAKEN HER TO JERUSALEM YET. He grew excited again, a tingling through his chest and head.

He tore open the telegram and gazed first at the sender's location: Buenos Aires, Argentina. He set it down, reflected, saw how she would never let go, never. He'd have to hire the gunman, not she. That's what she'd drive him to!

He read the message:

PLEASE ACCEPT OUR CONGRATULATIONS STOP YOU HAVE WON 1975 PAN AMERICAN LITERARY PRIZE FOR DISTIN-GUISHED ARTISTIC EXCELLENCE STOP A CADA UNO SEGUN SUS NECESIDADES AND FRENESI POSTUMO FIRST NOVELS TO WIN HONORS IN THREE YEARS STOP CAN YOU COME TO BUENOS AIRES ON SEPTEMBER 22 FOR AWARD CEREMONY STOP FULL LETTER TO FOLLOW

It was signed by Miguel de Santana, on behalf of the Pan-American Literary Committee.

Lionel put the letter down, looked out the window at the pigeons sitting on the power lines and expecting no telegrams. He read the message again.

He found it difficult to distinguish his neck burning from the excitement boiling inward. He did not know if the telegram was real, or what it meant. (Yes, the novel titles listed were real enough.) His first reaction was that, either way, real or fraud, it was a cruel missive. An ironic response to his pleas? A contemptuous note on his situation? What he did know for sure, as he went for water in the kitchen, was that his species and the times made it increasingly difficult to understand his life. Or to do too much about it; at least here, on this point of the planet. Perhaps things were clearer in Zanzibar, Peking, or even Tycho's Crater? He drank water, couldn't take it, switched to 7-Up, finally went back to Scotch. A strong urge rose in him to call friends to share in the sudden glory and champagne excitement. He lifted the phone and dialed Simone Best; but what if it were a fraud, a cruel Tippy fraud, no more? He put the receiver down.

In his study, he went to the *Columbia Encyclopedia* and checked out the prize. No mention of it, anywhere. He called up the Widener Library, reference section; the kindly European librarian spent fifteen minutes looking about, then called back to say he couldn't locate anything like it. Did he want other grants to apply for? Lionel smiled with bitter amusement. So: a brilliant hoax, or not so brilliant, to push his humiliation out into the open, to make him a public fool on top of being a private sordid victim!

He returned to his lecture . . . too despondent to think clearly, however. What he needed now was some of *their* hashish, some opium. To wander off toward oblivion, and white escape. And he knew yet again how clever and ingenious the girl was. Hit him where he hadn't expected it, and low, *low*. In his work. In his reputation. In his *literary kishkas*. Down and out for the past few years in his reputation, so you send him an award, you *tease* him with other writers' fruits! Oh, it hurt, it hurt! couldn't she have left him alone, just called him up and been obscene, been crazy and done dirty things to him, without the literary filigree? Without the shenanigans about novels, great writers? It was like taking a bum off the Bowery, buying him a suit of clothes and a decent meal, and giving him new hope—only to leave him then with a paid-for bottle of liquor, alone; so that when you returned, you'd know what you'd find: a drunken bum all over again! And so Solomon, a literary bum, staggered to the telephone to get help. From Dr. Lirič this time.

But he didn't get that far, since the telephone rang as he was two steps from it. Angrily, he lifted the receiver.

A reporter from the *New York Times* offering congratulations, and asking if he might answer a few questions, and also, if Lionel might pose for a picture or two? A *Times* photographer lived in Brookline, and could be there in fifteen minutes. They wanted to get the story into tomorrow's early edition, if possible. "If we've got the right info, you're the first winner since a writer named Gombrowicz in '67 or '68. And the first American winner since the award began."

His *picture?* "Why don't you use the old one?" he was

about to ask. Instead he said, with a certain calm, "Yes, she can come over, that would be all right."

The man thanked him, saying how he had always heard that Solomon was very difficult to deal with. He added, "I enjoy your work myself, very much." Lionel was grateful. "Now just a couple of questions, if I may?" Had he been awarded any prizes before this? Did they allude to any specific works in the announcement? What was he working on now, and when would it be finished? The first two easy to answer, the last difficult. "In between things," he offered.

"Stories, you mean?"

"Uh, no, not exactly."

"Autobiography perhaps?"

Yes, that was it, yes! Confession! "Uh, no, not that either."

Were there any South American writers who had influenced him, or whom he admired greatly? Would he be going to Argentina for the award?

"I haven't thought about going, actually," he said, and added that he admired the usual writers there, whose names were known. The reporter let him off then, thanking him again for letting the photographer come over on this short notice.

Lionel hung up and, on an impulse, went downstairs for some ginger ale.

The next day the photograph appeared in the "cultural page" of the morning *Times*, under the book review, as well as on page two of the *Globe* (UPI had called a half hour later). The photograph, looking like some odd daguerreotype, showed Lionel looking like a scarred war veteran, burned and bandaged, but steadfast, even slightly heroic. The eyes faced out at you straight and hopeful; both stories cited "a home accident" to explain the unusual face. The telephone immediately began ringing again; he let it ring. No point in going through the same explanation or lack of one again and again. Besides, he still had to look through his lecture pages and prepare for his last classes of the term. So, after the ringing stopped, he lifted the receiver off the hook and let it rest there buzzing protectively. While he thought about the novel, and his life.

At school, he parked in Lot E and walked in the warm spring air to his building. He wore his fine camel turtleneck, carried his briefcase, and thought it perfectly fitting when a young female student approached him with fresh flowers. "I don't know you, sir, but I wanted to . . . give you this." It had never before happened to him, and he took it with new delight, not old suspicion. "Daisies and paintbrushes," she explained. "Thank you very much. What's your name?" "Susan Garfield. I'm planning on taking your writing course next year. You'll be teaching, won't you?" Lionel paused, and didn't really know what to answer. "I didn't know paintbrushes could be gotten around here," he said, admiring the orange-red wildflowers.

Walking into Schiffman Hall with his bouquet, he tried to concentrate on *The Red Badge of Courage* and what was meant by realism in literature.

All was fine, students here and there turning (but he was prepared for that), until he climbed to the second floor and noted a crowd and small commotion around Room 217. Agitated suddenly, he thought of how a Brooklyn boy would respond. A Hopi. Neither suited. A colleague, a British historian, saw him, waved, said, "Let's have lunch soon," and Lionel was glad, twofold. He would take it like this Ronald H., with a polished amused surface.

Students, his, cheered when they saw him, then gasped. Cheered the prizewinner, gasped at the victim. He marched through them to the classroom. But once inside, to his horror, were strangers and cameras.

"Good morning, Professor Solomon, we thought we'd get a few shots of you actually teaching."

"How'd you get in here? Who got you per—"

"Mission? Cheesus, you really have had your troubles, haven't you?" the next newsman blurted out kindly.

"Oh come on, you're news, Mr. Solomon, news! The university knows it and has been very cooperative. Now what we wonder is—"

He had just put up his hand when a flashbulb clicked.

"Out gentlemen, please. Outside. I'll talk to you out there, if you will." He held the door open and walked out of the room into the hallway. They had little choice but to follow suit, protesting.

The students milled at the door and in the hall, along with the reporters, and Lionel changed from sunglasses to regular goldrims.

Two flashbulbs popped, and one reporter asked, "What's it like to be recognized in a foreign country after your last few books have been"—he shook his head—"pretty much flops here?"

Lionel's mouth watered, the years of frustration and envy and pain surged to his chest, the suicidal hours and depressions put a lump in his throat; the pentup rage rose in his stomach, at the philistines—moralists—cheap-shots artists—

"It feels good," he said.

"Will you fly to Buenos Aires to accept the award?"

He considered, and recalled the nice invitation of that young Spanish woman in his apartment. Ursula? "A trip to South America does sound appealing."

A third reporter asked, "Would you want to say how . . ." indicating Lionel's face.

Trembling, Lionel forced a smile. "Trying to shave in the shower does have its consequences. I think I'll go back to a beard."

"Could you be a little more specific?"

Lionel looked at his watch. "This class is about eight minutes late already, if you don't mind."

"Can we get one or two shots with your students grouped around you, Professor?" And they started maneuvering.

"I don't think so."

"Uh, sir," the student reporter from the college paper interceded, "where would you rank your place in American literature? Up there with the all-time greats—Hemingway, Fitzgerald, Faulkner? And are there any contemporaries you'd rank up there—Mailer, Pynchon, Vonnegut?"

Lionel felt the blood rush to his heart, and replied as softly as he could, "Oh, I think only time will be able to judge all that. If you'd like, we can talk about it another time," and he said to the young man, and to the reporters, "Forgive me gentlemen, but if you'd excuse me, I do have a class to teach."

"But you haven't given us anything!"

He thought, *a successful interview at last.* Turning away, he offered, "Next time, okay? Thanks. Excuse me."

Inside the classroom, he opened his briefcase, and waited while the kids settled down, in.

When he looked up fully, however, there was gasping, and silence.

"Where'd you get the flowers?" someone asked finally.

"A girl up the road," he said, holding up the bouquet. "Better than apples."

The class stared at him, silent. With more gravity, reflection. He didn't know what to do. Then Jeff Cohen, on the side, began to clap. And presently, gradually, the entire class joined in the applause.

Solomon felt tears coming. His face hurt from his attempt

to squeeze them away; his heart was moved, *terribly*. Crying, he turned away, and blew his nose, gently. Trying to recover.

Pam Z. called out, "We rank you up there with the best."

The class cheered.

His students, his friends! His daughter, his friend! There, in the clutch, when he needed them! He loved them, for sure.

Marc H. asked, "Can English 87a charter a plane and go with you to Argentina as your cheerleading squad?"

The class cheered, in verification.

Lionel laughed. "Yes. Do come."

He put his palms out to restore order. "Now, as to Mr. Crane's realism—"

"Just one thing," noted Derek, "could you tell *us* how you got those bandages? I mean, like was it a *Melville-type* wound?"

The shrewd, ambiguous phrase startled Solomon. Was the tone intimate, that of one in the know? His hands gripped the sides of the lectern.

The class of students stared, perplexed by the question.

*I got whipped by a young woman, may we go now?*

Waving a hand in the air magnanimously, he said, "Why yes, you might say that. Cannibalism, 1970's style. Yes. Just stay away from the wrong natives, Derek."

The bewildered tension loosened with laughter.

"Which are those?" Derek persisted.

"The ones that smile and carry knives in their teeth, of course." Nervous all the way.

At first they sat there, then came an affectionate hissing, finally gentle laughter at the irony. (Or did he just perceive it that way? Hard to tell anymore.)

"Nothing so dramatic I'm afraid," Lionel inserted, to quell rumors. "Shower stalls with glass doors are simply not worth installing if you're not used to them." He looked directly at the suspicious face, which settled slowly into sympathy.

"Now," adjusting his larynx, his courage, "Mr. Crane's little book on courage and cowardice in war, a starting point for American realism perhaps. A brilliant evocation of war without the author's participating in it at all, it turns out. To show you that not everyone has to have 'been there' in order to re-create it, very powerfully, in fiction."

Speaking more from rote than conviction, and letting the class talk almost at will, it all went fine, the storm points of life over and the skies again clear with harmless academic talk.

Later on in the afternoon, however, during his lecture, he

was neither academic nor calm, in that semicircular room holding about a hundred and fifty people. In fact his heart was pounding wildly as he spoke, though he was mostly reading from his prepared notes, only occasionally improvising. He covered topics such as intimacy in the novel, the decline in literary criticism and journalism, and pretty writing. The crowd was a rather unusual mixture of students, colleagues and outsiders. In all probability, the morning news had stimulated a larger crowd than he might otherwise have had, with undergraduates squeezing into every space on the floor, graduates standing, strangers wedged into the wooden window seats. Up front, he noted immediately, several tenured members of the department, whom he knew were eyeing him skeptically, to say the least. Skeptical already because of his ungenteel and troublesome novels—so unbecoming and undecorative for an English department—and now, also, because of his curious state of health. Not to mention the controversy, still going on, over whether he was to remain in the university. Which would win them over, the announcement of the prize or the dramatic mask of the wounded? this speech from a mummy?

And unlike the claims he had made earlier on in the Crane class concerning an author's imagination working for him in place of actual experience, he had an impulse near the end of his talk to consider the matter more closely. The matter of fact into fiction, of autobiography and fictional truth. "In other words, what does laying it on the line mean for a writer? What can be laid on the line and what is *better* held back? Is the real sometimes too much for fiction?" He began by reciting the Melville case, apologizing to English 87a for repeating the story. And as he came to the end of that, he considered his own recent life and present bandaged mask. Before plunging in there, he sipped some water, the glass shaking in his hand. Swallowing it, he was sorry he ever went into it in the first place, departing from the established text. Why, why?

"Of course I'm not sure that people in this country are as interested in pure fiction as they are, these days, in an author's personal life as it relates to the fiction. In part I think this is a genuine literary interest, in terms of the I-novels being written, and the confessional nature of the material. But in part I think there is another motive operating here, strictly *a*-literary. I refer to the new overwhelming interest in 'personality,' in America, in digging out the so-called secrets of a public person's life, in 'sharing' them with everyone, all spectators and readers, and along the way, in *exposing* the secrets. The cover used here is the 'pursuit of honesty,' the new native passion resulting from a climate of therapy and encounter groups; under this flag, a person, a fan, a reporter, is entitled *to rip through* the so-called facade of privacy and 'get at' the real inside person or story. Now I think no matter how innocent or amiable the motives of the investigators here, the result is a kind of cannibalism. The secret story, the private life of the individual, is transformed into the food for the curious; thus an author's life becomes a feast for the cannibal. Snooping, which has gone on recently at a rapidly increasing rate in American private and government circles, has now hit the literary fan, if you will; it has become the fashion. Directly and indirectly, I think this is unfortunate, and even potentially dangerous. Unfortunate, because the important thing remains the literary text; and dangerous, because sometimes there are *no limits* to the daring boldness of the investigator. Now of course there is one other important element here, and that is the author himself, *especially one who encourages* such inquiry, such *literary snooping*. For example, we all know of the very famous American author who has practically made his reputation, staked his reputation, on *opening his life* this way, exposing his chest, so to say, right there in his books. Not only inviting the critics to look at the life instead of the fiction—increasingly there's been less fiction, useful to note—but actually *advertising* the life over the work. The feast brought right out there and set on the table. Of course, need it be said, that the food here, the private details have been *very carefully selected*, so that what looks like absolute openness is really a *very censored* text. What appears to be spontaneity, is a carefully controlled and manipulated spontaneity. So there, the issue is not cannibalism at all, but rather, authorial rhetoric and old-fashioned conning."

Solomon paused, drank water, felt his neck warm, his heart pumping crazily.

"Now for the writer who continues to be interested in his work, his fiction first and foremost, there are enormous problems in presenting 'the facts' of his life just like that, unadulterated, in his fiction. There is his natural reticence, first of all, which in part is why he has chosen fiction as his life's work. There is also the knowledge and the belief that those 'facts' mean little, by themselves; that they are deceptive and even dangerous if presented as 'truth'; and that it takes the liberation of fiction *to transform* those chaotic facts into truth. To the life-question, 'What does it mean?' comes the fictional answer 'This, here, it means. Or may mean.' For the novelist is never sure of his truth, has no proofs as a mathematician does, relies on himself, his experience, and even then knows that uncertainty is the rule of the day, uncertainty and interpretation. And that what appears to be a fact turns out to mean something quite different, a piece in the jigsaw puzzle, not the picture. So that one is diffident before those 'facts'; or skeptical and even hesitant, knowing that they themselves don't *mean* too much, if anything." Then, on impulse, Solomon jumped to a different point. "So that if the question is put, how much of this is *you* here in the fiction, why the question itself, besides being beside the point, is also inaccurate; it's *unverifiable*, and unanswerable! There really is no way of telling, in all honesty, what the question means, let alone what the answer is. Am I clear?" Was he? Many in the audience looked puzzled.

Utterly sad suddenly, he leaned forward and pleaded, "Who would be mad enough to put one's life on the fiction line, plain and unadulterated? What would it get him but abuse, mockery, scorn, laughter, self-torment? Wouldn't you rather read about a chase after the whale than a lonely man sitting for thirty years in a customs house? And who, which writer, is fool or naïve enough to think that he is able to put his life down that way, plain and unvarnished, in his fiction? Why, the writer lives by means of his imagination, by means of his fictional lies, and the thought that he would resort to calling *everyday fact* truth, why it goes against his grain, his practice, his knowledge! He knows very well, in his blood, that he lives by his lying, tells the truth by his lying, and above all others, he knows the great folly of thinking that he could write or tell otherwise, or benefit in any way from becoming a mere factual reporter of events in his life. It is the one folly that he recognizes by his instinct, his smell, and needs no critic to remind him of."

He was rather exhausted, but he went on and made a few other points: Did art flourish or diminish in criminal times? (Answer, flourish.) Did the novel of enlightenment pass with the Age of Enlightenment? The first never existed, it was a myth at best. (Reading steadily from his note cards.) And then it was over, mercifully over. The reaction was rather mixed. The students, many of them, clapped vigorously, asked questions that showed their appreciation. Some strangers too. But there were assorted graduate students, and faculty colleagues, who were put off, or else came on hostile. A pleasant, well-dressed graduate student openly attacked his attack on the famous novelist, and claimed Solomon was envious and rather thick. An older colleague, whom Lionel liked, though he always managed to exclude Solomon's books from his contemporary course, gently mocked Solomon's "protective sense," asking if he wasn't being "slightly paranoid?" A friendly mockery which was sharpened by another gentleman, a visiting poet, who said that Lionel was underestimating the role of the ego and also acting rather disingenuously about his own self-importance. "We're all terribly interested in fame, let's come clean, it's the nature of the game," said the tall fellow snidely. "If our lives are available *to make* our careers, in any way shape or form, we will use them, as artists always have. I see it almost as sacrificial, and I wish you would come down off your high horse, a pretentious high horse, and admit the obvious." Perhaps the fellow was right, perhaps he was; who knew? Lionel at this point didn't. Had no idea. Sacrificial? That seemed right, he couldn't tell. "Look at yourself in the mirror, Lionel," the fellow called out suddenly, addressing him by his first name although he had hardly ever talked to Solomon, "it's a perfect metaphor for the kind of sacrifice that I have in mind, even though it may be totally unrelated to yourself as an artist."

A perfect metaphor in the mirror? Lionel repeated to himself. Ah, ingenuity, literary ingenuity! he thought, standing up there, seeing his face in the mirror of the morning. Suddenly, he smiled to the scorning, critical poet, smiled as widely as his bandages permitted, smiled peacefully at the new and rather novel interpretation of his wound.

# 9.
# Country Life

I am sure you will pardon this speaking all about myself; for if I *say* so much on that head, be sure all the rest of the world are thinking about themselves ten times as much. Let us speak, tho' we show all our faults and weaknesses, —for it is a sign of strength to be weak, to know it, and out with it, —

                              not in set way and ostentatiously, tho', but
                              incidentally and without premeditation. . . .
                                —Herman Melville, letter to Hawthorne,
                                          June 29, 1851

IN HIS STUDY HE GAZED out at Smarts Mountain and Mount Tug, foothills of the White Mountains. The air was clear, and rings of gray-blue mist drifted around the low mountains, as in a Chinese landscape. Morning serenity in New Hampshire. He had read yesterday's *Times*—one day's news as good as the next—and still could look forward to the Red Sox report in the *Globe* to come; once again, here in mid-August, the Sox hitting showed warning signs of failing. Next, he had gone through the *Weekly Market Bulletin*, a rural paper that listed prices and the availability of soybeans, apples, pigs, tractors, hogs; Solomon was looking for a goat, a milking goat. An exploratory trip into animals. He had listened to the two sides of the goat question: they were self-sufficient, interesting, and the milk was super, but also they could rip apart a yard, a fence, or whatever if they were ornery. Which most were. But Lionel didn't mind that quality. And ever since he had tried out the milk that summer, tasting its tart thickness and realizing it contained no cholesterol, he grew more determined to give it a try. (The right sort of goat of course—a female Nubian, say.) The search-project continued the morning ritual of humdrum and mindless busyness, perfect for relaxing him after breakfast, and for putting the world at the right distance.

Beethoven's piano sonata opus 101 played on the speakers, pushing him further into his journey of familiarity. He would take a record and play it over and over again, so it became a known companion. All getting him prepared for the day of writing, the lingering illness called writing a novel. The summer had actually proceeded quite nicely with this dull daily routine, his novella of letters doubling in length into a full-fledged novel, with new and unforeseen letters. The writing itself healed him, of course, at the same time that the occupation marked him for life. That was the paradox of writing books when you write for yourself and not for the marketplace. On the one hand it taxed you terribly and chained you; on the other hand you never felt healthier or more alive than when you were doing it, at work on a project of one to several years. Perhaps it was like a long, sustained intercourse, in which the pattern of compulsive attention and slavish attraction mixed with long-term ongoing gratification. The pathology and the pleasure which was made up of the need for daily invention, the impulse to originality, this oath to the self to keep the promise of a book. The occupation of the artist was for neither the hedonistic nor the impatient nor the indolent. But if one had the patience, and the faith, it returned you the dividend of making something the way you alone envisioned and wanted it.

Now in the weeks immediately after his great ordeal, the fiction had kept him afloat like ocean water. He had dived back into the work with a vengeance, and sure enough, as always, it had buoyed him up. Sanity and self-respect and working peace had begun to flow again. Sheyna and New Hampshire were also crucial nurses. In his awful helpless need Sheyna had come forth with open warmth and tenderness, announcing once and once only that when he wished to "tell her about 'the accident,'" she'd be pleased to listen. *If* he wished to tell about it. She had looked at him straight on with her wine-brown shining eyes of deep belief that night in the kitchen, and he was immeasurably and overwhelmingly grateful for that complete trust—the way he imagined a Catholic sinner is grateful for his understanding confessional priest. Only more so here because he didn't have to confess. She was not merely his girlfriend, but also his best friend. So what if physical desire had waned? Clearly there were more important things at various points in one's life. Qualities such as trust and companionship and steadfast loyalty; and it was these qualities that carried Solomon back to working order. And even to love.

New Hampshire helped too. There is nothing like the green (or snowy-white) routine of life and beauty that the rural life provides; for the sick it offers recuperation; for the dead, resurrection. Solomon, who had been both sick (in body) and dead (in spirit, soul), had been nurtured back to health by the countryside. A measure of health, anyway. There were the huge trees of the forest, which made him feel surrounded and safe; the birds that ate at the window feeders and cheered him endlessly with their colors and songs; the mountain air, bracing in its morning fragrances and evening coolness. For a gentleman of complication, of overtime consciousness, of memory and energy enough in his poor head for three full-size brains and hearts, the country was a resting place where nothing intruded or violated with distraction and noise, and where he could concentrate on the people and ideas in his head. Furthermore, there were also always projects in the country, even for a total incompetent like Solomon; this summer he was at work restoring the battered gazebo, overgrown with fruitless grapevines, and also finishing the job of resurrecting the clay tennis court, overgrown with grass and maple saplings. So he had spent a good many hours pulling up seedlings in the afternoon sun, neck coated with Cutter's in defiance of the mosquitoes, and then hoeing and raking the clay beneath. With the help of a teenager down the dirt road, and the guidance of a high-school teacher friend, they had actually gotten the court back to playing shape. Although it was still a good year or so away from being flat and fast and rain-resilient, it was a major triumph to hit the yellow ball back and forth and be able to count on a decent bounce, that first week in August.

Also, because of his new appreciation for the countryside, Lionel began for the first time to purchase land—a parcel of forty-one acres here with stone walls, springs and a running brook; a secluded hilltop there of thirty-seven acres with commanding views and several open fields; a side of a mountain like a side of good beef, about one hundred fifty acres' worth, of mature forest of maple and oak as well as old pine. It all seemed so pretty to him that he felt that money was better off there, visible and aromatic, than in a remote vault or invisible stock. He had taken to learning a bit about the woods, first from the county forester and then from the local surveyor and forester who advised about selective cutting and thinning. This interest, to his delight, put Lionel in touch with reality again—with surveyors and lumberjacks, bankers and foresters, trees and smells. It was real, and it was pretty. The smells of the forest, especially after a fine rain, were gorgeous, and provided much less trouble than erotic scents had. So he would write by day, and then, once or twice a week, take Sheyna to see land with the local realtor, a short Maine fellow who operated like a buzzsaw, never stopping from early dawn, waking time, to seven or eight in the evening, about half an hour before sleep. Wasn't it only animals who lived by such a clock? Anyway, he proceeded with his land and his timbering with growing satisfaction, and grateful feelings. Who could have imagined that timbering meant therapy? Or that he, a native Solomon, would inadvertently hark back to his Grandfather Alexander's domain of interest in White Russia? Did the woods run in their blood? (And, correspondingly, did a Minsky Tippy run into Zeyde Alexander's life?)

Now, as Lionel considered his first page for the day, and saw a note to call his friend Tom R., he recalled something else about this summer that had been curiously therapeutic.

For one reason or another, Lionel had become a kind of local priest, or country shrink, to assorted friends in trouble, or friends wanting to talk and who had no one to talk to. From city patient he had turned into country doctor, and it was refreshing. After a while you get tired of your troubles, bored with your own pains (and life) and *want out*. Playing doctor, naturally and inevitably without asking for it, gave him that out. In one case, this Tom R., a happily married man of forty who had a family of children and ran a small general store, suddenly fell into an inadvertent passion for a friend's wife; and there was his most ordinary life turned topsy-turvy. Yet, paradoxically, as he explained to Lionel beginning one March afternoon while they were stacking wood, he felt that for the first time in fifteen years he was *alive*, not dead. A gaunt Montana transplant who had hardly known a day's emotional turbulence in his life, he spoke slowly, low, with a slight twang, about the avalanche of chaos. Guilty over his wife and the possible family breakup, guilty over his cuckolded friend, yet crazy about the other wife, he was at a total loss as to what to do. Solomon, veteran sufferer, asked him what he *wanted* to do? "I don't know," the bearded fellow looking like Lincoln replied. "Gosh, I don't know. It's hell being at home and hell being up at Jodie's. All I know is that I've never suffered this way before." He shook his head in despair. And all Solomon could do, then and afterwards, all during the summer, was to see Tom, hear out the evolution of agony—as he went through the hell of telling his wife about the situation—and keep the secret between them only. Lionel was deeply moved. With another friend, the situation was not one of illicit passion, but rather of her trying to keep her head clear, above water, thinking straight. Emily L., a sophisticated literary girl who had dropped into country life and compost-pile discussions, made it a point to have regular talks with Lionel about most things in her life—job, marriage, family, future hopes, country versus city. Her husband, Eric, was a delightful fellow and a Lionel-friend too, but a very different sort: his loves were the outdoors—camping, skiing, Canadian geese and beekeeping. Solomon liked both enormously, found their dissimilarity (and arguments) most charming, and discovered the obvious point, that talking to each alone (which he did whenever possible) offered pleasures and disclosures not possible when they went out as a threesome. . . . People were lonelier in the country than in the city, Lionel had come to believe, the great empty spaces between homesteads acting as thick walls. And friendships worked, or consisted of, time put in, time in small turns accumulated, as much as depth or candidness of talk.

Now why was Lionel chosen for this particular role? In part because out here priests no longer really counted, and psychiatrists didn't really exist (and couldn't be afforded, financially). Also, Lionel was still single, could be visited alone, and *could keep matters private*. This was crucial in a tiny hamlet of under two thousand folk, as Jerusalem was; with fewer things to do, especially in the long winters, loose talk was a prime distraction. Most importantly, Solomon's books and his temperament indicated that he was open to the life of feeling, and private distress, without being moralistic, negative, or accusatory. To unhappy persons, such advice was like salt on wounds. And while at social gatherings he was gregarious and ubiquitous, friends began to see that up close, on a walk or in a room, alone, he was quieter, more reflective, and more given to questioning and listening than to providing answers or familiar slogans. When the heart was bursting and the brain turbulent, it was a great release to be able to come clean, blabber out your guts—knowing it would stay there, between the two of them and the walls only.

So it was not city stress that had necessarily driven people crazy or unhappy, as the popular culture and sociologists had suggested. Country life had its share of neurotics, psychotics, unhappy people, unwanted passions. No, not in honking horns or rude service was tension created and enflamed, but rather in people's lives at home, past and present. In families were the origins of health or disorder; and grass or asphalt, traffic jams or farming chores, were not going to alter things significantly. Be that as it may, the circle of irony was complete: Lionel, who got into so much trouble in his own life, was helping others in theirs. This was not unusual, of course, persons in pain frequently having more sympathy for others' problems and pains than those who pass over and through pain as if it were pudding. And Lionel, who had his work to speak to (and through), therefore needed no other ear.

Lionel opened the french door onto his porch, filled the feeder halfway, saw the white reflector telescope through which he and Sheyna had last night gazed at the stars. Back inside at his desk, he knew that above all it was his Sheyna who had put him together again, put the pieces back. Sheyna who had purchased the telescope as a surprise for the summer, and with whom he had stared at the "Big Jupe" as it rose in the eastern sky around 10 P.M. Looking at it in the lens on a clear summer night, you saw a yellow-orange silver

415

dollar with four golden moons hovering nearby, three on the left side and one on the right (though shifting), resembling a five-man touch-football formation of planets. Meanwhile, the earth's moon shone so brightly that Lionel had to don dark glasses to view it. A huge pale-yellow orb, with discernible smudges, cracks, indentations—the craters and mountain ranges. The more you stared at it, using dark glasses frequently upon its bright luminosity, as last night, the more you viewed a kind of interesting primitive face there, a Masai with tribal markings perhaps. In the larger lens, you saw only a sliver of it up close, the lens being too powerful—96 times the power of the naked eye—to take in the whole circle. (You could easily make out Tycho's Crater at the southwestern tip, as Sheyna had shown him.) And minutes later . . . the spectacular splash of stars, sparkling points tossed like silver tinsel across a black velvet cloth, signifying what? Extraterrestrial intelligence, life? All Lionel could do was gaze and wonder at this surface of miracle that beggared meaning, and his own small self and trials. So he had stared, selfless, joyous, admiring the young woman at his side, sighting the milky way from beneath. . . .

"No mail yet," interrupted Sheyna now, in cutoffs and purple jersey, the *kibbutznik* of Jerusalem, New Hampshire, "but here's the newspaper." Giving him the *Globe* from town, she then went through the motion of hitting the tennis backhand, in seeming oblivion. "Will you hit some for me as a warm-up for Lisa?"

Lionel adored the little actress in his saint, and smiled. "You've become a regular tennis freak, haven't you? It's just barely eleven o'clock."

But she was already in her darling follow-through, and only afterwards pretended to hear him. "Now all you have to do is hit the actual ball," he noted. "We'll see, 'Chrissie.' Now let me do a little work."

She took a step to him and lowered her fist playfully to his forehead, saying "Clunk!" in mockery of his own act. Then jumped away.

She left, closing the door carefully, and Lionel knew once again that right there was the engine of his smooth summer machine, his purring writing machine (him), that without her he never would have gotten back on the track so swiftly or stably. Certainly not this summer. (*Hold it, Doctor, I'm crying again. Forgive me, I must stop here a moment. I think of her, and it hurts, it hurts!*) . . . She and she alone had made it possible for Lionel the patient to pull through. That June,

416

July, August, an injured soul, he *knew love:* the complete forgiveness of error and mistake, physical nearness during physical-spiritual crises, the persistence of faith in the face of fear (hers) and betrayal (his). Not only hadn't she backed away from Lionel during those first days and weeks of his wounding—and hers too—she was there on hand stronger than ever. He recalled those first days of changing bandages and washing his cuts, preparing new pastas and Chinese dishes, and surprising him with summer gifts (Levi's jacket, tennis headband, beach polo shirt); treating him as if he had come home from the war and had not only been wounded in battle, but had witnessed scenes of horror. Never once asking him questions about those horrors, letting them heal in his mind first. Then, *if* he wished . . . and wasn't he like Hemingway's old soldier sitting there on the porch, rocking and watching and not speaking? Only the wars here were closer to home, the scars more humiliating; a civilian soldier of misfortune. . . . And sometimes, lying alongside the sleeping girl, her head tucked into the crook of his arm—his neck temporarily out of nuzzling-order—he found himself crying out of gratitude for *this girl's saintliness.* Oh he had known that she was *good* before, but it had taken this trial to test the mettle of *goodness.* . . . In his own eyes he was demeaned and dishonored and naturally no matter how much he sought to forget, he remembered. In the middle of the most innocuous contexts, flashes of that night and morning struck him—during dinner at the Parthenon, shopping in Filene's Basement, at an English Department meeting discussing honors for students, in the night just before dozing—and they would hit him like a flu chill, seizing his breath and making him shiver, so that he had to grab onto something if he were standing—a banister, a fence, a chair—to keep from falling. The present was blanked out at those moments, and was replaced by those Weimaeraner ocher eyes, the upper lip stretching with greed, the teeth edging forward, the wild color crossing her cheeks in excitement! . . . For how long would these images come back to haunt him? Would they ever leave off? Or were they part of him now forever, his own private baggage carried now down through adulthood and into the grave?

Did one have to go through unhealthy, unmentionable ordeals in order to experience love? Move through a literal Inferno to reach the illusion of Paradiso? Without this recent trial and punishment surely he wouldn't have appreciated Sheyna's depths or the full therapeutic uses of those depths.

Her *quality* was as fine as anything aesthetic or political; her *goodness* helped to heal, even to save. This therapy was the moral sense in action, and therefore most exquisite. And without the ordeal, her quality, and its uses, would have gone unnoticed, he believed. Presently, everything around here—the garden, the house, the spectacular air, the flowers, the sports, the whole sweet routine—all seemed in his mind a pale reflection of her resplendent inner life; a wheel of physical beauty spun by Sheyna's quality.

*Or, was this exquisite narcissist merely showing proper appreciation for the nurse who was bringing him back to the point where he could again manage his own self-love again? Was it his own feeling of shame which raised her so immeasurably in his eyes? A step farther: on her side, wasn't there something most attractive about nursing back to health a wounded loved one? He was not merely captive prey, you see, Doctor, but also, he was in your debt, subtly and surely. Nowadays, terms like resurrection and goodness must be taken with a sprinkling of skepticism. It's not to say he wasn't moved deeply by his Sheyna, for he was; but we must acknowledge the difference between what were grand truths for the nineteenth century, and what is considered more honest, prosaic reality in the twentieth. A man who has just been saved from drowning certainly has his own perception of reality, let alone of its merit.*

Yet, in this specific manner it may be said that her emotions for him helped him heal. Instead of the private voice whispering—sick, perverted, arrested, fetishist, masochistic—he was able to quiet the voice with phrases like "a strange incident," "a dangerous mistake," "an overheated affair," "a melodramatic night," "a *single* night." (Aided no doubt by the props of hash and an *extra* girl.) Words alone of course were cold comfort; warmer was the slow return to normal routine of work, reasonable feeling, regular sexuality. A month of climbing upward. Yet, paradoxically, while he wished to forget, he wished *not to*, too; he did not wish to bury the incident totally, write it off as if it were a case of leprosy. Rather, he preferred to retain it within him somewhere, deep down, like that exotic port of his youth, where he had observed fifty black shadows come aboard his freighter in the middle of the night like some amazing dream, only it was real, Africa, a reality which mingled with literature and fancy in his head, and remained there, mysterious. Similarly, he wished to keep his memory there, in the corner of his mind, as an ember of taboo excitement and terrifying pleasure that could be stirred to flame with the right wish. The ember that contained a journey to be remembered, learn from, be frightened of, yes; but not one to forget. Kept as a small weight of illness, if you will, alongside the larger weight of health, on the scale of experience. He knew too, however, that to pursue those feelings, that bold woman, was too dangerous; better to pursue the feelings but not the practice. Survival was what counted, this Veteran of Perverse Wars knew, survival, survival; not ruin through mental and physical degradation.

In love then this summer, with good reason, why not give his Sheyna what she most wanted, a child by him? Why not? Why save his semen for some demon when he could offer it to his saint? Why keep it for himself? What would he do with it—store it in a silo and sell it to the highest bidder? Put it in a Certificate of Deposit?

Back in the saddle now, the right saddle of contemplation, he could afford good humor, generous thoughts. Deeds too. Newspapers read, thoughts sifted, goats assessed (Angora, Tyrolean, Nubian), time wasted, wonderfully boring time wasted (with a vengeance!), he was ready to dig in, dig back down to despair, hopelessness, last appeal, in his "Last Letters." Here in green calm and mountain equilibrium it was easier to imagine back to suicidal moments, back to friends he missed, than when he was in the eye of a hurricane. Now Lionel wrote, based upon his earlier thoughts and notes:

Dear Karl,
   I miss you very much. Most knew you as this formidable intellect, a power in print, a strikingly authoritative figure, and were frightened to death. I knew you as a man of vast loneliness and vast shyness, a perpetual exile in whatever land you lived—Israel, England (your home), America; of course Germany of your youth. When you took your own life and the obituaries started flowing in the quarterlies, I was saddened to see how little they knew you, and how impersonally they wrote about you. Of course with many of your generation, the personal idiom did not come easy; it was a generation in which ideology and idea dominated, and the person always lagged behind, a suspicious creature. The question was, *What was his line, political line?*
   Would you recall our first meeting? A total stranger, I knocked on the door of your two-family dwelling in Hampstead, convinced of my folly, and was admitted by the landlord's daughter, who looked upon you as a good uncle; and you stood at your third-floor landing and asked who it was. I called up that you didn't know me, that I was a graduate student from Stanford University living in London while

writing a dissertation, and that I had read your work and wanted to meet you. With perfect naturalness, as if I were a distant nephew, you asked me up, shook my hand, and invited me in. In your baggy slacks and sport shirt and cardigan sweater, you were a leftist out of Eliot's "Gerontion." You put up the kettle for tea on the stove set in the bathroom—which startled me—and didn't seem at all surprised that I was in English literature, not politics; unlike many English professors, you had read Gissing, my subject, and thought him "not bad, a bit dreary, but underrated, yes." We began chatting about Stanford, where, it turned out, you had an offer to teach whenever you wished it. Meanwhile, I stared with fascination at what a lifetime of bachelor solitude and serious scholarly work produced in decorations: the green metal bookshelves in every room, the poignant attempts at "warmth" (a cookie and peanut plate, an innocuous landscape here and vase of old flowers there), the dominance of olive green and chocolate browns in chairs, curtains, rugs. Moreover, every room really was a thin disguise for a study, with those monstrous library stackshelves looming on walls. And while you, the terror of the theoretical gift, served me cookies and tea at the long dining table, I thought of what a perfect Gissing hero this lovely gentleman was, amidst this lonely setting. Right up to the point of the damage done to the eyes through years of reading: a page had to be held up to within an inch of your eyes. *Born in Exile*, Gissing's title, seemed appropriate.

Through that whole first meeting of two hours, you were astonishingly kind and open to that absolute youngster in his twenties, a contrast to your image fostered in those bruising polemical articles in the quarterlies which destroyed fools with high humor and offered the authoritative opinion on the situation with unassailable confidence. And remember, I was a complete nobody; an anonymous graduate student who, while recently interested in left-wing politics, was mostly interested in writing fiction! That the champion of the heavyweight division of the London-New York political left, the "foremost undogmatic Marxist" in the West, would talk easily and openly with that young anonymous enthusiast, and befriend him in a short time, was a testimony to your character, your unpretentiousness, your solitude.

I must say an immediate word, my dear departed friend, about the vast change in you from those first meetings in 1963, to my last visit, a decade or so later. The physical and spiritual differences shocked me. During those London visits, and the next year's regular San Francisco dinners, you were extremely youthful at fifty: the humor was ever-ready and sharp, the brown eyes glinted with merriment, quick emotion, fury and mischief, and the eyebrows never failed to rise to an exaggerated height at some "exotic" tale (meaning, woman tale); the cheeks were full and the bits of hair on the side kept up, neatly. You were a tidy dresser too, if not splashy at least crisp in shirts and ambitious in ties. In a matter of perhaps two years, there at the end, you were a changed man, suddenly on the other side of the hill, waiting to die. It was striking in one who had been so strong, so firm, so understanding of reality just the other year. (Not unlike Sidney's decline, by the way—though without his resentment.) In London in 1973 or so, on my stopover visit, the face had lost all its mobility and lightness, the eyes flashed not at all, the hair was abandoned and you, always formal in dress, saw me in an old bathrobe. That striped cloth bathrobe signaled it, backing up your words; it was all over, but, Karl, *I didn't really listen to you.* Couldn't quite believe what I was hearing about your not seeing my point in living. Not from you, Karl. And your intelligence too had changed, cynicism and cerebral thoughts replaced the old tactile feel of your intelligence; thinking no longer mattered. Now for a man like you, thinking had been a sensual experience; it was the difference between you, a passionate intellectual, and the modern breed of academic, for whom thinking is a passionless finger-exercise. The effect was so *sad*, Karl, that I didn't take the full consequences in! Will you forgive me, old friend?—But don't!

A concrete example of that decline. Very early on in our friendship, once you saw my absorption with women, over our dinners and lunches—appointments made via the mails, never the telephone—you shared a kind of secret with me. It concerned a "passion" you had been the subject of, from a younger female intellectual, a prominent American critic, who had seen fit to write you letters of adoration and admiration, calling you "the most prominent political intellectual in the English speaking world." (You blinked with embarrassment at such terms by the renowned lady.) And then, later on when you had met her, you found her "quite beautiful and charming," though you cared little for her writing ("pretty lightweight, I should say") and hence developed your own passion. (By that time, you had begun to court her avuncularly with flowers and European gallantry; real passion of bodies was out of the question, sadly.) Anyway, in those old days you clearly were vibrantly touched by the girl's attention; more, you *felt* the letters the way a less shy man, say, a less intellectual man, would have felt the woman's *actual touch*. But in the end, on my last visit through, you spoke four or five times about the "romance" as if it had occurred some fifty years ago. You held up to me the entire sheaf of correspondence (including your own "notes"), and, as if you were describing your life, you said it was all over, too late, gone by! (Besides, it was material fit for a novelist, not a critic.) In other words, by then, the *passion of the illusion* was gone too, it having sustained you the way an actual romance would sustain others. It upset me terribly to see the sudden absence of force in you, the abdication of authority—which had been like sexual power for you. You had given in. And you offered me up the sheaf not the way you told me stories over Chinese dinners in North Beach, asking me for advice, half in jest, half for real, but in resignation, in last appeal, the old energy and sensuality of authority missing.

I've felt guilty ever since, Karl, for not seeing you again as I had promised. Your voice of disappointment, when I telephoned from my London hotel to say I had caught the flu in Amsterdam and had to make my charter flight back to the States and couldn't see you, still stays with me. It was not your style to ask, as you did, "Can't you stay over and have a lunch or whatever?" But I, sick, exhausted, swirling with Amsterdam adventures, had forgotten your sharp decline and frightening words of ending; I *let them slide, Karl. And I didn't remember my own feelings, dear friend! I didn't gauge the depth of your plea! Forgive me, Karl!*

Lionel looked up, the British voice in his head, the lifeless eyes and shiny pate and wisps of hair left unkempt, the large man in the shabby bathrobe, and he was stung! Eyes grew wet. He blew his nose, got up and washed his face. Then he returned, for more.

Later, in a few months, when I saw the news in a local paper, a small obituary as befits the most intelligent in the ordinary world-at-large, I was flooded with guilt and remorse, and was assaulted by memory, especially that last memory! . . . And when the obituaries began to come in, in the idea magazines, there was *no you* in those words, no fleshy you, no living lonely man who had died, just some article-and-book machine that had suddenly broken down, lost a coil and been discarded. I recall especially your being hurt by an old (mutual) friend, who had in recent years broken from you. He told me when I asked why he didn't invite you to teach at B. that you "really didn't want to teach, and couldn't get along with students or colleagues"—though at Sanford you seemed to do fine and though you were very hard-up for money, still then after some thirty-five years of writing and editing some of the finest political articles and books. I was surprised and disappointed that he couldn't come close to the truth about you, or the truth that you had become enemies in the last years; after all, you had been his competitor and intellectual superior always, right up to the end. The wasteful pettiness of the competitive ego!

Why did you do it? The ostensible reason was that the world was so completely empty of interesting political regimes and serious ideas that there seemed no point in going on, and writing; especially after the idea of your life, Socialism, had been tried and betrayed totally (according to you), by Russia and China. Okay, I buy a truth there. I also buy the human connection, namely, that that old expatriate friend of yours, the woman professor at Manchester (?) who had come over with you to England thirty years ago, had herself died some six months previous (to my last visit with you). You told me then how you used to wake up in the middle of the night, and how out of habit and depression, you would telephone her in Manchester, only to hear a strange voice answer and ask you if you were crazy! Maybe you were, you wondered. (You, the Rationalist supreme, seriously wondering that! My God, what does the world do to us?) Only with the strange voice did you remember she was dead, and you were calling to someone who was dead, and there was no one else to talk to, to call, there in the middle of the night! In the midst of a depression! And then stay awake, depressed further. All those fifty-nine years for naught! There was no one out there! Only the grave, calling. . . .

I was amazed and delighted at your reaction to my novel, which I sent you in proofs, *Each According to His Needs*. Your observations were shrewd as well as interesting: "The 'racy' material, as you can imagine, rather overwhelmed me, but then I am of another generation entirely, and so look upon your Dean's miraculous adventures as a Martian looking in upon another species; but it was done with great humor, I must tell you. As for the political side of the novel, I found it caught the mood and mind of radical youth today in all its feverish activity and emphasis-on-action, another generational quality I'm out of touch with too, unfortunately (and fortunately!). I have no doubt that you will offend the New York literati and enrage some of The Famous Novelist's fervent admirers, but I don't look upon such outrage with anything but delight. The gentleman has been shooting his mouth off unmolested for years, and it is about time someone has taken him up on the nonsense he spouts. But you will not be liked for it, nor for your playful mocking of other cognoscenti. If you can take the reviews with a measure of calm, I dare say you will have a good time with the furor you may cause. As for your professor and his girls, I had no idea that the rather reasonable young man with whom I had taken so many dinners, could fill his life with so much chaos! You certainly are most active. If I may be so bold as to inquire, was that charming artist whom we dined with in San Francisco perhaps a model for one of the young ladies, or is this a professional secret? In any case, you must give me some pointers on acquiring mistresses; I have trouble enough keeping one!"

Lionel smiled, rereading the letter here, remembering the good-humored friend in contrast especially to the later bitchiness of those "cognoscenti." A democrat in his leftism, Karl had turned out to be seriously literary concerning sex in literature; his literary morals were not bourgeois prudish. (So different from Sidney, the Leninist and prude.)

He remembered something else now, and wrote an extra paragraph:

> I recall this apocryphal story concerning you. Time, 1949 or 1950; place, a nice restaurant in Jerusalem. In walks a blond knockout, and accompanying her is you, Karl, the young left-wing philosopher earning a living as a journalist, who is known for his bachelor-shyness and distance. Everyone wonders, Is this what has kept the brilliant thirty-five-year-old a perpetual bachelor all these years? Only later is it discovered that the seemingly young lady is your mother. . . . Is it true, or apocryphal? And what happened to her? To my great regret, I never asked you about your parents, beyond learning that the family included one of the founders of Zionism and a famous rabbi. All such material needed to make it a self-made novel was a beautiful blond Jewess, right? Karl, why didn't I pump you more when I had the chance? . . . Or should I write the novel and *imagine* the truth?

Sheyna had opened the door without knocking—uncharacteristic—and walked in.

Lionel, still with ghostly friend, looked up in a writing-daze. "What's up, pal?"

Her tanned face drooped in pain, near tears. She was trying desperately to control her tears, childlike, and not doing well. "This . . . came for you."

He stared at her, bewildered. He had wanted to tell her about his old friend, so vivid now; what was she talking about?

She held out two copies of *Esquire* magazine, evidence. And passed them to him. "That . . . cunt! How can they publish stuff like this? It's untrue, isn't it? It's a lie, isn't it?" Indignant and hopeful.

Holding the magazines now, looking at his loved one, he

suddenly couldn't lie to her! For some reason, he just couldn't tell her it was untrue; *didn't want to*. It had gone too far, and she had been too good, and he was too . . . tired?

And when he conveyed all this in a look to her—admission, cheating, humiliation—disbelief crumpled, and the tears flowed. She shook. And Lionel, who would have ordinarily held her, comforted her, sat and looked at her pain, and took it.

A long minute passed, while Sheyna cried. "This *shitty* life," she said.

Lionel squeezed his lips to keep his own tears in. His head swam wildly; who knew what was in the magazine? There'd be time for that.

Finally she fumbled out, "I . . . better go." Halted. "Don't forget to pick the beans." Shaking, trying to breathe. "If they're not picked, they'll go by." She held out a pole bean for him. "I picked it before . . ."

The full import of what was happening struck Solomon as he took the long crooked bean. "Going? Where?" He stood up. "Look—"

"*You* look!" pointing to the magazine in his hand as if it were manure. Face crunched up, tears running. "Why'd you *have to lie*"—she broke off for shaking and crying, forcing the tears out of Lionel too—"all the time? Why'd others have to find out *before me?* The whole world before me!" Her whole upper body trembled uncontrollably, and she huddled in her own arms, trying to console herself.

"Sweetie . . . Sheyna . . . I . . . I . . ." But what could he say, do? And what could there be, *in print,* in a public magazine that could break apart his life? Did his own novels ever have so much power?

Sheyna finally managed to unglue herself, and left the room. He glanced down. A paper clip with a card from an editor he knew there marked the place. The magazine opened right there, on the two-page spread, and it was entitled: "LIONEL SOLOMON AN INTIMATE PORTRAIT." And subtitled: *Notes Toward a Democratic Literary Criticism.* Huh? What's that? . . . And that bizarre epigraph?

> Finally, one day he [Flaubert] fell stricken, against the foot of his work table, killed by HER, by LITERATURE; killed as are all great passionate souls by the passion that fires them!
>
> —Guy de Maupassant

425

Was this a compliment or a warning? And was Her—Literature—Tippy? He hadn't had such full-scale publicity since his second novel! On the right side of the page there was a series of photographs, several immediately recognizable from that April day in Rockaway, others he hadn't seen for years. (Two from his high school days, for example, little mug shots of the crew-cut school sports columnist. Another was of him at the age of four sitting in his mother's lap; another, a graduation picture from the sixth grade in P.S. 189. And under the inscription "Writer's Pacifier," there was a closeup of his CLUB IROQUOIS jacket.) On the left side of the page was the text, with a small-print comment from the editors. It said in effect that this was a most unusual piece, suggesting a possible new breakthrough in literary criticism and living psychohistory, and the editors felt that, despite the controversial content, it was "too exciting a venture" to keep from publishing the piece. But the most astonishing thing was the byline, someone named *Pandora J. Armstrong*. Who? Shaking his head, he turned the page frantically, and saw there the box with the contributor's note:

> Ms. Pandora J. Armstrong is a Ph.D. candidate in American literature (and American studies) at Yale University, under Professor Harry Stark. With the aid of an Andrew Mellon Foundation Grant, she is working on a study of the image of women as portrayed by male novelists. This section, on the life and novels of Lionel Solomon, is part of the larger study, to be published by Pantheon Books.

What did it mean, who was this girl? At *Yale*, with that flashy clever professor who would consider anything new and apocalyptic? Desperately he wanted to race to Sheyna, plead with her to stay and explain what a fake this was! A criminal! But he was confused, startled. And he didn't want to "convince" Sheyna, manipulate her feelings. Leave her be.

Suddenly he noticed a small photograph in the back, at the end of the magazine article, of a girl sitting across a small Japanese motorcycle, helmet in her lap and hair wild; it was she! But: P. J. Armstrong???

Now the thought of his being up there all alone, in the country, with his book to finish, hit him in the chest and throat.

But his eye, now on the actual text, made him abandon those fears. For the issue seemed more serious than that. And paradoxically, he was satisfied; it was not all a bad dream, a dangerous projection, but real. Bad in a real way had its plus sides. His paranoia was justified now.

With outward calm he put the magazine on the bookshelf, sank back in his writing chair, stared at his manuscript waiting, at the chickadees at the feeder, at the mountains.

The engine in Sheyna's Saab revved up. He thought about his friends, his daughter, his mother, his students, his colleagues, reading the article. Thought about the word traveling through Cambridge, and his university, like an electric message. His job, previously on the line, was a joke now; all the pure Solomon-haters in the department would now have their picnic. Okay. His eye caught sight of the calendar; he judged that *Esquire* wasn't out yet, it would probably be a few weeks more before it was available to the public. Could he get the issue held up, legally?

Weakly, he got on the telephone, and weakly dialed his tough lawyer in Pollutionville. Marty Kaufman was in a Manhattan court all morning, however, and tied up till four o'clock. Could Mr. Kaufman call him then? Lionel nodded, feebly, and said yes. Hung up. Realized that he hadn't even read the piece, how could he speak to Marty about whether it was legal or not? But he *didn't want to have to read it!*

He got up, ran water from the washbasin faucet into the coffeepot, trying to stay calm, put the pieces together. All right, she was using a pseudonym. Clever. Was there a Tippy Matthews at all? Or just the clever name? Who *was* who in America? Did she do it all for the money? For plain old vengeance? How much could she reveal, how much would the magazine permit her to say? He tried to admonish himself: *What did it matter, Lionel? Get on with the serious work at hand. Forget the silly media stuff. It's* Esquire *Talk, grist for Manhattan dinner parties. It won't kill you, it won't influence the quality of your work. Would Stendhal be deterred by Ms. Pandora J. Armstrong's article in* Esquire?

He settled back into his chair and tried to read his last manuscript sentences, but realized he was breathing with difficulty and perspiring. Your girl has left you! Your best friend and companion!

But he knew that that was only part of the trouble, and not the cruelest part.

Like a prisoner being awakened in the middle of the night for his execution, Lionel got up and took the few steps to the bookcase for the hot print. The "essay" was very long, starting on the two-page spread and moving into endless single columns in the back, on pages 124, 126, 128–129, 130–132,

427

140–42, 143, and ending—with *Esquire* irony?—alongside a virile male model advertising shirts, on page 145. He couldn't read all that; who could? He would glance at paragraphs. But not inside; out there on the open porch, where there was clean air, birds, space. He needed lots of space and country air while reading it, he felt. Sitting on the white railing, he said aloud the name, "Pandora J. Armstrong." Repeated it. Tippy for Pandy, was that it? His eye wandered. . . .

Doubtless the social sciences have stepped far beyond literary criticism in terms of critical techniques. The main advance there has been the attempt, wherever possible, to work from firsthand research. Similarly, disciplines like history have recently departed from established procedures, to pursue the truth more precisely. Witness historical quantification; witness new perspectives on history from point of view of the bottom up, that of the workingman. And witness, perhaps the most exciting of all, new work in psychohistory, motivated by Erikson, fulfilled by historians like S. Friedlander, Binion and Mazlish. The lesson, learned from the great Freud himself, was to deal with the very specific in order to develop more general ideas and overall interpretations. One enemy, then, in all of these relations and studies, has been *distance*. Distance between the object or puzzle in question and the observer. More and more the critic here—the analyst, the historian, the social scientist— has tried to enter more directly into the closed private realm of the subject, his mind, his body, his gestures. Even the novelist himself has attempted this, trying to bridge the gap between himself and the reader. (And trying, too, to bridge the distance between his work and his life—see Mailer, Roth, Dazai, Mishima, et cetera.) To my mind, it is only the literary critic who has lagged far behind, in the pursuit of a franker, realer, more valid criticism. In a word the literary critic has remained in the last century, while his brothers and sisters have moved forward into new realism.

. . . The distance between the critic and the writer has always been a large and unfortunate one, but especially so in modern times, when novels and reports in first-person narration predominate. Now, if we use for example the analogy between the analyst and the patient, we see the enormous shortcomings for testing reality, and literary reality, in the critic-writer relationship. In part what I have attempted here is to bridge that distance; to enter the writer's personal world, his private rooms, in order to see the fictions more clearly and deeply. And, it is hoped, to help the writer see his own fiction more clearly.

428

Of course, Lionel said, nodding, of course, Pandora J. But wasn't this distance a fact of life? A useful fact?

Can a psychohistory of a living novelist tell us more about his *literary* characters and structures? Can we begin to discern more closely the motives for fiction, and the proportions therein of fantasy, wish-projection, reality? What is meant by a "writer's sincerity"? Obviously, I cannot hope to answer such weighty questions with full answers, especially here in this limited space. But I do hope to open up these lines of inquiry, and in a fresh manner.

It will be asked, is it fair to use sexuality for—and in—such a study? Fair to use the private life when analyzing a public fiction? First, let's not be too fussy about mingling genres here; the present age of criticism knows well enough that the lines between fiction and reality in our lives are thin indeed. Furthermore, if men explore—and abuse—our lives in their writing, can't we in turn explore their writing by means of our real lives? Can't we fight against words, deceptions, lies, by means of empirical realities? Simply put, can't we use our bodies in the service of our minds and soon-to-be-projected images? Real performance versus fantasy-act; personal ambush versus standard fiction attack; hard female facts up against soft, programmed male fictions; is all this not fair? If one aim of the new feminist criticism is to play the subtle guerrilla against crude (male) fictional imperialism, then terrorist attack by means of our bodies is a most useful weapon in the struggle. To put the matter in a more traditional literary way, can't character be headed off at the fictional pass, before it enters that sacred permanent land of the text guided by the male rider alone? Can't the protagonist be turned first into a more wide-open territory, where she is challenged by the real character herself? I submit the present tale in this spirit—*a character calling out to an author in search of her real self in his fiction!*

Example: Shouldn't Louise Colet have had the right to check herself out before she was turned into Madame Bovary? Maybe Louise wouldn't have been as dumb or self-destructive as Emma, for the sake of Gustave's ART? Maybe if Louise had had her affair in the novel, she would have handled it better, more discreetly, more cleverly? And hence saved herself in the bargain? To the criticism that this was Flaubert's business, *his choice*, the new critic would answer: perhaps some imput from the real person would have added profoundly to the fictional character? Maybe the image of this lady would not have been projected, down through the history of fiction, with quite the same connotations of pathos and self-destructiveness? Maybe even she could have gotten into the reasons why a writer

429

with Flaubert's technical gifts was so continuously turned on by this silly little melodramatic fantasy? and thereby aided the writer to make himself better, bigger, stronger? Not that it should all go in one direction, this beneficial flow. Why didn't Flaubert *use* the scene in which Louise, in her passion, goes after the writer with a knife? Was it too loaded, or what? And if Flaubert didn't use that scene, what fictional scene of violence will Solomon invent? The combinations for deception are endless, obviously. *Always* for the writer's good, *obviously*. Maybe, just maybe, a woman needs to coax and handle an artist, her creator-to-be if you will, the way she handles him sensually in life— with knowing care, with proper heat, with equal participation? Otherwise, what you will have—*and have had in Western fiction's male history*—is the sweet but unpleasant story of *man as boy, author as boy, playing with himself and creating from onanism instead of playing with* THE OTHER, *and creating from participation? Not more male masturbatory novels, but novels of love, serious love, are what the new feminist criticism seeks.*

*Wants.*

*Will get.*

It goes without saying that all citizens in real life who are about to be used and exploited in an author's fiction should have the moral and philosophical right to check themselves out *before* they are turned into characters. The use and exploitation of friendships for purposes of "Art" is a con game that's gone on for far too long. I happen to believe that the interaction between citizen and character, and ultimate confrontation between character-to-be and author, can only prove healthy in the long run. It is not enough that the author is an actor/liar in life, he must also recognize the roles he gives to his performer-friends. It is a process that goes on in drama all the time, of course, between director and actor. That the literary author should think himself sacrosanct, or beyond such interactions, is not merely literary pomposity, it is also a piece of literary infirmity. The spirit of Pirandello must be transferred to the world of straight fiction, so that the old Dictatorship of the Author is brought to an end, and an invigorating literature of democracy replaces it. To my mind, although I don't have the space to go into it here, the old writing is no more than a corollary of the old economics—that is, Monopoly Capitalism—and it is high time that literature step out of the philosophical confines set down by the worlds of commerce and business. *In such a literary democracy, men and women alike will be liberated from their former positions as slaves in an author's fiefdom. There is simply no gauging the new horizons or possibilities in a future of such literary freedom.*

What better place to start than with a writer who has pictured women prominently in his novels, and who has written one novel wholly from her point of view? Also with a writer who is in his mid-career and who quite possibly could benefit from such an open and intimate critique? Let me make clear here that I sought out Lionel Solomon as much out of a personal and literary attraction as out of a desire to test a thesis, obtain pertinent data. Not only did I think that fair to the novelist; I wanted also to be *involved* myself as a critic, to have my own critique imbued with personal feeling and commitment; if I was "testing" the writer, in his life, I would also test the critic, PJA herself. Essentially, then, I wished and needed an openly tactile relationship with the author who wrote *Post-humous Thrills, Rosen at Fifty, Journey to Manhattan, Each According to His Needs, Pamela: Self-Portrait;* and wanted, too, to find out how much fantasy-confession, autobiography-facts, deliberate lying-fictional distortion make up his fictions.

Only a radically democratic literary criticism, derived from an empirical one-on-one intimacy with the author, can explore in depth crucial male-female scenes in novels written by males. Take for example, the rape scene in Solomon's portrait of a woman, *Pamela.* In that scene, written with especial care, to be sure, the heroine walks in the Cambridge Common with a keen desire to have her body violated, which in fact is precisely what occurs (conveniently enough). Now while the two young boys violate her, Pamela regards the event in her mind not without sympathy and furtive pleasure, the entire brutal act turning into something approaching aesthetic interest. One begins with the obvious interpretation that the male fantasy is operating at full scale. But one can go further here, armed with relevant empirical data. This same author, I must confess here, several times attempted the same sort of forced seduction with me, *believing in his heart of hearts that I—like any woman, or his fantasy of women—secretly desired the act.* Resisting him was a serious matter, and not a very pleasant one. But in any case, it will be most interesting to see how, the raw desire frustrated in real life, the author will eventually treat the scene, in fiction: according to objective truth, or according to male-wish-fulfillment-fiction (MWFF). I am sorry to say that if he opts for the former, he will be missing out on the more powerful aspects of the situation. I refer of course to his own condition of the time: the pathos and degradation of the desire; the helpless and impotent fury of his frustration; the painful self-awareness of his pathological urges. In other words, I sincerely hope that Solomon will not skip over and euphemize the powerful anatomy of his own neurosis and possibly cultural neurosis. It would be a shame if the surface sensationalism of popular mythology replaced, for this serious author, the deeply felt and agonizing probing of his own violent and unquenchable fantasy-life. *A great fiction requires great honesty; I believe that Lionel Solomon has it in him to put forth both.*

Lionel smiled here, admiring. And skipped down through lines talking about trying to tie up psychoanalytical techniques with feminist criticism.

My own private experience with Lionel Solomon confirmed one common cliché about the artistic personality, namely, that he is both more and less than his literary characters, and that in his private life there is more deep frustration, pain and suffering than in the ordinary citizen's existence (excluding of course those ordinary citizens who live in asylums, or who *should*). That he is willing to trade injury and insult for the sake of Experience; that joy and high feelings are always double-edged states; that sado-masochism dominates the sexual and emotional life, out of boredom and exhaustion as well as need; and that finally he is much closer in his regressive-narcissistic states to a child than a god or adult. The dominant figure in this artist-boy's life who remains paramount is the Mother Figure. And the fantasy-life here is so swollen that it parallels at times that of a serious psychotic; its grip is so firmly embedded that the line between the real and the wished-for is at times hardly grasped.

Lionel, heart gasping, grasped the porch railing. The space of meadow and forest seemed to vanish; and in their place loomed the printed pages, larger than 8 × 11. Larger than life, even; like a movie screen blocking out the meadow. He read:

I was also fortunate enough to receive permission to look through some of Lionel Solomon's notecards and annotations,

Lionel blinked, recalling something said in jest: "Sure, look through my things if it'll help your studies." He had said something like that, yes; but then did every sentence you uttered in your life count as literal? Weren't some joking, kidding, ironic? Surely judges and lawyers and courtrooms allowed legal space for irony?

annotations which concern the transfer and transformation of real life into fiction. And what we see here, what I shall

432

show briefly but emphatically, is the way the author manipulates each real-life situation into a fictional possibility, barring none; I have also taken the liberty, for the sake of the whole truth so far as I could get at it, of telephoning several old friends

Oh? Which ones? Name them please; "old friends," a code name for enemies?

to check with them what the possible real-life events were like that were later put into fiction; and have tried to piece together here those basic elements that form the work of art—the "objective reality," the subjective perception, the precise nature of the transformation. All helping, in conjunction with my own private experience with the man, to construct a fuller sketch of the working materials for what Professor Crews of Berkeley has called "psychoanalytical criticism." If any of this following material is helpful in placing another step in that as-yet-unformed path, then the venture will have had, to my mind, a large success. And I want to stress here that the personal aspect of this fragile and exploratory enterprise is the least important, on the deepest level; if you put the name Dostoyevsky or Melville, Bellow or Mailer, in place of Solomon here, the reader will have a clearer perception of my true aim and goal; an attempt at a scientific inquiry of literary artifact, and not a private gossip forum about a living novelist. Above all, I wish Mr. Solomon himself, to my mind a great if crippled artist, to understand my essay in this larger, impersonal context.

Boy oh boy, as his mother might have said, did this girl know her business! The "larger impersonal context," like her "subtler level." He had underestimated her all the way down the line, in talk, in games, in disguises (mental and in print). And that last disclaimer was the best of all: concern for Solomon! She was Doing It for Science, Lionel. When Sheyna reads about the way Tippy drops her nightie over her head like a chute, or what she permits and what she doesn't in our play, Sheyna will nod sympathetically and understand that I'm doing it for ART and Miss Matthews-Armstrong is doing it for SCIENCE. Of course. Or when daughter Rachel reads the notes about her father's ambivalence about having a daughter, or his ideas for a short novel about the situation, she'll laugh it off and call up Daddy and say, "Oh Dad, your antennae are a gas! And Tippy, for informing me and everyone else, well she's really a FIND, DADDY!"

# SPECIFICS
### Enough general remarks and now on to specifics.

Lionel caught himself from falling over into the high bushes! Head dizzy, he held the white column tightly. In a minute he relaxed, and stood up. *Specifics.* Was there a more slashing word in the language just now? His chest and head were pumping too strongly. He put the magazine down on the redwood chaise in the kitchen. And, for the second time in his life, he drank liquor before five o'clock. It was now not even noon. A straight shot of Scotch, without ice or water. The burning of the alcohol was most welcome, and he understood alcoholics better.

The pole and bush beans, right now. Outside, the sunshine was warm, wonderful; those porches kept the house cool, the weather a mystery. He wandered down to the garden, carrying his collander and wearing his straw hat. Pretending nothing was unusual. The pole beans were indeed huge, seven or eight inches, and getting obese; he bit into one, its sweetness emphatic. In a daze he started to pick from the first pole, high above his head. Mosquitoes buzzed. From below, Xana, four, said, "Hi. I came to help." "Okay," he said. "You start down here," and as he crouched to show her, she reprimanded him, *"I know how."* She began pulling off the beans, carefully and correctly. Lionel went back to his pole. "Where's Sheyna?" It hurt. She loved her too, and vice versa. "She went for a ride." "Oh." A pause. "To town?" "Uh . . . I'm not sure." "Well she better get back by three," Xana said sternly. "We have to make a pecan pie." Lionel nodded, and with a handful of beans in his collander he proceeded out of the jungle of green and back toward the house. "You just started," she called out to him. "That's not enough, Lionel!" But Lionel was reeling too much to respond.

Back in the house he returned to the porch, took up the magazine, and brought it inside to his standing desk. He nibbled on his beans as he turned to the section. They can't print this stuff, he thought, seeing the subtitle "Specifics." Where's Marty? If I sue for two or three million, will they stop the presses? The mailings? Sure, he answered, if you have twenty-five thousand and three years to give up, sure. *And then lose!* He suddenly had huge sympathy for the Meyer Levins, driven down the drain by their own cases while everyone smiled and looked the other way! . . . Read it first, he said aloud to himself. Maybe you're the one who can be sued by her! . . . Lionel worried about the future of his sanity.

The power of the words was awesome, something like chemotherapy. The prospect of friends looking into his note-cards, real and fabricated, as if they were laymen looking into his mouth to extract wisdom teeth, jolted him. Perspiring, dizzy from excitement, he swayed against his standing desk; no, he didn't have the energy to speak to Marty Kaufman after all. He'd have to fly to New York, he'd have to pay fifty bucks an hour just to tell his side, and then go through the legal involvement itself. He couldn't. Naturally, the *Times* would get hold of it, and call him to verify it—no, no, he couldn't. Not now. He'd have to wait, rest up, consider. What he *really* wanted to do, he realized, was to sink into the ground, fold up into the cellar of his pre-Revolutionary house and bury himself there along with the brave but dead pioneers and pilgrims, forgotten now along with their errors. He was as dead as John Allen, and Tippy was his Priscilla.

> . . . it is in the tiny details of everyday life perhaps that we should begin to discover the inner man; and in those everyday rituals you will find L. Solomon a mixture of the petty and the amusing, the rageful and the vulnerable, the compulsive and the humorous, the confused and the unhappy. What looks efficient is actually quite neurotic. Small errands drive him into disproportionate emotions of fear and anger. Watching him shop, for example, is like watching an Ahab reduced to chasing after a squirrel, not a whale. Getting a new registration for the car, waiting for a slow telephone operator, having a secretary slip up, sets him not only off course, but into deep waters of turbulence. For just below the civilized efficiency machine, there is a disturbed vulnerable creature living. Consider an extended example: shopping for a pair of boots at the Harvard Coop. . . .

Solomon's temper is a thing-in-itself, something like Kant's *Ding an sich*. A pent-up fury like his, ready to be let loose at any moment, is a source of fear and anxiety for him perhaps, but a piece of unusual theater for the spectator. A value. How often he bursts out at the slightest interruption of schedule or routine. How frequently a serious molehill becomes a comic Moby Dick in small situations. [Touché, Tip!] How many times he winds up falling into deep soup from exaggerated anger. Comic, pathetic, farcical, yes, of course. And yet, temper in a man, in a writer, is not without its encouraging sides. Here, an antibourgeois factor of no little importance, as I read it. Symptom of fear and

435

insecurity. Solomon's temper is also a badge of protest, unease, dislocation. He is a dissenter as well as a disturbed person. Important. Right?

The dirty candid camera! The filthy piglet! Lionel took deep, deep breaths, counted to ten, twenty, sixty, looking up at the pictures of friends on his bulletin board. Back at the piece, he skipped quickly through the details of the shoe-department catastrophe, embellished with phrases like "machismo boots," "preening walk," "desire for abasement," "rituals of humiliation and suppressed fury." Ending with, "When I came to his help, he kissed and hugged me like a kindergarten boy once again in the arms of his momma, crying." Kiss? Hug? Cry? Not quite, Tips. Machismo boots? Possibly. Maybe just a change of shoe styles, however. Have trouble shopping? Yes. Inefficient salespeople compound the trouble, though. He read on in the section called "Personal Habits."

> . . . little bank envelopes with twenty pennies for the Mass Pike tollbooths, readied in perfectly miserly fashion before driving . . . the ancient ghetto and grad school style of dress (striped gray pajamas, vest undershirts) . . . unconscious hypocrisy and contradictions at night (calls police concerning rock-band noise on Massachusetts Avenue, but by day listens to rock music, and at night usually has radio and television going simultaneously) . . . anal-compulsive squirrel type (hoarding old letters, pictures, elementary-school notebooks; keeping up correspondence with girlfriends of ten years past; continually clings to albums of childhood memorabilia . . . Semitic superiority complex masks deep inferiority fears, and hatred of Christians . . . prideful about his neurasthenia and hypochondria, afraid of driving, flying, walking at night . . . a total tightness about routines, from morning cereal with sliced bananas to students arriving late after bell, flying into a rage at any break in solipsistic world . . . penny pincher, teetotaler tries to disguise this, but get drunk in front of him as I did!), sports freak (devises "strategies" for his favorite teams, and actually sends them off to the coaches), physical coward, moral trimmer, closet paranoid, frightened fucker, depth narcissist . . . masturbator, voyeur, ass-smeller, nose-picker, lip-puller, pleasure-preverter, liar, actor, melodramatist . . .

Lionel stopped. Enough. The mixture of the real and the made-up was ingenious. Yes, he'd have to sue. It would mean the end of his writing in this country, for sure. So what? But he was impressed with the notes she had taken. Oh, graduate school was not wasted here. How could she have, unless she had a tape recorder or camera? Lionel now remembered Mr. Dylan singing, courtesy of Sony. He smiled, two tears rolling down his cheeks; just two. Hadn't he long ago gotten used to being the object of envy, fantasy, hate, desire in others' fantasy-imagery? Wasn't he used to having a public item called Lionel Solomon held up to abuse and scorn? Didn't old girlfriends deride him in letters around the country (and to him occasionally), colleagues at gatherings mock him privately, to his friends, and even at a party given in his honor an editor from his own company gossip maliciously about him? . . . Could he go on parking all this in a slot called envy, and leave the lot casually?

But this was a new type of slander, a new type of assassination, a new type of character-and-personality-shrinking, done in bold print, spread nationally, and called reporting. He wanted desperately to cry more, but wouldn't, not yet. So his chest congealed, and his eye went back to its task.

> In sexual matters Mr. Solomon is not impressive but most revealing; competent at best, and only at times; he suffers from premature ejaculation, occasional impotence, fear of fucking, the results in part of hypochondria, arrested needs, a basic lack of trust in (or fear of) women.

Lionel felt punched in the chest! He didn't have the will to go on. Couldn't. Voluptuous pleasure with a young woman, now turned around . . . premature ejaculation? Possibly the first time, yes; natural enough. And maybe he came too soon another time. But isn't fifteen to twenty minutes sufficient erection-time, Miss Matthews? Impotence, when? Hard to breathe. And did you check it out *with others?* But that wasn't even the point! Was this fit material for print? For a literary or biographical study? For publication in a national magazine? For a university?! Tears came now. Steadily. He returned to reading.

> It must be said that S. knows zilch about the clitoral game. This is a foreign-news broadcast to him. Of the old school, the Edwardian, he believes essentially that woman's pleasure is in her orifices alone, and that that pleasure does not have to include orgasm. Or, his yes, ours no. And when I suggested to him my own manipulation, or even a vibrator, to help him out, he acted as if I were challenging his manhood. This is relevant indeed to his descriptions of sexuality in the novels. Again and again there you have the delights of the vagina imagined with a headmas-

ter's innocence and a pupil's rhetoric. Wearing modern dress, the Edwardian novelist parades about completely impervious to real woman's needs, and to his own reality-set. No wonder that his Imagining Game suffers terribly when it comes to this area, below the belly and in the mind. And the worst of it is, of course, that in this transference from life to fiction, his innocent views are turned into dangerous myths, whereby male inadequacy is treated ultimately with reward, not to mention impunity. . . .

Solomon tried to remember . . . vibrator? "God you're vibrant!" she may have uttered, he thought, that first night. Did he hear wrong? . . . Purposely? . . . And didn't she orgasm, many times, or was she faking them? But why? For this . . . TEXT?!

Without special fondling and maternal encouragement his bothersome impotence would undoubtedly be much more severe.

*What impotence?* His not wishing to try for more than three orgasms in one night? His soreness and ordinary stamina called *inability?* His constitution called dirty names? Liar!

Clearly when it comes to the bedroom Lionel Solomon is a "mama's boy," desiring maternal comforting more than adult sexuality.

Can't you be fondled, and look for tenderness, without being a mama's boy? Did he suck his thumb, take a teddy bear to bed with him? Or is that coming up next?

Sex in his fiction should be viewed within the difficult biographical context. Later on I shall look briefly at several Solomon heroes and their female partners. . . . The author's preference for buggery strikes a strong homosexual note, but when pressed on the issue, he begged off.

Huh? What? He had done that boardwalk stint with great flair, and at her urging! She had never pressed him about homosexuality—oh no!—as he now read:

It is clear here too that his guarded hostility toward the homosexual in his fiction is a reaction to his own fears and past experience. In his youth there was a young man with whom homosexual relations of one sort of another—either active or latent—occurred, a Joey Z. How this repression gets transferred in the fiction is of great interest in the

438

characters of Lily R. in *Posthumous Thrills* and Angela in *Each According to His Needs.*

Oh, he saw that coming, and it came. Poor Joey. Poor Lionel. Poor Lilly and poor Angela, about to get buggered critically too. The facts of these characters immediately twisted; Lionel skipped.

> Of course this sexual impairment is paralleled by an emotional arrest. The real-life Solomon is cold, aloof, protective, deeply indifferent to other human beings—though on the surface he is genial, polite, and apparently "feeling." This brutal indifference, which extends to daughter, mother, girlfriend, has less to do with the writer's conscious meanness, but rather, worse I'm afraid, with the unconscious viewing of all human relations as no more than "potential fictional material." He disguises (to himself) this impervious indifference as scientific interest, his haughty dismissal as artistic and necessary distance. And when he is emotional, it is a maudlin sentiment, centering mostly on the self and a lost past. One might call this syndrome . . . the autistic emotion of the down-and-out narcissist.

You mean like Mr. Proust. Yes, I see.

> In all honesty it would be unfair to Lionel Solomon if we didn't cite another critical factor here, physical handicap.

For a second Lionel looked down at himself, checking to see if anything had been amputated, and he had forgotten about it! His limbs, well, *seemed* intact.

> Lionel Solomon turns out to have only one real adult testicle, the other being a poor atrophied fellow the size of an old walnut. Not very pretty or very functional.

What was it supposed to do, my friend, a tap dance? Be tossed around the infield?

> It also affects his performance during intercourse, directly and unfortunately; and I wouldn't be surprised if it weren't a major factor in his writing as well. The author claims here a congenital hernia situation, which is not uncommon, *if* this is true.

Who do you propose, a testicle shrinker?

> For example, he is most anxious when engaged in foreplay or intercourse, that his testicles he protected and *if* handled,

439

that it be done with the utmost delicacy; if you should grab
him in a friendly way, or in play, he cries like a baby. And
when asked why he won't perform any more than once or a
few times

How many was that now, ma'am?

he refers guardedly to his handicap, implying how he
doesn't want to push "it." Now of course this honest writer
has never really written about the matter, though he has
written about the others' defects (see Jay Plesch in *Posthumous Thrills,* Hannah Grunbaum in *Rosen at Fifty*); but
what are the consequences of this repression? How does
this embarrassing injury manifest itself in the unconscious
in his fiction: To what extent *do women in his fiction* pay
the price for this personal predicament? For example, in
our own relationship there would be a certain begging pauper quality in relation to those testicles, and childish scrotum, like a child whining to the mommy for the nipple
perhaps. I would hope, in my longer project, to explore the
relation between autobiographical scar and fictional dis-
placement in the novels, as a kind of paradigm for writings
by males.

Lionel shook his head, sympathetic to his poor testicles
now taking it publicly on the chin. Would she get a federal
grant to explore his "autobiographical scar"? He skipped, and
couldn't help beginning to mark the margins of the pages, as
if it were a student's composition.

I state these very personal factors not to entice <u>Fame-
Fuckers or Sensation-Seekers,</u> but rather to investigate more
empirically the points of convergence and variance between
an author's life and his work. I am interested in seeing
where and exactly how <u>the male</u> constructs fictions about
the female, to see how permanent (not temporary) or
essential images of the female are implanted in the culture;
and to inquire about the place that vengeance, wish, ego-
ideal, and <u>anal-oral infant needs</u> play. Or even, in Lionel
Solomon's case, <u>how male humiliation and injury serve to</u>
<u>spur a fictional picture of Amazon Female Aggression.</u> Of
course I don't believe that Lionel Solomon is solely responsible for this AFA complex; for he is after all, a member of the Male Corps of America; his primitive fears and
fantasies are cultural, not merely personal and psychological;
whence his imagery of the female arises as much from the
male culture role, and its exhaustion, as from personal,
psychosexual impotence. →oh, I see ....

Now I must come to a set of scenes painful indeed to

*[Handwritten margin notes, left side:]*
NFL teams? of course
Tippy of course
chimpanzee
3 yr old's Need to write a Novel, yes
We always break to show leg to the power of the opponent

have gone through, and to have to relate here. Unfortunately, it is necessary to give the scenes in some detail before we try to discuss and analyze certain patterns in the Solomon literary canon. I wish to relate here a situation in which I personally participated, to my discomfort and surprise; a situation which seems to have been misunderstood by the media, with help from the author himself; a scene which pains me to recall, and for which I feel nothing but enormous sympathy for Lionel Solomon the man. Please remember in what follows that we are speaking here about an "artist," not an ordinary gentleman: Consider the disconcerting facts in the context of ultimate "artistic creativity," and the only humane responses are those of empathy and compassion for the suffering and shame involved.

Lionel looked up, took deep yoga breaths; in, holding it, then out; in, holding it, out; in, holding it, out.

*— werewolf??*

On the night of May 15, beneath a full moon, a friend and I visited Mr. Solomon at his invitation for dinner and literary conversation. My friend, a graduate student in comparative literature at the University of Mexico, was keen on meeting Mr. Solomon, whom she had read in Spanish. I could detect early on in the strange evening that something was up when Ursula tried to talk about Cortesar, Márquez, Fuentes; Mr. Solomon would answer cursorily, and instead, turned the conversation to Ursula's intimate life. Especially did he want to know about my friend's loss of virginity. Afterwards, he invited Ursula to join us in his apartment, and before a half hour was gone, it was clear he had other activities in mind than literature. Perhaps, in fairness to the author, it was the influence of good grass that moved him that way; clearly he was a novice at smoking. But I believe that the grass only loosened his real feelings. In any case, he made overtures to us about dancing, and when we began, it was clear that it was for *the two girls* to dance, and Lionel Solomon to watch; well okay. But after a while it became clear, too, that he was after a heavier scene, for us and for him; well, it so happens that Ursula and I are pretty loose about each other, so it was cool there. What came next on Solomon's part, however, gave away his number. How shall I put this without embarrassing the writer personally? Perhaps the simplest is to say that the long-standing metaphor "writer as voyeur" is, in the Solomon case, not a metaphor but a literal fact. *That* was his dominating interest. When he went so far as

*Noticed Tip*

*Subtle*

441

pen and pad, though, it went too far for use; we stopped his game and asked him to join ours. Here, I'm afraid, he was discomforted, surprised, and most uneasy; immersion in the real was not his game, or attraction, you might say. In short, what came through was the writer's proclivity for watching and observing; his fear of direct encounter; his reliance on pen and paper and brain in place of the natural flow of libido and limb. Now here we must remember this paramount fact of the preference for *watching over participating*, and see, later on, how this crippling and arrested need affects crucial scenes in the fiction; and also, how it determines treatment of and outlook toward female characters.

Lionel stopped, thought: the extra girl was all the evidence Tippy would need in litigation. For pleasure and for legal matters, Ursula came in handy. He bit into another string bean, and chewed slowly.

Move on. With my friend gone then, a whole new scene and change of role came down onstage. After an unpleasant verbal fight, and several Solomon slaps, I was forced to act out a scene which caused me great discomfort (as my own shrink in New Haven can testify). In point of fact, I proceeded to fulfill Lionel Solomon's inclinations—out of my own anger, and whathaveyou—by beating the author across the face and body with a tall avocado plant and also, I'm afraid to say, an instrument for such purpose that Lionel Solomon had on hand. This was done with the full if frightened cooperation, and satisfaction, of Lionel Solomon. (Resistance came only later on, after the brutal whipping, as I shall explain.) Needless to say, it was an experience and an emotional trip that I shall not easily forget; and one which I fully expect to reappear somehow in Lionel Solomon's fiction. For various reasons, then, it is most useful to get the *facts* on the record now, and hope that the interested reader will keep them in mind when—and if—they become transformed into literary artifact at a future point; manipulated, of course—inevitably, shrewdly, perhaps unconsciously—for male/writer Solomon purposes. In fairness to Mr. Solomon let me elaborate with sympathy on motive and scene.

The magazine slipped down off the desk onto the floor. Lionel found it hard to see now. His eyes burned, strangely, and his legs cramped. He needed air badly, and staggered out the side door, seeking oxygen.

There, on the grass, he kneeled down, and put his head be-

442

tween his legs, in the baby-posture. Smelling grass; crying. He stayed there for about five minutes, back eased, chest tight. Could he bury his head for good?

Finally he lifted his head, and then got up. The sun was still there, the trees tall and green; they remained untouched by this human calumny and printed filth. Something drove him back inside, and he obeyed, on weak legs. Once again he picked up the magazine and gazed through the last paragraphs, pages.

*Call her*
*Mommy*
*Tippele*

I must say a few words here about the person most important to Mr. Solomon, a person I spent several visits with, Mrs. Belle Solomon, the author's mother. Not only is she a warm and wonderful woman, a woman of common sense and keenness, but she too has a sense, I believe, of her son's extraordinary attachment to her. The relation here, at the ages of thirty-eight and sixty-eight, is not very different, I'm afraid to say, from when the author was eight, and his mother thirty-eight, and beautiful too. In other words, he is "a mama's boy" in all the diverse, complicated, rich, and debilitating connotations of the term. Let us probe this relation more deeply. . . .

Too much for Solomon. Couldn't take this. His eye skipped down, down, past three long paragraphs on the subject. Well, Mom, you made the news. How does it feel? Except that you'll probably think it's lovely, what's wrong with a little publicity?! Sure.

While we cannot pursue in great detail here the political ramifications of Solomon's condition, a few words in passing are in order. Once a socialist, he is now a decadent and a capitalist. Does the evolution of this author, from public idealist to private imperialist, owner of private property and private aberration, tell us something about the social condition of the male nation? In other words, does the Essential Pig—the imperialist male ego, the firm solipsist, the sadomasochistic capitalist reflect to some degree the larger order of things, here displayed in extreme? Have the very best urges of the male creative mind been themselves turned and twisted in the hopelessly sick climate, so that when he seeks to create, he is in fact making creations of disorder and serious neurosis? Does the instinct for sado-masochism here, and in the fictional patterns, reflect the insane asylum called male American society? With Solomon acting out roles of patient, orderly and doctor all at the same time? Prescriptions for further illness, disguised to the givers as drugs for health, can only make the sick sicker, sadly.

What can be done, except to point out to these infected and contagious doctors the nature of the illness, short of locking them up in quarantine?

Lionel considered the lunatic paragraph; an American Lysistrata of the 1970's? Instead of locking up her box, she'd lock up his penis? But maybe it wasn't a bad idea, to cool things off a bit? A Taft-Hartley Bill for sexual negotiations? Yes, it was worth considering. Under "Literary Analysis" he checked in again, here and there:

> . . . Of course we would be naïve and crude if we didn't admit frankly the literary possibilities of the personal wish or fantasy. Speaking critically, the important question is *not* whether something has been completely twisted for the sake of the novel, but rather, if the fantasy has been *liberating* for the fiction. Has the motive found the right fictional vehicle? Take the obvious case, the male chauvinist hero of *Each According to His Needs,* wherein the Dean-professor creates his harem of mistresses and then supposedly provides for them A to Z. Now what is interesting here is the energy of the fictional voice, at the same time that the man and situation remain obvious fantasy, a see-through wish-projection.

Lionel, chest burning, said aloud, "But that was real, real! Some characteristics from one girl to another switched, that was all. The trouble perhaps was that I didn't make up enough, reduce six to two or three perhaps!"

> . . . Whereas, in contrast, the portrait of the psychiatrist in trouble in *Rosen at Fifty,* living in the doldrums of his chaste monogamous marriage, clearly suffers from a lack of the made-up; the voice of Rosen is exact to the point of drabness it is stiff with the yoke of *un*transformed reality, a reality controlled by a prudish and closed personality; the failure here is clearly one of the imagination. . . .

But the whole thing there *was* fantasy, was *made up*, for worse or for better, probably for worse too. Why must she get it so wrong, so opposite?

> . . . Again, the problems operating here in the sodomy of Pamela in *Self-Portrait* have obviously to do with the latent homosexual wish unleashed here without any governors whatsoever, and so we are asked to believe that this formidable young photographer, in the midst of her

444

painful *moral* dilemma, is still ready to engage in her brazen pickup aberration? No, that won't wash at all, except that it reveals about the author. . . .

Lionel, remembering the incident in life and how he had tamed it down for the sake of fiction, shook his head. Then he remembered something else: there was no sodomy in the pickup scene, she's confused scenes!

> . . . I must repeat here, as I approach the close, what I said earlier. Above all I wish Mr. Solomon to understand that I would never have journeyed on this quest if I didn't think at the outset that he was a most interesting novelist with a chance for literary posterity. Everything that happened between us, regardless of how it may look in bold crude print, was understood by me in this very special context. And now, *more than ever*, I happen to *believe* in Lionel Solomon; I happen to think that he is a great if crippled man, whose eccentricities and obsessions are no more than the other side of his accomplishments, or perhaps even the spur for it. (Whether he is able to turn such obsessions into permanent materials of art, or suffer beneath their enormous weight and be driven into future silence or failure, only time will tell.) Therefore, I hope that he, more than anyone, understands this project *on all its levels,* and my own tremendous respect for him. Right from the beginning he was willing to adventure with me, a perfect stranger, a wide-eyed fan; he was curious enough to let himself loose with me, take a heavy trip at an age and station when most men stand on their hindlegs and back off, into safety. And just as one day I imagine he will use the adventure (and any future adventure) with me for his "creative" purposes, so I here have tried no more than to use it for my own, notes toward a more wide-ranging literary criticism, embracing personal involvement along with traditional procedures. (Or Notes toward a More Empirical Female Literary Criticism, if this is not too encompassing/pretentious.) To use a Solomon phrase, it goes without saying that I hope he does indeed transform me—his white whale, and our experience—into a (tall) tale, for *only then will my own project be rounded off fully, and be ready for final remarks of verification.*

*[marginal annotations: "where's your editor?"  "ah, that word!"  "Schlick and the Vienna School?"]*

Some artists are ordinary men, some are narrow and provincial, some are miserable, petty, and puerile; I want to confirm here and now that Lionel Solomon is none of the above. It is for this reason that I believe that he will understand what I have done here, why, and with what genuine sympathies. Revelation, insight, and higher literary principles have been my aim, not petty exposure or low gossip. This intimate portrait has been drawn with sympathy and appreciation, as well as with criticism and truth.

Mr. Solomon, please believe me when I say, I await eagerly your response to this portrait and project, whether that response is a fictional one or a straight one—one from the heart as well as the brain. You've been good for me, and I hope I've been good for you—with my honesty if nothing else. Is it the wrong place to add—or to announce, should I say, my dearest friend and novelist—that it is a measure of my respect and my believe in you, my love for you and your work, that I am now carrying within me the seed of a new Solomon?

At first dazzled, Lionel smiled: a warm smile. He put the magazine down and sat down by his typewriter, scratched his chin, burned.

*Doctor, to read about oneself, much as the anonymous desire it, can be a most unsettling experience. To be lied about in print, sir, is not an easy matter, no matter how much you once told me to forget it, go on with my work. To know that the magazines will print anything that will sell, under the heading of nonfiction, is a scandal. The great Flaubert was right when he said that if Napoleon would ban all magazines and newspapers he, Flaubert, would crawl on his hands and knees to Paris, and kiss the Emperor's ass. I would not be averse to considering a similar journey and reward, if our President decided upon a similar ban. Yet, to be vivesected in print is one thing; but to have your future stories prejudged and predetermined in a fixed false way adds a new modern twist of literary calumny. For this vile dart is aimed at one's true potency, at one's literary balls if you will. And it was felt by Solomon as such; not wrongly, I believe, Doctor. Little wonder then that he was helpless before the guerrilla's cunning new ambush, and perfectly ready to admit now, fully and firmly, that she was the stronger.*

He composed a note to the young critic.

Dear Miss Matthews,

Thanks so much for your words about me, and your invitation to respond.

I wish only to add to your forthright and well-meaning account a few observations. The evening was May 16, the whipping was with a cat-o'-nine-tails, my repertoire includes T-shirts as well as vest undershirts.

You are a most gifted lunatic, and I read with macabre fascination your distorted and lying version of our times together.

In case of death, may I put your name down as a possible eulogy speaker? What was your *name* again?

Do give Ursula my best, you two made a fine pair. Perhaps you could dissertate together?

Congratulations on your exciting news and expectations. What a charming place to make your little announcement. If you should need some mother's milk, by the way, try a real mother in any local hospital, don't bring the little tyke up on Carnation.

Sincerely,
Lionel Solomon

Briefly, he checked "Specifics" again, to the pages about the night and morning of darkness. His life and reputation were squeezed between Smirnoff's vodka and Cardin's leisure suits. He read the first few lines, but put it down. He wiped his wet brow, stood up, found his tennis wristband and put it on.

The telephone rang.

He went for it. He'd put it simply to Marty, she wrote a slanderous account with moments of truth in it—

It rang again. Sheyna? No, no more personal relations for today.

The slender beige princess purred a fourth and fifth time. Tempted, in controlled panic, he recalled that that's how it all began, how this Woman from Albuquerque had first come to interrupt his life. Not by knocking on his front door.

*She* rang again. He left the room, and the house.

Outside, he walked the length of the porch. Two large maples, one with clamps on it to keep it from splitting in winter, provided shade. To his left, down a mild slope was the old sunken garden with the freshly painted white gazebo; and up to the right, beyond the house, the weed patch that had become a usable tennis court. Two projects of resurrection. (Unlike himself.) Back across the porch, past gallon gasoline cans (for the lawnmower), garden tools, an aluminum stepladder, brooms, neat stacks of birch and maple, Xana's tricycle and baby-doll carriage and assorted trucks and dolls. This porch, her playhouse on rainy days. At the two white barrels holding kindling, he stopped, and wondered if he could climb in there, and live like Xana did in her games? *For a moment he was back with those wooden barrels by his father's counter, filled with sours and half-sours and briny water, and he shivered with despair. Smelled his hands to check.* Oh, to be in Tucson, Lima, the Marquesas. . . . He walked back the other way, stunned by the brilliant sun falling on the green lawn and trees, crazed by the events and reading of the past hour. Could *an hour* mean so much in one life?

He took hold of the long tool leaning against the corner post. To himself, he inquired, "What is your desire just now?" And he responded, "To dig a hole, climb in it, and stay there."

He was walking off the porch when Xana, running toward him, said, "Where are you going with the shovel?"

"I have to take care of something." He strode across the lawn toward the town dirt road, and the steep embankment. On instinct he turned about and sure enough, there was the little girl, with her two dogs, following, like a game. "No, you better go back, I'll see you later, okay?"

"Okay," she said, then, alert to his habits of gardening or painting, "Gonna take your radio?"

"Good idea," he said, starting to walk back.

But she was already running saying, "I know where it is, I'll bring it to *yah!*" with her four-year-old New Hampshire accent. The small ebony dog dancing in front of her, the shepherd-collie Hank by his side, as he followed along.

In the kitchen she climbed on the chair and gripped the large transistor with her two hands on the handle. "Can I put it on?" she asked, and he let her. She pushed down the fourth chrome button, and lit up with pride as "God Knows I Love My Music!" jumped on.

He sat down and exchanged his crepe-soled shoes for his work boots, took his hat and mosquito repellent, and told his "Little Miss Peppercorn" goodbye. She thought he was "acting foolish."

Taking his implements, he left the house and retraced his steps across lawn, dirt road and up through the high meadow on the far side of the road. He passed the abandoned chicken coop, the shell intact, passed the pretty but obsolete well, and entered onto the old logging road which snaked beautifully through the thick forest. Sunlight dappled the dirt path, and he realized that he had once been on this road, a while back, for different purposes. Cracking brush and twigs, he recalled a splendid afternoon out here, back a year ago, with the state's county forester. A burly fellow in his thirties down from Woodsville, Richard Pendleton had walked the length and width of his forest, answering all sorts of questions for Lionel—tree nourishment, wildlife trees, the age and health of particular trees, and the forest itself—and suggesting that a "selective cutting" wouldn't hurt any. The service was more like a private tutorial in forestry than an opinion on whether to cut or not. A courtesy of New Hampshire, it made one a patriot of the state. But this was another day, however, and instead of being in kindly, knowledgeable hands, he felt in the grip of more cunning forces. So he trudged on with his shovel and his radio, hat on, through the pine stand and then the hardwoods, feeling loose, lunatic, purposeful. The smell of pine scented the air, and the sun created glinting patterns of design and light upon the green. Why did everything terrible in life happen on glorious days, while in literature storms raged and seas turned? What was good for symbolism was not very true to reality. At the edge of that same lovely clearing—where he had composed mentally a while ago—Lionel stopped. Upon a huge tree stump he set down the radio and his repellent bottle, and began to test the ground with his long-handled shovel. Of course he was an amateur at this, his only holes being those made for small bushes or seedling transplants, and so he found himself testing three areas before beginning. Every time the questions came to him—what are you doing, and Why?—he put them away immediately. He had *thought too much*, had been hurt too much, and what he needed now was a hard labor, a definite task. Perhaps there he'd find a solution, or consolation.

At first it was fun, then it grew difficult, after that painful and arduous, and as the day passed, murderously punishing.

He dug straight down at first, simply using the shovel edge to lift the earth out of the hole. But as the hole grew, he had to use his foot on the shovel edge to dig down, and discovered that it was a small art not to slip off. Solomon, artless and therefore doubly ineffective, tried hard, dug down and shoveled dirt out; a dumb brute, slowly he dug down and dug out. Perspiring enormously after a half hour or forty-five minutes, he removed his work shirt and tied his handkerchief around his neck. When his chest would pound too strongly, he stopped, stood straight, walked a step or two. Gradually the birds' trills bored him, and he got a rock station from

449

Portland. For tough rocks or small "boulders," he had to go down on all fours, and, with his hands and fingernails, work them out of the ground as best as he could. His hands, innocent of hard labor, hurt, blistered and bled as a few hours passed so that at times he had to leave the grip of the handle and massage his palms with grass and dirt. (They were getting alike, actually.) Finally a granite stone was just too tough to remove, and he was stymied. Breathing slowly and deeply, he quieted the tiny voice within, which warned STOP, and decided the only thing to do was to return for an ax, and hoe, and whatever else. It was a good break anyway, he assessed, retracing his steps in the piney air with a more wobbly gait. It was a warm afternoon, but not overbearing, thank God; but he did feel warm inside, warm, strange, calm.

Back at the house he stopped by the shallow well, pumped cold brook water into his cupped hands, drank, threw water on his face, neck, brow. Wonderful! Sure, he'd fill a canteen and take it back with him; along with the ax, hoe, and a long-handled spade; also a pair of work gloves. Surprisingly, perhaps, he was practical enough to make himself a ham and cheese sandwich, wrap it in wax paper, and put it in a brown paper bag, as in junior-high days. Once again, however, the little girl Xana sighted him from her tricycle and asked if she could come with him now? He advised "later," and she asked, "About three o'clock?" He nodded, smiling. She didn't know the difference between three and seven, but used the numbers anyway. Then he was on his way, his feet tired, back to his curious task, which somehow satisfied him now. He was grateful that his work was not out here in the open meadow, beneath the hot sun; and he was glad that he had found a suitable project, though he didn't know its full purpose. Just hoping, as he heard the tinny sounds of the radio jarring through the quiet woods, that he'd be able to complete his work and somehow find a meaning therein, within. . . . But what did "completing it" mean?

Anyway, the new tools certainly made it easier. He was able to pierce and break the earth with the hoe and forked spade, or longhandled weeder, while keeping his back fairly straight; and when the rock was embedded in crabgrass or even, as at one point, in the trail of a tree root, he used the sharp ax. The practical progress pleased him, gave him some hope. Just as the gloves made it much, much easier. And at another point when he looked around and saw the mounds of dirt he was making, it suddenly came to him that perhaps what he was constructing was a kiva of sorts, his own special underground chamber for peace and prayer and ritual. That pleased him too. Still, the enormity of the task increased; the effect of the digging was taking an immense toll out of him. When he sat on the stump to eat his sandwich, he found, for example, that his hand shook terribly when he tried to unwrap it and he had first to lie flat on the ground for some fifteen minutes before he could muster the control to try it. And even then, as he ate, his biceps twitched mercilessly and his heart didn't stop its severe pumping all the time he was eating the sandwich. It tasted very good indeed, like the first bites of food and delicious water he had once had, on a Houston oil rig, after five days of not eating, when he was sixteen. He wished he had brought more, but he couldn't go back again. (Ever?) The work scared him now, and he resettled himself to the earth, putting his shoes in his shirt for a pillow, and lay there, resting. . . . The three o'clock news awoke him several hours later. Another terrorist raid on an Israeli village. Times were bad everywhere, he saw. Against his body's wishes he raised himself, with a kind of sadistic joy, feeling the sharp assault of fatigue and hurt. He did a few backrolls, pierced by twigs and pine-cones, to keep his back loose. It helped.

Finally he made it to the point of working from within the ground, tossing the dirt out as best he could without climbing and lifting it, a burden to the back. But this was difficult, another art not to have half the shovelful fall back into the rectangular hole. working on the sides he would then switch to depth, and back again, wondering how in the world coalminers did this day in, day out, or ditchdiggers. Also, the act of lifting his arms and the shovel had grown steadily more taxing, like lifting bags of cement. And then a most curious thing occurred as he tried to copy his sports habits and work through his fatigue to new energy; he worked through his fatigue but discovered at the other end *active pain!* What was previously tired, now turned into soaring, shooting *hurt;* engulfing him! . . . But he would push forward regardless, he decided, at least another foot, so that he could at least lie in it, somewhat; with a certain feeble ferocity he began chopping away, before he realized he was losing control, and needed patience. He wanted a drink of water badly, but since it meant boosting himself out of the hole, it was a major decision. He decided for it, reached out and grabbed the canteen, and brought it back to his earthpit, where he poured the remaining water over his head and neck. Wiped his face smooth with his shirt.

Dug on. And on and on, and on . . .

He wasn't sure *what* happened next, or *how*, except that he recalled the sun becoming a bar of filtered gold, and the flies and mosquitoes buzzing all around him. His body felt very light, gravity-less; the music had returned too. Steel Ice Band, George Harrison, the Eagles. The earth smelled aromatically, and he was in a crumble in his hole, exhausted.

And he wasn't sure quite how it happened, in his twilight consciousness, but he sensed someone approaching, a dog barking somewhere (?), and when he opened his eyes he saw first a little girl's smile, *then his old friend, with her wolfish smile and ocher eyes. "Tippy!" he formed with his lips, barely speaking it. Facing him on her knees, chin on palms, she gazed at him as if he were a silly boy in trouble again. She paused to sip her ginger ale through a straw from a white mug, licked her lips, and then laughing, got up. To the tunes on the transistor she began doing her little boogie steps, in fun, to please him. She was wearing a brief denim skirt and narrow halter-top, and her bare midriff was tanned. Was that a Beatle tune she rocked to? Oh, it was fun, a break from pain, and he wanted to kiss her with gratitude for showing up here like this, but he was too exhausted to budge. After a minute or two she lay back down, on her belly, and gazed out over the edge at him, palms cupping cheeks and temples. And Lionel, seeing this wonderful girl turn up in his hour of need, forgot about what she had done to him and wondered instead what she wanted from him—more? "I give in, Tippy," he said, "I do."*

*"You're* SILLY," *she said, moving a handful of dirt with her hand in teasing fashion, "Sol-o-mon's Fol-ly!" She giggled, shoving the pile over the edge, onto Lionel's legs. "Playing all these* SILLY *games," she repeated, pouting slightly,* "YOU JUST DON'T WANT TO GROW UP, DO YOU?" *Carefully she had gathered another castle of dirt and pushed it toward the hole, and over, her face spreading sensuously as it did when she ran her nail down his chest. Hypnotically she repeated this act, gathering the earth and pushing it over, spreading it onto Lionel's bare chest, face, head.*

*Like being buried alive in the sand in Coney Island, he thinks. Or, beyond his time, he recalls the life lived by his Uncle Morris and Miriam, and their two small children, all around White Russia. He had never understood what they meant when they said that for two years the family moved from one hole to another hole, or cave, in hiding from the Nazis, and from the frightened, anti-Semitic Russians. Along with three other families, they would find an area near a village, dig a hole for the four of them, and live there for several months, stealing potatoes and bread from the village or taking it at gunpoint. (Sometimes a village was kindly, and gave them provisions. But living in real holes and hopping from one to another? He thought only the Viet Cong did that; were Russian Jews guerrilla exiles too, hunted by everyone? Holes?)* Now he knew.

Dirt brushed down his forehead and nose.

*And he remembered too, in Brownsville, being chased down a mechanics' pit in a gasoline station by a couple of Italian hard guys, who called down to him, "You stay there, Jewboy! We don't wanna see you come up tonight, little kike!" And he had stayed there for hours, shivering in the dark dank pit, smeared with grease, worrying every minute about a rat brushing him! Cold and alone and terrified with his fielder's glove they had wanted.*

She was smiling greedily now, those teeth edging forward, as she shoved dirt with two hands down upon him.

*He feels the sacred Hopi mud spread upon his cheeks, and smiles fondly. Yes. Yes. Perhaps this too was a fertility rite, in its bizarre way?*

Dirt fell.

*Another underground scene slips into focus, when he's eight or nine and comes to help out at the appetizing counter for the first time. Downstairs in the dirty cellar, his father in filthy apron and thick black shoes, is using all his strength to roll a half-sour barrel toward the giant freezer. And as Papa sees him, he opens his arms out and the boy runs to him. But as he is held and kissed, the smells of fish and ox and half-sours mingle to create a repellent odor, and make him want to escape quickly! His father senses this, his eyes go wild with betrayal, Lionel feels crushed with bad feeling and tries to make it up, somehow. "So it's not good enough for you, heh? Very nice. Very nice indeed." And Lionel stands there, wanting to help, drenched with remorse, helpless! feeling cramped and suffocated as he backs amidst huge bags of potatoes that seem to have a thousand eyes. Helpless!*

In his pain now, in his shame now, he gazed up at the lovely young oppressor, for whom this was all a game. The dirt came down like a soft drizzle, everywhere, onto his bare chest and inside his trousers; knowing he was too exhausted to lift a finger to protest, sensing too that it would all be over soon. And as he understood this and faced it squarely, a kind of peace swept him, spread through his senses and brain, and made him feel easier. Tippy was smiling oddly (nervously?), chattering at him somehow, asking him questions from a distance, and looking just like a little girl in a jumper as she moved the dirt, though just now she hesitated, halted. Oh, don't stop, end it my friend, end it, I accept it! He gulped for air in the heat, and caught dirt in his mouth, and began to cough, and cough rather violently, shaking his body terribly so that he couldn't see anymore or think or talk, but was blinded by the shaking and the couch and the dirt, and he felt about to burst from lack of oxygen and trembling!

And then there was a great hollow of blackness, no more, nothing.

He didn't know what time of day or night it was as he opened his eyes, or if he was alive. It was charcoal gray, quiet, smooth. He turned his head slightly and felt his nose brush cotton, not earth. His fingertips reached out, felt . . . wool? No longer in his grave . . . a bed? Where was he, how did he get here? He lifted his head slightly, an effort; a crack of yellow light beneath the door. His bedroom? A hospital room? He tried to get up to see if there was a clock on the far night table, but his body tore in resistance, and took him back down, dizzy.

Dropped into quick sleep, deep dreams. In one he couldn't find his way out of an elevator subway station, and was pushed and cramped by masses of people. In another it was an opening at a painting exhibit, and he wound up in a bathroom that was tiny and hot, and people began entering, crowding him! Delighted suddenly when someone pulled open his eyelids and began to shine a slim beam of yellow at his pupils, blinding him momentarily. The British accent inquired, "Who are you?" What a fine question, who was he?

Lionel responded, "Who are you?"

"Doctor Hargrave, Mary Hitchcock Hospital. And you?"

Should he tell the truth or make up a name? Use Babel's? "Lionel Solomon."

"Where are we, do you know?"

Lionel looked about, the beam following him, a soft light on now. Saw his mantelpiece of books and Indianhead bookends, and above, Simone Best's watercolor. "New Hampshire. In my bedroom." Spoken slowly. Forgot the name of the town actually.

The long-faced man with the checked shirt and knit tie nodded, asked, "How old will you be on your next birthday? When is it?"

Naturally he said, "I would have been thirty-nine, next month, September."

The doctor smiled. "You will be, don't worry, Mr. Solomon. Just a bad scare, and a blackout. What the hell were you doing out there? Just rest now and in a few days you should be up and around again. Are there any family or close friends you'd like me to contact? Or a doctor?"

Lionel tried to think; it was too hard to figure out all that, and shook his head. The doctor explained that the girl next door, Mrs. Franks, would be happy to take care of him for a few days: Or he could have a nurse in for a day or two: Lionel, used to nurses, opted for the latter. How did it all happen, get here? he wondered.

"Would you raise yourself up for this tranquilizer? That's a good fellow." As he raised himself up he moaned irrepressibly, or his body did. He took the pill beneath his tongue, drank the water, and swallowed. Once again a doctor was advising him about a nurse and a follow-up examination. "You take it easy now. When you're feeling better you really must tell me what you were . . . building out there." Light and understated.

History repeating itself so swiftly in his life.

He had wanted to die powerfully, cleanly, and now he was limping back to life, a wounded body again, a sick soul. Why?

The room was very pleasant this way, with the bedside lamp revealing the room's familiar contours. The walls were papered in pale yellow with a small design; the curtains were simple and white, like the window shades; a glass vase with a maroon flower growing in water, and Simone's vibrant watercolor of the house and hills in summer, gave color. A fine gable gave atelier charm, and he slept beneath the sloping ceiling, feeling tucked in. Clothes were flung over an armchair, his dungarees were over the footstool (covered by Sheyna), a slim digital radio sat on the bureau (the clicking horrible when he was well). In his childhood he had never had a room of his own, but shared the living room with his sister. So this room had become special to him, with all its ordinary objects and habits. (A room with habits? Yes. The way the light slanted; the shade that didn't work well; the wallpaper edges that had come loose; and of course the fireplace that welcomed bats through every spring as if they were in spring training.) In peace like this, in soft light, the room got its full share of his attention, and it was worthy of it. Just the crickets outside, an occasional whippoorwill calling, and

Lionel absorbing it, in his bed. It gave illness a compensatory edge, as when you stayed home from school in childhood.

*Lionel lay there and was not there, but back, sliding into a cozy memory of boyhood. He saw his mother sleeping, on her left side, on the brocade-covered couch while he listened to the Lone Ranger on the radio. She had washed the dishes, he had dried them, she lay down and fell asleep to the deep baritone voice while Lionel printed his homework in the Composition Notebook, filled with gold stars. Her face was light and beautiful in repose. . . . Next he was with his own Rachel, showing her some newborn lambs in a friend's barn in California; with hesitancy and delight she stroked the back of a week-old lamb that Lionel held in his arms, with Rachel's eyes lighting up at the lamb's little baa cries. With the goat afterwards, however, she was much more frightened, and had to be held up by Solomon. Four years old, she was like those lambs, and asked to go back again and again, watching them swiftly. . . . He turned his neck, missing his mother, his daughter, himself as a boy! . . . His eye caught sight of Sheyna's burlap footstool, and he recalled the way she curled against him in bed, and said seriously that she wouldn't be able to sleep anymore, she had "too many worries." Making him laugh aloud. Recalled the scraping of her violin at Beethoven or Bach in her study; he'd stop and listen on the way to the kitchen, thinking how it was the right sort of scraping noise. . . . On the night table he saw the cube of photographs, one of Rachel wearing a long white dress at age three, just like Mama (Blossom) at the cottage in Palo Alto; recalled how she would whisper to him that he "promised" to tell her the next chapter of Ollie Bump II and Captain Chippers. A story which she stayed perfectly alert to, and in reward, hugged him tightly around the neck, kissing his lips goodnight and snuggling in his arms, using her tiny hands. . . . His father was playing him chess when he was four now and—*

He was thirty-eight, he was supposed to be in the pink and prime of his life; instead, here he was in the black and blue, in shame and pain, in solitude and disgrace. What was the good of getting older only to make worse mistakes? To suffer more?

A shaft of light slanted downward. . . . Lionel saw something. Felt something. An illumination? . . . Perhaps he was wrong. Perhaps he had imagined it all; or at least imagined it *his way.* A rip in the shade, it should be fixed by Sheyna. . . . Yes, perhaps the girl was right, and he, Lionel, had gotten it wrong. Remembered it wrong. Saw it wrong. Wrote it wrong. Felt it wrong. Yes, that last, there: *felt* it wrong. Maybe the facts were nothing but so much tinsel, next to the feelings imparted. Maybe all along she had been experiencing one set of feelings and one set of perceptions, and Lionel quite another set. And what were considered "the facts of the matter" were no more than a basic disagreement about boundaries, realities. Putting it badly now. He gripped the bedpost, tried to squeeze it; solidity was real, for sure, out there. Had he in fact tried to rape her? Whipped her somehow, without knowing it? Acted more violently than she, and therefore, was more ill? . . . Who knew what in fact did go on, when actions between two persons alone were so intimate and so hot? . . . Now this new line of reasoning, this unlooked-for and injurious revelation, frightened Solomon, and he turned and twisted to escape it. For it meant a whole different way of assessing the situation. Instead of being right, or being sure, or knowing how to behave toward the girl, he knew nothing. Was sure of . . . nothing. Had in his possession . . . nothing. Not warning systems to the self, not rules for the future, not lessons from the past. All of this self-therapy manual material was suddenly erased, irrelevant. He was back to square zero, concerning what had happened; or worse, how to act in the future.

But then too, weren't the girl's words appropriate? Why shouldn't she write her own "story" about him and call it nonfiction? Tit for tat, yes? Tit for betrayal, you mean.

He hit the pillow with his closed fist softly, too weak to do more.

But wasn't it just what he did?

No! A thousand times no! If he used friends in fictions, it was with friendliness only!

Come now, pal, cut it out. You'd do anything for the right story, trade any friend in for the sake of Art. But didn't Joyce? Didn't he use *real names* even? Don't I use my own life to a humiliating degree of exposure?

The lady has her rights then, no?

To *lie* this way?

He pulled the sheet and light blanket up over his head, to resist the assaulting ideas.

But these new thoughts and doubts and fears traveled through his body like a form of electricity, shooting chills up and down his spine and numbing his thinking. His heart staggered and reeled uncontrollably, because there was nothing he could control it with. His main weapons—his reason, his lessons from the experience—had been removed from his arsenal by his own hands, new illuminations.

And didn't the article itself *prove* what Solomon had come to feel: namely, that there was more to the girl than sensuality, that her attractions were deeper, more subtle? Or that her madness included a keen intelligence, distorted and comical as that may be? In other words, wasn't that very article, destructive in many ways, nevertheless a document testifying to his own sanity? Supporting his feelings that the girl was deeper than he was allowing for in his ego-bound consciousness or bourgeois moral judgment? Oh, the irony was real, was ever so poignant, even though at his expense now!

And then another thought, fine and original because of its perfect madness, struck him: Did he love her? Was that what it was about? Was it love that he resisted and didn't understand and didn't want? *That* love, anyway? Did you have to *like* the love when it came your way, hit you in the face? Passionate love, that rare sort. Was it the passion in fact that disguised the love? Was he so passionate about her—so stuck on her unique bravado, her overwhelming breasts, her erudite cunt, her genius pelvis—that he was blinded to his deeper feelings? deepest feelings? his crazy love for her? . . . Warm tears coursed slowly down his hot cheeks, and onto the pillow. He had turned onto his stomach, like a baby, nose pushed into the pillow. The thought of his loving her just made him cry and cry.

Presently, *Mr. Babel approached, wearing a short-sleeved shirt and wide trousers, of the thirties. He said, "You wanted to experience everything, didn't you?"*

*Lionel clenched his teeth, to avoid crying more. Nodded.*

*"I understand. I know. I was the same way." Behind his eyeglasses he blinked, a half-smile forming on his lips. "People don't like you for asking so many questions, do they?" he noted. "For being intensely curious. For wanting to know everything. I understand." He paused, considering. "We writers are all brothers, Lionel. We all get PUNISHED for our thirsty curiosity. For our desire to be freer with ourselves. For our desire to know." He removed his eyeglasses, exhaled upon the lenses, wiped them with his handkerchief, carefully. "Somewhere, sometime, perhaps we'll all get together, my friend, and share our stories. . . . And our persecutions." He put the glasses back on, one stem at a time. "Only watch out." He raised a finger, but spoke softly, "You mustn't let go*

*. . . prematurely. Observe it all, record it all, patiently—even though you may be burning."*

The words hit Lionel, and the tears flowed. He tried to stop them, but couldn't. He reached for a Kleenex, hit the bedpost with his elbow, collapsed in pain.

Two days later. Gray light seeped into the room, and the sound of rain splattered on roofs and off drains. He was most grateful that he could get up now, and around, even if he couldn't yet perform his morning ritual of yoga exercises. But he was good enough to come downstairs, take his own meals, walk about, mending. No work yet, however. He understood. In his long kitchen, he squeezed his oranges, ground the beans in his electric grinder and made fresh coffee, and sat with his cold cereal and cut banana at the oblong table, gazing out at meadow and mountain. Handel cheered from the kitchen speaker, and there was yesterday's *Times* to read. (Two *Times* per week gave him time to read all the nice furtive features on Zambia, Trenton, organgutans, old synagogues in the Caribbean, new pleasure centers in the brain, et cetera, et cetera . . . )The nurse had left yesterday, and soon Sue from next door would join him for coffee if he wished. And Xana would bounce in, after her morning TV shows, in her blue bathrobe, most careful about having a full wardrobe. A chickadee was on the window feeder, dropping sunflower seeds down to the ground for his buddies. Oh everything seemed in order again, even the light rain, refreshed. (Watch it, Lionel, he warned himself; watch it.)

He had learned yesterday what had happened. Suffering from exhaustion and shock, he had not been fully conscious when the little girl had come out into the woods to find him; it was only after a little while of playing at his hole, playfully throwing dirt in fun, that she realized that something was wrong, really wrong, and how strangely off were his responses. He had jabbered to her, it seemed, and she had taken that as a signal to keep playing, trying to cover him with the dirt; only finally getting scared, and with smart Mr. Hank the shepherd at her side, she ran back home and told her mommy. Sue and Walter had gotten him out of the hole, and bore him on their shoulders back home. Called the hospital immediately. The exhaustion was severe, however, and at the end of the week he was scheduled to come to the hospital to take various tests, including EKG's. But meanwhile he had responded well, according to Dr. Hargrave, and there didn't seem to be much to worry about, *physically*. "But I do think you ought to speak to someone, old chap, as to what you were doing out there." And so Lionel would write his note to Dr. Lirič, who was at the Vineyard for the month of August (his secretary on the telephone).

"Can I have some banana?" called out Xana now racing into his long kitchen and memory with morning energy and trust. "When's Sheyna coming home?" she inquired, already reaching onto the shelf to get the fruit down.

"Come here, you little golden retriever!" he said, cheered by her energetic little presence despite her daily punishing question. "I'm not a *golden retriever*," she protested, climbing on his lap with the banana, like a chimpanzee in a bathrobe. He whispered, *"You retrieved me, didn't you?"* She nodded, quite solemnly, remembering the experience, and paying homage to her task.

Three days of mail awaited him. Bills, postcards from Maine and Israel, a few personal letters (one from an ex-student), a *Sporting News,* a university letter. He was about to leave it all, when he noted the chairman's name on the return address, and opened it. Professor T. wanted Lionel to know that the department was going to meet "on your situation" at the end of September or early October, and was there anything else that Lionel wanted to add to his dossier? ("Any work of yours about to come out this year, or even, any discussion about your work by a critic?") As Lionel knew, his "case" was very much "controversial," and any news to "tip the scales in your favor" would help a great deal. Lionel liked the sturdy gentleman, who did his best to be fair: an old semi-pro catcher, he was also a keen St. Louis Cardinals fan, dating back to the days of Terry Moore, Marty Marion and Mort Cooper, and they had exchanged knowledgeable baseball notes every now and then. This present letter, with its news and request, came at a most fitting moment indeed. The *Esquire* edition with Ms. Matthews's appraisal, he realized, was the October edition, out about September 10–15; perfect. Far from trying to hide it, the proper thing was to have the department make note of it. Yes, yes, yes, Lionel: the mediocre of the world generally won out in the end defeating the good men around them. Those tenured members who wished to assassinate him would have their picnic, eat him up alive. Take it like a man, right?

But didn't he deserve it? Didn't he warrant it now? Ask for it?

No.

He had asked only to write and to teach, and they were not going to allow it. A vulgar wife, on top of his "vulgar novels"—as one member of the department had summed them up—was all that was needed to put him away for good. Okay: Lionel gave in. It was all right.

He read quickly through the ex-student's letter, telling of the M.A. at Iowa, and asking if he would have time to look at a novella of his? Lionel smiled. He thought of only one last irony, that if it were Mr. Joyce they were going to let go, Mr. Joyce would have his revenge later on, in his books. Naming actual names, and putting the professors in the right comic situation. This same Mr. Joyce, who, years later and dead,was revered by the same types. Rule of thumb: dead authors were the best for academics, but if you had to take live ones, you made sure they were safe and respectable and stayed away from convulsive experience.

He was suddenly grateful for his present wounds and condition; it made the school situation pale in comparison. Just one more Lilliputian dart to puncture his skin, make him bleed slightly. Nothing compared to the serious injuries done to his body and soul recently.

Later, in the afternoon, he was sitting on the screened-in porch, on his redwood chaise, reading, his sore body hurting every time he moved. Twice in one year, this body ache and soreness; was this how a boxer felt? After a few hours with *The Secret Agent* of Conrad, he had eaten his lunch (served here by Sue) and now he turned to light reading before a snooze. He picked up the innocuous American Express magazine, *Travel and Leisure*, with the piece on Ecuador travel by an old Stanford professor who wrote like a charm on nature. Lionel was enjoying the beautiful prose describing that (familiar) Oriente jungle he had once visited, when his eye was caught by an advertisement, a face, a name. An ad for whiskey, showing a young pretty woman, hair tied up and wearing bifocal eyeglasses at the tip of her nose, peering out from behind a typewriter and a mound of books on her desk. The room was a handsome book-lined study, and what looked like a Navajo rug hung on one wall, and two kachina dolls stood on a mantel. Below the photo, there was a small profile, beginning with the name. That name. The unforgettable name of his friend, though the photograph was that of *another woman*. With a sudden tense fascination Lionel read the sketch:

DEWAR'S PROFILES

TIPPY MATTHEWS

HOME: Santa Fe, New Mexico.

PROFESSION: Anthropolgist and archaeologist.

HOBBIES: Reading, walking, the American Southwest.

MOST MEMORABLE BOOKS: *Zuñi Self-Portraits* and *Sun Chief: Autobiography of a Hopi Indian.*

LAST ACCOMPLISHMENT: Elected to the Hopi Tribal Council (only Caucasian member); helped draft congressional legislation that would award some $80,000,000 to Pueblo Indians for ongoing cooperative ventures. Her monograph *The Longest Struggle*, a brief history of the oldest Americans, the Pueblo Indians of the Rio Grande valley, recently won the Bancroft Prize.

QUOTE: "As we approach *our* 200th birthday, it is worth remembering and honoring our older citizens, the *Native Americans,* and their 1,200th year."

PROFILE: Quiet. Determined. Exciting intellectually. One of the outstanding young anthropologists in the country, and the foremost young scholar on the southwestern Indian. Holds the distinction of being the youngest anthropology professor in the history of the University of New Mexico.

SCOTCH: Dewar's White Label.

---

You couldn't do that with ginger ale, could you, Pandy? She looked so scholarly, *this* Tippy of monographs and bifocals and slender chest. Who was she? Who *was*—

The telephone rang, and Lionel reached over and picked it up, expecting anyone.

"Hello, sonnyboy, how are you? I thought I'd give a call and say hello."

"Hi, Mom. I'm fine, thanks."

"You're working, yeah?"

"Uh, I'm taking the day off, actually."

"You, the day off? Go on, will ya, I don't believe it!"

"The afternoon, I mean."

She laughed. "That's more like it. Sheyna is well too?"

"Yes, she is. Fine."

"Is she there now, Lionel?"

"Uh, no, Mom, not just now. Went to town."

"You should see what I'm making her for the winter, the prettiest afghan. Do you remember how Rachel loved those winter booties?"

Lionel nodded, and said he did.

She went on to speak in her plaintive voice about her arthritic leg and arm, her trip to the Jewish camp in the Poconos, and her planned visit to Solomon's, for the upcoming September holidays.

Lionel said, "Sure, Mom . . . except you know I just may be in New York then, so maybe I'll see you there."

"Without Sheyna? Come on, I want to see her, do you mind?"

"Sure, sure. We'll talk."

"By the way," she shifted, "what happened to that nice Tippele? Did that article she was writing ever come out, *epos?*"

Lionel felt choked, coughed, gazed at Dewar's anthropologist.

"Lionel . . . Operator?"

"Sorry, Mom, I got something in my eye. No, no article yet. But if and when it comes out, I'll let you know."

She chatted on about an ancient poker-playing friend she had seen recently, and finally said, "Okay, sonnyboy, *I* can tell when you're getting *itchy.*" She laughed. "Be well now, and don't work too hard, please? Take some time off for recreation, yeah?"

"I will, Ma, I will." Like promising to wear his cap outside in bad weather, at age seven. "I'll talk to you soon, and let me know if you need anything."

"I will my *schein Kind!* Here's a kiss, because I love you!" She kissed him loudly. "Goodbye, sweetheart."

They hung up.

He felt a lump in his chest, and looked out the screen at the gray mountains, which didn't have to bother with human relations. Could he get through the day without work? Without Sheyna? Get through the next week or month, in this loneliness, despair? Through the endless shock and reverses? How could he?

Immediately he was back on the telephone, calling for Miss Matthews in Santa Fe. When the operator said there was no listing, Lionel grew irritated, remembered his earlier try, and said, "None at all? But operator, I'm sure she lives there!"

"Oh," she said, as if he had known all along, "there's a number sir, but it's an unlisted one."

"I see," he said. Why could Tippy get his, but he couldn't get hers? He called the University of New Mexico, waited through three or four connections, and got no answer. He called Western Union, and sent his own telegram. To Professor Matthews at the Anthropology Department, asking her to contact him, it was urgent! (Why was it, though?)

Having done what he could, he returned to Ecuador and tried to concentrate and stay together. It was very difficult, if not impossible. Only the typewriter and work could cure him, and that was out for now. Too much mystery and incongruity in the air; too much body soreness grounding him. Besides, he wasn't yet *allowed* to work—doctor's orders. And how could he concentrate if the weeks ahead appeared like some long dark tunnel, through which he had to crawl, alone? *Alone*. The word, which had sounded like any other word before, now struck him like a train whistle and departed train and empty platform, and himself standing there.

The telephone rang again. With a new expectancy he went for it. He'd have to chat more, socialize more, *accept* more. When you were down and out . . . black and blue . . . in lonely solitude . . .

"Hello? Are you there?"

"I'm here, yes."

"*Hi*, Lionel, how are you? It's *me* again. I wanted to know how you were. I wanted to tell you about this piece I've written—about you and me and literature. I wanted to see you again."

Lionel admitted a smile, not really surprised any more.

"Well, I've been . . . a little under the weather lately."

"Yes, I know."

"How?"

"I called the other day, from Arizona. They said you were too ill to answer the phone. Are you feeling better, sweetie?"

His word. Aloud, he wondered admiringly, "And how did you get *this* number?"

"Oh, Mr. Solomon, isn't that where we started?"

Lionel nodded, remembering. "I guess so. *How?*"

A strange low buzzing, like an airplane flying in too low, blotted out her voice.

"Sorry, what was that?"

"Where are you calling from, what airport this time?"

"Uh, it's a Lincoln, I think. Heading north. We're still in Tennessee, I think!" A giggle. "I just looked out the window,

464

to check a billboard!" She squealed, at herself. "The gentle-man who's giving me the ride has a telephone in his car. It's a gas."

He felt like a great fool, pursuing reason. "How'd you get this number?"

"Oh, *fuck*, and I promised too." Her voice taking a dive. "Lanie Rosenblatt, *if you must know*."

His mind clicked, checked. Came up with a dark-haired senior of several years back, a Jewish girl from the Dakotas who had intrigued him. Yes . . . she had called him up here once, he seemed to recall. But how the hell—did these under-graduate ladies keep up a private grapevine around the coun-try? Publish a Coed's Intimate Guide to Select Professors? My God, what powers!

"Lionel, I'd really like to come up and . . . be there with you . . . write my book there, with you. And—" (FADEOUT) *Write her book, what about his?* "Take care of you, you probably need someone now, don't you?" Did she know about Sheyna too, somehow? Was his house bugged? "Have your baby there, Lionel."

At that Lionel gasped, but retorted, "Yes, this is a good place for children."

Two sets of swallows flew in crossing patterns, their sun-tipped bellies dipping and soaring in artless splendor. Who cared what she said, claimed, wrote?

"Mr. Solomon, I'd also like to bring this piece up with me, it's part of my longer project, concerning you." (FADEOUT) *What a novice he had been at Alexander Bell's invention!* " . . . *Esquire* next month, and I'd like very much to go over it with you. Share my ideas, hear your criticism."

What charming phrases! He couldn't resist. "Why'd you lie that way?"

"Huh? Didn't get that."

"Lie, Tippy. Why?"

To his foolish charge she responded appropriately.

*"Mr. Solomon what are you saying?* I didn't lie. That's un-fair!" (FADEOUT) "Maybe, just maybe it was *you* who was wrong, *you* who forgot, *you* who don't want to face facts! Oh, Lionel, I'm not saying I was *totally* right in my interpre-tations, or totally satisfied with everything I wrote there, but when did you feel totally right with a novel you've written? . . . I was *trying something difficult*, you ought to know what that's like, so why can't you show some empathy, instead of coming down so hard?"

"I think the word is sympathy."

"Do you have to lecture me by *long distance?*"

"By the way, *Pandy*," rolling the name as if it were a Cuban cigar, "I was very impressed with your friend Tippy's recent accomplishments. Did you bring along her monograph on the Zuñi?"

There was no answer. Flat. A blank fadeout this time. He was about to hang up when the gravelly voice returned, "I can see we have a lot to talk about, Mr. Solomon. I look forward to it. God, I've missed *talking* with *an adult man*. With you." (Clear and composed.)

Lionel suddenly remembered the putative gentleman, driving. "Is *he* listening to all this?"

"Who, Nelson? No, he's *driving*, I told you. I'm *in back*, silly."

Lionel nodded. Sure, why shouldn't he become *her* critic, *her* fan? And her child's Daddy? Granddaddy?

Besides, all these were just words, words. With Tippy—she would always be "Tippy" with him, after all, the real Tippy—it was not words that counted, but stripes, spots, new colors and skins, her tail. It just so happened that this particular leopard wrote magazine articles.

In a lower voice she murmured intimately, "Mr. Solomon, I've missed your prick, terribly. I wish I could hold it here while we talked. Forgive me—for speaking out this way."

We come full circle, Lionel surmised. "You forgot to mention that desire in your article, Tippy."

"Touché," she said sweetly.

Before he knew what he was saying, he asked, "Are you really pregnant?"

"*Really.*"

He wouldn't bother to advance that ancient chestnut, disclaiming his part in the affair. Not here, anyway.

She said, "I've brought you a present, and I think it'll surprise you. Could you give me the directions once we hit Jerusalem?"

Lionel trembled at the name of his town. Why continue this charade? "Is he bringing you *all this way?*"

"Sure, he's a *neat* guy. You know what? He loved *Rosen at Fifty.* Not bad for a rather straight wasp lawyer." High cheer changed to sober statement, more touching than ever as the squeaky voice mingled with the gravelly connection. "Oh Lionel, you'll *never* never understand this, but I like you now more than ever, since we've been apart. I *really* do. That's why it's worth having the baby . . . *worth loving you.*"

Lionel considered that. No, he never, never would understand it, or her. How could she use that term? Did she have her own Conception of loving, a perverse version of Immaculate? (Or was it a more ordinary conception, that included a man's spermatozoa? *His?*) For some reason his cool vanished, and inner life surfaced. "I'm hurt, Tippy. My body . . . aches. I'm dejected . . . in trouble."

She was right there, with him, changing tone. "My *poor poor Lion*. I know, I know. It *breaks my heart* the trouble you get into. Maybe it's because I get into some myself. I'll cheer you up, I promise. I'll feed you myself and make you stronger. Honest, you'll see."

Did she understand? Would only someone as troubled as she truly understand?

Without quite knowing it, he gave her directions, calmly. He was about to hang up, when he had an impulse. A nice unfair impulse. "May I speak to your friend for a minute?"

*"Who?"*

Here we go, Miss Liar. A nice way to say no, to stop the act now. "Your chauffeur friend."

"Are you kidding?"

"No."

"Sure, hold on a sec."

There was a movement, an ear-splitting hollow crack, and a man said "Hello? Nelson Atwater here."

Lionel, put off by the noise, then the poise, said, "Oh, hello. I want you to know it's awfully nice of you to give my friend a lift this way. Are you sure it's not a little out of your way?"

"No, I'm heading up that way, to the coast of Maine. Go up there every August, a family thing. So this is really on the way, according to the map."

A sharp buzz and then it was clear again.

"When do you figure you'll get up here, Nelson?"

"Oh, it'll be a week. I have to make a stop in D.C. Monday, Tuesday? . . . By the way, your friend's been delightful company. If I may say so, I envy you."

He was on the verge of saying,"Why don't you take her all the way through to the coast with you, and I'll envy you." Also: "Don't you lay a hand on her at night!" But he said neither, feeling hopeless, humble, alone; and open now to anything. Anyone. Pandy or Tippy or whoever. Open and alone, the one gentleman on the porch in New Hampshire said to the long-distance driver on the highway in Tennessee, "Well, it's very decent on you, Nelson. Goodbye." Like speaking to a father of Rachel's friend, after a squabble.

"Nice talking to you, too. I'm an admirer of your work, did Tippy tell you? Would you like to speak to her again?"

"No need . . . you might tell her her ginger ale is waiting."

He was about to hang up, when she came back on. "Hey, dynamite—catch this—it's a favorite of mine—ssshh!" The receiver moved, and the voice was speaking slow, stately, solemn, faintly British:

> *And indeed there will be time*
> *To wonder, "Do I dare?" and, "Do I dare?"*
> *Time to turn back and descend the stair,*
> *With a bald spot in the middle of my hair—*
> *(They will says "But how his arms and legs are thin!")*
> *My morning coat, my collar mounting firmly to the chin,*
> *My necktie rich and modest, but asserted by a simple pin—*
> *(They will say: "But how his arms and legs are thin!")*
> *Do I dare*
> *Disturb the universe?*
> *In a minute there is time*
> *For decision and revisions which a minute will reverse.*

Melodramatic voice: "Isn't he too much?"

Lionel was fixed at the moving paragraph, at the august voice, the whole poem's resonance. "What?"

"Oh I knew you'd dig it! I carry him everywhere. Eliot and Dylan and you, my heroes! *Except I don't have you on tape*—not reading your fiction that is. But I'm bringing up some blank ones; we'll record you. Then you can be with me everywhere too, on the road. Does your car have a cassette?"

He shook his head.

"You're my Prufrock, and I love you for it." Voice grew low, somber: " 'Do you dare?' " She threw a kiss, and there was a click, a pause, a dial tone. Gone.

This Prufrock put down the receiver, got up slowly, and walked the length of the long porch, past the Ping-Pong table, to peer out at the fields and woods. Through the tiny myriad squares of the porch screens, he saw the very fine drizzle and the bluish bands of fog. The poetry returned, "In a minute there is time/For decisions and revisions which a minute will reverse." Well, he would have several days, a week, to recover, put back some weight, get stronger, make his decisions, revisions, run off, whatever. She knew her game didn't she? Was it real, that conversation? He could perhaps buy a gun, so that if rural love didn't work out, rural murder? (*Of whom?*) A turn of the tables that she might appreciate, work into her critique? Or else he might indeed help her out with her projects, about him and other chauvinist novelists, about him, her and literature? Perhaps even, to show he held no grudges, write some pages for her? Coauthor a chapter? Why not?

He went to the telephone book, flattered by the company of Eliot and Dylan, and looked up Guns and Ammunition in the yellow pages.

But when he found the actual section, with a dozen listings nearby, he perceived the folly of it all. With reality bearing down upon him, he had only the armor of folly, fantasy, and illusion to protect him. Sad. Here he was, a lucky survivor of his own death attempt, idly dreaming on his porch that he was going to get a gun to knock off the agent of his despair (and pleasure). Was that what he was driven to, the act of the primitive? Was that what she was teaching you, How to Be More Primitive in Three Easy Visits? How to lose consciousness and reason, sanity and novel writing? A literary-and-life capitulation for the sake of her thesis? her whims and unusual talents? . . . Isn't she better than that, Lionel? Aren't you?

*You know, my dear Child Lionel, that the gun is for you if for anyone. Merely a steel replacement for the hole you dug the other day, which, by some small inadvertence, you escaped being buried in. Now, can't you be more inventive than guns? Can't you be more true to your despair, more precise to your predicament?* He wished he had great claws to rip through the mesh screen and escape.

Because the terms now were too too hard, he sensed as he left the porch and walked slowly toward his civilized hole. All was in order at his desk. To his left, the portrait of Einstein in rumpled sweater and baggy pants, at a blackboard; over his desk, a Burpee seed calendar, showing two huge ears of sweet corn for this month; over his standing desk, the large picture of Dostoyevsky, a Russian reproduction from a painting (gotten by Sheyna), with hands on knees, pose thoughtful. He *couldn't* write just now; he *couldn't*, he bemoaned, as he put on water for coffee in his study, he *couldn't* as he sat down, behind his desk, in his slave seat. The typewriter keys were oars, for him to lift and to pull. Focusing his brain made his lip twitch as he began to whip his will and mind to the task. Out of shape from lack of work, and weak from injury, the effort to concentrate was excruciating.

To his old friend, the novelist Dan S., away for the summer, he mused:

"Dear Dan, I'm afraid old chum I've gone too far this time. I'm in the midst of falling. It's scary. My emotions alternate between . . . numbness and degrees of terror. There's also some pleasure in being able to 'function' in the face of panic. Soon enough, you will read the . . . indecent exposure and intimate lies about yours truly in *Esquire*, composed by a shrewd young lady who showed up at my door one day and whom I took in, for a few scenes' worth. Her current act of print, on top of the actual scenes of bizarre and comic/tragic nature—mingled with strange pleasures, to be sure—all of it has accumulated into a power too cunning for me to handle. (And you know I'm not a total innocent in these affairs.) Oh, I was a fool, but give credit where credit is due; this young lady is an expert dealer. Dan, beware of literary fans! Beware of coeds! Beware of dissertation-diddlers! For those hungers, we writers are no more than sitting ducks, awed does, fat pheasants! . . . Most curious is my sitting here, *waiting,* after just speaking to the young lady, and giving her directions to my house. Can you imagine this sort of folly?

"Yes, I did try to get in touch with Dr. Lirič from Boston, but it's August, and therapy is out to lunch, at the Cape. And I don't really have the stomach, or stamina, or time, to start with a new one now. Perhaps you were right when you suggested that I try serious psychoanalysis a long time ago. Perhaps. But look, I've seen you inside of it for nearly a decade now, and consider your own recent life, the pain and confusion. (Which is one of the reasons I haven't wanted to bother you with my own turmoil.) At least you have your son for comfort. But here I sit, alone, waiting. Though thank God Rachel is in Israel just now—on a dig, actually. Curious. With a possibility for something more curious in the offing— my beautiful fiend turning up pregnant with a fetus caused by my (innocent) sperm! Nice last twist? . . . Perhaps it'll look to the world as if I'm a 'responsible' sort after all, waiting here this way. A fine irony. Actually, I did try to take my leave the other day, once and for all, but a resilient four-year-old friend rescued me from my dug grave. Too bad. As you can see, I've had my adventures. And I'm glad too, to be around for the new turn of events, to see what new number Lady (Tippy) Macbeth is ready to perform on me. She's a kind of genius of the obscene—perverse whims, powerful limbs, ingenious talents (pen and paper, dirty talk, special games). You wouldn't think of it, from her angel looks. Perhaps she strikes me as so singular because we've never lived together? Maybe we can remedy that now. . . . Falling. In between emotions. No desire to 'save myself,' or even, just now, to end myself. Is it that I'm trying to give in to her 'flow'? As you can gather from her article, this flow—no, no, enough.

"Now while I've been working on a novel for a good while, I am no longer interested in that genre, when ordinary lies are passed off as truths nowadays much more readily and regularly. Fictional disguises seem like so much child's play next to this new . . . genre. Was it Montaigne who once said that the crime of *lying* deserves punishment of fire? Several hundred years and one magazine article later, I second the motion. Speaking frankly, I'm not sure I know definitely what the truth is anymore. Or where it resides. Or how to get there. I used to, but no longer. Oh, I think I know the 'facts' of the affair, and shall attempt to write them down—but as to the *truth* of it? I decline; no opinion. I should have taken your suggestion of long ago, and used a pseudonym, beginning with *Each According to His Needs;* for as matters stand now, I've lost my desire to see my name out there, to see it toyed with or abused, to have some dangerous crackpot-called-fan grow enchanted with LS and seek to use him—me—in her controlled experiment. As you know, I always had the impolite habit of asking people questions, pushing them, and now that curiosity has come back to haunt me. Just as several of my books have returned, in unforeseen ways, to stick it to me. How odd, to feel anxiety about not being taken seriously, and then to be taken *too seriously* . . . is there no equable in-between? . . . My desire now is to remain in the background for the next ten or twenty years, working at some anonymous job, having a family (with whom Lionel? the Sheyna you've driven away?), *and ceasing to be Lionel Solomon anymore.* Now how's that for a birthday wish?

"My pleasant fantasy has unfortunately been complicated, obstructed, by this recent 'Intimate Portrait' by the girl. Not only am I visible there, but my life and name are spread and smeared like rancid peanut butter; and there's Rachel to consider, my 'reputation,' even myself. (Paradox? Contradiction? Fine!) The teaching job is beyond my recall, at this point; the healthy gentlemen of tenure will not wish to have on their hands my sort of dirt. Who can blame them? First the books, then this life! So: what the young lady is forcing me to do, what her scandalous genius performance is forcing me into, *is*

471

*to sit down now and write out the fucking sordid mess from
beginning to end as best I can without resorting to fiction.*
Resorting only to the facts as I know them, including names:
real names, given names, assumed names, whatever. This is
difficult enough when the facts are nothing short of embarrassing and humiliating. Imagine what it's like with my body
aching, stamina weak, my will almost gone? The only consolation—or is the word reward?—is that I won't have to invent,
just report.

"If I don't make it through, pal, I want to say a word to
you. *Thanks.* Is there anything higher in life than the continuous acts of loyalty, generosity, companionship at the right
time between isolated souls called human beings? Especially
when the other pal happens to be in the same illness-business
of writing, and therefore subject to all those petty, neuras-
thenic germs found under the heading of jealousy, envy, competition? Somehow or other, we managed to be free of those
germs during exchanges of manuscripts and literary discussions, which added to their usefulness a certain nobility, I
think. If during the years I came to drop some of my own al-
batrosses of bias and prejudice concerning literature, people,
morals, it was in great part due to you, dear pal. Your criticism was always first-rate, and even when I disagreed with it,
it was a force I had to think about and confront. There was
something substantial for me to grapple with, instead of my
going to the mat with soda pop and cornflake brains. Even
during the recent years, in which we've more and more gone
our separate ways in terms of literary taste and feeling for
each other's work, the trust and the companionship have remained. (I'm even tempted to think that my current distress
has been a kind of homeopathic illness, coming as it has during your own year of sadness.) You've been a good and loyal
friend!

"Another irony. I am scheduled to teach in just a few
weeks, but I don't think I'll be able to make it. The desire
and the strength are gone. So that which I loved and which
sustained me is shot. I won't make it this time. And doubtless
the lady's article will close down my job for good. (After my
strange talk and appearance last spring, it was shaky at best.
Who wants a mummy *and* a perverse lunatic around?
prizewinner or not?) But here's the irony: all those years of
teaching hot, vital texts—Kafka, Dostoyevsky, Mann, Musil,
Chekhov, Mishima—and suddenly, when *I'm* caught in the
middle of one myself, why I can no longer carry on! With
myself in the scenes of trial and pressure, ordinary life is im-

possible! I can't teach or write or see people or eat dinner, for my stupidity! my pain! my shame! Oh, God, it's hell, Dan, hell, when it's not literature but real! Why didn't these stupid incidents stay put between bindings of books, and not jump out suddenly to life? *My* life?! To destroy it. . . . How shall I put this? I see now how little I *felt* those literary texts, how I experienced them from the outside looking in only. Not from the playing field, but from the academic sideline, and now it's too late, too late. And yet, paradoxically, now with my life as the hot text and myself as the protagonist, I can do nothing but feel trapped. By myself as much as by any fate or girl. Yes, the author and the victim of the trap at one and the same time! . . .

"Dan, forgive me for carrying on like this, forgive me. I know this is not your style, really. And I know too that the rise and fall of a single 'bourgeois writer' of little import will not shake worlds, change lives. But the saddest part of it all perhaps is that I cannot now make the material into a novel; 'Intimate Portrait' has closed down that avenue, permanently. Furthermore, I am simply not strong enough, now or in the immediate future, to move in that direction. The energy it takes to invent, to imagine! And further: I'm not strong enough to ward off the inevitable criticism of such a book, the vile gossip and vile distortions and vile misunderstanding and vile politics that it will inspire, and that will be called book reviewing. The only thing I can do is to write it all down for the record, adding my reflections here and there, and send it on to . . . you? . . . Dr. Lirič? . . . keep it in my drawer? (Though with the girl on the premises, this is dangerous. She'd find it somehow, and do worse than burn it, far worse.) Why don't I just take off for Wyoming or Amsterdam and forget all this? Because I can't budge, Dan, can't forget. And Tippy is on her way up, from New Mexico or Tennessee, on the highway right now, in a Lincoln with a gentleman who 'likes my work.' The comedy proceeds. . . .

"She will show up, in this huge car (or on motorcycle?) with the gentleman perhaps (and perhaps not), and I will look at her and be immediately enthralled by her beauty. In overalls or jeans or skirt, she is like some great wild bird, stopping you. Dan, has the world ever invented a more deceptive mask for the executioner than that of the young American graduate student in literature (and AmStud)? Ph.D.-to-be? mother-to-be, searching for a subject-to-be? Was the CIA or KGB ever more deceptive? I shall help carry her bags in, taking the light briefcases of her manuscripts because of my weakness, and we will chat pleasantly. I shall be dazzled by her youth and her beauty, even from behind, and she will chide me for my paranoia, hypochondria. And inside, walking through the vestibule to the colonial dining room, she will turn all SERIOUS, ALL SINCERE, handle my penis as if my soul, and tell me how much she's missed me! And how she was afraid that her article would offend me! And how she worried desperately over whether I was 'man enough' to take the piece in all its complexity! Caressing my 'childlike scrotum' (magazine lit-crit), while asking me to understand her literary motives! Levels! Dan, how much defamation under the heading Complexity can I take? how much pleasure under the heading Defamation will I allow?

"I know your advice in these matters: get yourself in the hands of a doctor fast, and scram! . . . No, not now. No time, no strength. I wait.

"And take up the typing. Trying to get it down, for some record or other, my side of the affair. If I perish while not publishing here, would you mind very much if I appointed you my literary executor? I think you are clearly the best suited, being my toughest critic as well as closest friend. Thanks, yet again. . . ."

He broke off, wondering if he'd ever get to write this letter, knowing that the novel-in-letters, the novel-to-be, was gone, finished, once and for all. He got up, resigned, for his coffee at the high end-table. Sugar and creamer in the cup, stirred it, then back down. Warmed up now, his brain. A fresh piece of paper in the machine and he was ready to put down the facts of the affair with the girl Tippy, a truthful account to defend himself—posthumously if necessary. He gazed outside and realized that he'd like to be jogging right now, jogging all the way back to his adolescence, when he'd run and run from day into night, worrying only about basketballs with his endless boyhood energy. Jogging the way he did that first day in March. He'd start there, yes. And he was about to, when he had another impulse. An odd one. But why not, he thought, getting up? *Why not?*

From the pantry he took several cans of paint, and a brush; from the spare study a Hopi kachina doll; and carried them upstairs, to the outside porch. There, in the warm sun, he removed his clothes, and put on the pair of brief khaki shorts that Sheyna had brought from her kibbutz. Setting down the kachina on a webbed chair, he got to work. Using the edge of the two-inch brush and a small mirror which he affixed to the screen door, he began to paint his face; under the eyes and along the cheekbones he made slashes of black and fire-red enamel. Next, from his memory, he painted long strokes of yellow and cobalt blue on his inner thigh, upward from the knees. The smells of paint and turpentine filled the air with an acrid pleasantness, sending wasps above the doorway into crazy fits. Upon his forehead he used the width of the brush to paint a thick band of white latex. It was odd indeed having the stuff stick to you. He did it in ten minutes or so, and next went to the bathroom, taking his doll. Sure enough, there were leftover toiletries of Sheyna's, and as best he could, he put on mascara and eyeshadow. The mascara moved, ran, burned. The blue eyeshadow smudged. Okay. On his pale cheeks he patted rouge, from a compact. Paleface was becoming redskin. Professor, chief; albeit comic chief. Observing the kachina, he realized that eagle feathers were out of the question, for the shoulders; . . . but he had a replacement. Downstairs again, from a tall white vase he removed five peacock feathers and cut the stems back; the silky feel of the feathers and the green-blue iridescence were quite magical, however. Taking his tennis headband, he then taped the feathers to the band, and took the improvised headdress upstairs. Comic, yes; but also something else . . . stagy, crazy. That was okay, too. In place of an eagle feather for every victory, as in a real headdress, a peacock feather for every folly. In the small cedar jewelry box of Sheyna's he found just the right items: the Hopi silver necklace, which he put around his neck, and the strong inlaid bracelet, which he squeezed onto his wrist, cutting the skin. Almost ready now. He found his embroidered shirt from Ecuador, buttonless and open at the neck, and his old leather sandals. He put those on too. In the mirror, now, he was no longer the judge or professor or writer, but this new sort of creature, a hybrid without a name.

Ready now, attired foolishly and appropriately, he took his seat by his typewriter and looked back, way back to that spring day when it began. He knew now, of course, that this had to be written to the doctor, for it was an account of illness, not of health. He began witn his preamble.

Dear Dr. Lirič:
   At thirty-eight, my senses upset but intact, my body sore but still capable, my will tampered with perversely—and I think irrevocably—and my other will made out firmly, I want you to know that I'm in trouble, deep trouble. And in pain, physical pain. . . .

He thought of a codicil to that "will made out firmly." To leave his timber rights to Tippy, his land and buildings to Sheyna and Rachel. The three knew each other by now, and they were all his daughters, weren't they?

He writes. In his jewelry, feathers and paints, he begins to record his ledger of illness, misfortune and mistake. His side of the ledger, that is. Shall we leave him there, then, at the thankless task of digging up his own dirt and making his own (spiritual) grave, using his best shovel, the typewriter?

Clack, clack, clack, types the sitting (writing) duck, stuck at his desk, his task. Chief Solomon quacking, if you please.

*Ah, Doctor, my last note to you.*

*Why that last act of dressing up? Is it not childish, melodramatic, foolishly vain, uselessly theatrical, primitive? All of these, and more? Somehow or other he felt in his bones the need to express visibly his decision of giving over, of releasing his will in the matter and letting hers, or another's, take over. He felt something like you, sir, taking that long walk with the Kommandant to the front gate of the camp, a soul whose fate was to be decided by another's will, not knowing if he were heading toward a cruel ending, or toward some strange new beginning. Putting on the new powder and makeup and dress was like putting on a new skin, for all— and himself—to see. Great crisis often makes one inert, and Lionel had work to do. Doctor, I am sorry, more sorry than you can imagine, to leave him in that sad state in his prolonged act of self-punishment, in his costume of self-parody. I wish that it might end otherwise! This ending, I mean. The one that I supposedly have some control over. Isn't this the important one, after all? Look, sir, the smuggled gun rests still in the bureau, not used, but having served its reminder purpose. I'm tired, Doctor, tired. At thirty-eight, exhausted by myself, distracted from fiction, tricked by truth.*

*Yes, he believed he was more open then, inwardly. Less slavish to the power of reason, to the force of intentionality, to morals and to writing novels (let the others write them). The price of writing had grown too high. Freer certainly from reputation, self-image, literary expectations. (Now, if you will forgive me, Tippy knew all this, I believe, teasing him that way at the hole in the ground, at the hole of his subconscious. She knew, and she knew that he knew, or believed these things. Shrewd and strong till the very end.)*

*The whole matter could be put another way: in his wait he began to feel in limbo, to feel the uneasy freedom of his limbo, his personality growing anchorless, suspended between* selves—the old familiar one he had built up for years, now having passed on, and the new one, approaching. I suppose it was something like a blind date, dressing up that way, awaiting a stranger you had heard much about. So: at that point he felt a certain calm, a positive lucidity. At the same time that he wondered if it were all a delusion, a grand deception, a last ditch self-defense?

Of course the answer lies, I think, in the mask, the picture. The man sitting at this typewriter and beginning a long journey with and within himself, in his feathers, paint, trinkets— had he not gone off the far end? Had he not exhausted all ways out and by finding none, by choosing to wait for the girl, exposed the darkest needs and twists of his character? Hadn't the stranger approaching already come, some time earlier? Why, of course. The scary part was just that, that there was no escape from meeting that crippled self; he was there on stage now. Next to that understanding, Tippy Matthews would be a relief, some outside fun.

# 10.
# Retiring Early

NOT TALKING, DOCTOR, FOR SEVERAL months, is an experience. At first, it is rather extraordinary, like fasting; afterwards, refreshing; and finally, like everything else, a habit. (Most surprisingly, this curious cycle ending in quiet takes but a few days to sink in solidly, not a few weeks or months. Or does this say something further about my condition?) Oh you talk to yourself, more than usual at first, but after a while, that stops too. But under the influence of silence, writing, I'm convinced, is somewhat easier. You look forward to it more, you get a little hungry for words. Instead of that same dull sentence to push up the mountain and down again, by day and by night (in talk), here words seem more novel. Count for more.

Outsiders have a mistaken impression of a sanitarium for disturbed persons, Dr. Lirič. At least I did, before coming here, on this extended stay. My dumb impression had been a circus of bedlam, with patients in loose gowns wandering about in total distraction, openly mad, disassociated, into themselves. And being set down there was like being thrown into a snakepit, without escape or relief. Actually, Swerdlow's is much more boring than all that. (Doctor, is everything more boring than its advertisements, in life? Except perhaps danger, madness, adventure—Tippy? If so, is this why one eventually opts for boredom?) No, at Swerdlow's it's routinely dull, peacefully, endlessly predictable, more like a Magic Mountain than a looney bin. Now I don't know about a state asylum, but here, in a private one, where the inmates are (mostly) self-committed, it's a fine and private place to work. Don't laugh or smile, sir, I mean this sincerely. And it's not so much a matter of one's own health, Doctor—after all, I don't have mine any longer, I don't even have the energy to get it back; when you're down this way, *even health is a project*, something to be struggled for and made, not taken for granted—no, not a matter of health, as much as it is one of a clear and defined task. Like trying to take a specific hill in battle. The conditions that prevail here, in an institutional way, are no more than the conditions that a writer seeks to set up for himself, on his own, usually without the same success. Here the routine is flawless, the nurses are one's family, and it all proceeds without one having to oversee it, or pay with mental energy; the patient doesn't have to be also a doctor, an overseer, a boyfriend. No need to worry about frozen pipes, ice on the roof, doors shrinking and expanding, in, obligatory social and sexual dates, a friend's moods, one hundred seven other items of daily life. Here, if you keep a low profile, and have work to do and are healthy enough for that one single task, why it's a rather fine existence. Add to all that your coming around to chat, to show concern, what more is needed?

Perhaps a visit from a comrade? . . . *The small balding man adjusted his eyeglasses, rubbed at the bridge of his nose, crossed his arms.* "I know you are in a predicament, my friend, so let me tell you a little tale of mine. Once upon a time there was a Russian short-story writer who, though he was a firm believer in the Revolution and a new system of justice and equality for all, which he thought to be Communism, also happened to be a Jew. This was most unfortunate, since the Leader of the Revolution at the time seemed to have constitutional dislike for Jews, perhaps stemming from his many years in the seminary. In any case, the writer* *fell into disfavor with the Bolshevik regime, though he was a most mild man, a Milquetoast you would call him I think, and he was hounded personally, his stories banned, and finally he was arrested. Not an atypical story, you understand. But what made matters worse, or gave the writer's situation an extra twist, if you will, was that of all things, the poor gentleman suddenly found a sympathetic soul in, of all people, his jailer's wife. Not just any jailer, mind you, but the grand jailer of all, the Chief of the Soviet Secret Police, a well-known barbarian. Certainly the writer's luck was not very good. Eventually, inevitably, the police chief discovered his wife's infidelity, and the source of it, and decided, before punishing the writer, to read his stories to see the kind of man he was dealing with. These short stories, not very impressive I assure you, Mr. Solomon, were noted for their brevity and their streaks of violence. You see, dealing with events in my primitive homeland, especially with gentlemen like the Cossacks, necessitated such themes. So the police chief read, and one fine day soon, the short-story writer was taken from jail to a private room, where his blouse and undergarment were removed and his chest bared. Two burly guards then tied him down to a table, flat on his back, beneath a glaring light. Next his eyelids were taped back, so that he could not fail to witness the event to occur. In a few moments, a long steel-mesh cylinder or cage was set across his chest, lengthwise, not heavy, you understand; and presently there was a movement inside. A flutter of light feet across his chest in the cage, and the writer saw a small white rat there, rushing to and fro seeking escape, but going nowhere; stopping momentarily to eye the writer beneath him. The eyes of the rat were tiny, black, and beady, but not without their beauty, and the writer, because of his imagination as much as his predicament, speculated that the rat and he understood each other somehow, had a kinship of sorts trapped that way together. So that while he was terrified lying there, and could feel his heart hot and pounding, he also felt as if there were a strange rapport between the rodent and himself, and he was almost grateful for him. Almost. Then, a guard moved, a piece of mesh scraped slightly the writer's chest in the region of the heart, and the rat stood still, afraid, transfixed. What had happened? Neither the rat nor the writer seemed to know. Presently, however, the rat grew calmer, and began poking around; suddenly he discovered for both of them, that a small area of the bottom of his cage had been slid to the side, permitting an opening. And when the rat inspected*

479

*there, he poked his face into soft flesh. He looked around
however, checking; he looked at the writer, checking; looked
at the room, just to make sure; and then in a blur he took
three quick little bites, making the writer jerk involuntarily,
and cry out! The rat scampered away, in fright, but only to
his corner; then he perceived that his newfound food was
there to stay, and could do nothing but jerk slightly and cry
out in response. Acting just slightly more confident now, he
returned to his hole in the cage for his feast, the writer hearing some laughs and a door close. . . ." The man paused
here, stretched out his arms, yawned, commented, "I think
that before passing out the writer heard the voice of the
Chief of Police, but I won't vouch for that. Sometimes one
gets carried away, and it takes some fifty revisions later before I am able to delete all the exaggerations and melodrama,
and not waste the reader's time." Babel looked at Lionel, and
smiled sheepishly, as if his story wasn't much after all, and he
hoped he hadn't wasted Lionel's time.*

Also, the range of persons here is remarkable, much more
variety than you get at a normal social gathering, and for a
novelist this too has its great merits—if not immediately, then
for later on. There is little Mr. Weatherby, frail, white-haired,
sixty-five or so, who gets furious if he doesn't get his daily
shave; otherwise he's as happy as a kite. And if you get him
really excited, he'll tell you about the high point of his life—
going down to New York City from upstate, upon graduation
from college, and "whooping it up with the girlies." Now although Weatherby has town privileges, or can leave the sanitarium to live with his daughter (who visits), he won't do
either. He's here to stay now, preferring to walk around here
like a penguin in shirt and tie, show his marvelous false-teeth-
disappearance trick to new inmates, or mutter a few words
about the stock market. When he goes out to stay, he gets too
depressed; his wife's death some years ago did the poor fellow in, and there's no help for it, period. No fancy therapies
or wise words to change things. Then there's the ex-baseball
pitcher Randy R., who's just left to return to his family. Did
you know him at all? (I'm purposely avoiding your patients.)
He had a real major-league career ahead of him, when his
arm went bad; next thing you know his marriage went bad,
and after busting up his wife a bit, and then getting himself
busted up, he came to Swerdlow's. This was his third visit; he
stays for two months or so, and then returns. It quiets him
down, he explains, enables him to go a year or two "on the

outside." At first, it was touch and go with him and me; he felt threatened by me since I was the only other virile patient around, and don't think he didn't frighten me, with his teamster bulk and menacing eyes and laconic truculence. But after a week or ten days, and my quiet and isolation, he began to come around and say a few words, on occasion; and after a while, he just softened up and began telling me about his high school pitching days in Indiana, just start talking while I'd be at my typewriter, about playing in the minors in tiny towns and then in Double A, before the arm went; he cried, remembering it. Not a frantic cry, Doctor, just involuntary sadness, like remembering a dead child. He said he heard I wrote books, and couldn't wait to get out and read a few, and would I visit him in Amsterdam (New York)? He goes along fine, and then boom! gets violent, uncontrollable. Paranoid, my reading. The real stuff. Sad. And what about Mrs. Roberts, down from Vermont, a pretty, reasonable woman of forty, who simply cracks up every few years and comes down here for shock treatment. It's hard for me to *believe* that, Doctor. When I'd take breaks around four o'clock in the afternoon and sit in the television room, she'd come and sit by me, and show me pictures of the family (two sons, a daughter), tell me about her husband (has a John Deere franchise), and then suddenly, zap, for a couple of days, she's like a walking zombie. Doctor, forgive me, but it's incredible; there's enough sorrow and enough stories here for three novels! Why should I ever leave? . . . Carrie is the teenage girl from Poughkeepsie, whose parents are professors but who is right out of *God's Little Acre*. One day she's charming and polite and funny, and then the next hour she's on the prowl, hunting for a male stud to trap and to seduce. How much do you know about the inner politics of this place, Doctor? Did you know that the charming young nymph(omaniac) almost got the new young orderly fired? After drawing his sympathy, she next drew him into her room and got the door closed, a "no-no" (Nurse Charles' quaint phrase; in fact many of the nurses speak to us with a similar baby language; I can see their point). Anyway, when the young fellow resisted her advances, she began taking off her clothes, and screamed. Fortunately, her doctor had known her history, and also, fortunately, she had written the boy two lusty letters previously, which he had turned over to her doctor. I've seen Carrie's parents visit, in tweeds and graying demeanors, a pair of academic bookends bravely accepting their daughter's cursing sarcasm and scorn. I feel for both—daughter, parents. . . .

*Why am I going on this way, Doctor? To show you that I am still "reality-oriented" despite my period of imposed* quiet? *To show you what it looks like from the inside out, the child's view from the playpen? (Being attended to by simian creatures who haven't the faintest idea of the inner lives of their children?) A curious thing occurs when you don't talk—people start flocking around. Silence attracts. The other guests want to befriend me, help me, tell me their stories. Not speaking, am I their mirror on the wall? Among strangers, with the social controls of the outside gone, they give over their fears, reservation, repression, and monologue on and on. If one goes quiet on the outside, will it provoke equal outpourings of confession and lifestory?*

All of the above goings-on are accepted as perfectly natural by the community here, by the way.

What's refreshing is the absence of moral judgment, the tacit agreement not to pass sentence on others' affairs. (Oh there's gossip—what's life without that?—but no one actually *condemns* another for his having *behaved badly*, out there.) As I say, the talks are monologues anyway, but even so, the guests here are not out to interpret reality for you, to explain the world for you. They don't have, or have shed, the *presumptuousness* of the self-ordained priests in the outside world. It's a relief, Doctor. No middleman proselytizing for this politics or that position on marriage, for this morality or that view of "relationships," et cetera. In the new-event-per-minute environment we've created, do we need also to be *hit by twice as many interpretations* on what the events signify? Can't a reasonable man see and think for himself? Pass his own judgment on things? What's the point of going to school for fifteen years, if not for that? Are the middlemen really brighter than a thinking private citizen? Doubtful. Why take as "truth" what is, in most cases, a reflection of this unconscious bias or that hidden fixed view? Do you see my own case in the hands of these middlemen, literary and political? Why even I, to this day, remain puzzled about how to judge it, grip it.

Or what is one to make of the following story, Doctor? Unbeknownst to you, I have opened one set of letters, from an old college roommate, who got in touch with me after reading an early novel of mine. Donald Cohen had become a psychologist, lived in Atlanta with his second wife and two kids, was connected with a good hospital and also was editing a new psychiatric journal based on experimental therapy. A solid success story if there ever was one. Consider this turn of events, then, as portrayed in these recent (forwarded) letters. The first was a madly scribbled eight pages, handwriting large and unwieldy, narrating a story of how this same Dr. Cohen threw up family, job, city, and ran off with an ex-patient and her son, landing in Mexico; and there, under the influence of drugs, he turned violent and, according to her, tried to murder her! Believable? In life, perhaps; not in fiction. From a professional practice in Atlanta to a Mexican jail is a long, long way, sir. Anyway, with a doctor's title and American citizenship, they let him out, he was now in L.A., broke, alone, apart, ruined. Could I write him a few lines, maybe read something he wanted to write on the subject? A nice scene, don't you think, the shrink defrocked, at "General Delivery, Los Angeles," asking the writer turned patient, in Swerdlow's for aid? The blind aiding the deaf, yes? Three days later I received a manila envelope containing a sixteen-page short story, handwritten, entitled "Rosalie."

Now the circle area of the "R" was shaded in, childlike, and the "o" had a slash mark through it; in the upper left-hand corner of the page was a rectangle containing the four suits of cards, inscribed underneath "Tarot"; within a circle in the upper right-hand corner sat a man on a horse, aiming with a bow and arrow, the inscription reading "The Archer Queen"; in the lower left-hand corner, a circle containing a lion, labeled "Leo"; and sprinkled throughout, assorted five-pointed stars and astrological signs; in the lower right-hand corner, a circle enclosing "By" and then, handwritten, "Dr. Donald M. Cohen, Clinical Psychologist." The remaining pages were illustrated similarly, the handwriting was fourth-grade large and legible, and the story a clever eleven-year-old's gothic-romance fairy tale. Oh, I was on the verge of telling you about it, Doctor, and asking if you had a friend out there who could help out Dr. Cohen; but I didn't have the energy. Now is this sort of reversal of roles frequent in your professon, sir? Is the painful regression more common nowadays than yesterdays? To be sure, I felt my own troubles a little less severely next to my old buddy's. But how to judge his case, what to say about it? Without having been there, how could one tell? Certainly Dr. Cohen didn't seem to be able to tell. Could a doctor in the comfortable distance of his office, listening to one side, tell? The obstacles to judgment are many, I believe. I was moved but baffled, and remained silent; afraid, I'm sorry to say, to write him anything. Could you find out somehow if he's survived?

I like my room a lot. It's simple and tangible: the single bed with the institutional blankets rolled at the end, the knee-hole desk, the pull-chain lamp, the sturdy bureau, the window looking outside. It's all a man needs, especially one with sustained work to do. It simplifies life suitably, spendidly. In my own life there have come to be too many rooms, too many distractions, too many opportunities, and a single room in a large old house called a sanitarium cuts things down to size. The pine grove and patch of lawn outside, with the winding path to the woods, provides a most pleasant illusion of clarity in one's perception; and you, with your constant visits and steady determination, are also most comforting. I know you got terribly frustrated with my quiet, Doctor, do forgive me; I hardly meant it personally. I can still see you know, jumping up—not quite jumping, though—after ten or fifteen minutes of my sitting there, returning nothing, and walking the few steps across the room, stopping at the bureau and lifting the unopened mail and dropping it again like lost poker chips. What you didn't know perhaps was how I cherished not your meaning but your motions, if you will; I looked forward not so much to your reason as to your habits: the wide Windsor knots in your tie, still made at age seventy or so; the wild white hair made unmanageable by the slightest wind or movement; the double chin you never failed to pull at when in trouble (in homage to a past goatee?); the dramatics of your hands, making tents, ovals, diagrams to support appeals, arguments, demands. You have great hands, sir; now of course I see where I got Dr. Erikson's hands from, in that little fantasy scene. (Though I left out your pinky ring, that small blue sapphire that your wife gave you to replace the family heirloom the Nazis borrowed from you.) Was it your accent too that I half-borrowed, or the cadence; is Serbo-Croatian similar to Austrian? I especially liked the voice, you know, when it turned staccato (not often), in exasperation; unprotected it seemed richer, more full-bodied, than usual. Of course I "heard" the stories you were telling, about your "American" children, your son's amusement with my baseball knowledge, life in Zagreb as contrasted with Kentucky (your internship?), and so on. But I was really "listening" for other things. Do I have to *understand* the colors and words of a cardinal flying about my window in winter? Isn't his loyalty and beauty enough? Your gestures added to a sum of tenderness and concern, and for me, that was all the meaning I needed, my friend.

Doctor, did I ever tell you the full story of that trip down to Swerdlow's last August? Tippy took one look at me, shook her head, and said, "You poor baby," and advised that I'd be better off under "professional care" for a while. She smiled and kissed me warmly on the cheek. She next found out the pertinent information about you and the hospital, asked if there was anything necessary for me to take along (my manuscript) and then she packed solicitously the old Gladstone bag, and we were off. I followed her out to the car, thinking how pretty she looked in her loose summer dress (yellow with flowers), and how like an off-duty doctor with her briefcase, tote bag, dark glasses. She explained to her "ride" the situation, and he got into his huge car, waving to me (nice fellow in red slacks and sailing cap) and inviting me to Northeast Harbor when I "got out." With Tippy alongside me—and a vaguely familiar redolence in the air—I drove out my dirt road and through the tiny village of Jerusalem, and headed east, down Route 4. She continued to express her concern over my health ("You've gotten so *thin*, baby, you're all bones!") and the "dressing-up business," though, oddly—shrewdly?—she had done nothing about making me change, allowing me to drive in my paints and jewelry and feathers. (Was that perhaps so *you* could see, Doctor?) "You mustn't take this as anything but a temporary setback, *Lev*," she explained, gravely; "in the end it will make you stronger. You get a good rest, mellow out, eat your wheat germ. Later on, we can go through my article piece by piece." She smiled, having resolved that problem, removed a thread from my hair, and lit up a cigarette. I was myself too exhausted to pursue the article with her then, and anyway, she was acting so tenderly, why go and spoil it? No, I needed her tender just then. So tender that I didn't even mind when the smoke smelled sweetly, too sweetly. In friendship, I accepted a "toke" or two from her.

We had just taken the right fork heading for Concord, on that twisting southerly route, when there she was again, like old times in the Cambridge taxi, handling me, wonderfully, casually. Idly telling me how Nellie, her lift, had "really weirded out" when she had put Eliot on in his car cassette. Only this time, before I knew what was happening, and while taking a drag, she disappeared downward. I gripped the wheel tightly with both hands, glanced in the rear-view mir-

485

ror to check for Nellie, but under the strong influence I was being subjected to, I stopped caring. I tried to concentrate on the staggering white line of the divider. Soon, however, it became thrilling to the point where I lost all track of where we were, or what my responsibility was, and frames of that powerful evening returned, in which the girl greedily took control of me, and my heart shuddered further; and I'm afraid I pressed the pedal down as if I were blowing up a ball with a foot pump—and just missed jumping the road on a curve! The adventure was Tippy all over again, the solicitous maternal woman of ten minutes ago having disappeared into this dangerous sensual creature. I held on, and held on, and held on. Finally the wheel became like putty in my hands, and I had to slow to 40, 30, 20 (the speedometer gauge turning candy cane-colored on the old Mercedes dash), to keep the road. . . . A furious honking from behind, not Nellie, pushed me back to normal again. After licking me clean like a cat, she was back up in her seat, hair disheveled and face reddened with passion, and, as if she had been me, kissed me on the cheek. I loved that. I breathed deeply, and drove, while she began fidgeting for a comfortable position, bare feet up on the dashboard.

"Gosh, I almost forgot!" She smiled, and reached over and removed from her tote bag a small wrapped parcel, which emitted the most aromatic smells. Oh, her face shone with pride, Doctor, as she opened it and showed her baby, me, what she had brought: fresh lox, sturgeon, bagels. "See, precious, you're always with me," she cooed, the clever darling, and the two of us munched with surprising hunger. As we rode on, those strong ancient aromas filled the car with Brownsvilled resonance, father feeling.

" 'So it should be,' " she began in her best stagey voice, " 'that none but Antony should conquer Antony; but woe 'tis so!' " She turned to beam at me. I told her that she knew an awful lot of literature for a girl interested in Indian affairs. She took that seriously, reflecting, moving again. "Shit," she decided. "Literature is a trip." I waited, deciphering, then, smiling somewhat, said foolishly, "So's this." She gazed at me quizzically, made a scrunched-up face to indicate my hopelessness, noted, "Huh? Are you going *literal* on me again?" No, actually, I wasn't. I kept quiet, scooting among huge trees and crazy shadows, following the intricate road, thinking of this Antony, heading for Swerdlow's and silence; nothing as grandly heroic or memorable as martial death. But shouldn't I be the one, I thought momentarily, to be bringing

486

in this Cleopatra for examination and rest? She shifted yet again—hearing my thought?—this time slipping out of the top of her dress, and curling her lithe body up sideways, feet toward the window, head propped up on my side, knees up toward her chin. There in that fetal position, in her (breathtaking) nakedness, she seemed at last content, and I, curiously, felt content too. A sudden static, and a voice came up from somewhere on the floor, stately, unadorned, British, and I realized it was that same poet again, reciting slowly, about a patient, a table, insidious intent. . . . It was soothing, and slowly revelatory. We drove that way a long time, interrupted only once by Tippy turning over the tape, all the way down to the asylum, with passing drivers and tollbooth agents doing double takes. We didn't mind, though. Tippy remaining immersed in her deeper levels while I, the more literal, supported her, every now and then looking down at her—glowing face, shining hair, wonderful breasts (in repose)—feeling happy, unreasonably and unnaturally happy, and I didn't want the ride ever to end, ever. I remember perceiving too that I had never understood that beautiful elegy to energy and manhood as much as I did then, on the trip, or had ever been so strongly affected by it.

# Postscripts

### Afterword by Dr. Benjamin Lirič

I wish here not to present my own thoughts on this strange case and moving text, but rather to offer the reader some further materials to aid him in his own understanding and possible interpretation of the Solomon story. There are three documents here, all very different from each other, perhaps only one with direct relevance to the story. First, I've seen fit to reproduce a sampling of letters to *Esquire* in response to the Tippy/Pandora article. These speak for themselves, I believe, in representing the views of the general public to such private revelations. The second item is a letter from Rachel Solomon to her father, from Israel, which Mr. Solomon didn't wish to read, and never opened. After several weeks of sitting with that unopened mail on his bureau, I thought to open it, and gave the information to him; he didn't react, however, but just sat there. (I did not consider it wise to give him the gist of the paragraph on Tippy, which I think may be the most interesting now for the general reader.) Again, I am not sure of the relevance of this letter, but the reader will forgive me if I have acted on sentimental impulse alone; I hope I haven't. The third item is of obvious relevance, a true document. It is another letter, this one from Professor Tippy Matthews—may I say the "real" Miss Matthews?—written from her university, upon her return from six months in a Mexican Indian village in response to Lionel Solomon's plea for information. Unfortunately, Mr. Solomon never saw this letter, it being sent on to me, months afterward, a month after Lionel had left Swerdlow's. If it clears up certain mysteries and answers certain questions, it also coats the entire story with an extra veneer of irony. So what you will be reading are two pieces of mail that never reached Solomon, for one reason or another. An odd fate for letters.

The final section is made up of excerpts from two essays by the great French writer, Michel de Montaigne. They were selected and edited by Lionel Solomon himself, and placed at the very end of his own text, a postscript. It is here that I have taken my one liberty with Solomon's text, by shifting that postscript to the end of the whole book. I have done this in accord with Mr. Solomon's basic intention, namely, to leave the reader with Montaigne's words as a final coda. Did he do this as a means of putting some distance between the event of Tippy and his own torn feelings? As a means of justifying his own ambivalent interpretation, or lack of final judgment? or, very simply, as a means of substituting a voice of reasoned elegance for a voice grown tired with despair and confusion? In his own brief preface to the master's thoughts, Lionel provides his own clues. Again, it seemed amiss not to end with the final flavor of Lionel's feelings and deliberations about the whole strange affair, as he sat there in his sanitarium room, contemplating his recent powerful past and trying to imagine, somehow, a possible future. I hope it has not been a future of futility, but rather, one of temporary disrepair. His disappearance, as I have said earlier, can be used as evidence of either interpretation. As the months pass, though, the case for futility grows stronger and stronger.

But it is neither lie, nor the imagination, nor fiction, that Lionel Solomon is still a missing person, and the girl Tippy remains out there somewhere, wanted for questioning, and missing, last seen at the literary ceremony in Buenos Aires where she accepted the award on behalf of the novelist. For all we may know, as one friend suggests, the pair may be living "quite nicely" somewhere in South America, or in New England, writing books, a dissertation, planning for a child. I think otherwise. Tippy, I feel, will resurface somehow, in one guise or another. But as to Lionel Solomon, I remain skeptical, and worried; as time passes, I have less and less hope that we shall recover him, or see any more of his writing. Whether the story will remain a permanent puzzle, or develop into a serious legal case, or . . . Only time, and the participants will be able to tell. But where, how, in what forum—a courtroom, a critical study, a psychiatrist's couch? Will any one of these, by itself, satisfy?

The only word I shall add about Montaigne's work, from my own recent rereading, is how much insight he provides about the self at the same time that he writes about the world. In fact, the line there between the two frequently dissolves, though in a way quite different indeed from how the dissolution occurs in the long narrative you have just read. The difference in control is vast, of course, and the contrasts most striking—in the levels of pain and confusion, among other qualities. As Solomon himself observes, it is one thing to withdraw from the world at one's own will, quite another when the world forces you out; even if you imagine that world to be called Tippy.

# A Sampling of Letters
# to the Editor on "Solomon:
# An Intimate Portrait"

Three cheers for your magazine for your gutsy decision to publish Ms. Armstrong's all-out exciting article (October, 1975)! To my way of thinking, it is a breakthrough in literary biocriticism, a field that has long ago ceased to interest the modern critic. What Ms. Armstrong has done is to knock away the "time-honored" and "untouchable" pedestal called An Author's Privacy, and shown us the nitty-gritty of the man himself. It so happens that the man in question here is a little more sick than the average author, and this may scandalize many of your readers. It shouldn't. To one like myself who has in the past lived with a painter for five years it neither scandalizes nor surprises me very much, having seen up close the inflationary cost to everyone concerned of living in his presence. Congratulations, Pandora. Congratulations, *Esquire!*

Mary Lou Meachum
Critic
Cambridge, Mass.

Was that a put-on? Yet another setup to give publicity to some unknown graduate student and a second-rate vulgar writer? Or is someone with clout up at *Esquire* dating the chick, and hence the piece?

Ilene Watson
Croton-on-Hudson

... *Esquire*'s decision to publish the essay was a seriously mistaken one in every way. I am sure Mr. Solomon's attorney can speak to the legal matters involved, but as to matters of editorial sense and literary taste, it was inexcusable. ...

Georges Raymond
Literary Agent (for Lionel
Solomon)
New York

... there's no doubt that women have been on the short end of the proverbial stick from time immemorial when it comes to being "subjects" in men's fictions (and/or fantasies!), and the service performed by your magazine—and of course by Ms. Armstrong—cannot be overestimated. What we've needed, following Ms. Millett's and Ms. Ellman's work, among others, was precisely the kind of empirical critique and actual data, before the fact, so to speak, that Ms. Armstrong provides. For the first time we have considerable evidence in hand to judge the sort of manipulative powers and twisted chauvinist motives that parade under the conveniently safe rubric "fiction," when it comes to distorting a real-life experience involving a woman. What the article really says is, Woman, Beware! when you approach a man who happens to write or paint. He not only is liable to exploit your body and your mind, but also, later on, your spirit as well. To use a phrase taken from another sphere, "Never Again!" after reading Ms. Armstrong's liberating piece. At first I felt truly sorry that my own magazine didn't have first crack at it, but now, after all, I'm delighted that New York's official Magazine for Men has shown the balls to run it.

J.W. McWilliams
*Ms. Magazine*

Can someone please tell us what's going on in New York City? Are we to believe that a national magazine actually printed the piece we've just read? Are all laws and morals OFF once you cross the Hudson?

Does anyone really care whether Mr. Solomon has one testicle or two? And does this have anything in the world, on this planet, to do with literary criticism? . . . More than ever, I am in favor of cutting off federal funds and even, if things continue this way, communications with New York until an explanation for "Solomon: An Intimate Portrait" (October) is offered. The "reasoning" given by the author surely fits a chimpanzee, not an adult of our species.

Linda & Ralph Merriweather
Boise, Idaho

. . . certainly Ms. Armstrong's thesis or proposition is intriguing, and may indeed provide some useful clues to further fiction. It also opens up significantly the whole question of "material" for a novelist, especially when the novelist is a male, and the subject is a woman. However, I must seriously question whether or not the personal material is used here in a way that is particularly germane to literary exploration. Unless personal or intimate facts can be related specifically to thematic patterns or literary imagery, or specific characters, we shall have to remain somewhat skeptical about the uses of the material. The few paragraphs of example that Ms. Armstrong provides do seem abortive, in terms of persuasive argument; and she is quite right when she admits that "naturally it will take much more evidence from the actual novels to test sufficiently the basic theses." (Admittedly, *Esquire* readers are not that interested in close textual analysis.) So what I am saying is, while the attempt strikes me as potentially most interesting, it still remains to be seen whether it is of serious value in the long run. . . . As to Mr. Solomon's "future novel" on the subject, yes, it would be very nice indeed if he were to oblige us with one. Has he been properly asked?

Marjorie Samuelson
Author, *The Woman in Victorian Fiction*

. . . are we now going to be faced with a series of studies on James, Flaubert, Tolstoy, and anyone else who has used female protagonists, which will seek to catalogue their daily and personal habits in order to "expose" the "true" authorial purpose behind the characters? Doesn't the surface of the novels—characters, plots, language—count anymore, save as a shield for some "insidious" male design? . . . Who really cares what was secretly behind Daisy Miller or Isabel Archer, or what devious male motives lurked behind the creation of Anna Karenina? ...

Sam Pinsker
Assistant Professor of English
SUNY (Buffalo)

... May I add, as an old Solomon girlfriend from college days, and one who has seen her NAME exploited in an earlier novel, my own congratulations to Ms. Armstrong for her forthright article and insight. It seems that Lionel has not only not changed very much from the early days, being ungiving and near-impotent then, but has actually taken a turn for the worse. ...

Harriet Feingold
New York City

I've never met Lionel Solomon but I have read his books and all I can say is, I KNEW IT! I'd have bet my bottom dollar that the guy was seriously sick, and the article ty PJA proves it. Can't we get more of these male novelists out of their (artistic) closets and see them without their masks and mirrors? Can't we get the lowdown on Mailer, Bellow, Roth, etc., *before* they rip off more women in their fiction? (and lives!) At last a woman has gone out and stood up for herself—and for all of us!—instead of taking it on the chin and burying the whole thing with a drink or a shrink! The syndrome is familiar enough—from male novelist to male fiction to male shrink—how's that for the Complete Male Rip-off, at thirty-five an hour no less. To PJA and all other hitherto female victims of "male art," I say, Right On!

John P. Frances
Free-lance Writer
San Francisco

# Letter to Solomon from His Daughter

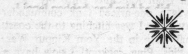

August 7

Dear Dad,

I hope the tennis court is ready by now, and that the sweet corn will grown well and escape the raccoons (though they have to live too), so I can try both when I return. (*If* I return this fall, but more on that later.) And be good to Sheyna—"You don't know what ya got till it's gone," sings Joni Mitchell. (Tell S. I'll write to her separately.)

Israel is so different from what I had imagined! Life is so terribly hard, there are so many everyday problems and tensions, and the pound is forever being devalued. Jews here have a harder life than in Cambridge or Great Neck. The other day there was another little explosion in a Tel Aviv cafe, and three kids are in the hospital in serious condition. Two weeks ago I went to a funeral with a friend, and I couldn't believe my eyes and ears; I had never seen Asian Jews in suffering before. The screaming of the old women terrified me, I had never heard *real screams* before. It's difficult to believe that they are of the same "tribe" as me, really. My friends by the way include a marvelous Kurdish girl, an old friend of Sheyna's, whose grandparents came to Palestine on donkeys from Iraq, at the turn of the century. She's so *alive*, and interested in everything American. She'd do *anything* for a pair of blue jeans or a new Billie Holiday record. Can you dig up either?. . . . My own dig goes well, if slowly. Sometimes it's hard to believe that what we are excavating is a real wall several thousand years old! Imagine that Solomon's Temple existed in fact, not merely in the Bible. (Will they ever excavate a wall from your temple in New Hampshire, Dad? Or maybe find your old Ping-Pong table in the year 3001?) It's very exciting. Except when a sandstorm brews.

Would you believe, by the way, that the hero around these parts is Kojak? And that the first aliyah has produced, several generations later, gangster and moll types, complete with wedgies and mascara? But most of this takes place in Tel Aviv, thank God. Here in Jerusalem we're still pretty much spoiled by the beauty, silence, etc. Something like your own Jerusalem, in N.H.

Yes, it's a little different from Radcliffe. Ditto my "love-life." My first "friend" was a one-armed tank commander who gave me a lift one day when I was hitching to the coast; he turned out to be a small hero in the Yom Kippur War, and also, married with 3 kids. Ping, jackpot! I now have a more sedate friend, a young South African socialist who, in a little hot water over that apartheid thing there, is now here, probably to stay. Louie Zeigenbaum, with blond curls and long eyelashes, Dad. Father a businessman in Johannesburg, but a lot of *meshpucheh* (?) here. He's really given me a crash course in Israeli problems. He's all the way on the left, naturally, and is in almost daily fights with the old kib-butzniks who are pretty conservative. I pick 'em, don't I? But he does think that social change is possible here, and wants to try. (I gave him *Posthumous Thrills*, but he didn't "get it." My boyfriends are not very literary, are they?) All he's after is to settle the Arab question, probably become a Knesset member, try to start a new party, that's all. Anyway, he has a sense of humor about it all; with me, anyway. All told, I'm thinking seriously about staying here for the fall semester, pos-sibly the whole year, what do you think? Mom thinks if I want to do it, why not? What do you think, Mr. Tenacious? Give me a break? Would it be a great loss to miss the Cliff for a year? Doubtful. I'm thinking of staying at a kibbutz for several months, then maybe try Hebrew University. Any friends there?

I didn't get a chance to tell you about a brief but fascinat-ing meeting before coming here. Guess who showed up at Moore Hall one day? Our old friend, Tippy. We had a sand-wich together, and it was fun and interesting; we really related. She's a much, much more thoughtful head than I gave her credit for. There she was sitting across from me, with her marvelous green eyes, asking if you were well, asking about my trip, giving me a name or two in Israel, in-cluding a member of Knesset(!) and I was feeling shittier and shittier for having attributed *to her* all that crazy stuff done to you back in June. I never felt so guilty! We talked about your books, which she knows practically by heart, and then when she laid that trip on me, about the visit to Grandma's, I almost fell off my seat. She bops around, doesn't she? You must send me a copy of the piece she's doing on you, ok? Although she wouldn't say anything, I think she was hurt at not seeing you anymore; did you drop her, Dad? (I know, it's none of my biz!) On top of everything, I think she's very modest. She's one of those people who gets to know about something—a person, a place, a movement—in a remarkably short time, and I got the feeling that she wished things were otherwise. As if she's superficial about knowing things. *I* should be so superficial! Personally, I think she's a very neat individual.

May I say one word here about your accident or incident? Or rather about the effect on me? I can't ever tell you what it meant to me to see you that way, hurt and bandaged and in trouble, and not being able to help you. It tore my heart out. I remembered one time way back when I was about 10 or so, and we went to that park on the West Side where you played in a pickup game of softball, and suddenly, out of the corner of my eye, I saw you run into that fence trying to catch a ball, and you went down just like that. I just stood there for a minute, paralyzed, while everyone ran out to you; finally, I was able to make it out there to you, and everyone was crowded around you. I stood there, quiet and anonymous, thinking maybe you were dead, and feeling helpless; I couldn't even cry, seeing your body folded over, I was so stunned. I remember I had my tennis racket, and just kept squeezing the handle and scratching at the strings, praying that you would *move*. And it was only when you did move or groan that *I* was able to move, and cry out, and acknowledge that I was your daughter! It was almost as if I was knocked out along with you, I think, and incapacitated the same way. Well, something like that happened when I saw you by the river that day; I felt paralyzed before I could run off and away. *You know, Papa, that I wanted you to know and prayed that you did know, and know that you knew, that no matter what had happened to you, and no matter what had happened between us, that no daughter ever loved a father more than I loved you.* But I knew, too, that there was nothing I could do, you didn't want me to do anything, and so I only wrote you that one line note, telling you that I loved you. At first it hurt me when I didn't hear from you, but then that passed, and I understood. My underlined lines still hold fast, Papa.

Last words about the Promised Land:

My first impression after several weeks is that this is a hard place to live in, but it may be worth it. The potential is here for a real *terrif* society. The mix is fantastic: the colors, the people, the landscape. Then there's the tension between fighting off terrorists and inflation on the one hand, and on the other, fighting to make a more egalitarian society. The tension and contradictions are wearying but impressive. You know what? I think it might be a nice change for you. In America, your life has become pretty routine, staid, even boring; wouldn't you like to try to pump back into it some of the old anarchist-socialist ideas? Feel some public involvement and tension in your blood again? Think about it, seriously Dad. Here, you know, if you've written books, you're really *somebody*. (By the way, how come you're not translated into Hebrew? Or are you? I've looked around for your books, but no luck.) You're near forty; why not start a whole new career? Maybe even, become a Jew? (Even Tippy thought that you had a great Jewish novel in you!)

Kisses and Love,<br>Rach

P.S. Just discovered *Rosen at Fifty* in Steimatsky's.

# Letter from Professor Matthews

Dear Dr. Lirič:

When I returned to the university in late January, after some eight months of fieldwork in northern Mexico—the Yaqui Indian is not big on relaying mail—I found two messages from Lionel Solomon awaiting me, asking me to get in touch with him (telegram) and by letter, asking, "Who is Pandora J. Armstrong?" and could I supply some "information about your relations"? I tried to telephone Mr. Solomon, but found the number given the wrong one, and his phone unlisted by information; so I dropped him a note, telling him briefly that PJA was my half sister, and that I was not in the habit of discussing family members with strangers. That was the last of it until I heard from you of Mr. Solomon's predicament and the magazine article. Under the new circumstances, disturbing and unusual as you describe them, I'm reconciled to abandoning this rule. I hope my information can be of some help to you.

I had known since early summer of my sister's involvement

with Lionel Solomon, from a mutual friend and from Pandora herself, in her inimitable way—something like, "Have you ever read any of Lionel Solomon's novels? No? Really, Tippy, you ought to!" a cultural indictment that signified, for my sister, a romantic affair with the gentleman in question. Pandy, as she's known to me, was not one to keep her affairs secret, especially (with me) if they involved a "success or triumph" on her part. The competition for men was always paramount with her, though God knows why in our case since she long ago won, and keeps on winning. Not that we "talk"; we haven't talked for years; mostly we are forced to deal with each other over family and financial matters, from time to time. Over trust-fund investment discussions, with our family lawyer sitting there, we exchange "remarks." Yet one is—I am—constantly hearing "news" about Pandy; she's always been that sort of person. It turns out, on checking the dates, that I have talked with her once since Mr. Solomon's removal; no word was mentioned about it from her, and of course I knew nothing of it; however, she did say this, "Well, Tippy, are you ready to be an aunt? I've decided to have a baby." That, I'm afraid, is Pandy-in-action with me. So you see I have not questioned her about the affair (or article), nor could I have. Pandy would not accept questions from me very easily. For her sake, I hope she is not involved in this Mr. Solomon's disappearance in any negligent manner, or worse.

Describing our history together to you is like going back to my own early sessions in therapy—it was *the* crucial theme of my sessions for two whole years. I first met Pandy when she was going on thirteen and I on fifteen, when her mother married my father, after a divorce on one side and death on the other. One curious thing about it was that we actually didn't look that different, though God knows we couldn't have been more unlike. She was a quiet, respectful proper young lady, while I was a rather rebellious and hypersensitive hellion.

How do I describe the change that occurred during the next two years, a change so radical that I still don't believe we were *those same girls*. But maybe we weren't. Being away at the eastern boarding school changed her completely. She became the stronger one; I, the weaker sister. The scared, virtuous, uncertain girl, who had followed me, sheeplike, in everything I did or thought or wore, had turned into the hellion, the troublemaker, the kleptomaniac, the devilish liar, the supertroubled teenager. Yet, what she was facing in me—who had gone to my own prep school, out there in the Southwest—was a changed Tippy too. I had grown reconciled to my new family situation, especially since I was away from it most of the time; and I suddenly had a whole new interest in school, which absorbed me totally: the American Indian. I have no doubt that it was that early, serious interest, motivated by an Indian friend who invited me to her reservation one holiday and continuing through college, graduate school and a professional career, which truly "saved" me, or put me onto the right track. At the same time, my sudden "career" killed Pandy. Once again, I was *one up* on her; I had jumped from girlhood to adulthood with one quick leap, having the great luck of geography and my good Indian classmate; my back yard and surrounding areas, and my new friends, composed my "interest."

So you see, she was a sister of tough breaks. By the time she was having her first man, about 14½ or so, I was publishing my first article, at 16½. I recall to this day my excitement when, after five months of sending the manuscript off and giving up on it, I received a letter of acceptance from the *American Anthropologist,* concerning my piece. "A New Dating of Antelope Ruins, Canyon de Chelly." When Pandy heard about it, from our parents, she wrote me from Vermont and said, "Congratulations on your attempt at sublimating your personality defects. You may trick our parents, but you won't trick me, or, I hope, yourself." It was the sort of thrust that she had become very good at, finding a vulnerability—in this case, my abysmal shyness and fear of boys—and saving it for special occasions. It took me years and years of therapy to become impervious to her powers.

Jealous over my father too, Doctor, for sure. We had a very solid relationship before and after my mother died, and to have the new woman enter it was a deeper blow than I could assess. And Pandy was attractive on many counts. Not only was she at 13 a *very* developed young woman, and also an exceptional athlete, but my father felt deeply for her loss of her own father (he had moved to California and abandoned the Armstrongs). Obviously, he was going to bend over backwards to replace her father, and aid her; but can you ever really replace anyone? Or "help" anyone if their need is overwhelming? Dr. Lirič, as you can see, there ought to be a law banning such marriages; they produce too many complications for the teenage children. *Half* sisters is the wrong terms for such as we; *unnatural* sisters is much better.

Either you're family or you're not; either you're allowed to sleep with someone, or you're not.

When she returned from Putney one Christmas, she was a changed girl, and a changed daughter for him too. She then began to take the upper hand with me in several ways, calling me Miss Clean for my tidy ways—she was just the opposite—and Tippy Wippy for my new scholarly interest and lack of boy interest. Also, she began to punish me severely with my father, by playing up to him shrewdly, playing on whatever sympathy or attraction she could command. It was a masterful job, as only a clever teenager could pull off, who's not "responsible" for her actions, or who "doesn't know" what she's doing, or who "doesn't mean things the way they look." (My father's terms of placation.) When he got home from work she'd take him out for a set of tennis or a swim, insisting that he needed the exercise; she'd walk around the house casually in a bikini or her underwear; she'd buy him small presents from Vermont and surprise him with them, privately like a lover (I'd find out later, by chance). Wanting her to feel wanted at home, he became rather easy prey for her cajoling, I'm afraid; fortunately, he was not the sort of man who could be physically seduced—her erotic inclinations were very much *there*, at the surface, without very much disguise. But he was strong, as well as naïve; the line between paternal tenderness and male passion was a very clear line indeed. I know this from the way he talked to me about her and the way she'd be frustrated with him, and make fun of him *to me;* I could tell that it was because he *didn't* lust after her or give in and play the role of lover to her. And you know what? She blamed that on me too! Accused me of talking behind her back, against her, to Daddy. Not true. I never did, cross my heart. I kept it all in, *whatever* I felt about her; kept it in to the bursting point. This was one of my main problems, as I came to learn with my doctor.

Pandy responded to my academic successes with fake congratulations and clever tauntings. When I'd be going off with an Indian friend, she called me Miss Pocahontas, or, if I was publishing something, I was Tippy-Grind. (Also, on social occasions with young men, she referred to me as "Chesty," in honor of my lack of breasts and her own premature development; she frequently stole a high school or college date from me, using her looks and breasts with vengeful pleasure.) She accused me of trying to "save" the Indians, and alternately of using them "selfishly" to promote a career. As I've suggested to you, however, my involvement with Indians stemmed from friendship and schooldays, in Flagstaff, when I was 14 or so. I also wound up spending two whole summers on Navajo and Zuñi reservations. (With the Navajo, for example, I lived in a hogan in Canyon de Chelly, where I first learned about the Basket Maker culture, from the pictograph drawings and ancient stone ruins along the canyon walls. That's how I happened to write my first article, at 16. I also first became acquainted there with the rending and nearly unsolvable dilemma of the Hopi-Navajo land dispute, taking the Hopi side; whenever Pandy saw me studying a map of the reservation, she'd comment, "Oh, are we divvying up the territory again, Miss Red Riding Hood?") One summer, I returned home from Zuñi with a special present, a pair of Zuñi fetishes of mountain lion and bear, made of natural stone formations; fetishes are objects in which spirits are said to dwell, which can give supernatural power to the owner (for the southwestern Indian); they were the best presents I had ever received! And suddenly, one night I came home and they were gone from my shelf, vanished. Oh, there were a few other things missing, but I could tell that it wasn't a real theft, because the forty dollars I had in a drawer was still there. When I asked Pandy if she took them, she just smiled at me, looked all happy and innocent, and then asked me how I could think of such a thing! I cried and cried for weeks over that, with a teenager's helpless fury, and have never forgotten it. In therapy, I learned that I could have been quite mistaken about who the thief was, and that it was just very easy for me to attribute the theft to Pandy. In my heart of hearts, if not in my mind anymore, I have little doubt, however.*

What was she like at Putney and then in college? She was forever going from one interest or subject to another. One day she'd want to be a painter, another a writer, another a dancer; at Bennington, she did all three, and did them well from the little bit I could gather, or witness. Then it would be history or anthropology for three months (after dropping anthropology, she said to me something like, "The great anthropological work has already been done, it's mop-up time, Tippy, and I'm just not very good at being a janitor"); law

* In Mr. Solomon's possession I found a small figurine which Ms. Matthews refers to here as "mountain lion," which was left in Solomon's apartment by the other Ms. Matthews, according to his text. With the permission of Mr. Solomon's executors, I have returned the Zuñi fetish to Ms. Matthews, who thanked me in an ensuing letter, most movingly—making me feel like some family detective.—Lirič.

and literature, too. She stuck with law until she saw that Daddy, himself a lawyer, wasn't influenced one way or the other by her choice, and then she called law study a "drone's apprenticeship." Along the way she changed schools as often as she changed topics; and yet always managed to do a stint of performance work—modeling, acting, dancing—in a professional way. You see, Doctor, the truth is she's a *very* talented person, maybe too talented; it seems that whatever she did pick up, she'd master in a very short time. Then leave it. (One day I saw her in a national magazine, after she'd been modeling for a month and she was called a "model's model.") With men, she was the same way; just as changeable, just at talented. She had *all* sorts of lovers, from a famous football player to a college professor to her psychiatrist—who actually left his family of five and moved across town in Berkeley to live with Pandy! It lasted about six months before she moved on; but you see she was *that* attractive to men, smart men especially; from Daddy she acquired a civil rights colleague, and from me, a young Hopi friend; and on and on, into the dozens, maybe hundreds. I'd get a message at the university to call my sister Pandy at the Waldorf Astoria, and she'd ask me on the telephone about some dress that she claimed was hers, along the way slipping in the information that a well-known doctor, with a penchant for the "kinky," was putting her up there for a few days. Another time, she woke me at 3 A.M. to tell me what an exciting party she had gone to that evening in Lima, Peru; and when I didn't sound too enthused, she blamed me for always being a wet blanket on her fun, and foiling her attempt to get close to me! Oh, she's talented, for sure. I've had to change my number because of her, and then get an unlisted one. (No help.) When she'd ask me about my men friends, it came out, "Who are you fucking now, Sis?" Knowing full well that I didn't have that many lovers, if any, and that I was unable to use that sort of language in any case. One year she passed on to me two of her old lovers, from brief affairs; it was terribly humiliating, Doctor, in every way. One of them believed I was a nymphomaniac, and the other, that I was a pathetic frigid creature. Both had been led to believe that they could get back to Pandy *through* me. It was a betrayal of generosity on my part, she claimed, when I told her not to pull that stuff ever again. Doctor, she has never let me alone!

Am I being too hard on Pandy in all this? Perhaps. But perhaps not hard enough. I can go on and on and on. However, with the exception of (petty) thievery, which I haven't really gone into here, she has never been involved in any "criminal" action *that I know of*. Though at one point she was very much into forging letters, from Dad or her mother or teachers, to use at her convenience. (Sometimes I wonder if she herself knew who had written them, so convinced she became of their authenticity.) This latest episode, *using my name and my life* in her affair with Mr. Solomon, has frightened me all over again. I have decided to go back to my therapist, and to take certain other precautions. But where and when will it end? I wish she were less clever, less talented; I'd be less afraid. Or I wish that this new "success" of hers, in *Esquire*, and at graduate school, would make her feel easier; I know this is unfair to Mr. Solomon and his name. I have been terribly shaken by this experience and the new revelations, and I'm afraid it will take me several months at least to sort things out in my own mind. I really don't know what to do about her anymore, Dr. Lirič, and if you have any thoughts on the matter, or further information, please let me know. In the meantime, I hope my own scattered impressions and disorganized thoughts are of some help to you, in your sorting out. May I add that after reading your own long and kindly letter several times, I trust you fully with this information, and authorize you to use it as you see fit. I thought somehow that I had been rid of the "major" difficulties with my sister, and once again discover my naïveté in the matter.

Yours sincerely,

## Solomon's Postscript

Some last words. An addendum of wisdom. By Michel de Montaigne, the successful judge who, at the age of thirty-seven, decided to retire from his active worldly career to a life of contemplation in his château in the Dordogne Valley. How nice, to withdraw at your own volition and not at the world's. Doctor, I find his words here, on these twin subjects of lying and imagining, most intriguing in light of my own experience. And truthful. How? They present to me something of a mirror, a theoretical mirror perhaps, to the perplexity in my own mind governing the situation. Or interpretations thereof. Sitting here, in one piece, gazing out at the orderliness of Swerdlow's in winter, I keep thinking, did it—or did Tippy—happen to me? Did she *really*? To say, *I believe* she did, and *therefore* she did, is one way of approaching the dilemma. I still have the magazine picture of her slouching by her motorcycle, along with the article itself; and also the advertising photograph of the other Tippy, sitting peacefully in her study. Then too there's the quaint picture of yours truly, wounded and bandaged. So some objective reality exists, verifiable you might say, on paper. Now how much of the rest is the result of my own active imagination? Or how much due to the girl's superb performance during every act? I barely know anymore. But to my great interest, I have discovered that Montaigne has put forth his own speculations on the general subject. It appeals to me very much that the master should see fit to inquire into the two different but bordering territories, trying to discern where one line zigzags across the other's land, and back across again.

There is something appealing too, Dr. L., in returning to a gentleman philosopher in this age of professional though plebian psychology. Certainly the old masters knew as much or more about the human being and his capacity for truth, deception and ambiguity as do the current journeymen and apprentices called clinicians. (No offense intended, Doc. But I consider you a European gentleman of letters, after all. By now you have read Kleist's stories and Stendhal's diaries, yes?) That so eloquent a writer as Montaigne should take the time to reflect seriously, and amusingly, on the subject of the overexcited mind and ever-ready (though unpredictable) member pleases me enormously. It seems to me that the gentleman must have been touched personally by his own Tippy somewhere along the line; or else, perhaps, his own imagination and fantasy sought her out longingly. In either case, I do wish he had written about her concretely, and saved me the trouble. For if I may say so, I believe that it is a more difficult, and a more painful, chore to get her down personally, so to speak, than to muse generally about the problems she presents. Be that as it may, his eloquent considerations about the life of deception stir my spirit and lift my feelings. That is why I wish to end with his words. Words which strike my ears like the singing of the birds in the morning, during a New Hampshire spring. And while it is still winter here, still night, and promises to be both for me for a long, long while, my heart is with spring. Does this sound like more folly, Doctor, more dangerous folly?

There is no man so unsuited for the task of speaking about memory as I am, for I find scarcely a trace of it in myself, and I do not believe there is another man in the world so hideously lacking in it. All my other faculties are poor and ordinary, but in this I think I am most rare and singular, and deserve to gain name and fame thereby.

Besides the natural inconvenience that I suffer on this account—for assuredly, considering how necessary it is, Plato was right in calling memory a great and powerful goddess—in my country, when they want to say that a man has no sense, they say that he has no memory; and when I complain of the shortcomings of my own, people correct me and refuse to believe me, as if I were accusing myself of being a fool. They can see no difference between memory and intellect.

This makes me look much worse off. But they wrong me, for experience shows that, on the contrary, excellent memories are often coupled with feeble judgments. They also wrong me in this, that the same words which indicate my infirmity, signify ingratitude as well—and I am nothing if I am not a good friend. They blame my affections instead of my memory, and turn an involuntary defect into a willful one. "He has forgotten this request or that promise," they say, "He doesn't remember his friends. He did not remember to do this, to say that, or to keep quiet about the other, for my sake." Certainly I am prone enough to forgetfulness, but as for neglecting, out of indifference, a service which a friend has asked of me, that I do not do. Let them be content with my misfortune and not turn it into a kind of ill-will, a kind quite foreign to my character.

But I find some consolation, first because I have derived from this evil my principal argument against a worse evil, which might have taken root in me: the evil of ambition. For lack of memory is an intolerable defect in anyone who takes on the burden of the world's affairs.

Then, as several similar examples of nature's workings show, she has generously strengthened other faculties in me in proportion as this one has grown weaker. I might easily have let my intelligence and judgment follow languidly in other men's footsteps, as all the world does, without exerting their own power, if other people's ideas and opinions had ever been present with me by favor of my memory.

Again, my speech is consequently briefer, for the storehouse of the memory is generally better stocked with material than that of the invention. If my memory had been good, I should have deafened all my friends with my chatter, since any subject that calls out such powers as I have of argument and development warms and extends my eloquence. This would have been lamentable, as I have learned in the case of some of my intimate friends. In proportion as their memory gives them a complete and firsthand view of their subject, so they push their narrative back into the past and burden it with useless details. If the story is a good one, they smother its virtues; if it is not, you curse their fortunate powers of memory or their unfortunate lack of judgment. Once one is well on the road, it is difficult to close a discourse and break it off. There is no better way of proving a horse's strength than by pulling him up short and sharp. Even among men who keep to the point, I find some who would like to break off but cannot. While they are searching for a place at which to stop, they go maundering and trailing on like a man who is losing strength. Particularly dangerous are old men who retain the memory of past events, but do not remember how often they have repeated them. I have known some very amusing tales to become most tiresome when told by some gentlemen whose whole audience has been sated with them a hundred times.

I find some consolation, also, in the reflection that I have, in the words of a certain ancient author,* a short memory for the inquiries I have received. Like Darius, I should need a prompter. Wishing not to forget the insult he had suffered from the Athenians, the Persian king made one of his pages come and repeat three times in his ear, each time he sat down to table: "Sire, remember the Athenians"; and it consoles me too that the places I revisit and the books I reread always smile upon me with the freshness of novelty.

Not without reason is it said that no one who is not conscious of having a sound memory should set up to be a liar. I know quite well that grammarians make a distinction between telling an untruth and lying. They say that to tell an untruth is to say something that is false, but that we suppose to be true, and that the meaning of the Latin *mentiri*, from which our French word for lying derives, is to go against one's conscience, and that consequently it applies only to those who say the opposite of what they know; and it is of them I am speaking.

Now liars either invent the whole thing, or they disguise and alter an actual fact. If they disguise and alter, it is hard for them not to get mixed up when they refer to the same story again and again because, the real facts having been the first to lodge in the memory and impress themselves upon it by way of consciousness and knowledge, they

* Cicero, speaking of Caesar, *Pro Ligario*, XII.

507

will hardly fail to spring into the mind and dislodge the false version, which cannot have as firm or assured a foothold. The circumstances, as they were first learned, will always rush back into the thoughts, driving out the memory of the false or modified details that have been added.

If liars make a complete invention, they apparently have much less reason to be afraid of tripping up, inasmuch as there is no contrary impression to class with their fiction. But even this, being an empty thing that offers no hold, readily escapes from the memory unless it is a very reliable one. I have often had amusing proof of this, at the expense of those who profess to suit their speech only to the advantage of the business in hand, and to please the great men to whom they are speaking. The circumstances to which it is their wish to subordinate their faith and their conscience being subject to various changes, their language has also to change from time to time; and so they call the same thing gray one moment and yellow the next, say one thing to one man, and another to another. Then, if these listeners happen to bring all this contrary information together as a common booty, what becomes of all their fine art? Besides they trip up so often when they are off their guard. For what memory could be strong enough to retain all the different shapes they have invented for the same subject? I have seen many in my time who have desired a reputation for this subtle kind of discretion, not seeing that the reputation and the end in view are incompatible.

Lying is indeed an accursed vice. We are men, and we have relations with one another only by speech. If we recognized the horror and gravity of an untruth, we should more justifiably punish it with fire than any other crime. I commonly find people taking the most ill-advised pains to correct their children for their harmless faults, and worrying them about heedless acts which leave no trace and have no consequences. Lying—and in a lesser degree obstinacy—are, in my opinion, the only faults whose birth and progress we should consistently oppose. They grow with a child's growth, and once the tongue has got the knack of lying, it is difficult to imagine how impossible it is to correct it. Whence it happens that we find some otherwise excellent men subject to this fault and enslaved by it. I have a decent lad as my tailor, whom I have never heard to utter a single truth, even when it would have been to his advantage.

If, like the truth, falsehood had only one face, we should know better where we are, for we should then take the opposite of what a liar said to be the truth. But the opposite of a truth has a hundred thousand shapes and a limitless field.

The Pythagoreans regard good as certain and finite, and evil as boundless and uncertain. There are a thousand ways

508

of missing the bull's-eye, only one of hitting it. I am by no means sure that I could induce myself to tell a brazen and deliberate lie even to protect myself from the most obvious and extreme danger. An ancient father* says that we are better off in the company of a dog we know than in that of a man whose language we do not understand. Therefore those of different nations do not regard one another as men.† and how much less friendly is false speech than silence!

## On the Power of the Imagination

"A strong imagination brings on the event," say the scholars. I am one of those who are very much affected by the imagination. Everyone feels its impact, but some are knocked over by it. On me it makes an intense impression, and my practice is rather to avoid it than to resist it. I wish I could consort only with the healthy and the cheerful, for the sight of another's anguish gives me real pain, and my body has often taken over the sensations of some person I am with. A perpetual cougher irritates my lungs and my throat; and I am more reluctant to visit a sick man to whom I am bound by duty and interest than one who has a smaller claim on my attention and consideration. As I observe a disease, so I catch it and give it lodging in myself. It is no surprise to me that the imagination should bring fevers and death to those who allow it free play and encourage it. Simon Thomas was a great physician in his day, and I remember meeting him once at the house of a rich old man who suffered with his lungs. When the patient asked him how he could be cured, Master Thomas answered that one way would be for him to infect me with a liking for his company. Then if he were to fix his gaze on the freshness of my complexion, and his thoughts on the youthful gaiety and vigor with which I overflowed, and if he were to feast his senses on my flourishing state of health, his own condition might well improve. What he forgot to say was that mine might at the same time deteriorate.

Gallus Vibius so taxed his mind to understand the nature and periodicity of insanity that he completely lost his senses and was never able to recover them; he might have boasted that he had gone mad by learning. There are some who from fear anticipate the executioner's hand; and there was one who, when they unbound his eyes so that his pardon might be read to him, was found to be stark dead on the scaffold, slain by no other stroke than that of his imagination. We sweat, we tremble, we turn pale, we flush, beneath our imagination's impact; deep in our featherbeds,

* St. Augustine.
† Pliny, *Natural History*, VII, i.

we feel our bodies shaken by its onslaughts, sometimes almost to the point of death; and fervent youth grows so heated in its sleep that it satisfies its amorous desires even in dreams,

> *Ut quasi transactis saepe omnibus rebus profundant*
> *fluminis ingentis fluctus, vestemque cruentent.**

Although there is nothing strange in seeing horns grow in the night on foreheads that had none at bedtime, there is something memorable about the case of Cippus, King of Italy. During the day he had been a passionate spectator at the bullfight, and all night long he had worn horns in his dreams. His forehead had actually sprouted them by the power of the imagination. Anger gave Croesus' son† the voice that Nature had denied him, and Antiochus fell into a fever because Stratonice's beauty had become too deeply imprinted on his mind. Pliny says that he saw Lucius Cossitius change from a woman into a man on his wedding day; and Pontanus and others record similar metamorphoses that have occurred in Italy in more recent times. By his own vehement desire and his mother's,

> *Vota puer solvit, qui femina voverat Iphis.‡*

Passing through Vitry-le-François, I was shown a man whom the Bishop of Soissons had confirmed under the name of Germain, but whom all the village's inhabitants had both known and seen to be a girl, and who had been called Marie up to the age of twenty-two. He was then old, had a heavy growth of beard, and was unmarried. He said that as he was straining to take a jump his male organs appeared; and the girls of that neighborhood still sing a song in which they warn one another not to take long strides or they may turn into boys, like Marie Germain. It is not very surprising that this sort of accident happens frequently, for the imagination is so continually drawn to this subject that, supposing it has any power over such things, it would be better for it to incorporate the virile member in a girl once and for all, rather than subject her so often to the same thoughts and the same violence of desire.

.  .  .  .  .

It is probable that the belief in miracles, visions, enchantments, and such extraordinary occurrences springs in the main from the power of the imagination acting princi-

---

* "As if they were performing the entire act, the mighty wave gushes forth and stains their garments."—Lucretius, IV, 1035.

† According to Herodotus, he had been dumb from birth, but had found his voice when he saw his father in peril of death.

‡ "Iphis as a man fulfilled the vows he had made as a woman."—Ovid, *Metamorphoses,* IX, 793.

pally on the minds of the common people, who are the more easily impressed. Their beliefs have been so strongly captured that they think they see that they do not. I am also of the opinion that those comical impediments which so embarrass our society that they talk of nothing else are most likely caused by apprehensions and fears. I have personal knowledge of the case of a man for whom I can answer as for myself, and who could not fall under the least suspicion of impotence or of being under a spell. He had heard a comrade of his tell of an extraordinary loss of manhood that had fallen on him at a most inconvenient moment; and, when he was himself in a like situation, the full horror of this story had suddenly struck his imagination so vividly that he suffered a similar loss himself. Afterwards the wretched memory of his misadventure so devoured and tyrannized over him that he became subject to relapses. He found some remedy for his mental trick in another trick; by himself confessing this weakness of his and declaring it in advance, he relieved the strain on his mind and the mishap being expected, his responsibility for it diminished and weighed upon him less. When he had an opportunity of his own choosing—his thought being disengaged and free and his body in its normal state—he would have his virility tested, seized, and taken unawares, by previous arrangement with the other party. He was then completely and immediately cured of his infirmity. For once a man has been capable with a certain woman, he will never be incapable with her again unless out of real impotence.

This mishap is only to be feared in an enterprise where the mind is immoderately torn between desire and respect, and particularly when the opportunity is unforseen and urgent. There is no way of overcoming the trouble. I know someone who found it a help to come to it with his body already partially sated elsewhere. Thus the heat of his passion was allayed. Now, in old age, he finds himself less impotent because less potent. And I know another man who was greatly helped by a friend's assurance that he was furnished with a counter-battery of enchantments, certain to protect him.

. . . . .

It is wrong of women to receive us with pouting, querulous, and shrinking looks that quell us even as they kindle us. The daughter-in-law of Pythagoras said that a woman who goes to bed with a man ought to lay aside her modesty with her skirt, and put it on again with her petticoat. The mind of the assailant, disturbed by so many different alarms, is easily dismayed; and once the imagination has subjected a man to this disgrace—and it never does so except at the first encounter, because the desires are then more turbulent and strong, and because at the outset one has a much greater fear of failing—the fact that he has be-

511

gun badly throws him into a fever, and vexation at his mischance carries over to succeeding occasions.

Married men, with time at their command, need not hurry, nor need they attempt the enterprise if they are not ready. It is better to accept the disgrace and refrain from inaugurating the marriage bed when feverish and full of agitations, and to await another more private and less disturbed opportunity, than to be thrown into a perpetual misery by the surprise and disappointment of an initial failure. Before possession is taken, one who suffers from the imagination should by sallies at different times make gentle essays and overtures without any strain or persistence, in order definitely to convince himself of his powers. Those who know their members to be obedient by nature need only take care to outmaneuver the imagination.

We have reason to remark the untractable liberties taken by this member, which intrudes so tiresomely when we do not require it and fails us so annoyingly when we need it most, imperiously pitting its authority against that of the will, and most proudly and obstinately refusing our solicitations both mental and manual. Yet if on being rebuked for rebellion and condemned on that score he were to engage me to plead his cause, I might perhaps cast some suspicion on our other members, his fellows, of having framed this fictitious case against him out of pure envy of the importance and pleasure attached to his functions. I might arraign them for plotting to make the world his enemy by maliciously blaming him alone for their common fault. For I ask you to consider whether there is a single part of our bodies that does not often refuse to work at our will, and does not often operate in defiance of it. Each one of them has its own passions that rouse it and put it to sleep without our leave.

How often do the involuntary movements of our features reveal what we are secretly thinking and betray us to those about us! The same cause that governs this member, without our knowing it governs the heart, the lungs, and the pulse, the sight of a charming object imperceptibly spreading within us the flame of a feverish emotion. Are these the only muscles and veins that swell and subside without the consent, not only of our will, but even of our thoughts? We do not command our hair to stand on end, or our skin to quiver with desire or fear. The hand often goes where we do not send it. The tongue is paralyzed and the voice choked, each at its own time. Even when, having nothing to cook, we could gladly prevent it, the appetite for food and drink does not fail to stir those parts that are subject to it, in just the same way as this other appetite; and it forsakes us just as unseasonably when it chooses to. The organs that serve to discharge the bowels have their own dilations and contractions outside the control of the wishes and contrary to them, as have those that serve to relieve our kidneys. And though, to vindicate the supreme power of our will, St. Augustine claims to have seen a man who could command his bottom to break wind as often as he wished, and Vives, his commentator, caps him with another case from his own days of a man who could synchronize his blasts to the meter of verses that were read to him, this does not imply the complete obedience of this organ. For usually it is most unruly and mutinous. Indeed, I know one such that is so turbulent and so intractable that for the last forty years it has compelled its master to break wind with every breath. So unremittingly constant is it in its tyranny that it is even now bringing him to his death.

But let us take our will, on whose behalf we are preferring this charge. How much more justifiably can we brand it with rebellion and sedition, on account of its constant irregularities and disobedience! Does it always desire what we wish it to desire? Does it not often desire, to our obvious disadvantage, what we forbid it to? Does it let itself be guided, either, by the conclusions of our reason?

In short, I ask you on behalf of my noble client kindly to reflect that, although his case in this matter is inseparably and indistinguishably joined with that of an accomplice, nevertheless he alone is attacked, and with such arguments and accusations as, seeing the condition of the parties, cannot possibly appertain to or concern the said accomplice. Wherefore the malice and manifest injustice of his accusers is apparent.

Be that as it may, protesting that the wranglings and sentences of lawyers and judges are in vain, nature will go her own way. Yet she would have been quite justified in endowing that member with some special privileges, since it is the author of the sole immortal work of mortal man. For this reason Socrates held that procreation is a divine act, and love a desire for immortality as well as an immortal spirit.

. . . . .

But all this may be attributed to the close connection between the mind and the body, whose fortunes affect one another. It is another matter when the imagination works, as it sometimes does, not on one's own body but on someone else's. Just as one body passes a disease to its neighbor, as we see in the case of plague, smallpox, and pinkeye, which one person catches from another—

> *Dum spectant oculi laesos, laeduntur et ipsi*
> *multaque corporibus transitione nocent,* *

* "When their eyes behold others in pain, they feel pain themselves, and so many ills pass from body to body."—Ovid, *De Remedio Amoris,* 615.

513

so, when the imagination is violently disturbed, it launches shafts that may hit a distant object. The ancients believed that certain women in Scythia, if aroused and angry with a man, could kill him with a single glance. Tortoises and ostriches hatch their eggs merely by looking at them—a proof that their eyes have some ejaculative power.

. . . . .

For the anecdotes that I borrow I rely on the consciences of those from whom I have seen them. The inferences are my own, and depend on the evidence of common reasoning, not of experience. Anyone may add his own examples, and if he has none, the number and variety of the occurrences being so great, he may still be sure that plenty exist. If my own comments are not sound, let someone else comment for me. In this study of our manners and behavior that I am undertaking, fabulous incidents are as good as true ones, so long as they are feasible. Whether they happened or not, in Paris or in Rome, to John or to Peter, there is always some turn of the human mind about which they give me useful information. I note and draw profit from these anecdotes, whether they are shadowy or substantial. Of the various readings that the histories often provide, I make use of the most unusual and memorable. There are some authors whose purpose is to relate actual events. Mine, if I could fulfill it, would be to tell what might happen. The schools are rightly permitted to invent examples when they have none. I do not do this, however, and in that respect I surpass the most faithful historians in scrupulous reverence for truth. In the examples which I am drawing here from what I have heard, done or said, I have refused to be so bold as to change even the most trivial and unimportant details. Consciously I do not falsify one iota; I cannot answer for my knowledge.

In this connection I sometimes wonder whether it can be right for a prudent theologian, philosopher, or other such person of precise and delicate conscience to write history. How can they pledge their word on a popular belief? How can they answer for the thoughts of unknown persons, and advance their own conjectures as valid coin? They would refuse to give their own sworn testimony before a magistrate concerning actions involving several parties that had actually taken place before their eyes; and there is nobody whom they know so intimately that they would undertake to answer fully for his intentions. I consider it less dangerous, however, to write a chronicle of my own times. They consider that I view things with eyes less disturbed by passion than other men, and at closer range, because fortune has given me access to the heads of various factions. But they do not realize that I would not undertake the task for all the fame of Sallust; that I am a sworn foe to constraint, assiduity, and perseverance; and that nothing is so foreign to my style as an extended narrative. So often I break off for lack of breath. I have no proper skill in composition or development, and am more ignorant than a child of the words and phrases used for the most ordinary things. Therefore I have undertaken to say only what I can say, suiting my matter to my powers. Were I to select some subject that I had to pursue, I might not be able to keep up with it. Besides, the liberties I take being so complete, I might publish opinions that reason, and even my own judgment, would find unwarrantable and blameworthy. Plutarch would readily tell us that if the examples he cites in his works are wholly and in every way true the credit is due to the other writers; if they are of use to posterity, on the other hand, and are presented with a brilliance that lights us on the way to virtue, the credit for that is his own. An ancient tale is not like a medicinal drug; whether it is so or so, there is no danger in it.

A man of many parts, don't you think? Who appreciates the power of folly in our affairs with an amiable reason and worldly sympathy.

Oh yes, speaking of folly, and danger. One other development has taken place which the gentleman from Dordogne would appreciate, concerning the gentleman from Cambridge. (And Doctor, please forgive me for not mentioning this item to you personally, but it struck me as an amusing footnote, no more.) Of late, in the last few weeks or so, coinciding with the last snowstorm in fact, a daily emission of seminal fluid has dripped from my penis. Also, sores or chancres have emerged about the head, and there is a sizzling pain when I urinate. Ah, the noble spirochete has leased out my body! *Treponima pallidum* is her official name; a germ with a tail. *T. pallidum* for short. (*Tippy pallidum?*) At first I was alarmed, naturally, but then I calmed down and viewed the matter more philosophically. (Which raises all seedy affairs to serious heights, yes?) In my innocence I believed that such symptoms and diseases belonged to a previous time, and previous conditions. And to low contacts—to prostitutes, say, not graduate students. Yet, how fitting that it should have been my dear friend who deposited the tiny devilish creature in me. In any case, if the infection is left unchecked it can lead to all sorts of nasty consequences, I understand, lesions and inflammations, fevers and chills, etc. At the end the entire nervous system is affected, and the flesh itself may crack, shrivel, even fall off. An odd prospect, don't you think? To be truthful, however, I doubt that I'll have the courage or fortitude to proceed straight through to that end, with my

515

present policy of nonresistance. But just now I derive some consolation, if not pleasure, from contemplating the appropriate exchange, if you will. Tippy's spirochete for Solly's sperm. . . . And if there really is an "offspring" on its way, what sort of very wild Indian or crazy Jew will it be?

Looked at from another angle, I take a certain firm pride in the company I now find myself in. The history of gentlemen anointed in this fashion is long indeed. And offhand, the list includes some of the most noble—Baudelaire and Nietzsche, Maupassant and Gauguin, even the master Flaubert was touched. Not to mention those who suffered its wounds by means of misnomers (aneurysm, say) or euphemisms. For after all, what better mark of the adventurous soul than the infamous spirochete crawling around your body? . . . And, if at the end, it is only madness that awaits, the derangement of the brain and the dissolution of the senses, isn't all that somewhat anticlimatic? Unless of course my friend Tippy can find a use for it, in her own unique work, and on her own level. What's hard for me has always turned out to be easy for her, right? Easy.

# About the Author

Alan Lelchuk was born in 1938 in Brooklyn, New York, received his B.A. from Brooklyn College (1960), and his graduate degrees from Stanford University (Ph.D. 1965). A graduate fellowship gave him a year at University College, London, and he was a Guggenheim Fellow in 1976-77. He joined the English Department at Brandeis University in 1966, and is Writer-in-Residence there. For two years he was associate editor of *Modern Occasions* (edited by Philip Rahv). Both fiction and criticism by him have appeared in various magazines and quarterlies, *New American Review, Transatlantic Review, Works in Progress, Sewanee Review,* etc. His first novel, *American Mischief* (1973), was a Book-of-the-Month Club selection, translated into eight languages.